Orphan in America

—

Nanette L. Avery

ISBN: 1495433404
ISBN 13: 9781495433405
Library of Congress Control Number: 2014902391
CreateSpace Independent Publishing Platform
North Charleston, South Carolina

I dedicate this book to
Craig

———

A special word of thanks to my editing team from Miami to Nashville!

"In 1853, a minister by the name of Charles Loring Brace and a group of social reformers founded the Children's Aid Society. Its purpose was to care for homeless and neglected children by removing them from their present homes of poverty and placing them with farm families in the West and Midwest. The assumption was that by situating these children away from the slums to work on farms, they would inherit a better life. The manner of travel was aboard trains; the Orphan Trains."

Nanette L. Avery

———

"The founders of the Children's Aid Society early saw that the best of all Asylums for the outcast child, is the farmer's home."

Charles Loring Brace, 1872

———

"Yesterday, agents of the New York Juvenile Asylum brought to the city seven boys and five girls, which had been rescued from the streets of New York. All the children were between six and ten years of age. The children were nearly all disposed of yesterday to well-to-do farmers in this vicinity."

The Burlington Hawkeye, 1898

Chapter 1

He was only four or five years old when he saw his mother sleeping with death. Alex couldn't remember much about his early life except he did recall her lying real still and quiet upon a sheet of snowy linen. She was heavenly in her crisp white dressing gown which hung down below the bedding, but still revealed the tiny lilacs embroidered upon its hem; and though her skin was pale and ashen, her cheeks remained pink and rosy from the flushing the fever had provoked. Her eyes were sealed shut and a faint hue of grey encircled the closed lids like marble. But she wasn't asleep, just resting peacefully among all that white; for even the sky outside the narrow window was pale and colorless, while a veil of haze shrouded all prior memory and clarity of thought.

He overheard the doctor tell his Pa that "she was at death's door," but he didn't really understand what that meant so he sat in the portal guarding the room like a faithful watch dog. Occasionally when no one was looking and his whereabouts were not in question, he would hold on to her limp hand and squeeze it tightly between his small palms. Then he would balance on tiptoe, lean forward, and stare at her motionless face, waiting patiently for her to awaken.

Sometimes he would play a game with himself. First he would think of a number, then close his eyes and slowly count upward until he reached his number, whereupon he would open his eyes to find her gazing back and she'd laugh out loud, "Now, what are you doing, my sweet little boy?" But this game only proved to be a child's dream that he could win only in his mind.

One day the little boy had a most terrible scare. He couldn't remember if her eyes were blue or green, and he waited patiently by her bedside for her to awaken, yet she never did reveal them to him ever again.

———

It was a yellow sun-washed morning in August, a time when great blocks of ice arrive like a welcomed summer guest and restless voices float through the windows sharing exploits and troubles and domestic quarrels over kitchen tables. Judging by the start of this day it had started forth on an aimless course until there sounded the harsh rapping on the door like a woodpecker's drumming except it was louder and the fervent sound seemed to be so much more impatient.

"When Pa opened it a pair of sweaty men and a fancy lady started talkin' real fast. They told him that it was best if he were to give me up to another family on account that some other folks could care for me the right way. Pa warned them three to keep away, and he tried to stop them two from comin' round and pesterin' us. But it didn't help cause next mornin' they came back with a policeman and a stack of papers for Pa. It was the fancy lady who pushed her way in, grabbed me up, and carried me down the stairs. Pa was fightin' and yellin' that they had no right to take me! I was screamin' and kickin' with all my might to get free! But next thing I know, I was starin' out the window of a big train, sharin' a brown leather seat with another boy.

The train was a ramshackle relic, shakin' like a tired old man, and it smelled sour like day-old milk. I remember there were babies wailin' and lots of kids cryin' too. It took plenty of days, but when we finally pulled into the station the train made a loud cracklin' noise as if it were spitting fire. We had been cleaned up with brown soap and a scrubbin' brush before the trip so I felt like a shiny penny. They marched us off the train and onto the platform. It was pretty cold and the wind was kickin' up, so we huddled together like a bundle of cats to keep warm. But it wasn't long before they lined us up again, and we carried our bags to a big tent filled with chairs, one behind the other. Everybody got to sit on their own. At first I thought we were gonna see a show. But after a spell grown people started walkin' around. Some ladies were smilin' and some just shook their heads. Others came up to talk to us. A few of the children looked real scared 'cause they didn't speak English so they couldn't answer when they were asked a question. Then there were the men that glared at us with beady fox eyes and round powdered faces. Folks from the train brought out important lookin' papers and started writin'. When they were done I was pulled away from the rest, picked up, and put in the back of a dusty wagon. I heard the man who was drivin' them two horses say, "Gid'up," and we trotted away. I watched them kids by the train til my eyes burned from starin' so hard, and soon they were too small to see. But I never did cry; I was all cried out."

———

Randle and Betty Forester purchased their land from Joshua Coiner, who had procured his real estate during the 1820s Missouri land patent deals. However two years prior, he belonged to a different class of people, serving as headmaster of an exclusive private academy. Now, it just so happened that the son of a senior Senator in Congress was in attendance at this very school, but unfortunately for the Senator, while other students were positively drafting their futures, his young son was not showing himself to be a very apt student; in fact one could say he was somewhat dull. In preference, he took to play rather than giving much attention to his teachers, whereupon Joshua Coiner had the foresight to take the boy under his wing and seized the opportunity with a vengeance. As several months passed, he soon found that with the healing influence of a strict hand, tempered by the addition of individual direction, the boy was capable of passing his classes and would move up to the next level with the rest of his classmates. In exchange for "tutoring" his son, the grateful Senator provided Joshua with a few "inside" tips about government land that was selling cheaply. With his newfound connection, the

headmaster was able to acquire 160 acres from the Missouri government for $1.25 an acre. Upon purchase, he exchanged his notice of
retirement for the start of a new life and headed into the rugged
existence of homesteading.

However, not long after his move, Joshua Coiner soon realized
that he really knew nothing of rural life and was more a scholar
than a farmer. The land he had purchased was pocked with scores
of tree stumps and the soil was far more stubborn than enterpris-
ing. After several failed attempts at growing corn, he had the land
resurveyed, resold parcels, and returned back to St. Louis in his old
post as headmaster. "These hands of mine were bred to write and
not accustomed to plowing the tough soil," he wrote in a letter to
his lawyer. As a result, the Foresters found themselves on the receiving end of securing their parcels for $3.00 an acre, thus providing
Mr. Coiner with a nice profit.

———

Randle and Betty Forester always made due with "just enough" and
were content with the notion that they were self-sufficient. Both
having been raised in the Missouri territory, they were accustomed
to the old ways of the West. But times were quickly changing and
with the industrialization of farms Randle began to notice that his
neighbors were becoming more modern. When John Deere, back
in 1837, invented the steel plow, light enough to be pulled by horses
instead of oxen, the Foresters were not interested even though Don
Griffin insisted it was going to lessen his load. "You're just a dern
fool, Forester, if you think I'm using that 'ol plow that my daddy
left me!" he exclaimed trying to woo his stubborn friend. But it took
almost a dozen years after McCormick invented the mechanical
mower-reaper, a modern miracle that could yield the work of five
men, for the Foresters to finally buy a new steel plow, which in very
little time proved to be far better than iron. However, the approval
to venture into the industrial age was not the admission of prudence,
but rather the simple fact that their robust youthfulness was now

bowing to age. So, coupled with their new plow came another necessity, horses.

The idea of employing horses in the field was novel to the Foresters. Not knowing what to buy, they enlisted the advice of the livery's stable hand. "Get yourself two Belgian draft horses, they got the temperament of a gentle giant, but don't git fooled. They rather work than be idle." Such was the recommendation whereby an amicable transaction commenced. The Foresters petitioned Johnston Livery to find and negotiate the sale and within several months Delilah and Dandy were bought and delivered from a horse auction in Jefferson County.

The Forester barn was built from oak and ash timbers. Its joints and pegs interlocked like pieces of a jigsaw puzzle. Randle was mighty proud of this barn since all the lumber had been hand hewn. The east end was commissioned for storage of farm tools and silage while he kept the west end for his two milk cows.

"Can't have no farm without a sow and a couple of good milking cows," reminded Betty to her husband whenever he got an inkling to sell any of the animals. Consequently, in addition to cows, pigs were kept penned to sleep, but often set free to wallow about. A corncrib stood by the side of the barn for storage after harvest. Its narrow crate kept the shucks from molding. Behind the corncrib was a small blacksmith shop where Randle would sharpen the plow points and forge his tools. His anvil and bellows had been handed down to him from his father that had been handed down to him by his father before. The work was brutally hot; the fire with its lapping flames of the forge scorched the very breath taken in, and the soot from the embers would freckle his tanned face and arms.

There was an involuntary surrender to the pre-dawn bustle that roused the early risers to the rhythm of the farm. The rooster knew not of daybreak and his crow summoned the sun to rise. From the moment your ears sensed the high pitched solo of Henry, the rooster, so then would the farmer's day begin.

Betty Anne was a tall woman of 5 feet 8 inches. Her face was long and her skin tawny from the harshness of years working in the fields. And although she looked directly at you when she spoke, her eyes wore the expression of being in a faraway place. Her often severe and strict appearance might have been the result of wearing her hair tightly pulled back into a bun. She followed the philosophy that required little interpretation; want not more than you can fit in your cupboard. As a result she supplemented their income by sewing and mending clothes, which she sold and repaired for the townsfolk and neighbors. Because of her industrious disposition, she expected others to be the same. As time went on, the twenty acres of land proved to be difficult work for the aging couple who never had any children of their own. They were tired people, getting on in years, and decided that a way to alleviate some of the chores would be to adopt a child. This is how Alex came to live with them.

Although the child was only four when he arrived, Randle and Betty believed that they should never mention his unfortunate parents again. By withdrawing into a great silence, they acknowledged their new responsibility by immediately changing his last name. From that day forward he would be a Forester.

Betty and Randle selected a handsome little boy, with fair gray eyes, a tiny pinch of a nose, full round cheeks, and a crown of hair as yellow as a field of hay that curled about his head like wisps of dandelions. He was a small-framed child and came with few belongings being as that he owned very few possessions. His only valise was an over-sized carpetbag that in spite of being quite well-worn had been handily patched with quilting, swatches of brocade cloth, and assorted remnants of material that had availed themselves to the mender.

Alex proved to be quiet and mild mannered, more so than the Foresters imagined a little child would be. And since neither of them had any experience with children, they did not really know what to expect. Betty had fixed up their small storage room next to the kitchen for the boy to sleep in. It was a dark and windowless space, particularly somber and dull for the likes of a small child, but being clean and functional it had been deemed suitable. Randle constructed a wooden cot from scrap lumber, whereupon Betty stitched a mattress and stuffed it with hay and buffalo hair and laid it upon a "bedspring" made of hemp tightly strung into a platform of mesh. The cot was far from soft, simply serviceable, and would keep the boy up off the floor, away from bugs and vermin that may creep his way. A pair of wooden crates had been stacked one on top of the other providing ample space to store his few articles of clothing.

Like a rabbit entering its burrow, Alex warily paused to take note of his new quarters. First he set his sights on the keyhole with the intention of learning if the door could be locked from the outside. Secretly relieved at finding no key hanging from either side, he shifted his attention to the floor and then ventured up along the wall and across the beamed ceiling where a sliver of sunlight had found entrance from the outside. He followed the thin beam as it threaded its way down the opposite wall, across the floor, and into the opposite corner settling itself like a sunny nest. A low wooden stool with three uneven legs was sandwiched between the foot of the cot and flush against the wall, strategically balancing a metal wash basin that clumsily teetered on the seat. A fresh white linen cloth lay neatly folded over the rim stealthily linking the importance of cleanliness with daily chores.

Having convinced himself that it was safe to enter, Alex prodded his bag into the room and immediately squatted before the cot. Then with all his might, he leaned forward and mashed down upon the weathered carpetbag with his tiny palms positioned flat against its side; as he pushed, the weight of his body gradually compressed its meager contents until it slowly deflated becoming much flatter and thinner than it had started out as. The child offered no explanation, but with a concentrated look in his eye he finally pushed the squashed bag into the crawl space beneath the cot's low frame. A little tired, perhaps suffering from a bruised hand but no real ailment, he suddenly detected something of a predicament and promptly sat down on the hard earthen ground with the full intention of concealing his stowed belongings from sight.

Randle and Betty watched and made no attempt to question the child nor did they endeavor to take away his bag. The unruffled woman took her husband's rough hand in her equally rough hand and gave it a tight squeeze. Then she released it, advancing closer to Alex. "Now there boy, we ain't gonna take that bag from you. Why don't you come with me and git somethin' to eat?" She held out her hand to Alex as she spoke hoping he would accept her invitation by following her into the kitchen. "You must be real hungry after your long trip," Betty cooed trying out her new motherly voice. Randle leaned back against the doorframe with his arms folded across his chest allowing his wife to try to reason with his new son. But Alex just sat with his legs crossed and his head leaning forward, while his questioning eyes fixed intently upon this strange woman's face. And try as she might, Betty could not coax the little boy out of his tiny room.

On the first day in his new home, the child had found a hickory twig just about the length of a quill pen and spent his time sitting in front of the cot etching pictures in the dirt. He discovered that if he pushed hard enough he could replicate a man, a woman, a boy, and anything else he wanted to conjure up. The earthen floor made an excellent canvas. Yet, whenever Betty came back into the room, he would quickly skirt his hand over the ground erasing the dusty pictures; allowing the images to remain only in his mind. Then, when she turned her back to go out, he would begin again. Time and space began to evaporate as the day grew into evening and before the room was completely flooded by the blue-black ink of darkness, Alex pulled the blanket from off the cot and coiled it around him like a caterpillar encased in a cocoon. For several minutes he stared up into the beams hunting for any bits of light that might have found their way in through the timber cracks; minutes slid by as a sense of weariness took over his whole, his lids grew too heavy to lift, that magical quality of peace overcame him, and he finally fell into a thankful slumber.

For two days and nights Alex kept to himself and could not be cajoled to leave his tiny quarters. But finally his hunger won out over his timidity, and he found the courage to slip away in search of something to eat. Possessed with curiosity, he wandered into a windowless corridor that led him into a good-sized room where his craving of hunger would soon be appeased. He stood just inside the doorway and feasted his eyes on its entire splendor, for never before had he ever been in a room that was filled with such an assortment of exotic things and smells. There was a large table surrounded by walls of shelves, counters, and a cook's hearth. Under the table was a multicolored floor covering made from tightly wound scraps of cloth that were coiled around and around until they formed into a huge oval; an asymmetrical hodgepodge of calico, plaid, paisley, and gingham. He wondered if it was soft enough to sleep on and decided that it would be better suited in his small room rather than where it was now placed. Alex peered about and detected a large collection of ceramic crockery of all sizes and shapes lined up in an orderly manner from shortest to tallest, glass jars with lids, those without lids, and finally wooden boxes. Paddles and beaters to tenderize meat hung from heavy iron pothooks forged from wrought iron; in addition S-hooks and trammels were strategically positioned near the fire at altered heights. A round cast iron cooking kettle with squat stubby legs and a hooped bail stood aside the inlaid arched brick of the open hearth. And the shelves; they were arranged and stacked with a plethora of items that dazzled his young imagination. He eyed a red earthenware jar about 8 inches tall, pewter moulds to make compote from nougat, and another that resembled a knitted hat. There were dark wooden butter prints and shiny copper moulds, even an apple corer carved from bone. A wooden butter churn stood in the corner alongside of a small table covered with a half-dozen pancheons, which Betty employed for the setting aside of fresh milk while she waited for the cream to surface to the top. A brass skimmer, in need of polishing, rested wearily against the wall.

As for the aromas, depending upon where in the room one stood determined what scent wafted by. There was a blend of salted and cured pork, clover, cinnamon, yeast bread, and laundry bluing. Alex would later find out that the bluing would make his eyes sting for it was terribly caustic and emitted an ugly smell.

The boy circumnavigated the table where he found the door open to the outdoors and Betty sitting on the porch step with her back facing the house. She was leaning over her bent knees that had formed two bulbous mounds under her full skirt. Her dress and apron were pulled down like a loose sling so that the form beneath the material resembled the outline of a dromedary camel. She was surrounded by a disorderly stack of corn and piles of freshly ripped green leaves that had been removed from their husk and haplessly strewn about her bare feet like a discarded carcass. Strands of corn silk clung to her yellow gingham apron and the hem of her cotton dress. Alex shyly peeked out and watched as she shucked the corn. With gusto she stripped back the thick outer leaves, and when they were all removed she ran her fingers along the disrobed cob picking away any stubborn silk. Strands scattered everywhere. Timothy, the napping tomcat, was awakened by the noisy splitting of cornhusk, and sent an irritated glare down from the rocking chair that he had adopted as his own. Raising his lazy head, he surveyed with one eye open and searched for the source of the noise without making any effort to move any more of his body parts than necessary. However, when he found nothing of particular interest to a crusty old cat like himself, he stretched lazily, accentuating his prickly hunting claws, and then shifted his front feet under his large head, and promptly fell back to sleep.

With new interest Alex eased forward and meekly stood behind Betty. He caught a piece of floating corn silk and nervously wrapped it several times around his finger until he had made a glossy ring and then proceeded to unwrap it again.

Betty felt his presence and glanced round to speak to him. "So, boy; you hungry now?" she asked and scooped up a batch of the hardy maize and dropped the lot into the wooden bucket placed beside her. The pail was brimming full of cold well-water and with each careless toss a bit of water splashed over the sides. The small pool was immediately soaked up by the dry earth like puddles of raindrops during a sun shower. "You come and help me now husk this corn and then I'll fix you bread and butter. Got to earn your keep," she said as she continued to keep her attention on the chore before her.

With silent obedience, Alex picked up a coarse green husk and examined it in his small hands. He rotated it several times, turning it over as though he were searching for a loose thread. Methodically Betty tugged on the stiff green leaves and ripped off the protective layer. Bright yellow kernels revealed themselves like rows of crooked teeth. Alex mimicked her actions by peeling back the tip of his husk and used small forceful tugs. One by one, he tore away the fibrous leaves. Within a matter of seconds, he had successfully freed his first ear of corn from its earthly swaddle; however, if he were looking for motherly approval, he received only a simple nod and a finger pointing toward the bucket, intended as a reminder of where to drop his contribution to dinner. Good work was rewarded with more, and at the Forester's there was always plenty to be done.

Chapter 2

In the earliest hours of the morning, Betty would school Alex in the rudiments of reading and writing. She had borrowed a primer, slate, and slate pencils from a neighbor whose children had long grown up and moved away. Sitting side-by-side at the kitchen table, she would drill him with the utmost patience, and regardless of how meaningless the words were to the child, she was determined to teach him to read without stammering. The little boy listened to her with the absolute intention of pleasing, while bearing the insufferable monotony of the lessons without displaying boredom or ill humor. And without her knowledge, he put forth the greatest effort to comprehend much of what she and Randle were saying since their regional pronunciation was quite different from the one he had inherited. Yet it would soon come to pass that with each hour, each day, and each week that turned the page of the calendar, he adopted the speech and diction of his surroundings and without notice gradually left behind his former accent like the melting ice in the spring.

Since his arrival six months ago, Randle and Betty rarely heard the child speak freely. At first they feared that perhaps he had been born hard-of-hearing and incapable of producing much speech; however, they quickly dismissed that notion when at night they began to hear the uttering of faint murmurs like the whisper of an angel coming from his quarters. But to whom or what he addressed left them only to wonder, for although he could talk, he only responded when answering their questions, which always proved to be quite short and simple. Then, without anymore remarks he would lapse back into silence.

———

Alex managed to be a help to his new parents and despite his small size and young age, he never complained about the difficult work and completed his daily chores without interruption. Scarcely would the hands of the clock reach eight o'clock before he was dismissed from his lesson and surrendered to the fields. In the hours that slowly passed, he would cast aside any intention of frivolous play or distractions. On a farm there was always work to be done, and so in the mornings he could be found on hands and knees digging up potatoes or pulling weeds, toting water, feeding livestock, tending to the chickens, and gathering eggs. When the sun cut a path into its afternoon descent, it was time to clean the pen and to mix the slop for the sow and her piglets. But of all the jobs a boy of five could manage, his favorite was helping with the work horses, Delilah and Dandy. Next to these large and muscular chestnut beauties, he was but a tiny imp however; he never feared their superior size for he only felt their gentleness.

At the end of each workday, Alex would help lay down a clean bed of straw in their stalls right before Randle would lead Delilah and Dandy back into the barn. With a spirit of adoration, Alex would watch and admire these hard workers as they swat fat blue bottle flies with their long flaxen tails or rippled their muscles while Randle currycombed their tired limbs. Then when Randle was finished, Alex would stay behind, treating both horses to bits of apple or carrots that he had picked out from the hog slop and hid in his pockets. Yet, what the two adults did not know was that when he was alone with Delilah and Dandy, the little boy would freely speak and in his meek and hushed tone he would narrate to them all his secret thoughts. He found the two great beasts to be excellent listeners and trusted that they would never reveal to anyone what he said. Gently, he would rub his small hand across their velvet noses feeling the hot air released with each exhaled breath. "Don't tell a single person, Delilah," he would whisper as he rested his cheek against the large mare. "You, me, and Dandy are family. There's nobody else." Both horses would make a snorting reply and shake their great heads as if they could each understand; and he had great faith that they understood everything he confessed.

The month of October was harsh, and its sharp gusts of wind bit faces and boxed ears unless hat brims and flaps were pushed down over ear lobes and woolen scarves were wrapped around noses and mouths.

"Alex, where are you boy?" cried Betty as she hurried across the barnyard. Her cotton frock, too light and flimsy for this brisk autumn day, blew up around her knees as she scurried, and except for a grey knit shawl draped across her broad shoulders, she was not suitably dressed to protect herself from this unusually cold weather. She cupped her hands closely together so as not to reveal its contents or drop what was obscured between them. "Alex, come along boy, got somethin' to show ya!" She shouted again but more sharply and this time her remarks pierced the wind like a thorny briar.

Delilah and Dandy pinned their ears back when her shrill call made its way across the yard and into the stalls. "Don't forget what I told you," Alex reminded Delilah and with a tender hug he nestled his cheek against the mare's warm nose. "I've got to go!" he whispered and releasing his grip he darted away from the stalls towards the impatient woman. "I'm in here!" he shouted, "comin'!"

Betty turned to catch sight of the small child heading round the corner at full speed. Clumps of dry dirt and broken sticks of straw kicked up behind him as he scampered in the direction of her summons. "Now what were you doin' in there?" she demanded and tossed her head in the direction of the barn. "I was lookin' all over for ya!" Her brow was furrowed and the sour look of displeasure was quite clear as she tapped her large foot like an impatient hare. However, as much as he wished to answer, the poor child was unable to speak for the agitation in her voice combined with the haste upon which he ran in hopes of pacifying her irritated tone had caused him to become quite winded and out-of-breath; and when he opened his mouth to speak only ragged spurts of air like steam from a boiling kettle escaped from his mouth as rapidly as his breath was drawn in and out; so he simply shrugged his shoulders as if to say, "Nothing!" However, by now the woman was paying little attention to his physical state and did not wait nor seem to care for his explanation. Instead, she knelt down and held her clasped hands close to her chest as though protecting whatever it was she was hiding. "Got somethin' that you're gonna like to see!" she said in a gentle tone that seemed to have come from a different personality.

Without hesitation, Alex kneeled down too. All timidity towards the woman had momentarily disappeared. The blustery wind had untamed Betty's neat bun and several strands of long brown hair had tumbled down upon her shoulders and with each heavy breath of wind another thin strand would fall. "See here?" she asked the child. She stretched her arms out and slowly as her hands began to unfold Alex could hear the faint cry of several weak chirps. "Come, put your hands out, Alex," she commanded. He now sat pitched back on his knees with his feet dug into the earth to keep his balance. He cupped his small cold fingers together and with the utmost care Betty deposited a downy soft chick into his palms.

Alex bent his head forward to get a better look and immediately closed his hands together to keep the precious cargo from falling. At first it seemed to him that the chick was not moving, but in a matter of seconds he could feel it try to release itself from his grip, wriggling its frail body by twisting and squirming. Suddenly, it let out a rather sorry chirp.

"Careful now, you don't want to squeeze it too hard," said Betty as she took hold of his hands and gently pried them open a small bit. "Got to give it a little air, don't want to smother it."

Alex looked up at her and then back down at the chick; his eyes were smiling but his mouth remained in its usual stoic expression. He could see between the slots in his fingers the damp fledgling sparsely covered in brown and yellow down.

"This little chick is from that fat brown hen, but she don't seem to be takin' to it so it's gonna be your job to be sure it gits enough scraps. Even though it hatched just a short time ago, it can walk and eat by itself. It's a tiny one." Alex looked innocently at the woman. She repeated, "This here little chick is gonna be your responsibility, make sure it don't get picked on. Think you can do that, Alex?" Betty glared at him, questioning his countenance. Then, standing up and dusting the earth off her tired knees, she readjusted her shawl to keep it from falling off her left shoulder. She grabbed the two ends together with her hand and pulled the cloth closer to her body trying to keep the cold out, but what little warmth she felt, it was not enough to prevent an exhausted shiver.

Alex looked up at her long stern face. There was earnestness in his eyes that she had never noticed before. The boy pursed his lips together as though he may have had something to say but wished to keep words from creeping out of his lips. Then, he looked away and lowered his eyes over his tiny bundle of responsibility. The chick now felt very moist in his sweaty palms, and he wished he could open his hands and dry them on his pant legs, but he dared not allow himself this privilege for he feared that if he loosened his hold the tiny fledging might tumble out of his little nest.

"Go along now, you need to git this little fellah back to the brooder," advised Betty, and with a slight coax she leaned over and gave Alex a nudge with her hand. "It's time to see if it will eat."

Alex turned his eyes up at the stony faced woman he never called mother and nodded affirmatively. He put his cupped hands up to his ear and listened to the chirping complaints between his fingers. Betty regarded Alex for a few seconds, and then pulling her shawl even tighter around her she started back to the house leaving Alex to his job as caretaker.

Alex cracked his fingers opened and gently showered his warm breath upon the tiny captive. "Don't worry little chicken," he said gallantly. "I'll take good care of you." And with full allegiance to his charge, Alex escorted the little bird away towards the barn.

Chapter 3

The mother hen was roosting aloft on one of the lower rafters. She was the largest brown hen in the barnyard and easily identified not only by her stout appearance, but by her crown, a rich crimson comb, and her pale peach wattle. Although she alluded to be resting, she was actually keeping an eye on everything below her. Alex folded himself over the wooden rails and set the chick into an apple crate that had been set aside as a brood. He then sat cross-legged with his head framed between the rails and watched as the chick unfurled its wings and began to take a few ungainly steps. It stopped, pecked at the straw that was covering the bottom of the crate, and fell among the rest of its brothers and sisters that were huddled together like a yellow pile of fluff to keep warm. Their downy feathers fluttered up and down in unison with each breath much like dried dandelions quivering in a gentle breeze. Alex did not notice the plump bird sitting directly overhead for he was mesmerized by the tiny chicks, but the ornery hen was very aware of her surroundings; and, it was only a few minutes after Alex had placed the little chick into the crate when a piercing cry that sounded almost human-like emanated from above. Without warning the fat hen sprang off the beam making her intentions quite apparent, for as she descended she screeched and squawked; flapping and fluttering her short wings with such vigor and ferocity that it appeared as though a torn feather pillow was tumbling to the ground with its contents scattering like autumn leaves! And in spite of the belief that hens are not the best of flyers, she landed directly and squarely next to her pile of chicks. At once she began to shoo her clutch into the opposite corner from where they were resting, blocking her favored children with her corpulent body from the intruder. With its animal instinct the chick tried to follow the brood and stumbled behind, only to find that its presence was not wanted. With deliberate provocation the mother turned promptly toward its undesirable offspring and began to peck fervently as though she were trying to rid it forever from the rest. She was a hammer, her head raised and lowered over the little chick like a walnut that needs to be cracked.

"No, no," cried Alex shivering as he realized the terror that was about to be unleashed. Pulling himself over the wooden divide, he jumped between the chick and the angry mother. But to his surprise the hostility was now no longer addressed towards the baby but had been redirected towards him. Astonishingly the irritated hen flew upward and with outstretched wings she batted and swatted, she squawked and complained; for she was determined to prove to Alex that he was no match for her. Horror-struck by the hen's offensive moves, the frightened boy raised his arm to protect himself and turned his face away from the angry beak. He possessed only one thought whereupon he scooped up the tiny chick with his free hand and fled across of the barn with the angry mother hen still ranting and hopping up and down.

Now it just so happened that during the loud commotion of his ill-natured mate, the rooster was comfortably perched on a low rail and felt no reason to either move nor interfere since it was not uncommon for the hens and pullets to get into a spat. Henry was an old timer, a buff colored Leghorn with a single rose comb, which he wore high like a Sultan's fez. He was the oldest member of the barnyard and had earned the respect and fear of all the other animals.

For the moment, the brown hen had grown tired and disheveled for she had lost many of her feathers, which only added to her tousled appearance. But still having not satisfied her restless discord, she was continuing to feel very discontented and persisted to stomp about the barnyard; when suddenly she emancipated a repertoire of disharmony that was so loud and piercing that she finally gained the attention of Henry. However, it may not have been the attention she expected, for at once he expelled a sensationally loud and royal crow that frightened the fat hen so vehemently that she flew back to her roost for the duration of the afternoon. As for Henry, he could finally get back to his rest.

———

Tears were streaming down Alex's flushed face and although it was cold in the barn, beads of sweat were dripping down his temples and small grains of dirt stuck to his cheeks and gathered in the creases of his neck. He wiped his face with the sleeve of his jacket smearing the dirt even more across his forehead. He peered upon the limp little bird he was guarding in his palm; it lay so silently still and help-less. Frightened that maybe he had squeezed it too hard during the rescue, the worried boy placed it back down on the ground. At first he tried to set the chick up on its spindly legs, but all it would do was collapse like a rag doll. Alex leaned over and watched it for several moments, which held the full bearings of turning into a disastrous outcome. Bending down closer, he suddenly thought he saw a tiny bit of motion. Sure enough the round belly of the tiny bird was stirring in and out; it was making all attempts to regain its breath-ing. Alex continued to watch when finally, unprovoked, the little ball of fluff stood itself up and began to peck at the ground searching for grubs, seeds, anything to eat. Such a transformation of sadness to happiness could not have been delivered more quickly! Playfully, Alex scooped the little bird up and cradled it in the curved crook of his arm. "Nothins' gonna hurt you no more," he promised the tiny bird. At once he scrambled to his feet and began to search about the barn for a safe dwelling to rest the tiny creature in; all the while keep-ing an eye on the ornery brown hen that had returned to its roost and, quite exhausted, had fallen asleep.

There was now a great necessity to hurry, for the chick was appar-ently quite hungry, and as it began to peck at his arm the incentive to locate a suitable shelter had amplified. Alex followed his intuition and headed for an unused corner of the stable where he remembered seeing an old and tattered saddle blanket. He approached it cautiously as though it was a sleeping snake, and then with his free hand yanked it off the ground. Dust flew from the tight weave as he tugged it up and away from its resting place of so many years. He winced to keep from getting dirt in his eyes, and turned his head to the side as a billow of fine dust particles sprinkled down upon him with the vengeance of a sandstorm. Buried beneath the blanket was a perfectly intact crate; and although it had originally been used as a storage bin for glass jelly jars, it would make a suitable corral for the slats had been nailed tightly together and the sides were high enough to keep the fledgling from climbing out. Alex placed the bird in its new home and then sprinkled the bottom with broken straw. Pleased with his excellent find, he picked up the crate and carried it to a more secure location; all the while the tiny bird stared back up at him as if to say, "Thank you!"

Setting the box down beside the stall he turned to its occupants and exclaimed, "Now, you keep that mean momma bird from peckin' this baby. I'll be right back!" When Delilah heard the soft voice of Alex, she twisted her head to see him, and swooshed her tail as though to reply, "Don't worry."

———

Alex hastened his way up the front porch, but stopped before reaching for the door. He stomped his feet with the good intentions of shaking free most of the dirt from his shoes, and briskly brushed himself off with the palms of his small hands. When satisfied that he was as clean as he could get without using water, he took a deep breath, put his ear to the door, and listened. The only sounds he could hear were his own breathing and an elusive quail peeping in the elder bush. Alex lowered the latch with the utmost care, slowly, gently; he pulled down, wincing with each tiny creak. Hoping that his entry would remain unnoticed, he continued to gently nudge the door open. But in spite of his precautions, the rusty hinges that were in need of oil suddenly cried out as if in pain.

"That you, boy?" called out Betty. Wiping her hands on her apron, she dismissed herself from the warm kitchen at the very same moment that Alex, who thought perhaps the coast was clear, had successfully edged the door shut behind him. But, as he veered round, he was startled by the face-to-face encounter of a rather somber countenance he had hoped to avoid. Betty stood stalwartly, and with an increased glow of disapproval, she held Alex fast with her eyes. "Now looky here, what in the world?" Her large hands clenched and fisted now rested heavily upon her hips as she examined him from head to foot. "You look like you've been wrestlin' one of them turkeys out in the barnyard," she exclaimed with a laugh and straightaway plucked several tawny feathers out of his tousled hair. She dangled the ruffled plumes by their bony quills and waved them up and down before the boy like a fan.

"That brown hen, she's mean," Alex grumbled and brushed his hair back with his dirty hands.

"Yep, that's what I was afraid of. She's not takin' to that new little chick, but it sure looks like she tried to take it out on you," added Betty with a smidgen of understanding in her voice. She ran her fingers up along the vane to the tip of the feather and smoothed out the ruffled barbs.

"I'm making a new brood and need to find something to keep water in. I put the chick in a crate with straw and Delilah is takin' care of her."

"Good thinkin'," agreed Betty in a voice that was trying so hard to sound motherly. "So, what else do you think you need?"

Alex shrugged his shoulders with a gesture of uncertainty. Betty leaned over and patted the child on his head, and then turning her interest back to her chores, ushered him towards the kitchen where she knew the kettle pot would soon be bubbling with needed attention. "Here, let me help you take off your jacket," she said as she yanked his sleeve and then tugged the opposite one freeing his arm from the tight fit. She hung the jacket up on a low nail beside the cupboard. "I want you to go on and wash up; you can better think about what you'll need after yer clean," she said pointing to the basin filled with cold water. Alex nodded and began to roll up his shirtsleeves. He had already noted that the tall woman had exchanged her concern for him to something else that was drawing her attention. The kettle was now making a fierce clamor and the bubbling of hot liquid spit and hissed angrily. Betty dropped the cast iron lid down closing up the opening as if sealing shut a volcano before an eruption. Then, she slid the lid aside so that some of the steam was released; upward it twirled towards the ceiling and slowly fell, hanging like a low cloud on a rainy day. The woman wiped her face with the hem of her apron as drops of perspiration dotted her tan forehead. She turned from the kettle towards Alex and shook the wooden paddle she was holding as if striking the air with a firm warning. "Now don't you get too attached to that little chick, I don't want you to name it 'cause we don't want to eat no pets," she instructed and walked back outside to cool off.

Alex knew exactly what she meant and made it a point of never becoming too attached to any of the livestock. Except for Delilah and Dandy, he rarely spoke to or tried to make friends with any of the animals. The hogs and their piglets were not finicky eaters and as they became adolescents they would consume almost anything fed to them; household scraps, plants, grains, berries, even fish. And as they began to age and grow fatter and plumper, they were destined to become Sunday night dinners, Monday morning sausages, and weekly side dishes. Alex never watched the butchering; it was bad enough that he knew in advance when its time on earth was to end. For a few weeks before the butchering, Randle would feed the unsuspecting hog extra corn and fermented mash, which was supposed to add flavor to the slaughtered victim. The extra weight also made it easier to catch. Alex wondered if maybe the pig had thought he was being given something extra to eat because it was special or because it had been a very good hog. Sadly, he felt that the poor animal was being unfairly tricked to eat more than its usual ration.

Alex rummaged about the kitchen looking for something that he could use as a container. It could not be too tall or too fragile; it had to be shallow enough so a tiny beak might retrieve water from it. The Forester kitchen was the focal room of the house; a place where all the important decisions were made. At night when Betty and Randle thought he was asleep, Alex could hear the two talking in hushed voices or with quick grumbles that stirred and unsettled the air. Deeds, expenses, and "that darn bank" vexed them the most. He could hear Betty slide her chair away from the split-log table Randle had made for her from his wife's explicit specifications. Then, she'd open the door and step out into the pitch black night to fetch water so she might put coffee on the stove. Other times he could hear her dipping candle wax way past midnight The smell of the paraffin would waft through the rafters into his storage room, choking the air and making it so thick to breathe that he would become fearful the odor would harden in his nostrils and smother him as he slept.

Like a hungry beggar, Alex hunted about the shelves and even on the floor until he happened upon a jar lid lying alongside of the broom. It appeared as though it had been swept up and forgotten. Alex eyed the lid as if it were a piece of lost gold from a treasure chest. He brushed it off on his pant leg and examined it carefully, turning it over several times in his hand. "Can I have this?" he asked Betty who had slipped back inside from shaking the dirt off his jacket. He handed her the lid and she exchanged it for his jacket. She turned it over in her hands.

"It's no good, see this dent?" she remarked pointing to a small depression. "You can have it," and she tossed it back to him. "Make sure you check the hens for eggs when you go back to your chores, and put on your jacket, winds pickin' up." Then she turned sullenly and walked back to refuel the hearth.

Chapter 4

With the cleverness of a tightrope walker, Alex deftly balanced the water-filled lid all the way from the hogs' watering trough across the barnyard back to the stalls, where he found his tiny charge happily marching about its confinement as boldly as a miniature soldier and pecking curiously at the crannies and crevices of its enclosure. He gingerly set the lid down into the crate, making the most considerable effort not to spill a single drop of the precious liquid. However, the little bird seemed to take no notice of the boy's effort for no sooner was it positioned, did the little creature defiantly hop directly into the water as if it were meant for swimming.

Poor Alex, having never been in charge of a new chicken swooped the bird up and promptly began to dry its wet fluff with his own shirttail. Then, when he felt it was sufficiently dry, he placed it back into the crate. Again, the bird swiftly ran into the water and began to gambol and peck about, but this time with glorious vigor. Subsequently, as if mocking his keeper, the chick mechanically halted, turned around in the opposite direction, and promptly stomped about its tiny tin pool splashing happily. It toddled impishly, bobbing its head up and down, while poking enthusiastically at the water. Alex wondered if perhaps this was some sort of baby bird game, for being soaked did not seem to trouble the little chick. Alex thought for a moment and then dug his hand into his pocket and picked a few crumbs of bread that had settled into the corners of the material. After breakfast he would often stuff his pockets with pieces of bread to save for later in the day. With a few sprinkles he scattered the hard remains into the crate and only had to wait a few moments for a sudden shifting of scenes to take place; for when the tiny chick caught sight of the morsels of bread, it scampered out of the water greedily scavenging at its meal.

Seriousness faded from his face as a sudden burst of happiness overcame him; a feeling that he rarely seemed to display. And the longer he watched the more he found himself smiling and laughing at the bird's innocent and ungainly antics. The young custodian leaned over the crate and allowed himself to freely be entertained. But, as the day began to grow, so would the afternoon soon mesh into evening, and he knew that he needed to finish his last chore. "I got to git to work. You stay put and I'll be round with feed later," he whispered. And then ever so gently, he stroked the little bird with the very tip of his index finger. However, the chick was too busy searching for crumbs between the shafts of straw to acknowledge.

———

The wind moaned as the sky shifted from pale blue to ashen gray and darkness blanketed the spirit of the barn. Alex looked out from the inside; Betty had lit the first evening lantern. A wavering beam of light projected through the glass chimney and pierced the darkening sky like a full moon. Alex rooted around the customary nesting places searching for eggs to place into his basket. His thoughts were drawn away from his chore as he envisioned the fat brown hen. He squeezed his eyes shut and shook his head as if to rid the very image out of his brain. Fortunately, she was perched higher in the rafters than usual and wasn't in her customary nesting spot.

"Come on in now, Alex," remarked a tired voice. The weary tone belonged to Randle entering the barn from a day out in the field. Methodically, as he had done every evening for so many years, he leaned his pitchfork in the corner, tongs up and rested it alongside of the hoes and spades. "I believe we're in fer some cold weather, sky looks angry."

Alex crooked his neck back and peered up at Randle's face; without speaking he nodded affirmatively and followed Randle back toward the farmhouse carrying his basket with four newly lain brown eggs.

Randle was a long, lean man who kept himself and his farm in an orderly manner. He arranged his tools like he arranged his life; everything had its place and its reasons. Otherwise, it wasn't necessary, and he didn't need it. With this philosophy, he and Betty had been able to manage through tough financial times and even harsher winters. Randle did not take to politics however; he was seen as a fair man who believed in the good of the country and the state he lived in. As the head of his house, he treated his wife fairly and would never impose any rules upon or over her, even if it was his lawful right. When he was younger, he wore his hair cropped short and never sported a beard. But now his hair had grown sparse with age, and the wispy black strands were laced with gray. In the summer his skin turned brown like sienna, and around his eyes tiny spokes like the wheels of a wagon were etched into his skin from years of working in the sun. But these lines defined the man he was, and as a farmer he wore them like an insignia of membership in a club. In the winter he lost his cinnamon color, but his skin tone remained tough and leathery. "You can trust a man who has coarse skin," he would tell Alex. "For a man who is smooth doesn't really understand all his fellow men."

———

The sun set early in the October sky and as the orange glow dipped between the hilltops supper was ready when Randle came in from the fields. His place was at the head, while Betty and Alex sat opposite one another on either side of the table. Since Alex was of small stature, Betty placed a wooden box across the bench for him to sit on so he could better reach the table.

"Betty told me that the brown hen gave you a piece of her mind today," Randle remarked, heaping several boiled potatoes on his own plate and dropping a piping hot potato on Alex's plate.

"Yes, Sir," he replied meekly; and though he was listening his eyes followed the pale skinned spud as it slipped across his plate.

"She can be mean and feisty, but a good layen' hen, otherwise she just might be on my dinner plate right now. Ain't that so, Betty?" Randle added, looking up at his wife.

"Yep, she sure is plump, but as long as she does her job, we'll keep her out of the stew kettle." Betty smiled and dropped a piece of boiled turnip on Alex's plate. It rolled alongside of the potato like a steaming billiard ball.

Alex looked down at his food, but suddenly, even though he was famished, all he could make out on his plate was the outline of a brown hen set before him; the very thought of eating even that mean old bird made his stomach sour.

"Eat up, ya worked hard today; got to git your strength up for tomorrow," remarked Randle. He eyed the boy and noted that he was quietly rolling the steaming potato around his plate with a fork. Hoping to cajole the reluctant eater, the hungry man stuck out his hand that resembled a huge crooked hook. Between his thumb and fingers he offered a piece of thickly sliced bread.

Alex's senses suddenly leaped into attentiveness like a cat in anticipation of a rat. He knew that if he did not eat he would certainly go hungry until the next day. "And, after all," he thought, "he wasn't eating the fat brown hen; why she was roosting somewhere and probably sound asleep." Putting his mind at ease, Alex leaned forward and reached across the table to retrieve the bread that was being offered.

A tired hush fell over the room. Suppertime was not just a time for nourishment, but also a break before the remaining chores had to be completed. Only an occasional clang of a platter being passed across the table, the slurping of soup, or the stir of restless feet shifting under the table interrupted their silence. On occasion Betty might push her chair away from her setting to get up and replenish a bowl or platter if it was emptied, but other than that the time spent eating remained somber and subdued. Each of the three persons reflected upon their day's work or pondered over which remaining chores needed to be completed before they could retire.

Alex's eyes flitted from face to face. Randle sat back in his chair and pulled a toothpick from his pocket. He massaged his gums with the pointed end and darted the tip in and out between each tooth. There was a large gap where two opposing back molars had rotted away, and he was careful not to poke the area that remained tender even after a year of having lost those teeth. Betty, who was clearing the dishes from the table, moved slowly and every now and again would sigh loudly and heavily. Both went about their business without even noticing that Alex was still at the table, and the more he waited the more he wished to finish his evening chores.

Darkness now blanketed the earth and he knew that only the moonlight would help him trace his steps to the barn. He sat patiently, but could hardly remain still much more because he noticed a prickly feeling in his foot; and the longer he sat, the more this uncomfortable sensation grew. He tried to ignore it, but what he hoped was just a passing feeling, he soon realized he could not suppress. Trying not to attract any attention, he began to lightly kick his foot against the bench rail, which only proved to be a futile attempt at shaking free the pins and needles' sensation from his foot.

"Bang, bang," the bench rattled. He shifted position and began to hit his foot against his other in hopes of muffling the sound, but it was too late for he was acknowledged by an irritated stare across the table.

"Alex, what are ya doin' rattlin' about on that bench?" questioned the annoyed woman. Betty still wasn't used to having someone else around the house besides Randle.

"My foot, it don't feel right. I think it's what you told me once before; it's gone to sleep," he muttered sheepishly.

She tried to ignite a more motherly and tender side, which did not come naturally, and suddenly realized that they had ignored the child for what must have been an interminable amount of time. "Come on down and let me see," she said, turning her chair away from the table. Obediently, he climbed down from his wooden perch and limped toward her. "Now, hold on to the table and lift your foot up," Betty suggested.

Following her directions, he balanced himself on one foot and allowed her to reach down and remove the shoe. As she pulled his foot free, he could feel his sock begin to slide forward and away from his heel. "Why, what's in here?" she asked quizzically and peered into the little shoe. Like a baby stork, Alex teetered on one foot and tugged at his sock just as Betty began to tilt his shoe and pour out onto the floor a pile of dirt. Alex lowered his stocking foot to the ground and quickly squatted down; for as the rubble dumped out before him, he had spotted something other than ordinary pebbles and grains of sand; something different that had tumbled into the mounting pile.

"Why, you must have brought in most of Jefferson County in your shoe," laughed Randle who had watched his wife deposit yard dirt from the boy's shoe.

But Alex was too busy excavating the tiny pile to hear the two adults chuckling in the foreground. Dirt stuck to his fingers and side of his palm as he swooshed the soil back and forth along the floor. He bent closely over the pile and picked through its contents as meticulously as a gold miner. He fingered the earth and rolled it between his fingers until he ferreted out a small smooth object of oblong shape. He flipped it over several times and wiped it clean against his pants. Then, satisfied with the results, he stood up and centered his find in the middle of his outstretched palm; which he promptly placed directly before Betty.

Chapter 5

The carefree listlessness of the English countryside had taken a sharp turn as the age known as the Industrial Revolution established its roots in Great Britain by awakening the grand country's potential as a manufacturing giant. Prior to this industrialized development, most all production was of goods assembled by hand. However, due to the invention of new technologies, such as the mechanical steam engine, changes were rapidly taking place. For Great Britain, having been blessed with natural resources such as coal and iron, it was soon recognized that these reserves were exactly what were needed to feed the voracious appetites of the manufacturing furnaces. As a result, fuel consumption grew; but those who were to extricate the ore from beneath the ground encountered problems. As time went on it became evident that steam engines embodied the very solution to the problem of water-filled mine shafts. Now they could be pumped free of water and pave the way for more mining. It was a bonanza for some well-connected entrepreneurs, for as the increase in the production of goods flourished, the expansion of modern factories in the cities became a catalyst to employ more workers.

Consequently, the textile industry in London and Manchester was on the rise ever since the invention of the power loom. Those individuals who had only known a rural existence found that the factories' need for more workers would draw them out of their sleepy crossroads and villages and into the cities. On the other hand, what they did not bargain for was the dramatic change this would bring to their lives. For in spite of the manufacturing boon that served to make a few rich and corpulent, it did not take long for an ugly shadow to be cast upon anyone who found themselves entombed within its mills and factories. For as many traveled from hamlets and countryside to find jobs, the living quarters for working families of the mills were overcrowded, cramped, dingy, and unsanitary. It was not uncommon for several families to share only one or two rooms. Too often such squalid conditions lead to domestic quarrels, crime, and neglected children. Among other grim effects, workers living in these confined quarters were often afflicted with the deadly typhus disease and small pox.

———

Amanda Piccard prided herself on being a hard worker and as a reward for her tenacious efforts, a miserly portion of good fate was portioned out; she rapidly worked her way up from a thread picker to weaver on one of the mighty power textile looms in Manchester. A fair-haired young woman with great determination and gusto, she lived alone in a sparsely decorated room that was housed in the city's slum district. Rows and rows of sad houses were becoming part of the urban landscape. They were built without windows in the front and purposely devoid of any backyard, which greatly increased the amount of dwellings that their owners could profit from. Due to their constricted design, they had acquired the infamous name of "back to backs".

Amanda worked half of her ten hour shift the day she gave birth to her only son. It was a cold October day, and she had already resigned herself the morning of the 10th that she could not possibly work on past noon. Her labor pains had already begun hours before her shift at the mill, and it was only a matter of time before her supervisor had no choice but to find a replacement for her on the loom and to send her back home.

On this hastened exile the wind held fast against her back, pushing the young woman forward along the broken sidewalks, urging her towards her quarters. Shifting uneasily, the frigid air bristled and snapped like a dog baring its teeth, and she grasped her arms tightly together to protect herself from the mighty gusts that tore at her shawl and whipped her stockings. Amanda grasped her wrap, pulling it up around her neck and mouth, anything to keep from losing warmth and dignity. Her eyes began to tear, and she was not entirely sure if the drops falling down her cheeks were because of the wind in her eyes or the pain she now bore. She quickened her pace and bowed her head beneath the shawl, casting a dark figureless shadow that barely resembled a woman's form. Upon finally reaching home, she signaled her elderly neighbor with three strong blows on the door, ensuring that help would be imminent. Mrs. McGlaugland was a fixture in the district. Her years of practical experience granted to her the unofficial standing as the best locale midwife. Although aged only by her gray hairs and hardened features, she remained youthfully robust in stature. She was comfortable with the notion that babies were content to stay put until she had fetched water and linen. After that, when she was ready, they could make their entrance into the world.

The elder midwife went about her routine as she had done so many times before. She gripped the taut rope handle of her tin bucket and walked calmly outdoors towards the community water pump. It was the only source of water for all the neighbors and the only fresh supply.

Amanda lay upon the narrow cot with her knees slightly bent. She positioned herself on her right side and tried to keep her pain at bay by tightly folding her arms around her enormous abdomen. The blanket had been kicked to the foot of the bed, exposing the clean muslin sheets, and the door had been deliberately left unlocked and ajar, acceding to the midwife's arrival. Cued to every noise around her, even the faintest of sounds resonated up through her body and thumped wildly in her temples. With each grind of the pump handle moving up and down, with every stream of water that was dumping into the bucket; the mother-to-be felt that she was getting closer to the birth. The rusty pump crank squealed and complained, and she grit her teeth as she waited for the older woman to return.

Narrow and bleak streets surrounded the "back to backs" and very little sunlight could penetrate the billows of grey coal clouds that hovered above. Behind the doors and beneath leaky roofs was an unwritten belief prescribed to by all who lived in these crowded and desperate conditions. All understood that the birth of a child was only successful with the help of earnest prayers, a seasoned midwife, and a healthy strong mother; only these three things could bring the new life into the world. Amanda retained all three.

Two hours after arriving home, her son was born in spite of the odds that the poverty of Manchester offered his mother. The midwife ferreted about the room and found some newspaper, which she blanketed around the newborn so as to insulate him from the damp cold English air. And as Amanda nestled her tiny treasure in her arms, she looked down upon her son and whispered to him his name, William.

———

Like baby Moses, baby William was cradled in a reed basket and lay at the feet of his mother as she worked the looms. Life for the young boy began in misery, spending dismal days in the gloomy and noisy factory, often in periods of isolation whereby he was placed in a penned area away from the looms. When he grew old enough, he earned his keep as the mill's scavenge by crawling about the factory floor searching beneath the machines to salvage any pieces of cloth that could be reused. The whirl of the motors and the deafening sound was frightening at first. However, as a young worker he learned to keep steady, and the hours spent watching others soon taught him to keep his fingers clear; for the loss of a limb was far more frightening than the noise itself.

Life outside the city of Manchester was unknown to William; his only familiarity with the outdoors was smoke blanketed streets and open drainage ditches. It was a breeding ground for poverty, crime, and disease, and had all the makings to become a curse upon the boy. Amanda forbade her son to leave their home alone in hopes of preventing him from befriending street-wise urchins whose lives were so desperate that they became pick-pockets or thieves. Horror was lurking in all corners and alleyways, and she constantly feared that if life as a mill worker did not destroy him, there was always the dreaded fear of an outbreak of small pox in the city that would surely bring about his demise. Even as William got older, the young mother continued to be haunted by her own fretful apprehensions; and as the love for the child grew she was ever more determined to seek out an escape for her son, even if this meant they would have to be separated.

So, when a flyer was posted recruiting male workers to move away from the cities and out to the farms of rural England, Amanda entrusted her son, who was now sixteen, to the butcher, Mr. Rumble. You see, it just so happened that as a result of the industrialization in the cities, Mr. Rumble had the foresight to take advantage of the situation, and knowing that farms were always looking for strong cheap laborers (and that he would be finely rewarded for each young worker he placed) he became the middleman for those boys looking for an honest way out of the mills and factories. Among a myriad of uneasiness, but well within the boundaries of motherly love, Amanda gave her son, Will, as he was now called, over to Mr. Rumble, knowing that she was trading away his only source of family for a single life of great uncertainty.

———

Libby Dowling had been raised on a dairy farm with her father, mother, and dear Grandmother Analiese, the farm's primary mortgage holder. Several years after the older woman's husband had died from typhoid; she sold off a few parcels of the precious land and paid off all bank debts. The tracts were considered prime pieces of real estate and unmistakably their sale allowed the family to continue living a reasonably comfortable lifestyle.

Libby could be labeled by most as a lucky child for those who loved and cared for her maintained the unconventional principal that she should expand her immediate horizons beyond that of the farm, whereupon her mother sent her to the local school regardless of her gender. It did not take the bright young girl long to learn to read and write as well as complete her studies at the top of her class after finishing the eighth grade. Her interests in learning and a desire to know more about the world followed her even after her schooling, so her parents decided to indulge upon her the rare luxury of buying and owning a great many books.

Libby was a quiet child, who in spite of adult attention, longed for youthful companionship. She secretly wished that she had a baby brother or sister; however, since her mother had lost two infants in childbirth, she dared not ever repeat her desires. Libby was regarded as small for her age and being rather delicate and petite in stature, if ever there was any malady or illness to contract, she sadly seemed to always succumb to its scourge. Subsequently, at the age of thirteen, she contracted scarlet fever. Her health rapidly declined, and she was summoned to her bed for several months. Devoted to the child, her grandmother remained vigil, staying by her bedside day and night during her convalescence. When the feeble child gained her strength and was able sit up, the kindly old woman spent her day teaching the child to cross-stitch. Finally, when Libby was well enough to leave her bed, it was deemed necessary for her mother to air out her room. The windows were cranked open to the outside, but the child's door remained closed from the rest of the house. All bedding, bedclothes, and books, anything Libby had been in contact with during her long illness, including her needlepoint, had to be destroyed.

Dried oak branches were placed crisscross in a heap upon the earth, far away from the lovely hazel tree, a favorite because of the nut it produced. This was the very tree from which Mother would pick the ripened seed kernels and remove their dark brown skin, roasting the nuts on the hearth or grinding them into a fine paste.

Her father, Mr. Dowling, extended a flaming torch and with his out-stretched arm, swooped over the top of the kindling and set the pile ablaze. Libby trembled as she watched and listened to the cracking of branches; dried twigs snapped and howled as they became consumed by the eager fire. As though stoking a furnace, Mrs. Dowling flung her daughter's possessions into the flames and immediately they were ferociously devoured by the hunger of the inferno. With each new item that was offered, the fire's rage grew, extending its flames upward. A tempered breeze blew charcoal grey smoke towards the heavens, and Libby lifted her eyes following the thick haze until it dissipated, blending into the cerulean sky until slowly the world around her was clear again. Her father had explained that burning her things was the only way to prevent the dreaded scarlet fever from spreading. So holding back her tears, she had nodded in agreement and bravely stood by the burning pit until all that remained was smoky ash. She tried to tell herself that they were only "things" but days later when she came upon bits of charred needle-point that had been blown up and away during the fire, a heartbreaking ache was rekindled once again in her heart.

———

Months after the great catastrophe, when the weather had grown warm, Libby delighted in sitting outdoors under the poplar tree where she would spend her hours either reading or sewing. During the spring and summer the old tree looked especially grand; her flattened leaves catching the first sunlight, casting a blonde shimmer upon her elegant canopy. And if the wind blew, she would toss her agile branches about as though sparring with the breeze. During the colder months, Libby was confined to the house where, like a sentry, she would watch the poplar disrobe its verdant green attire to sport a golden hue. And as the days grew shorter and colder, it seemed silly that this poplar wholly shed its cover, only to reveal her bare limbs and branches that soon would be dusted with snow as fine as confection.

To bide winter's time, Grandmother taught her granddaughter to weave and quilt. Libby was a disciplined student, and by the time she was seventeen had become as adept as her grandmother in the craft of quilting and creating intricately colorful patterns. Her hands were physically nimble and having slender fingers she was said to be a "natural".

Life on the farm was tempered with the ordinary, for living far from the city and several miles from the nearest hamlet, the young woman had few friends her own age and seldom did anyone ever visit. So when a horse-drawn buggy drove up the dirt road one autumn morning, Libby peered through the window like a curious canary peeking out of its cage.

———

Mr. Rumble was pulling back on the leather-worn reins of a rather weary looking mare and leaning forward as though he himself was going to topple upon the bedraggled beast. The stout man's awkward mannerisms revealed to any on-looker that this was not his usual mode of transportation. Likewise, the young man sitting next to him did not possess the demeanor of a local, but rather appeared considerably unsettled as he was holding on to his seat quite decisively, while keeping his foot firmly propped up against the dash rail with knees solidly locked.

"Hello," called Mr. Rumble as he collected himself by setting the reins down upon the lap of his passenger. He tilted his head like a dog as he listened for a reply, waited a few moments more and then tried again, this time with more vigor. "Anybody home?" he cried.

Libby's father had eyed the buggy riding up the dirt road and was making his way from the around the back of his house towards the front. He rambled slowly, but deliberately towards the waiting buckboard and wondered who and what had come onto his property.

"We don't get many travelers coming up our way," replied Mr. Dowling, now wiping his hands with a clean handkerchief, which he had pulled out of back pocket. "What can we do for you?" he asked, gently grabbing the bridle of the old mare and shooing a fly away from her eyes.

Mr. Rumble, trying to act as though he was very adept as a driver, grinned widely and, in a carefree manner, began to hop down from the buggy. However, not being accustomed to its height, he hooked his boot on the edge of the small step during his dismount, at which point the portly butcher found himself dangling by one foot and displaying a most ungraceful gesture, while simultaneously turning the color of a ripe tomato. Most fortuitously, he was able to latch on to the side of the buggy and catch his balance just in time to prevent a most embarrassing tumble.

Libby continued to spy out the window, capturing Mr. Rumble's impromptu egress. She held her hand to her mouth keeping herself from bursting aloud with laughter at the rather comical Mr. Rumble; and all the while wishing she could hear the conversation taking place. But all she could do was follow their gestures, as the butcher now appeared to find his land legs again and was once more fully in control of his own feet.

"This is fine looking buckboard," extended Mr. Dowling, now releasing his grip on the mare and running a smooth hand over the rail. "Hickory, isn't it?" Then answering his own question he added, "a fine flexible wood." The questioning Mr. Dowling returned his eyes towards the driver of the buggy, "You aren't from around here are you?"

"Actually, no, I am Jacob Rumble and this is young William Piccard," replied Mr. Rumble now pointing to the lad who was feeling quite out of place up on the seat of the buggy. "We are looking for the Hartford Farm; young Will is from Manchester and has relocated to the country to work as a farmhand. I do believe," continued Mr. Rumble fumbling with his hair, which had blown every-which-way during his trip, "I say," he restated, "I think we may have taken a wrong turn back a-ways."

"This is a lovely buggy," said Mr. Dowling ignoring the statement and now examining the cart more closely, "This wasn't made here, was it? Couldn't be from England." His matter-of-fact tone made him sound like an expert rather than an ordinary curiosity seeker.

"Oh, the buckboard, no, it was brought to London and transported to Manchester by an American for an exhibit. I suppose the owner decided not to take it back, and it landed with me. I am only borrowing it from a lawyer friend to take the young lad, William, here, to the Hartford Farm," he replied pointing up at the buggy seat. "I dare say, can you point us in the right direction, and we'll be off?" added Mr. Rumble hoping to divert the conversation away from his buckboard and back to his original concern.

Libby's eyes were fixed on the young man in the wagon. She was rather intrigued as to what he wanted as well as being hungry for news about any place other than this boring little hamlet. She spied upon the young stranger with an added interest; clearly he was not from around these parts for she would have seen him in town. Unwittingly, her eyes meet with Will's, who had at that very same moment turned towards the lovely delicate face staring out the window. Being rather shy, he quickly looked away and down at his feet, whereupon he noticed that his boots were particularity shabby and worn, and he tried to hide them out of sight by crossing them beneath the buck seat. But Libby, who was feeling bold, after all it was he who was in her territory, continued to stare. Will looked back up and again their eyes met, but this time he did not pull away, but was magically fixed upon her. "She is like a porcelain doll," he thought, "yes, a doll; for something so charming could not really be alive." He was enchanted and could not help but smile rather bashfully at Libby, who turned her head to the side and smiled back. She then touched the pane of glass with her graceful fingers as if she were stroking his face. Will meekly raised his hand back and waved to her.

Mr. Rumble, more carefully this time, climbed back up and took the reins from Will. The old mare however, had no intention of going anywhere until she was given a sharp slap on the back with the buggy whip and was persuaded to lumber onward.

Mr. Dowling lazily sauntered back towards the barn as soon as he saw the buggy head down the road to the neighboring Hartford Farm. Mr. Rumble began to mutter excessively, exonerating his earlier wrong turns by explaining how in these parts of England every road looks the same. As for Will, he listened to Mr. Rumble but heard nothing. He was still at the Dowling dairy and was quite thankful for Mr. Rumble's erroneous sense of direction

Chapter 6

Alex held the lantern straight out in front of him and fixed his eyes on a golden path of light that led him across towards the barn. He pushed his free hand into his pocket and fiddled about until he could feel the smooth object concealed in the fabric. His pace quickened as a desperate urge to share his treasure with Dandy and Delilah seemed more urgent. The night air snapped cold as he hurried along with his shoulders tightened and hunched against his neck. The raised jacket collar shielded the wind from blowing down his back, and he bowed his head into his chest, preventing the wind-tossed dirt from blowing into his eyes. The lantern swayed frivolously as he scurried quickly, while a flurry of Luna moths darted back and forth, zigzagging in and out of the glow as if keeping the boy company. He trampled over some overgrown weeds as he approached the far side of the barn and fingering the splintered wood, found his mark and pulled aside an unnailed board, swinging the base upwards; it swayed as though it were hanging on a hinge. The hole it produced made an entranceway big enough for Alex to squeeze through. Randle had said that he needed to nail shut the shifting board so that a clever fox could not gain access. All farmers knew the menace a red fox might create; they were shifty animals that liked to hunt at night eating small animals such as the chickens and even the eggs. "They're right smart those fox, might even double back to confuse the enemy hunting their tracks." Alex reminded himself of Randle's warning as he swung the loose board back over the opening.

The boy stood just a few feet from the opening and listened for any unfamiliar noises. Hoping that he would not encounter any such animal, he decided it would be best to make his presence known. "It's only me, Alex," he shouted. Then he waited again. The two horses were bedded for the night but the sound of his tiny voice resounded with pleasure to their ears. His gentle call reminded them that man did not represent only work, and within some humans love could be found.

Alex was careful to set the lantern down before entering their stall. Its short wick burned brightly casting a twinkling halo that illuminated around his small frame. He came upon them quietly as not to scare the two resting horses. Delilah stirred a bit and shifted her weight from left to right. She rubbed her long silky nose against Alex's hand, giving him a nudge as he stroked her lovingly. "Wait until you two see what I got!" he whispered enthusiastically. He reached down into his pocket and pulled a very tiny oval-shaped object. Carefully, he displayed it between his third finger and thumb. "Ever seen one of these before?" he asked and held it up to her eye. "It was in my shoe, and I didn't even know it," he continued to explain. "If I come close to you so you can see," he warned, turning to the other horse, "you can look, but it's not to eat." Dandy gazed sleepily back at Alex and as if understanding him blinked. He placed the object before her. "Know what it is?" he asked and as though he was holding a precious gem, snapped his fingers shut and returned the object to his pocket for safekeeping. He brushed his hand down along Dandy's nose and continued to whisper, "Betty told me it was a seed. She said that it was a special seed from a tree we don't have round here. How do you think it got here?" Both horses stood silently as if waiting for his response. The boy continued to speak in a hushed voice. "Randle said that a bird may have dropped it, or maybe it was stuck on the fur of a squirrel." Both horses now swatted their tails back and forth as though they were listening intently. "He said that it looked like it was a seed from an apple." Alex paused and stuck his hand in his pocket and turned the seed over several times in his fingers. "To tell ya the truth, I don't really know what a apple is? Betty said it was a fruit, but all I ever seen of a apple was in my primer, *A for apple*. There is a picture of a round looking thing drawn real big under the letter. 'A' is the letter that apple starts with." Neither horse seemed the least bit impressed. "Well, I got to get back to fetch water. I'll see you two tomorrow. I love you Dandy, I love you Delilah." Then, depositing a small kiss on each of their long noses, he turned away, picked up the lantern, and burrowed out of the barn the same way he had entered.

———

Alex had been living with Randle and Betty long enough to know that he was now six or seven years old. Often at nighttime as he lay in his cot before falling asleep, the memories of his train ride would ignite his curiosity, and he'd wonder about the fate of those other children aboard that fitful ride. His attitude toward his involuntary departure left him thinking. "We were all taken away and left at the same station, but we all ended up alone and living with strangers." He loathed the harsh reality that he had not been afforded an opportunity to make friends with any of the other children for their time together had been too hurried and too scheduled. There was so much confusion and too many adult voices ordering them to "be quiet" or "stop crying." Yet, even with only fleeting glances back and forth amongst them, the scared expressions and saddened eyes had been freed from obscurity, and the vivid images of those same children on the train frequently came back to visit him in a dream.

But for some reason this night was different and as Alex lay on his cot with his blanket tucked beneath his legs, he returned back to the time he had journeyed west. He stared up into the dark room, his eyes bulged a little and he wondered how this memory could have presented itself so clearly. There was a small girl, about his age, sitting next to an older girl in a seat near his on the train. The younger child was clutching a doll, which resembled a lady. Its porcelain face was painted with dark oval eyes, tight scarlet lips, and pink blushing cheeks; and its painted black hair was styled like nothing that Alex had ever seen. It was dressed in a fancy purple gown belted at the waist with a bright blue sash. A lacey petticoat stuck out below the hem of its fancy dress. He could see its legs were clothed in a white muslin pantaloon and the feet were painted as though she was wearing ebony boots. Around its doll neck was a painted necklace of tiny white pearls. The little girl cradled the lady doll as though it was a baby, but in fact the doll could have been the mother.

Alex couldn't recollect the exact features of the little girl or the older girl who may have been her sister. But he could clearly envision the doll lady that seemed to stare at him throughout the entire trip. Even when the little girl leaned her bonneted head against her sister's shoulder to find a soft spot to sleep against, the doll was propped up, body resting forward against the train seat. The neck and head were erect and the dark eyes watched Alex, or so it appeared.

Alex turned over in his cot and closed his tired eyes. Was this a dream he had fabricated or had the doll been real? If it was a doll, he wondered if the little girl still carried it about or if the doll now remained alone, bent at the waist, sitting on an abandoned shelf in some strange house. He continued to thread his way back and wondered what became of the two girls? He hoped that they had not been separated. A feeling of despair began to well up within his little body as he contemplated all the children he had encountered. What if no one wanted them, and they were still at the train station waiting for a grown-up? He pulled his blanket over his head shuddering at the thought of being alone in a cold and unfamiliar place. His little heart began to race. He leaned in towards the wall making a tight cocoon within his nestled blanket. He listened to his own breathing and soon became more relaxed, until he finally dozed off with the face of the doll lady being his last vision before he was asleep.

———

When Alex awoke early the following morning, he tried to move his legs but something was preventing him from shifting about freely. As though a weight had been placed across them, he tried again but continued to find they were being hampered by what appeared to be a rather heavy knobby object. The sun had not yet risen, and it was still very dark in the somber little room. Curiously, he reached down and tapped at what he now recognized to be a soft lump. "What's ya doin' here?" questioned Alex, now aware that the heavy object was Timothy, the tomcat, that had decided to bed down with him sometime during the night. Now most farm cats were used as "ratters" and Timothy was no different. It was not uncommon to find a half-eaten mouse tucked away in a corner of the kitchen or on the stoop. Alex pulled his legs upward and wiggled them free from being used as a cat cushion. "You're supposed to be workin' like the rest of us. Betty won't like it if she sees you sleepin' when you're supposed to be catchin' mice," whispered Alex. By now the old cat had been disturbed enough whereby he rolled over on his side and stretched almost another half a cat length. It opened its jaw and yawned, displaying four sharp canine teeth and a set of equally sharp incisors, which would have intimidated any self-respecting mouse. "You sure are lazy," continued Alex as got up out of bed, trying not to capsize the cat that was now lying very close to the edge of the cot.

Alex decided that today was the day he would plant his seed. The frost had not yet set in, and the earth was still soft enough to allow him to dig a deep enough hole to securely plant. He had learned from being on a farm that the crows could be his worst enemy. They liked corn seed, and now he asked himself what would prevent those cackling pests from picking out his precious seed too. Randle had taught Alex that the Forester land had a soul and that the corn and crops that were planted also had a soul. "If you tend to your land as you tend to yourself, then it will be one with you." Alex was a little confused by all this talk of land and souls, however he solemnly promised to take care of it. So, taking Randle's words to heart, the boy wanted to make sure that wherever he planted his seed, it would be a spot where it would get much attention. However, as the little farmer looked out towards the flat of the horizon, he soon came to the troubled conclusion that all this farmland certainly must be filled with souls because it ventured way beyond any visible stopping point. All of this devotion was a bit worrisome, yielding a fear that if he dug too deep he might hurt one of these souls. After all, Randle said that their land had soul. How would he know where to put the seed?

All morning long as he went about his chores, Alex was tormented by the question of where to plant his seed. At first Betty thought that the furrows between his brows were because the half-bucket of water he was toting was too heavy. But something in the way he carried himself told her it was more. "Why you sure look like you own a problem, Alex," she commented with a note of interest in her voice. "What's got you today?" He set the bucket down with two hands, trying not to allow any more than usual to spill out. Betty bent down and heaved it up effortlessly and dumped its contents into a vat she had set aside to make soap. Anxiously, he looked up and shrugged silently although he was preoccupied with the seed and reached back into his pocket.

Betty looked hard at him, stirring the contents in the vat with a stick. "Still got that seed?" she asked. He nodded 'yes' and hoping not to get into trouble for not paying attention, slipped his hand out of his pocket. "Ya know," she paused for a moment and then continued, "I cleared some land away for Randle, and if you're gonna plant that seed, I think I know a good place; it's all away by itself." The water sloshed violently against the container as she swirled the stick around.

Alex cocked his head to the side like a small bird and pursed his lips together as he often did right before he would speak. "What 'bout the souls?" he asked timidly.

From a smaller tin bucket Betty poured out a conglomeration of lye into the vat of water. Wispy billows of vapor rose as the mixture swirled and belched from the caustic reaction she had provoked. "What's that you said?" the woman demanded. She rubbed her face against her sleeve; she was hot and the chemical reaction frothing in the vessel sizzled like fatty bacon.

"How 'bout the souls, what happens if I dig and trouble one?" Alex wondered aloud with even more concern trailing his question.

"Souls?" Betty stopped and rested the stick against the side of the cauldron. She wiped her hands on her apron and then placed them on her hips. "What are you talkin' bout?" she questioned more fervently.

Alex proceeded to explain what Randle had told him, parroting back to her the exact words imparted as he spoke in nervous staccato. Betty listened with a silent stare and when the small orator was finished she unleashed a shriek of hilarity that was harder and louder than any laughter the child could ever remember hearing. Naturally, he had no idea what was so amusing.

"Just like your Pa to say somethin' but not explain just what he means. That Randle, sometimes he forgits that you're just a little boy," she snickered. "Now listen here, you don't need to worry 'bout stirring anything in the earth. Only thing you might run into is an old gopher." Alex listened as Betty tried to reinterpret Randle's ideas. "A farmer must respect all kinds of life that we share the world with. The crops give us nourishment and feed our souls. We are here together with the land and so you just take care of what you grow and it will take care of us." Having nothing further to convey, Betty reclaimed her position and tended back to her vat, continuing to mix with renewed intensity

The little boy pondered her words and decided that what she said now made better sense, and the general dread was slowly being extinguished like a soft rain smothering a camp fire. He put his hand back into his pocket and clutched the seed. A shade of genuine relief fell upon him. He would take the seed and plant it. It was something that he knew was important; he was now part of a chain. He picked up the handle of the water bucket and started toward the pump to refill it for Betty; and as he walked, he vowed to take good care of his apple seed.

Chapter 7

The year had freely drifted away during which time Will had matured into a hard-working and tireless field hand. He toiled from dawn to dusk and at night slept in a field house with other young men from different cities in England. And although they reconvened each evening like travelers meeting up at four corners of a well-traveled road, they remained a quiet lot and did not share much of their past. Perhaps it was their suspicious nature carried over from an earlier life of poverty that compelled them to keep to themselves, or maybe it was just that by the end of the day all were too tired to talk. When they were finally permitted to lay their heads down, sleep was the only thing that they wished to resume.

A day did not go by that Will Piccard didn't find his mother's image suddenly appearing like a soft breeze on a windless day; she would come to him in his thoughts or present herself outwardly in the form of a stranger who had adopted her mannerisms or demeanor; and her tired gray eyes would penetrate into his. He wondered if she spent wakeful nights haunted by her decision to forsake him. Did she realize having him sent away from the harsh mills of the city was the most unselfish act a mother could give? Yet with all her good intentions and sacrifice, the young man was discovering that regardless of where one lives, to escape England's poverty was like trying to free one's self from a labyrinth. And though he had been liberated from the bleak conditions of the mill, he couldn't help but wonder how this life was much better.

Mr. Hartford was an old widower; a vintage farmer tangled in the clutches of a changing society. He had lost his wife and two sons to typhus fever, which he continually blamed the dreaded disease having been brought over by Napoleon's soldiers who emigrated to England after the war. The Hartford farm had been passed down to him from several generations, and these Hartfords before him had always been productive and prosperous. His fields were blessed with soil that extended deep into the ground; rich loamy dirt veined with stiff clay and sand. Coveted by other farmers, his wheat grew tall and flourished during the hottest weather. His turnip crops, though often bitter, were cultivated and cooked to nourish the farmhands and feed traversing beggars. For as tight as the money was, Mr. Hartford would never leave a man hungry that passed through his property.

Nevertheless, with industrial changes embraced by the English, all farmers, including Mr. Hartford, were feeling the financial pinch. Small family farmsteads were being bought up and combined with others to make larger more lucrative farms. In addition, it was becoming more and more difficult to hire dependable hands, for so many were lured into the cities by what they believed to be a better wages. In a time when aspiring young men were scarce, those such as young Will Piccard were the only hope of keeping a handle on present existence.

———

Will had earned his position as a favorite work hand and though he was not sure why he had deserved this status, he began to see its benefits. Perhaps he acquired his reputation as a stellar worker because of his constitutional fortitude; he seemed to be able to endure the hardest labor without complaining and always gave one hundred percent even though the meager diet of bread, cheese, and bacon was hardly enough to satisfy his craving for more. If there was no tea to drink, he would soak his burnt toast in hot water without objection, and although others grumbled and complained, he took it in stride knowing disapproval would only fall upon deaf ears; so why bother.

Consequently, one crisp and rather misty fall morning, Will accompanied Mr. Hartford to the barn where he instructed the young man to hitch the sire Draught, Gally, to the wagon and make the twenty mile trek to town with a supply list. The speaker paused a few moments and then continued as though the prosperity of the world would now rest on the messenger's shoulders. The list was to be handed over only to Augie, a peculiar old local whose livelihood was negotiating trades and bargains between the businesses and farmers. Augie was considered an ethical and reliable gentleman and had gained his honorable reputation years ago after giving away his last pence to another. "The lad was worst off than me," he claimed, and having heard this story Mr. Hartford only entrusted Augie with getting his supplies at a fair market price.

An unprecedented feeling of adventure peppered Will's sur-roundings like a cool morning dew after a humid night. A trip such as this one was not often awarded and Will readily gave up the monotony of a day in the fields for a few hours alone; solitude was a luxury that one seldom encountered on the farm. He found himself listening to the elder farmer with complacent appreciation and after absorbing all of Mr. Hartford's instructions, he soon gave way to an experience of delight as horse and man rode through the open gate and into a shroud of mist.

In comparison to the first time Will had ridden on top of a wagon beside the stout butcher, Mr. Bumble, he was in complete control. He leaned forward with the reins cradled loosely in his hands and his hat tilted downward; he looked as though he had been born on a farm. His only poor decision was not wearing his work smock, the daily outer coat of most all the country hands, for as the damp air was getting chilly, he knew that the ride back may be even colder.

Gally was a large bay-colored gelding with white markings on his feathered legs. In spite of his standing over seventeen hands, his steps were especially light, for he too seemed to realize he had escaped the tedium of pulling the plough up and back the same plot of land. Today's tramp was euphorically different.

Thick clouds continued to hang low and mocked the early morning as though it were later than a mantle clock would chime. The landscape of the uplands was a tidy blend of moors and dales. Low dry stone walls established artificial boundaries built by laborers of wealthy landowners. The buckboard's wheels turned steadily along the coarse country track. Years of wagon and carriage travels had created a permanent impression in the earth, which formed a natural wedge and trail to follow. It was as though Gally knew the way, *clip clopping* along, snorting a bit, shooing his tail, and enjoying the freedom of the day.

They had been travelling for only a short time accompanied solely by the peacefulness of the landscape when in the hazy distance Will spotted the silhouette of a lone figure walking along the side of the road. At first glance he could not make out any of the details because the heavy mist obscured the clarity of his vision and as an apparition appears like vapor, so did this ghostly outline. He gave Gally a sharp tap with the reins and the horse picked up the pace. "Hello there!" Will shouted with the full intention of stirring the attention of the walker. However, the figure continued with an unbroken stride, its head looking forward without a twist of curiosity. The man and horse were now gaining on the small cloaked figure and being that the road was very narrow the wagoneer was concerned that the traveler might not be aware of their impending presence. With greater pronouncement Will cried out again, "Hello there; wagon and horse behind you!"

This time the figure clearly heard the break in the silence, for it quickly snapped round and stepped back off the dirt road and into the dew-laced grass to permit the wagon and horse to pass. (It was an unwritten law that in such constricted circumstances the moving object would have the right of way.) The figure, adorned in a scarlet wool cloak and black boots, stood back, expecting the wagon to pass, but rather, to its surprise, the rider pulled back the reins, instructing the reluctant horse to come to a halt. "Good day," greeted a most cheerful voice. "Would you like a ride? It's a rather nasty morning to be walking," he added and gestured to the empty space beside him.

Such an opportunity does not often arise and Gally immediately took full advantage of the unscheduled stop and stretched his neck over to the roadside discovering a wealth of grass sprigs and dandelion greens to nibble. Will tilted his hat back and peered curiously down upon the invited stranger whose face was still obstructed by an oversized hood. Evidenced by the demure stature and tiny boots that were exposed beneath the flowing cape, he knew the concealed identity would reveal a lady. Will tried to gain attention once more. "You seem to be traveling my way, would you like to join me?"

"Well, Sir, I don't believe that would be proper; we haven't met." And with those words, she brought her hand up to her face and pushed back the head covering revealing her fair and lovely features.

With immediate recognition, the young man tipped his hat again. "I believe that you and I may have met before," he exclaimed eagerly. "I am Will Piccard."

"And who may this lovely beast be?" she asked toying with Will for she now turned all her attention over to the horse.

"Oh, this, this is Gally. He belongs to Mr. Hartford."

"I see," the fair lady replied and approaching the sire, she reached over and began to stroke his long neck. "I am Libby Dowling. I don't believe we have formally met, have we?" she asked and looked up offering Will a smile.

Will was now looking upon the face of the prettiest young lady he had ever seen, and he could feel his palms begin to sweat as he clasped the reins tightly as though they were a lifeline. "No, not formally," he said, "but I do believe that I saw you when I first arrived from Manchester. I would never have forgotten you." Suddenly everything he said was designed to yield to her delight.

"Why, Mr. Piccard," replied Libby pretending to be shocked. "That is quite a bold statement."

They say it is stunning how a moment in time can change instantly and the feeling of excitement turns to uneasiness. So did this happen to Will for at this moment his innocent attempt at being friendly had been interpreted as being overly forward. Like one who puts too much salt in the cook pot he was not quite sure how to undo his mess. "Oh, I never meant to offend you. Please forgive me, why I only meant that you are..." but now under these embarrassing circumstances, finding the right words failed him. "What did I mean?" he said utterly fumbling for the correct thing to say. Will was now obviously flustered and peered innocently down from his wagon seat only to see she was laughing. "I meant no harm," he repeated.

"I am sure not, but I must insist that you drive along and permit me to go on my way. I am not usually on this road alone and especially talking to strange men." She continued, "I am on a mission of mercy to the Widow Parker: I have to pick up some clothes to be mended. She has not been well and finds herself unable to sew her own hems and buttons."

"Would you like a ride? Gally and I could use, I mean, we would be honored, Miss Libby, if we could drop you at the Widow Parker's. Why, you could sit here," he said tapping the board upon which he sat. "I will get down and lead Gally."

"Thank you, Mr. Piccard, but I have only a short distance to travel. It is just over there," and she pointed across the road. Libby now was feeling bold. "Do you remember where we first saw each other?"

Will felt his heart take a little jump. "Why yes, you were looking out your window when Mr. Rumble and I had lost our way. We happened upon your farm and your father kindly set us straight."

"That is correct," she smiled. "You were on your way to Mr. Hartford's to work on his land." She paused and continued, "Well, it is getting late and the widow will think I have lost my way. I must get along." And she reached behind her head to pull up her hood, which had folded back and was resting upon her shoulders.

"Miss Libby, I hope I am not too insolent to ask if it would it be possible for us to meet again?" Will requested as he picked up the reins that were resting on his lap.

"Perhaps my father may need an extra hand now and then," she suggested.

"Thank you, Miss Libby, that would be fine," he said with an appreciative smile and with all the upbringing of a fine gentleman, he removed his hat and added a gesture of good manners towards the lovely cloaked figure. Then, without any further adieu, he gave Gally a tug leading him away from the grass and with a light slap with the reins, the wagon slowly picked up speed and rolled along towards the market town.

Libby watched the wagon as it rambled away and turned at the bend in the road out of sight. The fog was finally beginning to lift although it continued to lay heavy against the horizon. Fixing her attention back to the widow, she lifted the front of her cloak slightly as she started back down the road with the vision of Will Piccard as clear as a looking glass in her mind.

Chapter 8

Betty Ann and Randle had never traveled farther west than the western border of the Kansas territory. They had heard that the land boomers were seeking free acreage and settling in what was always considered Indian Territory. They knew that 'The War' with Mexico had dislodged any boundaries in the Southwest and flocks of people were heading to Oregon to find new and fertile soil to farm. Local flyers and newspapers informed readers that workers on the Sutter Mill had discovered gold in the American River. "It's a gold fever, the whole country has caught it!" claimed Randle hearing the gossip about residents just leaving and abandoning their homes to secure their fortunes. Yet, in spite of all the temptations to head west, the Foresters remained content with their homestead.

The practical couple reassured themselves that drifting from one place to another made little sense as contrasting rumors trickled back to the Midwest and the East. Sensational news recounted expeditions of half-burned wagon remains, skeletons of men and animals being bleached by the sun, and grave markers that were now the only reminders of those who had ventured west. No, they were not feeling any of the adventurous spirit. They were pleased to stay put for they had made a comfortable existence for themselves by most pioneer standards.

Their homestead was near enough to the Missouri River so that the surrounding land was laden with timber. However, in many other locations further west, building materials were not so commonly found. In the prairie, a dugout or sod house often became permanent shelter. "If we had to live in the side of a hill in one of those dugouts, I think I'd have taken a train east," sighed Betty to her friend Georgina Shafer one day when they were passing through and stopped for a short visit.

"Can you imagine living with a roof made of poles and sod blocks leaning back into a hill with just layers of dry prairie grass to hold in the earth? Why every time it would rain, puddles of muddy water would be in the middle of the floor! I shudder to think of how those dugouts are dark and damp," added Georgina declaring her disproval.

"No, Randle would not have gotten me in one of those! I would have pitched such a fit that the whole state of Missouri would have come out to see what the fuss was about!" exclaimed Betty.

Georgina Shafer was a long time friend of the Foresters. She and her husband, John, owned a small but prosperous molasses mill along a wooded stream. It was a simple operation whereby the water mill was designed to squeeze the juice out of sugarcane stalks. In the beginning years, John bought Chinese sugarcane that was brought in across Missouri; however, he soon realized that by growing his own crops to be converted into syrup at his molasses mill it would prove to be much more lucrative.

Betty and Georgina welcomed the companionship of each other's friendship since neither woman had neighbors nearby to gossip with or confide in. So when Randle and John headed out to the barn that afternoon, both women felt like a pair of giddy schoolgirls attending a secret club. "Where's that little fella you got from the East?" asked Georgina with a rising infliction. She munched on a molasses cookie that Betty had baked with the remaining syrup from a previous delivery.

"He's out pullin' weeds," she replied pouring her friend a little more coffee.

"Ya got your little boy in school?" asked Georgina and lifted the hot tin mug to her lips as she blew on the surface to cool it down. Georgina was a small woman in comparison to Betty. She sat contently as the hot liquid and the enjoyment of her friend's company was beginning to warm her up. She removed her spoon bonnet, revealing a long neatly woven braid that was spun up and pinned to the back of her head.

"He's such a little thing; he got some learnin' from me but now with winter comin' we won't need him in the fields as much," replied Betty almost as though she were contemplating the idea aloud.

"This ain't the same community that we settled years ago," remarked Georgina. She stirred her coffee around so the settled sugar was remixed again. "Why look how much it's growin'. Ya got a schoolhouse just 'bout two miles, and now that it's almost November, it's time for class to start."

"I've been thinkin' it might be good for Alex to get better learnin'. He don't talk much to Randle and me, 'cept he sure likes to talk to them two work horses and that little chick he's rais'in. School might help him make some friends," agreed Betty to her friend.

"Well if he was my boy," Georgina now hesitated as she took a small sip of her coffee as though she were a high society Easterner; she patted her lips with the cloth napkin she was given, "like I was sayin', I wouldn't dither about this decision and you go and send him to school."

———

Georgina and John had come by the Forester's to leave off some molasses and pay a short visit. But now the glow in the Midwestern sky was diminishing as the rim of the red sun settled. The two women embraced like sisters departing for the first time, and they made promises they knew they couldn't keep, vowing that they would get together again soon. John and Georgina climbed up into their buggy. The wind's bite was harsh and suddenly Georgina felt a sense of urgency to get back home before dark. Shielded against the cold in a boarskin coat and woolen muffler round her neck, Betty rested a horse blanket over her legs, allowing it to trail below her feet. In spite of this attempt to keep warm Georgina continued to shiver. She was a thin and frail woman and indeed sensitive to the slightest change in temperature.

The sight of Georgina bundled from head to toe reminded Betty of the winter of '48, when her friend nearly died. Georgina had become gravely ill with the grippe at the very time she was due to give birth. Confined to her bed for weeks, a small bag of sticky paste consisting of raw onions, rye flour, and vinegar was hung around her neck to render some relief. Regardless of the remedy and help of a midwife, the baby was stillborn. Georgina convalesced while she rebuilt her strength, however, the illness and emotional loss took an enormous toll, leaving her forever barren of child. Through time she was nursed back to health with the exception of guilt that she could never fully expel.

Betty shaded her eyes as she watched the buggy head back along the dry road, kicking up dirt and rocks as it slowly rolled along. She looked up at the sky and wondered when it would rain. Then her thoughts were drawn to all those families whose homes were of sod who would awaken with mud in their hair because of the rain that soaked into the dirt roof and dripped muck. After a storm everything inside would have to be hung out to dry. Some homesteaders would line the walls with newspaper. "It surely must be hard," thought Betty. With her arms crossed in front to brace against the wind, she turned and walked up the steps into the house. Firmly she shut the door behind her, setting her mind back on her own chores. She was too busy to let a momentary sense of loneliness intervene.

———

Alex had spent much of the morning pulling the remaining weeds that had not already turned brown and withered from the first autumn cold snap. He knew that for his seed to grow into a tree he would need to start with a patch of land that would be greeted with daily sun and free from stronger plants that could threaten the little sprout when it became a sapling. Not all of the land that belonged to the Foresters had been cultivated. Randle told him that if he could find a place to grow a tree then it was mighty fine with him. With strategic insight, Alex was determined to create a special place where it would be safe and secure from accidental trampling. The best land was away from the house, barn, and anyone or anything that might cause it undo harm. He had helped Randle furrow rows for sowing crops and now he understood the correct proportions to dig the hole, neither too deep nor too shallow. He had carried a bit of compost and chicken droppings in a bucket on account he had seen Betty use this combination when planting her herb garden and knew that it helped provide the plant's nourishment. He also remembered that too much could be poisonous to new sprouts. So, like an experienced farmer he dug a hole with the spade he brought and replaced the soil back into the bucket. Then he mixed the soil with the compost and droppings together. He then dug into his pocket carefully removing his seed. He placed it on his soiled little palm and rolled it about. Next, he bent down and arranged his precious find into the hole with his thumb and index finger. He gave it a gentle pat with his other hand, stood up, and as though he was burying a loved one, delicately shoveled his compost mixture on top until it was refilled.

When he was finished, he reviewed his work recalling how he had previously surveyed this spot. He had paced twenty-two steps starting at the foot of a kingly size boulder to where he now planted. The boulder looked way too heavy to move and so Alex felt assured it would remain untouched. However, just to be on the safe side, he positioned a broken off branch upright with one hand and tapped the flattest end into the ground with the back of his spade next to the newly filled hole. This was his own tree marker; bare-leafed, somewhat crooked, but would do. Alex wiped his dirty hands on his pant legs and felt content. He promised himself that he would be sure to water his seed every day until the snow began to fall, and then, his seed would have to care for itself.

———

The little seed was not the only item that needed tending to. Alex picked up his tools and began to hurry back towards the direction of the barn so he could feed his young chicken that was growing larger by the hour. Its once soft down was now beginning to be replaced by stronger adult feathers. During its first weeks of life Alex was especially concerned that it would not get enough to eat. He had seen Betty put sugar into the drinking water for the other chicks, so he followed her lead. Whenever he could reach up to the table, Alex would pinch into his pocket a little sugar from the sugar bowl. What did not cling to the lining, he sprinkled into the chick's water.

Betty had told him not to name the chicken, but the more he cared for it the more he thought of it as a pet and not just another barnyard fowl. At first when he came to feed it he would simply call out, "Here, chick chick." But as it began to grow and recognize his voice, Alex noticed that the little chicken was developing a personality of its own. Maybe it was because it did not resemble its plain brown-feathered mother who was mean and contrary. Rather, her discarded offspring was producing feathers with charcoal penciling while its plumage was streaked with silver lace. Alex found that when he brought feed to the now adolescent chicken it would come racing over to him with almost a cheerful "clucking" in its throat. As a result of the bird's affectionate interest in its surrogate father, Alex could not help but feel that it needed a proper name. He decided to call it, Yazhi, the Navajo name meaning "little one".

As Alex continued to daydream about his chick he suddenly realized that he had not paid much attention to where he was walking. He had journeyed further away from home than usual and the landscape was not familiar to him. He paused to glance up at the sky and stopped to read the clouds. These were "mares tails", wispy, light, and beautiful. He had listened to Randle recite a rhyme, which Alex now repeated aloud.

"Mares Tail, do beware
But fluffy clouds, hopes are fair"

The day was aging. Before long the sun would set and the temperature would gradually begin to lower. Alex didn't want to admit it, but he was sensing that he actually might be lost. He figured that he could retrace his steps back to where he had planted his seed and begin his way home again. However, though the idea may have been good, the gusts were now more blustery and any trail that he may have left had become dust in the wind. Alex was weary from carrying both the spade and bucket. He shook his hurt hand free from the wire handle and noticed the blisters on his palms. "I don't need this thing now," he said giving the bucket an angry kick with his foot. He watched as it tumbled over. Hitching a ride with the wind, it began to pick up some momentum, clanging noisily away.

Overhead a solitary raptor polished the sky with its expansive wings. Alex tilted his head back and tried to make out if it was a hawk or a falcon. Both possessed sharp beaks for tearing at flesh and strong talons for killing and holding its prey. "It must think somethin's 'round here to eat," thought Alex. "It ain't dumb, that's fer sure." The bird glided with the wind and then rapidly beating the air with its enormous wings sought to fly higher. "I wonder where it's headed?" Alex marveled as he trailed it across the sky, but soon he abandoned the dark object to ponder his own dilemma. "If I don't git home soon I know I'll be out in the dark alone!" Alex continued to walk a bit faster, leaving the bucket behind, but decided that Randle might be angry if he didn't return the spade. He looked about, turning left, right, and behind him, but nothing looked familiar and he felt small, tired, and very hungry. He did not realize it, but the only creature that could see him was the hawk that too was keenly observing the surrounding area. Alex remained a single figure, not much taller than the prairie grass. Who could see him now?

———

The earth continued to spin on its axis and regardless of fears, emotions, hopes, and prayers, this rotation was constant. And regardless of a tiny boy now alone, the positioning of the earth to the sun remained a constant; that is, time would go forward and the brightness of the daylight must become twilight. Twilight, the time when natural light and the sun do not help illuminate the sky. It was now this celestial time and Alex could not help but feel an almost mystical presence. His vision was becoming obscured and a hue of violet haze enveloped the landscape before him.

He shuddered with every crack of the twig or branch he stepped on. The dry tinder resounded in an almost silent world. Tears began to well up in his eyes, and he could feel himself grit his teeth. He would not allow himself the freedom to cry even though a lump was swelling in his throat. His jacket now seemed to provide little defense from the crueler wind, which was battering his small body; and as his nose began to run he took his sleeve and wiped it dry.

Twilight prepares us for dusk as violet hues transcend into an amethyst sky. Alex careened through brush, striking out in front of him with the spade. Dusk had diminished and night was now upon him. Groping in the darkness Alex stopped and knelt down to rest. He picked away a small rock that gouged his bony knee. His heart was beating so quickly that he felt like he would be sick. He leaned his upper body against the spade handle as the pointed blade was now lodged into the earth. Without warning, he caught a noise that was not the familiar moan of the wind. At first he thought it might have been his own grasps for breath. So he tried to hold his breath to listen more intently. Still unsure of the source, the sickness in his stomach frantically changed to an overwhelming feeling of panic. Something was nearby but he could not see what it was.

Approaching desperation, he dropped the spade and curled down like a ball, tucking his face into his hands. Clumps of dirt dropped into his hair when the spade toppled, losing its grip with the ground. Alex listened with all his might and tried to siphon out the unknown noises from those of the wind. He trembled, twigs and fallen branches snapped around him. Slowly and cautiously, something was approaching. He unmasked his hands from his face and placed them over his ears. He couldn't stand the anticipation that materialized as the sounds came closer. What he now thought he imagined was true. He picked his head up and opened his eyes. He could not see anything but was sure it was the panting of an animal. He quickly assumed the same position, except that this time he folded his arms under his forehead, resting his head, face down on his sleeves. His eyes were sealed tight and he tried not to whimper with fear. The smell of cold damp earth and animal musk was caught in his nostrils. Pieces of dead grass poked up between his folded arms tickling his face. He wanted to scratch his cheek but he dared not move. Suddenly, something wet and cold pressed against the back of his head, inhaling and exhaling, sniffing his hair and nosing along his back. He felt what he thought was a snout pushing harder against his neck as though it was trying to pick up a scent. Alex knew that he must remain as still as he could but he was fearful that his pounding heart would give him away. He was now sure that this "something" must be a wolf!

Chapter 9

"Randle, is that boy with you? He ain't here. I've looked everywhere," announced Betty in a worrisome tone to her husband as she heard him push open the door. An icy rush of cold night air pushed past him instantly chilling the room. Randle had returned for the evening from the chore of twisting hay for fuel. Some time back, he had learned of a rather ingenious invention by a man in the Dakota territory who had taken a couple of upright pieces of wood, a roller, and crank handle, hooked the hay, and wound it up around the wood to make a solid stick of fuel. Randle fabricated a similar design and was able to keep the Forester's hay-burning stove well stocked with an ample supply of pyre before the first winter storms.

Randle was rubbing his hands together with a small amount of goldenseal oil to help heal the tiny cuts he obtained from the small sharp pieces of hay. "What do ya mean he ain't here? He went out long time ago to plant that seed he's been keepin' in his pocket." Randle stopped rubbing and reached for a cloth that was neatly stacked with several others on a narrow sidebar beside the cooking pans and utensils. He uniformly wiped them to remove any residual oil and continued, "It's cold and dark out there, I better go look in the barn and see if he's talkin' to the animals."

"Now you don't suppose he's still out and lost?" Then without waiting for a response she answered her own question with her actions by slipping on her warmer coat and buttoning it up to the collar. "I'm goin' out!" Suddenly she paused and looked wide-eyed at her husband who had not yet removed his own jacket. "Randle, there's no tellin', he might…"

But Randle interrupted her for he did not want to hear aloud what he had already surmised. "Now you stop that kind of talk, he's probably in the barn. Besides, he knows this farm mighty well." He was squeezing Betty's arm as he spoke. "I tell ya what," he continued releasing the hold he had on her. Trying to sound reassuring he lowered his voice, "We'll both go on out to the barn. Go get the other lantern and meet me, I'll check on ahead." And with those words Randle took up the lantern that was set on the table and hurried out.

———

By the time Betty had joined Randle he had already scoured the barn. Roosting fowl and resting animals, too tired to give him much of a welcome, were all asleep. Two dim lantern lights illuminated the barn casting an enormous shadow of the couple. Their faceless silhouettes framed the barn wall.

"Did ya look out in the corn crib?" she asked realizing that Alex had not been found in the barn.

"Alex never goes out there after dark, he's afraid of the rats," Randle said in a matter-of-fact tone.

"Well, I'm gonna check," said Betty turning away and scurrying out. Randle stood alone fantasizing the worst. He knew that children could easily become lost and that any number of hideous results could befall them. It did not take Betty long to return alone.

"We better head back to the house, the wind's pickin' up and no use all of us out there on a night like this," he explained cautiously. "It's too dark to be walkin' around and first thing, when day breaks, I'll go and bring him home." Betty did not reply she just listened. Her large body now grew smaller as she stood with her shoulders hunched over, trying to keep warm. Randle continued, "If he don't turn up, I'll go to town and head up a searchin' party, like they done for the Juarez boy few years back."

Betty now stood upright and straightened her shoulders, "Why, you remember what they found, that Juarez boy was found all tore up by mountain lion, or wolf, or heavens knows what it was," answered Betty in a more controlled voice.

"Now there ya go, lettin' your imagination run wild," said Randle trying to comfort them both. "There ain't no way we'll be able to find him tonight."

In a last attempt to satisfy her quest, Betty wandered over to the horse stalls, guided by the lantern beam. There was no child to be found.

"Come on now, Betty," urged Randle, "no need in getting up your hopes here, come along and we'll start fresh in the mornin'."

"I suppose you're right," she agreed turning back to her husband. "I suppose you're right."

And with one last look behind her, she followed Randle back to the house.

———

It was a long night for Betty and although she was tired from the day's chores she could not fall asleep. She listened to Randle as he slept. With each breath he exhaled she counted to five and sure enough, she heard the hoarse vibration of a snore. She wasn't sure if her keeping count of the intervals or the actual noise produced by Randle was keeping her awake. Most nights his snoring did not seem to trouble her, but tonight every breath he took kept her alert. And then, there was the howl of the wind rustling and shaking weak branches. Timothy the cat was on a prowl and even he, who was generally stealthy, seemed clumsy, as he jumped up and down from the furniture creating more of a ruckus than usual. But it was Alex who was the real reason for her unrest. Any justification she came up with that he must be somewhere safe was countered with a more plausible reason that he was in danger. She wasn't sure if she had really loved the child, however she knew that she was very fond of him and wished him no harm.

Betty slipped out from beneath the covers and placed a shawl around her shoulders. She tiptoed into the kitchen and bent over the stove, stoking the embers with an iron poker, she then added another hay log. Its dry shafts immediately caught fire and she began to warm her outstretched palms. She pulled up a chair in front of the stove and sat in silent contemplation, listening to each and every creak.

———

The sun had not yet come up but being a farmer, waking did not coincide with morning light. Randle awoke to find Betty had fallen asleep in the chair. He gave her shoulder a light shake. "What's ya doin' out here, Betty Ann?" he asked.

She woke immediately upon feeling his hand on her. "Randle, oh, you startled me," she answered. Leaning forward she noticed that she had a rather uncomfortable stiffness. Holding her back with one hand she stood up and tidied her shawl, which had slipped off her left shoulder. "I couldn't sleep, so I came out here. Guess I drifted off. Is it mornin'?" she questioned Randle who was now adding more fuel to the stove.

"Yep, better get dressed. I'll put on some coffee and after we eat, I'll head on out."

Betty, still a bit dazed from having been so abruptly woken, remembered the mission that was ahead. She said nothing back to her husband who was busy lighting a lantern. "I'll be right back, gonna git some more water." She heard the door open, shut, and then silence. She proceeded to the wash basin and began to clean up and dress for the day.

———

Alex felt like he had been lying face down on the ground forever. He knew that if he dared try to get up it might be the last movement he ever made. Trapped, cold, and hanging on to a desperate desire to be rescued, his emotions were overwhelming. He no longer could hold back an uncontrollable urge to cry. Tears streamed down his face and he began to sob. The presence of an animal was definitely not his imagination. The pawing and sniffing continued until he heard an unfamiliar voice.

"Sergeant, back!" roared a raspy shout a short distance away. Instantly the pawing stopped. Alex heard a low distinct growl, which could only be interpreted as a threat from a large and toothy animal. He could hear footsteps approaching. "Good boy, good boy. What's ya got there?" boomed the voice again. Alex turned his face to the side and a thin beam of light shinning towards his direction broke the darkness around him. The beacon illuminated the area and the footsteps trudged towards him and then halted. The lantern now was blinding him with its light.

"Sergeant, sit!" a command summoned. Alex craned his neck upward but could not make out the face that belonged to the voice. "Now, what do we have here?" asked the voice poking Alex's back with the end of a stick. Still jabbing him, the voice continued, "What's ya doin on my property? This here is private property. You're darn lucky I don't sic ole Sergeant on you. Git up!"

Alex obeyed. The light continued to be aimed directly at his face and as he started to stand he could hear the low moan of Sergeant. "What's your name boy?"

"Alex"

"Alex, got a last name?" demanded the harsh voice.

"Alex Forester, I'm lost," he replied.

The lantern was now raised up and down so the person holding it was able to get a full view of him. "Well you don't look bigger than a minute. We can't leave ya out here, the wolves would eat you!" he continued. "Ya want to be wolf feed?" he asked jabbing Alex in his ribs playfully with the stick.

"No, Sir," answered the child meekly.

"Well, you come on with me and Sergeant or else you'll find yourself dead in the morning," demanded the voice.

Alex seemed very perplexed. He was too scared to stay and now very frightened of the future. He stood rigidly as though he was mechanically unable to take a step.

"Here, hold on to this. Sergeant will lead you back with me." And the voice placed a tattered piece of rope into Alex's hand. He felt a slight pull and now recognized that the dog was tied to the other end of the rope. "Home, Sergeant," roared the voice. And with that order the three started away.

———

Alex stretched his arms over his head and found that he was butted up against a large animal. He saw next to him a dog, a very large dog that now opened its eyes and then sleepily closed both lids without stirring even its tail. "Sergeant?" whispered Alex. The dog replied with a thumping of its tail, still not moving. Alex found that he had an old saddle blanket covering him. He wiggled his toes, which were still locked into his shoes and folded back the blanket and sat up. He remained still while he surveyed his surroundings. The room he was in was small and dank; it did not resemble the house that he now lived in. The floor was dirt and moist in the corners. He could tell by the darker color that they had recently been wet. A speckled goat and small white pig were eating from a bucket together; both animals making snorting noises of contentment. But it did not take long until he noticed that the goat was the aggressor of the two and managed to get most of its face into the opening, preventing the pig from its share of the contents. As a result, the bucket tipped over with a clamor and rolled to the far end of the room. The pig dashed over for the remains as the goat cleaned up any of the scraps that had spilled its way. Sergeant remained asleep.

No sooner had the animals finished eating than Alex's attention suddenly was drawn away. Someone was entering the dwelling by way of lifting the buffalo robe, which hung in lieu of a traditional wooden door. In the sunless room all he could make out was a figure carrying a stick in one hand and a rifle in the other. "So, ya decided to git up, eh?" stated the figure. Alex recognized the voice as the same raspy one from the night before. "Alex, that's right ain't it?" asked the man standing in the darkness.

"Yes, Sir, I am Alex," he replied now trying to stand and not fall over the blanket which was caught under one foot. Sergeant, too, rose when he heard his master's voice, trotted over next to the man and plopped down with a "humph."

"Hungry?" he asked. Alex nodded "yes". He dared to take a step forward, fumbling with the blanket, which he now had gathered up in his hands.

"Ever been in a sod house before? It can be kind of dark on account that it doesn't have any windows. We had a door once but a bear tore it down and I never did get a chance to fit one in its place." The man grinned at Alex who, upon the words "bear", appeared wide-eyed. "Come to think of it, I ain't sure if it was a bear; found it off its hinges one day and decided that it was more of a nuisance to fix. Besides, ole Sergeant likes to come and go at night."

Alex looked more relieved when the idea of a bear was stricken.

"Go on outside, you'll see a barrel on the side of the house. You can wash up. When ya come back in I'll fix something for you to eat. Then we'll talk some," directed the owner of the crude dwelling. "Go on now, it's cold and you'll need something hot in yer belly." He placed his hand alongside of a worn rag carpet, which was hung in the center of the room, indicating that there was another small room beyond. Then he disappeared to the other side.

Alex walked over to the entrance and stroked the tanned hide. It was heavier than he thought and it took a bit of persuasion to lift it high enough to walk under. Sergeant bolted past him into the outdoors and away from the house. Seemingly enjoying the cold morning air he could be seen sniffing and playing with anything that stirred in the wind.

Upon the boy's return from outside, the man pointed to the wooden crate. "Sit on this; it's just your size." Alex continued to dry his wet hands on his breeches as he sat down. He had used his jacket sleeves to dry his face. A dry goods box fashioned a table where placed before him was a tin cup and a trencher plate. "You like goat milk?" he asked Alex, pushing the tin cup towards him. "It's fresh."

Alex picked up the cup and drank. It felt warm on his lips and tasted sweeter than the cow's milk he was used to. He emptied the cup and his host immediately refilled it. Alex reached over and took hold of the larger of the two corn pone cakes that had been prepared for him.

Sergeant pushed aside the buffalo robe with his head making his entrance known with his heavy panting. The man threw the dog what looked like scraps of fried meat. The dog devoured the food and sat waiting for more. Again, pieces of meat were thrown and the dog scrambled for the food. Neither the pig nor the goat was in sight. Surely neither would have wanted to get between Sergeant and his breakfast. "Good boy, good boy," the man would repeat each time the dog would catch one of the tossed pieces of fried meat before it reached the floor. With all the excitement, dirt was being broadcast and strewn about as the dog became more and more excited with the prospect of food. Alex continued to eat and drink, watching the action, realizing how very different this scene was from the Forester mornings.

"Sergeant, sit!" roared the man and with great obedience the dog went to the corner and lay down.

Alex completed his breakfast, wiping his mouth on his sleeve. "Thank you, Sir," he said.

"Don't call me Sir, it reminds me of being in the army. You can just call me Tully," the man said, pulling on his beard. He was a scruffy looking fellow, unkempt but not dirty. One would be hard pressed to know his age by looking at him. The sun and long hours working outdoors hardened most men who worked the land. So the clue to his age was that he had once been in the army. One could surmise that he could have battled during the War of 1812, or he may have been in a more recent conflict, the Mexican-American War. Whichever it was, it was evident that neither had left Tully with much more than a distasteful memory. As for Alex, he would not have known the difference, for to him the clue lay in the threads of gray woven into his beard, which made the man look old enough to be his grandfather.

"Well, now that you're fed, slept, and rested up, let's find out where ya belong. I imagine somebody must be wondering where you are."

"I bet Delilah and Dandy must want to know where I am," agreed Alex in a meek voice.

"Now who might they be, yer folks?" questioned Tully who had now pulled up a box and turned up the wick in the lantern to brighten the room.

Alex could now see Tully more clearly, as that he was sitting forward. He noticed that the older man had grey eyes and corn pone stuck in the mustache of his beard.

"No, they're my best friends," said Alex.

"Brother and sister, now we're getting somewhere," replied Tully. "They older or younger than you?"

"They ain't my kin," said Alex, "I don't know how old they are but I miss them somethin' awful."

"Well, I bet your folks are missing you, too. What'd ya say their names were?"

"Betty and Randle Forester, but they ain't my real ma and pa. My ma and pa are up somewhere East." He paused for a moment and grimaced as if in pain before he continued. "But some people came one day and took me from Pa, said he couldn't keep me no more. So I came on a train with some other kids and ended up livin' with Betty and Randle." Alex was looking down and began to fiddle with the button on the cuff of his jacket.

Tully said nothing. He had heard about the transporting of orphans out to farms from the north, but had never met any until now. "Sergeant, come here boy," he called.

Sergeant, who was sleeping in the corner, heard the call and immediately obeyed. He lumbered over and then sat diligently waiting for the gentle stroke of his master's callused palm across his back. Then Tully turned to Alex and spoke. "You're like Sergeant here. When he was just a puppy I found him yelping, cryin' for his ma, but she was nowhere. Found him in the brush right over by Miner's Bridge. He was just the size of a minute, like you. So, I took him in and we've been family ever since. Ain't that so, Sergeant?" The dog wagged his tail and rested his face on Tully's lap. "You're a stray, but you'll grow strong just like Sergeant here," said Tully to Alex.

Alex looked up and caught a glimpse of a smile behind the wooly face. He thought he saw a smile on Sergeant's lips, too.

Chapter 10

Will became a most favored worker on the Hartford farm. He minded his business, ate only what was put on his plate and never asked for more, although he would willingly have taken another mouthful if it had been put before him. Mr. Hartford was getting on in years, set in his routine, and no longer enjoyed traveling into town for necessities. The notion of having to partake in small talk with others he may meet up with was an unpleasant social activity he would like to ignore. He decided that Will could be entrusted with specific jobs and therefore was the farmhand who would drive into town whenever the need arose.

Will, on the other hand, took delight in the long rides alone on the desolate countryside, which he easily transformed into a pastoral landscape painting. Gally and he were the subjects of the brush strokes, discreetly painted into the foreground as they rambled aside miles of verdant green pastures with whitewashed cottages nestled between wooded fields and meandering streams. Will trusted Gally the same way that one would employ the friendship of a confidant. In the evenings after a day on the road, Will would remain in the stable to groom him. He would begin by rubbing him down, curry combing and brushing his neck and forehead. He would slide the coarse bristles with a side-to-side motion, carefully dislodging any dirt or dust. Will would massage his tired limbs and then take a cool bucket of water and sponge his coat, resurrecting it from dull and dry to a lustrous sheen. Gally enjoyed the human interaction, or perhaps it was just the attention from Will that he found pleasurable. As though posing at attention, he would stand erect and gallant, more like a military steed than the farm horse that he was, until Will was finished.

Will had been born with an innate compassion for animals; showing particular lenity towards those domesticated brutes that helped plow the land or carry the loads. For Will, though his own skin seared and cracked from the punishing rays of the sun and his muscles ached from the burden of labor, it was Gally who had rarely found satisfaction from the toils set before him, and therefore deserved to be pampered for his hard work. So it became a custom that after the evening grooming, after the young man gave the horse a gentle stroke across its long nose, he would often wander back into the black pitch of night to bunk down in the stables until morning, when it was time to start all over again.

———

It was another gray afternoon, as so many are in England during fall. Will had been sent to town to pick up a neck yoke that was to replace the one that had fallen victim to years of wear. He had just finished loading the wagon and paying the livery manager when he heard a sudden outburst. It was a fearful cry. It was the lament of a young woman.

"No, no, shoo, shoo, go back!" trembled a plea from the voice. Will turned an about-face but saw nothing unusual, certainly no one who seemed to be in distress.

Again, an alarmed plea could be heard, "No, go away, go away!"

This time it was followed by a low and threatening growl. Deep throaty snarls forewarned its victim.

Gally, aware of some pending danger drew his ears back like feathers on an arrow. It was evident that he was uneasy for he shook his head, snorting and hoofing the ground, all the while pulling back from the hitching post he was tied to.

"Look, over there!" shouted a man pointing across the road. "It's a girl! She needs help!" he exclaimed and in mid-sentence ran in the direction of the distressed voice as he frantically tried to draw the attention of anyone who might follow. Again growling became more pronounced. "Someone bring a rifle!" the man yelled as he fled towards the open doorway of Hurley's Tavern.

All at once the frenzy of the situation seized him, for Will, having just arrived in town, happened too to be in earshot of the desperate cry for help. Knowing that he was not in the possession of a gun, he instinctively tore off the tarp, which had been carelessly tossed over the backend of the wagon and rummaged feverishly through the box of unwanted tools until he came across what he was looking for, the handle of an ax. "She's over there! Near the alleyway!" cried out a townswoman to Will as she scurried past the wagon towards the sound. "Hurry, boy, hurry yourself!"

A gathering of about a half-dozen people now poured out into the street to bear witness. Each was fueling a bit of drama to what would ordinarily have been a most dull and colorless afternoon.

Upon hearing the commotion, Sidney O'Dell stormed out of his tavern fortified with a wooden club, ready to assist. When asked how he had one so readily available, he revealed that he kept it in the back of his establishment for unruly customers. Jessica Brown, eager to comfort anyone who may become wounded, assured Mrs. McLaud that she had training as a nurse. Toby and Julian, the Derby twins, just wanted to see what all the fuss was about and sat right down by the two ladies' hemlines waiting for some action.

"That animal might have "the mad dog" disease," warned Sidney O'Dell as he approached Will, who was now trying to push his way through the curious onlookers. "Comin' down out of the countryside, he's lookin' for prey! That animal could kill anyone who it bites. That's all it takes, just one puncture, get the saliva into your bloodstream and you're meeting the maker." A unified gasp was sounded from the bystanders, and the twins crossed their fingers hoping to see a bit of action after such a bold proclamation was made.

Will turned angrily and faced the assembled small crowd. "You people aren't helping the situation. Now be quiet and stand back. Unless you have a gun, someone needs to sneak up behind the beast to free her. We don't want to scare the animal into believing that it's being threatened. It will become ever more viscous if it thinks it is cornered!" instructed Will, trying to establish reason.

"O.K. everyone," cried O'Dell. "You heard the young man, get out of his way!" He stretched out his arms as if to hold back an unruly crowd, when in fact he was the only person who was not heeding his own advice. O'Dell continued to creep behind Will on cat paws while the others, fearful of the imminent possibilities, obeyed. Suddenly, detonating from the alley, there exploded a series of hideous barks. Will's hands, already wet with perspiration, clenched the wooden handle evermore tightly in anticipation of offering a deadly blow. Muffled hissing could be heard between momentary lapses in the ferocious growls. With deliberate and slow steps, Will headed away from the group to the alley. All eyes were perched on him in anticipation. Mrs. McLaud and Miss Brown huddled even closer as the Derby twins stood up and dared to slink towards the noise, until O'Dell pulled both lads back by their coattails.

Before Will entered the alley he took a deep breath and repositioned the ax handle in his right hand giving it a light tap on the palm of his left hand. He took a small apprehensive step toward the snarling predator. There before the girl crouched a wildly angry dog; its back end reared upward ready to lunge forward as if on a spring, and its coarse yellow hair bristled, standing on end. He could not see its menacing jaw, but he could see a small pool of saliva floating over its front legs as a result of it barring its teeth and feverishly pitching forward and back. A terrified young woman, obviously shaken by the events that were unfolding, clenched her handkerchief to her face, obscuring her petrified features. She had found herself in a deadly predicament, trapped with her back against a brick building with no options to escape in this dark alleyway. Her eyes were locked on the ferocious beast, until she was drawn away for a moment by a black shadow cast upon the wall that was slowly growing larger and extending itself over the loathsome animal from behind. As the shadow swung the handle up over his head, the young woman covered her hands over her face to shield her eyes from what was about to happen. An instant before Will brought the handle crashing down upon the hideous beast he cried out, "Run, run, run away!"

Mrs. McLaud shrieked. The canine burst out a woeful "yelp"! Will jumped back watching its every move. The dog that had lost its footing fell to the ground and then sprang back up. It had been more stunned than hurt by the glancing blow. Turning round, it locked its eyes upon Will and then to the axe handle the man was clutching. It folded down as if recoiling, but within a flash retreated. It raced past the witnesses and fled towards the dirt road, sprinting away from the town, leaving only a trail of footprints behind.

"Young lady, you gave us all quite a scare, why it's a miracle that you were not torn to shreds!" exclaimed Mrs. McLaud, embracing the young hostage.

"Yes, you're very lucky, Miss," added Sidney O'Dell, swinging his club side to side as he spoke. "Lucky indeed that this young lad came to town today. Of course, I would have come to your rescue if he hadn't," the braggart boasted in his Irish brogue.

"You, Sidney O'Dell, an 'ero? That I would have liked to hav' seen!" laughed Jessica Brown. "I remember a fox had you cornered in the old belfry the time you decided to 'elp clean out the starling nests."

"It startled me," he said defending his honor. "Just snuck up behind with its pointy little snout and black pellet eyes! It looked evil!"

"Now both of you, can't you see the poor child is trembling?" replied Mrs. McLaud. "She's been terrified."

"Are you all right dear?" asked Jessica now turning her attention to the young lady who was now being smothered by the concerned woman's embrace.

The now composed young lady gently pried herself away from the overprotective woman.

"Yes, Mum, I am fine now," she said nodding her head "yes". Then looking about asked, "Where is the young gentleman who so gallantly saved me?"

"Don't know if 'es a gentleman, but 'es over there by the wagon," piped up Toby, the taller of the twins who was waving his hat in the direction of Will and eavesdropping on the adult conversations.

Curiously, she turned away from the group just in time to see the back of Will as he was repositioning the tarp over the wagon as he had found it earlier. Gathering up her cloak in a lady-like fashion so she would not trip over its great length, she hurried over to where the wagon stood.

"Excuse me, please, wait!" she cried out as she approached Will, who had now gotten up in the wagon and was sitting on the planking. "Please, I must thank you," she said. "It is you, isn't it, Will Piccard, correct?" she said a bit out of breath. She still held up her cloak with one hand and took hold of the side of the wagon with the other as if to prevent it from leaving.

"Yes, and you are Libby Dowling," he replied tipping his hat to her and now feeling his cheeks flush pink.

"Please, I must thank you. You put yourself in grave danger to help me. Let me repay you, I insist!" she demanded.

"That is not necessary," he answered looking down from his towering position upon her weary face. "On the contrary, you must be very tired. Please, let me take you home."

"Oh, no, it is I who needs to repay you. I could not take advantage of your good nature," she exclaimed.

"Please, Miss Dowling, Gally and I would like to. Besides, who knows where that dog could be at this time? I would never forgive myself if it were to threaten you again," his voice sounding most sincerely concerned.

Libby said nothing and paused giving herself time to reflect. She frowned back at the road where the animal had escaped to. This time, without hesitation, she reached out her hand and allowed Will to help her up into the wagon.

———

This chance meeting of Libby and Will took place not more than two weeks after their encounter on the road. Libby's family was eternally grateful for his act of heroism. They found him to be a polite young man with ambitions of becoming independent. He had earned a standing invitation Sunday nights to join the Dowling family for supper, upon which Will graciously accepted with the understanding that he needed first to obtain permission from Mr. Hartford. As it happened, the industrious Will owed Mr. Hartford less than one more year of labor to remunerate him for the food and shelter he had provided. As soon as the debt was paid, the young man had decided that he would leave the unprogressive life of rural England and move to America, the land of uncharted opportunity.

As the months passed, Libby and Will grew to know one another. They enjoyed each other's company and found that they were quite compatible. Libby learned of Will's early childhood and how his mother had given him up in hopes that his life would be better apart from the harsh conditions of the city. As for Will, he learned of Libby's delicate condition and felt a need to protect her from any harm. However, what he did not realize was that he would have to take her far away because her greatest threat was right under the very roof she lived in. It was Mr. Dowling, Libby's father.

Chapter 11

At age seventeen Libby Dowling had grown into a bright and seemingly happy young woman. Those who came in contact with her could not fail to become intoxicated with her kind and dear disposition. However, behind all her sweetness one would never know that she concealed gloomy fears and uncertainties which were infecting her life like tainted water. Libby drew affection from her mother and grandmother; while her father's cold and detached temperament repeatedly left her uneasy. And although Jonathan Dowling may have demonstrated his affection in the privacy of his wife's company, his mannerisms were stoically reserved and fastidious. Cordiality was a trait exchanged in the Dowling household, but it was her father's unpredictable temper that provoked Libby's apprehension.

It was not uncommon for her father to unleash his temper at what would seem frivolous or minor situations. His controlled behavior would suddenly explode without warning. To Jonathan Dowling, a mere slurp of soup at the dinner table was cause for extreme measures. One such incident occurred when Libby, who was merely four at the time, demonstrated such a behavior. Her tea was too hot for her small baby lips. She had barely lifted the spoon to her mouth when she sipped the liquid from the edge of the spoon. Fearful that the contents might splatter, she slurped, trying to prevent it from spilling. Mr. Dowling instantly cast an evil look across the table at the small child. Her mother, knowing her husband's temper, at once began to pass a plate of freshly baked scones to divert his attention. However, it was too late. "Stop that noise now!" he roared leaping up from the chair. He marched over to where she was sitting and pulled her up by her arms and away from the table. Consequently, her small foot knocked over the tea-filled cup causing it to spill.

"Do you see what you… you little messy child have done now?" he bellowed carrying her away. "You are not fit to sit with us at the table!"

That was the first remembrance Libby had of being locked in the woodshed.

———

Libby's mother was not afraid of her husband's temper for she had grown to anticipate his irritations and therefore knew what to avoid. She was however, most fearful for her daughter, for the little child unknowingly became much like a splinter under his skin; it would fester and fester and then abruptly ulcerate.

Libby had not been a well child and spent much of her time indoors. She often was confined to her bed or the common room where she would play with her few toys. One winter, the year she was ten, or maybe nine, a most unfortunate incident occurred. Her father had come in from the dairy barn. Days turned into dusk earlier as the sun set low in the English moors. A dim coal lamp was burning in the corner, leaving the rest of the house rather ashen. Libby had been playing with Maggie, her doll, and had taken off her shoe to use as an imaginary carriage. When it was time for bed, she and Maggie retreated to her small bedroom, however; she had not picked up the "carriage".

Mr. Dowling, tired from his day's work, mechanically walked into the common room, and unwittingly stumbled over the shoe. His crash to the floor caused the whole house to shudder when all came to realize the unfortunate accident had occurred. Although Mr. Dowling was not hurt, he was enraged that the shoe had been left out where it did not belong.

Mrs. Dowling, wearing a rather somber personality, came running in just in time to see her husband nursing his bruised elbow. "Where is she?" he bellowed wagging the little shoe at his wife. Libby's Grandmother too had come to see what had happened. With her crochet needles still in her hand, she waved them about like two tiny batons as she spoke.

"Johnny, dear, don't be upset with the child," she urged trying to calm the angry man, for she feared what her son might do.

"Where is she?" he shouted again ignoring the old woman; his eyes bulged and there was wildness in his expression.

"She has gone to bed, John," his frightened wife answered tenderly, all the while trying to mask her quivering voice. "Here, give that to me," she said reaching for the shoe. "Come and sit down!" and pointed to the only armchair in the room.

But he would not listen and paced about, with Mrs. Dowling trailing him like a puppy and the elder not far behind. "She knows better!" he groaned, "and needs to mind not to leave her things about." With those words, Mr. Dowling stormed away leaving the two women hoping that he would calm down.

That night the young Libby and Maggie were locked in the woodshed, not to be let out until morning.

———

Although Libby was considered an adult, she admitted to Will that she did not like to sleep without a small light burning. "I guess I am afraid of the dark," she confessed one day while they were out walking together. "Now you tell me, what are you afraid of?"

Will stopped to pick a primrose with its delicate pale yellow blooms and bright green crinkly leaves. "Do you see this flower?" he said to her. "It promises that spring is around the corner," and he handed the little spray to her.

"It is lovely," she said taking it and sticking it into her hair.

"You are an angel, Libby Dowling," Will smiled as he watched.

"And you have not answered my question, Mr. Piccard." Libby felt carefree and happy as she sauntered ahead of Will. She twirled about like a top, her hair spinning and her pink skirt catching the wind. "Don't be shy," she toyed with him. "Tell me, what are you afraid of?"

Will put his hand out and she grasped his in hers. This was the first time that they had held hands. "If I tell you, do you promise not to laugh?" he asked pulling her closer.

"Oh, yes, I promise," she whispered. Libby, petite and delicate stood facing Will. He now clutched both her hands in his; her skin so smooth against his rough palms.

"I am afraid that I might lose you," he acknowledged. "Libby, I want to tell you something," then a moment's pause came between them, "I believe I am falling in love with you."

———

The gardener is humming,
Trowel in his hand as
The sun casts rays upon
the milkweeds.

Days in rural England are often only remembered as damp and gray unless you are able to appreciate the splendor and beauty they have to offer. Foliage dipped in cream, rose, and burgundy, a kaleidoscope of colors mottles the countryside. Vine-covered arbors, plants tumbling over walkways and great masses of yellow-petaled Black-eyed Susans have inspired the artist and the poet. Libby and the flowers are both children of the fields, and where she wanders they seem to grow ever grander. Each blossom displays its grandeur only to please, asking nothing in return. Libby had come to personify each flower. The wild iris awakens hope, the lily ignites virtue, a chrysanthemum cures sadness, while the rambling roses with their thorny stems contemplate no harm, only passion.

And as twilight sits on the edge of darkness
A lone gypsy's mandolin performs
Til' the promise of daybreak

Mr. Dowling did not mind Will Piccard and often accepted his offers of helping on the dairy farm when the young man was not working at the Hartford's. "I've known Mr. Hartford for some time now, and he is a decent man, but getting on in years. Eh, Will? Do ya like 'em lad?" Mr. Dowling asked one Sunday afternoon when Will had come by to help with a broken fence. One of the rails had rotted and needed to be replaced before the canker spread to the healthy wood.

"Yes, Sir, he has been good to me since I've been with him," replied Will dutifully.

"I imagine he's been more than good, kept yer belly full and gave yer a roof over yer head each night," proclaimed Mr. Dowling.

"Yes, Sir," replied Will. He did not want to engage Mr. Dowling anymore than he needed. It was difficult not to remind the man that he had in return given him years of labor and often went to bed hungrier than he should have. Will did not mean disrespect since he knew that had he grown up in the city, his life may have been much worse.

"Don't ya forget that, Will; ya could have been brought to the O'Bentley farm. Never would have seen the likes of my little Libby if that had been yer destiny."

"I think that is the farm some miles from here with the red silo, is it not, Sir?" asked Will now wondering what was the problem there.

"Now, I never tell a man how to treat his hands but Timothy O'Bentley, he can be tough, mighty tough. No free time for those lads. Sun up to sun down, sleep, work, all discipline. They don't get time off and never to go visitin' with the others. He gets his work out of his boys and then some. There," announced Mr. Dowling putting the last board in place, "I believe we're done." He stepped away from the rail to examine the work.

"Is that all, Sir?" Will asked. Consciously aware that the job was complete, he stooped over the tools and began arranging them back into the wooden box Mr. Dowling used for his jobs around the farm.

"Just one more thing, boy," replied Mr. Dowling picking at a few splinters from the newly placed rail. "You might want to say yer goodbyes to Libby, she'll be leaving."

"Where is she going?" asked Will, innocently.

"She's getting married," he snapped.

Will stopped and stood up. "Married?" he parroted back incredulously.

"That's right, it's time she stopped livin' off her mother and father and start a family of her own," he replied in a tone that was quite matter-of-fact in nature. "Now, come along and carry the box back to the shed. Ya can wash up 'round back and join us for dinner," called out Mr. Dowling as he turned away from Will and headed toward the shed.

"Mr. Dowling," Will shouted, "she can't get married!"

The farmer stopped abruptly and as though fanning a fire with his voice, turned and demanded. "Now son, tell me why she can't!"

Boldly, Will edged towards him as he spoke. "Because Sir, I wish to marry her!" he blurted out.

And as if those words had severed a vein, Mr. Dowling's face began to turn red for he was not used to being challenged. "You, you want to marry Libby?"

"Yes," Will replied. "I was planning on speaking to you at a later time however; it is clear that I had better speak quickly. Mr. Dowling, Sir, I would like to ask you for Libby's hand in marriage." For a moment it seemed as though time had stopped; for hearing such sincerity emanate from the brazen lad's voice gave the elder man reason to take pause. Mr. Dowling solemnly approached Will and when the two men were only several feet apart he stopped, removed his leather-brimmed hat, and wiped his forehead with a cotton handkerchief that he pulled out from the back pocket of his overalls. Will stood and watched as the menacing father took his time, drying his brow, then his neck, then his entire face. Finally, Mr. Dowling shook the damp cloth and then meticulously folded it back into a neat square, and shoved it back into his pocket. He looked directly at Will and replied in a most louring manner, "Do you think I'd allow my daughter to marry a farmhand? A farmhand who was dropped on the doorsteps asking for a handout? You wish to marry my daughter with nothing to offer? Now, do as you have been told. Carry the tools to the shed. It's getting late and supper will be ready." Mr. Dowling turned his back and briskly walked away, leaving Will behind.

Chapter 12

Sergeant was comfortable as he lay by the feet of Tully. The goat and pig both had returned from the outdoors to seek the warmth of the little house and immediately began to nibble about the dirt floor trying to scavenge up any remains of food. The crafty pig rooted around the spot where Sergeant had been eating his meat scraps, hoping for a small reject of gristle.

Alex looked down at the dog. "You can pet him if ya want. I think he's taken to you," said Tully to the small boy. Alex climbed off the chair and squatted beside Sergeant who was breathing deeply in a sound sleep. Alex cautiously stroked the back of his head pulling down towards his muscular neck. Sergeant's russet coat was not coarse, rather short and glossy, his skin loose and wrinkled. "He likes the attention, he's a good ole dog," remarked Tully as Alex gingerly continued to pet the large animal. "Well "little minute," I think we had better take a walk back to see if we can find where you belong. Ole Sergeant and me think it's time for you to find your own family," stated the scruffy man. "If we don't, they'll have the whole town out 'round these parts and I don't take kindly to folks meddling in my affairs."

Then, without warning he called out, "Hey yup." This sudden outburst startled Alex who at once jumped. However, the cry was an apparent signal to Sergeant who must have been used to the command. He lifted his head and too stood up. Tully pulled on the lead that was hanging over the back of the chair and hooked it on to the rope collar, which was settled around the folds in Sergeant's wrinkled neck.

"Take off your jacket and give it to me," demanded Tully to Alex. Bewildered why he would have to remove it now before he was going out, he did as he was told and handed it to Tully. "Here Sergeant, find the scent, boy, find the scent," he repeated as the rolled up jacket was placed under the nose of the "hunter." Sergeant sniffed and snorted at the jacket as Tully continued to wave the object under his nostrils. "Here it is, find the scent, boy." Sergeant plunged his nose into the material and when he emerged tugged toward the exit. Tully hung on to the rope with one hand and tossed the jacket back to Alex. It was cold in the dugout and a sharp wind blew in as Sergeant led Tully outside, pushing aside the buffalo hide, which framed the entrance of the doorway. Alex hastily put back on his jacket and followed the two without looking back. He now understood. Sergeant was going to help him find his way back home by using the scent from his clothes. However secretly, Alex wished they would never find the way back.

———

"I've searched every speck of the farm, turned over every dead leaf, even stuck my head into a gopher hole! I believe that boy has gone and got himself very lost," said Randle to his wife as they headed back from the potato fields. The early morning hours had been spent following each dusty trail and every little hiding place that a small boy could creep into. Randle wrapped his arm around his wife who was obviously cold and weary. "Don't worry though," added Randle in a comforting tone. "He's a tough little guy, not much of a talker but determined. Why he just might be back in the house right now." His voice was low and he was trying to mask the lie that he was telling. Randle was sure that Alex was not safe in the house; there had been too many cold nights where he himself was glad that he was not wandering around.

"We better get Delilah hitched up and drive into town," Betty remarked. "We're gonna need some help. This spread is too big to find one little boy by ourselves." Her pace had quickened, she was eager to get back home. Although she appreciated Randle's heroic attempts to relieve her from dread, it wasn't working. "Soon as we get a search party together, why he'll be found and be just fine, just fine," she whispered under the heave of a great sigh. She retied the corners of her shawl, pulling the front snug against her body and tried to pocket her hands inside. Her hair, once neatly pulled and smoothed back into a large bun on the back of the head, mimicking her relatively simple clothing, began to unravel from being battered by the gusts. The long hairpins were no match for the wind. She lowered her head to keep the dust from flying into her eyes. Randle kept in step with his wife as he shielded his eyes with his forearm.

"Go on in and bring out a blanket while I go round to the barn!" exclaimed Randle to his wife.

"Blanket, ain't there one in the back of the wagon?" she questioned.

"We might need an extra, we don't know what kind of condition we may find him in," answered Randle now more matter-of-fact.

Betty now looked up at her husband pushing back the fallen strands of hair away from her face. "Condition eh, ya really mean dead, don't ya?" she said turning away and hurried towards the house.

———

Like a chocolate curtain draped behind the Forester house, a rocky knoll was pitched, shielding against harsh winter winds but also obstructing summer breezes. Its terrain silently eroded during spring rains and now it stood rocky, barren, and treeless. Neither Randle nor Betty had noticed the appearance of two bent figures and a dog descending slowly down the side of this hill. "I think Sergeant has found it. Is that where you live?" asked Tully, who was being led by the canine scout, tugging and sniffing like the hound dog that he was.

Tully did not hear a response and turned to see the boy had stopped to dump out several pebbles that had settled in his shoe. He tried to do this while standing on one foot, but the ungainly surface made it too difficult, so he had to sit down. Tully gave Sergeant a swift jerk with the rope and he halted, but his nose continued to burrow in the soft earth. "That your place way over there?" Tully questioned Alex again.

"Yes, Sir, but how'd he find it?" asked Alex who had now gotten up and was dusting off his dirty hands on his pants. He raised his head and started back down the hill, stumbling a bit in an attempt to catch up with Tully and Sergeant who were waiting for him several yards away.

"That's his job, he's a hound dog. Why he can track a man or animal for almost 100 miles! I've seen one hound dog save its owner from a mountain lion! See him, look how he's pulling really hard. Sergeant doesn't like to be on a lead, when he's on a scent nothing will stop him. Come on, you're almost home."

Alex followed diligently down the side of the slope at the heels of Tully who was behind Sergeant leading the way; dislodged rocks coasting ahead of them all. They had hiked midway down the slope when Tully pulled Sergeant's lead signaling him to stop. Panting from his hard work, the big dog wagged his tail happily as he saw Alex come up behind.

"This is where we part, "little minute". You don't need us anymore. You can see your place from here." Tully stroked Sergeant on his head as the dog sat down awaiting the next command.

Alex looked at Sergeant and pet the dog on his nose. The happy beast licked the little hand. "Sergeant took a likin' to you," Tully continued, "he doesn't always take a liking to strangers."

"He's the best dog I ever have known," whispered Alex. "Do ya think he would help me again?" he asked looking through his own sad puppy eyes.

"Well that depends, what did you have in mind?" questioned Tully who now squatted down on the craggy rise.

"Well, I thought maybe," he hesitated before he started again, "that he could help me find my real dad, on account that he's a hound dog."

Tully looked into Alex's eyes and found an earnestness that was genuine. For some moments the man had listened and with a sincere penetrating look he answered, "I see."

"You said he could find anyone or anything, and I sort of got to thinkin', that is if he don't mind, we could look for my real Pa." This time there was an almost desperate tone in his voice.

"Well Alex, that's a pretty tall order for even Sergeant," replied Tully pulling on his beard in contemplation. Sergeant hearing his name in the conversation stood up and nestled his head next to Tully's shoulder.

"Yea, I guess so," replied Alex remorsefully.

Tully continued to pull on his beard; he was not quite sure what to reply. He got up and looked away from the boy and out towards the horizon. He was visibly still, like a sentinel on watch. He began taking in deep and long breaths of the crisp air. Alex stared at him and tried to follow his eyes to see what it was that Tully might be looking at.

"I do believe that we're in for a cold winter soon. See that," he pointed to the north, "it's a favorite wintering spot for eagles, bald eagles." Tully stopped talking and turned to Alex. It was quieter now; even Sergeant seemed more content as he aimed his large snout into the wind.

Tully broke the silence; he knew that it was time. "You better get goin' or they'll have the whole town looking for you," he reminded Alex.

"Thanks for seein' that I didn't git eatin' by a wolf." Alex smiled at Tully, trying to hold back tears.

"Now get on down and be sure that ya don't lose your way again." Tully turned away and started back up the hill. "Home, Sergeant," he commanded.

For the first time in awhile Tully felt something that he had not experienced in a very long time. There was a heavy lump, a swelling, forming in his throat. He had a sickened feeling of … he wasn't sure… but now suspected that it was sadness. He turned back round in time to witness Alex making his final descent down the hill and scamper towards the Forester farm.

———

Alex slid down the last few yards of the slope and upon reaching the bottom ran towards the Forester's just in time to see Randle leading Delilah out of the barn. She was hitched to the wagon. Her bridle was aligned with a raised noseband, and she was wearing blinders to prevent her from becoming visually distracted. Betty was the first to notice Alex. "Randle, Randle, looky there!" she shouted shaking an extended arm and pointing at the child.

Randle, who had been preoccupied with his task, cupped one hand to his ear to better hear his wife. "What's that?" he shouted back.

At that very moment he felt something tug at his shirttail. "Randle, it's me," Alex said.

Randle looked down and let go of the bridle he was holding. "Well, I'll be!" he exclaimed. Then he shouted to his wife, "Betty, hurry up, Alex is back!"

Betty called out as she quickly scrambled towards the barn, "That's what I was tryin' to tell you." Winded by the excitement and rushing, she grabbed Randle's arm with one hand while patting her chest with the other. She started up again. "I seen him runnin' towards the barn. At first I wasn't sure, but then I knew it by his curly hair all jumbled and flyin' around."

In all the excitement neither of the two adults noticed that Alex backed away from them and had stepped directly in front of Delilah so she was able to get a full view of his return. Wearing her blinders, all vision to her left and right was blocked. "I'm back Delilah, and I missed you," he whispered rubbing his face against her velvety nose. She must have understood what he was saying because she began to rub her long face against his shoulder almost knocking him over with affection.

"Alex, you come over here and let me see you," remarked Betty. "You gave us some scare. Why, when you didn't come back last night, we thought, we thought ..." Betty stopped what she was about to sputter.

"You thought some old bear or wolf ate me," announced Alex walking back over to her.

Randle looked at his wife and she back at him. Both were amazed at how unfettered the child appeared.

"Well, we really were not sure what happened, but I see you're all right," Randle added peering down at him. His arms were bent at the elbows and his fists were resting on his hips. "Got lost did ya? I thought ya went to plant the seed you've bin carryin' around in yer pocket. How could ya git lost?"

"Now Randle, he's just a little boy, this is a mighty big spread," interrupted Betty. "We can't be hard on him." Betty turned to Alex; "We just want to know where ya were last night so it don't ever happen again."

It was the dawning of a cold day. The sky was clear and colorless in harmony to the brown barren earth. The barnyard fowl now wandered about pecking the ground for grubs and insects. They were cackling and clucking, flapping their wings all the while complaining that they were hungry.

"So tell us boy, what happened to you yesterday that you were gone all night?" demanded Randle. He was leaning against the wagon now with his hands folded in front of his chest waiting for a reply.

"Well, I went out to the acreage, like ya told me. I took the spade and a pail of chicken manure like ya said to." Alex looked at each face; both were stony and expressionless so he continued. "I found a really good spot to plant the seed. It's gonna be a great place for a tree. I did like ya said, dug a hole, not too big, not too small," he looked at them again, but was stopped abruptly by Randle.

"Alex, get to the part when you were lost. Where were ya last night?" he asked again holding back his impatience.

There was a chill in the air, the wind blew across their faces and picked up the dust and tossed it upon their feet. Delilah pulled her ears back as though she was trying to keep the wind out of them. Betty began to blow on her hands to keep them warm. Alex pulled up his jacket collar and commenced again. He spoke of the scared feeling he had, how Sergeant and a man had found him. He recounted his predicament with the most accurate details that he could remember; simply he had been aided, sheltered, fed, and brought back home safely. He explained it all and had nothing more to say.

Betty and Randle exchanged glances when Alex had completed his narrative. It was Randle who spoke first. "So tell me again, what was the name of the man?"

"Tully," exclaimed Alex. "And the dog, a hound dog, a really smart dog, Sergeant! You'd like them," he added with a smile. "They have a goat and a pig sleepin' in the house."

Randle said nothing; he just turned his back and started to walk up to the front of the wagon.

"You come along and let's git you somethin' to eat now that we know what happened," Betty commenced gently patting Alex on the back. "Randle," she said turning to her husband, "meet us back at the house and I'll fix ya somethin' to eat, too." On that note, Betty headed back with Alex skipping closely behind.

"Well, Delilah, looks like you're not going for a walk after all," and Randle led the great draft back inside the barn.

———

Betty prepared a basin of tepid water, laid out clean overalls, a muslin shirt, and undergarments for Alex to change into. "Look at you Alex, why you're a ragamuffin."

Alex stared back up at her face to see if she was angry, if there were any lines forming between her eyebrows and on her forehead. But she didn't seem out of the ordinary. He wasn't sure what a ragamuffin was but he imagined that it couldn't be anything good. He remembered that he heard that same word used by Betty when a peddler was passing through selling pots and pans.

"You hurry and get yourself cleaned up best that you can and come on to breakfast," she directed and gave him a little pat on the head and left him to dress.

He lifted the sand colored shirt by the shoulders and frowned when he looked at all the buttons. Buttons always gave him some trouble; they never seemed to cooperate when he was in a hurry. Some of the buttonholes always managed to be a little smaller than the buttons were round, so fitting them through took more than a struggle. If he asked for help, that was even worse. Betty seemed to fiddle so long that he grew tired of standing, wishing he could just sit down. She would say, "Now Alex, if you would just stand still I could button this for ya."

As for Randle, he was no better than Betty. His ring finger on his right had been caught in a reaper and even though it had been wrapped, it had never healed properly. As a result, it remained crooked and bent like the toe of a chicken. So asking him to button was not a good idea.

Alex squeezed out the remaining water from the white muslin cloth that he scrubbed himself with. He began to dress and as he did his mind began to daydream. Maybe because he was putting on clean clothes he began to think about Betty's soap-making days. The smell of lye stuck in his nostrils with the mere suggestion, and he instinctively wiggled his nose as if to eradicate the fictitious image he conjured up. Betty mixed together and saved all leftover bacon rinds and fat from scraps of meat, drippings of lard, and marrow from the soup bones, which she stored in a crock. She always stored it away in the cupboard so that Timothy couldn't knock it over and steal a portion for a snack. Sometimes the cat would paw at the cupboard because the smell of renderings would waft into the air. She also saved ash from wood or corn stalks in a leach barrel. When it was time to make soap she would take the ash-filled keg and raise it at one end, pouring water into it. The ash would soak up the water like dry mud on a rainy afternoon. Finally, after about a day, the liquid would slowly flow out a narrow slit in the leach barrel. Alex remembered her very firmly telling him, "Now boy, you stay away because this is poison and even the fumes will burn your throat." But in spite of its hazard, it is the crucial ingredient, lye.

Alex pulled up his woolen overalls and buttoned a strap over his shoulder. He squirmed a bit sensing how scratchy the material felt against his skin. "Wouldn't it be nice if they were as soft as Timothy?" he thought. Then his mind wandered back and he laughed to himself as he pictured the fat cat rubbing himself on Betty's leg as she removed the fat from the crock and dropped it into a kettle with boiling water. When it was time to melt the fat into tallow, Betty would pick Timothy up like a kitten, tossing him by the scruff of his neck into the barnyard and out of her way. This happened every time. "You would think he would learn by now," Alex said to himself and shook his head fiddling with the other strap.

His thoughts drifted back to the picture of Betty pouring the poison lye into the tallow mixture. She would check it over and over again, all day, mixing the slippery mess. He wondered how come he wouldn't get burned if he washed with the bar filled with lye. When she first handed him some of the hardened soup it looked brown and oblong. He remembered he turned it over in his hand as though he were holding a brick. Betty promised him that the tallow she added weakened the lye so it was not as strong; a promise it would not burn.

He picked up a pair of dingy colored socks. The heels had been darned several times and were almost worn through. Betty constantly remarked that even blueing could not seem to get his socks white. It was funny to think that if she mixed into the wash water a little "blue" packet wrapped in cloth, that it could make the cloth less dingy. Betty said that white clothes turned yellow after awhile and blueing would help. But it didn't fix his socks. Alex placed a sock back down on the cot. He decided that he didn't want to put them on; his shoes were pinching his toes and right now he would rather have his feet cold than cramped.

"What's takin' so long, Alex? Bacon's ready!" Betty called out to him. Alex instantly refocused his attention and hurried to fasten the last button.

———

There was a clean oilcloth draped over the table. A small plate of fried mush with molasses was waiting for him when he sat down for breakfast. Randle was sitting in his usual spot at the head. "That fella who helped ya last night," inquired Randle as he sopped up the bacon grease with a piece of bread, stopping in mid-sentence to take a last bite, "you said his name is Tully, right?" Randle waited for a reply while licking his fingertips clean.

Alex looked up from his own plate. He hadn't eaten much since he had already had corn pone earlier and wasn't hungry. "Yes, Sir," he answered and silently wondered why this question had been repeated several times.

"Randle, I don't think we need to go into it now. Alex is home and he's got chores to tend to." Betty was clearing away the plates. "Alex, you didn't eat but a bite," she remarked noticing his full plate.

"I ain't finished with him yet," Randle glared at his wife. He pushed his chair away from the table, stood up, stretched, and readjusted the straps on his overalls. "You sure he said his name was Tully? Cause some years back, a kind of, well let's say, a different sort of fellah from the rest of us was rumored to have drifted around these parts. But he ain't been talked about for quite awhile. Matter-of-fact, most believes this Tully fellah was killed in the war."

Alex knew better than to question. His place was to listen and obey. Randle sauntered over to Alex, bent over and whispered firmly in his ear, "Understand, boy? I sure hope you didn't make it up since as sure as I'm sittin' here it wasn't Tully." The sternness in his voice was frightening. Alex did not move a muscle until Randle had stood up and backed away. Then, he nodded "yes."

"Betty, I'm goin' out. Alex, you better tend to the chickens, that little one yer raisen' is growing fast. Is she layin' any eggs yet?" he asked.

Suddenly Alex realized why this question had been mentioned. If she didn't lay eggs soon, she would be put in a small coop and raised as a "fryer!" Alex quickly replied, "I'm not sure."

"Well, keep an eye on her," he commanded. Then Randle slipped on his jacket and walked outside.

———

Alex slid down from his seat. The morning chores had been delayed due to his disappearance, however, now that he was home things were back in motion. It was as though nothing had ever happened differently. He pulled on his socks and squeezed his feet back into his shoes. He noticed that Betty seemed to struggle while putting on her boots and wondered if her feet hurt too. She was getting ready to set out and milk the cow. Everything on the farm was routine. After the milking, she would transfer it from the bucket into the crock and set it again in a barrel of water outside to keep the contents cold. As it cooled the cream would rise to the surface and Betty could roll it off the top like a pinwheel. She would put the cream into the butter churn. After that, it became his job to churn the butter, by pumping the plunger up and down until the cream turned to butter. But that chore was not until tomorrow. "Good," he thought recalling how his hands and arms grew tired from the constant motion needed to churn.

Alex pried open the pantry and pulled a shredded rag from the basket that was lodged in the back filled with remnants of gingham and calico. Wrapping the scrap around his palm, he clasped his hand tightly to prevent the rag from slipping off. He noticed that Betty had left the front door ajar with the slop bucket set in its usual location, on the bottom step. The bucket made of wooden staves was heavy even when empty. Alex grabbed the wire handle with the hand protected by the rag. Then he set out, dragging and lifting the heavy contents to the pig trough. Squeals and snorts trailed through the air, becoming louder the closer he neared the pen. "I'm comin'," he shouted to the hog. She was a square-headed Duroc sow with reddish bristly hair, a long tail, and droopy ears. Her twin piglets were exact miniatures, hearty, stout, and spent their days rooting.

Alex set the bucket down as he always did and lifted the gate handle to let himself into the pen. Randle had erected a small wooden shelter where the three pigs could settle in and away from the cold weather. This morning the pen appeared empty except for the nosey guinea hen that had decided to forage for leftovers. "Such a small head on such a large body," thought Alex as he dragged his bucket to the trough and dumped out the contents. Instantly, the resident sow scrambled out of her sleeping quarters with her little ones in pursuit. Alex jumped away from the narrow trough when he saw them approach so as not to be accidentally pushed in. Unprovoked by the boy's presence, they grunted with content as they gobbled their breakfast. He took a rickety rake that was resting along the fence and scratched the surface, trying to even out the hay floor so that it was not thicker in some spots than others. He knew that the pigs would shift the hay when they walked about; nevertheless, he wanted their pen to at least be a little neater. When he was finished he unbolted the gate and left taking the empty bucket with him.

In the meantime, the guinea hen had been keeping her eye on the whole affair. In a halfhearted attempt at flying, she flitted over to check out the trough, however, was too late for there was not much left but a few rogue scraps. Being a foolhardy bird, she jumped right into the feeder and began to clean up any small bits that the three pigs may have missed. Alex knew that the guinea hen might seem unfriendly to most others, but her unusual scream was able to chase even the most determined hawk away at night. So, he thought, she does have her place.

———

Last night was a *once upon a time* dream; a shadow of events that Alex continued to roll over in his mind. "What did Randle mean when he said that Tully was different than other folks?" He tossed the image of Tully back and forth but didn't come up with anything unusual.

Although he hadn't come across many others, the people he had met were all about the same. Alex set the empty slop bucket back on the house step and turned to see Betty coming towards him. She was carrying a full milk bucket, walking slowly so that none of the milk would slap over the sides. Her large tall frame tilted towards the heavy side as she trudged and her feet seemed to crisscross as she walked with the unwieldy load, something Alex never noticed before until now.

The sun was trying to warm the land but those days were gone for the next six months. A hint of a large object rolling down the dirt road came into view with the noisy rumble of its wooden wagon wheels.

"Who's that comin' down this way?" thought Betty as she tried to see but her failing vision did not allow her to clearly focus on the faces. "Alex, can ya make out who that is?" she shouted to him.

Alex had already turned toward the noise of the approaching wagon when he heard Betty calling out to him. The rumble of the squeaky wheels and the jingle of the harness bracket accompanied the sight of a woman wrapped in a gray woolen blanket. She was seated next to a capped boy who was handling the reins of the one-horsed cart they rode in. The large mare plodded along until it stopped when the boy pulled back on the reins. Betty had reached the side of the house and lifted the milk bucket into the quarter-filled barrel of water.

"Well, if it ain't Belle Tarson and her son, Joseph!" exclaimed Betty pulling her shawl more tightly as she walked up to the boy's side of the wagon. "What brings you out now?" Betty questioned. "Come on down here Belle, here, let me help you!"

Joseph, a lad of about eight, jumped down from the cart and hurried over to his mother's side to help her. Alex noticed that Joseph walked with a limp and wondered if it was from an accident? He also thought that Belle was a silly name for a person and glad that no one had named him something like that.

"Joseph, git back up here, I didn't tell you we were stayin'." Belle Tarson glared down at Joseph who meekly apologized and limped back to the other side of the cart and pulled himself up. "So Betty, this is the boy you got from back east, eh?" she asked of Alex.

"Yes, this here is Alex, he's turned out to be a fine boy, quite a help too," replied Betty. "Come on over and meet Missus Tarson, Alex," she coaxed, waving her hand toward him to approach. Still standing on the step, he timidly walked over next to Betty, who continued to talk. Alex's eyes met Joseph's and they stared at one another but neither spoke. "So, what brings ya out?" she asked.

"Just came to tell you that the schoolmarm is back and stayin' with us. So, if you want to send yer boy, he can come over after morning chores. By the looks of him he's old enough," she added inspecting Alex as she spoke.

"Why that would be very nice; we were just talkin' bout school. Wouldn't that be nice, Alex?" Betty asked in a tone that demanded an affirmative answer.

Alex nodded "yes" but the idea of going to Belle Tarson's for school seemed out of the question.

"Then it's set. We'll see him in the morning. Have him bring a slate if he has one. We'll get together some time soon, Betty, but now I must get along," and with that Belle elbowed her son to get the mare moving.

Alex stood for a few minutes watching the cart roll away. It was a rickety old thing and teetered back and forth as it was pulled along the bumpy terrain. "Get on out to them chickens, Alex!" Betty reminded him as she handed him the burlap bag of feed. Then she went into the house to tend to her other chores.

———

Alex approached the barn door, and as he entered he was immediately stormed by several of the more brazen chickens. The leader of the siege was the fat brown hen, promptly followed by one of her offspring, another fat and brown but smaller chicken. These two were the first to peck at the feed Alex scattered about. He scanned the floor in search of his chicken and saw her feeding off by herself.

Alex dumped the rest of the feed carelessly about and followed Yazhi. She had grown large and round, considerably more robust compared to the first time he had held and protected her as a tiny chick. Now Yazhi seemed to fit right in; she looked like an ordinary chicken and demanded food just like the others. But nothing had really changed and the fat brown hen, Yazhi's mother, didn't pay any attention to her; that is unless there was a larger scrap and then a squabble would ensue. The brown hen always was the winner. Alex's eyes followed Yazhi, her bandy legs strutting about until she found just the right seed to peck. Alex squatted down and as he watched her endless pecking and bobbing he knew that he would have to come up with a plan to keep her from becoming Sunday dinner. "If that happens," Alex thought, "I will never eat another chicken again."

Alex stood back up and walked over to the stables. He liked it the best of all the places on the Forester farm for it made him feel safe. If he closed his eyes he could follow a scented trail of hay and sweet alfalfa which could lead him straight to the horses. He leaned against the wall of the empty stall and picked at a splintered piece of wood that was sticking out. He wished that Delilah and Dandy were not with Randle, he needed to ask their advice on a few matters. Then, he took up the pitchfork, the one with the handle that Randle had shortened, and began to muck the stalls. Alex had done this so many times that he hardly had to think what to do. Maybe that is why his mind always began to drift away.

Suddenly, he stopped what he was doing. Soon it would be 'tomorrow'. His throat began to close up as a nauseated feeling erupted, and he felt as though he could throw up. "School?" he pondered the word. "School, pool, tool, fool, yes, fool, I feel like a fool 'cause I never bin to school." He made a little face at the idea that he had never played with other boys and girls. Maybe that was what made him skeptical. He had overheard Randle telling a neighbor about a couple of "bad" boys who had thrown Mrs. Chang's cat down the well. "If you go to fetch water at the well you can hear a low and ghostly spirit down at the bottom. The spirit of the cat was so angry that its ghost became possessed by the phantom of a mountain lion." Betty told him that was not true, but how would she know, she didn't like Mrs. Chang either.

Suppose those boys were at the "school" and didn't like him? His heart began to race and he imagined he was cast into a well, headfirst; wild and hideous laughter trailing behind as he vanished into a void of blackness. Alex flinched, trying to erase the scene he had called up, but it was the rustling of wings that brought him back to the barn. He looked up where the sound came from and in the rafters he caught sight of a heart-shaped face and dark eyes staring down. "Maybe an angel?" he thought. Alex craned his neck backward trying to get a better view but it was gone. He sighed and continued to replace the hay in the stable with the fresh batch. It didn't matter if they did like him or not 'cause he was goin' to school and that was already decided.

Chapter 13

Summertime is free and clear
Autumn brings the winds that shear
Springtime rains help flowers grow
And winter snowflakes make the snow

Libby tried to recollect all the times her grandmother would recite this poem and as the verse lingered in her mind it helped her from projecting forward into the future. But right now the present did not seem like something she wished to dwell upon either. Libby echoed the poem over and over as she stitched and tacked the calico smock for Mrs. Dowling, whose fingers were bent from years of toil, and her eyesight too poor to thread her own needle. A month; that was all she had left. "Ouch!" Libby pulled her hand back and saw that the needle had drawn blood. She reached for a scrap of material and wrapped it lightly around the throbbing finger. "How can something so small hurt so much?" she thought.

She stuck the threaded needle into the pincushion and noticed that a tiny bit of blood had spotted the smock she was mending. Quickly, she pulled it off her lap and dunked the soiled hem into the ewer filled with water. She watched as the stain began to disappear. "If only my fears could be fixed so quickly," she mused, rubbing the barely visible blemish with the brown soap. She set the smock aside to dry and walked over to the window, drawing the curtain back. Libby stared out and saw her father who was chopping wood for the stove. She backed away so he could not see her and returned to her mending.

"I must think of something else, I must not ponder on what I cannot fix," thought Libby as she picked up her mother's covering and placed it upon her lap. She turned the torn pocket inside out and pictured her mother wearing the linen pinafore looking like a grand lady. It is stained with the labor of her daily chores, no longer rough like when it was new. Libby ran her hand over the muslin material, its threads worn in the spots where mother wiped her coarse hands dry. All women's hands became coarse and red over time. Libby turned over her hand and stroked her finger along the palm. It didn't look or feel worn, not yet. Why would it matter now anyway? Her destiny was marked.

> Butterfly, ladybug, and tiny yellow bird
> Tell me, tell me, what have you heard?
> The King and the Queen have eaten all the pie
> Now the hungry children sit and cry.

Libby hunted through the sewing basket for thread that would match her mother's garment as she continued to recite the rhyme. But her mind would not tear itself away from the idea that was haunting her. "You will be leaving for Scotland as soon as the end of this month. Erskin Mackenzie is a good honest man, a widow, he is. He has no children, but many fine sheep." She could hear her father's commanding voice over and over in her head and no matter how hard she tried, she could not seem to replace his words with any positive outcome. "Butterfly, ladybug, and tiny yellow bird, tell me, tell me, what have you heard? Libby and the old man will marry straightaway, so send for the boat and cast her heart astray."

She knew her father was stubborn and could not imagine how she could convince him that marrying a man who was already twice her age was not a good idea. "He needs a young wife, Libby, and is willing to give yer mother and I a handsome sum. He's goin' to throw in a couple of sheep for the winter, even without a dowry for you." Libby was not surprised by her father's decision. Many young women were sent away to be married and not many of them were coupled for love.

Libby sat back in her chair and set her eyes away from the work. She shut them for a moment and immediately Will Piccard came to view; young, fairly handsome, and most of all, he was devoted to her. She opened her eyes and frowned. "Oh, that Will Piccard, why did he ever have to leave the city? He should have stayed where he belonged and not befriended me so he could steal my heart. It would have been so much easier to leave. How can love cause so much pain?" Libby heaved an enormous sigh.

The sunshine was radiating through the partition of open curtains and spilled upon the wooden floor. She moved her chair into the rays to cast more light upon the smock she was mending and continued to work, but noticed that she now could not get Will Piccard out of her thoughts. Libby leaned forward attempting to fool herself that she was intent on her work and had no time to think of foolishness. But in due course she found herself making larger than usual stitches and needed to tear out the threads that she had been heedlessly tacking. Unexpectedly, the natural light she was relying upon was suddenly diminished by a looming shadow cast upon her and her work. "Those are not the kind of stiches I taught you to sew," spoke a voice.

Libby looked up with a start, "Oma, you frightened me!" said Libby in a startled voice.

"Enkelin, it is not like you to work with such large stitches. You are not minding your work, no?" asked Grandmother Analiese.

"Oh, Oma, I am unable to think or concentrate," moaned Libby. She did not wish to trouble her old grandmother with things that no one could help her with. Libby's grandmother, Analiese Helm, was a wise and hardy woman. She had been born in the Empire of Austria and lived in the great country during difficult times. When she was a very young child, her county was waging war with Russia. Analiese's father was commissioned into the military and as a result, he sent his child and wife to England in an attempt to shield them from their uncertain future. When the Russians were defeated at Pruth River, Analiese's father was rewarded with several days off. He and three other officers of the army could foresee the future. Peace in their county would not last. So, in the dead of night with their money pooled, the four clever soldiers bribed the captain of a cargo ship destined for England and stowed away. Before his life in the military, Analiese's father had been a successful and prosperous farmer. However, with the current sense of uncertainty looming, he traded his livelihood for freedom.

"Remember," he would say reminding the young Analiese, "if you have your vits, you vill succeed!" In their new country Analiese's parents managed to become the caretakers of a small farm and were given a plot of land as their own. They built a home fashioned after the one that they left behind. Utilizing a method of popular architecture called fachwerk, its design consisted of a construction system of heavy timber framing that is filled in with brick wall nogging.

"This is sturdy house, no one vill take it from us," stated Analiese's mother to those who questioned their decision. "It is fachwerk; it is strong and vill stay put!"

Analiese was taught to read and write, and when she turned seventeen met a young carpenter, Jewel Dowling, who lived in the village near the farm. He was an orphan who was raised by his spinster Aunt Florence. Jewel never liked his name and instead called himself J.J. In fact, Analiese never knew her husband's real name until one day, years after she was married; she heard the story of how he was named from Aunt Florence upon her deathbed.

Jewel's mother, Ophelia, always wanted a child, however was unable to bear children. At least that is what she had been told. So, she and Jewel's father, Douglas, had come to terms that a child would not to be a part of their family. However, when Ophelia turned forty years old she discovered that in nine months she was to bring a baby into the world. Both the expectant parents wept with delight upon hearing the news and promised that they would cherish the child as a precious jewel. Hence forth, when he was born he was named Jewel. But as things do not always turn out happily, not long after the blessed couple brought the new baby into the world they were tragically killed in a road accident. Their wagon overturned one foggy night, and it was reported that nothing could have been done to save either of them. The only fortunate circumstance was that Jewel had not been with them, but rather was being minded by their neighbor, the mid-wife who assisted during his birth.

"Oma, I just can't seem to feel as though things are going right," sighed Libby to her grandmother who now sat in the chair beside her cheerless granddaughter.

Analiese closed her eyes and let the sun shine upon her old and wrinkled face. She said nothing. She had been thinking about her own youthful love affair with her dear husband. Libby waited patiently and then spoke again.

"Oma, did you hear me?" she repeated giving a little shake on her grandmother's knee. "I just cannot feel as though things are going right!" the young voice lamented.

The old woman raised herself up, supported by the arms of the wooden oak chair. Although she was old, she did not walk hunched or bent like so many elderly women and men. "I was just thinking about dein Opa. We were so in love," she said smiling when his name passed her lips. "We lived here in dis house, the house that I grew up in, like now you, and your Mutter und Vater all live in." She paused. "It is a great house, strong and mighty like the family that lived before." Analiese sat back down and placed her hand under Libby's chin. She pulled it towards her and looked directly upon her granddaughter's face. "Something has happened that is trying to change the future, and I must stop it now." She lifted the young woman's face lightly towards the sunlight and then took her hand away.

Libby looked back at her grandmother perplexed and cocked her head to one side. "What do you mean?" she inquired setting her stitchery aside and leaned forward to catch every word that her elder was about to reveal. She knew that her grandmother could be filled with mystery, but somehow there was urgency in her voice that she did not recognize.

"You must leave home tonight, Libby; you must kiss your Mutter und your Vater goodbye. But you must not tell them that you are setting out and going away. It is your Vater; he will try to stop you."

Libby looked at her grandmother in a most perplexed way. "Oma, what are you saying?" She clutched the old woman's hand and clasped it tightly.

"This is your only chance for happiness my child. Please, put your trust in me," whispered the elder. She leaned forward and placed her finger to her lips and then continued, "However, after tonight, I too may never see you again."

Chapter 14

Alex walked along the twisting dirt road toward the Tarson's farm. The neighbors considered them "high-tone" because their frame house was constructed not of rough timber, but pre-cut timber from the mill. The plans for the house were brought in from Illinois and the house was referred to as "the one with the Chicago construction". Greg Tarson had moved his family from the East and decided that the fresh air of the country would be healthy for his wife and child. Little did he realize that nothing would seem to please Missus Tarson. It may have been her strict upbringing, which she passed along to her method of child rearing, or it may be that she was just plain ornery. Whatever it was, no one, especially her own family, wished to cross her. She was rarely seen without a switch and was willing to use it on any youngin' that contradicted her or her belief.

Perhaps this was why she was asked to house the schoolteacher and the children until a new schoolhouse could be built. It was only six months ago when the building caught fire. At the time, the Frontier School, as it was named, was barely a year old. Great community pride and hard work had established the school. It consisted of one classroom and another small adjacent room erected for the caretaker who lived there. The floor was bare and a wood burning stove was set right in the middle of the classroom. It had a well out back and outhouse too. Students often sat three to a seat on the wide planked benches that were joined to the desks. The youngest members sat in the front of the room. The "black board" was made from wide pine boards painted "black" with the alphabet written above in cursive. Slate was too expensive and needed to be shipped in, so the "black board" would have to make do. Students learned respect, manners, discipline, and the basics of reading, writing, and arithmetic.

It was recess and the children had been playing out back behind the school just minutes before flames roared across a nearby field. Witnesses exclaimed that without warning, tiny embers flew out of the sky like fireflies and fell to the ground where they rolled together becoming bigger and bigger until they were swept up by a gust of wind and cast into the dry grass by the schoolhouse. Within minutes flames jumped from blade to blade like hungry locusts, and suddenly ignited the entire building, devouring the wooden construction with relish. That was enough of an excuse for the schoolmaster, Mr. Briggs, who was a transport from Virginia. The very next day he was headed back East, claiming he had enough of the smell from farm animals, tapeworms, and ill-mannered children. "Guess he didn't take too well to the country life," exclaimed Missus Tarson when she secured him a ride back to Jefferson County. "It takes a strong man to endure life here, and that Mr. Biggs just doesn't want to trade his fancy britches in for overalls."

Betty reminded Alex not to dawdle along the way, not to stop to catch any insects, or stray off the trail after a rabbit. He walked along reflecting about the morning, how he fed the chickens and spread hay down for Delilah and Dandy. He was cold and wished he could have hid in the stall all day. Both horses were large and the heat from their strong bodies always seemed to keep him from being chilled. Alex tried to squeeze his hands into his jacket pockets but they had grown too large and parts of his palms were sticking out. Betty had packed him a satchel and carefully placed in it a broken slate pencil, a writing slate, and a piece of wool cloth to use as an eraser. She wrapped in paper a brown-skinned boiled potato and a large slice of bread for lunch and told him to ask the teacher for water to drink.

The serenity of the walk was laced with the past and the present. The trail he followed now began to become inhabited by more trees and saplings. The smell of winter ash, maple, and oak was increasingly prominent. Alex looked upward to find the "ghostly" image he had seen in the barn. However, the barren tree branches stretched across the sky, tangling one with another in a web of confusion. "Keep following the trail and you'll come upon a covered bridge. I ain't sure what the name of it is but it's known as "the kissin' bridge! It's been said that more than once a boy has snuck a kiss on his sweetheart," Betty told Alex before he left.

"You been kissed at the bridge before?" Alex had asked innocently.

"Can't say that I have and can't say that I haven't. But I know that its got the power to grant a wish. Ya got to hold yer breath the whole length of the bridge from one end to the other," Betty had remarked when she handed him his satchel. "Now git on so ya ain't late fer the first day."

Alex practiced holding his breath as he rounded the bend, and just as Betty had said, there it was, the 'kissin' covered bridge. But what he did not expect was to find a structure so very large. He followed the trail up a short incline to a clearing where the bridge provided a safe crossing. Its paneled boards were fitted securely together creating a hooded rectangular building. It looked very much like a narrow barn that had been erroneously erected over flowing water. As soon as he entered the covered portal he could see that the bridge was built to withstand whatever was set before it. The large posts and crisscrossed braces extended from top to bottom. The floor was planked wood, which showed just enough daylight between each board to see the rushing river below. He bent down and put his ear to the ground and could hear the water talking in babble; a language so quick that a human's ears can only decipher it as a charge or flood of movement.

He stood up and forgot to hold his breath because the excitement of the day had overtaken him. He began to run through the dark tunnel and as his eyes adjusted to the darkness he continued to keep his sights set on the light ahead. His feet pounded against the uneven planks and as he ran he wondered what would happen if the bridge collapsed and he fell into the rushing water below. Would anyone know where he was? The thought sickened him and he stopped as he exited the opposite end of the bridge. He bent over to catch his breath, holding one hand against his cramping stomach.

"Hey shortie, follow me." Alex looked up and saw a tall thin lad with a gray satchel slung over his shoulder standing a few yards in front of him. "Hurry up or you'll be late," warned the boy who was now heading up a clearing which led to the Tarson farm.

Alex did as he was told, still holding his aching side and scrambling to keep up with the long strides of the older boy.

"What's yer name, kid?" asked the youth who turned round and walked backwards so he could see Alex.

"Alex Forester," he said trying not to show that he was in pain.

"I'm Zachary McNary Rucker, my friends calls me Zach. But you better still call me Zachary until I see what you're like."

Alex said nothing and actually had no intention of ever calling him anything at all, especially now.

"We're almost there. Hurry up and be sure that ya git yer tail inside before they ring the bell so ya don't git a whoppin." And with that brief encounter, Zachary McNary Rucker turned and hurried away.

Missus Tarson was nowhere to be seen but instead there was a large heavy set woman standing in front of the barn. She appeared to be much younger than Betty, wore a russet brown cotton dress with a rounded white collar that was heavily starched. The sleeves were gathered at the shoulder seams while the cuff and frocked front panel were fastened with ten little hooks and eyes. The tips of her brown boots stuck out from the bottom of the hem and she stood straight and erect. Her Bo-Peep style bonnet framed a full and round face and a coal-colored woolen shawl was strewn about her shoulders. She clasped a large hand bell, which she began to feverishly wave about. The clanging bell pealed loudly and suddenly as though a hive had split, a rush of children like a swarm of hornets streamed out from behind the barn where they had been playing. Two lines queued, one for boys and one for girls. It was apparent that there was an undisclosed pecking order, for the younger children lined up behind the eldest.

Alex needed no formal introduction to this matter and immediately followed the crowd of children, finding himself situated behind a sandy-haired boy not much taller than he. A total of fifteen children were ready for their day and as the schoolmistress stepped aside each child filed passed her reciting, "Good morning, Ma'm." Boys who had forgotten to remove their hats before entering the makeshift school were quickly reminded with a simple snap of her hand behind the head.

A portion of the barn had been set aside for the school as a provisional partition of stacked crates kept the stalls from view. One wondered if the barn had been used for other functions in the past, such as community meetings or town hall assemblies. In the front of the room was the teacher's desk and chair on a raised platform so she could see everyone very clearly. Behind the desk hung a large painted blackboard with writing on it that looked like this:

GOOD MORNING
MY NAME IS MISS HENSHAW
NO TALKING, WHISPERING, PULLING, POKING
NO CARVING ON THE DESKS
No Hats for boys inside
Firewood schedule will be assigned each week

As soon as each child entered they stood in the back of the room waiting for a seat assignment. Alex, having been in the back of the boys' line now stood in the front of the row of children. Without talking the schoolmistress tapped each child and pointed to a bench and table; four to a plank, that was the arrangement, with the younger children sitting in the front of the room. Boys sat on the left and the girls sat on the right side of the class. Alex waited patiently since he was now in the very front and one of the youngest. He didn't know what to do with his satchel so he kept it draped over his shoulder and clasped the bottom of it securely. At first he followed every move the teacher made as she glided back and forth ushering the children to their seats. But then he began to examine the building. Like most barns it was made of wood and the floor was lightly dusted with straw. However, the walls of this portion of the room which he sat in were lined with shelves. There were a few books, slates, some slate pens, and cloth, which Alex assumed had a purpose. There was a ball, a few ropes, and then suddenly, there on the shelf was something that looked very familiar. It was a doll, a lone doll that had been deliberately propped up against a twisted tin cup. Alex craned his neck to get a better view. He wished to get up and examine the object but feared reprisal if he dared move even an inch off his assigned seat.

Daylight streamed in through the open doorway allowing some brightness to fill the somber room. However, as soon as all the children were seated it was necessary to keep the room shut, barring against the frosty November wind. Several wall lanterns had been hung and when lit, they cast a dim light about the dingy room. Fractured sunbeams poked through cracks in the plank walls. Splinters of light caught dust particles that peppered these blond rays and floated aimlessly about.

"Young man," sounded a stern voice, "it appears that something besides the front of this classroom has your attention!" Alex, startled, turned and mechanically stared forward not moving a single muscle. He felt the presence of his teacher standing behind him; he could hear her breathing more heavily as though she had some sort of respiratory ailment which caused her to wheeze slightly. She said nothing else and glided to the front of the room. All eyes were now upon him and Alex recognized a silent mixture of both sympathy and ridicule. Zachary McNary Rucker, a few rows behind him, threw a scornful gloat that stabbed his neck and sent a chill up his spine. Alex stared ahead and never took his eyes off Miss Henshaw. She must have been reading what was on the board because she was using a yardstick and with each spoken word she pointed at its written twin. But all Alex could hear was his own inner voice telling himself to relax.

"We begin the day with devotional readings and a song," began Miss Henshaw. "I will ask everyone to please stand up." Immediately, scuffling feet, benches being pushed back, and the feeling of restlessness blanketed the room.

Miss Henshaw stood in front of the room for what seemed to be an eternity. Alex repeated when he was told to "repeat" and he "listened" when he was told to listen. He stood when he was told and sat diligently when he was not asked to speak. But all he heard on this crisp Monday morning was," Blah, blah. Blah, blah. Blah, blah. Blah, blah and then Blah, blah. Blah, blah

Blah, blah. Blah, blah

Blah, blah. Blah, blah and

Blah, blah. Blah, blah

Blah, blah. Blah, blah and

Blah, blah. Blah, blah

Blah, blah. Blah, blah

Time for lunch!"

Suddenly there was a roar of "Hurray" which resounded in unison. In addition to the jubilation, several students added some revelry in the form of "cattle calls" which were advancing from the back of the room.

"Children!" shouted Miss Henshaw who grabbed a willow branch from behind the desk she was standing beside and walloped it upon the table. "I will not allow this noise!" Silence now cloaked the room. Although short and pudgy, Miss Henshaw became a larger force not to be underestimated. Rounding her wooden desk with the willow branch held like a cavalry riding crop, she patrolled the room slapping the switch against her other palm. Venom oozed out of her eyes as she dared anyone to cross her path. Alex trembled as the teacher started towards him. Her long flowing dress accidentally brushed his foot as she walked past, and he felt as though his heart would pop out of his chest and she would step upon it grinding it into the earth.

"Now let's do this correctly," she bellowed, turning her back on the children and slowly making her way to the front. "Aaron," she said pointing to a boy of about fifteen, who still did not read any better than some of the youngest.

"Yes, Ma'm," he replied in his most earnest voice,

"I will dismiss you to fetch a bucket of water from the well. It is to be left inside the door for drinking." Then turning her attention to the rest of the students she added, "I hope you all remembered to bring a tin cup."

Several of the older girls replied in unison, "Yes, Miss Henshaw!" while others simply nodded "yes".

Miss Henshaw continued, still holding the willow switch as she spoke. "It is too cold outside so everyone is to remain indoors to eat, that is unless you need to visit the privy. Am I clear?"

Again there was a resounding, "Yes, Miss Henshaw!" But, is that the response everyone replied with? Could someone have dared defy her? Instantly her stoic expression transformed into a sour and scornful scowl like someone who has been eating something woefully bitter. Someone in the back of the room had bleated out in a rather mocking tone, in a louder and most belligerent manner, "Yes, Miss Heehaw." Unfortunately, everyone else heard it too and smiles of approval were donning many of the children's faces. Young boys and girls tried to mask their snickers by putting down their heads or covering their smiles with their hands. She could not be certain whom the culprit was but she now was determined to find out.

Miss Henshaw stood firmly and her stern expression did not waver. "I certainly will not tolerate such behavior!" continued the teacher. "Let this be fair warning, if I hear such insolence again the whole lot of you will be punished. Now, you may be excused for lunch."

The schoolmarm marched back to her desk, sat down, and proceeded to pull out of a rather large bag what appeared to be another muslin sack with bread and butter. Her porcelain mug decorated with a spray of lilac violets and green leaves sat on the edge of her desk next to a metal pitcher that had been filled with water.

As soon as Miss Henshaw began to eat, a fervor of low conversations began. Alex was unsure of what he was supposed to do so he followed the actions of some of the children he was sitting with. Tin molasses buckets and sacks were opened and spreads of buttered bread, jam, and bacon were strewn about. He opened his own sack and laid out his food in front of him. Another small boy next to him, who was named Michael, too had spread out his lunch. It was a tin of stew and a boiled vegetable, which he claimed was a turnip.

Alex did not say much, for Michael had turned his back and was facing another child and they were now both engaged in a conversation about who could count higher. Alex now wished that he had brought a tin cup whereby he could fetch some water too, but did not dare ask Miss Henshaw if there was one about that he could borrow. As he picked at the small crumbs that he tore off the bread he continued to glance about. The children ranged in age from about six to eighteen. All the girls were dressed in a similar style, long fashioned tunics, some still kept on their coats or shawls because the heater in the center of the room barely kept everyone warm. Most of the boys had leather-tanned skin and a rugged physique from having spent most of their youthful years working outdoors.

Alex continued to scan the room when across the sea of children he spied a pair of eyes which he thought he recognized. They belonged to a small narrow face, as though outlined in brush strokes upon a wash painting in Indian ink. He tried to jog his memory of where he could possibly have seen her before today. Her chocolate colored hair was woven tightly in a pair of identical braids, which were tied off with large yellow bows on either end like a horsetail that had been plaited and decorated with ribbons before a show. Her cheeks were rosy, probably from the cold, and she quietly inspected her surroundings too. Alex followed her eyes that were now fixed upon the actions of a cheery and animated older girl who wore her hair in one long honeysuckle braid that bobbed up and down whenever she laughed and swayed from side to side. Alex looked down at his bread so that he would not appear to be staring. He continued to pick at the dry crust and made himself seem interested in his own lunch when he felt someone come up from behind him and roughly shake his shoulder. He turned with a start.

"Hey kid, so how's your first day?" It was the prying voice of Zachary McNary Rucker, still holding fast to his shoulder. Michael, the small boy next to Alex, turned to see who was behind and immediately pushed himself as far away from elder as he could.

Two other ruffians about the same age, ten and eleven, who were surely part of Zachary's band of cronies, flanked either side. "This here's Alex," the leader said turning to his two friends. "He's never been to school before."

"That so?" asked the shorter of the two.

Alex nodded timidly. A most dreaded feeling of claustrophobia now arose as the three intruders encircled closely behind. They hovered like vultures eyeing him so intently that if the poor little boy wanted to get up it would be virtually impossible.

"What are ya eatin'?" asked Zachary, who now picked up the cold potato that was set before Alex and rolled it about in his palms like a toy. Alex wanted to grab it back from him, but didn't dare. "Mind if I have it, I ain't got much of a lunch today," jeered Zachary.

Alex started to shake his head "no" but even before he could refuse, the insolent lout had popped the entire boiled potato into his mouth. He smiled like a cat that had just eaten a mouse. Alex sat with his hands clasped together on his lap. He was afraid that if he put them anywhere near his bread one of the three may take notice and eat that too. Zachary's neck bulged like a python swallowing a rat as he wolfed the potato, and it slowly slid down his throat. "Thanks, kid," he muffled, wiping his mouth on his sleeve. "We'll see ya later," he snarled, and the three swaggered back to their seats.

By the end of the day Alex had managed to learn the names of many of the students, especially those whom Miss Henshaw had to chastise, for they were the names that she constantly called upon, due to their disruptive behavior. He learned Michael was one of six other children and lived not too far from the Tarson farm. Missus Tarson's son, Joseph, whom Alex had meet earlier at his own home, was not in school but in bed with the grippe, and as for the mystery girl, he still did not figure out her identity

Alex scanned the pages of a well-worn small book titled, *McGuffey's Eclectic Readers*, which Miss Henshaw handed out. Each page contained a series of printed pictures and words. Alex assumed that the pictures went together with the words and traced the letters with his fingers and then on his slate. He held the book in his hands and wondered who else may have read this very same book. "You may leave your books on your desk, children," announced the teacher at the end of the school day. "I expect everyone to be here on time tomorrow."

"Yes, Miss Henshaw," they all repeated.

"Please stand so you may be dismissed."

And like a small infantry regiment, they stood and awaited the next command.

"Those boys whom I spoke to are to bring in firewood, lest we all freeze. You younger children may please leave first."

Miss Henshaw opened the door for the first time since the ringing of her morning bell. Immediately a flood of radiance filled every dark crevice. Alex was drawn to the light like a moth, and he squinted his eyelids to become accustomed to the brightness. Fresh crisp air quickly replaced the stale earthy smell of grain and bales of hay stacked neatly in the stalls that must have once housed livestock. There was no sign of animal life now except for a worn-out looking harness balanced on a large nail.

Alex had not removed his jacket, and as soon as he stepped outside he reached for the buttonholes and fumbled awkwardly to fill each with a button. A trail of students followed closely behind but Alex looked frontward, not daring to look behind him as he trampled down the hill towards home. He was gratified that he could escape before Zachary. All he wanted to do was to reach the covered bridge; if he crossed in one breath his wish would be fulfilled.

It was gloomy and the steely grey sky created an unearthly mood. Several children had stopped to play along the way and so Alex was no longer in hearing distance of the others. As he approached the opening of the bridge it looked like the mouth of the whale that swallowed Jonah, black and cavernous. Alex hesitated for a moment, held his breath and started to run. The satchel strap was draped over his shoulder and the pouch slapped against his hip as he ran. He could hear his feet pounding the wooden trusses beneath him. The thumping of the boards echoed through the dark tunnel; he continued to hold his breath, his cheeks puffed and lips sealed, all the while he longed to exhale and suck in a fresh breath of air. He kept running, still holding his breath, with the growing intensity that his chest would burst from lack of oxygen. He chugged towards the approaching exit when for some unexpected reason, at this precise moment in time, he cast his eyes upward to behold a rather subdued spectacle. Alex stopped in such haste that it nearly caused him to trip over his own feet. Yet his eyes never looked away from the grand sight and he opened his mouth in awe, releasing his breath, and stared into the darkness.

It was those round button eyes, the same set that was in the Forester barn. Alex, panting like a tired dog, collapsed as he tried to catch his breath. His sight wandered upward and when he blinked he thought "it" blinked too. Was it following him, waiting for him, or was it just a sixth sense? He didn't hear anything except his own dogged pant that was finally abating. He respired aloud, his little heart fluttering. Releasing the satchel, the exhausted boy leaned back against the ridge and batten board, mesmerized by the prospect of something above, all the while he continued to gaze up towards the "eyes". Clearly he could follow the rafters crisscrossing and supporting the beamed roof. Two small but fundamental window frames, neither cradling any glass, permitted patches of daylight to enter. A small coal-burning lantern was hanging aloft in the center of the bridge emitting a stream of artificial light, but not enough for Alex to secure a clear view of the image above.

A sudden gust of cool wind passed over his face and he closed his eyes, only to find that when he reopened them a sinewy figure was leaning against a pole at the end of the bridge. Instantly, Alex scrambled to his feet. He didn't look up but sensed something watching him from above. He could feel this visionary shadow, this invisible spirit as he gathered his satchel and proceeded out.

Alex felt as though he recognized the stance before him and then realized who it was when the figure's companion entered the bridge wagging its tail. He picked up his pace and ran towards the large hound dog. "Sergeant, Sergeant!" he called, arms outstretched and ready to embrace the droopy muzzle.

"Why look who it is," the raspy voice called to the dog. "It's that little minute."

Alex bent down on one knee and was having a difficult time getting his arms around the neck of the large dog that had decided to lie down and lap up all the attention. His tail thumped the wooden floor as though he were keeping beat on a conga drum.

Tully sauntered out from the entrance and into the covered bridge where boy and dog were uniting. He carried a long pole with a hook. "We're here to refill the coal-lamp," he continued. "It gets mighty dark in here at night and there was already an accident few months back."

Alex let go of the dog and stood up. He smiled heartily at Tully who was now heading back to the center of the bridge where the lantern hung. Sergeant followed the man while Alex remained where he was and watched. Tully held the end of the pole reaching up at least 14 feet. He maneuvered the device like a fisherman baiting a hook and then carefully lowered it towards the floor. The light was dim, an indication that just a moment of oil remained. Alex continued to watch, but now the light had given out and with the lantern no longer lit the two figures melted into a pair of silhouettes against the darkening backdrop of the opposing entrance.

As soon as the chimney was cleaned and coal oil refilled, the lantern was returned and a bright steady glow illuminated the darkening chamber. Tully strolled back towards Alex and the three exited the bridge. With the pole stretched vertically across his shoulder, the man shifted his attention to the boy and began to speak. "So, where are you headed?" he asked Alex, who was quickening his step to keep up with Tully; as for Sergeant, he was busy snooping around the grounds ahead.

"Goin' back home from school," he replied rather sullenly.

"School, over at the Tarson place?" he asked even though he knew the answer to his own question.

"Yup," was the reply.

"You don't sound so keen. It's good for a man to be able to read and write. You don't want to be ignorant, now do you?" asked Tully eyeing Alex.

"No, it ain't the learnin'; that's o.k.," he replied and pressed his lips together.

Tully continued to walk and glanced over at Alex who was grasping his satchel with both hands. "Looks to me like you could use a little good news. Tell ya what, follow ole Sergeant and we'll take a shortcut home," he proposed. "There is something I want to show you!"

Alex smiled up at Tully who didn't need a verbal reply to notice the sullen boy's mood immediately perk up.

Chapter 15

Sergeant, the watch and ward, remained close to his master and young companion. His course zigzagged as he followed the earthy scents that kept him from tracking a straight trail. Only when a sharp wind delivered a new odor did Sergeant stop to hold his snout high up in the air and flair his nostrils in and out like a train whistle. The three ascended an embankment. The hard packed earth ribboned with frost displaced the once thick carpet of grass that held the mound from eroding. Sergeant raced ahead to chase a fox squirrel that was wearing a thick coat of terracotta fur for the winter. "Looks like Sergeant found a friend to annoy," laughed Tully as he stopped to watch the squirrel outwit the dog. "It probably nests in the wedge of that old tree there," he remarked pointing to a dense wood, coarse and gnarled at the base of the trunk. "That fox squirrel sure has got a bushy tail, wide enough to shade them from the sun, don't ya think?"

Alex replied with a nod and watched the squirrel suddenly dive into a hole at the base making itself invisible. Sergeant's tail wagged violently as he rose up on his hind legs and rested his front paws against the trunk. With a boisterous "woof" he started to bark eagerly not understanding that his invitation to play was threatening to the little animal. "Come on boy, it ain't comin' out now," commanded Tully. Obediently Sergeant backed down and proceeded upward towards their destination, tail still wagging.

———

The three reached the flat hilltop and with sudden recognition Alex burst forth with enthusiasm, "I know where we are!" The landscape of the hill hit his senses with dramatic intensity as he ran up to the large boulder that was situated directly ahead. He tried to put his arms around it as if it were a long lost friend. Sergeant, not the least bit impressed by the great rock, came upon it and walked past with not much regard. Then Alex took notice, shouting to Tully who was not far behind. "Look, why, it's grown so much!"

Alex lept away from the boulder and raced up to a sapling; his tiny apple tree was not much more than a foot tall. It was enshrined within a circle of small gray stones all about the size of Alex's fist. Tully sauntered up and knelt down beside Alex, who now sat cross-legged beside it. "Sure is a fine little tree," said Tully.

"You did this, didn't ya?" asked Alex turning towards the man. "You've been watchin' out for it!"

"Now what makes you think that? I just wanted you to see how much it has grown," said Tully.

"Why, it's been tied to this stick, and I ain't the one who did it," remarked the boy pointing to a piece of wood supporting the lanky sapling. "I can see that you helped him stand up." Alex looked up with gratitude then back to the little tree.

"It is a mighty good lookin' tree. See how strong he is all by himself? You must be a genuine Johnny Appleseed," suggested Tully.

"Who's that?" Alex asked.

"He's a pioneer named Johnny Chapman, but most everyone calls him Johnny Appleseed. He became a hero planting and caring for apple trees. Wherever he wandered he planted apple seeds in neat rows, growing trees and giving starters to settlers to plant on their own land. He even built fences round the saplings to keep out animals," explained Tully. "He tended the land just like a good farmer would."

"Maybe I can be like Mr. Appleseed," said Alex. "But first, I need to keep field mice and rabbits away from this here little tree."

"First, you got to get on home, don't worry 'bout this tree," added Tully. "Come along." And with those words he stood up and clapped his hands together. "Here boy!" Tully cried out as he sauntered away from the tiny sapling. Alex gently stroked the spindly branch and watched as it seemed to shiver with his touch. Quietly, he rose and followed behind, tossing the strap of the satchel over his shoulder. Sergeant came bounding toward them, slowing down his pace as he met up with his master, and the three silently headed back toward the Forester farm. The wind began to pick up while the day aged with each hour. Not a word was uttered as they came upon the end of their time together.

Tully and Sergeant watched Alex trudge down the rocky slope home, carefully digging each foot into the terrain of the embankment so he would not lose his footing. Tully kept his eye on the boy until he saw Alex stop at the bottom and wave goodbye. Then he scampered towards the barn and Mr. Forester. From above Tully could see Alex slip the strap of his satchel on the fence post, and pick up a slop bucket before rounding the corner of the barn and disappearing out of view with Randle in the lead. "Time to go, boy," Tully called out to Sergeant and both proceeded back up the hill and away.

———

Several shivering months had passed and the days were cheerless and gloomy. Alex had become accustomed to his routine and walked back and forth to school, but only on the days that the trail was open. "Maybe this is why we got school at the Tarson's," thought Alex to himself as Betty wrapped his feet in gunny sacks. "Otherwise Joseph couldn't go to school. He sure would have a hard time in the snow, on account of the way he limps." Alex sat attentively still contemplating the situation he dreamed up, while Betty cloaked and tied the sacks up to his ankles as to prevent his shoes and socks from becoming too wet in the snow. He was envious of the boys and girls who wore snowshoes; they seemed to glide to school as effortlessly as an ermine refashions the color of its fur for the winter season.

Alex had adapted to the rigid and tough manner of his teacher, Miss Henshaw, a woman who remained unblemished by even the most insolent of children. It was not more than a week after school had started when a most bold and daring event occurred. The school bell had rung and all the children were in their places. Miss Henshaw had instructed the children to copy the lesson off the board. She circulated the room and stopped every few feet to examine the writing of particular children. She inspected their manuscript like a fly hovering over a picnic blanket. Suddenly the door opened and a cold wind rushed in like a dam bursting. The contour of a matriarch stood within the portal. All heads looked up as the figure headed indoors followed by a small limping shadow that shut the door behind him.

"Good morning, Miss Henshaw. This is Joseph, and he is here to join you today," a dignified voice stated. Everyone recognized that it was Missus Tarson.

Miss Henshaw, now aware of the intrusion, turned to greet the proud mother and her son. The class continued to stare at the three as Missus Tarson proceeded; "As you know, Joseph was ill with the grippe and unable to keep down a thing in his stomach, weren't you, Joseph?" she said directing her attention to the boy who wished that he could melt into the ground. It was bad enough that his mother had brought him to school; it was bad enough that the school was in his barn, but for her to publicly speak about something so private to all the children, he felt miserably humiliated.

"Yes, Ma'm," he mumbled, daring not to disagree.

"Miss Henshaw, I hope that you have all that is needed to teach these children to read and write," added the persnickety woman.

"Everything is quite in order, thank you." replied Miss Henshaw. Joseph continued to stand awkwardly by his mother who seemed to consume his every move. The once noiseless room began to stir with restless feet and hands. Some children began to draw caricatures of Miss Henshaw on their slates, snickering and giggling as they compared each others' roly-poly renderings. The schoolteacher sneered at several children with an evil eye, as to stop the misbehavior without wanting to verbally interrupt Missus Tarson who continued to prattle on.

"Do you have a separate bucket of water for drinking and one for washing?" she asked. "And have you sent out the boys for wood?"

"It is all in place," acknowledged Miss Henshaw, satisfied with her own efficiency. "Zachary and Wilhelm, those two boys," she remarked turning towards their seats, "have returned with kindling, and we are setting right away to start the heating stove."

"Wilhelm?" questioned Missus Tarson, "Is he the boy who is from Germany? Where is he?"

Miss Henshaw walked over to the boy of about age 16. He immediately stood up, greeting her approach at attention. She looked him up and down and then noticed something out of order. "What is this? You have come to school and your hands are dirty!" scolded the teacher pointing her finger up at his face.

Wilhelm, who himself was just learning the English language, was not so sure he understood what she meant. He did not say anything but one could tell that he was interpreting what she had said as fast as his broken English would allow. "Did you hear me?" repeated Miss Henshaw. "What did I ask you?"

Missus Tarson now took an interest in what was going on and walked between several rows of younger children to get closer to the back of the class.

Wilhelm answered loudly in a thick German accent, "You have come to school vit a dirty head!"

The entire class broke into a howl and even the indifferent Missus Tarson could not help but turn her sour lips into a smile. Wilhelm, who had not really understood what would have caused such an outpouring of laughter now thought himself a sort of hero. After all, he had gotten the attention of the entire class.

"Children, stop it this instant! This is no time for such laughter." She clapped her hands together and immediately like orderly dogs the students resumed their attentive positions. All turned and twisted to face the action. The room grew quiet again as Miss Henshaw continued, "I can see that Mr. Hildebrandt has a lot of work to do if he wants to succeed in our country."

Suddenly someone called out, "Hidelbrandt! What kind of name is that?" and there followed another uproar of laughter.

However, this time it was quite clear that Wilhelm knew what had been shouted. His smiling face of innocence turned into a mask of vengeance. His deep set blue eyes, usually so gentle, became enraged. "Vat do you mean? Hildelbrandt, it is a name that has been passed down from my grandfadder. Vat is vong vit dat?" he hollered.

Miss Henshaw clearly understood that though some of the children were unable to read, they were quite capable of beating up one another. These were the offspring of rugged people, they endured daily hardships and a fist in the eye would not be a new use of hands. She plainly understood that she had to get control of the class back under her reign.

Outwardly stunned by the angry outburst, several of the younger children appeared frightened, cuddling together on the benches where they sat. Little Amy Lou Hanson, only six, could be heard whispering to her companion that she wished to go home. However, the greatest distraction arose as several of the older boys, seated in the back, began tapping their knuckles on the table tops. At first, one could notice the tapping as more of an annoying undertone, however soon the rapping grew into a threatening demonstration.

A sick feeling came over Alex as he witnessed the events taking place. What would happen to him if the others found out that he was not from around these parts? What would happen if they discovered that he had been brought here from the East on an orphan train; that he had been taken from his mother and father. What if it became known that they were not from New York? Alex pondered this with fear. He did not know where Germany was but he knew it was far enough away that you had to come by boat. He also knew that his mother and father had come by boat from England. Were the two places nearby, Germany and England?

Alex's fears grew even more as he realized that his name was not really Alex Forester. That was the name Betty and Randle leant him.

He grew more anxious and wished that he could go out to the privy and throw up. What was his real name? He pursed his lips together and wished he knew. What if it is something like, Brinkerhoff, Allendorf, or even Van Piggy! He put his hands to his head and held them there for a moment. He would have to run away if that happened. He would have no choice.

The tapping of a few knuckles increased as others joined in. It did not take long for the entire two back rows of students to take on the role of percussion section from an orchestra. The dull pounding of wood agitated an already upset Wilhelm, and he clenched his hands by his sides into tight fists, digging his nails into his skin. Missus Tarson backed up and stood beside her son so she could usher him out at the first sign of any unruly disturbance. It was up to Miss Henshaw to maintain discipline and order. An unprecedented mindfulness and scrutiny weighed upon the teacher as though she was Joan of Arc.

The thump, thump, thump, which spread from the back grew into an unnerving pounding and finally Miss Henshaw covered her ears with her hands and marched through a sea of benches. "This is uncalled for young man!" she exclaimed to an older, pock-faced boy, who seemed to be the leader of much of this commotion. Apparently having been the victim at an earlier age of small pox, he now wore the scars of survival. Miss Henshaw placed her hand over his thumping fist preventing it from taking another beat.

"Now," she said turning to another shorter yet stockier lad who was sitting beside him, "I do not see where Wilhelm's name could be so amusing." She released the fist of the first boy and proceeded to the front. The makeshift schoolroom remained silent.

"John," she said pointing her fleshy pointer finger at a tired and dark-eyed youth, "your name is McCleary and your father was from Scotland. And you, Zachary," her finger still in the air but now shifted directions at another, "I believe your mother is Irish. Is that not true?"

"Yes, Ma'm," he agreed shrugging his shoulders and turning his lips downward. The teacher, who now turned her back on Zachary, overlooked his aloof manner. She then began to address Wilhelm.

"Well then, Wilhelm, I believe that you are in good company. We have many students that have forgotten their own heritage and unfortunately too have forgotten their best manners. Lest we forget that we are in the presence too of our benefactor, Missus Tarson," added the teacher. Miss Henshaw pivoted and nodded to her employer, who presently stood steadfast, not having changed her stoic and gloomy expression since her entrance. Miss Henshaw continued to circumnavigate the room. "We will move forward with our lessons for the day with no more disturbances, unless the whole lot of you would like to experience my switch!" Silence prevailed as Miss Henshaw scanned the room with a look that would have scared away a hungry wolf. The notion of being swat at with the switch was an immediate deterrent; remembrance of such pain is not easily forgotten. However, the humiliation of such a beating was often more agonizing than the pain, for it survived long after the sting. Not a child in the barn had ever been spared a thrashing, since during these times the switch was used to discipline children. As a result, every student could depend on the teacher to keep her word.

Wilhelm was still standing and waiting for permission to sit. His hands were relaxed now and his flushed cheeks gradually lost their angry rosy color and became pallid once again. Miss Henshaw approached and began to speak in a low and gentle tone. This time she pointed to her own hands as she redirected the question, "Why have you come to school with dirty hands?"

"Vell, Ma'm, you vanted sticks for ze fire, so I bring dem vhen I came. I had no chance to vash before you ring da bell to come inside!" The reply was earnest and straightforth. Even Missus Tarson appeared to be taken in by the sincerity in his voice.

"Very well, Wilhelm," said Miss Henshaw, "you may go outside to wash now. Thank you for the wood."

———

Alex, ensconced in his daydream, was suddenly brought back to the present by the voice of Betty. "There, you're ready," she said as she placed the last tug on the string around his ankle. "Try not to step into too deep a drift even though you won't be goin' to school today. No matter how cold it is them poultry needs to be fed."

Alex slid off the wooden stool and glanced down at his feet. Both were wrapped like two pieces of meat and tied up with twine. He had been adrift in his own thoughts and fancied that he would never have to go back to school. Betty helped him put on his jacket and new brown mittens she had knit for him. Leaning forward, she took him by the shoulder and tugged him toward her holding on to the left sleeve. "Now look at you, yer growin' like a weed. Step back." He did as he was told and scooted several steps backward. "Them britches are short, too!" she exclaimed yanking at the pant's hem.

Alex bent down at the waist and examined his feet. He felt like a stuffed scarecrow. His jacket too was short and the sleeve shoulders were gripping snuggly under his arms. Betty pulled him forward towards her again as she wrapped a woolen scarf around his neck. "Now, pull this up over yer mouth, the wind today will whip the teeth right out of yer jaw." She pulled the scarf up over his mouth and his disguise was not unlike a bandit. The wool itched every fiber of his skin, but he knew that the wind would have a far worse effect.

He shuffled towards the door, kicking up dirt like a human floor sweeper. Though simple, rustic, and austere those who lived a paltry existence appraised the Forester farmhouse as highfalutin'. As a birthday present to Betty a few years back, Randle surprised her and laid wooden planks down on the barren floor raising her up out of the dirt. Although the wood was burdened with knotholes and not milled smoothly, its elevation was able to keep the dampness and cold from seeping upwards. This was a far better prospect than the hard packed clay floors of most homes. At least when it rained the water that dripped from the leaking roof did not form mud puddles. In addition, the planks could be swept, which allowed the home to be maintained with a decorum of cleanliness.

Alex slid the metal latch and inched the door open. A gust caught the edge of the door creating a situation not unlike a sail snared by the wind. He hung on tightly but in spite of his effort to keep standing, he was propelled forward, tumbling head over heels into the bitter snowy outdoors.

Chapter 16

Will employed his wits and good sense of direction as he searched for the location of the prearranged meeting spot; a razed oak trunk lying on the side of the road. The old tree had never gained any approval and in fact was often criticized as "an eye sore" or "blemish" upon the countryside. However, at this moment the rotting wood fell upon the young man with the same appreciation as an upright beauty for either vertical or horizontal, it held the distinction of being the starting point of a new beginning.

He looked up towards the heavens and cast his eyes upon a celestial haven. There were the usual twilight sounds from above and below, a hoot owl, stirs from the underbrush of insects finding shelter, and small rodents burrowing beneath the dead leaves deep into the ground.

Alone and filled with anticipation, he sat down and rested upon the gnarled log. It was dusk, a time which is neither night nor day. It is more like limbo, a state of uncertainty and wonder. "How appropriate is this!" thought Will as he reflected. "My eyes wish to play tricks for it is not too dark to see but not light enough to see clearly. I believe I am in an altered state. I have heard that the stars give off a magnetic fluid that bathes all individuals on the earth. Perhaps something has interfered with this magnetic flow because I cannot believe my eyes!" For out of the emptiness a sweep of clear sky had assembled a female image and drifted towards him as though she had snuck in on a cloud.

She was dressed in a fine azure gown of cotton voile. Her tight fitting bodice was elongated into the shape of a V and elegantly cinched at the waist with a royal blue sash of silk. The pelerine collar was made of fine Irish lace and it draped over her shoulders like a short cape. In contrast to the slim fitting bodice were full billow sleeves that fluttered as lightly as butterfly wings as she moved. Her skirt was gored into individual panels and the ruffled hemline had been stuffed with horsehair, gradually sloping a full six inches down the back of the skirt. Upon her head she wore a coal scuttle bonnet tied with a grey velvet ribbon that ran over the hat and fastened under her chin, while a wreath of daisy flowers twined around the crown, such as a fairy princess might wear round its head.

"Will, it is me, Libby!" sang a sweet voice as she drew closer. "We had better hurry; Grandmother is waiting for us at the fork in the road with Judge Carson."

Upon hearing her voice Will jumped up and hurried towards her. "You are beautiful, but you would be beautiful in a gunny sack," he exclaimed. They stood, one before the other, and everything around them seemed to cease to exist. But now seeing Libby so finely dressed he began to wonder if perhaps all that Mr. Dowling had put forth to him on the afternoon they were fixing the fence may indeed have had some merit. And as he mulled over those hateful sentiments the young man suddenly felt terribly inadequate. Doubt rained over his thoughts flooding his happiness; would he be able to provide her with the things that she was so accustomed to? "Libby, are you sure this is what is best for you?" he questioned as uncertainty trailed his voice.

The big yawn of evening was swallowing the daylight as the two young people clasped hands. "Will, are you having doubts?" she asked in a most direct manner.

"Heavens no!" he exclaimed. "It's just that..."

"It's just that if we don't get moving my father will find me and then all will be ruined. Will Piccard, I love you. There!" she announced with a most matter-of-fact tone.

Will picked up her hand and drew it to his lips, kissing it as though he were a knight and she the damsel he was saving.

Behind the bend Judge Carson's filly gently neighed. "We had better get to the wagon. No one heard me leave, but if my father finds my bed empty he will surely come looking for me," Libby reminded Will in a soft and temperate voice. Then, she took up his hand and led him away towards the wagon.

———

The ceremony was performed at the comfortable summer cottage belonging to Judge Carson; a man of distinction. He had a long sallow face, gray around the temples, but for a man of his age, he remarkably still had most all of his hair, though it had thinned quite a bit over the years. In spite of the fact he had been retired for over a decade, he still retained all the legal rights of any practicing civil judge in England. He was not much younger than Grandmother Analiese and being that he was smitten with her; he had readily agreed to conduct the marriage of Libby and Will.

Libby embodied classical grace. She handed Grandmother her bonnet and daintily replaced it with a wide veil of silk chiffon with a rolled edge. "Was this the little girl she helped raise or an imposter angel?" Grandmother thought as she pinned the veil on her granddaughter.

The wedding was simple, as simple as their love, as simple as their need to be together: sealed by the words, "Til death do you part" this simple phrase now united Libby and Will forever. Neither of the young couple owned anything of value yet both had everything to offer. Will held Libby's petite hand in his and slipped a simple narrow wedding band on her finger. He had taken a handful of silver coins that he had saved to the blacksmith, where they were melted and forged into a plain silver band. The ring was crude though smooth and though it was not as ornate as one that would have been crafted by a jeweler, it was the best that Will had to offer his young bride.

When the two were pronounced "man and wife" a kiss was bestowed, sealing their marriage. Judge Carson turned to Will, and ushering him aside, proceeded to administer some fatherly advice. Grandmother Analiese handed Libby an envelope sealed with wax. "Dis letter is from die Mutter, Libby. She wanted you to read it before you went to America."

Libby turned it over and read the familiar scrolled lettering of her name, 'Libby.' "But I thought mother did not know that I was leaving," she questioned her grandmother.

"Here, sit down." She pulled her granddaughter next to her on a small settee. "Read and you may understand." She sat back and fanned herself with her laced handkerchief as Libby carefully unsealed the envelope and unfolded the parchment. She lowered the correspondence towards the illuminating lantern and transfixed her eyes upon her mother's words.

My dearest daughter,

When you were born I was so filled with delight. I had lost two other children, both boys, and I knew that you were a gift. You were as tiny as a fledgling but miraculously survived.

I always imagined giving you a large wedding where we invited everyone in the village and danced until dawn. Never did I envision that you would have to quickly marry and then steal away into the night. I never thought that your wedding day would be a secret like this.

I have tried to be a righteous mother to you; however, I am weak for allowing your father to have his way and for not standing up against him when he instilled fear in you. But, I am his wife first and must obey. He is not an evil man, yes, melancholy at times, harsh at times, but he is a good provider and head of this family. Libby, you must understand that your father has never been able to accept the fact that I lost his infant sons.

Forgive me for not being with you today and for not being able to say goodbye to you in person, but it is for the best. For you my child, I pray that you get away before your father finds that his only daughter has left his home without his knowledge or permission. Please remember, I will follow you with my heart and my soul will be with you and yours forever. You may not understand this now, but maybe someday you will.

I will always love you,

Mother

Libby turned to her grandmother and her eyes welled with tears. This was the happiest time she could remember and wished that she would not cry. She stared at the dear handkerchief that she often used to blot her eyes upon when she was much younger. Its soft cotton with familiar lace trim stood for more than a snippet of cloth that one would discard when it aged and yellowed. For Libby, this was a token of stability, always arriving like a white flag on the battlefield. She gestured for it once more.

"There, there Enkielkind, no tears on your wedding day," whispered her grandmother handing her the lacey handkerchief. "Now, haste, we must get you and Vilhelm away!"

But no sooner had she uttered these words did she cease to speak. Unexpectedly, as though a winged pixie had been obscuring itself in the rafters and flitted off only to reveal their sacred secret into the ear of a tyrant, a terrific blow battered the front door. It was supplanted by frantic pounding which one could only surmise as being directed towards those who inhabited the pastoral cottage. Libby could only imagine the hideous anger which would lead a person to assail such rage and vehemence, and she clutched the handkerchief to her heart and began to tremble.

———

A winter morning benumbs all sensations. Its cold paralyzes anyone and anything that dares to tread out of doors. It holds hostage small rodents and insects beneath the ground while above, an innocent layer of frozen earth is covered by a snowy quilt. White, many deem is the blush of purity, of peace, of innocence. Others search northward, towards the place from where the white eagle comes and grants the visionary powers to heal. This wintry whiteness promises a future palette of springtime, a season of flowering and rejuvenation.

Alex lifted his head and tried to regain his feet floundering like a bass out of water. He leaned his hands back and struggled to lever himself up, only finding that his arms sank deeper into the snow, all the way up to his elbows. He lay back again; tiny crystals of snow beginning to find their way down the back of his shirt and slowly melt into a cold wet spot. He looked up but became blinded by the whiteness around him. He squinted, and peeking between his lids he was fascinated by his ability to create a prism. Separating white light passing through a spectrum of sunbeams and flickering off geometrically perfect films of ice, it paraded slivers of colorful rays that seem to have been dropped from red roses, bluebells, and yellow daffodils.

He continued to toy with the rays of colors as he remained as lifeless as a fallen angel. The sky was not blue but almost white and therefore it was difficult to tell where the earth and heavens separated. With no variation in the colors there was not any discernible horizon. Then, without provocation, Alex thought that he was being watched. He tried to open his eyes wider, however the sunlight remained too strong and he winced; blurred before him now were spotted crimson stains.

Rolling over onto one side, he finally found he could lean over, bend his leg and pull himself up with enough balance to stand. Brushing himself lightly as one dusts a pan with flour, the first soft snow flickered off his pants. The gunny sacks were still secured round his feet, however meager an attempt they were in keeping his shoes and feet dry. Alex shaded his eyes with his hat brim, pulling it lower on his forehead and leaned his head back slightly. He scanned, but the eyes above that were minding him had evaporated into the whiteness of the morning.

The barn was solidly secured; both double doors sealed tight whereby only the cry of the wind permeated its barricade. Small openings high up under the ridge of the gable ends provided the only breach in its solid foundation. Here sunlight could cascade downwards like a series of spotlights. It had stormed much of the night and new fallen snow had blown up against the barn. Alex trudged his way towards the side where he always entered. There the wooden slat could be shifted to create an opening wide enough for a slender and wiry person to slip through. He pulled his mittens up and tried to tuck his cuffs into them so that snow would not roll down into his shirtsleeves. Remembering that Betty had remarked how he had grown, it was futile, his jacket sleeves were too short. He crouched down leaning into the drift and began to burrow like a dog uncovering a hidden bone. Alex easily cast the new fallen snow behind him. In no time he had scratched out enough of a recess allowing him to yank the wooden slat aside.

But as soon as he crawled inside he sensed that he was not alone. He remained low, hoping that he had not been seen or heard. He waited and listened. The snorts and shifting of Delilah and Dandy in their stalls were all too familiar to Alex. However, this anticipation, this feeling which now consumed him propelled a terror through his tiny nervous system like needles shooting out of his fingertips. Was he agile enough to crawl backward through the very hole that he had just entered? Alex's salvation was to sneak away and find Randle so he could rid the barn of whatever evil lurked. But at the very moment that Alex was to put this credulous plan into action, a melodious whinny sounded from the stables. More curious than frightened that the mysterious visitor had penetrated the stalls, Alex crept forward on all fours, slinking low like a ferret. His knees and palms began to sting as he inched along the hard and dusty barn floor. The earth beneath him was cold, solid and unyielding except for the thin shell of dirt that puffed upward like a cloud of grime and settling upon him as he moved. He wanted to rub his eyes, but knew if he dared this might only create more of a dilemma being that his mittens, wet from the snow, were laden with dirt. Grit entered his nostrils, and he could feel himself blinking incessantly, trying to flick out the specks of dust.

The barn was like his second home and he knew all its nooks. If he could reach the wagon without a disturbance and manage to creep underneath it, then a birds-eye view of Delilah and Dandy would be accomplished. However, being that Alex was seven and a half years old, he had not thought out his plan to full circle. And although he was by most standards an exceptionally bright little boy, his logical thinking skills were just beginning to become engaged. The prospect of finding the intruder was one thing; however, what he would do if such a scheme developed was a calamity that Alex had not contemplated.

The wagon was parked in the midst of the barn; its horizontal crossbar to which the harness traces connect the horse to the wagon had been lowered and rested on the ground. Alex crept like a cat following the line of the barn wall with only a slight detour to round several stacks of wooden crates and tilted sacks of grain neatly arranged in rows. Randle was fastidious and proud about the way he kept his barn; everything set in a particular order and place. Alex's thoughts flashed back to a few months ago when an acquaintance who lived in town was heading back from his travels and stopped by the Forester's for a midday meal. When he had finished eating the visitor sat back in his chair, for he had been quite satisfied with the hospitality, and took on an air of superiority. This pasty-faced man had stared for some time at Betty's tawny face and then appeared to fixate on Randle's callused palms. "Tell me," the man had asked haughtily, "how is it that you have spent your time working so hard? Why don't you sell this place and live more easily and comfortably in the village or the city?"

The room remained silent for several moments as the guest's words were digested by the host. A slight discord arising from the hush was generated by Randle as he picked up his fork and jabbed his cooked potato with the spiky tines until it was transformed into a plateful of white confetti. Then, he wiped his mouth on the linen cloth that was tied around his neck so he would not spill food on the shirt that Betty had washed and ironed for him. Randle stared for several long minutes at the man and finally replied, "Put work aside, the barn lays still, for it is with the farmer that the richness of life stays alive."

Alex never understood what that meant until this very moment! A particular wonderment arose within him with an instinctive premonition to protect the barn. The lonely neighing of a horse echoed through the stillness sending a shiver down Alex's tiny spine. He crouched lower and set his sights upon the wagon. Slowly, ever so slowly, he began to crawl towards the hollow between the large wooden wheels. But suddenly, without warning, a set of claws grabbed his back. Alex toppled as though a weight had fallen down upon him from the rafters. A shrill sound pierced his ears! Alex sprung up and reached behind blindly pulling at whatever it was. He tugged off his mittens, grasping wildly behind his head. A chorus of squawks and cackles joined the clamor. Alex ran wildly, tripping over his own feet, which were still encased in the cumbersome gunny sacks. Frantically he tried to yank the burlap bags off, managing to only lose one shoe and sock in the process. With one bare foot and the other fettered in burlap, he clamored up the wooden ladder leading to the hayloft. At the top rung he threw himself into a mound of hay. Alex was breathless as he rolled upon his back and stared up into the dark rafters. He reached behind him, stretching back to pull some hay behind his head as a makeshift pillow when to his dismay he felt the cold flesh of a hand grab him by the wrist.

Alex gasped as he spun round, the hand losing its grip on him. Dry hay scattered, sending bits of straw about like shrapnel. The frightened boy desperately attempted to escape, and not knowing who or what it was that seized him; he was frantic! The loft was a large structure, housing fodder for the winter. Bales of hay were stacked forming a miniature mountain range. Alex scrambled, slipping on the loose pieces of hay; he glanced behind him but saw only a powder of dust. The distressed child, openly alarmed, sought refuge as he slid behind a mound of dried alfalfa. Breathless, he clutched the mound tightly as though he might be able to melt into its porous surface. Its brambly texture scratched his soft cheek as he leaned his face against it and peered meekly round the corner.

Alex remained vigil during what seemed to be an immeasurable amount of time; all the more intent on staying anchored behind his impenetrable fortress. But impatience began to get the better of his judgment and rather than remain concealed, he decided to snatch a peep. Releasing his grip he tipped forward, bending at his waist, and supported his weight on one foot, the foot which bore the shoe. His hands were now repositioned, and he grabbed hold of the coarse bale. In order to find a better view, the small boy reached one arm forward hanging on with a tight grip, but no sooner had his fingers begun to secure themselves did he feel the slap of another more powerful hand latch on to his, drawing him away from his hideout.

Petrified, Alex gasped with fright realizing he was in the custody of a stranger. Instantly, he flashed upon that harrowing experience when he had been taken from his real mother and father, and he became overwrought with panic and dread. His words rang out in a strong youthful voice! "No, no, let me alone!" he shouted pulling with all his might as he tried to see who was responsible for this vigorous hold.

Chapter 17

The powerful hand restraining Alex's wrist relaxed, releasing the boy from the firm grip; and though Alex had been set free, he still remained trapped for the stranger was blocking his only escape. "There, there, little fella, I didn't mean to scare ya!" said the voice. "I was sure that ya might fall out of this loft. It's a long way down and you were scamperin' around like a rabbit bein' chased by a coyote."

Alex looked up at the man, his face was bare, not a whisker could be found on his chin. He was a wiry and thin fellow, and he leaned casually against a stack of hay. He was bootless, and he curled his toes as he stood in stocking feet. His yellowed cotton shirt and woolen pants were rumpled, as though he had been woken abruptly and had no time to straighten himself up. Thick dark hair was laced with pieces of hay, obviously a result of having been laying on an arrangement contrived as a bed made from the dry and brittle straw found strewn about.

"What are ya doin' in my barn and who are ya?" asked Alex, his fears having been slightly abated by the gentle and concerned manner of the intruder.

"My name is Wade, Jack Wade, but most call me "Pinto Jack", the young man replied running his fingers through his hair like a comb. He picked out small broken pieces of straw that had clung to his hair during his sleep.

Alex regarded him curiously and wondered why he would have two names. He knew that the only other name that he had ever been called was...he paused. At school some of the older boys called him "shrimp" or "mutton" but those were not names that he would tell anyone. His memory tried to resurrect his short-lived time with his real parents, but his memory did not call up the nick-name his mother would coo at him. Suddenly, his private thoughts were interrupted with a question.

"So, you know who I am, what's your name?" beckoned the stranger.

Alex became mindful again of this most extraordinary situation. He turned away from the stranger and inspected his dirty foot as he formed tracks in the dirt with his big toe.

The stranger started again, "I heard ya shooin' away that brown hen, she's got a mean streak in her!" he laughed. "She sure got your attention!"

"Alex, where are ya boy?" an abruptly familiar shout bellowed up into the loft from below.

Alex recognized that it was Randle who must have entered during the transfer of informalities with the stranger. "He's up here in the loft, Mr. Forester!" called back the itinerant guest.

"Well tell him to git on down, and you too, if ya want somethin' ta eat," replied Randle gruffly.

Alex looked blankly at the stranger. He was dumbfounded that so many of his thoughts about this person were so erroneous. The man bowed in a perfunctory manner. "Alex?" he asked and then paused momentarily, "that is you, unless of course there's another Alex up here with us?"

"Yes, that's me," he replied automatically as he tried to reconcile the notion that this person, who called himself Pinto Jack, was indeed not a rogue.

"I believe that we had better get down, wouldn't you agree?" He walked over to the corner of the loft and produced from under a rather worn and dingy blanket a pair of leather riding boots which he easily slipped on, indicating that they must have been his correct foot size. This was a luxury that in his young life Alex had not yet encountered; shoes that were neither too loose nor too tight. The man smiled, grinning and displaying a set of very white polished teeth. He turned now towards the ladder, backing down its narrow and uneven rungs. Alex watched, kneeling at the opening, steadying himself so as not to accidentally plunge down head-first. The boy was impressed with the ease and dexterity of this Pinto Jack who seemed to glide effortlessly, unlike Randle who would descend in a most labored exhibition of downward strides. Alex was determined not to show any awkward manner as he now turned to secure his bare foot on the second to the top rung and alighted downward from the hatch opening.

Both Randle and Pinto Jack were at the bottom of the ladder when he made his final step off the last rung.

"Well, look at you boy, what in the name of typhoon happened to you?" questioned Randle, shaking his head in dismay. But without a moment given for a reply he started up again. "Wait 'til Betty gits a load of you. Why you don't even got yer shoes on! And them chickens!" he pronounced placing his hands on his hips. "Squawkin' so loud, they might have raised the dead!" complained Randle. "What was the raucous 'bout anyway?" Randle's query however was solely an outward declaration of frustration rather than one which sought an audible response inasmuch as he recognized Alex was a child of very few words. He simply gestured with a look of utter disgust. Pinto Jack stood aside and watched the interaction between the boy and his father for he understood it was not his place to intervene in the way a man wanted to bring up his son. Although, he hoped that perhaps he would get a chance to come to Alex's defense if the right time and conversation traversed his way.

"Alex, go fetch the blanket out of the wagon fer Jack," grumbled Randle. The compliant child immediately obeyed and disappeared around the corner. But no sooner did he scamper away when he came upon several pesky hens, including the cantankerous brown hen that was pecking feverishly at the gunny sack, which now revealed his lost shoe. Alex kicked the burlap away, snatched away his lost boot, and tried feverishly to force the shoe back on. In the process, he managed to tug the gunny sack off his other foot. With his feet free from the cumbersome coverings, he found it much easier to climb up into the wagon to retrieve the blanket.

Randle's voice resonated as he addressed the man, "It's too dern cold to go on out with just yer shirt. Betty ain't finished mendin' yer jacket."

Alex returned and handed Jack a well-worn but still colorful quilt, laden in rich patterns of emerald and violet triangles, stitched together in neatly fit patterns. Its once taut trim now bore frayed threads of cotton tabby. "This is fine, thanks," retorted a most grateful Jack, who immediately began to drape the quilt over his shoulders. Then fashioning a hood with the balance of fabric; he completely engulfed himself in the cocoon with the sole purpose of captivating some warmth. Randle had already started out, leading the way with the younger man following so as not to miss out on a warm meal. However, before leaving he glanced over his shoulder, pushing back the cloak from his face, only to discover the little boy had melted away into the melancholy mood of the barn.

As far as Alex was concerned there was an unwritten law in nature that man, woman, and animal were to live in harmony. But like most things, there were always exceptions. The brown hen, for example, did not abide by such legislation for she often violated the rules. His chicken, Yazhi, Alex decided, was not the most quick-witted of birds and so he excused her for any liability that she may generate on account of her heedless actions. Timothy, the cat, was a tireless sneak and therefore Alex conceded that this feline could not really be trusted. Though Timothy wished to coexist in accord, just by the nature that he was a cat made him not responsible for his actions. Delilah and Dandy were forever securing their end of such a peaceful coexistence, and he especially loved them for that.

Alex was a child who had not been tempered by the hardness of life but rather delighted in his own findings. The farm was laborious and the rawness of its surroundings was often savagely rugged. But in spite of his frail beginnings, Alex managed to peel back the world's tough hull and glean what he could use. Randle had filled the wooden pail, allowing only a paltry ration of seed to be scattered for the birds. Alex was careful not to cast all the feed at one time, knowing that the domineering and aggressive would surely take all, leaving only a few husks for the others to scratch away from the earthen floor. Its mixture of shelled corn and ground grains were greedily gobbled, and during the winter Randle would add alfalfa meal for added nourishment during these greenless months. The boy knew that these birds were not being well treated because of the symbiotic relationship between man and animal, but simply because the fatter the chicken the...! Alex didn't want to think about that next statement for unless they were laying hens their destiny included a butcher knife. Unknowingly, they pecked and scratched with vigor while Alex bemoaned each morsel they relished. He tossed the last handful of food and backed aside.

The barn was teeming with life and it heaved and creaked as if drawing in a breath. He raised his head upward where out of nowhere those curious large round eyes again reappeared. Alex exchanged glances, as he was now becoming accustomed to its visual gestures and was finding nothing strange about its random materialization. Then as quickly as they appeared, were gone.

Having completed feeding the poultry, he scampered across the barn into the stalls where he came upon an unexpected visitor. "What!" exclaimed Alex aloud; for there before him stood a horse of such grandeur and magnificence that he felt a sudden tinge of guilt for having such immediate devotion to it while in the presence of the resident tenants, Dandy and Delilah. Alex was overwhelmed with awe. He had heard talk of such animals existing but never expected to see one in his very own barn! It was white with splashes of round gold markings, and its legs were as white as the fur on an arctic hare. Alex was familiar with the largeness of his drafts, however this horse was so much different. It wasn't the fact that it was smaller, maybe 15 hands he estimated, though he wasn't very good with weights and measurements yet, but rather statuesque in appearance and had a most dignified presence. "This horse wasn't fit for farm work. It must be doin' somethin' very very important!" Alex thought in the most private part of his mind, not allowing Dandy or Delilah to hear him, lest they have their feelings hurt.

Both Delilah and Dandy snorted and called affectionately to him as he circled the new guest and greeted each most enthusiastically. "So, looks like you have company!" he said grinning happily. He walked up to the horses and one by one stroked each smooth and velvet nose. "I see Randle fed you already. I am sorry that I was late," he added noticing two empty feed bags slung over a hook. "You know I love you the best and no horse, no matter how fine it looks could ever take yer places, right?" He clung tightly around the muzzle of Dandy and closed his eyes dreamily. Feeling Delilah nudge his shoulder, he opened his eyes and turned to give her an equally affectionate embrace.

He shifted his attention to the visiting horse, its painted coat shined and the long ebony mane was curried so well that it gleamed even in the dull lighting. He wasn't so sure how this champion might take to him, so Alex decided to gently admire it from several steps away. He yearned to stroke its long neck that blended smoothly into the withers; the shoulders, overlain with lean flat muscle that too were perfectly proportioned. "What are ya doin' here, girl?" Alex asked, now having decided that "she" was most certainly not a "he". "Guess ya must of come with that fella." Alex paused as if waiting for a reply. "I bet you were cold last night. At least Dandy and Delilah got some meat on their bones, but you ain't got much fat to keep ya warm." The young child's voice was sweet-tempered and serene like the whispers of the horse spirit. There was a peculiarity about Alex that defined him unlike other children, for he used his benign disposition intuitively. The guest was not a bit agitated by the attendance of Alex. In contrast, she held her head forward as though wishing to be stroked and her ears were flickering lightly as she listened to him.

"I got to git on with my chores, so you all be good. It's too cold out for a walk and too cold to git to school. That suits me just fine 'cause I rather be here with you anyway," murmured Alex. The trio remained still, their ears perked up high while the little boy delivered his words before he resumed his chores. His hurried steps made a slight pitter-patter as he went about his work, and they felt comfort in hearing his presence. But as the hour passed, he moved with his chores and was too far away for even their keen senses.

———

"Long long ago, in the days when the forests were so thick a starling could walk from branch to branch without ever taking flight, the roots of the Great Tree of Wisdom stretched far out whereby chieftains of many tribes would feed upon the knowledge. Berries, nuts, and fruits sustained life from neighboring plants and nourished all whom dwelled in their midst. Upon the Great Tree was a silver bough with silver branches that bore the most beautiful and delicious hazelnuts, and these would feed the stallions and mares, for they were the graceful creatures. Alas, the land was cleared away and the stallions and mares no longer would be able to feed upon the beautiful and delicious hazelnuts, and so they became difficult to tame and ran away from where once stood the thick forest they called home. Throughout the ages poets, farmers, and rulers tried to tame the graceful creatures, but to no avail. Until, as the story goes, a man entered from far away who, it was thought, held the secret from the Great Tree of Wisdom. This secret had been passed down from generation to generation, for one hundred generations. And until now the secret had never been told. But the root of the Great Tree of Wisdom must have penetrated his soul and he was the one who could tame the wild horse. He had the ancient knowledge of the "horseman's word."

Alex sat mesmerized as he sat and listened to Pinto Jack read his tale. He was taking in each word with such intensity that he became spellbound. Jack paused to moisten his lips, swallowing more of the cup filled with water. He laid the book on the table and was careful not to get the leather cover wet from the dripping of his cup. "Did he have a name?" asked a most quizzical Alex waiting patiently for more of the story.

Betty and Randle exchanged glances for they rarely heard Alex speak up unless spoken to and especially when there was a stranger around. "Now give him a chance to finish his breakfast, Alex," piped in Betty as she placed a corn pone cake on his plate.

"That's fine, Ma'm, I don't mind reading some more," he added, then turning to Alex he assured him, "I'm getting to that part." A white linen cloth was tucked under his chin, folded over much in the same way as Randle's, however not as grease laden as his host. Jack wiped his hands on the bottom of the cloth, picked up the book resting its spine on the edge of the table and opened it to where he had left off. Alex automatically smiled at the sound of the man's rhythmic articulation for he had never heard words sound so imaginative before, not even in school.

"Now, some believed that this secret was an incantation, a spell of those who practiced the sorcery of evil spirits and in the protection of amulets. Hitherto, those who trust in the Great Tree of Wisdom acknowledge the untruth and make bold the secret as it is; an ancient bond between man and horse."

Randle struck his fork down with such a force that it clanged against his platter, interrupting the reader and listener. "Now what's this nonsense you're tellin' the boy, somethin' 'bout spirits and secrets?" he demanded.

Betty padded over to Randle and rested her hand on his shoulder, rubbing him gently as she spoke. "Why, this is just an old tale, Randle, for amusement," she said trying to tame her husband who was obviously irritated. Then, throwing a gaze upon the guest she continued, "Ain't that so, Jack? This here is just a story."

Jack closed the book and placed a thin strip of cowhide between the pages to mark his place. "I didn't mean harm, Mr. Forester, I just thought that the boy might like this, since he's takin' a liking to animals the way he does. Anyone can see that this is a very special boy you have," said Jack and then repeating the man's name to affirm his position, "Mr. Forester."

Randle scowled with irritation across the table as Alex's fawn-like eyes darted from grown-up to grown-up as they spoke. "Well,

I guess it ain't got no harm, just as long as he ain't gonna be scared at night. We can't have him awake and not sleepin'," he paused, "on account he's got chores to do."

Randle calmed back down as Betty poured black coffee into his tin cup. She placed one for herself and then poured a cup for Jack. "Hope ya like it strong," she added.

"Thank you, Ma'm," he replied after she had sat back down in her seat.

"Go on, Jack," murmured Alex. "What happens next?"

Jack gathered up the book and commenced to read. "There was an ancient bond between man and horse. Now this man, his name was Filib, was only sixteen when he came upon a lone and hungry stranger sharing the same path as he. 'Young man, if I may walk with you and barter for a meal, I would be most grateful for your kindness,' the Old Man professed.

"Now as the story goes, this man wore a countenance with skin weathered and creased, and his form wilted and bowed. He labored as he hobbled along the path with slow and deliberate steps. Filib was accustomed to beggars; however this vagabond was odd, more exotic than the usual paupers he had ever encountered. Filib nodded and slowed his gait as to keep step with his companion.

'I have carried something for a hundred years, and as you can see it makes my back arch and my legs tremble beneath me,' he continued in a low tone.

Curious and generous, Filib asked the man if he wished any help whereby a reply was returned that he desired some nourishment. Filib, as stated earlier, was both curious and generous, and therefore led him straight-away to the village inn where they might share in a meal of rabbit stew.

A steaming bowl was set before them with a pewter ladle to dish out the meal. Filib watched with uncertainty while the aged man positioned himself in a most unnatural pose. His elongated chin nearly rested on the edge of the table and his face, so close to his dish that he neither required a fork nor a knife. He lapped the food much like a hungry dog and sopped the grease with the crust of the bread. When there was no more to be had he licked his fingers and wiped them on his ragged clothes. 'Now my young friend, I wish to divorce myself from this load and bequeath it unto you. But first you must take an oath, an affirmation to use it discerningly, by you and only those that you trust.' He grinned with the utmost satisfaction, as though he had been waiting to present this recitation as far back in the number of years as he had aged

'I have no reason to profit from you, Old Man,' replied Filib. 'But if I may help you unload that which weighs you down, then by all means employ me and allow me the honor.'

The Old Man, his spine angled like a fish hook, gripped the edge of the table with his bony clutches and pulled himself up and away from where he sat. He lumbered over to Filib, who was sitting across from him, and put his lips to the young man's ear to divulge his secret. The words oozed from his mouth and seeped directly to the core of his beneficiary. Was Filib captivated by this knowledge he now possessed, or was he perhaps spellbound by the secret he must now shield?

'There, it is done,' the Old Man chimed as he patted Filib upon his head. Thereupon, he composed himself upright and sauntered blithely out the door.

By and by time passed and the artistry, which Filib had acquired, became well-known around the land; for he became eminent, the one who could tame wild horses and calm their terrified souls. He was the one who commanded the "horseman's words" and these secrets that he swears by are today yet known only by a few."

Alex watched Pinto Jack close the book, set it back on the table beside him, and give a stretch up towards the heavens. "Is it true?" asked Alex.

"Is what true?" questioned Jack, knowing very well what the child meant but wanted to toy with his imagination.

"Is it true that the man in the story could tame a horse with his secret words?" he asked again.

"Now there ya go, Alex, talkin' nonsense," piped in Randle. "Didn't yer Ma say it was just a story?" he snapped.

Alex stared down at his plate still littered with the corn pone he had not eaten and bit his lower lip. "Yes, Sir," he said and shifted uneasily in his seat.

Jack looked at the child and wanted to answer his question. He wished to explain that he really was unsure, that maybe the words of the horseman were some magical power or maybe it was simply the bond that some special folks have between man and horse. But he knew better then to meddle with the upbringing of a man and his son, so he remained quiet.

"Now git on and finish yer chores, we got a farm to run and it ain't gonna happen on its own," continued Randle. Then addressing Jack he turned and asked, "So, if ya want you can stay a day or so til' the weather tames down."

"I sure am grateful to you and Missus Forester, don't know what Cally and I would have done if we hadn't run into your place last night. Might have froze to death or been eaten by wolves. Let me help with some work, I'm pretty good choppin' wood."

"Why don't you follow Alex to the barn, he's got to tend to some chores and I bet he'd like to have some company," added Betty. "He could use some help too with his schoolin' maybe later. You got yerself an education don't ya, Jack?"

"Yes Ma'm, my mama was a teacher and my daddy was a businessman, so they believed that schoolin' was mighty important when I was young," he added.

"Business, what nature of business?" asked Randle half-listening as he tossed onto the floor a leftover nibble of fried pork rind to Timothy. The large feline may have been lazy, but by being patient someone would usually forsake a sampling of their meal to him. He gnawed the scrap with gusto at the feet of Randle in anticipation that more food may rain upon him like manna.

"He was kind of an investor. He owned a cotton mill in England and when they moved to America my granddad invested his money in cotton. So, my daddy did the same, that is until he lost it all in the great disaster," admitted Jack, not sounding a bit unhappy. Randle now appeared more interested and lightly kicked Timothy away, who had decided to rub against Randle trying to either thank him or persuade him to relinquish more food. The latter being the most probable reason for the excess of affection.

Jack continued, "Yea, the Panic of 1837, as I was told, became the ruin of so many families and their livelihoods. Anyway, when banks went out of business, so did my daddy."

"Well, we didn't have much to lose," replied Randle. "Everything we could make was from the hard labor of our backs. I never did trust the banks anyway. But I do recall folks that were desperate. Why, we fed many a family that might pass our door, on account that many came west." There was a tinge of nostalgia in his voice as he leaned back in his chair. "Ain't that so, Betty?" But when Randle shifted his focus to his wife, there was an empty reply for she had disappeared from the conversation and pulled out her darning basket.

Chapter 18

S chool was in session during the spring and summer, that is if folks did not need their youngsters to help with chores. When it was time for the fall harvest the classroom was most often vacant, while the impassable winter made it a season of little formal learning. Following a scheduled calendar was unpredictable for if a storm did not keep the students away, epidemics of cholera, measles, and other diseases often spread within a community propelling an almighty fear of contagion that surely would keep even the most dedicated of learners away. As a result, schooling was often severed, suspending any harmony with learning that a child may begin to tolerate.

This pale winter day the desks were not filled with the motley crew of gunny sack-footed scholars, and allegiant dogs were not patiently awaiting the return of their young masters. Today children remained home, near-at-hand to oversee that hearths were fueled with kindling enough to keep the fires hot, or adjacent to bubbling cauldrons filled with lye for the making of soap. The paths leading to school remained idle except for an occasional rustle of a soft-footed rabbit. However, quiet as it may have appeared, darting behind gray barked trees, two stealth figures lurked about the wood.

The snow was deep and with each step they marked, a crisp outline of a print was embossed. Neither was concerned by this identification of their whereabouts, for they were on the prowl and only concerned themselves with the tracks of game. Red cedar harbored animals that indulged in its berries and hid amongst its pyramid-like frames. In addition to sheltering small creatures and winter birds, the fullness of the juniper also concealed the duo. Small mammals liked to scurry about and their light-footed gait barely broke the surface of the crusty ice that glazed the landscape.

In spite of the attempt to hide behind a screen of branches, it did not take the hunters much time to spot several pheasants that had let their guard down. Lowering the muzzle of the guns, they held steady, taking deliberate aim. With a deafening crack an eruption of buckshot exploded into the tree spraying the innocent birds where they sat roosting. A small bouquet escaped helter-skelter, wings flailing in terror, leaving behind a small male that one of the young hunters managed to bring down. Its limp body now hung on the belt of the youthful huntsman who wore the game like a trophy. Long sweeping tail feathers, tapered with black bars, glistened in the sun's light, for the kill was still fresh.

Alex was keenly aware of the presence of hunters, for he had heard the echo of the shots ricocheting from tree to tree. Although the blasts were not foreign to him, it flagged a signal of darkness even amongst this pure and wintry whiteness. He managed to look up at the bluff as he was trudging back from the house towards the barn. He was sure that the noise came from that general direction, the same direction that he often traveled on his way to school. Again another a shot resonated through the air, except this time it was much more powerful; it was approaching and whoever the shooters may be, they were clearly within striking distance of the Forester barn.

Instinctively Alex felt a necessary urge to take precaution and keep at bay anyone that may decide to harm the barnyard, especially the horses. He was not sure what he needed to do but figured he must investigate the source. The snowdrifts were so high that they could easily have buried him if he had not taken a poled-switch to stick into the snow like a measuring device as he trudged upward. Anywhere that he felt might be too deep he would have to make a trek to either the left or the right, creating a sort of zigzag trail. The sounds of gunshots had subsided and as he distanced himself from the barn a feeling of déjà vu overcame him. He remained still, permitting the solitude to wrap around him like a cloak. He had not felt this way since his day on the hill with Tully and Sergeant. Alex kept his eyes closed and listened to the nothingness.

"Crack!" he blinked his lids open as a violent rush of fright soared through his small body. The sound of the shotgun was so sharp that he himself felt woozy, as though the spray of lead had struck him. Any harmony that he had felt moments ago instantly melted into the snow. The shot vibrated through the stillness of the countryside while the caw of birds in mourning sang out for a fallen comrade. Alex threw his entire focus upward catching the sorrowful birds. He followed his instincts and tried to reach the summit as fast as his snow-bound legs would carry him. But as he approached the crest he was stricken with horror to suddenly encounter a thin trail of crimson stained snow.

The fresh snow hampered his pace, and he tried to plod through as fast as he was able but his feet, once moderately protected by the gunny sacks, were wet, cold, and numb. He could no longer feel his nose, even if he wiggled it, and he imagined it was pink and raw from being bitten by the wind. It wasn't more than ten yards from the start of the red trail that he noticed something lying in the snow. At first he thought it was a small mound, maybe having been built by an animal. But no sooner did he get about a yard away did Alex determine its actual identity. There before him lay a wounded white rabbit, no more than several months old. Its little ears still trembled as did its tiny pink feet. Alex walked up to the small creature and bent down to take a closer look. Its side, which was facing upright, was furry and white; it blended in with the purity of the landscape around it. However, the side it was laying on was no longer snowy white, as the crystals of ice were dispersing red liquid. It was now quite apparent that the tiny rabbit lay in its own scarlet bed of blood.

"Git away from that rabbit," cried out a harsh voice. "It's my kill!"

Without waiting for a second bidding, Alex turned towards the voice only to see the muzzle of a shotgun aimed directly at his face!

"Now git up slow and easy like, and I won't have to make yer mama cry tonight," warned the vengeful voice. The boy behind the gun held his weapon steady. It was most obvious to Alex that this was the voice that shot the rabbit; and anyone that could shoot such a tiny creature probably meant exactly what he threatened.

"Go on, I dare ya to pull the trigger, he ain't nothin' but a mut-tonhead anyway!" another cried out. A shorter and younger boy, try-ing to run in the deep snow, came up at the heels of the voice behind the gun.

Alex remained stunned but traded his fear for himself towards the little rabbit that was quivering with its last fight for life.

"If you touch that rabbit, I swear, I will blow your head off!" screamed the boy again.

Alex looked away from the rabbit. He looked up at the two. The boy bearing the gun squinted his left eye while focusing his right eye on the front sight directly at Alex. His head was bowed and his finger was clearly clasped round the trigger. Alex quickly threw his sight on the companion who was donning a large grinning smile and a raccoon skinned hat, which he wore twisted round his head so that the long furry tail jingled back and forth next to his left ear. "Go on, don't be yeller, pull the trigger!" the younger boy called out mocking his friend.

But just as these words darted from his lips, there uttered nearby a low and deathly growl, a sound so menacing that it made the earth around one's feet vibrate.

"Drop the gun boy, unless of course you want this to be the last act you perform on earth!" demanded a more threatening voice.

———

The ominous tone of a growl continued to grow and a large hand placed itself on top of the muzzle of the shotgun, pushing it away from where it was aimed, at Alex.

"Now, you need to give this to me." There was a definite tone of ultimatum in the statement. The large hand pulled the gun away from the boy who now stood in dismay.

Alex stood up from where he had been stooping over the blood soaked body of the small rabbit. He wiped his eyes with the sleeve of his coat, trying to mask his emotions. He stood as though pinned to the spot, dismayed by such an act of brutality. Overwhelmed with emotion, he fought back tears. "I think it's dead," whispered Alex.

"Course its dead, I shot it and its mine!" challenged the angry boy protecting his game.

The younger of the two stepped next to him and added, "Sure was a clean shot, why that rabbit didn't have a chance. Zachary had him in his sights and "boom!" The next thang ya known that fellah was stew meat! Course we got to cut off his foot for good luck."

Alex stooped back down over the rabbit, which now lay perfectly still. Its eyes seemed to stare back at him but he knew that it was no longer alive. He sighed and bowed his head when he suddenly felt a nudge from behind. "Sergeant, why Sergeant!" he cried out taking hold of the dog.

"Now, you two, pick up your game and git on home," demanded a firmly spoken voice. "Here's your shotgun. I've got a mind to keep it but I know that your Daddy probably needs it." He waited until they both nodded affirmatively as he handed the weapon back. "Tell ya though, if I ever hear you pointing a gun at anyone again, well, you'll wish you never heard the likes of me!"

Zachary sauntered over to Alex, who was still nestled in the fur of the large dog. As he reached down to grab the limp carcass, a low menacing growl followed his moves. "Git that dog away, will ya mister," petitioned the boy in a more remorseful tone.

"Sergeant, back," Tully commanded. The hound immediately sat down in the snow; he remained back as he was told, but did not take his eyes off the boy.

Zach bent down and picked the rabbit up by its ears. Alex turned his face away so that he would not have to see the gaping hole on the side. It was now clotted with drying blood. "See ya in school," he sneered back as he deliberately swung the rabbit in front of the disheartened boy. The two young hunters turned away and began to follow their own footprints back towards the trail that they came from. The younger boy slung the shotgun over his shoulder as Zach stomped ahead of him with his fist clenching the ears of the dead rabbit out in front. As they plodded away the cheerless breeze carried with it the lively chatter of the younger boy, "This sure will make a fine stew, won't it Zach?" The reply was too faint to be heard.

Alex fixed his eyes on the place where the little rabbit once lay. He cupped his hands and gently tossed fresh snow upon the sight that was mottled pink and red. "It was just a baby," said Alex now looking up at Tully who stood over him. "He was just a baby rabbit."

"I know, but things happen in the wilderness that we don't have any control over." Tully wasn't sure if this answer would help.

"Why did he have to kill the rabbit?" he asked, continuing to cover up the spot in the snow.

"Well, Alex, sometimes in life we have to satisfy our own physical needs in order to carry on. It appears that those two boys were taking home dinner for their ma and pa," he tried to explain. "You are unique and see things in a special way. I believe you seek the simple truth, which goes beyond those of other boys."

Alex looked away and continued to lament. "But it was just a baby, Tully. It never did git to grow up!"

Tully ferreted through his mind for words that would console but decided that his remarks were now useless. He understood that out in these parts of the country a boy is raised with a gun and that hunting was as ordinary to wilderness life as taking a breath. "Come on," he said putting his hand on the child's head; and he began to walk up and away from the newly hallowed spot.

Alex pressed one last mound of snow together and strew it upon the bloody droplets. Sullenly, he stood up and followed the man and his dog.

Chapter 19

"Open this door right now, Libby. I know that you're in there!" bellowed the voice, continuing to hammer upon it with furious blows. The wooden door was the only element that now separated father and daughter. Libby was horrified. In a matter of only moments she must make a decision that would leave a scar forever.

"Quickly, you must be swift," whispered Judge Carson appearing by her side. "My home is well-built and of solid construction, but this door may not be able to secure your safety if it becomes compromised!" Will, alongside of the benevolent Judge, held fast his bride's delicate hand and bid her to follow closely behind the elderly gentleman through a stony narrow passageway that led outside to the carriage house. Grandmother Analiese queued after the entourage but paused just inside the doorway.

"Grandmother, I can't leave you here, please, you must come with us!" begged Libby, who had abruptly stopped and turned to look behind her.

"We have no time to waste, you must leave her behind," called out the Judge who was several meters ahead. Will remained with Libby in the darkness where the only light present was the glow from within the cottage illuminating the old woman.

"There is no place for me where you are going, Libby!" Grandmother assured her. Her voice, though she was old, was still strong and alive with the spirit of adventure. "Leave now, kinder, dis is your time! I will contend to your father. He will not be pleased with me, but I am still his mother and he would never harm me!" And with those determined words she turned away.

As tears flowed freely down her face Libby cried, "Grandmother, Grandmother, I love you!" Will coaxed her gently, reminding his bride that she must hurry. The clamor of hooves and the rattle of the wagon suddenly jolted Libby into the present.

"Come now, girl!" shouted the Judge as he pulled alongside of the two. He was propped high up on the seat and his large body slung forward as though he could topple head over heels if by chance he released the reins. "This wagon is no match for your father's maverick!" he exclaimed. "Here, help her up!" he called to Will. The fury in his voice betrayed her father's dangerous wrath. Libby knew that she must take flight; this was the only salvation from a life of regret.

Will vaulted into the wagon and bent forward towards Libby's outstretched arms. Firmly he grasped her, holding her steady so she would not become unbalanced. With ease she climbed into the wagon and moved towards the back. She sat down and taking hold of the sides braced herself. Then she called out, "All right, Judge Carson, I'm all right." But in spite of this reassuring call from Libby to proceed, if an onlooker had overheard her sweet voice at that moment, he or she would not be certain where the true source of her response had come from; was it the heart or the head?

"Get on!" shouted Judge Carson, snapping back his buggy whip. Immediately, the sharp crack of the leather commanded the horse into a vigorous trot. The oversized wheels turned without faltering, chipping clay and earth as they rolled away. Small clouds of dirt rose up and settled like whey as the wagon broke into the blackness taking the young newlyweds towards an obscure future.

———

Their arrival was without fanfare; no rousing display of grandeur, no one eager to send them across the Atlantic with good tidings. Rather, the early morning deemed itself rather gloomy and bleak. Though green hills and freshly sowed fields bid good day to the country dweller, the same morning greeted the sailor with a pungent smell of gray sea and brine.

Libby was escorted down from the wagon and felt her legs fold beneath her from having been sitting for such a long period of time. She smoothed her hands along the bodice of her wedding dress and attempted to straighten her wind-blown hair by fiddling with the tortoise shell combs that kept her strands up and away from her face. "Oh, I am a mess, aren't I?" she questioned Judge Carson, who was now standing beside her. He had summoned a young porter to keep charge of his horses and wagons.

"Nonsense, you are as lovely as you are sweet," consoled the elder. However, unlike Libby, he had not been able to unfold so unsullied. In contrast to his usual well-kempt self as a blue-blooded gentry, he now resembled a disheveled coachman. His gray and silver hair had been swept about every-which-way and his black satin cravat had twisted crookedly about his neck.

"You are such a dear man," smiled Libby. "Here you are so far from home and caring only for my Will and I."

Will came up alongside of his bride and took hold of her shoulder. "Are you sure you truly want to go away from England?" he asked her. "You know that I will love you always even if you decide that you now regret this hasty decision," he added.

"Oh, Will, we will never be able to be together if we do not leave at once. And if I remained, I would be forced to leave England and be married away to the old Scotsman. I should rather die than live such a life!" She spoke with such passion and determination; there was no question of remorse in her voice.

"Then we must hasten and get you aboard; the ship leaves for America at noon and you do not want to be lolling about the dock if your father would by chance find you here!" reminded the Judge. Then, he grabbed his hat from the wagon seat and slipped it on, buttoned the few pewter buttons of his frock coat, and flipped sixpence to the youth holding the bridles. Will had already unloaded Libby's belongings and since he did not have much, their three bags were not a burden.

Princes Dock read the signage. It was cloistered in a massive wooden frame and extended high above their line of sight. They entered through a gate and came upon a pair of square buff sandstone piers. The design took on the style of Greek Revival, an architecture which delighted the eye in contrast to the unfamiliar smells of fish and ocean.

"This is the famous Princes Dock!" exclaimed the Judge. His voice drifted off into a sigh of delight. He continued like a tour guide. "This is the first dock to have a boundary wall, for security purposes naturally. Masterful, wouldn't you say?" Then without waiting for a reply he added, "London was always the star for trade but as you may not know; our Princes Dock of Liverpool is bound to pass her quickly." Both Will and Libby kept pace with the elder as he hastened his step, waving his arms about and pointing out the sights as they hurried along. "Cotton, silk, food, and tea come in from Asia. See that building?" he questioned, "it is a newly constructed transit shed built to protect the goods awaiting the fine gentry and ladies of our great country."

"Why Judge Carson!" said Libby delightfully, holding her skirt up above the tops of her shoes so that they would not rub along the cobblestones as she hastened, "you do know so much about all this."

"A hobby of mine, my dear." Then he halted and looked about, gesturing for the service of a young scruffy sailor bearing a burlap sack over his shoulder. It was an unfortunate person to stop, as he was obviously struggling to keep his load balanced. "I say lad, could you please direct us to the vessels bound for America?" the Judge paused and then started up again. All around them was an awesome spectacle, bare masts assembled like a forest. "The ship's name is…" then he fumbled in his vest pocket and pulled out a scrap of paper. "Ah, here it is." Then turning to Will, he handed the slip of paper to read, "Haven't got my spectacles, what is the name of the ship, it has left my memory."

Will read the name aloud, "Elijah Swift."

The lad, obviously disgruntled from having been intruded upon, remarked in a surly manner. "Well, me lord," speaking directly to the judge, "yer luck is in place, she's not but a fathom from ya!" and as he pointed he continued away, dismissing the three with a snarl of indiscernible mutterings.

"Why look!" cried out Libby, for not more than twenty meters away was their escape. The Elijah Swift was a three-mast vessel called a barque. Her distinctive rigging was identified by three masts, the "front" two (the foremast and mainmast) square rigged, the back mast (mizzenmast) rigged fore-and-aft. She had been built in Maine, an American state noted for its long-time maritime residents, and registered in New York.

"Well, I suppose this is where I must leave you two," decided the Judge. "We have found your vessel and your destiny now lies with the Captain." He paused and looked away. "I am not one for long farewells," he continued. "You have what you need to get aboard. I am no longer needed here." Though he attempted not to seem sorrowful, there was a definite sound of wistfulness in the elder's voice.

"How may we repay you?" asked Will feeling pitifully poor. "You have been more than a friend."

"Hmm, let me think!" he said rubbing his chin between his chubby fingers. Then in a joking manner he replied, "You may name your first son or daughter after my father. I never had the privilege of having a family of my own. Now his memory may live on, naturally in name alone."

"Granted," Libby whispered squeezing Will's hand tightly. "Tell us, what name was he given."

"Alexander," touted the judge. "Naturally, if you bear a baby girl, Alexandra would be a grand name. And if you have a male, why not call him, Alex?" Will and Libby looked at one another and nodded in agreement. Both remained sincerely indebted to Judge Carson, and they promised to honor such a reasonable request.

"Well you had better be off," announced the old gentleman. "Be sure to send me a note or two when you get settled. You have the name and address of an old acquaintance of mine who should be able to get you lodging when you arrive. I have already sent ahead in anticipation of your arrival in New York."

The next few moments were spent trading heartfelt farewells, exchanging hugs, and dispensing pats on the back. Will and Libby departed from the kind old gentleman who was nodding with approval as they walked timidly towards the plank that led to the Elijah Swift. Will tossed a fleeting glance towards the Judge but only his shadow remained visible as it bled into the dark cobblestones. The apprehensive traveler proceeded forward as a chilly gust of sea air pushed him from behind, as though it were a reminder to him that there was no turning back; he was leaving England forever.

———

Alex tagged behind the tracks left by Tully. He had so much on his mind that he wished he could erase it all and start the day over again. The alabaster trail he followed converged with the landscape. It was whiter and more achromatic then he ever remembered. This path was a partnership of man's steps and animal paw prints. As they ventured forward Alex paused with a sudden recollection of his surroundings that lay as quiet as a grave before him. "Tully!" he called out fearfully, "it's not dead, is it?" Tully raised his hand up signaling the boy to carry on and without turning around forged ahead through the snow. Sergeant, not a bit tempered by the winter weather, backtracked, wagging his tail in pure glee; it was his attempt to get Alex to hurry. Alex interpreted the man's gesture as a positive response to his question.

The familiar boulder remained steadfast in its usual location, not that it could ever have moved itself. Tully stopped and waited for Alex to catch up. The snow was at least a foot deep creating a most cumbersome walk, particularly for a child. Tully stretched his neck back and faced the sun as it aspired to angle itself into an overhead position. Fervor poured from the rays and spilled upon his face, warming his heart, not his body. Both boy and dog romped together and settled beside the boulder and as quickly as he had approached, Sergeant scampered away to toy with his shadow in the snow.

"Come over and take a look!" welcomed Tully as he prompted Alex. There, in full view, it stood. Alex clamored across snowy grounds to where his sapling had once been secured to a pole to help keep it upright. In its place stood a small leafless tree; thin branches raised towards the snowy heavens. "I bet it's as tall as you are," Tully said as Alex gently stroked the thin bark. "Here, let me see. Turn your back and I'll measure." Alex did as he was told as Tully took his palm and held it over Alex's head parallel with the top of the tree.

"Well, well," replied Tully.

Alex shot round, "What's the matter?" he cried out.

"Looks to me like you and your tree are just about the same size; 'course in a few months when spring comes round it might get a head start. Soon as the rains fall, why your apple tree is bound to sprout up even more!"

"Think so? It's healthy ain't it, Tully?" asked Alex again for reassurance.

"Why, it won't take this tree long before we'll be enjoyin' sweet apples," smiled Tully.

"Just like that Mr. Appleseed?" asked Alex.

"Yup, just like Johnny Appleseed." Tully paused as Sergeant scrambled back to Alex and then stood attentively waiting for the next command.

Alex began to pet Sergeant and then spoke with apprehension in his voice. "I think I know why we came up here," he said. "On account of that little rabbit, wasn't it?"

"Why's that?" probed Tully.

Alex took his arms and wrapped them round himself trying to keep out the cold. A light flurry of flakes began to blow about, settling gently on any and all things. "I kind of think it has somethin' to do with nature," he began again. "Maybe 'cause my tree is growin' so nicely, some things grow old." Alex looked up and twisted his head in a quizzical fashion. "And some things never get a chance."

"Somethin' like that, Alex. Somethin' like that." Sergeant wagged his tail as though he understood.

The three started back toward the Forester's house as snowflakes powdered the small tree, the lonely boulder, and the barren land. It fell upon them, erasing their trail with each new footprint. And in spite of the newly falling snow, the retreat back was seemingly less arduous than the initial journey. Tully and Sergeant watched while Alex walked alone down the last length of the trail. When he reached the bottom of the hill, he was met by a man who had been awaiting his arrival. Tully watched from afar as the man appeared to greet Alex with a friendly tap to the boy's back.

Tully tugged down on his hat brim, endeavoring to shield the sun away from his eyes. He concentrated on the man who was bending towards Alex as if they were speaking to one another, and then he followed as the stranger escorted Alex towards the Forester home. Tully shifted his feet as he stood and watched. Cold air blew out of his nostrils and he rubbed his hands together and then hooked them under his arms. He could barely make out the figure of Betty who half-heartedly unlatched the door to permit them to enter and just as quickly as it was opened it shut again. Tully turned away from the distant scene with Sergeant by his side and walked back up and away, disappearing like a pale mirage into the whiteness.

———

Pinto Jack didn't ask Alex, but Betty did. "Where have you been?" Her voice hinted annoyance. "I sent you out to find some kindlin' and there you go, off by yerself again." Betty did not wait for a response from Alex who was pulling off his damp jacket; its snug fit distracting his attention. She cast aside her inquiry and with undisturbed composure continued anew. "Pinto Jack wanted to know if you'd like to go with him to rub down his pony." Alex looked up and nodded approvingly with a definite yes. "Good, but first you better drink some hot cider, you look stony cold; you're cheeks are pink and yer feet have got to be wet. Right lucky if you don't come down with the grippe."

Without waiting for more instructions, Alex plopped on the floor and immediately began by tugging fiercely at his wet shoes; whereupon their removal only exposed his wet socks. These he found to be even more difficult to peel off since they were too small and cramped his toes. He yanked and pulled on the soggy socks, stretching the grey soles that had been darned at least half a dozen times, being as they were hand-me-downs from Belle Tarson's boy, Joseph. Like holding up a prize fish, he dangled the limp pair in the air; displaying his catch. Pinto Jack awkwardly stood by and watched as Betty handed Alex a piece of cloth to dry his shriveled and wrinkled feet. Jack found himself in the middle of the two so he took the cloth from Alex when he was done and handed it back to Betty. She mechanically exchanged it for a warm cup of cider which Jack handed to Alex. Betty turned away and lifted a basket filled with odd socks, ribbons, yarn, and pieces of cloth. In spite of her efforts to find a pair, Betty knew that once he put on his shoes his feet would get wet however, the luxury of multiple pairs of shoes did not belong to the Foresters even though they were far better off than some folks in the winter.

Alex by now had wiggled himself into Randle's larger saddle back chair and sat crossed-legged, adjusting his feet to tuck under his knees. He looked comfortable as he molded himself in the boar skin seat. Jack handed Alex the cup of cider to drink and then, leaning against the sideboard, stole a moment to look about the room. His quick appraisal chronicled the Foresters as a couple with more sophisticated taste than many who lived in the wilds of the country. He peeked under the linen cloth and rubbed his hand across the smooth surface of a cherry oak table. He bent his head to see it was designed with a breadboard siding. "This is a fine table," Jack said to Alex.

Alex, never minding much of the table except for practical purposes, set the empty cup down. "So, I could use a hand with Cally," Jack proposed, "and seeing how good you are with the animals, I thought you might want to give me a hand."

Alex nodded and picked up the dry pair of socks Betty set out for him before she sat down in the corner to mend. He pulled on the pair and wriggled his toes, deciding these socks were too big but at least they did not bind his feet. He wiggled down off the chair to ask Betty for permission to go out. She was seated in the rocker and bent forward busily tending to her work. Her fingers sailed up and down as she stitched the tiny holes closed. Some tatters were the product of having been worn so many times and others were made by moths and beetles. Other tears were caused by accident; too much lye was in the soap or the very simple explanation of "knee bursts," too much abrasion on the knees of pant legs. Hardly a moment went by where Betty wasn't setting out or doing a chore.

Alex was stealthy in his stocking feet as he approached her. She never looked up and worked diligently as he stood steadfast as a soldier awaiting a command. After several moments Betty set her work on her lap. "Did ya feed the poultry?" she asked him. He nodded affirmatively. "How 'bout Dandy and Delilah, did ya clean the stall any today."

"I'm gonna do that now when I go help Jack with the pony," he murmured, shifting his feet and tucking his toes under.

"That's fine, then bundle up and go on ahead. And while yer in the barn, check on that little hen of yer's. Is she bout ready to give us some eggs? Randle was askin' and I told him that I wasn't sure," Betty asked barely taking a breath between her words.

Eggs? Alex grew suddenly very uneasy. He had seen enough killin' for one day. He remembered that if Yazhi didn't lay eggs, then she would have to be fattened and slaughtered for dinner. What could he answer Betty, she was waiting? She was staring at him and it felt as if these eyes could read his mind. They were not angry eyes, just curious, the kind that wants to know "right now" what the answer was or the kind of eyes that could see that "you were hiding something".

Alex bit his lip and was about to speak when, CRASH! A loud and unexpected disruption erupted from the pantry shaking the shelves within it. "What was that?" shrieked Betty, pushing her sewing off her lap and into the adjacent basket. Pinto Jack followed the noise and pulled open the pantry door only to discover Timothy the cat dashing out after a small and terrified four legged creature in the lead.

"No, Timothy, no!" screamed Alex as he followed close behind the two. Mayhem ensued as Betty grabbed the corncob broom and raised it over her head in an attempt to be ready to fire it down upon the head of one or all of the unsuspecting parties.

At this point Jack was a bit perplexed, for he was not sure if Betty was going to clobber the mouse, the cat, or the boy. All four followed in pursuit of the mouse, who had skillfully headed to the nearest hollow in the wall. Obviously he had used this tiny hole as a point of entry and escape and had found that it was still most suitable for the latter. Timothy, not realizing or admitting that he had been outwitted by a paltry mouse, remained crouched before the tiny hole. His tale slowly wagged back and forth and his ears were like arrows, pulled back on his head.

"You're a bad bad cat, Timothy," scolded Alex, wagging his finger at him. The cat did not move nor acknowledge the boy. "Shame on you, the mouse was cold and now he's outside," cried Alex in a most frustrated manner.

Jack stood by and watched as Betty lowered the broom and leaned it up against the wall. She stood posturing over Alex with her hands on her hips. "Now listen here, Alex, we can't have no mice in this house. Timothy is a ratter and doin' his job 'round here. Everyone on the farm got to do his part, even old Timothy," she explained. The cat remained vigilant, still waiting for his prey but now he almost appeared to have a sinister smile on his cat face, as though he approved of Betty's words.

Alex bent down and stuck his face next to Timothy trying to claim the same vantage point. The cat shifted closer to the hole, trying not to allow Alex to get in his way; his tail continued to wag back and forth but a bit more feverishly. "You're not really a bad cat, Timothy," Alex whispered in the small cat ear. Suddenly, Timothy stopped wagging his tail and his whole body appeared to relax. "You were just protectin' the vittles in the pantry," the boy said stroking the cat's furry back. Timothy seemingly forgot what he was planning and rolled over affectionately displaying his fluffy and fat underside. His purring became almost like a hymn as he put up a paw at Alex. "You're a good boy," said Alex as he continued to stroke the cat under his chin.

Meanwhile, Betty had left the three in search of a rag to stuff the hole with. "There's always so much to do 'round here," she grumbled returning with a wad of calico.

"Here, Ma'm, let me try," and Jack took the cloth and attempted to push a tiny snippet of the material a bit at a time until the hollow was filled.

"Now, git yer shoes on, Alex, them animals ain't gonna get tended to by themselves!" reminded Betty.

Without hesitation to this predictable advice, Alex rose from his spot leaving Timothy in the same location; however now the relaxed feline lay sprawled out on his side and had contently fallen asleep.

Winter children are muffled in anything and everything that will protect them from the cold. But no matter how frigid, many go outdoors in playful attempts to capture the sunbeams within a fruit preserving jar. Like a firefly in the summer, a sunbeam could cast a glow that would light up an entire room. However, as hard as one tried, most clever sunbeams would not allow themselves be captivated.

The barn was a point of refuge from the cold. Small animal tracks led up to its entrance whereby it was not uncommon for a slinky ermine or lissome squirrel to survey the perimeter, hoping to find, by chance, a breach in the mighty structure. However, if they are acrobatically able, they would discover a series of rooftop ventilators that served as a portal for fresh air and windows for light. Without these vents, the barn would be a sad and stagnant void. A clever person must too become most resourceful, for during this time of year the days grow short and will slip quietly into eve, taking with it all natural light. When this transpires, if one were to take a single twisted piece of cloth and allow the end to become ignited, naturally permitting the coil to rest in a saucer of melted lard, its lovely illumination would seethe over the vessel's edge casting a most pleasurable glow. And if the moon would cordially position itself in a most satisfactory manner and shoot its beams through the vents, this radiance, perchance, would flow and settle upon the very same spot as the saucer of light. If one were to witness this infrequent occurrence, they would for sure believe that it was the work of an omnipotent being; for nothing could be more beautiful.

———

Alex waited patiently as Jack pulled open one of the double barn doors just wide enough to allow them to squeeze through. Chores were waiting for Alex and no matter how much he would rather be elsewhere, he set out to work. The Forester barn had taken advantage of its location and was well designed; built into a hillside so that manure could be efficiently stored in a basement below for fertilizer. "Maybe I could help you, Alex," suggested Jack picking up a pitch fork. "Then you could help me with Cally, she'd sure like that!" Jack sounded sincere and began to tend to the stable area. Maybe it was the child's tired eyes or the fact that Alex was a serious child and did not find much time to spend on play or just that he needed to repay the Foresters for allowing him to stay a few days; whatever the reason, Jack felt compelled to assist.

Alex didn't pay much attention to the man. A great burden was weighing upon him at this moment. The death of the tiny rabbit began to manifest itself in his mind. He recalled its limp body hanging off the belt with a loosely tied string, exhausted of any life. Alex cringed and tried to shake the image away. He continued to pitch the hay and meticulously leveled it like a blanket upon the barren earth so that the animals would all have a proper amount of cushioning to keep them up and off the frozen ground. He trampled upon the hay, pounding it down with his steps, walking to and fro, back and forth, whereby his thoughts aimlessly drifted to the imagined dinner scene.

He and Randle were waiting to be served, it was cold and only the small fire from the hearth kept them all from the bitter chill. Betty approached the table with the cast iron pot. She was holding it, cupping the sides with two hands, which were encased in two scraps of cloth, the only elements that prevented her from burning her palms. Randle sniffed the air like a dog in anticipation for the meal. Alex watched himself as he slid down in his seat, as though if he plunged any deeper he would blend in with the white oil covered cloth. Steam rose up and over the brim as Betty set the pot down, grabbing the ladle to dish out what had been stewing for hours. She began to stir its contents, Randle savoring each smell which wafted his way. Like a snowflake from an open window, a tiny feather rose from the floor and found itself twirling about the hot vapors that grew from the pot. It danced up and down, tossed about from the rising steam, then, as if exhausted from its flight, it hovered for a moment and descended, only to drop down upon the table.

Alex continued to observe himself, and as he gently fingered the feather he suddenly recognized its origin. He drew his hand towards it and clasped the downy feather in his palm and quickly stuffed it into his pocket. He looked at Betty, whose eyes were still drawn into the pot and then he shot across at Randle who had pierced his meal with the fork and was cutting with the same back and forth motion that one saws white birch. Alex reached back into his pocket but this time retracted his hand finding it was empty except for a loose thread. "You sure look like you're in another world," interrupted a voice that brought Alex back into the present.

The distant boy glanced up from his day-dreaming as one recovers from being lost. Then setting his pitch fork back to the corner he replied softly, "I better go fetch the eggs, Betty is waitin' fer the eggs."

"That's a good idea," Jack smiled and continued to pitch the hay.

Now, a laying hen usually drops her eggs where it is soft, comfortable, and out of the way of other beasts that would like to make a meal from her troubles and in a barn the size of the Forester's a hen could be most resourceful. Alex had been collecting eggs for quite a time now and knew the location of each ones' nesting spot. That is, all but his own hen's hiding place and he was now in the belief that maybe she was not capable of producing breakfast for the family.

Yazhi had grown accustomed to Alex's comings and goings and like a dutiful pet she would come out from hiding whenever she heard his voice. No longer resembling the tiny chick or even the adolescent chicken he had grown to love, Yazhi was a full-grown hen and by farm standards was expected to act as such. "Where are you hidin' your eggs, Yazhi?" demanded Alex. In his wicker basket six albumin eggs that he had gathered up from the other hens lay in a circular cluster. He set the basket down and called out again, "Here Yazhi, where are ya?" In hopes that she was perched in the loft, Alex scanned upward, only to catch a glimpse of what appeared to be a scurrying mouse racing across a beam. "Only chance that mouse has is if the barn owl stays asleep." Alex noticed Jack too watching above.

"Who are ya lookin' for?" asked Jack, who now had finished one set of chores.

"It's my hen, Yazhi, she's supposed to be a layin' hen, but I haven't been able to find any eggs," replied Alex, who had retrieved the basket and was fumbling with the bounty that lay carefully within its confines like babies in a bassinette.

"They can be sometimes allusive, finding the eggs that is," replied Jack. "I remember once a chicken that laid an egg right inside my father's hat!" Alex looked at him suspiciously. Jack continued, "Of course, it wasn't on his head, the hat that is." Alex smiled at Jack's attempt at humor.

"She usually comes out when I call her," explained Alex.

"Well then, that is a fine sign, a mighty fine sign," assured Jack. "I bet she's settled into a fitting and cozy spot to lay her eggs." He paused hoping for a positive reaction from Alex, who was continuing to rearrange the collection that was in his care. Jack resumed, "We have to think like a hen, or actually a crafty hen. Now if you were her and you wanted to keep your eggs hidden, where would you hide?"

Alex stopped sorting the eggs and pursed his lips together. This was a rather large barn and a hen could stow away in a number of any pigeonholes or alcoves. She most likely would select a hollow large enough to sit in for a spell and away from most of the daily traffic. He had to think, but think fast in order to keep Yazhi out of that unspeakable cast iron pot.

But no matter how much he wished to find her, Alex realized that he had to finish his chores. The sunbeams were now streaming in from the north end of the barn, which meant that it was growing late. "Jack, we better tend to Cally, she's been waitin' fer ya," exclaimed Alex. "Betty said that I could help ya, and maybe Yazhi will come on out when she's hungry." He understood that it was futile to try to lure the hen if she didn't want to be found.

"I know Cally would like that a lot," agreed Jack, placing his hand upon Alex's thin shoulder. Alex lifted the basket and secured it with two hands, and then guided the man towards the stables. Alex surveyed the barn as he walked. He played a game, hunting streams of light that crept into the dull barn whereupon a particularly golden beam of yellow light caught his attention. This resulted in him pursuing the ray upward and following the sparkling shaft as it protruded higher, leading him directly to those now familiar dark eyes. Then, in an instant the eyes blinked and the strange and lovely spectacle disappeared and was absent from his sight.

———

Each person adapts to loneliness in his or her own way. Jack would fill his quiet void by whistling, and as he walked he followed his tune that drifted ahead. Cally was now aware of her rider's presence, and she shook her ebony mane and swished her tail as though deliberately keeping up with the chorus that Jack was whistling.

"What's the name of that song?" asked Alex as he set the basket down under the rail. The child had been listening with great earnest for he was unaccustomed to hearing such pleasantries.

"Song?" Jack seemed almost surprised that someone noticed. "Let me see, that was a tune that I picked up on the trail." He continued, "I do believe it's called 'Gentle Annie'."

"It's nice," remarked Alex and then turned to greet his best friends. "I see that you've been fed. Let me take off yer feedbags," he whispered. He pulled up a small step that Randle had assembled for him and climbed up. With a gentle tug he pulled off the burlap bags, one by one, around their soft velvet ears. The horses snorted releasing small bits of feed that had inadvertently become lodged in their nostrils. Delilah and Dandy had not only been fed by Randle earlier in the morning, but he had found the time to dust off a well-worn pair of woolen blankets and cover each broad back. The wind could be cruel and no matter how determined Randle was, it was impossible to patch every opening in the barn; preventing the winds from seeping into the tiny crevices was hopeless.

A burgundy saddlebag had been strewn aside and lay on the ground near Cally. It must have been purchased from another part of the country because Alex had never seen nor felt such beautiful Latigo leather. Jack slipped open the billet straps and reached inside for a curry brush. The small wooden handle was designed to brush the contour of a horse's body such as on the head and around the legs. Jack had to be extra gentle not to accidently tug the soft hairs around her nose and eyes. Cally stood enjoying the attention, just as she had done so many times before, permitting Jack to remove dried sweat, caked mud and dirt from the trail, or to whisk off water after a bath or wading in the streams.

"Would you like to brush her?" asked Jack.

Alex had been watching from the corner of the stall; he was intrigued by this horse which seemed small in comparison to the two drafts in the neighboring stalls.

"She is sure pretty," remarked Alex stepping gingerly forward.

"She can be kind of skittish, but doesn't appear the least bit nervous with you around," noted Jack handing the brush to him.

The boy began to gently stroke the horse. It was plain to see that he held her attention for she instantly appeared to become mesmerized as he began to speak softly to her. "You're a good horse, Cally girl, you need to get better so you can get out of here and do what you like best."

Cally shifted the weight off her hurt foot and while she was being brushed she allowed Jack to reach down and raise it off the ground. The frozen trails had been difficult for the pinto to follow and during the arduous ride her hoof had become bruised and sore. Alex stepped back and dropped the curry brush onto the saddlebag for he now redirected his interest towards Jack. "What's that?" he asked, referring to the sticky salve concoction Jack was dispensing.

"It's a mixture that contains the flowers from the arnica plant," the young man began to explain. "It grows in the mountains even though it looks something like a prairie sunflower. I always keep some particular herbs like this one in my possession, especially during the winter. See here," he said pointing to the area of discomfort. "In a day or so Cally will be better." He continued to apply the sticky dressing with a short blunt stick. When he was finished he scraped the remaining salve into a small sepia colored jar which housed the rest of the arnica flowers, olive oil, and melted beeswax mixture. Then, he resealed the container with a tightly fitting lid. "This kind of mishap occurs a lot and you never know when you need a bit of help," he said giving the jar a little tap of assurance.

Alex stared curiously at the gloppy covered hoof and hoped that Cally would not try to lick it off. He envisioned her tongue sticking to the gooey mess.

"She's got a beautiful coat," remarked Alex, stroking her neck with his small palm. He felt her skin ripple lightly as he continued to pet her with a gentle downward motion. "She was specially picked to wear these fine colors." Alex nuzzled his cheek against hers. "Not all horses get painted so fine." He was speaking with a voice of authority. "When she was a young foal her coat was plain and showed no special markin's. But all things changed the day she raced through a field of wildflowers. They were so pretty; all in bloom and grew tall and waved in the breezes so they appeared to whip across her shoulders like a blanket of colors while she ran. It was a real hot summer day and then the flowers started to wilt as the noon sun baked the earth; and the colors began to melt off the soft petals. But instead of flowin' to the ground, the colors stuck to the plain horse." Alex looked at Jack. "That's how come she got her colors," he whispered. "She's very special."

"How do you know that?" Jack asked; for the story that the boy recounted with such powers of imagination now roused his interest.

"Because I saw it happen," Alex replied in most dreamy manner. He looked at Jack with an expression that confirmed that he too was perplexed and repeated his answer. "I think I saw it happen." Jack did not ask Alex to explain what he meant. It was very clear to him that there was something very special, very unique, and very innocent about this little boy.

Alex stroked Cally on the nose, and she blew back hot air through her nostrils. He rubbed her again on the side of her neck, and as he did she flicked her tail up and onto her back. It was evident that the pony liked Alex; she remained calm even though she was having her hoof treated and most likely would have preferred to be left alone had she not been with the child.

Alex sauntered over to a short bale and sat down. He picked up a piece of straw and aimlessly began to pick around the thin tier of hay which had been strewn about.

"Ya know, you remind me of a man that I heard about. He actually must have been a hero, but I never myself met him," Jack remarked to Alex, who had now discovered a barn beetle and was watching the insect try to bury itself beneath the ground. Alex poked a slender path to help the beetle. He looked up and pursed his lips together.

"Why was he like me?" Alex asked.

"Well, he was a good man and had a way with animals. As the story goes ..." Jack stopped for a moment and began to gather up his medicinal herbs and ointments that he had set aside. "This man was a Texas Ranger, the time back when Texas was an especially unsettled and harsh frontier. Bandits and rustlers found it to be a place where they were able to blend in without much concern." Jack paused and looked up from putting his jars back into the saddlebag, noticing that Alex had made himself more comfortable and surrendered the brittle stick back into the bale, placing all his attention on what the storyteller had to say.

Jack continued talking while at the same time fumbling with the insides of his bag. "Now, these Texas Rangers are a proud and brave group of men and the particular unit this hero, which I speak of, fought alongside of his friends in the Mexican American War. They were commanded under General Taylor, a renowned and wild maverick. As the story was relayed to me, the 1st Mounted Rifles were sent into enemy territory and ordered to take control of the enemy's artillery. Positive results would naturally save the life of many Americans and put the enemy at a serious disadvantage." Jack refocused his attention to the interior of his saddlebag and located the item he had been rooting around for. Concealing a small object in his palms, he tossed the bag aside and leaned back, his legs crossed and outstretched in front of him. "You might be wondering why this man is a hero when there were many heroes in the war. Well you see, he had a special gift; he had a gift with horses."

"Is that why he was considered so important for the Texas Rangers?" Alex questioned, mesmerized by the story.

Jack found the boy's attention entertaining. "Well, that is probably one reason," he replied continuing with the tale. "But a most unfortunate development occurred the night before the siege was to take place; an enemy soldier snuck into the Rangers' camp. Everyone was asleep, surely resting up for the attack that lay ahead. The sentry was on patrol, completing his rounds. However, the saboteur was so stealthy that not a single break of a fallen branch underfoot was heard, nothing at all. Suddenly a fury arose from the corral, the black night choked in smoke. A fire had been deliberately set and the first blaze began to consume everything in its path. All the horses were being surrounded by what was quickly growing into an inferno. Immediately the Rangers sprung into action, but no one, they say, as quickly as Marcus."

"Who's Marcus?" interrupted Alex.

"That's the hero's name; I forgot the most important part!" Jack laughed.

"Go on, what did he do?" The story was getting most interesting and Alex was himself caught up in the drama for every word was laden with excitement.

"Well, Sam Walker, the second commanding Ranger, barked out orders. It was a priority that they were to free the trapped horses. Everyone knew that if the horses did not make it, their horrific fate would not be the only loss the Texas Rangers would endure. It would be impossible to surprise the enemy with the attack they had planned."

Alex reacted to this predicament by folding his arms in front of him as if to protect his thin frame; for at that very moment, whisking across where he sat, an icy gust claimed all in its way and settled itself as if it had been purposely placed to add a bit of macabre to the story.

"Volunteers raced towards the corral and each man was determined to be the one to release the horses. The raging fire was blinding, smoke spilling over the tips of the flames making it a dangerous and almost impossible feat. However, what no one had taken into account was that once the terrified horses did escape, what would keep them from running helter-skelter into the night! A frenzied panic terrorized the animals so that it seemed they were out of control!"

"Stop!" shouted Alex, in his own panicked plea. "Tell me, did they all die?"

Jack suddenly realized that the heroic tale that he was unfolding in his mind was a nightmare to Alex. He felt miserable and irritated with himself; he should have recognized that a sensitive boy like Alex would take the story to heart. "Now, don't worry, Alex, I think you're gonna like the ending. Is it okay if I finish?" A nod of "yes" acknowledged the story to proceed. Jack lowered the tone of his voice so it wasn't quite so sensational.

"Now, like I said, it was pretty hectic and the main idea was to free the horses. One of the new recruits was commissioned by Sam Walker to cloak himself in a soaking wet blanket, which was prepared by having been dumped into the rainwater barrel. Two others helped retrieve it, for it was now pretty heavy. They helped the young private shroud his body in the wet armament. With all energy breaking free, he ran directly into the fiery arena, while dodging and outwitting the hungry flames. He could barely see for the smoke and darkness made an impassible veil. The seconds seemed like minutes, but finally the men heard him shout out through the haze that the blaze was as high as the tree branches and had not yet found a way to the inside of the corral. With an outstretched arm he reached over to the locked fence and covered his palm in the wet blanket, for the iron bolt which kept the horses captive was now scalding hot. And, as dynamic as the opening of a dam gate, the horses thundered out of their enclosure with a force that mimicked the flood of water being released. Racing wildly into the night, they were finally freed!"

"Wow, that was lucky!" chirped the young listener spinning out of his spell of dismay.

"Ah, but I haven't gotten to the part that is the most incredible. This is why I started the story," replied Jack. "The horses were running uncontrollably and there was now great fear that if they continued galloping in a straight direction they would fall off the mesa and plummet down into a measureless cavern. Now," said Jack taking a breath, "the thundering of hooves and the snorting of nostrils echoed through the night. The men were scrambling about trying to come up with a way to turn the horses around. With no sound solution, many began to chase behind the charging beasts almost as wildly and equally as disorganized. The horses' pace had not slowed even minutely since the remarkable breakout, and they continued to follow their deadly course with full vengeance.

While the action of the frantic men, though with good intentions, were fruitless, it just so happened that Marcus had the fortitude to solve the problem before most men even had a chance to see trouble in front of their noses. For right about the time that the horses were to be released from the corral, he grabbed a lantern and headed towards the edge of the precipice.

Well, as the herd charged across the mesa heading for the great fall; amid the incredible clamor of beating earth and snorting gasps, a high-pitched whistle, which could only be heard with the most acute and keen hearing, resounded through the night. It was accompanied by the flicker of a yellow glow which illuminated the blackness with a soft radiance of quiet solitude. And miraculously, as if the horses had been instantly hypnotized and placed under a trance, their full gallop began to slow down to a canter, to a trot, and finally a peaceful walk.

When the Rangers arrived, convinced that all the horses had raced blindly into the cavern below, they were shocked to find Marcus calmly stroking the neck of a Palomino, and whispering softly."

"How did he do it?" asked Alex. "How did Marcus keep the horses from running into the cavern?" Like a cow greedily pasturing before the rains, he was hungry for an answer.

"Now that, Alex, is the mystery. He had a gift that only a few men or women are given."

The boy gave the story teller a cursory nod and took a few moments to ruminate the tale. "So, how is that like me?" Alex did not understand the connection.

"I think you have the gift, Alex. I see how Cally is with you; she can be a pretty feisty gal. But with you, she is a princess." For the first time since his arrival, Jack noticed that Alex imparted a smile, a real smile, not a half-hearted grin. "How about doing me a favor?" Jack continued. "I need someone not too heavy to ride Cally. I want to watch her walk to see how that hurt foot behaves, and it would sure be great if you could do that for me."

Alex did not have to be persuaded. He waited patiently as Jack retrieved a grey saddle blanket hanging off the stall rail. He watched as the kindly man spread and then folded the blanket on top of Cally's back; deliberately positioning it forward over the withers, and then slid it back into place to ensure that the hair on her back would lie flat beneath the pad. Next he lifted with two hands the leather saddle upon her back. "You have to let this fall lightly or she could become spooked and never let me saddle her again," Jack advised Alex who was noting each step.

He pulled upon the stirrup and adjusted the length so that the boy's short legs would not hang down idly, allowing himself enough slack as to tighten the girth adequately so it would hold the saddle firmly in place, but making sure that it didn't pinch the filly by mistake. Jack had been bitten a few times by a horse who didn't like to be girthed, and he wasn't taking any chances, even with Cally.

"Come on over here and take a look, are there any wrinkles under the girth?" he asked Alex pointing to the underside of the horse. "Tell me if you see her skin wrinkling." Alex crouched down and examined her underbelly while Jack lifted Cally's leg to be sure this action would not cause the girth to show any restraint. "I think she's ready for ya," claimed the cowboy, standing back around as he dropped the horse's leg.

If there was ever a time for a heartbeat to call into action, it was at this moment. This was not the kind of beating that one feels if they become frightened or scared, not the rapid thumping when hands grow clammy and the pink in the cheeks turns to alabaster. No, this was a skipping the heart does when it is happy and excited, when it anticipates wonderment. Alex was suddenly touched by this new sensation. For his little heart had rarely experienced this intrinsic physical phenomenon.

"Why, you look like you belong up there!" exclaimed Jack as he watched Alex maneuver the pony about the barn. "O.K. bring her round towards me so I can take a look at that foot," and with each step Cally took, Jack watched to be sure that the horse was not favoring any of the others.

The boy and the horse made several laps round the barn until they came to a stop. Without any help Alex slid easily out of the saddle and dropped down. Still grasping the reins in one hand, he pulled her close and nestled his head against her soft neck. "You're a fine girl, Cally," whispered Alex. "You're the kind of horse that someone can be proud of."

Chapter 20

Many people believed that Belle Tarson was an ornery woman. She didn't talk much and had an impatient streak for those who gossiped. She kept a neat and tidy home, expected her workers to abide by the rules, and though fair with the wages, she was frugal. But in defense of her shrewish personality, it was noted that even the most mild-tempered woman who was able to survive the harsh and lonely times in the wilderness, or the prairie, could turn temperamental.

Belle and her husband, Greg, traveled from Pennsylvania in a Conestoga with their only son, Joseph, when he had just turned three. Little Joseph was crowned with chestnut hair and fair skin that was silky smooth. He spent the better part of the trip confined to the back of the wagon, in hopes that the canvas top would protect him from the brutal sun, which beat down mercilessly. However, the family had journeyed only a month out on the trail when the poor and curious child met a most unfortunate accident, toppling out of the moving wagon when his folks thought he was asleep. They had traveled almost a mile before anyone noticed the child was missing. Alas, when they backtracked retracing their steps, Belle discovered that her little boy had been accidentally stepped on by the oxen, which had been tethered and shadowing behind the wagon.

They came upon him sitting by the side of the trail showered with prairie dust and doused in fear. Belle frantically tried to comfort the terrified child, who was clearly in pain. His tiny foot was twisted in a mangled mess. She gently stroked the contorted appendage before relinquishing the child to her husband. He held the tiny ankle and heel firmly in his hands and yanked the little foot straight. In spite of his hideous screams and constant struggle, they managed to splint the foot. However, by the time they arrived in St. Louis, Joseph had managed to wriggle free from the restraint so many times that it never healed properly.

Could this have been the catalyst that transformed Belle Tarson from a genteel Eastern lady into a cantankerous Western woman? Perhaps that innocent act of having neglected her toddler son during what seemed to be just a short moment in time, managed to permanently wrench her soul and stain her forever with guilt. For no matter how much she had tried to erase the wrong, his ever-present limp took her back to that painful accident

It had been many years since the Tarsons left Pennsylvania, yet in all this time they never surrendered their reasons for having left a well-to-do city home for a rustic wilderness life in Missouri. At first, rumors were spread in the hush of the livery stables. Some argued that Tarson had made his money during the Mexican American War trading arms, while others waged bets that Belle had inherited her money from a spinster aunt. But regardless of the truth or the allegations, they did not care to reveal the past and the curiosity of the unknown made for good gossip.

The Tarsons remained a private people who made education a priority. Both Bell and Greg had been well-educated back in the East; she having completed high school and Greg almost completing a university education. It was not difficult to understand that both were determined to ensure Joseph would be well-schooled, at least as best as they could in such a "forsaken and desolate place." Therefore, when the local schoolhouse burned down, and even before the last smoldering ash dispersed into the earth, did the Tarsons loan the use of their roomy and underutilized barn towards the education of the neighboring children.

Word of illness spread like grease floating on the surface of water. It was not uncommon for children and adults to die after taking sick. So when "the fever" struck the Tarson's, the dark fear of doom cloaked the homes in the surrounding areas. If there was any luck to be found in the midst of all the ugliness, the deep winter barred students from forging a path to school. Fittingly, it had been closed for a week and not a visitor nor vagrant had been able to reach the Tarson place even if they had wished to venture out into the snow.

Doors and windows were shut up tightly. Even the curtains remained drawn preventing any cold that might seep its way in by means of minute fissures in the walls or unsealed windowpanes. Only a winter red robin, who happened to settle itself upon a branch outside the window, could hear the horrible rasping and choking emanating from the thin shell of a child who lay helplessly alone upon a bed of soft goose down pillows. Carelessly, its lively black eyes peered into the lodging where the child's air passage was slowly being engulfed and strangled by a clear and gooey membrane. The bird continued to stare through the opening where the curtain folded away from itself exposing the child. In a momentary glance of curiosity, the bird appeared to share in the seriousness of the situation. Was it empathy or merely instinct driving it to take refuge within the warm shelter? Its reasoning for where it perched will never be revealed, for a startling and abrupt cough scared the bird back out into the snowy morning.

———

"I heard there's fever over at the Tarson's," remarked Randle in a noticeably matter-of-fact tone. He often spoke in such a manner when trying not to alarm his wife. He pulled off his wet boots and threw them aside. Then reclining back into the wooden chair, he rested his head against the cushioned back and tilted his stocking feet towards the hearth warming his toes. Halfheartedly he lowered his arm over the side of the chair and fumbled with an equally haphazardly heaped pile of corn cobs. Grabbing one of the dried cobs, he tossed it into the diminishing fire. A small blaze was immediately rekindled. Light embers were displaced throwing them upward and then gently sprinkled downward joining the smoldering ash.

"What's that you said 'bout fever?" Betty now took an interest in what her husband had to say. She put the mending down on her lap. "Who did ya say told ya 'bout the fever?" she asked with misgivings.

"Roy Flanagan came on by to borrow some feed; claimed he heard someone's takin' sick up at the Tarson place." Randle paused calculating how the next bit of news would be received. "He said he thinks it's fever." Randle turned his head towards his wife to catch her reply, but was surprised that she did not appear to flinch under the weight of his words.

"Roy Flanagan, how did he know that?" Betty frowned, her lips automatically curled downward when she spoke the name. She was not fond of him as she found him a user, continually borrowing farm tools, animal feed, even candles or soap. Her lips relaxed as she contemplated this raw thought. Suddenly she felt a bit selfish; after all he was a widow. She softened her tone. "How is Roy?"

"Suppose okay, good as anyone in this winter: his heifer is 'bout to calf and he didn't want to be short on feed." Randle turned back toward the hearth and lobbed another cob.

There was a lull in the conversation; Betty picked up her mending and continued to sew. Darkness was spreading, but the unfaltering crescendo of yellow glow emanating from the hearth warmed the room. She reset her work back into the basket and rose to light the lantern that was set upon the table. She opened the little hinged door and pulled toward her a limp piece of cloth. Clasping it in her fingers, she twisted the wick so it became more tightly spun. Randle watched as she selected a piece of kindling and knelt down by the hearth, placing the narrow end of the stick on a glowing ember. She waited as it began to ignite. Holding her hand close to the flame, she cupped her palm to protect the tiny flame from any intruding breeze that may cause it to extinguish. She returned to the table and gently touched the flaming stick to the lantern wick, which immediately caught fire.

Betty placed the kindling close to her lips and blew the flame out. A spiraling thread of grey smoke levitated, climbing a trail of hot air above her head. "So," she continued as she moved about the room, setting the charred kindling stick by a short stack of tapers, "which Tarson is it that's got the fever?"

Randle was afraid of this question but not nearly as afraid of the rebuttal he was about to receive when he gave his answer. He sat up from his reclined position, "Didn't ask, and he didn't say." He bent toward the warm fire and began to rub his hands together

"Didn't ask?" Her voice seemed to escalate with annoyance. "Now, ain't that just like a man?" Betty rumbled back, obviously irritated.

Men; she rolled the gender over in her mind. They were inadequate with acquiring information, content with one syllable answers! Ask a woman to find out something and you come away with history! Why a woman would have found out who was sick, when it happened, what the Tarsons were doing about it!

"Fever, that's what he told me," Randle added hoping that by replying it would add something new to the conversation, even though it wasn't.

Nothing else needed to be answered or asked and both Betty and Randle knew that what was unknown was really of no consequence to the outcome. Whoever contracted it was in grave danger. Betty sat back down and picked up her mending; Randle leaned back staring into the fire. She looked up at her husband and smiled. She knew that he didn't mean to be short with his answers; after all, he couldn't help it. This was the nature of his kind.

—

Belle Tarson entered the sickroom where the child lay listlessly. She dropped a chunk of snow into the basin of water that lay on the small wooden table next to the bed and watched as it broke apart into smaller pieces, icy splinters, and eventually dissolving into its original state, water. It was one of the first times that she was pleased to have winter all around her. The child's tiny waif-like face was rosy in color. But it was not the color of April pink that comes from the sun's warming of velvet petals among sweet wildflowers. It was the color one incurs when stricken by a rise in body temperature from an invading army of disease. Even in the coldest of days, perspiration moistens the bed sheets and cheerful twinkling eyes now glare back, dull and spiritless. Belle dropped a clean linen cloth into the water and let it soak for a moment. She raised it above the basin and squeezed it, allowing the water to gush like a miniature waterfall. The sound alerted the child who turned its head towards the noise and then back again as though encased in a tomb, looking straight forward, melting into the down pillow. Belle folded the cloth into a rectangle and placed it upon the narrow forehead. The face, so small and oval appeared to be straining under the weight of the cold compress. Belle moved the damp cloth away and dropped it back into the cold water. She followed the same procedure, replacing it once again back on the tiny forehead.

She had sent word to Doc Foy, who upon a punctual arrival, examined the child and prescribed a local medicine to help with the cough. There was not much else that he could do, not with "the fever." Belle never felt much confidence in Western doctors. As far as she was concerned, they were not much better educated then a shaman and by now an East coast physician would have had the child up and feeling better.

The child closed its eyes. The lids were either too tired to remain open or too burdened by the placement of the wet rag that lay upon the brow. Belle dried her hands with her calico apron and pulled the straight-backed chair from the hallway into the small room and brought it round to the side of the bed. She had not felt this helpless in a long time. She picked up the child's limp hand, a lifeless appendage attached to a bony frame sticking out of a mannequin-like body and held on to it; not with the tenderness of a mother, but more like one who had an obligation or duty. Still holding the listless hand she released her grip on it and lightly placed it back on the bedding, as though it were fragile enough to shatter if not set down gently.

"What was I thinking taking on another child?" Belle mulled the decision over in her mind as she stared at the little face. It seemed like a lifetime ago that she and Greg had stepped foot on the platform. Like frightened puppies, small groups of children were huddled together. But this one, she stuck out from the rest. Was it cruel not to have taken the sister, too?

Belle couldn't think about that now. The sister was years older and naturally was happier in a home where she would not have to compete for affection between she and her younger sibling. Belle continued to console herself in her usual levelheaded manner. Besides, it would not have been right to take two children when she really only needed one. She regretted now having treated the child like a stray dog. She should have been more attentive to her when she brought her to school. But how could she have been different? This child was fully able; she was fully capable of getting to and fro. No, this child was not like Joseph who needed special care.

Belle's thoughts suddenly switched course like a two-tracked train rail. As soon as they realized the onset of any infection, she sent Greg away with Joseph. The risk of disease and all the horrors it would bring gave Belle mixed emotions towards the little child who lay sick and helpless. Part of her was angry for bringing this child into her home, for allowing a stranger to upset the balance of their family.

She stroked the little girl's hair and brushed back a fly-away strand from her hot pink cheek. She was still burning up. Belle removed the wet cloth and again dipped it into the cold water. But when the weight of the cloth was lifted, her head effortlessly rolled to one side and a pitifully meek plea suddenly surrendered from the dry and pale lips of the sick child. "Mindy, where is Mindy?" The delicate fingers groped along her side and feebly about the bed.

Belle ascended from the chair and reached up to retrieve a lovingly worn doll from off the thin wooden plank. "Here she is child, she's with you now," whispered Belle placing the doll in the tiny fingers. Instantly, a sense of unprecedented exaltation occurred as the little hand recognized the doll. A moment of sublime emotion transpired through the frail body; maybe only for an instant, but Belle was sure that the child had found peace. However, as quickly as that sensation materialized did the fever rebound, only to deny any pleasure of physical comfort. The child exerted herself, laboring to twist her face towards Belle. She wished to fully open her eyes but was able to marginally oblige for they refused this meager act and remained at half-mast. She could make out the image of Belle sitting beside her through the slats in her lids, and she could feel a trickle of water find a path down the contour of her face. It was hot, growing ever so hot even though it was the dead of winter. She held her doll fast. Its lifeless body's cold porcelain felt familiar in her hands, and she dared not let go for if she did she may lose it again and loss was something she was becoming far too accustomed to, even at seven. Finally, she found within the strength she had been searching for and with all the energy she could muster she faintly murmured, "Thank you."

———

Upon their return from grooming the horses and cleaning the stable, Alex and Pinto Jack were greeted by the aroma of fat smoldering and the sound of chitlings splattering in the red-hot iron skillet. The table was set with crockery and covered with a clean oil cloth, the hearth was glowing, and Betty was busy scurrying about. Randle rocked in his chair, his hands rested behind his head in a casual manner. But in spite of what one could assume was a languid setting, no matter how the room tried to convince those who entered that there was harmony about, the feeling of apprehension consumed both man and boy.

"Sure smells good," exclaimed Jack, who decided that he should not move far from the threshold of the door. Alex, not understanding this reaction, tried to coax the man into the room by gesturing him to 'come in'. He motioned with a bent index finger and wiggled it up and down a few times. Jack remained politely waiting for a more formal invitation and decided not to follow the little boy.

"Set your jacket on over the hook, yer welcome to have some supper with us," greeted Betty. Her voice trailed behind as she left the room and entered the pantry to retrieve a bit more lard. With vigor she plopped a dollop of the grease into the pan, causing it to sear the fat of the meat releasing a fury of crackles and spatters.

"Yep, we got some unfortunate news today," Randle piped in. He set all four legs of the chair back down, stood up, stretched, and turned his back to the fire. "Get all the chores done?" he asked Alex, changing the subject.

Betty's hand was cloaked in a white cloth as she began to wipe away the grease that had splashed out along the sides of the pan. Watching Alex with one eye, her jaw began to clench tightly. Then without provocation she barked, "I don't want you standing there with a wet jacket!" She commenced again, "Here, take it off and let me hang it next to Jack's." She moved the skillet and set it upon a clay trivet on the table and positioned it next to where she sat and could also serve. The fat in the pan was sizzling like an angry snake locked in a box as she brushed her hands on her apron and grabbed Alex's jacket sleeve. She tugged furiously attempting to help, but proceeded in a most annoyed and gruff manner. Alex looked up in horror as the woman seemed so intent to remove the clothing. It was as though she were skinning an animal. "How many times have I told ya, don't keep wet clothes on?" complained Betty as she yanked on the snug sleeve.

However, hard as he tried, Alex actually couldn't remember ever hearing her tell him that. He was going to remind her but in her present state all he could do was wince as she clutched his arm by the shoulder and tugged on the material. By now no one in the house would have been surprised if she took her foot and braced it up on the wall so she could get better leverage on the boy's sleeve. Yet, in spite of her zealous efforts, the sleeve did not want to release the child.

"Betty, you want to wrench that boy's arm out of its socket?" Randle asked his wife, tapping her gently on the shoulder.

Startled by his presence, she let go of the cuff and stood there just looking at the child. "Well," she exclaimed in a manner that was more fitting for a wrestler who had just taken down an opponent, "take off that jacket, boy, it's time fer supper."

Now on all other comings and goings, Alex was perfectly capable of taking off his own clothes. He always had done it before and wondered why Betty was taking such an extraordinary interest today. Randle turned away from the scene and sat down at the dinner table, not saying anything to the curious child, who had carelessly wriggled free from his own damp jacket. The wooden bench was resting against the entrance wall; Alex pulled it away and stepped up, hanging his coat on the hook next to Jack's. Then, in all attempts not to disturb the already tense atmosphere, he stepped down and pushed the bench alongside of the table and catlike, sat down for dinner.

Jack tried to blend in with the wall and stood as far from the congestion as he could. It was not his place to interfere. Situations like this reminded him why he enjoyed life in the saddle. "Sit down, Jack," commanded Betty. She nodded her head for him to take a place at the opposite side of the table from Alex. He was hungry and the smell of a hot meal would not be refused, especially since this would be the last he would enjoy for a long time.

———

Silence now overshadowed the imminence of doom which had precluded the events that took place before dinner. Jack wondered what Randle had on his mind when he had mentioned the unfortunate news. However, unfortunate news was not uncommon in these parts and the younger man reminded himself that it was more a curiosity than a concern that lay fresh in his mind.

"So, how's yer pony? She ready for your trip West?" asked Randle, sopping the grease up with a piece of bread.

"Seems pretty good; she got plenty of rest enough and now that the snow stopped, we'll manage just fine," he looked over at Randle who nodded his head in agreement. Jack glanced over at Betty, who was consumed in something other than the meal she had prepared.

Alex heard these words and though keenly aware of Jack's plans to leave, the actual pronouncement of departure was the final scene in a Greek tragedy; a veil of melancholy fell upon him, the last actor on stage.

"There's fever in these parts," Betty broke the silence.

Jack looked up as her words taunted misfortune. The bleak expression on her pale face gave hint to an unspoken qualm. Betty continued, "We're not sure who, but up by the Tarson place, somebody up there got the fever," she added.

Alex's eyes rose from the plate. He shifted his look from Betty to Randle hoping one of the two would continue.

"That's serious, how long?" asked Jack now with a personal interest. He was not sure where this Tarson place was but he was certain that he didn't wish to go anywhere near.

"Not too sure, we just found out today." Randle pushed his plate away towards the middle of the table. This was his method of telling Betty that he was finished with the meal.

"Alex, you ain't to go near the Tarson place, ya hear?" Betty added with a stern look.

He responded with an affirmative nod. Jack now understood why Betty was so determined and upset before. There was always the presumption that keeping wet clothing on, especially in the winter, would increase the odds of someone contracting an illness.

"Good," Betty replied recognizing the non-verbal response that she usually received from the boy. "Now, go on and git ready to go to bed. Jack has got to get his rest so he can head out in the morning. Besides, you got chores to tend to in the morning."

Alex, who always obeyed, scooted down off the bench and stepped back from the table. He was noticeably disturbed by all the events that had occurred and Jack was aware of this even though neither Betty nor Randle seemed to take in the child's feelings at this time.

"Don't you worry little fellah, I'll be sure to let you say goodbye to Cally before we set out," said Jack as he pulled his bench away from the table and stood up. Alex remained frozen surveying the man. He appeared so much taller and so much wiser than he remembered from the first time they met. Could a grown-up grow in a matter of days? He had heard Betty say that he was 'growing like a weed'; could that have happened to Jack? Alex wished he could rush up to him and clasp his hands in his. He had an ache which felt as though it would burst if he did not blurt out for Jack to take him too; to save him from being so alone. He was so desperately ...so desperately what? Suddenly, powerless to find the correct word, all Alex could muster was the idea that he was desperate, but not sure what it was he was desperate about.

And though he screamed inside, "Jack, don't leave me here!" he simply stood by silently as Jack thanked Betty for the meal and thanked Randle for letting him stay for a few days. Engulfed within his painful silence, he watched this traveler retrieve his jacket, slip it on, and walk out into the black and grey eve, back to the barn where he would sleep until awakened by either the first light or the first frost.

Alex listened to the door shut and then bid good night to Betty and Randle. He could hear them talking as he managed to get himself ready for sleep; an unintelligible mumble emerged like idle chatter one hears unconsciously. Timothy was already taking up most of the little cot, and Alex gently pushed the fat and lazy cat to one side to make room for himself. He lay down and reflected on the day, on the cold, and on his existence. He brought the blanket up to his chin and turned over onto his side. With his closed eyes he envisioned Jack in the barn, sprawled under a blanket, resting with his clothes still on and a covering of hay beneath him. He turned these images over again like pages in a picture book when he suddenly remembered that he had something to give Jack before he left. He leaned over Timothy who was now coiled up in a round fur ball. "Don't let me forget to get something important for Jack," he whispered to the cat. But Timothy did not even stir; he would not even give Alex the satisfaction of a miserly and perfunctory yawn; after all, he was talking to a cat.

Chapter 21

The carpetbag remained intact, stuffed securely under the cot. It had never been opened nor disturbed since his arrival. Alex recalled for an instant that infamous day when he first set eyes on the tiny storage area that had been earmarked as his sleeping quarters. He bent down on all fours and twisted his head to the side to see under the cot; however, this time he reached beneath to retrieve rather than hide. Grabbing the bag by its black leather handles, he pulled with one hand and steadied himself with the other. Giving a mighty tug he managed to slide it closer towards him. However, the space beneath the cot was tight and cramped, and did not wish to liberate the bag without resistance. It was clear; a change in strategy was necessary. Alex sat facing the cot with his legs bent upward and grabbed the handle with two hands. He bowed at the waist like a folded rag doll and with several vigorous pulls, he managed to tug and slide the bag free from its secret spot. It lay in front of him like a sleeping badger and was no more dusty than he imagined. What he didn't take into account was the thin layer of cat hair which the bag was wearing like a fur coat. "Timothy, you left yer fluff all over this thing," whispered Alex to the cat that was still fast asleep at the foot of the cot.

Though black as pitch outside, a path of silver threads from the waxing moon shone through the open door. Its illumination was so dazzling that the light seemed as though it was seeping up from beneath the earth rather than lying upon it. Cross-legged, Alex pulled the bag to him and unclasped the buckle. He began to rummage through its miserly contents, feeling around for the object he had set his sights upon. Because of the bulky nature, it was easily the first item he seized, and like a pirate delighted with a cache of gold, so did Alex feel when he pulled out his own treasure. He wrenched it from the bag, brought it up and buried his face within the folds of the soft cotton. It held a familiar sweet odor of which he tried to remember the origin. Was this the smell of a food that he liked to eat when he was very young? He shrugged his forgetfulness aside. She will love this and it will keep her warm, he thought continuing to stroke the small quilted blanket. And though it was still too dark to make out any of the details, he could follow with his fingers the designs and patterns of stitchery sewn into the fabric.

Alex set the quilt aside, secured the bag shut, and then pushed down upon it, mashing it much flatter than before. Then, he negotiated his feet against the bag, bent his knees forward, and with one good shove managed to cram it back under the cot. On this occasion the absence of its bulky object made the job substantially simpler. Alex leaned back against the edge of the cot; it was still too early to get dressed. Although not really tired, he had nothing else to do except get back into bed. He bundled the quilt into a ball and used it like a pillow. It was much more comfortable than his own headrest and no sooner had he placed his head down than he noticed that it had attracted the affection of Timothy, wanting a piece of the quilt for himself. "Don't git used to this," he whispered to the cat, "cause in the morning it ain't gonna be here."

———

Henry never failed to do his job and today was no exception. The senior rooster, though getting on in years, was still king of the barnyard. Henry was the custodian of dawn and his divine ability to tell time with a proclamation of the day was indeed a unique predisposition. Some farmers believed that if one hears a rooster crow at night it is a bad omen. Perhaps this is why there are farmers that are restless, listening for that ominous prophecy. However, all the Foresters slept soundly, perhaps owning this to the trustworthy nature of Henry. Even though he was a king, he did not flaunt his falsetto voice nor show off his fine and rich colors like a peacock. He did not fly as high as a Thunderbird or exhibit auspicious behaviors. But even a bird of great virtue is not without fault and being a cunning bird he was prone to display an aggressive side to both man and beast. So, on more than several occasions, it was his misfortune that this proclivity had him under the blunt end of Betty's broom.

When Alex crept into the barn, he was met with two distinct and separate whinnies from Delilah and Dandy. They were accustomed to Alex's early comings and goings, however this morning the first light had barely been introduced into the stables. "I know it's early," he whispered, "but today Cally and Pinto Jack are leaving." Delilah was the first draft to be greeted and Alex stroked her long nose, nestling his face against hers. "You are a good girl sharing the stables with a stranger." Alex turned and stroked Dandy who was ready for a morning greeting. "You know that you and Delilah are my favorites, don't ya?" he reminded the horse patting her neck. Both animals acknowledged that they knew he would never abandon them for another horse and gave an affirmative whinny.

Cally must have heard the reply for at that moment she piped in with her own neigh. "That you, Alex?" a voice called out from above. Alex looked up to see Jack backing down the ladder, his hair still mussed from having been sleeping in the hay and his shirttail half tucked into his pants. He was fully dressed, sporting a shabby woolen blanket around his shoulders. "It sure is cold right now," he added as he stepped down from the bottom rung. "This morning frost gets your blood going. I've been spoiled for the past several days," he said approaching Alex, who was watching what appeared now to be a walking blanket with legs. "Sleepin' here in the barn shelters a man from the elements." Jack stopped and readjusted the blanket. "So, what are ya doin' here this hour of the morning? Why it's early for even you Foresters."

"It's on account of you leavin'. I have something fer Cally." But as soon as he had spoken he realized that maybe he had hurt Jack's feelings, having a gift only for one. Wishing to retract his sentence, he piped up again, "What I mean is that you can share it with Cally, but you already got one," he said pointing to the blanket the man was donning.

"I see," replied Jack in his most gracious tone. "That is very kind that you thought of us."

"Here, let me show it to you." Alex scampered back into the stalls and retrieved a soft bundle that he had tossed into the hay when he came in to greet the horses. He unfolded it so it was now fully open, dragging it over the ground as bits of hay trailed behind. Placing his arms out he offered the blanket to Jack.

"Mind if I take it over to the light to get a better view?" Alex shook his head "no" and followed him to the open door. Jack examined the counterpane like a man who had just been handed a treasure map. He ran his fingers along the fabric and examined the patterns. The brilliant colors had most likely been produced from mordants, a kind of fixative that was combined with pigments imported from across the eastern hemisphere. Fabrics dyed using a slow and arduous process could only have been used to create these lively patterns; deep blue made from the indigo plant and imported from India, red and rich from Asian madder's root bark, brown from red oak bark and walnut hull, and yellow from peach leaves. There was a particular sheen on this quilt; perhaps it had been finished with a glaze of egg whites or honey. After having passed his hands across the design for a few minutes he handed it back to the boy. "Alex, this is your blanket, I don't think that you should give it away," he stated in a troubled voice.

But the child only pushed it back. "It's been in my bag for a long time. I don't need it and Cally, why she's got to have a warm blanket when yer on the trail." Alex's reply was deeply sincere and at this moment Jack felt as though he was in a very weighty dilemma.

"Whoever made this took a lot of extra care," Jack mumbled to himself and then pointed out several designs embedded in the material.

Alex was not at all impressed with this bit of information. "I always had it fer a long time. Its been in my bag stuffed under the cot.

But I don't need it on account that Betty gave me another blanket. I want Cally to wear it," he pleaded.

Jack shifted to another patched area of design. He wanted to follow the labyrinth of patterns, to uncover the hidden designs sewn into these beautiful motives, but Alex was too excited to allow time for such examination.

"It was in my bag when I had to come on the train." He paused to collect his thoughts.

Jack wasn't sure what to make of it all. "I believe this is an heirloom," he offered him as an explanation.

Alex appeared puzzled at those words. "Hare loom, what's a hare gotta do with my blanket? I don't think it was made from a hare. It's soft, but not like a rabbit or a hare, Jack," replied Alex satisfied that the man had definitely made an error.

"No, not hare like the rabbit; it's a different word, H-E-I-R-L-O-O-M." Jack spelled out the letters, one after the other.

Again, Alex was not amused by the response and simply smiled. "It's for Cally, she needs it more than I do."

Jack continued to examine the blanket. It was evident that the creator of this quilt was skilled in their art. He held it gingerly in his calloused hands and began to mindlessly fold one half over to the other, continuing several times over and over until it was packed into a soft bundle. He held it in his arms, stroking the fine needlework gently as though any slight disturbance could cause it to tatter. He looked at the small child who stood before him and it all became quite clear. To tell the child to take it back would cause more harm than good. There was no way that he could not accept the gift. He was not going to be the one to break the child's heart. "Sure will be a perfect fit for Cally!" he exclaimed. "Come on; let's see how she likes it." Jack unfurled the snug bundle and now draped it carelessly over his shoulder and gestured for Alex to follow. The quilt hung down his back like a colorful poncho and swayed freely as the man started towards the filly.

"That is a fine idea, Jack, let's see if it fits!" flitted Alex, now skipping ahead. Jack followed behind the delighted child however he knew there was something not right in taking this present, and began to wonder why he just couldn't shake this ominous feeling that was baiting him with doubt.

Alex caressed Cally and gently whispered that the blanket would protect her from the cold. The morning light had finally made its way into the stable, casting a spotlight upon the boy and the horse, encircling the two in an ethereal bond. Jack abandoned his feeling of uncertainty as he watched, and then walked up to Cally and arranged the blanket upon her back. The horse seemed to comply with what was happening and affectionately nudged both her master and the child with her velvet nose.

"I think she likes it, don't you?" asked Alex as he gripped the edge of the blanket and began to tug downward to remove any visible wrinkles.

Jack nodded in agreement and added affectionately, "I believe she does, Alex, I believe she does." At that moment, any ideas that he had, any doubts he may have thought, were now eradicated. He knew that he had made the right decision to accept the gift for Cally.

Chapter 22

M aking a transatlantic journey is not for the faint or cowardly; for discomfort and even tragedy often stowed aboard
the most well-scoured vessel. Just conjure up the poor souls who
set sail aboard the SS Forge upon that fine and sturdy ship in the
Scandinavian Line. For if by chance any of the 409 men, women,
or children had survived, they would reveal their most treacherous
voyage. It was the 5th of February, 1849, when the seasoned Captain
Northrop, a staunch and crusty sea-faring man sailing from Oslo
bound for New York, suddenly was drawn into a dramatic change in
weather; whereupon the wind was blowing over leagues and leagues
of ocean and began pulling up a tremendous monster of water.
The SS Forge measured about the same length as the distance between wave crest to wave crest, wobbling and drifting upon colossal
rollers. The sea, a landscape of cobalt mountainside, was capped
in white froth. Several crew members and the captain struggled to
steady the wheel; however this unforecasted windstorm overtook
their course. Gusts of cyclonic force blew the ship causing great
stress to her hull. Ice had formed on the ship and created an even
more unstable situation. Though every exertion was made to save
her, the assault was too great, resulting in her breaking apart. The
hapless passengers and crew all drowned, leaving behind only a
floating pile of kindling.

———

The Elijah Swift weighed anchor and was one of the first ships to leave port. The coastline of England began to gradually melt away; dissolving into the horizon. She made an excellent run out of the channel, and in about a week was hugging the Cape Lands. The passengers had all kept to themselves for the first several days since many were too seasick to find the companionship of others. Will tried to keep the story of the SS Forge from finding his new bride, but in spite all his good intentions, rumors traveled quickly. Like a line which is tied together at opposing ends, there was nowhere else for the story to go but around. And in spite of her fragile and delicate appearance, Libby was not easily frightened by secondhand tales and dismissed the misadventure as just that, a horrible act of nature. But the Monday morning of the second week out, all aboard were wakened by the startling shrill of an alarm. This was unfortunately not a rumor; a fire amidships had been accidentally set and though extinguished quickly by a lively young crew, it was copious enough to create a thrill of horror in the minds of some, succeeded thereafter by the thought that this accident was an omen of doom.

Keeping busy on this long excursion would retard any suspicious feelings of dread. There was little to amuse one with and so passengers had to become creative. They strolled the decks, reminisced about their lives, and projected the future in another continent. Some read such publications as *Lancaster Hive, Harpers New Monthly Magazine,* and *Scientific American.* The latter became a most favored publication with unfailing interest; it engaged the reader beyond even the most avid naturalist. One of the passengers, known only as Sven, earned distinction as the resident docent, for this was his second trip to America, and was well-equipped with worldly sophistication fitted for his role. He and other elders would lounge on deck chairs and enjoy the open sea air, stolidly smoking pipes while their wives crocheted, knit, or gave motherly advice to anyone who would listen. Boys and young men set up a game of cards, while young girls encouraged the more musical to entertain them with out-of-tune melodies on the harmonica. But those grim days, when the weather became angry, all would seek refuge below deck. As with all long journeys this was the most disagreeable way to spend time, for within the closed and cramped quarters, anticipation and expectations of disease grew. Recirculated stale air mingled with the uncontaminated, thus providing a perfect breeding ground for even the mildest illness. The potential for a ship-wide epidemic hovered like a kettle of vultures.

Weeks passed and the transformation of time could be marked by a display of daily watercolor washes that had been brushed above and below the horizon line. Violet sky branded with the figure of a hinging sun, red-streaked clouds lightly stroked aloft the cold sea drenched in the dull ashen color of a cod fish. The next day that very same sky was a hue of coral like the paint in your first watercolor set. Will and Libby spent hours during charcoal grey days watching the ocean and sky fill the entire porthole in their small room, except for a subtle effect of light and shade upon the tips of the waves. Through the powdery haze of the clouds they managed to keep their spirits high. Libby, like many of the other women, occupied her time by quilting a small blanket. Sometimes she would sit with other women on deck and they would share ideas about how one appliqué might echo another appliqué pattern. Many of the older women were in awe of her dexterity; however she easily explained that her talent had been inherited from Grandmother Analiese.

"So, Mrs. Piccard, what are you going to do with your blanket when it is finished?" asked Madame Beaumont, a French widow who was heading for New Orleans. "Is ze blanket for decoration?" (Her voice raised up an octave at the end of the word.)

"Actually, Will and I have been thinking …," she paused and gently stroked her stitched work like a hummingbird ruffling its feathers, "and we would like to start a family when we get settled in America," replied Libby blushing.

"Very wise, ze bebe will bring you happiness, and you are young zo why wait? No?" Madame did not wait for an answer and continued, "Then it is settled, ze blanket is for ze bebe," she smiled and patted her hand upon Libby's. But the conversation was suddenly cut short as a strong wave abruptly tossed the ship, allowing the great bow to plunge, dousing them lightly with the cold ocean spray. Both women were taken aback by the surprise shower that lifted them onto their feet. Libby hung on to her basket of quilting notions, protecting them from being pitched overboard.

"Ah ha, a sign, a very good sign indeed," laughed the French woman who had her goods bundled in her arms.

"What kind of omen?" asked Libby as she reseated. The ship having now settled itself moved more steadily on its course.

"It is said that zer is a tree called the tamarisk, a hearty species that germinates under za harshest weather conditions and survives by growing near ze coast. It is the spray from the sea water that moistens its leaves." The woman paused to rearrange her hairpins intercepting the coiled bun as it flopped to the left side of her head. "Maybe you are like ze little tamarisk tree, Cheri."

Libby smiled timidly at Madame Beaumont and resumed sewing while Madame folded her hands across her lap and tilted her face back towards the open sky. Then, much like a content cat sitting in the sun, the elder lapsed into a secret silence. It was strangely quiet and the lapping of the waves against the sides of the ship became hypnotic. Libby frisked her mind to uncover a similar childhood resonance, but she could find none that resembled this maritime sound. The newness of the excursion gave her a tingle of excitement; she smiled, but only meekly, for she held within her a fear that if she was to express too much happiness it may suddenly perish, like a fish that moments ago lived its carefree life only to find itself plucked out from the seas by a hungry gull. Libby shuddered at the image of a poor defenseless fish being swooped up and away. Her fingers fumbled as she tried to resume her needlework.

Ironically, at that moment a flock of sea gulls, like an explosion of fireworks, ascended towards the waves in perfect unison. With a grace and precision of movement, they were ballerinas, an ethereal vision costumed in long white tutus. "Maybe I was too harsh on them," Libby muttered to herself as she watched these creatures wing and glide in magnificent choreography.

The cawing of delighted birds disturbed Madame who sat up and began to speak. "Another sign," she whispered, trailing the birds with her eyes. She gave pause and continued, "There is land ahead, Cheri. I hope you are ready."

Libby said nothing in reply; the strangeness of her deck companion offered enough of a reason for her to quiver with uncertainty.

———

Built on the shoreline of the Chesapeake, Fells Point served as a major maritime port during both the War for Independence and the War of 1812. The land had been purchased in 1763 by William Fell, and his son, Edward, plotted the layout of the village. Because of the deep water harbor, unlike its neighbor, Baltimore, Fells Point became a favorite port of entry. During the 1700s, multitudes of clipper ships favored this port and like 100 years before, the Elijah Swift finally anchored in the harbor of Fells Point, 45 days after she had set sail. The captain had made this voyage time and again, and upon their docking advised the passengers from the first class down to steerage that the end of the trip was not final. No one would be permitted to disembark until they passed through a series of immigration inspections.

Lines of passengers began to wrap around the deck of the ship. Libby looked woefully upon those who had spent the majority of their time in steerage. Their only misfortune was that they were poor. It was no wonder that so many were dreadfully tired and many now sick from the long arduous crossing. These wretched passengers had resided in overcrowded conditions. By law they were entitled to 14 square feet of horizontal space and a berth measuring six feet long and eighteen inches wide; but the primitive sanitation, foul air, and poor food during their journey to America caused the illness of 1 out of every 6 persons. Libby watched as the immigrants clung to bundles of their own bedding, for none had been supplied during the trip. They had to clean their own rooms and cook their own food, which consisted mostly of herring, potatoes, rice, dried peas, salted meat, and bread.

"Keep moving, young lady," cried a Gaelic officer at Libby. Though he was nothing more than a shipman, she felt compelled to pay heed lest she loose her place next to Will.

"I can't bear standing idly by while there are those two poor little children over there," Libby pointed sadly and continued to shuffle away from them as she moved in line with the rest of the first and second class passengers. "They are in need of a doctor," she lamented to Will. Indeed, a pair of doe-eyed youths not more than six and seven years old stared blankly into the crowds. Banded together like Siamese twins, they shared a tattered shawl over their thin shoulders.

"Don't worry, Miss," said an elderly gentleman donning his fine Sunday dress. Having overheard Libby's concern, the man continued to address her. "There are appointed physicians that will check on us all. Those little urchins will be tended to when it is their time."

Will had set their bags down and straddled them between his legs. He knew that they could be pinched from the very spot where he stood if he was not careful. Will stroked Libby's back trying to ease her concern. "Don't fret, Libby," he whispered bending down and placing a soft kiss upon her cheek.

"I don't see anyone who appears to be taking charge of those children," she bemoaned. "They look as though they are alone. See how no one is even taking time to ensure that they are moving along with the others!" Libby sighed suspecting the worst inflictions would assail the young travelers.

"The authorities will take care of them when they board the ship," interrupted the elderly man again. "I am afraid that their mother may have been one of those unfortunates who died along the way. Tuberculosis," he muttered. "Yes, I bet it was tuberculosis," and he repeated the disease as though he had some inside informa-tion as to the death. "As for a father, one cannot tell if he is still back in Europe."

Libby gravely looked upon her husband with horror and then back in the direction of the crowd however, the orphaned children were no longer visible, inferring that they were somewhere amidst the forest of people.

Unlike Libby, Will's pain stemmed from a different source. For as he looked across the ship into the masses of steerage passengers, he knew that his only distinction had been the tickets purchased by the kindly judge. If it had not been that salvation, he too would be amongst the more ill-fated. Will scanned the group honing in on a man about his same age. There was something about the fellow that drew him in and as Will continued to stare he was able to link eyes with this young man on the other side. An unmistakable recognition of kinship was immediately acknowledged though words were not exchanged. A cold sweat overcame him; an affirmation of own reality was staring back and the only honor of difference was his location on line.

Public health inspectors boarded the ship and the single procession of first and second class passengers was quickly routed into several lines. The process of physically inspecting the passengers for illnesses like typhus, cholera, smallpox, tuberculosis, and trachoma was taking place. Fortunately, the captain had advised his passengers not to bathe in seawater. This practice would cause red eyes which many of the inspectors often would mistake as trachoma. Upon the completion of physical examinations, bags were prodded for contraband and although most everyone's belongings were inspected, it was seen but not mentioned that an exchange of money replaced the opening of several large valises.

"Welcome to America, Mr. and Mrs. Piccard," greeted the officer upon the end of their inspection. "I see you have a satisfactory letter of introduction, and therefore you are permitted to enter the United States." The pasty-faced officer handed back to Will his letter upon which the new arrival fed it into the lining of his jacket for safety. "Now, if you follow the others you are free to exit down the gangplank. I believe you will find the city of Baltimore one of vast opportunity." And with a half crooked smile, or perhaps it was a sneer, he turned to the next set of immigrants and resounded again, "NEXT!"

Many who had left Europe had their sights set on a westward migration, looking for adventure and a new life where they could farm and prosper on rich fertile land. But Libby and Will never tabled such a notion. They were determined to seek out a Mr. Jack Philander, whereby they hoped he could supply them with an opportunity to secure a place to live and subsequently the ability to earn an income would then quickly follow. Unlike New York where competition for jobs was more stringent, Baltimore was in need of cheap labor making hopes of a better life more obtainable. Will and Libby followed behind the others who were disembarking. Two orderly lines of people suddenly dismantled themselves into a disorderly horde that now rushed about seeking familiar faces and voices. Libby grabbed Will's jacket and the two snaked their way through the throngs, scouting a means of escape from the zealous crowd.

"Mr. Piccard, Mr. Piccard, over here!" a high-pitched male voice was heard bellowing above the rest. Will pulled Libby as he heard his name again being called, "Will, over here by the gas lamppost!" An arm was waving feverously for attention.

Both Libby and Will agreed that luck was on their side since after having taken the seafaring voyage; the overland journey beginning from this point of landing was disheartening for so many others. All during their trip passengers were warned that they needed to heed dangers that awaited them. Emigrants who preceded their arrival narrated tales of having been victimized by dishonest innkeepers and swindlers selling counterfeit tickets to destinations after arriving at the port. Others were cheated by high pressure jobbers who offered to take them to a safe lodging, only to find instead disreputable inns or rooming houses where they could be fleeced by a wicked assortment of ruffians, thieves, and other immoral people. Will had carefully secured their letter by having Libby sew a pocket into the lining of his jacket. This would prevent a pickpocket or rogue from slipping it out unnoticed. He believed this document guaranteed the opportunity towards their success.

"Oh, I had a time finding the correct dock, but it appears that you have safely arrived. I am Jack, Jack Philander," greeted a pencil-mustached fellow putting out his hand in a friendly gesture.

"Pleased to make your acquaintance, Mr. Philander, but how did you know that we were the Piccards?" questioned Will.

"Actually, I had no idea at all. I just figured that if I called out your names long and hard enough, someone would come down the plank and claim themselves to me just as you had. It was merely a game of chance, and after all, isn't that what life is, chance?"

"Well, just not to take a chance, let me show you our letter of introduction," agreed Will, and he began to open his jacket and reveal his secret pocket.

"If you don't mind," requested Jack and flashing his hands about in a hurried manner, "I've been waiting here for rather a long time and developed quite a thirst. Why don't we take our business across the way; I could do with a pint, how about you two?"

Libby, who had been standing meekly by her husband spoke up for the first time, "Mr. Philander, I don't suppose you might find your way to lead us to an establishment that may serve a spot of hot tea?" she asked sweetly.

"Tea, you want tea, eh?" This was not exactly the refreshment that had crossed his mind. He repeated the request cocking his head to one side as though he had heard incorrectly, "Hot tea?"

"Yes, if you don't mind, a cup of English tea would be lovely."

"Lovely. Tea? And I suppose you want tea, too?" Jack turned and dubiously asked Will.

"Whatever Libby would like is fine with me," Will nodded in agreement with his wife.

Jack paused for several moments running through his mind where he would be able to find a reputable establishment and to make matters even thornier, one that served "tea". After all, they were on the docks, besides, he had his reputation!

"Well, would you look at this," Jack piped up after having pulled out his pocket watch and fumbled with it for a moment. "Oh, my, I believe that I must have forgotten. I have an appointment that I am already late for," he fibbed. "But I promised Judge Carson that I would lead you in the best direction. Let me suggest The Cambridge Arms. It is a boarding house not too far from here and would be a fine start for you two. Yes, here," and he pulled out an envelope and handed it to Will. Then he continued in a hurried manner, "It's a short missive that states that I met you and find you both honest and can produce respectable references."

"How did you know that before you met us?" asked Libby.

"Honestly, Miss, I didn't, but the Judge sent me enough of an incentive that he knew I would not let him down. But after meeting the likes of you both, anyone who could travel across the Atlantic and wish to quench their thirsts when first arriving in the great country as the United States with simply tea," he shook his head woefully and continued, "I can sincerely believe that you will surely make a fine addition to the population of Baltimore." He pulled his pocket watch out again and retorted, "Pleased to meet you both, good luck!" Then with a cordial tip of his black bowler the hasty man turned away.

"Now, I do believe he was rather odd," stated Will watching the man swagger hurriedly away.

"Rather," Libby agreed.

———

The atmosphere bustled with a flurry of excitement which consumed and devoured the ship's passengers. The last group of families had been ushered off the gangplank which cleared the way for the yelps and jovial play of the salt-stained crew whose immediate destination was the nearest pub. It soon became most apparent that Fells Point was a place of important enterprise. Eight to ten shipyards intermingled among the wharves. Libby and Will found themselves wandering along the cobblestone of Thames Street, which angled and turned left and right. A surly policeman with a thickset neck and ruddy cheeks swayed back and forth alongside of an open alley way. "Excuse me, Sir," said Will getting the attention of the police-man. "Could you please direct us to The Cambridge Arms Rooming House?"

"Cambridge?" he repeated directing his attention to the matter at hand for he had been curiously absorbed in the business of a young lady and gentleman that had just stepped into an alleyway door. "Let me see," he grumbled and cleared his throat. "Well, everyone knows the Cambridge, still run and owned by Mrs. Elizabeth Cambridge herself. I suppose you're going to stay there for awhile?" he questioned, but did not wait for a response and continued with much authority as one would expect from a policeman. "Well, most of this area west of Broadway is pretty new, since you immigrants need quarters," he said tapping his billy club on his palm. "You're heading in the right direction. It's not too far but you got a little more walking to do." The policeman's head bobbed up and down as he spoke, and he swayed back and forth on his heels appearing to lose his balance, but immediately gained it back on the forward motion. Will listened intently taking mental notes of the directions the policeman was fir-ing at him and then thanked him greatly for his help. The officer nodded approvingly but not without a stern warning that they had better not get into trouble. An assurance was promised by Will; they were by no means those kind of people, thereupon Libby awarded the policeman one of her sweet smiles that could have melted the most callous of hearts.

They were to head to the outskirts of Fells Point known as Washington Mound. Since immigrant settlers had already populated the upland area that makes up the southeastern and western region, Washington Mound was now being occupied by the most recent newcomers. Will walked beside Libby, quite pleased with the news, however, the young bride at this point didn't much care about its history as long as she could rest; her feet swelled and blistered from her shoes, clearly not made for the hard cobblestone streets. White twisted columns and alabaster marble stairways coaxed curious pedestrians to peruse this residential neighborhood of two story row houses. Libby and Will scanned both sides of the narrow crooked streets; reading the signage neatly lined up like laundry and nailed above the portal of each doorway.

Abruptly Libby stopped. "C-A-M-B-R-I-D-G-E," she called out to Will. "Why dear husband, I do believe that we have arrived. Above the doorway an ornate letter "C" had been molded and embedded into the wall emphasizing the individual importance of the owner's name.

Will turned to study the façade and amazed by its great size, unlike the other homes on the street, this one was colossal. The exterior showcased a newly constructed building, sturdy, brick, but rather plain in a classical style. A tall cast iron fence surrounded the property, which seemed to imprison the building like a Bastille. An iron gate, the only accessible entrance into the secured fortress, displayed a most unusual bell. Cast in the shape of a partridge, its body was notched with grooves and scallops resembling feathers. Fire spewed from its beak distinguishing it from ordinary birds. Hidden beneath the mouth of the bell, its metal clapper dangled, daring any visitor to pull the chain so it might summon the proprietor.

Libby gingerly clasped the long chain and gave it a tug. Immediately a loud but surprisingly gentle tone was emitted. Both stood and waited for a moment, eyes peeled upon the secured wooden door within the gated portion. No one appeared.

"Here, let me have a whirl," said Will, as he tugged more firmly. He repeated the gesture for several moments unleashing a continual ringing as one peals a church bell. Again they waited except this time the lock of the gate was released and the gate automatically slid open. Had either Will or Libby been more vigilant, they would have noticed a small metal chain trailing up from the gate, leading to the door and then skillfully pulled through a tiny mail slot. The gate was hooked in a rather ingenious fashion allowing a party within the house to give a tug to the tether, which would adeptly unlock the gate. Upon admittance, the gate would swing back into its locked position as soon as the chain was given slack.

"Someone is rather clever," smiled Will as he gestured for Libby to enter past the open gate; he following behind.

"Or very lazy," she laughed. The gate shut immediately behind them and at the same time an undetected niche in the door slid open, revealing the pupil of a midnight blue eye.

Chapter 23

Overhead in the rafters where a powdery haze of sunlight floats listlessly, sheepish eyes gaze upon all the dwellers below. "The angels are crying today," whispered Alex as he pressed his cheek on Dandy's soft muzzle. He tried to fight back the tears, but managed only to stain his own face with the salty drops. He lifted his fingers and pinched down upon his closed eyelids with a failed attempt to keep himself from revealing his feelings.

"Well, come on over and say goodbye to Jack and Cally," called out Randle to Alex as he watched Jack give a last tug to the stirrup before mounting. "So where are ya headed?" he inquired of the traveler, who was now sitting up in his saddle.

"Heading to St. Joseph, I hope to get a job as a Pony Express rider," he answered.

"Well, you got the build, light and wiry. They like that in a man; can't put too much weight on them fast ponies. Think Cally here got what it takes?" asked Randle, giving the horse a light stroke.

"If she's healed like I think, she just might be one of the best ponies they could get. Course I wouldn't get to ride her all the way to California, but we'd meet up just the same. Ain't that so girl?" Jack leaned forward in the saddle and stroked the filly lightly on her ears. Cally flicked them as though his touch tickled.

Alex's demeanor perked up when he overheard the words, Pony Express. The idea of racing across forbidden lands in the wake of danger was a newly romanticized notion. He had heard talk of it from the older boys at school. Timidly, he crept out from his safe spot and approached Jack and Cally: his eyes burned from the salt.

"Why you all teared up, boy?" asked Randle, who immediately noticed Alex's red nose and stained face.

"I believe that Alex got a speck of dirt in his eyes when he was helping me earlier," Jack hastened to reply.

Randle continued to look disapprovingly at Alex who was blinking feverishly to prevent himself from tearing, but the sheer emotion of Jack and Cally leaving became overwhelming. Suddenly, he lunged forward and united himself with man and horse. "Please, please, take me with you, please!" he sobbed uncontrollably, holding on to the reins which were dangling loosely. He craned his neck back and looked up towards Jack who was towering above him.

Randle was aghast, astonished, for he had never heard the child ever call out and this display of grief was most unprecedented! Feeling helpless and unaccustomed to such a demonstration of emotion, he set out to pull the child away. "Now, what is going on?" demanded Randle, who had managed to remove the reins from Alex's tight grip and held the boy firmly with both hands planted upon the tiny shoulders. At once Alex was jarred back to a familiar feeling, it was that sickening sensation of helplessness that he had experienced when the abductors carried him away from his father. Randle continued excitedly, "Stop that whimpering, I don't know what's got into you." Jack, unable to interfere with a father and his son could only watch as Randle pulled the boy back.

Alex's tiny shoulders continued to heave with sobs of anguish as he desperately managed to muffle his cry. Overcome with sadness and misery his entire body and soul ached. The cold ground drew itself upwards from the frozen earth and the grey feeling that comes with a chilly winter day reached out to variegate everything in its midst. Like dormant boughs and branches that anticipate the first thaw, Alex stood frozen in the spot, his vision blurred from grief. He was numb and bewildered and helpless. Randle released his grip and spoke again, this time in a more gentle tone. "Now Alex, come on over and say goodbye. He's got to get a start before long. You know that St. Joseph is a ways away, don't ya boy?"

Alex heard the words and nodded in agreement. He wiped his eyes again with the sleeve of his jacket and tried to regain his composure by quietly inhaling and exhaling tiny sighs of woe.

Cally shifted her feet and shook her head gently. Jack squirmed a bit in the saddle; although reluctant to dismount he began to speak. His voice was soft, and it appeared to almost crack under the emotion of the morning. Leaning down towards the side he supported his weight with his boot firmly pushing against the stirrup. "I was meanin' to give you this before I left," he said stretching his arm and hand out towards the sad boy.

Alex's quivering little body stepped forward to see what it was that Jack had displayed for him. He peered into the man's palm and pawed the tiny item like a timid woodland creature examining a nut or berry before eating it.

"Go on, it's for you," assured Jack.

Alex accepted the gift and immediately stuffed it into his jacket pocket. "Are ya sure?" he exclaimed with the excitement of having recognized the precious handout.

"Absolutely, I am sure," Jack stated as he repositioned himself straight up in the saddle. "I know that it will be safe with you." Then he picked up the reins again and gave Cally a gentle tap with his heels. She began to walk slowly toward the front of the barn.

Randle had already anticipated the timely departure and opened the doors. A magnificent blaze of sunlight reflecting off the whiteness of the snow was dazzling. Alex followed behind and then stopped, leaning against the portal. Cally gave a shiver as she stepped out into the frigid air, her feet made a crunching noise as she broke the glaze which varnished the surface of the land. Jack pulled back on the reins and twisted his body again towards the barn. He opened his mouth to call out pearls of wisdom but all that diffused was a whisper of cold vapor which dissipated into the air with the same nothingness that his voice had found. In lieu, he simply raised his hand to his hat brim, tugged on it a bit, and nodded. Alex reciprocated with a gesture of a small hand waving goodbye.

There was no pomp and circumstance to this departure as Jack pulled up his collar with one hand as to keep the wind from creeping down his back and turned away. Alex remained vigil, watching the gentle tapping of the rider's heels while Cally obeyed, proceeding towards the snow covered trail which led into the vast, white open space.

Alex began to swing on the door, balancing his feet up along the wooden crossbars and straddling the edge of the support like a sail. The lightness of his body weight permitted him to coast back and forth, and each time the door would begin to stop, he would put his foot down and push back so that it would swing backward again catching another ride. He rode the door back and forth, back and forth, never taking his eyes off the man and horse. But soon the clear outline of the two images began to gain upon the horizon and what was once a vivid picture now materialized as a blurry shadow. Alex hung on the door, his hands holding fast upon the latches with each back and forth motion its hinges moaned like a tired old man. He stared out into the ivory emptiness, and his eyes penetrated the chasm so bleak and void of life that he wondered why that entity in charge of the world would let this season called winter rest itself upon the earth for so many months.

———

"Well, looky here!" a gruff voice called out breaking the silence. Startled by the intrusion, Alex hopped off the door ride and ran towards the loud intonations. With hands and arms fixed akimbo, Randle stood before a shoddy burlap sack partially filled with coarse grain feed. Its contents had been disturbed and the sack, once capable of supporting its contents like a stout mushroom stalk, flopped slightly to the left away from its original upright position, contouring a folded funnel in the sack's rim. Tiny increments of seed created a steady cascade settling upon the ground.

"I never thought I'd see this, but I've been wrong before," Randle announced displaying its contents. Nestled comfortably and most relaxed sat Yazhi. Her body melted commodiously into the feed and with her wings fastened to her sides, only the wobble of her head clued the observers that she was indeed a live creature. Dark pellets for eyes quickly darted from Randle to Alex, then back again to Randle, and her expression, if hens were able to have expressions, was one of surprise, clearly a declaration of having been caught.

"Yazhi!" exclaimed Alex with such jubilation that a passerby might have believed the salutation had been meant for a relation who had been away for years. "What's ya doin' here?" Alex appealed to her, overjoyed to have discovered her nest.

Randle kneeled down and grasped her wing with his left hand and gently settled his right hand beneath the bird's body. Her feet dangled awkwardly, hanging in mid-air until he repositioned her so she rested on the flat palm of his hand. Gently, so not to terrify the poor bird, Randle lifted her away from the temporary domicile, allowing Alex to peer into the burlap sack. There he immediately spotted two chalky white eggs resting side-by-side. The unblemished shells were a bright contrast to the yellow and brown feed and their purity in the dingy and melancholy barn accentuated their innate characteristic of luster. The only evidence of Yazhi having sat upon them was a dash of lightly sprinkled corn bits and millet

Not being accustomed to being confined in the hands of Randle or any other person, the pullet began to grow quite agitated, whereby she strained her neck forward and back like a coiled spring. Twisting it about, she began to open her beak with the sudden intent of deciding to peck her way free. "Go on boy!" Randle summoned, "pick up them two eggs so I can put her back down." He held her fast, but it was obvious the feisty bird was giving him a fuss.

Alex looked at the eggs and touched one of them with his forefinger, petting gently as if he were to disturb the shell something might miraculously awaken and crack open. However, Randle was becoming impatient with the boy and in a torrent of agitation he once again commanded, "Go on, this hen don't like to be up, now git those eggs!"

Immediately Alex did as he was told. He carefully reached into the sack and with both hands timidly clutched the eggs. They were still warm to the touch, but noticeably larger than the other eggs that had been laid by the rest of the brooding hens. Removing the two from their refuge, Alex secured an egg in each hand, judiciously mindful that if they had grown any larger and rounder his small palms would have been out-sized by the enormity of the pair.

At the same time Yazhi was expressing her displeasure from having been uprooted and created such a squawking and cackling that several of the other barnyard fowl descended upon the premises; this included a robust turkey who should have remained anonymous, for upon his entry Randle commented, "Well, that Tom Turkey sure looks as though he's ready for the butcher knife." A brood of tiny chicks were hastily ushered towards the commotion as though this was a perfect lesson for a mother hen to instill upon her young, where not to nest.

Randle replaced Yazhi back upon the feed sack and shooed the on-lookers away, but not before catching up with Tom Turkey to offer him a bit more feed. Alex looked on knowing that this bit of generosity was not imparted out of kindness, but rather a method of fattening up the bird for a Sunday dinner. Randle turned to Alex who was still holding each egg with extreme caution. "Let me take a look at these beauties," he stated dusting his hands off on his breeches and then reaching out for Alex to relinquish one of the eggs. Randle raised it up towards the open barn door as though he were examining a diamond for any impurities. Sounding more like a gemologist than a farmer he continued staring up at the egg. He rotated the egg around in his large hand and shut one eye like a watchmaker using a loop to heighten his sight. "This sure is a beauty," he proclaimed again. "Wait til Betty sees these two," he smiled and then set his free hand upon Alex's shoulder. "Looks like you raised a fine layin' hen, don't ya think?"

Alex tipped his head down toward his egg-laying victor, who continued to reposition herself upon the coarse granules and with every wriggle of her thin feet and underbody, she would disturb the surface upon which she sat, and lowered the contents of the feed like the tipping of a basin of water. Alex then contemplated the egg in his hands with the same appreciation as the lad who had held the golden egg that had been laid by the goose; for this was the first time that he had actually felt as though maybe Randle thought he had done something to be acknowledged. "She done all the work," the child replied holding the egg out for further inspection.

Randle eagerly plucked the egg from the boy's hand. "Well, Alex, maybe so," he affirmed. "But you took care of her when even her own mother didn't want her." Then as though he realized that he might be sounding sentimental, Randle turned and briskly started away towards the sunlit doorway, leaving Alex standing by himself. However, as he reached the portal, he halted as though he had suddenly remembered the child and made an abrupt about-face. "Come on boy, we got chores to tend to," he bellowed loudly and with a quick step, he completed a full circle, shuffled his body forward, and hastened out into the snow. Alex scampered behind.

———

Betty attended to the large iron skillet by bending over and forking each clump of fat from one side of the pan to another; beads of sweat began to form around her lip as the heat from the fire rose up and enveloped her head like a hood. The cast skillet was a favored cooking tool, and she cradled its contents as tenderly as if rocking a babe. Years of curing cast iron meant filling the pores and voids in the metal with grease, and as a result she had serendipitously also cured the cracks in the walls. For whenever the hearth was kindled there was a smoky reminder to all who secured its warmth that this savory-seasoned skillet would come back to life. Acrobatically, Betty maneuvered about, anticipating each spatter of fat before it was ejected from the sizzling pan.

The twin eggs rested together in the wooden bowl, destiny lay in the hands of the cook. "Come on and sit!" yelled Betty to both

Alex and Randle who were individually awaiting the midday meal in separate locations of the house.

"What's ya shoutin' fer? We heard ya the first time!" Randle announced entering the room and pushing his chair away from the table. Upon sitting down he promptly tucked the gingham cloth under his chin. Alex followed deftly behind and scampered up and onto the bench to await his meal. However, he always felt silly placing his cloth under his chin and rather allowed it to hang half-way off the table next to his cup.

Betty's lips soured as she wished to fuss back at Randle, instead she mumbled indiscernibly at the pan and took it out on a piece of fat, stabbing it several times with the tines of the fork. Then reaching for the eggs, she pulled one out of the bowl and turned to Alex. "This is a beauty, Alex, a real big egg!" She smiled at him showing off the egg and then turned back towards the skillet.

Alex waited with anticipation, half believing that as soon as everyone had tasted Yazhi's eggs, they would be proclaimed the most delicious eggs in all of Missouri. He rehearsed in his mind the conversation that would take place, "I cannot believe my mouth, I have never in all my days tasted such an egg!" or "This is by far a dish set for a king!"

However, it was the sounds of eggs cracking and a sudden, "Oh my, oh my!" uttering from Betty that erased the happy scene he had manifested for himself. Randle pulled away from the table to see what it was that had created a lull in the cooking. Again, but this time with more vigor Betty proclaimed, "Oh my!" Her spatula now dangled limply in her hand, grease dripping from the edge dropped slowly onto the floor. Out of nowhere Timothy appeared, lapping the droppings by Betty's feet.

"Step aside woman, what is it that's got you so shook?" Randle, honing in on Betty's territory, peered into the skillet. "Well, I'll be!" he cried out.

Alex's heart thumped wildly as though it was preparing to fly out of his chest. Not daring to move from his place, he impatiently sat and waited. The fat hissed and sizzled as the smell of fried eggs waft through the kitchen. "Well, go on," Randle said turning from his wife and retrieved his position at the head of the table. "Serve it up!" He was grinning with the hungry look of a toothy canine.

Betty gently booted Timothy who scampered away, taking asylum in the corner of the room and proceeded to lick his front paws with the utmost satisfaction. "I think that you should have the first pick," Betty said as she stepped to the side of the table dangling a platter in front of Alex. "Do ya want one or two?" she asked. Alex looked upon the large plate and then up at Betty. Bewildered, he said nothing. "Go on, count em!" she suggested prodding the platter again under his eyes.

Alex followed her command and pointed, "One, two, three, four?" There are four yolks!"

Betty grinned and Randle laughed so loud that it scared Timothy towards the back of the house. "I have heard of one, but never seen one! Alex, you raised yer self a hen who can lay eggs with two times the yolk. Why I do believe you are a farmer, a true farmer!"

Alex looked upon the serving dish that Betty continued to suspend before him and gingerly slid one of the double yolked eggs onto his plate with his fork. Like a pair of yellow eyes protruding out of a slick white blanket, they coasted to the center of his plate. He pushed his finger over the top of one protrusion and could tell that it had thankfully been cooked for a long enough amount of time so it was not too soft. For unlike Randle, who liked to sop up the runny yolk with bread, he preferred his eggs cooked well. Alex placed his fork on the side of the plate and waited until Betty stepped away to serve Randle and then herself. Then when she was seated, he cut himself a small piece and took a bite. An unfamiliar sigh of relief was suddenly released like steam out of a kettle as he chewed. For the first time since his arrival he finally felt as though he had done something special to contribute to the Forester farm. A sense of satisfaction dominated the table; eggs never tasted so good.

Chapter 24

A sturdy and plain paneled front door swung open exposing a rather dark and colorless foyer. Directly to the immediate right as one stepped off the front mat, there stood a carved oak hall bench with a beveled glass mirror and winged griffins rising above. Acanthus leaf accents and a cartouche crest dominated the design advertising that the owner was a person of means or recipient of a generous inheritance. "Well, don't just stand there gaping, enter, enter!" a woman's shrewish voice snapped. "You're letting in the cold! Shut the door."

Will quickly did as he was commanded and lightly kicked the door shut with his foot for he was quite loaded down with all their possessions. The two weary travelers stood in attendance and with the exception of a single flicker of brightness entering from a half-open interior door, the room was eerily dark. Several moments passed quietly until they heard the door groan as it was slowly being pushed all the way open exposing behind it a dark hallway. The woman's voice bit at them again, "Follow me, follow me, and don't dally." Then, the bidding halted and was exchanged with the thump of three separate steps resonating up a twisting stairwell. Will and Libby obediently followed and soon found themselves being led by an elderly white-haired woman guided by the tapping of a wooden cane. She held in front of her a tallow candle which was the only visible means of light, and as the three made their way upward Libby made note that if the elderly woman had decided to retreat in the opposite direction and go back down, it would be up to her to lead for the narrow stairs had not been built with more than single file in mind.

"Wait here," demanded the white-haired woman when they reached the top of the stairway. She pointed her cane at a small arched nook that was set back in the wall. Still there was no visible means of securing any outside light which led Will and Libby to wonder if this building had any windows that were not shuttered closed. Will clutched their possessions with both hands and neared closer to Libby as she began to fan herself with one of her calf-skin gloves she had removed. Her hat, once sitting pretty and erect upon her head, slid slightly to the left and she wished that she could finally find a place to sit and recuperate from their travels. Both pairs of eyes followed the trail of light, and they listened to the tapping of the cane strike the floor until it was silenced as the old woman stopped before one of the doors lining the long corridor.

The air was musty and stale and lingered in their nostrils. Libby felt herself become woozy from this mixture of stench and her fatigue, and the more she felt faint the faster she fanned herself. She leaned back against the wall and allowed it to support her tired body.

"Come along, come along," cackled the elder again. Will, who was now leaning flush against the wall, stepped forward and turned to see her silhouette disappear through an opened doorway at the end of the hall. The only flicker of light followed along leaving the two arrivals pursuing the whereabouts of the white-haired woman in a void of darkness.

Libby felt her way along the corridor with the palms of her hands and counted seven closed doors before reaching the eighth door which had been left ajar. Will gently kicked the base with his foot, and its hinges ached with a painful creak as though it had not been stretched open in a goodly amount of time. The smell of mold and tainted air reinforced the theory that the room must have been shut up for some time. Upon a small round table the same tallow candle they had pursued had been placed before a bent seated figure being propped-up by a wooden cane. The tallow flickered more brightly than before since it was now sitting stationary in its holder. The old woman with the alabaster hair glared up at Libby and then Will. "Drop your bags and let me look at the two of you foreign vagabonds!" she stated in a voice surprisingly strong in contrast to her frail looking body. And at the same time that she began to inspect the weary travelers, so too were the Piccards creating their own opinions of the speaker. Her hands, bent and gnarled at each joint, clasped the cherry wood handle firmly allowing it to support her body as though, if removed, she would fall over limply with the same degree as cutting the taut strings from a marionette. Although it was midday, she wore a pink silk gauze dress with draped folds and appliqués on the short puffed sleeves, trimmed with lace that had frayed with age. The gown was a fashion of an earlier era and was marked with the yellow age of time, and though it may have been tailored to her fit during the more carefree years in her life, the present state of her physique barely filled its flowing material. Protruding from beneath the hem of the dress were pink satin evening slippers, decorated on the vamp with a monochromatic pattern of narrow pale rose stripes and bouquets of tiny flowers.

"So, you are Libby and Will," she announced leaning forward on the cane. "Come closer and let me look at you!" she demanded pointing at Libby. Libby obeyed and bowed her face towards the white-haired woman. "My, my," she resumed staring up at the younger; "you are a pretty thing, aren't you?"

"Thank you," replied Libby now backing away as Will reached into his coat pocket and produced a stiff envelope.

"Mrs. Cambridge, permit me give you our letter of introduction," he said handing the letter to the elderly woman.

The white-haired woman plucked it away and toyed with its contents for a moment before continuing to speak. "This is a formality," she said shaking the envelope with her free hand, "I knew to expect you both. Now," she exclaimed using her cane as a pointer at Will, "you are Will Piccard and this is your new bride, Libby." She paused to give the two enough time to nod. "Well, I hope you find the accommodations suitable," she proceeded and as she spoke slowly began to raise herself up off her chair. Will immediately sprang forward to assist, for he half expected the aged lady to find it quite difficult to resume standing. Vehemently, she pushed her hand forward and gestured for him to retreat. "I don't need your help, never have and never shall," she barked. "Now," she said steadying herself with her cane, "since I am the proprietor of this rooming house I will be the one to whom you will direct all payments. Naturally the Judge made all the necessary prearrangements for you whereby your first month's room and board has been paid in full."

Will and Libby continued to stand at attention as the flickering tallow seemed to be desperately trying to keep from becoming extinguished, however; it was growing shorter by the moment. Libby spoke up, "I do beg your pardon, Mrs. Cambridge, but would it be possible for me to open the window shutter. I fear that the tiny candle is growing low as we speak."

The ashen woman looked down at the candle and then brought it closely up to her face. "Can you see me better now, my dear?" she laughed in delight. "Do you find me pretty?" she asked coyly allowing the light to dance around her white head. She paused, watching Libby struggle for words and knew the younger would not wish to offend her. Again the old woman baited her with the question, "Come now, am I lovely? Here," she urged pointing her gnarled finger toward her. "Look at my face, pretty eh?" she chimed. Then without warning, she released upon them both a most hideous laugh, simultaneously drawing her rounded body up towards Libby like a serpent. Provoked by this unexpected howl, the younger stepped back and found herself pressed against the wall as the white-haired woman laughed wildly, all the while slowly advancing. The questions, the pungent odor emanating from this melancholy room, a sudden rise in temperature was all too overpowering and suddenly Libby shrieked in fear, gasping for a breath. The ghastly shadow of the old woman's figure against the broken wallpaper began to come alive and without warning the young bride fell back upon Will and fainted.

When Libby awoke she found herself lying on the bed with Will sitting by her side. "You gave me a fright," he whispered, gently stroking her hand and lifting the cool compress from her forehead.

Libby smiled up at him and touched his hand with hers. "Why, this is the biggest bed I have ever seen!" she exclaimed turning her head from side to side admiring the large four poster bed. "I could get lost in it," she laughed.

"Are you feeling better, Libby?" an unfamiliar voice asked. Startled, the exhausted young woman tried to sit up to see who it was that spoke. She struggled to lean back upon her elbows to support herself.

"Lay back down, Libby" whispered Will, noticing the look of fear returning to his wife. "It's all right, here, let me introduce, Katrina, Mrs. Cambridge's housemaid," he said as the middle-aged woman approached the bed.

"Do as your husband tells you, Libby, you'll have time soon enough to be getting up. You need your rest, deary," she uttered, tapping Libby lightly on her leg. Katrina, a tall and robust woman stared down upon her with dark eyes that were framed under equally dark brows. Her thin lips were a natural crimson color, and she wore a scarf tied behind her head, knotted just below the hairline. Her chestnut hair was braided and pinned back under the flap of the scarf. She might have been a handsome woman in her day however; years of toil wore heavily upon her, which was accentuated by particularly large hands, chapped and rough from the lye of soaps. She spoke again with the weighty tone she executed when speaking to the rest of the staff, "If you need me, I will be downstairs. You both may come down to the kitchen when you are hungry." Then, not waiting for a reply, she turned out of the small room.

Will shimmed open the shutters. The staleness of the room began to seep out and escape into the courtyard below. Baltimore was not a bright city, and its sooty streets and grey tones muted any sunlight that wished to cast upon its boulevards and back alleyways. Libby stretched lazily like a cat and obeyed by closing her eyes while Will sat upon the edge of the bed and waited anxiously until he was sure she had drifted asleep. He hesitated a few moments and then stealthily picked up the newly lit candle which had been secured in a bronze holder on the fireplace mantle, and tiptoed away to explore their new residence.

———

The winding stairwell escorting Will downward did not seem as difficult as before, now that he had become accustomed to the obscure lighting of the flickering candle that he held straight out before him like a beggar's cup. Upon reaching the landing, he stepped into a small deserted corridor where he readily opened a narrow door and soon discovered that it led into another dim hallway similar to the floor above except this time he was drawn towards a wide-open portal like a moth being attracted to the light. Since he was no longer in need of its guidance, he blew his candle out. To his surprise he had entered into a rather ostentatious room; its dining table large enough to seat ten. Upon a mahogany buffet, a silver tea service, one bone china teacup and saucer, and a waste bowl for teapot warming water and used tea leaves awaited the daily ritual. Will eyed an adjacent platter of crème filled pastry and raspberry scones, which promptly roused his stomach and triggered pangs of hunger. Moving closer to the tray; he contemplated removing one of the smallest tea sandwiches. "How would anyone notice a morsel of bread out of this heavenly stack of sweets?" He dug into his pocket and estimated that there would be enough room to secure the sandwich without turning it into a soggy mush.

But before he could extend his hand upon the crustless aperitif and stow it into his possession, he was surprised by a raspy voice that called out, "By the horn spoons! What are you doing in here?" Will, startled by the clandestine stranger, turned round to witness a crusty looking man. He was a large fellow with shaggy brown hair that he wore long to his shoulders.

"I was just looking around and happened to come upon this room and…"

The intruder interrupted to complete Will's sentence. "And you thought you just might have a little nibble, eh?" The man poked at the pastries and selected a crème filled tart; with two fat fingers he grabbed it up and dropped the entire delicacy into his mouth, savoring each bite he chewed with gusto and then licked all his fingers clean of any butter fat before wiping them dry upon his shirt. "These are Mrs. Cambridge's sweets and tea. Every afternoon you can find her in this dining room and every day she perches herself over there," he said with authority and pointed his chubby finger at the head of the table. "Occasionally, she invites one of the high paying room guests to join, but not me. I rent my room cheap and come and go as I please." Will regarded the man with great interest and allowed him to continue. "We all got our reasons for bein' here and we all got our secrets." He smiled and exposed a mouth full of tired teeth. "So, what's yours?"

"Mine?" Will began to feel as though this conversation was not headed in any positive direction, but inasmuch as the man seemed to be a permanent fixture in Cambridge Arms he certainly did not want to be on his negative side. "My wife and I are from England and wish to find work."

"Baltimore is the place then; you want to work, it's work you'll get." Then the man demanded, "Let me see yer hands."

"My hands, whatever for?" Will pulled them back as though he feared the man would tear them off the very wrists they hung on.

"Are they working hands, are they afraid of hard work?" the question needled him.

Will heeded the words and like a summer storm that comes in without warning, he found a wave of acrimony striking him. For the first time since he had left the English port he was provoked to anger. Emotions overcame his senses and his thoughts jumped about impeding all rational thinking. He brooded as he wondered if now, in America, he would have to prove himself worthy of work; that he would have to display his hands to validate he was honorable!

"These hands!" he exclaimed exposing them in a most emphatic gesture and shaking them violently. "These hands have known work before they were old enough to hold a spoon. These hands," he stated again displaying the open palms, "if they could talk, they would cry out in pain! Yet all these hands can do is reach out and find dignity in work that is often regarded as toil for the unworthy, the poor, the reprehensible." Will's hands were no longer posed open, but now tightly fisted and clenched by his sides. He idly dug his fingernails into his palms.

"Good," the man said smiling, not the least faltered by the sudden outburst. He reached over and popped another dainty into his mouth. Each chew was exaggerated with a swoon of delight, and he savored its sweetness with loud smacks of his thin lips; and as though mimicking a gentleman, he primly slid away any remaining crumbs that were wavering about the corners of his lips by dusting them delicately with his oversized index fingers. Taking his last swallow, he began to speak again. "Dear me," he replied, "we haven't gotten off to a very good start, now have we, chum? That is what you English call each other, isn't it? Well then, no more shall be said on the subject. Now, I do have many acquaintances here and if you wish I can ask around to help find you employment. If you're willing to work more than ten hours a day I don't think you'll have a problem." The man smiled apologetically and waited for Will's response.

Will's tension relaxed and he now stood more at ease. "I'm Will Piccard," he introduced himself. "My wife is Libby, and we're in room number eight."

"Room number five, Nicholas Biddle, but you can me Nick. Here, have a scone but by all means don't let the old biddy know that we've trifled with her teatime biscuits." He laughed and elbowed Will carelessly. "Now, follow me and let us leave this room before we get caught making off with the dainties. Permit me to take you about Cambridge Arms, not everyone takes to foreigners as I do," he added as he offered himself a scone, winked at Will, and gestured for him to follow.

The recommendation was received with caution as Will slipped back into the darkened corridor directly behind his new acquaintance.

Of all the places investigated there were two locations that roused Will's interest. The first was the small courtyard garden sandwiched between a square brick enclosure in the back of the building. Under the boughs of the hawthorn tree sits a pair of rickety wooden benches. They had been replaced several times in earlier years because of weathering however; the original benches had been built by Mrs. Cambridge's son. It was revealed to Will that Nick had only come to stay at the Cambridge Arms because he was a childhood friend of the boy. This backyard was once a favorite spot since it was her son who had planted and cultivated the garden. In the milder months of spring and summer, rows of wild indigo, golden aster, strawberry bush, and pasture rose took turns enticing the visitor with its colors. Maidenhair ferns were plotted about like green tufts of hair. But now that he was no longer living in the house, the summer garden vines had strangled the flowering plants and the strawberry bush, no longer pruned or cared for, grew leggy and bore only nettles. The maidenhair fern was boundless in its propagation, wildly overgrown and untamed.

Nick tried to recreate this period as Will artfully weeded through his descriptions seeing past the presently chilly brown, mustard, and grey garden and envisioning its more glorious past. "Does Mrs. Cambridge come out here anymore?" he asked.

"Not that I am aware of," Nick replied picking up a tiny pebble and pitching it aimlessly into the barren plot. "She really has never forgiven her son for leaving."

"What happened to him?" Will wondered aloud.

"He was drafted into the military and though Mrs. Cambridge said she could call in favors to keep him from serving, he believed that would have been dishonorable. So, he went off with his assigned regiment and never returned home," Nick explained bluntly, and declared nothing more.

The tiny cubical adjacent to the root cellar proved to be the most bewitching room in Cambridge Arms; not because of its dark and dank interior, but perhaps because of its tale of reticence. During the War of 1812, Baltimore harbor was "a nest of pirates". One such pirate captain, who called himself Blackbeard after the infamous buccaneer during the late 1600s, intended to transfer silver he had stolen to a British warship for transport to London. However, during this exchange, one of the shipmates plotted against him and the secret mission was foiled. Naturally, the blood-thirsty plunderer sought refuge and discovered by chance an exterior tunnel which led to this very room in the Cambridge Arms.

"Why didn't you show me the tunnel from the outside?" asked Will as he walked behind Nick who was leading them both with only the glow of the flickering tallow.

"That entrance was boarded over years ago, and this is the only passage I know from the inside," he whispered twisting around back towards Will. "Be sure to bow your head when we go through the door; the ceiling is lower down here."

The temperature gradually became cooler and the walls grew damp and moist to the touch as the two men descended below ground level. Nick directed his candle towards a wooden door, "This is the root cellar, but this way," he remarked and redirected his candle to an opposing wall, "this is the chamber." At first glance Will was unable to detect anything that could resemble a doorway. However, he watched in the scant light of the tallow while Nick fumbled about, feeling the rough blackened wall. Small pieces of rubble and slag crumbled to the ground. He continued to grope, sliding his hands over the rough surface. "Ah, I know what the matter is!" he laughed as he crouched down and proceeded to scan the wall again. This time it took only a moment before he found a wobbly rock and pulled it out from the wall. At once he reached in and was able to locate what seemed to be more loose rock, which turned out to be neatly camouflaged panels made from planks. Nick gave it a jolt and the panel released itself from the wall, exposing a small cavity. "Well, it sure was bigger a time ago," he said standing up. "When Cambridge and I were young this made for a good place to play. I remember one time young Cambridge, myself, and the cook's son, Dell, decided to pretend we were pirates. You see, the tale of Blackbeard was a legend that had been etched in our minds. Naturally, if we were to

be certified as true pirates we had to do something bold and daring."
Nick stood up and brushed his hands on his pants.

"Naturally," agreed Will waiting to hear the rest.

"Well, it turns out that Dell, bein' as he was from, let us say, the
bottom rung of the social ladder, was willing to take up the role of
pirate quickly and freely. He was about nine and Cambridge and I
were about six," he said. "No," Nick pondered, stroking his chin.
"Actually we were seven years of age. Well anyway, we needed to
commit a misconduct that would have been worthy to the character
of plunderers and marauders. Here, take a look in," he coaxed Will
and stepped aside.

Will took the candle and crouched down to peek into the little
room. Clearly it must have been enchanting to a young boy.

Nick continued, "Now, Dell, you see was a buck that was beat
more than once a week, so he had grown hard and scared of nothing.
The scheme was concocted whereby Dell was supposed to climb up
onto the roof and plug up the kitchen chimney. Then, when cook
started the next meal..."

"I see what you are getting at," Will laughed at the thought of
such a childish prank.

"Yes, we would smoke out the entire place! It was shear genius;
however that is what we thought! You see, Dell, not bein' the bright-
est of lads, decided to make his ascent to the chimney by way of
the hawthorn tree out back. He hadn't gotten more than his head
and torso up into the first bough when he was caught red-handed
by Mrs. Cambridge. Standing directly under the tree, she shook her
fist and demanded that he descend without delay from her property. Having no other means of egress, he reluctantly submitted.
Immediately upon placing his first foot on solid ground, she boxed
his ears and pinched his nose. I'll never forget the howl that boy
released! Unsurprisingly, Cambridge and I did not want to tarry in
fear that Dell would betray us and confess under the tyranny of Mrs.
Cambridge that me and her son were part of the foiled prank. We
cowardly scurried down here to hide and held up for a least half a
day."

"Did Dell ever reveal you as conspirators?" asked Will most curiously.

"Dell was a true pirate and had not divulged our whereabouts. He took the beating for us all and then was sent away to work with his father in the shipyards. We rarely saw much of Dell again. When we finally got too hungry to stay hidden, we unearthed ourselves like a pair of terrestrial moles. As fortune would have it, Mrs. Cambridge forgot about the incident since she was too busy attending to the affairs of the home." Nick bent down again to examine the small opening. "Now there is no way I could fit comfortably in there anymore," he jested as he patted his oversized posterior.

"I see what you mean," agreed Will, who tried to imagine the frightened countenance of two little boys and the integrity of young Dell for not telling on his two friends.

Nick handed the candleholder to Will as he set back restoring the wall to its original manner like a skilled mason. "Let's get out of here before we lose our light," he exclaimed as he patted down last section of wall. "This candle has not much life left in it."

Chapter 25

Belle Tarson hadn't slept but a few hours each night, and although most of the folks thought of her as headstrong and thorny, she had mothered the child back from the grips of sickness with the best of care. Mindy, the doll, lay between the limp fingers of the small hand, eyes wide-open and arms outstretched, the doll was ready for play. Belle unfolded the tiny bent fingers of the child and pulled the doll away from the clenched hand. She twisted the toy legs at the joint and positioned Mindy to sit stiffly upon the wooden table like a watchful angel. Belle stroked the sleeping child's pale face; finding it was no longer warm to the touch. She pulled the woolen blanket up towards her chin and dabbed the cool compress to the pale forehead.

Dr. Foy had finally broken through the snow drifts like a vole burrowing through the snow. It was a gloomy afternoon when he took up his position by the child's bedside. He conjured up a remedy in the proportions of one part black mustard seed to four to six parts of linseed meal. Belle was instructed to apply the mild mustard poultice to the child's tiny throat and chest, but not to keep this pasty compress on for more than a quarter hour at a time. He prescribed a teaspoon of elixir mixed from thyme and sarsaparilla every four hours to ease her brassy cough. She was to remain in bed for at least another week, to be fed warm broth, and not to be excited in anyway, lest her cough would resume again.

Belle had little faith in either remedy and her lack of confidence in any Western trained doctor seemed to only ignite her cynical nature. Regardless, the child was examined by Dr. Foy and proclaimed no longer in grave danger. Feigning thanks for his accomplishment, Belle sent the doctor off in good spirits with a gold piece in his pocket and a basket of canned peaches for Mrs. Foy. "Give my best to your family," Belle insisted, as she eagerly escorted the elderly gentleman out the door. However, before bolting it shut from the inside, she peered curiously through the slightly open doorway and watched as he mounted the buggy. The harsh wind had died away and resurrected in its place was a halcyon breeze; but still the winter sky remained cold and crisp and when the doctor snapped the whip back, its loud crack electrified the air and sent a sharp echo through the trees which roused the old mare. With yet another neighbor boy to tend to, the elder physician hoped to reach their homestead before dark set in.

Belle pushed the door shut, drew the gingham curtains together, and lit the coal lantern. She paused momentarily. Savoring with satisfaction that she was not the one traveling through the cold and impending dusk; she then settled down into the wooden rocker in the parlor. She found herself wishing that the day was over so that she would be able to lie down. She tried to cast away her feeling of loneliness, closed her eyes and expelled a deep sigh. The natural light was fading. The tired woman slowly rocked as though she were slipping away between these light and lurid moments of time. Amidst the incandescence of the coal lantern she thought that she saw her little dog, Bailey, spring out from behind the bushes; Bailey, her childhood companion that would wander about while she fetched chestnuts and ripe beechnuts. Shadowing behind is Adam Hixon, the little boy that likes to scratch around in the fallen autumn leaves and the frisky pup rolling about collecting pieces of broken twigs and burs in his fur. Auntie Fay, carrying a bucket of slop, comes out from behind the shed; she is calling forth, "Where are you?"

Belle hears the voice again, "Where are you?" it cries, but now it sounds farther away than the first time. Bailey frolics and romps round Belle's feet as she moves towards the river's edge. Bending down to pick up a chestnut that has rolled out of her full basket, playful Bailey leaps up and knocks the basket out of her hands.

Frantically, trying to keep her gathering from falling into the rushing water, she throws her hands forward only to find that she is losing her footing. Automatically, Belle tries to break her fall, but it is too late. As she tumbles downward towards the river below, the cascading earth slides beneath the skidding Belle who is dangerously close to the water's edge. Adam Hixon is watching, jumping up and down. He is laughing and runs off to catch a squirrel. Gasping with terror she now recognizes not herself but her beloved puppy, Bailey, being sucked underwater by the rapid current. "Where are you?" the voice calls again, but this time it is muffled by her inability to catch her own breath, too helpless to retrieve the dog who frantically struggles to keep its nose above the rushing surface.

Dazed and confused Belle is suddenly awakened by a jolt of adrenaline. She grabs hold of her blouse collar and tries to loosen the snug fitting lace trim by tugging upon the stiff material with her fingers. She sets her eyes upon the mellow flickering of the coal lamp and is transported back to the present; realizing this moment's lapse was simply a dream. Brushing her hands over her skirt as though dusting and flicking this illusion away, she promptly regains her composure when she hears the familiar cry, "Where are you?" Then, removing the coal lantern from the table, she follows the trailing voice of the little child back into the sickroom.

———

Never had a winter's day seemed so fair as today, Belle concluded as she slid the secured wooden plank away and cracked open the sealed window shutters. Despite the frigid cold, fresh air was a welcomed event and it quickly circulated about the house emancipating a sensation of new energy. Joseph, her dear sweet Joseph; Belle's vision embraced that of her son, and she relished the idea that her husband could finally return with the boy. These few weeks had been Joseph's first experience away and though it had been less than a fortnight, surely, she thought that it was possible for him to have grown at least an inch.

Belle scurried about insuring that his return would be met with all his favorite fixings: corn bread, butter, fried bacon, and milk. The hired hands had also been permitted to return however; it took some convincing from Missus Tarson to persuade the superstitious cook, Beatrice Winston, that the sickness, which had been the cause of all the evacuations, had truly been exterminated. "That child still looks like she's got the poison in her!" cried Beatrice through chattering teeth. Swaying back and forth while trying to keep herself warm, she raised herself on tiptoe, hardly able to balance her rotund physique, and peeked through the cracked shutter at the sleeping child. Terrified that the fever demon still lurked about in an invisible form, Beatrice would only reenter the home if both garlic and onion bulbs were hung about to stave off any such infection-bearing creature. An exasperated Missus Tarson was eager to relegate all the cooking duties back to Beatrice, and immediately set about gathering sprouting bulbs from the root cellar and hung them about the kitchen with twine and yarn like Christmas decorations.

The hearth was ablaze with activity, the table was set with the fine Sunday ware, and as the house moaned and hummed with the ordinary labors of daily chores, Missus Tarson became galvanized, instructing and mandating tasks, and before the end of the day's light, Tod, the cook's younger brother, scampered up from the barn all out of breath! "He's here, he's here, Miss Tarson, I believe I see the wagon comin' up the trail!" the eager boy shouted as he pushed open the front door, nearly toppling a full basket of freshly laid eggs from its post on the counter. An enormous surge of northerly wind blasted into the cozy warm house, causing the window shutters to slam shut with such a thud that poor nervous Beatrice burst forth a startling shrill of fright.

"Tod!" scolded an unnerved Missus Tarson, who too had been alarmed by this sudden explosion of dissidence. "Shut that door! And next time, come in through the help's entrance!"

Tod, who had believed he was only delivering a message of good will, hung his head like a shamed dog, did as he was told, and slowly muddled his way towards the kitchen where his sister was preparing the big meal. However, as soon as the nervous woman laid her eyes upon him, accompanied by wet tracks of melting snow that followed behind, she immediately withdrew her wooden spoon from the large bowl with the same finesse as a swordsman pulling a cutlass from its sheath, and proceeded to lay several strikes upon him in retaliation for scaring her "half-out of her wits!" The simple lad took his licks in stride, and although he did not feel they were justified, he let his sister have her way with him, when suddenly the cast iron pot, dangling over the hearth, began sputtering fat like firecrackers. Beatrice, springing into action, released her full attention away from the lad and now aimed it towards the sizzling suet. Fortuitously, with the spotlight turned from his direction, the catlike lad snuck outside, hastening lickety-split towards the barn, all the while nursing his battered shoulder as he fled. Now, just how simple is our Tod is a question to be pondered, for directly prior to his stealthy escape, he most cunningly spirited away several yeast buns that had been set aside for the young Tarson's reunion.

———

Indeed, a wagon was approaching the property, but when Belle opened the door and peeked out the wagon had already been hitched and three bundled figures had dismounted. "Don't worry, Delilah," a small hushed voice whispered. "We won't be long, promise."

Belle recognized the visitors as the Foresters and immediately beckoned to them with an outstretched hand; her body served as a blockade and prevented only a minimal amount of winter to enter. "Randle," she shouted, "take the draft into the barn, Tod will tend to him! Betty, come on in and bring the boy!" she commanded.

Although the Foresters were only planning on a modest visit, none would have disobeyed Belle for her forceful manner was not easy to oppose. Alex followed behind Betty and felt a firmly placed hand propelling him forward. "Don't dawdle, Alex!" exclaimed the churlish voice of Missus Tarson. "Remove that coat and your shoes." Hurriedly, he looked at Betty who too was heeding the commands like a child of eight. "Now, go stand over by the fire." Missus Tarson softened her voice and took the heavy coats and draped them on a large row of neatly hammered pegs. Betty felt rather awkward for she had not planned on staying but for only a moment and certainly did not wish to remove her shoes to display her winter stockings. Her mind tried to reflect back on the morning as to which of the several pairs of stockings she had put on. Betty wiggled her toes hoping this would help her to recollect and thankfully she recalled that the newly darned stockings were the ones that she wore.

"Beatrice, Beatrice!" fussed Missus Tarson to the cook, "go and put on another three plates, we will have a real party for Joseph." Then she turned to Betty who was still standing awkwardly by the front door. "I insist that you three stay," continued the emphatic Belle. "Why, won't that be fun for everyone?"

"Fun for who?" mumbled the cook. Beatrice entered the living area wearing a sour disposition and a greasy apron, for upon hearing Missus Tarson she was not at all pleased with the amended meal plan. "Miss Tarson," scoffed Beatrice, "what do you want me to serve up? Why you know that I planned on four!"

"That, Beatrice, is why you are the cook!" stated the mistress of the house. Visibly annoyed but not daring to disobey, Beatrice turned to where Alex was sitting and threw back at him a vexed glance.

The glowering scowl of the angry servant lay heavily upon the naive boy, and he suddenly grew terrified that he was going to be poisoned by the angry cook! Deeply troubled, he began to toy with the notion that Beatrice had probably taken straightaway to concoct a dish laced with arsenic, or worse, maybe at this very moment she was taking revenge and frying a field mouse because she had nothing else in the house to prepare. No, she had caught a rat and it would never be detected because all she had to do was chop off the tail and ears, and after it had been cooked it could easily be disguised as meat within the gravy. Alex became revolted as he contemplated the angry woman serving this rodent-dish to him because she knew a child would dare not complain and, after all, it was his fault that she had more people to feed.

The more Alex tossed this picture about, the wilder his imagination grew! Panic crept inside and all he wanted to do was run from the house. He wished to recount this horrific premonition to Betty; however, she was now engaged with Belle in what sounded like a trivial conversation about winter storms and the projected spring thaw. A cold feeling of nausea overcame him as tried to peer around the corner of the kitchen portal, when Beatrice grabbed him by the scruff of the neck and squealed in delight, "Never play cat and mouse games if you're the rat!"

Alex gasped, he was caught spying by none other than Beatrice herself and now surely he would die by the hands of this clever woman! "What are ya doin' peering in at me, eh?" Poised with one hand on her hip, she violently shook the wooden spoon as if it were a paddle.

Fearful, Alex shifted back and forth shoeless, his sock bearing a hole exposed his big toe and he was wavering like a flimsy dandelion. Beatrice could not remain harsh anymore and smiling, she settled the spoon back in the bowl for a second time that evening. "I bet yer hungry," she said. She stood with her hands outstretched. "Want to have a piece of fried fat and meat?"

"Fried meat?" These words were immediately revoked by his brain and replaced with a petrified expression which could only be interpreted by the receiver as an obvious decline, for Beatrice responded heartily with, "I can see ya ain't got an appetite." She busied her fingers and turned her attention to a cutting board with an assemblage of sundry pieces of raw victuals. He stared timidly as Beatrice took up the sharp cleaver and skillfully drew down upon the strips of pink and white flesh, dropping the smaller chunks into the vat of hot grease.

However, no sooner had his trepidation began to retreat when the house was disturbed by a loud knocking upon the door. It did not resemble the usual rap that one produces with bare knuckles, but rather a series of sharp strikes with a blunt object. "That don't sound like Randle," said Betty now wondering to herself what was keeping her husband.

The rapping continued but now it was even louder and a voice was mixed along with the strikes. "Open up, Belle! It's me!"

This time the urgency and tone of the voice and the repetition of strikes had an opposite effect on the woman. With regal composure and serenity she gathered her skirt and slowly meandered to the door. The door rattled with impatience and the louder the voice behind the door grew, the more slowly Belle appeared to be walking. By this time Beatrice emerged from the kitchen to investigate the ensuing commotion. Her stout girth masked the entire portal as she leaned against the frame. Alex too wished to find out what was going on however, only a small sliver of space within the doorway was granted for him to peer through. He crouched down and prudently slid aside the ruffled material of her full skirt like one who peers between the thick velvet stage curtains to watch a performance without paying.

"Belle, hurry now, unlock the door," called the harried outsider.

Missus Tarson clasped the latch and gingerly released it, allowing the voice behind the door to dart in. A gloved hand emerged, hooked the edge of the door and shoved it open, erratically knocking with the wooden cane that was fixed in the opposite hand. "Belle!" The flushed face of a man shaken and filled with anxiety appeared before her. It was Greg Tarson, wet, breathless, and trembling.

"I know what you are going to say!" replied Belle as she stepped aside allowing her husband to enter. "I know what you are going to say!" Her voice was calm and low and she kept repeating the words, "I know what you are going to say, I know what you're going to say."

"How would you know what I am going to say!" he cried out. "There has been a terrible accident!" he echoed, while nervously fumbling with the same cane that he had used to rap upon the door.

Belle turned her back to him and glanced up towards the heaven, "Because," she replied, "I just know."

———

Beatrice remained within the portal of the kitchen, one hand on her head and the other braced upon the frame as she groaned and moaned, "Oh me, oh me, the demon is still in this house!" Alex, now particularly eager to break free from behind this large obstruction, made great attempts by trying to jostle past. Getting down on all fours he pushed her legs which caused a shift in position, and quickly he scurried along like a dust mop. "Oh me, what will become of this house," wailed the woman who now fanned herself with the greasy gingham apron she was donning.

"How do you know?" cried out Mr. Tarson, who wore signs of an accident. Though he was once dressed for a special occasion, he now resembled a pitiful buffoon; he sported a waterlogged woolen coat with black dress collar and brass buttons. The pleated frill of his shirt wilted under the soggy weight of water, and the tied bow of the now limp silk cravat dripped onto his breeches that had been tucked into leather boots laden about the soles with hardened mud. The appearance of Mr. Tarson would have been most comical indeed had the situation been less grim.

Alex finagled an amicable escape from the kitchen without having been accidentally stepped upon by Beatrice, who continued to bleat mournfully. He successfully crawled across to the far side of the room undetected because at the same time Randle entered the house, the door still slightly pitched open.

"There's been some sort of an accident," Betty whispered to Randle who had not been privy to the present situation. She darted around a drenched Mr. Tarson who had collapsed into the empty rocker. Alex watched as each adult reacted to another, imitating a performance of marionettes. Their arms and heads remained limp until one began to speak and mechanically come alive and then grow limp again. Strangely, they did not interact at the same time, as though they were being moved by a single puppeteer. Still in the doorway, Beatrice wailed pitifully in unintelligible tongues, Missus Tarson stood by the window wringing her hands and nodding to herself and every once in a while whispering, "I knew it, I knew it." Greg Tarson placed his head in his hands and habitually ran his fingernails through his drenched tousled curls as though trying to eliminate the pain he seemed to be carrying, while Betty quietly recalled to Randle the few moments he had missed. And although everyone was in the same room, no one seemed to take any notice of the small child who had entered.

"Where's Joseph?" called a meek voice.

Alex looked around at each adult face, for the child who'd spoken was obscured from his sight. The voice repeated the words that no one had dared ask. "Where's Joseph?"

Beatrice moaned louder and cried out when she saw the little girl standing in the bedroom doorway, "Oh, what a miserable state is borne by these wretched souls!"

The child hugged her doll tightly and stood frozen as though having been scared stiff.

"Now, look who's here?" said Betty walking over to her. "You're all better, ain't ya?"

Alex peered out from his safe corner of the room to catch a glimpse of the brave voice that uttered the burning question that needed to be asked. But as soon as he saw the child he stood up aghast as though he himself had been struck by an apparition. Cold winds brushed through his hair, spiraled about the room, and then floated upward. Randle felt the cold wind too and inferring that it came from the outdoors, he unglued himself from his spot to secure the front door.

"Don't touch that door!" screamed Belle furiously, startling all.

Betty placed her hand upon the little girl who now was holding Mindy in one hand and allowed it to dangle freely by her side.

"Why Belle, I just wanted to keep the cold out," Randle started to explain as he picked up the board and placed it against the door.

"I said," Belle bellowed again racing towards Randle, "don't touch it!" and she hurled her body against the door and threw her outstretched arms to keep anyone from tampering with it.

Calmly, Randle stepped aside. "Here, Belle, let me open it for you," he replied in a hushed tone. Belle maintained her outstretched pose; her eyes looked back at him, blank and expressionless. He waited for several minutes wondering if his appeal had been sent to deaf ears. Finally, Belle lowered her arms to her sides and shrank away permitting Randle to unlatch the door. He leaned the board up against the wall saying, "I'll just set it right here, Belle. Right here, where nobody's gonna mess with it," and slowly backed away as though she was a rabid animal. Now Randle didn't believe in the supernatural, but right at this moment Belle may have changed his mind.

"Thank you, Randle," she replied in a calm and mechanical voice. "You see," she continued, "he might need to get in, that is, when he comes home and we might not hear him knock. He is a little boy, and he knocks gently, on account of the fact that he's a little boy." Belle smiled and tossed the curtain aside so that she could stare out the window into the darkness.

Beatrice moaned again, "What is happening to this house. What is happening?"

Mr. Tarson threw an angry expression towards Beatrice, and he nervously continued to claw his fingers through his hair. "Shut yer mouth foolish woman!" he called back at the cook.

"Beatrice, why don't you go on in there and make everyone something hot to drink," Randle suggested as he approached the sniveling woman. Taking her arm he pried her out of the portal and scooted her back into the kitchen.

"The demon's here, Mr. Forester, the demon's shadow is scorning us!" she hushed.

Alex remained dumbfounded as he stepped curiously towards the little girl who now was standing in her own doorway. Betty had tried to coax her back into the bed, but the commotion was too much to allow anyone to get any rest at all.

Those eyes, they were staring right into his soul and were becoming imprinted in his mind. Alex tried to recollect where he had seen those beady dark eyes. He scooted a little closer and tilted his head. They never blinked, never made any attempts to look away. If he moved his head upright, the eyes mirrored him. The sleepy little girl turned away, her chocolate hair, plaited in two burgundy braids dangled down her back. The doll had been hanging stiffly alongside until she picked it up and allowed it to rest upon her shoulder patting it gently as though burping a baby. The doll rested comfortably upon her small shoulder and its eyes remained fixed upon Alex. Links of disjointed facts were now beginning to surface; the hair, the eyes, they were not pieces of one person but strangely embodied the same memory.

A memory is like lake water, the more you stir up the bottom, the more blurred it becomes. But if you run lake water through a sieve it becomes more pure. Alex's memory was a sieve, filtering away obstructions so that he could reproduce and replicate events. The murkiness slowly filtered away and he blurted out, "I remember!"

Chapter 26

Guided by her cane, the bent-over elder hobbled down the creaking stairs into the dining room for her afternoon pot of tea. She sat down at her usual place at the head, rested her stick upon the edge of the table, and drew the tea service towards her in the same ceremonial fashion that she was so accustomed to. "One, two, three, four, five, six, seven," she counted, pointed, and then scowled. There were always ten delicacies arranged upon a linen pastry doily however, today the silver tray displayed only seven. Yesterday nine delicacies were tallied. Mrs. Cambridge was now confident that she was sharing her four o'clock teatime with a filcher. "Let me see," she pondered. "It could not possibly be the aged Admiral Ringgold in room 4 because he was presently at sea. The last time Cadwalader Ringgold had returned from his expedition of surveying the Southern Seas, he found it most favorable to spend his afternoons eating canapés with Mrs. Cambridge; for she was a most willing ear upon which to narrate his tales. But this most recent expedition to San Francisco Bay had kept him away from the Atlantic coast for over six months. "No, he could not possibly be the culprit for the most obvious reason," she thought.

Positioning the tea sweets now in size-order on the tray with her long bony fingers, she slid her index finger across the doily, scrounged any loose confection and licked her sugar-capped finger; then began to reconsider alternate boarders. Her thoughts transgressed to Miss Wanda Bourdette; a rather imposing figure of a woman, who resided in room 6. Miss Bourdette, who liked to think of herself as ageless, was seldom seen before the sun had set. Her occupation as the "headline singer" at the Six Tankards Music Hall kept her engaged until the last round was called. Entertainment reviewers branded her an "Obtruding Coquette", for her rousing songs were as colorful as her costumes. However, regardless of her occupation, one could not denounce the fact that she was a good-hearted woman, for during her younger years she volunteered as a "nurse" caring for wounded soldiers. Her arrival to the Cambridge Arms was accompanied by five large steamer trunks, a set of velvet burgundy drapes, an oval rug woven in an Herati motif of cherry, brown, and ochre, a large brass featherbed, a mahogany armoire inlaid with a tulip and poplar design, and matching dressing table with full-length mirror. It took half a dozen of Baltimore's fine young men to carry the load up the winding stairs, but no one seemed to mind for there were free passes to Miss Bourdette's performance that very evening. "No," decided Mrs. Cambridge, "Miss Bourdette may be given many titles, but thief was not one of them. Besides, she was probably fast asleep or engaged in her room." The grey lady picked up the smallest scone and dunked it several times into her Earl Grey. Soggy morsels crumbled into the brew before she could take a bite of the spongy scone.

Mrs. Cambridge shifted her thoughts to the newest set of boarders, Will and Libby Piccard, and confirmed that their most recent arrival placed them as being the least likely. Having just settled into Baltimore they would not even know about her scheduled teatime. The help were all too loyal or too frightened of her, so she could dismiss them as suspects. The only presumptuous answer rested with Nick. Mrs. Cambridge smiled as she settled upon the name, "Nick, that good for nothing boy," Mrs. Cambridge thought and fingered another scone. "Well, let him eat my treats," she laughed, "he may think I am a foolish old woman, but soon we will see just who the fool really is."

As the light dwindled into obscurity, Mrs. Cambridge settled comfortably into the feathered cushion of her dining chair. Teatime was a leftover ritual from her early years as a child and then a young lady in Europe. When she came across the Atlantic so many years ago, she never relinquished this part of her social graces. Americans were a crude rugged people, especially when it came time to eating and table manners and although she adopted the country she refused to adopt the habits.

Her eyes caught those of her late husband, Allister Cambridge. She never thought that the portrait captured his true essence and spirit, but it did capture the likeness quite well. Perhaps no one really knew his spirit like she did; how he married her without any questions and brought the boy up like his own. She closed her eyes and allowed his tenor to remain cast upon her. How he came to this place was in itself a miracle after surviving the great invasion at sea. She reopened them to see if he had looked away, but as always, he remained faithfully hers.

"1800 was an ugly time." Mrs. Cambridge recalled her husband's declaration. The four Barbary States; Algiers, Tripoli, Tunis, and Morocco were conducting piracy within the Mediterranean and the mighty powers in Europe were forced to pay a tribute in order to protect their commerce. The young United States at first agreed to meet these financial demands. However, when the Pasha of Tripoli increased the American's protection rate, there was no choice but to declare war. Allister Cambridge, a young naval lieutenant, was called to service under Commodore Edward Preble of the Mediterranean squadron. Their mission was to sail into Tangiers to rescue a number of Americans, 307 prisoners to be exact. Cambridge was ordered to partake in a secret mission along with another young lieutenant, Stephen Decatur. The mission involved a prodigious raid in which they were to sneak aboard the captured U.S. frigate *Philadelphia* with the mindful intent of destroying the vessel and decommissioning it permanently out of enemy control, the Tripolian Navy. Although they were successful in burning the captured American vessel, sadly, the crew was not able to be rescued.

The war's future ensued with a land advance into Tripoli and heroic commendations for Decatur. Cambridge, on the contrary, was wounded by falling debris during the fiery raid and having nearly lost his leg from a ghastly infection, he was deemed unfit to be part of the soon to be won battle. He returned home only to read of the final victory in the newspaper, and although honored by his men, Allister was never able to shake his feeling of having failed.

Mrs. Cambridge dunked another scone with a fresh cup of tea as she mused about the antics of her husband. The memories of him were alive, and so she insisted that this room remain in the likeness of him.

Allister had worked alongside of his father learning the trade of shipwright as a little boy. By the time the young man was in his teens, he had apprenticed on the docks and had gained in reputation as a fine carpenter. Therefore, upon returning from the war, he easily reestablished himself and worked his way up as Master Shipwright, over-seeing the day-to-day runnings of the shipyard. A short time passed and young Allister became more ambitious, leaving his present job and taking on larger endeavors. The Chesapeake Bay was a natural port from which farmers could ship their produce; establishing Baltimore as an important Eastern port and an optimal harbor for shipbuilding. Taking advantage of his wit and location, he borrowed money from private investors in England and purchased the Chesapeake Maritime Company. The need to employ those skilled in carpentry, sail making and rigging, caulking, and rope making quickly made him a locally popular man. Those workers coming from outside Baltimore needed somewhere to live, and so he extended his ventures and bought a building, converting it into the Cambridge Arms Rooming House.

Mrs. Cambridge pushed her tray towards the center of the table, twisted herself about and pulled the gold cord behind her, summoning Katrina. The tall woman immediately appeared as though she had been waiting outside the door, and reached across the table to remove the silver tray as she had done so many times before. "Don't go just yet," declared the grey woman grasping her arm.

"Ma'm?" she responded curiously pulling her large hand away from the tray.

"Katrina, do you know that for the past two days we have had a pilferer in our midst?" Mrs. Cambridge questioned the housemaid.

"Why, what do you mean, Mrs. Cambridge?" she responded artfully. Katrina was aware of her mistress's ability to ask a seemingly innocent question and upon hearing the response place you into a snare like a captured animal.

"I have noticed that for the past two days my lovely dainties have dwindled in number indicating that someone has helped themselves. I don't suppose you know anything about it?" she questioned; her prying eyes now honing the younger woman's face like those of a bird of prey. A crown of wrinkles trimmed the upper lip when she smiled.

"I will certainly question the staff about this, Mrs. Cambridge, as for me, I do not know who would take your dainties." Katrina, satisfied with her simple answer, contemplated it again over in her mind; direct, to the point, however not curt. She smiled stiffly, waiting for Mrs. Cambridge to dismiss her.

"No, I suppose not, thank you my dear," Mrs. Cambridge sweetly said. Then pointing to the tray, "Please, take this away when you leave," and she shooed the woman with her hand.

———

It was nearly 5:00 when Mrs. Cambridge rose from the table. The elder trundled towards the mahogany case clock, a reliable and steadfast sentry guarding the corner of the room. The rat-a-tat-tat tapping of "three legs" upon the wooden floor brought Katrina back into the dining hall. "Would you like anything, Mrs. Cambridge?" she asked.

Mrs. Cambridge turned slowly, pivoting about the cane as though it were a wheel hub. "Yes, my dear," she warbled, leaning yet more onto the wooden support. "Go upstairs to the new boarder's room, the Piccards, and ask them to join me for dinner. Tell them the mutton is to be served at 6:30 sharp. Then, when Nick returns from the docks tell him that his presence is expected."

"Certainly, Mrs. Cambridge. Will that be all?"

"Tell cook that we will have port in the parlor this evening," replied the white-haired woman.

"In the parlor?" the voice repeated. Mrs. Cambridge nodded turning back towards the face belonging to the clock. "Shall I have an additional chair placed?" Katrina questioned. "I believe the wing-back would fit quite comfortably," she suggested. The parlor amply accommodated four, but since the departure of her son for military service it was rarely frequented.

"A good choice, Katrina, have it placed near the hearth." Katrina nodded affirmatively and departed on her errand as Mrs. Cambridge peered up to examine the clock's "lunar dial", carefully incorporated into the main dial plate at the very top section of the arch. How many times had this spot been set upon? "Hundreds," she thought. The carpet itself was slightly worn where feet stood, perhaps shuffling or pacing about. Mr. Cambridge had relied upon this dial when winter nights matured early in grey afternoons to determine when the light of the moon would be available for travel; or when the tide was right so a coach could ford a stream. Its smiling face, ripe like a tawny peach, shines innocently down over anyone who leers upon it.

———

Libby and Will made their way down the stairs, greeted at the bottom by Nick, who appeared to have taken the opportunity to freshen up, for he was well-groomed and dressed for dinner. He had tied his hair back, and it hung behind his head like the tail of a terrier.

"So, this lovely lady must be the Missus?" he trumpeted, while reaching his hand out to help Libby down the last landing.

"And you must be Nick," she exclaimed allowing herself to be assisted. "Will has told me that you and he have become friends, as I hope that we too will soon become." Nick winked at Will and gestured for Libby to take his large arm. Will followed behind his charming wife. She looked more delicate than ever as she was ushered into the dining room by her rugged escort. An angel-like creature, she was garbed in pink and white taffeta. Finely stitched pleats choked her tiny waist in contrast to the bishop sleeves crimpled with gilt-edged stitches. Will trailed them into the dining room and upon his entrance suddenly perceived the piercing eyes of Mrs. Cambridge probing him. Did she covertly witness the thievery of the afternoon pastries? "Why, Will, what is the matter, you looked positively flushed?" remarked Libby as she turned noticing that his demeanor was rather unsettled.

"I bet the old boy is just a bit hungry, aren't ya sport?" asked Nick with a sly and mischievous look.

Will smiled at his wife trying to reassure her that perhaps Nick was correct. He reached his hand into his coat pocket to take out what he thought was a handkerchief, but instead felt not the piece of linen cloth but rather a mushy wettish object. He removed his hand and found pieces of crumbs clinging to his fingers, the very crumbs of a dainty that had been snatched off Mrs. Cambridge's tray earlier that day. It became immediately clear to him that Nick must have snuck a pastry into his pocket upon leaving the room.

"Why dear, what is the matter?" Libby questioned again as she noticed a look of horror that now overtook her husband. However, just as he began to brush his hand against his jacket to remove the sticky evidence, the rat-a-tat-tat of the three legs interrupted him. Quickly, Nick looked at Will and tilted his head forward to encourage him to glance down at the floor where he revealed a small ring of pastry crumbs now scattered about his feet and on the tops of his newly polished shoes. Hoping not to give himself away, he began to do a sort of two-step, trying to stamp ever-so discreetly upon the bits of food and wiping his soles against the back of his pant legs, like a stork wiggling on one foot.

As Mrs. Cambridge entered Nick dashed in front of Will, almost bowling him over! "Dear Auntie, you look ever so divine this evening!" he cried out. "Here, let me escort you to your place at the table!"

"Nick, what has gotten into you? Move away and let me have a look at our new boarders, step aside, step aside!" she demanded shaking her cane at the young man.

Slowly shuffling back, Nick purposely scuffed his feet along the rug, mashing any rogue crumb in his path. "Very well, Auntie, go ahead and hurt my poor feelings," he teased and sauntered away allowing the elder to confront the two.

"So, we meet again, young Mr. and Mrs. Piccard," Mrs. Cambridge greeted, edging as far forward as her cane would permit. Her angular form was hidden in the thick folds of her gown and the cashmere shawl draped over the shoulders reaching the ground made her appearance evermore frail under the weight of the material.

"Please, call us Will and Libby," proclaimed Will, and he reached forward with a cordial token to allow the aged one to take his arm.

"No need, no need, I can manage," she piped in straightening up a bit and resumed hobbling past the three; only then allowing Will to pull her chair away from the table for her. She settled quite comfortably and handed Nick her cane, which he set resting against the table at arm's length. "Libby," she said pointing to the seat on her right, "that is usually where Miss Bourdette sits, however she is not dining with us so you may take her position. As for you, Will," she commanded, "please position yourself next to your lovely Missus, and Nick," she stated turning to her left, "take your usual place next to me."

The table had been set with an ironstone service. Will lowered his eyes upon the ermine white plate set before him and fingered the spray of pink violets that swirled merrily about the center of his plate. "Thistles would have been better suited," he thought as he looked across the table towards his dinner hostess. A fresh loaf of bread was placed next to Mrs. Cambridge coupled with a small matching plate of fresh butter pats and a glass jar of clover honey. When all three had become settled, Katrina entered carrying a large tureen and wearing the same suggestive grin one exhibits when giving a gift. Then, in keeping with her grand entrance, she raised its lid pronouncing the beginning of dinner. A waft of steam sprang out and at once its liberation began to fulfill its mission. The titillating aromas of stewed mutton, sliced potatoes, and mild onions floated about the table and working their way into each inhaled breath of alternating nostrils. Mrs. Cambridge watched Will as his eyes widened with the abundance of food exhibited by the maid. "I see you're not accustomed to this, Mr. Piccard?" stated the white-haired elder contemplating his every expression while she snatched the first thick slice of doughy bread.

"Well, Ma'm, where I am from the working man did not eat very well, except sometimes we fared better on Sundays when a share of prime fat mutton with baked potatoes might be served. I suppose I'm not familiar with such luxury in the middle of the week," he added as Katrina held the steaming tureen beside him and heaped several meaty piles of stew upon his plate. Will wasn't sure if the maid deliberately gave him an extraordinary helping because of his comment or because she was used to serving such generous portions.

"I do remember that roast meat was my husband's delicacy, as it was the principal dish for me as a girl. The English appreciate better than any other people the art of properly roasting a rib or a joint. Americans are most uncouth when it comes to meals. Don't you agree, Libby? You don't mind if I call you Libby, do you dear?" She directed her question to her right. The younger woman had stopped Katrina from overloading her plate and now sat before a dish which displayed a quantity much more in portion to her petite size.

"Oh, please do. Actually, as to your former question, I cannot really say, Mrs. Cambridge, for I have not truly entertained the habits of my new countrymen," smiled Libby diplomatically.

"Well, take my word for it, if you know what is good for you, do not abandon your old ways entirely."

The meal continued silently with the exception of knives cutting and scraping along the plates. Everyone followed the lead of the hostess and remained discreetly vigil. Will was pleased with the formality of the meal for he found himself lacking conversation and hoped that his new friend would not say anything that might jeopardize Mrs. Cambridge's impressions of her new boarders.

Nick ate with relish and saved his bread for the last, sopping up the greasy remains which became a wading pool in the center of his plate. Mrs. Cambridge too had a glorious appetite for an elder, agreeing to seconds when Katrina circled the table with the tureen. In contrast, Libby rearranged her mutton several times upon the plate and taking only the smallest bites possible so as not to offend the hostess.

"I hope that you find your time here suitable to your needs," piped up Mrs. Cambridge to Will and Libby. "Meals do come with the room; however, I hope you don't expect to dine with me every evening. I usually eat later, isn't that so my boy?" she said turning to the young man.

Nick looked up from his plate. "That is true. Auntie's meals are served to her here in this very stately room." One could not tell if he were mocking her or simply being sterling. "But don't worry," he continued adding a chuckle, "you won't starve; Katrina has the cook set a pot of food for the boarders in the kitchen. By this old clock you'll find breakfast precisely at 5:00 a.m. and 5:00 p.m. for supper. You can help yourselves." He smiled and hoped that his response would not have given the impression that he thought himself an elitist. He added, "Why, the dining room is fair game if you want to eat in here, isn't that so Auntie?"

"Fair game?" she paused at the phrase. "That is an odd way of putting it, Nick. Yes, if anyone wishes to eat here before 6:30 p.m. it is fair game," she agreed. Then, without any warning, she reached for her cane and began slowly to unfold as she raised herself up and out of the dining chair. "Follow me," she commanded giving the stick a sharp tap on the floor. "We will toast to your new home in America."

———

"My husband was a genteel man who was both creative and industrious," said the elder shaking her head over her glass of port. "Do you share any of these qualities, Will?" asked Mrs. Cambridge sipping her port and settling the glass lightly upon the laced doily.

"I suppose I do. I haven't really reflected upon it, but I always do what has to be done," he replied. He tried to keep the small glass steady in his hands hoping to steal a moment when he could relieve himself of it. Yet, not wishing to chance a spill, he thought better of reaching across to set it upon the small table beside the elder.

Instead, he decided to balance it upon his knee, however awkward it was.

"And you, my pretty, are you creative and industrious? A fine quality for a young lady wishing to find work," Mrs. Cambridge turned her attention now towards Libby. Her hawkish eyes focused upon the young face and her tone demanded a quick response.

"Well, I am quite good with the needle and so, I do believe I am all that you ask," she replied sitting with hands folded upon her lap. Libby had not taken the port for she herself was not feeling well and thought it better not to accept after dinner drink.

Nick slung down and leaned comfortably into the wingback chair. He was accustomed to these inquiries and found himself quite entertained as Mrs. Cambridge chose her sparing partners. "Nick, I would like you to take Will down to the docks. I am sure we can use another good man in some capacity," said Mrs. Cambridge and pointed her finger towards the empty glass.

Will saw the gesture and wished he could hand his glass to the old woman and say, "Here, I really never wanted this swill, but just was being polite and took it." Instead he put the small glass to his mouth and sipped the acrid liquid. It tasted like turpentine. He licked his lower lip hoping to remove any of the residues that stained his mouth.

Nick lifted the bottle and poured the mahogany wine into her glass. Then he poured himself more, swirled the glass by the stem, and sniffed its contents. His entire body appeared to be inflated during this gesticulation for while he sucked up the aroma, his large figure grew taller as he inhaled most of the air around him. Will watched and anxiously anticipated the moment that Nick would have to exhale, hoping that he did not create a change in the atmosphere when he did. "Ahhhhh, quite the smell!" he expelled with delight.

"It's a bouquet, you oaf!" snapped Mrs. Cambridge.

"Bouquet?" remarked Nick sheepishly.

"Yes, bouquet! Bouquet, that's what you call the smells that develop with age in a mature wine," she explained scolding him like a schoolmarm to a dunce.

"So, then, should I say that you have a delightful bouquet upon your person?" asked Nick as he winked at Libby.

Libby dropped her head and could not help but smile when hearing the question.

"Certainly not!" cried the white-haired woman. "You are rather insolent or rather stupid, neither of which is becoming!"

"Now Auntie, I was only toying with you," Nick cajoled and placed a kiss upon her sunken check.

"Well then, I would like for you to take Will with you tomorrow and speak with John Henniker, see if he needs some more help."

"Why you dismissed Mr. Henniker just last month, Auntie," reminded Nick.

She paused for a moment. "Yes, that is right, that Henniker was not fit to work. Well, take him to whoever you want, just show him about!" she exclaimed. "Now, as for you, my dearie," muttered the elder to Libby, "what would you fancy?"

"Well, I am quite apt and nimble with the needle and jenny, so I thought perhaps I could use these skills to my advantage." Libby fingered the pleats on her skirt as she waited for the reply.

"Well, I would like to have a young pretty thing about the house, perhaps we could find piecework for you, eh?" grinned the ancient one.

Libby looked to Will, and they exchanged glances of uncertainty at the proposal, however both knew that this was not the time to reject an offer of work.

"Good, then it is settled," added Mrs. Cambridge surveying the two for any sign of disagreement. "Since there is no better offer, I will assume that you agree. Get some rest, both of you, for Baltimore is a city with opportunity if you know how to find it. Now if you will excuse me, I believe it is time to retire."

Will, though still nursing the small glass of port, rose as the elder inched upward. Nick handed her the cane and waited attentively as she seemed to unfold and reassemble herself into a walking position. Then, she grasped her gnarled fingers round the handle and allowed Nick to accompany her upstairs to her chamber.

Will set his glass down on the table adjacent to the two empty ones and exhaled a sigh of relief for he was quite pleased to finally be rid of the wretched little impediment he had been holding most of the evening

"Well, dear," said Libby when she finally heard the thumping upon the stairs diminish, "I suppose we will call this place home." Smiling gently up at her husband, she took his hand and squeezed it tight.

"I guess so," he agreed, "I guess so."

———

Dreary, dreary, cold and dreary
Morning's tenebrous woolpack droops
Bleary and smoky city coughs
Clearing a place for the sun

By 5:00 a.m. a well-scrubbed kitchenmaid, Marthe Govertsdatter, was warming a tray of sticky dough buns and stirring the coarse porridge. She lifted the large ladle and plopped a formidable helping of the slop into a wooden bowl, handed it to Will and motioned for Libby to set forth her bowl. "Oh, no thank you," replied Libby who was quite content with the buns and hot tea that were set out.

"Nooo?" doubted the young maid as she allowed the spoon to dangle in mid-air, permitting Libby a moment to change her mind. Thick globs of porridge began to slowly fall back into the pot.

"No, no, thank you!" insisted Libby with a blunt gesture of her palm.

Marthe plunged the ladle back into the large pot and stirred its thick contents again. "Very vell, very vell," she sighed. And in a care-free manner she shrugged and grinned happily back at Libby, exhibiting her large and strong teeth. Then, she swiped the wooden ladle handle with the muslin cloth that was strewn across her shoulder and set about frittering like a dormouse. Marthe, a simple woman of twenty-six, had traveled alone from Trondhiem across the North Sea to Great Britain. Having decided to meet up with her Uncle Isack, she purchased a rail ticket, traversed England, and boarded a ship from Liverpool destined for America.

Isack Govertsdatter, a carpenter by trade, had reached New York shores months before and wishing to settle down in a climate more like his native Norway, he pressed north to the prairies of Canada. Unfortunately, not long after his arrival, he met his untimely death; for shortly after walking across what he believed to be a frozen pond, he fell through the thin ice, submerging and never surfacing from the freezing waters.

Poor Marthe, she had only a bit of American money and a pocket full of "spesidaler", currency from Norway, which proved to be worthless. She was a farmer's daughter who had never learned to read and was barely capable of writing her own name. Despite her lack of schooling, she managed to stay out of harm's way while she wandered about the docks of Baltimore with only a handful of English words, a battered suitcase, and a calico kitten that she befriended.

"So, you have found your way to the kitchen and Marthe, I see!" called out a raspy voice. "Coffee my dear, straightaway!" jeered Nick to the young maid as she quickly ran over and poured him a mug.

"Good morgin, Nik!" she grinned handing him the steaming mug.

"So, you've met our Marthe, quite a good worker, and makes a great sticky bun!" he said grabbing the gooey sweet roll and stuffing it into his mouth. Then, licking his fingers he pulled the cloth from off her shoulder and completed the task of wiping his hands.

"Vie, Nik, you are a pest, no?" smiled Marthe grabbing her cloth and repositioning it back on her shoulder.

"Come along you two, stop gawking and follow me!" he called to Libby and Will. Both now realized that they were staring at the situation that was taking place as though watching a show from the wings of a theater. Marthe dished out a bowl of porridge, sprinkled several teaspoons of brown sugar upon the hot slop, and handed it to Nick. "You take good care of me!" he winked and dallied out.

"Ya, see you later Nik," she sighed and returned to her frittering.

Nick pulled out the chair that had been the place Libby sat during last evening and allowed her to sit before taking his usual spot at the table. This morning Will took the liberty of finding himself a chair next to his wife. A lone lantern had been set upon the credenza and illuminated the room with a willowy glow.

"Marthe is a good lady, found her wandering about docks 'bout a year ago. She had barely any money, and no family; only a crumpled letter from her Uncle's employer detailing his death. It was pretty ragged and can't imagine that she understood much of it on account of the language." Nick took a slurp of the hot porridge, smacked his lips with apparent satisfaction, and dropped the spoon back into the bowl. "She hadn't a plan as to where she would find work and being as naïve as I think she was, trouble was bound to find her. Well, I suggested that she come back here with me; couldn't let the girl roam around the docks without a chaperon, and implored Mrs. Cambridge to give her a small allowance in exchange for work in the kitchen. She agreed to take her in, minus the kitten."

"Kitten?" asked Libby putting the sticky bun down to inquire.

Nick continued to stir the porridge and looked up from the bowl, "She had this little kitten, but the ancient one is not too fond of small animals. So before it was turned out into the streets I returned the tiny fellah to the docks. Actually, not such a bad place for a stray, plenty of rats and mice to keep it fed."

"Yes, I suppose,' agreed Libby still picturing the dear little kitty being cast out in the cold.

A quiet now replaced the conversation and the three remained solemn in their own thoughts. Will raised his eyes up from his bowl and noticed Mr. Cambridge staring down upon him like a Great Horned Owl. The master possessed eyes that no matter where you stood or sat, he appeared to be watching. His countenance portrayed an expression of being earnest, successful, and perhaps even a bit cocky. "If only I could see his hands," Will thought looking back at him, "then I could really tell what kind of man he was."

"So, the old man interests you, eh?" asked Nick, interrupting Will's private review.

"I didn't think that it showed. Am I that transparent?" he asked.

"Most who dine in this room eventually find themselves drawn into the elder; he has a way about him even in death," mused Nick.

"Was he as successful in his private life as he was in business?" questioned Will boldly. He felt that he could be candid with Nick.

"To tell you the truth, it depends on who you ask," he replied speaking with an air of authority. "The old man was at the pinnacle of his success before he passed away. He was meticulous in his thinking; kept a chronicle of every detail pertaining to the business. He knew the names of all the men who worked for him; whether they were a sawyer, caulker, smith, or apprentice sailmaker, everyone was important. He learned that trick when he was just a purveyor, ordering the supplies as a young lad. 'Make everyone feel important and they'll be loyal.' He had a memory as sharp as an awl. I suppose that's why he and the ancient one got along so well, she is as shrewd as he was. Loyalty is the most important character trait she looks for, don't forget it."

"The son, what happened to him?" Will remarked after contemplating the idea that there was nothing about the boarding house that would suggest an heir ever existed.

Nick got up from the table, tiptoed over to the hallway and peeked from side to side. He closed the dining room door, returned to his seat, and put his finger to his lips in a hushed gesture. "We don't talk of him anymore. He's as good as dead to Mrs. Cambridge. If ya know what's good for ya, don't mention him again."

Libby looked to Will and a most disturbed expression came over her. "No," she whispered, "I should say we really don't need to know. It is none of our affair, is it Will?"

Will pursed his lips together and then shifted his chair closer to his friend. He could not truly agree with his wife. "Is there something you're not telling me that perhaps I need to know? After all, if I am to gain her support as a loyal employee," he emphasized the word "loyal" when he spoke in hushed tones, "then I beseech you to bring me into your confidence as your new best friend."

Nick looked at Will and studied him for a moment. "Well, when you put it that way, if we are to be stuck together in this great old place, and we will be working closely, I suppose I can trust you. But let me warn you; never make public that you heard these truths from my lips for I shall deny every word that you claim and have you renounced as a scoundrel."

And thus it was solemnly promised the following story was never to be uttered after this time forward.

"Mr. Cambridge became intrigued with Elizabeth not for love or beauty, but because she was ambitious. He was fascinated with her sharp mind and confident manner. 'Any woman that would cross the Atlantic with nothing but her certitude is a woman for me!' They were married after a very short courtship and almost six months to the date of their blissful union a baby was born. Neither parent had decided upon a name so they called him simply Boy for several weeks. However, as time grew, the baby earned its name, Marcus Tullius Cambridge; after the great Roman Orator, Marcus Tullius Cicero. It was said that the child cried and squealed day and night, thus earning his moniker.

Marcus grew up to become bright and sharp like his mother and stepfather, however he would circumvent building boats for hiking deep into the woods and hills, seeking refuge away from the sea and city. It wasn't that he didn't want to learn, it was just that there was something in his temperament that made him restless to roam the most unchartered territories.

I was about six and he, the same, when we first met unwittingly on the Wilk's farm. My folks were sharecroppers and I would work right alongside of them. It was an ordinary blistering summer afternoon, as usual; I was out digging in the fields when I happened to look up and not far from the edge of the fields I spotted a boy, not much bigger than me, walking freely about. Well, at first I believed it was one of the other boys skipping out from doing his work! So I grabbed my hoe and ran as fast as my legs would carry, striking the air and shouting, 'Come on back here you lazy lout!'

Poor Marcus, he must have thought he had done something terrible 'cause when he saw me running and swinging my hoe, for I was heading straight for him like a medieval knight with a javelin, he took off. But, no sooner had he scrambled away than he tripped face down, landing flat out in an irrigation ditch. Before he could gain his composure, I came upon him and with my foot pressed against his back deliberately kept him pinned to the ground. At once I could tell that he was no farm boy, his hands were not tawny enough to have been working in the sun, so I let him up. I asked him what he was doing around the farm and he told me he was on a hunt for jack rabbits. Yet, he didn't carry a gun so I was kind of suspicious. He replied he just liked 'em and wanted to see how they lived. I must admit that he sounded so sincere that I truly believed his intentions were simple and curiously refreshing so I promised that if he would return on Sunday, I would reveal to him where I knew there was a warren and we could watch them together.

That was the beginning of our friendship. At first, the ancient one didn't like the idea of her son keeping company with a sharecropper's boy, however, Marcus didn't care, for he was interested in the person, not his breeding. He enjoyed our friendship and so, as time grew, he would invite me into his home more and more often. The Wilks didn't care as long as my field work was complete, and they had one less mouth to feed when I was gone. Either the ancient one knew that there was nothing that she could do about her son's choice in companions, or she felt sorry for me since my parents had left me behind while they headed west looking for better wages. Whatever her reason, she finally relented and consented by allowing us to openly play together. Years went by and our friendship grew. However, shortly after Marcus turned fourteen, as most young men who are groomed to become gentleman, he was sent away to attend military school.

I never thought that I would see him again for his departure was abrupt, and I was unable to give him a parting farewell. Several weeks passed and naturally I was feeling low when my luck suddenly changed. A renewed clamor of hope was regenerated when Mr. Wilks brought me a message with an invitation requesting that I spend the weekends at The Cambridge Arms. Naturally, being the opportunist that I am, I packed all my meager belongings, hitched a ride with anyone who would carry me into Baltimore, and ended up at their doorsteps. Weekends became weeks and weeks became months; I became the step-son of convenience, a symbiotic kinship had been formed. I tagged beside Mr. Cambridge to the docks, learning the trade and doing whatever he and Mrs. Cambridge wished. I earned my keep and have become forever indebted, after all, I was the son of a sharecropper, and my family knew nothing else but debt of one sort or another."

"What about the Wilks, how did they take your departure?" asked Will.

"The Wilks were good people, but I suspect they were remunerated for they never tried to stop me from leaving." Nick paused and drank heartily from the water glass set before him, and then he continued. "Marcus would return for holidays and was earnestly happy that I was always there for him for I seemed to buffer the inevitable conversations that consumed the dinner talk. Upon his graduation, he would join his father in the family business, continuing their legacy.

However, Marcus was determined to be his own man, and he had no intention of obliging. To seal his fate from his mother's iron will, two weeks before he was to graduate, he enlisted in the army. He was ordered to report to the Texas Territory for duty in a month's time."

Nick hunched forward as though concealing himself from an intruder who may have inconspicuously snuck into the room to steal this bit of information. "Let me back-track for a moment and parlay a bit of unknown about the time the "Mrs." was a "Miss". Her lone sail from England to America was consummated not because of a deep desire to fulfill an adventurous spirit. No, she escaped because she could not bear the malice brought about by her own brother; a self-righteous man, arrogant and hard, who swore that he would have her lover arrested and thrown into prison for the shame that they brought upon the family. As a result, she felt she had no other choice than to disappear from England and rematerialize as a new woman in a new country." Nick stretched his back for a moment and then began to carry on with the tale. "Now Marcus, his character is different from any man or woman that I have ever known. He completed his tour of duty in the army and rather than returning home decided to travel about the country on his own. But his heart was too big to be alone, and he met a woman, fell in love and was married. When Mrs. Cambridge received the letter of his matrimony, well, it was the day I learned that not scarlet blood, but rather dark scorn flows through the veins and into the black heart of that woman!" The storyteller's voice rocked with anger as he continued the tale. "After she finished reading his letter, her pinched lips oozed repugnance and abhorrence for her son. I will not repeat in front of Libby what hateful words the elder spouted. But be assured, I am pleased that Marcus was not there to hear."

"Surely, you may stop now, Nick. We can see that retelling this story is upsetting to you," replied Libby reaching forward and placing her tiny hand upon his as she tried to comfort him.

"No, you need to know more about the woman under whose roof you now reside." He rose from the chair and walked over to the portrait of Mr. Cambridge, the man who had opened his home to the son of a mere sharecropper. "The old man was dead at this time; he passed away peacefully in his sleep several months after Marcus enlisted. So, he was spared this ugly scene. He was spared the fact that the boy he called son could never return home." Nick faced his friends and leaned his arms upon the back of the chair that he had occupied. "You see, it was not the fact that Marcus had married that angered the elder, but it was to whom he married. Sadly, his wife was unacceptable to his mother. 'This wench is beneath him!' were her exact words. You see, Marcus fell in love with a young woman of the Niúachi Tribe, she was an Indian."

Libby ran the words over in her head and could not imagine that the white-haired mother could have grown so bitter. Suddenly the nightmare of her father, her hasty departure from England, the escape to America, and each of her own fearful events began to resurface. She looked upon her husband and wondered if he noticed her agitation. But Will was not minding her; instead he was regarding Nick with an altered appreciation. He had gained a new insight into the man whom he befriended. He truly understood why Nick remained at Cambridge Arms and why he had never left. For like so many other men, Nick was a prisoner of the economic times, financially indebted; for a man is nothing without his honor and honor was really all men, like himself and Nick, owned.

"You said that she was an Indian. Did something happen to her?" asked Will most astutely.

"You are very observant, my friend. Actually, his wife of less than a year became quite ill and though she was young and hardy, she died," replied Nick. A beam of light had grown proportionally with the time of morning and encircled the floor with its unceremonious brilliance. A strange and awkward stillness now filled the room. Nick looked up at the great timepiece that was the keeper of the day and lamented.

"It appears that we are obliged to set out to the docks. Are you ready?" asked Nick pulling away from the table. He stood up and gave Will a hearty slap on the back. It was most apparent that his present mood was clashing with his former grim spirits.

"I am," replied Will also pulling away from the table. He got up and bent over to his demure wife. "Goodbye, my dear," he whispered affectionately, kissing her check tenderly.

She reached out for his hand and squeezed it tightly, for this would be the first time since their marriage they would be apart for so many hours. "Have a good day you two, and don't mind these dishes, I will tend to them straightaway," she sweetly replied.

"Just give them to Marthe, she doesn't like anyone messin' in her kitchen. Mind that the ancient one doesn't scare you, Libby, she is rough," Nick cautioned.

Libby remained at the table until both men had left the room. She could hear the jovial tone of Nick's voice, but could not make out the conversation as they strolled down the hall. Sitting alone in the great room, she began to contemplate her day.

Chapter 27

Pinto Jack pulled his collar up against his neck and hunched over the saddle horn trying to keep the snow from completely obscuring his vision. "Cally, we got only a mile or so to go, girl, just a little more 'til we get to the station." Tucked securely into his vest pocket was an article cut from the *St. Louis Republic.* He had folded and unfolded it so many times that the newsprint was now barely legible; but it didn't matter since the lone rider had it completely memorized. There is a saying that "a picture is worth a thousand words", and so it stands true for the drawing in the advertisement. A slim and determined cowboy riding a spirited horse raced across the wrinkled paper with enough realism that one assumed they could leap right off the page. The headline, "Wanted, Riders with Experience!" sent excitement all the way down to Jack's toes that initiated a feeling of impatience, for which he gave Cally a little nudge with his spur to get her going. But despite his degree of eagerness, the snow continued to make it difficult for the horse to walk. Whispers of cold air circulated about her nostrils as she breathed in and out. They were lonely figures in a well-shaken snow dome.

Jack shifted his weight from one side of the saddle to the other and began to mull over the quote, "*A great crowd had amassed on the streets of St. Joseph, Missouri. Flags were flying and a brass band added to the exaltation. Finally the crowd is hushed and as the moment of departure approaches, the doors swing open and a lively horse and young rider of barely 19 is led out. Both rider and horse share in the newest form of overland mail delivery, the Pony Express!*"

"Think of it Cally, why soon enough we can be part of the most exciting job offered any man!" exclaimed Jack as he brushed the snow off her long mane. The enthusiasm of his prospects seemed to overshadow any sensation of cold and hunger, for they had been riding for hours and not much appeared to change as miles of white snow shrouded the landscape. By her slow and methodical pace, Jack wondered if she shared his excitement. "When we get to the station, why we'll bed down, and I'll cover your back with the blanket little Alex gave you!" Jack leaned forward and stroked the horse gently, but she did not wish to reply with a usual nod of her head or a flicker of the ears. None of this seemed to be of interest to the young pinto, and she trudged along reluctantly following her master's lead of the reins.

Now they say that depending upon the mood of winter the falling of snow expresses its personality in the most diverse of ways. For example, there are the gentle star-flakes that drift about shyly landing upon you with the utmost apology; the larger lace-like flakes fall softly but with more impudence, while icy crystal balls convulse in a most churlish manner. However, as the two crossed the mute land a light flurry fell uniformly with anxious fervor. Jack's brim was encased in a thin layer of icy crust that pierced every crease and cranny. With every movement of her foot, Cally lanced the thin sheet of ice that had formed like petrified wood.

St. Joseph is unlike any other place in Missouri. She has it all, or at least claims to have. She resembles in some respects an all-inclusive city assailed by prosperous merchants, thousands of inhabitants, and at present maintains the excitement of energy from river boats and railroad lines. As the jumping off spot to the West, the California-Oregon emigration continues to fuel great fortunes made by outfitting those journeying west. Others cross the river and encamp on the west side in the Indian Territory lured by the prospects of finding precious metals that once had been gold fever of '49. She contains four good-sized hotels, about two dozen stores, and the balance is made up of groceries and bakeries.

Pikes Peak Stables, the sign hidden behind a screen of continually sprinkling snow hung above eye level and was firmly nailed to the building's facade. Jack had dismounted half-way into town and leading Cally by the damp softened reins came upon a bystander who unbeknownst to reason had ventured out into the cold. "Looks like you two could use some help," said a muffled voice escaping from behind a tightly drawn woolen scarf. A thrust of a tiny cloud followed directly, escaping out from the wrapping round his mouth.

Jack's head bowed low away from the direction of the oncoming wind. He retrieved the question from out of the cold and responded diligently as he turned to see the speaker. "I'm lookin' for the Pony Express Office; I was told that if I went straight on it was in this direction, but maybe I missed it?"

"Look up boy, see where you've stumbled? Right over here is Pikes Peak Stables," mused the man pointing at the sign. His words were barely audible, but by now Jack was looking past the pointed finger and shuddered at the fact that he was so unobservant. Surely this local would think he was a fool.

"Right, I see, over here," Jack mumbled back at the man, and humbly tipped his hat. "Thanks, for the help."

However, the man did not wait for his gratuity for the snow was falling fast and he had already continued to lumber slowly across the road to a destination known only to himself.

The double stable doors were shut tightly and bolted from the inside. It was an impressive structure; Jack figured it must be at least 125' long with a 60' frontage. He scoured the front of the building and peeking through the window could make out a dimly lit interior with rows of stalls. He tapped lightly with his knuckle, waited, and then hoping to stir anyone who may be inside, rapped again with more vigor. But despite his effort, he decided that if there was anyone inside, which he imagined there must be, they could not hear his knocks.

The air was wet and cold and the front of the building did not provide much refuge from the wind. Cally swooshed her tail and flicked her ears at the falling snow. Jack stepped away from the facade and noticed that to the very right of the stables was another entrance, much narrower and less obvious to a passer-by. The flurry finally began to abate as he led Cally up to the newly discovered door; this time he proceeded with a much more vigorous knock. He waited a moment and then tried the latch, which to his surprise easily disengaged. Jack knocked again and opened the door just wide enough to allow his head to enter. The strong mixture of horses, hay, and warm lamp oil instantaneously filled his nostrils. "Hello!" he shouted. Still there sounded no response. "Helloooo!" he bellowed once again, placing a greater emphasis on the last syllable His call ricocheted off the timbers that separated each stall. Then inching in from outside, he stood in the doorway and glared. "Will ya look at that?" Jack thought aloud. He could not believe it; over one hundred neatly aligned stalls filled the front of the stable.

A large shadowy figure slowly began to materialize from the farthest end. "I'm comin', I'm comin'!" a man's low voice grumped. As it neared closer, Jack heard the man again, who also appeared to quicken his step when he realized that someone was standing outside. "Come on in fella, too cold out thar to be carrin' on a talk!"

"I can't, I got my horse out here with me!" repeated Jack opening the door even wider.

"Why didn't ya say so! Walk over to the left of the stable; I'll let ya both in." But perhaps the man thought better of his actions, and he paused cautiously and asked, "There's just you and ya horse, right?" his voice wavered with distrust.

"Yep, just me and my horse," replied Jack assuring the man that he was not going to be tricked. "Just me and Cally out here."

"Cally? O.k. then, just be sure to pull the door tight behind ya, eh?" and he traversed across the stable towards the larger entrance.

Jack listened and waited for the unbolting of the great doors. After several long minutes he was able to detect that someone on the opposing side was taking great lengths to push it open for much thrusting, groaning, and grumbling was taking place, but to no avail, it could be pried only an inch. "It won't budge on account of the snow!" shouted the man through the crack that he wedged open. "Ya gotta git the snow away from the bottom of the door!" he continued to instruct in a more emphatic tone.

Sure enough a small bank of snow had gradually piled up against the door preventing it to open outwardly. Once again Jack thought that he must have appeared foolish for not having anticipated this problem. "O.K." he called back. Sizing up the job ahead, he looked down at his hands and was especially grateful for his gloves. Then, like a burrowing gopher, he leaned over and began to feverously toss the snow aside. As the mound diminished and enough had been cleared away, he stomped about the area he had unblocked, flattening any remaining chunks of ice, and smoothed the frozen ground into a flat surface with his boot. "I think it's ready to try," he called through the breach that had been earlier forced open and then backed away. Cally stirred and gently nudged her nose against Jack. He waited and shivered; every bit of his body was growing numb. He tucked his arms tightly together; turning his toes up and down in his boots to be sure he could still feel them.

Finally, one of the great doors edged slowly open, sliding and screeching as if in pain against the frozen ground. "Hurry up, don't want no more cold gettin' in!" a voice bellowed. It belonged to a faceless unnamed man.

A passable clearing was made as Jack led Cally into the enormous stable. Small lanterns hung on pegs hammered into the posts above every other stall, each casting a pinch of illumination. However, because of the generous number of lanterns circling about, they brightened what would otherwise have been a very dark and gloomy building. Heat was generated by half-dozen or more wood burning stoves efficiently placed in the center of the building, proportionally apart from one another. The smell of hickory and horse dung permeated the entire structure. The large wooden door swung shut and a man about 6 feet tall emerged from behind. He was well-groomed; clean shaven with ruddy complexion and beneath his tight shirt and pants posed the anatomy of a classical Greek figure. His brown leather boots were detailed with an emblem of a hawk stitched on either side and by their fine condition you could tell he owned more than one pair; these were not ordinary boots but cobbler made. As he approached, Jack noticed another man coming up from behind one of the stalls. "What ya got thar, Mitch?" the man called to the other who stood in front of Jack, concealing him from his sight. His was branded by a distinctly southern drawl. He was of a much heavier physique, not nearly as well built; this was a man who enjoyed his food and drink, perhaps the latter more than the former. By the swagger in his gait he was marked with the pretense of being a person who was used to asserting himself.

"A cowboy and his horse, they're comin' in to git warm," he called back. "Ain't that so?" remarked the man to Jack, affirming his answer.

The other speaker neared them cracking his knuckles as he walked; a toothpick hung from one side of his lip, and he shifted it about his mouth from side to side. Jack watched as the burly man removed the pick and poked the splintered end between his teeth.

"What's ya name boy?" the questioner asked, sizing Jack up and down.

"Jack, Jack Wade, but most folks call me Pinto Jack," he replied pulling off his wet gloves and putting out his hand in hopes that one of the men would reciprocate.

"Well, Jack, pleased to meet ya. I'm Mitch, in charge of this stable," he said exchanging the handshake. Jack was immediately impressed by the mighty strength of this man for his grip was exceptionally firm like no other he had ever encountered, almost bone crushing. "This here is Big Pete, he's our head blacksmith," added Mitch turning to the larger fellow.

Pete didn't say anything, only sauntered over to Cally and gave her a gentle stroke. The soggy end of the toothpick hung limply from his lips. "This ain't no livery, ya know? There's a livery not too far where ya kin bed this horse down. The Patte House is 'cross the street if you can afford it, otherwise there's always a bed of hay," Pete advised.

"No, I wasn't lookin' for a handout," Jack replied hastily. "I'm might obliged to be inside where it's warm. Me and Cally have been traveling for quite awhile when we were unfortunately engulfed in snow, but lucky for us it wasn't a whiteout."

"En-what? What ya say, engulfed? What's that?" Pete elbowed Jack.

"Oh, I mean we were passing into some mighty heavy snow," Jack clarified his words and realized that he had better heed what he said.

"What brings ya here to St. Joseph? You talk like city but ya don't look like a city boy?" remarked the fat man who was now using the dry end of the toothpick to clean his nails. "This ain't no livery," he repeated again.

"Don't take no offense but, I gotta agree with Pete here, are ya heading west? Most folk come to St. Joseph and join up with a wagon train," Mitch added.

The two men stood glaring at the newcomer for a long silent moment. Jack, who was now completely exhausted and hoping to just sit down, maybe be offered a tin of black coffee, some fried bacon crisps, and a bag of oats for Cally, listened to the wind scratch the window. The numbness in his feet had disappeared, probably because his body was responding to the weakened sensation of fatigue. The warmth in the building penetrated every pore in his body and he fumbled as he unbuttoned his jacket, his fingers still stiff from having gripped the reins during those long arduous hours. He reached into his pocket revealing the warn article that he had been securely sheltering up until now. He unfolded the sheet and ran his hand over the wrinkled paper.

"This is why I'm here," he said as he lightly shook the paper and handed it to Mitch for inspection. "This should explain my reason for coming here," he revealed, wishing he had taken up a more determined sound, but by now he was too exhausted to be as exuberant. His weary thoughts and tired legs weighed heavily upon him as he waited for the response he hoped to hear.

"What's it say?" asked Pete, who was watching his partner silently reading the information. Mitch complied and read the words aloud.

"Wanted -Young, skinny, wiry fellows not over 18, must be expert riders, willing to risk death daily. Orphans preferred, wages $25 per week."

Mitch looked up and handed the paper back to its owner. "Carrying the mail can be dangerous work," he began to explain. "Ya gotta be willin' to work harder than you've ever imagined; sometimes entering through mighty threatening country. Some of our riders were hunted by Indians or accidently killed along the route."

Pete charged into the conversation wishing to impart a bit of his own news. "Why just last June," he paused momentarily and corrected himself, "no, come to think, it was July 'cause we just had seen fireworks on account of the 4th of July. Well anyway, one of the station keepers out of Kansas sent word that a rider on his way back to St. Joseph had been thrown from his horse and killed while crossin' the Platte River." Pete glared at Jack watching for signs of faltering, but the interested rider did not seem fazed.

Jack had acquired the attention of both men and decided that he must seize the moment. This was his opportunity to explain why he had traversed across the countryside during such deplorable weather. The words spilled easily out of his mouth for he had rehearsed them in his mind at least a hundred times before. "I've been reading everything I could get my hands on about the overland rides." He began as though he was being interviewed. "I know that the Pony Express is divided into five operating divisions. The first runs from this station in St. Joseph to Fort Kearney; second division from Fort Kearney to Horseshoe; the third from Horseshoe Station to Salt Lake City; the fourth from Salt Lake City to Roberts Creek; and the fifth division from Roberts Creek to Sacramento. As far as I heard each one as treacherous as the next, especially when you get farther west where its desolate; between these home stations are relay rider stations set approximately twenty to twenty-five miles apart, but some can be as close as about fifteen miles. It takes about seventy-five horses to make a one-way trip from Missouri to California, so at each station relays of horses are plentiful."

Pete looked over to Mitch who was now walking around Cally. "I had a pinto some years back, called him Apache Charm, fine animal, except he wouldn't let anybody ride him but me."

"Well boy, ya been muckraking; finding out about how we work. Question is," Pete paused, as he seemed to do often when he spoke, "how do we know you kin ride?"

"My word," Jack said earnestly.

Mitch handed the advertisement back to Jack. "Sorry fella, but a man's words don't mean much 'round here. We get plenty of drifters, they come on in, tell us the same thing, all looking for good pay. But no sooner than they arrive at the first station they pull the mochila off the saddle, heave the mail out of the catina pocket and expect to take pay after the first run."

"This is a business," Pete paused again and cleared his throat. "Plain as that: on account as we can't take no chance on a bum rider, especially now."

Jack looked perplexed as he listened to this blunt excuse and examined the tone at which it was expressed. Although he was young he had acquired a sixth sense of reading into someone's words more than they often let on. Did this sloppy fat man have something to say, but took pleasure in baiting him? "What do you mean, now?" Jack asked quizzically.

"On account of competition," Pete cited abruptly and looked to Mitch to finish his statement.

"Ya see kid, the Pony Express is not a moneymaker, it isn't charity, and time and talent is what makes us the fastest way to send a letter cross the country."

Jack scrambled for the right words to say. "The Pony Express is a noble profession providing an essential service to the country." He caught himself sounding like a politician trying to convince his constituents.

"Listen kid, we think so," agreed Mitch, "but we're only hiring the best riders, light and able."

Jack began to unravel the article; its softened folds still clenched in his hand. "But it says right here," he pleaded pointing to the picture of the rider.

It was Pete who now stepped in. "You've been keeping that paper with ya?"

"From the first I saw it posted." Jack's voice rose as he answered as though it were a question rather than a statement.

"Got a proposal for ya," Pete paused again. "Say we take ya on, give ya a chance to ride for the Express, what do ya think yer gonna do with yer Pinto?" he walked over to Cally and facing the rear of the building, he leaned gently against horse's shoulder as he ran his hand down her forelimb; helping her to shift the weight to the opposite leg before lifting her foot. "She had an accident not too long ago." he said examining the underside of the hoof.

Jack now looked at Pete with more respect. This man, this adversary who upon first acquaintance appeared to be an ignorant stooge, now displayed an uncanny amount of knowledge about horses and had suddenly redeemed himself. "She's all healed now," Jack replied.

Pete rested Cally's hoof in his large palm. He pulled a toothpick from his pocket and began to poke around, removing any loose debris, and then set the leg down again. "Done a good job, but doubt she'd make it to the first relay without injury. This ride is fast, no breaks for man or horse, just straight ridin'. This pinto, she's got spirit, but long distance runnin' ain't in her no more."

The words collided with Jack's senses like a clap of unexpected thunder.

"Now if ya want, you could leave her at the livery or sell her, that is if we decide to hire you," Mitch stated. "Even if she was able, she would be left at the first station run and then you'd switch horses within moments of your arrival. Cally would have to rest and then take a run with some other rider. Might be that you'd never lay eyes on her again. Matter-of-fact, some ponies never get to its station," Mitch concluded, whereby he reached into his shirt pocket and exposed a tin container. He carefully lifted the lid and pulled a knife from his back pocket. Jack watched curiously as the open tin exposed its contents, plug tobacco. The cake-like substance had been pressed into a 3/4" thick slab, and he pried off a piece using the pocketknife and stuffed a chunk into his mouth, burrowing it with his fingers towards the inside of his cheek like a squirrel with a hazelnut. Then, just as meticulously as he had removed the tin, he reversed the process. "Got a sweet flavor of honey and molasses," he remarked to Jack, who was staring in wonderment at the slightly bulged jaw that shifted rhythmically with each articulated sentence.

His thoughts returned to the situation presented to him. "So, what you are saying is that if, just if," he was carefully choosing his words as to not appear too presumptuous, "if I was hired then Cally wouldn't be able to even make the first station." Jack tried not to sound doubtful.

"She wouldn't make it on that hoof, why she'd have to run about 10 miles an hour, at times galloped to 25 miles an hour," Pete remarked. "We got about 100 horses, each one picked for speed and toughness. Got to carry the mail at least 200 miles a day which means each horse got to do its part."

Jack turned to Cally. She had lowered her smooth silky neck; the reins dangling loosely skimming the ground. Her nose lay flush to the stable floor as she sniffed the ground in search of stray oats.

"Ya understand what we're telling ya? There's no way to ride this pinto. Best idea is fer ya to let her go. Why don't ya sell her, ya can probably get a good price at the livery even with that hoof." Pete sauntered over to the weary man and rested his hand on his shoulder. "Tell ya what," he continued, "we'll fix ya some grub, Cally can rest in one of the empty stalls and on a full belly you'll make up yer mind. But don't take long," he warned, "cause we got a bag of mail gotta get out to Calfornia, and its got some important letters."

"Does that mean that you might hire me?" asked Jack perplexed by all that was going on.

"You seem like an honest fellah, so I guess that's what we're sayin'," Mitch added as he turned away, but not before stopping to spit into a tarnished green spittoon.

Jack picked up the fallen reins and followed Pete towards the back of the stables. Cally trailed behind like an obedient dog unaware of her destiny.

Chapter 28

It had been several months since Jack and Cally's departure from the Forester's on that white icy morning. Alex would often try to imagine what they were doing. Sometimes in bed he would close his eyes and wonder where they were, but like seasons passing one into another, they too were melting away.

———

It was a tidy day, an ordinary day. Alex reached into his pocket and pulled out the flat round object Jack had given to him and offered it up. "You always got something in yer pocket, Alex Forester!" a tiny voice exclaimed with delight. "I don't know what I'd do without you if you didn't come over to keep me company," she said. The small hand accepted the trinket and like a museum curator receiving an artifact, placed it guardedly across her palm. "It's a coin! A might fancy coin," she proclaimed with wonderment. "Why it sure is shiny." She continued to examine it with interest by turning it over several times and stroking the frayed blue and red ribbon that was attached. "What kind of bird is this, Alex?" she asked handing it back to him.

"This is an eagle, see, the wings spread out a little. I ain't too sure of the words." He flipped it over revealing two oak branches, the stems tied with a traditional bow. "I like to keep it real safe," he said slipping it back into his pocket. "I never shown it to nobody, except you." Alex smiled meekly.

"Ever since Joseph died, Belle just sits by the window like she expects him to come walkin' through the door. I feel real bad for her, she don't talk, don't like to eat, nothing," the little girl explained with a sad remorse in her voice.

Alex didn't really know what to say. Fact was, the only time he ever spoke out or displayed any true feelings was to Delilah and Dandy.

"Mr. Tarson, he keeps to himself and don't like to bother Belle. I do believe he feels like it was his fault, the accident and all." She got up and skipped over to a small cluster of early spring flowers and picked two, poking the thin stems into her tightly wound braids. "Are ya happy that we're gonna go back to school, Alex? Sure has been awhile," she remarked.

He shrugged his shoulders with indifference. He didn't care either way, but if he had a choice he would not go; not because of the schoolwork, but because he didn't care much for the older boys. He stood up and headed up the side of the now grassy hill that not too long ago had been laden with snow and frost. She followed closely behind, stopping every so often to pluck dandelions. "Where we goin', Alex Forester?"

"You'll see, ain't too much further," he stopped and turned to see if she could keep up. "Are ya tired?"

"Why no, just cause I'm a girl don't mean I can't climb this hill." Her pantaloons stuck out from under her calico pinafore as she walked. She had taken off her bonnet permitting her long braids to sway as she frolicked up to where Alex was waiting.

"Come on, a little more," he said, and she trudged on, not daring to complain even though her boots were a bit too big for her feet. She had dressed herself with two layers of woolen stockings, but it was all in vain for they still did not fill the empty gaps where her toes lay.

Yellow and orange hues flowed down from above like a tangerine rainbow. Surrounding them was a blue haze. "There, see that?" he shouted and raced forward. "It's grown so big!" Alex could feel his heart thumping with excitement.

Not wishing to be thought a slow-poke, his companion tried to catch up but her boots prevented her from getting up much speed. "I can't believe it, why there are tiny buds, and she's gotten so tall, taller than I ever imagined. She must have liked the winter!" his voice proclaimed with exuberance.

"This sure is a fine tree, Alex Forester. I seen big ones like this, but this is sure a fine tree," added the little girl when she had finally made it up the hill. She smiled acknowledging his enthusiasm and tossed her bonnet onto the ground.

"I never told no one 'bout this, except Tully and Sergeant, but they're different from others," he whispered, protecting his words as though they could be stolen by a mockingbird and repeated on every limb.

"You sure got a lot of secrets, don't ya?" she announced.

Alex excused her question and slowly walked about the tree admiring it from all directions. Raising his head back, he peered up into the burgeoning treetop. Bursts of sunlight followed a path through the thin boughs and between knots of branches. His vision became blurred by the sharp rays so he squinted, relishing the height of his tree like a proud parent. But in spite of his handicapped vision, another sight came clearly into view, and it blocked the brightness of the sun so he no longer needed to squint. High above him, beyond the tallest branch, a pair of dark round eyes stared back as they had done so many times before. Recognizing the vision, he craned his neck back to get a better view.

"Alex, what kind of tree is this?" asked the little girl. She too was peering up and around with genuine curiosity. Her interest drew him away from the secret dark eyes.

"It's an apple tree, a real apple tree," he said turning his face towards her. He lightly passed his hand over a low set of leaves affectionately and sat down in their cool shade. She followed his invitation and imitating a proper lady positioned her calico outward like a lily pad as she tucked her legs under.

"I promise, I ain't gonna tell nobody. But I might have to tell Mindy, she never talks to nobody but me."

It was serenely quiet with an occasional stir from a sprinkling of gnats that meandered the outdoors like the clouds in the breeze. Winter's hard frozen ground had thawed giving way to tufts of spring grass. They sat for a bit, each in their own private thoughts when Alex was jostled by a sense of familiarity. "Walk away fer a minute," he exclaimed. "Stop when I say "stop" and then sit down."

Curiously, she obeyed and walked forward a few yards when she heard, "Stop!" She halted abruptly, twisted back around and promptly plopped upon the ground. "No, turn away from me," he commanded.

"What kind of silly game are you playin'?" she called back, now a bit suspicious that he was toying with her.

"No really, turn around!"

Satisfying his request, she spun herself about keeping her legs tucked up like a cannonball. Alex stared at her back for several minutes, and then, suddenly a deluge of memories flooded back; the pigtails, the tiny shoulders, the calico dress, and the doll. "It must be her," he thought. Could she be the same girl? He sat for another moment and stood up. Was it possible? Was she the little girl on his orphan train?

"What's ya lookin' at Alex Forester, yer actin' kind of strange." She walked back and sat down under the tree.

"What's ya name?" Alex asked. He sat back down, picked a blade of grass, and began to twirl it around his forefingers.

"My name, you know my name; Grace, Grace Tarson!" she pronounced, and she proceeded to pick a blade of grass, too.

"You sure?"

"What do you mean, am I sure? Don't ya think I know my own name?" she declared as she made a futile attempt to loop her splinter of grass like a ring.

"Here, yours is too short," Alex pulled a taller piece of grass and handed it to Grace. "Like this," and his nimble fingers crossed the blade into a knot. Then he looked up and repeated his question. "Are ya sure?"

"That's my name!" the lively child laughed, but after a moment's reflection launched forth another suggestion. "Oh you mean Gracie; some call me Gracie, but only folks I know. I always introduce myself as Grace; I think it sounds more proper."

Alex paused and wondered if he should continue with this track of conversation. Maybe she was content with the way things were. Why maybe he'd wake up a notion that shouldn't be stirred. "Just ferget what I said, I know yer name."

Grace looked inquisitively at him. "I don't think you'd say anything that you didn't ponder first. You've been actin' funny. Now fess up, why did ya ask me?"

Alex handed her a chain of grass all knotted together and stood up, slapped his pants clean of any debris that remained clinging and continued. "On account that I think you ain't a real Tarson, like I ain't a real Forester." There, he had said it. "Now what?" he thought looking for a reaction. Curiously, but grateful there wasn't one, at least not the kind he had expected; he knew that he was right.

Grace tried to tie the grass chain to her wrist like a bracelet, but found that it was not as easy as it appeared, so she tucked it into her pinafore pocket where she often stashed items she found; important things like buttercups or shiny pebbles. "No, but now I'm a Tarson, like you're a Forester. How come you asked?"

"I saw you, I saw you a long time ago, on a train and you were holdin' a doll! I saw the same doll at the Tarson place the same night we found out…," he stopped for a moment and wasn't sure if he should say it, he didn't want to be disrespectful.

"The night we heard that Joseph fell into the river and died?" she finished his sentence.

"It was yer doll, I was sure I'd seen it somewhere, but I couldn't get my mind clear, on account of the calamity. Then today, I remembered where I've seen ya. You were sittin' with another girl."

"Emma, her name was Emma. She was nice and let me sit next to her," she said.

"How come I didn't remember when we were in the school?" he wondered, though more to himself.

"I don't know about you, but I was scared to talk to anyone, especially a boy. Besides, why would ya?" she asked smiling as though she had struck a nerve.

Alex just shrugged his shoulders. "Where ya from, I mean before the train?" he questioned moving closer into the full shade of the tree. The sun was shifting overhead and the shadow was beginning to wane.

"Why, I think Chicago, or maybe it was New York, I ain't sure," she began.

"I'm from the East," he replied. That was one thing he knew for sure.

"I don't think about it very much, the train and all, but I guess we've got more in common than most." Grace looked up at the tree, "When do ya think you'll get apples?"

"Not sure," he replied also looking above.

"I've been thinking, maybe we ought to go down to the river and put some wildflowers in the water, for Joseph." Alex listened to Grace as she continued with her idea. "I mean, he never had a righteous parting and maybe we could make him feel better."

"We could I suppose," Alex agreed reluctantly. He had walked over the river many times through the covered bridge; the one Betty called the "kissin" bridge.

"It's real close by to my place. I'll pick some flowers that have grown up since the thaw and put them right here in my pinafore," she tucked her hand in the pocket to demonstrate its depth. The clouds had surrendered to the sun and released its March brilliance upon the two. Grace frowned at her bonnet and the thought of the ribbon under her chin. "I really don't like this silly hat, but it does keep the sun from withering me away like a plucked daisy out of water," she remarked fiddling with the large brim. "Do ya want to go?" she asked again.

"I guess we could." It wasn't exactly what Alex wanted to do, but Grace seemed so taken by the idea; he hardly wanted to disappoint her.

"We can't tell Belle about this 'cause just the very mention of her dear Joseph would put her into a deeper melancholy," Grace explained.

Walking downhill was not nearly as interesting as going up. Grace dawdled behind, stopping every few yards to pluck snowdrop flowers that bowed their delicate white heads, and salt and pepper flowers displaying their reddish-brown anthers against a pale parasol of petals. With the beginning of spring, small tracks of once hibernating animals dimpled the bare earth. Moles that liked to reel through the ground near the surface and voles that frequently use their tunnels as travel lanes would now become easy prey for red shouldered hawks. Alex kept vigil for any signs of wildlife and hoped that he did not have to witness such a demise of some innocent rat mole or the like.

"If we turn to the left up this way," she pointed, "instead of the way we came, lickety-split, we'll be along the bank!" Grace called to Alex with an air of excitement. "I've never been to this part of the river, it's like an adventure!" She skipped one foot in front of the other to catch up to Alex despite her oversized boots bridling her usual springy step. This would have been quite a simple task had she been barefoot. "Have you been this way before?" she questioned catching up.

"Yep," he said juggling a pebble that he had picked up along the way. But his recollection was not without misgivings; for these parts of the riverine grew steeper and more unsteady as it stretched beside the narrow dirt road.

Paralleling the bank, the ground was brown and coarse; river bulrush and bur reed hadn't yet grown up to hinder the course as they plodded and continued single file. The river narrowed, careening over and between sharp rocks that huddled together as foamy peaks collided against the stones, showing no mercy to anything in its way.

Alex shivered at the thought of the wagon wheels missing the roadbed; it would have been so easy for even the most skilled driver to overturn in the blackest time of night. The brightness of the day contrasted with his feeling of uneasiness. He wanted to turn round and head back to the apple tree where he was comfortable and familiar with earth's expressions. But in this setting, nature did not show her gentle side, in contrast, she was provoked and angry, laughing at his human frailty.

"I bet we could stop here, Alex Forester," Grace said peering into the raging water below.

Alex turned; grateful they did not have to carry on. She pulled out of her pocket a handful of well-worn flowers, still lovely in color but limp to the touch. "I do believe they still got a little bit of sweet smell," she exclaimed, putting them to her nose whereby small bits of yellow pollen stuck to the tip. "Wanna sniff?" she asked. But before he could decline, Grace had separated the fairest of her droopy bouquet and put it under his nose.

"Like it?" she asked pulling it away and giving it another whiff. Alex nodded but in actuality did really not smell anything that resembled a sweet odor.

"I bet we could get a little closer to the water, I don't think that I'll be able to pitch these in from here," continued Grace.

Alex looked down into the thrashing current and began to reckon how much of a drop it was from where they stood. By his calculations, there was a lateral tier, probably caused by erosion from the meandering river centuries ago. They could climb down and there was probably a ledge to give them room to stand. However, as he continued to look down, he imagined his feet slipping on the unstable dirt causing him to slide uncontrollably into the raging water while Grace stood helplessly above. He was hurled against the rocks gasping for air. Maybe it really wasn't necessary to consecrate this spot; she could throw the flowers towards the water from here. Besides, it was the thought that was important.

"Alex," she called breaking his concentration, "do ya think this is a good place to go down, it don't look too steep from here?" He glanced in the direction of her pointed finger. His immediate reaction was fearful reluctance; not the kind of fear that was chicken-hearted or cowardly, it was wariness, fear for the right reasons.

"Come on boy, you ain't afraid are ya? Be a man!" Alex winched and tried to shake Randle's voice out of his head.

"Sure," Alex replied trying to sound genuine, "but I'll head down first and you can follow me." It became immediately apparent that the slope was so steep that the only safe way to descend was sideways. They dug the sides of their boots and heels into the ground to keep balanced, unearthing small rocks and soil that propelled down into the river.

"I feel like a duck!" exclaimed Grace catching herself from falling over, "these boots are too dern long." Alex twisted around to be sure she could continue, although he wasn't quite sure what he could do if she did lose her balance.

The ledge was well above the river, the beating of the water against the rocks created a frothy spray to fly up and wash their feet with a cold mist. Sunshine floated upon the surface. "I think this is a perfect spot, don't you?" she laughed pulling the rumpled flowers from her pocket. "Here, you can throw some into the water too," and she started to hand Alex half of the bunch.

"No, you do it, besides it was yer idea."

Grace drew her hand back and held the limp bouquet against her chest as though she was praying. "Well, what do you think we should say? I don't suppose we should just toss them in without sayin' something," she replied with a request, so appealing and bearing such honesty that it did not seem as though it was coming from the voice of a child.

Alex looked down into the raging water below, its unremitting display of power stampeded in a most deliberate course. "Do you suppose this is what it's like aboard a ship in the ocean?" he asked.

"Never really thought about it, I guess it might be," she answered. The flowers were wet with spray; small beads of water formed a trail of droplets from the drooping stems to their curling leaves, dribbling drop by drop, one after another, onto her apron.

"What would a captain say if one of his men fell overboard?" Alex asked.

Grace pondered a moment, her lips pursed as though she knew the answer but wasn't able to remember. "I ain't too sure, I never was on a ship, but I did see a picture of one in a book."

"If you were on a ship," Alex stated, "you'd have to be very brave, you couldn't be afraid of the ocean. It would be yer friend that you'd get to know real well." Grace held the flowers tightly as she listened. "A captain wouldn't be too sad, since the person who fell over would just become part of the ocean." He looked over at Grace who seemed to agree and seemingly quite content with this logic. "On account that the ocean can't die, so he ain't really dead, just not around."

"Why, Alex Forester, that makes sense, real sense." And with that she stepped closer to the edge, allowing the front of her long shoes to tip over the embankment. Then with a great gesture she released the flowers tossing them forward. They glided slowly as if in no hurry; some were caught up in the light breeze and parachuted down into the water. Both of them watched as the river captured each stem, and violently carried them downstream. "Come on Alex Forester, let's follow the river until we can't see the flowers anymore!" she cried.

Forsaking his apprehension, Alex took chase along the narrow embankment. They were no match for the river, for it roared past them, forging ahead like a steam locomotive, sacking everything in its path. As the river began to round the bend, the two found themselves unable to continue, for their ledge had tapered, too small to walk upon. Alex craned his neck to see beyond the barricade while steadying himself against the earthen wall; the only thing that separated him from perpetual movement and the termination of a life.

Grace gazed about for several minutes, pitching a few loose stones into the river. "I guess we better go back even if it's purty round here," she exclaimed above the roar of the river. Then carefully she made an about-face. "Ain't ya comin'?" she called to Alex realizing he was not following behind. Silently he heeded her call and turned away from his thoughts.

They followed the same trail back, walking opposite to the flow of the river. It did not feel quite as treacherous compared to the start of their adventure. The sun beamed overhead and its warmth toasted the tops of their heads. "I fergot my bonnet up by the tree,"

Grace exclaimed realizing that perhaps wearing it did have some significance. "If I git home without it why Beatrice will have a conniption. She's kind of nervous now that Belle ain't herself." Alex walked in silence as Grace continued to gleefully chatter during their return.

———

The open clearing had been created by the removal of original forests by former generations of inhabitants. Even seedling trees were displaced for firewood and kindling. Having been abandoned for better woodland, its sparsely treed site became a mosaic of shrub thickets and forage grasses that took ownership. But in spite of man's influences and interference, the little apple tree was bringing hope to the survival of nature.

"There it is!" Grace noted, somewhat out of breath from the trek. "I do believe that the wind must have carried it away 'cause I dropped it under the tree." She picked up the bonnet and shook the dirt away before putting it on. "I do hate wearin' this thing, but I reckon it does keep me from burnin' to a crisp."

Alex was half listening; too intrigued by several ants trying to carry what appeared to be crumbs of bread. He bent down to examine them, amazed that such small creatures could carry a load twice their size. However, as he looked more closely, he discovered that there were several morsels of bread littered about. He poked around the dirt with a small stick, uncovering more crumbs, and began to wonder where these pieces came from since neither he nor Grace had been eating.

"Well, well, well, looky har, if it ain't the little yokel!" an eerily familiar voice echoed through the air. Startled, Alex jumped up and instinctively turned around. Within hailing distance the unmistakable outline of Zachary McNary Rucker could be seen. He was considerably larger than Alex remembered since the last time they were in school and had gained weight in equal proportion to his height. Flanked by his two cronies, both having grown in size, they sauntered with deliberate and intimidating swagger. Each boy clasped a hand-ful of bread and was eating with gusto, losing an occasional crumb as they chewed and spoke at the same time. It now became clearly evident where the ants had gotten their meal.

Zachary wiped his mouth on the sleeve of his jacket. "What's ya doin' up here?" he called out to Alex

"Ain't ya far from home, muttonhead?" snorted the shorter of the three. He was a scruffy boy and like younger siblings in a family, he was bestowed with hand–me-down clothes. His over-sized pants were too long so he rolled them above his ankles. For a belt he used a piece of cut rope tightened under the waist to help keep them from falling, but the bunched material kept loosening whenever he walked so he acquired a habit of tugging tightly at the knot. Likewise, his shirtsleeves were rolled up above his mud-stained elbows. His round face wore a ruddy complexion, speckled with orange freckles that matched his red hair. He had the reputation of being a scoundrel and enjoyed instigating fights in school. Only Miss Henshaw called him by his real name, Elijah, but would only answer to Lig by anyone else.

The trio walked slowly towards Alex, eyeing him like their prey. Dell Corny was flaunting a slingshot, pretending to take aim. With every other step he would straighten one arm, pull back the rubber band and let it go. "Got it!" he cried with enthusiasm. "Want to try?" he asked Alex as he pulled back and aimed the band at him in jest. "You kin knock a squirrel clear off a branch when ya practice."

"No, thanks," Alex replied. He was horrified by the request, but had learned that boys couldn't show any sign of being a mollycoddle if they wanted to keep themselves in one piece.

"Why, Dell Corny, that's the most terrible thing I can imagine!" Grace cried out running towards them. "Why would ya want to hurt a squirrel?"

"Why would ya want to hurt a squirrel?" he mimicked. "Why to eat it!"

Grace's cheeks flushed with exasperation knowing full well that she couldn't disagree with his answer. Most folks ate squirrel, some-thing that she herself was not party to since Belle Tarson was not one to have an animal in the rodent family served at her table. "Well, ya don't have to talk about it!" she said.

"Alex, tell her, tell ya little girlfriend ya like to eat squirrel!" Lig coaxed.

Caught in a dilemma, Alex didn't want to give into his true feelings. "Come on over here boy, I want to teach ya how to skin these squirrels that yer Ma's gonna' fry us up fer supper!" Alex thought he had buried these words, but they were now resurfacing; exhuming with it a hideous flashback. "What's ya doin', Alex? How are ya gonna hold this squirrel if ya keep turnin' around?" There was something biting and forbidding about the way Randle had tugged at his arm and dangled the piteous dead animal in front of him.

Zachary put his arm on the distraught boy's shoulder and gave him a hearty pat, "Course he's eaten squirrel, matter-of-fact, next time we bag a few we'll invite Alex here and little missy to eat with us!" Zach laughed heartily and the rest of the boys joined in like a chorus on cue. Alex surrendered a meek smile even though the thought repulsed him.

"Well, you can count me out, I ain't gonna eat no little squirrel," Grace replied and started away from the rest.

Silence fell upon Alex with all its weight. It was painful standing among the three, and he wished that somehow they would walk up the hill, giving him just enough time to escape. The grotesqueness of their gestures and talk, the ignorance in which it was exhibited troubled him greatly. "How foolish I am not to leave," thought Alex. But it was not long before they seemed to forget about him and began to wrestle and roll about, kicking up the dry dirt and parcels of new grass.

Grace was sitting under the tree fanning her face with her bonnet. She wished to take off her boots and run barefoot, but feared that if she came home with dusty feet it would be trouble. "Come on, Grace," whispered Alex

"Where ya goin'?" demanded Zachary standing behind. His face was smudged and the sweat sticking in the creases of his skin was etched with dirt.

"We gotta get goin', it's getting kinda late and I've got chores to do," explained Alex and then wondered why he was apologizing.

Running up along Zachary were Dell and Lig. They were shaking grass from their hair and brushing their soiled clothes with their hands. Lig tugged feverishly at his rope, tripping over the cuffs that had unfurled. "Hey, I never seen this before, have you?" asked Dell elbowing Lig. He circled the little apple tree and tugged at a low-hanging branch.

Zachary reached up and snapped off a tiny silvery leaf emerging from a new bud. "Me neither," he said pulling another.

Alex tightened his fists as he watched several buds drop to the ground. "What did ya do that fer?" he charged in an exasperated tone. Grace flitted about the tree like a butterfly gathering the fallen buds and dropped them into her pinafore pocket.

Wretched silence and a muted scowl foreshadowed the events to follow. The contemptible boy had been provoked by Alex's solicitation. Zachary reached down into his boot and removed a leather sheath. He cunningly pulled out a hickory handle and displayed the icy blade of a hunting knife that brandished a keenly tapered tip and sharpened point. "Know what I think," he said grinning like a swashbuckler, "I think this would make a fine switch!" and he held the end of the tiny branch and with a sudden whack it was dissected from its bough. "Here muttonhead, the first one is for you," and he tossed the cut portion at a mortified Alex. "Who else wants a piece of this tree?" Zach cried. "Why by this afternoon, I can hack the whole thing into kindling!"

Now, in the world when the injustice of a real truth is witnessed, a self-disciplined figure who abides by integrity becomes wildly emancipated. As such, with Alex, an unfamiliar feeling swelled up inside and with the greatest of force he lunged at Zachary with all his might, knocking the large boy off balance and causing the knife to flip. The heart within Alex's chest ached with each thump and with a broken sob in his throat he blocked his body in front of the tree. "Get away from here!" he screamed, "get away from my tree!" The young guardian was shaking with anger. His face grew crimson and the emotion he harbored for so long had finally erupted.

Grace trembled with fear that Alex's outburst had fueled the defiance within Zachary like bellows stoking a fire. Everything around her was heating up with an out-of-control intensity. "It's O.K., Alex, they're gonna go away, ain't ya?" she pleaded to the fallen boy.

All eyes were upon Zachary who was bent over on all fours. An eerie caw from a low soaring blackbird sounded from above; no one spoke. Slowly he stood up, rubbing his hand and picking dirt out of his skinned palm. "Go on Zach, give'm what he deserves, give it to 'em!" coaxed Lig dancing about with fists raised, punching an imaginary opponent. Dell smirked at Alex and nodded his head approvingly; the idea of a fight was enchanting

Alex remained fast, beseeched by the uncertainty of what he should do. He knew that his reaction was illogical considering the obvious consequences. His mind swirled and he began to get that sickened feeling in his stomach. Nervously he tried to reassure himself. "I had to defend the tree," he thought. "This is my tree, even if I do git my head knocked in, I can take it."

Grace stood to the side of Alex and whispered into his ear. "Alex, let's go! Let's go before they kill ya!" Her tiny voice flitted about like a moth dancing in a light beam, but in spite of her good intentions they only seemed to confuse him.

"You git, now Grace, go on, run home!" Alex insisted pushing her away. "Go on, git!"

Grace looked at him helplessly, but the earnestness in his eyes revealed something in Alex that she had never noticed before. Her impulse was to stay however; good sense told her that if she hurried she might be lucky and find someone along the way. Breathless from fear she obeyed. Time was against Alex, and she needed to get help. Her cumbersome boots kicked up large clods of soil like a slow, old mare. Grace stopped and looked back, just as Zachary was pointing his finger and saying something to Alex, but she couldn't make out the distant words. She bent down, pulling frantically at the laces with fingers that did not want to work. She struggled with the ties and finally slipped out of her boots. Her eyes continued to be set in the direction of the apple tree as she tugged off her stockings and stuffed them into her pinafore pocket. The cool ground under her feet gave way to her agility. She was a mustang speeding away, long braids streaming behind, and soon out of sight.

Chapter 29

The knocking at a door can be discerned by a well-tuned ear for the urgency of the tones amplified is different depending upon the method. For example, a loud impetuous strike comes from the banging of a brass knob usually by the repetition of three blows. The gentler knock is delivered in staccato by the knuckles, while a series of continual short curt taps is distinguished by the rapping of a cane. Such was the sound distributed by the visitor upon the door of the Cambridge Arms.

The peephole from the inside opened giving view to the caller who, while waiting at the door, was plucking a small rosy blossom from its thorny branch that had stretched itself from the garden into the covered portal, and placing the lovely bud into his lapel.

"How did you get through the gate?" demanded Katrina swinging open the door. "I got a mind to call the police or worse yet, Mrs. Cambridge." Her voice was threatening and always lowered an octave when angry or annoyed.

"Now, don't you look lovely today, done somethin' different with your hair? I do like it up like that!"

"Don't try to get cheeky with me, Jack Philander! I know that gate was latched this morning 'cause I done it myself!" she snapped back while pushing a loose hairpin back into her bun, wondering if he really meant the compliment.

"Well, Katy, I am afraid that the latch was not as secured as you believed it to be. Why look over there," he pronounced pointing his cane in the direction of the gate. "I would say that a bit of grease would help make that latch work better. Maybe you just didn't pull hard enough, being of a delicate gender and all," he said smiling all the while like a greedy crocodile and brought her hand to his thin lips.

A warm flush rouged over her face, but she quickly withdrew his advances. "You're a scoundrel Jack Philander. Now, do you have business with Mrs. Cambridge, she didn't say anything about meeting with the likes of you!"

"My Katrina," he said tapping the cane upon the tip of his boot, "I assure you that I will not be denied entrance if you simply tell Mrs. Cambridge that I have come to call on her."

Shaking her head, she reluctantly led him into the small foyer and promptly shut the door behind them. "Ya can put yer cane in there," she barked, pointing to a stand decorated with festoons of flowers. "And don't go touching anything while I'm gone," she warned wagging her finger. The room was grimly dark in spite of the time of day. He stood idly for a few minutes studying his gloomy environment, however soon became rather bored with this activity and commenced to buff the crooked cane handle against his sleeve jacket to pass the time. When he found its bronze coating to be sufficiently polished, he unscrewed the handle and gently slid a concealed blade from the hollow shaft. He didn't dare remove it entirely, but only partial way, glowering at it triumphantly. The heavy sound of footsteps trudging down the stairs awakened the wily man's senses, and he quickly slid the blade back into its secret compartment, securing the handle tightly just as the door pushed open.

"Ya look like yer up to no good!" Katrina scorned looking him up and down. "Well, yer lucky, Mrs. Cambridge has got time fer ya!" she snapped and beckoned for him to follow her through the narrow corridor and into the parlor.

Faded light peppered the small room. A pungent scent of lilac sprang from a fresh arrangement of purple blooms exposing the language of flowers. Clusters of pale petals symbolizing the "first emotions of love" roused those who encountered their loveliness and conjured up images of youth and beauty. But in spite of the sweet smell of youth that struck the nostrils upon entertaining the first step, one was immediately drawn into a clash of senses, for resting upon a white doily was a set of gnarled bony fingers.

"Come in, come in foolish man!" The old hag sat molded against the velvet wingback chair. "Katrina, close the door behind you my dear, I have some business to attend to with Mr. Philander," she said pointing to the man.

"Of course, Mrs. Cambridge, but you ring right away if you want me. I don't like the likes of his kind!" she said scowling at the man.

"Hush my dear, no word of his presence," and she shooed her away with a whisk of her rickety hand. The door shut behind her leaving the intruder standing before the old woman.

"You look lovely today, Mrs. Cambridge, and I think more refreshed and radiant than usual," Jack declared. He balanced his cane and swung it back and forth in his palms. Beads of sweat formed upon his brow and the stiff shirt collar was choking his thin neck.

Mrs. Cambridge glared, turning her lips down. "I haven't slept well in years and as for looking radiant, don't try to flatter me with your insincerity!" she growled. "Put your stick down and come sit close to me," she demanded and pointed her cane at the mahogany chair in the corner.

Jack Philander followed her instructions and pulled the seat next to hers and sat leaning forward into the cubby of the large chair she occupied. Surprisingly however, the white-haired lady reached over and rather than speaking, as he anticipated, she tugged with all her might on his left ear lobe.

"Ouch, what did ya do that for!" he squealed pulling away and cupping his ear in pain, fearful that she might attack again.

"That's because you don't listen to me and maybe next time you'll remember!" she scolded. "Now, I warned you never to come around here!" she said in a low and threatening tone.

Jack eased away and teetered on the edge of the seat. The room was growing warmer, and he wished to open a window, any window, but there was none in sight. Only thick brocade drapes hung like vestments against the parlor wall. "I have come for the rest of my money," he said.

"What's that?" she asked toying with him. "I don't believe I heard you."

Jutting a few inches forward he spoke up more slowly, enunciating every word. "I went to the dock just as you wished and as the two came off the gangplank they were easy prey. Ah, if the old magistrate only knew he would wish his beloved newlyweds had never been received by the likes of me, Jack Philander. Oh, the two were a gullible mark; directed them right to your doorstep. I can see the English fool now!" Jack laughed recalling the entire incident. Mrs. Cambridge nodded her head agreeably as he sputtered on. "So you see; I would like the rest of my money." His lips parted as he spoke, and then he slipped back into the chair like a snake.

Mrs. Cambridge followed his body language detecting a nervous tapping of his fingers against his knee. "Yes, my dear," she continued, "that you did. And I say, most successful in the mission." Her tone was low and her tongue saccharine. Jack watched and waited for her to speak again. She placed her wrinkled hands upon the arms of the chair and pulled her spent body towards him, placing her weight upon her cane. Her expressionless eyes looked hard into his and he wished to turn away but was drawn into them as though under a spell.

"Yes, you did follow my instructions," she hissed. "But, you will not be given another cent until the job is finished. Now, don't let me see you on my property unless you are summoned again. I will be the one to tell you when you will receive the rest of your payment." Upon those words she stomped her cane upon the ground with such force that had the house not been built with the best of timbers it would surely have lost a floorboard. "Katrina," she shouted. "Katrina!"

The shout of the elder shot through the maid's eardrum, for during the meeting in the parlor Katrina was bent over listening at the keyhole. She hesitated a moment to feign her location and then entered the room, presenting herself as if having hurried to her call. "There you are, my deary, you may show Mr. Philander out, he is leaving," the elder announced. Katrina smiled with new enthusiasm, gloating widely at the man as she beckoned the rogue to follow. Jack looked over at Mrs. Cambridge realizing that he was in no position to object and like a chastised dog, he obeyed.

She waited for the sound of the front door to close and called out for Katrina to ask Libby to join her in the garden. The shuffle of the maid's footsteps rounded the corner and ascended the stairwell. A most cunning smile settled upon her wrinkled lips at the anticipation of her young boarder. "How I do enjoy a good hunt," she remarked to herself and started to unfold herself from the chair.

———

Libby sauntered into the courtyard drawing a deep breath into her lungs. Several days had passed since she had been outdoors and although content with her small living quarters, she embraced the fresh air like luxury. The stately hawthorn tree was the oldest inhabitant of the garden and extended a welcome to the wrens and thrush. Its dull grey bark, rough and hewed with age, appeared most sorrowful in contrast to the light and delicate features of its human visitor. Libby took a seat upon the rickety bench that teetered on uneven cobblestone beneath its outstretched boughs. She turned her face upward towards the open sky and embraced the fresh air.

Perched upon a low branch, a grey squirrel rustled the thin twigs with its spinnaker like tail. Slowly, so as not to startle the little animal, Libby rose and drew closer to the branch. Delighted with this lovely creature she watched as it scampered to and fro from branch to branch until it stopped, as though frozen in time, and sat upright with its tail curved like an "S". It hovered boldly above, curiously watching Libby with a fearless notion as though it sensed that she was a country girl. But just as a clock shoos away time, this peaceful synergy between man and nature was suddenly vandalized.

"Don't encourage that vermin! We've got enough trouble with pesky birds!" warned Mrs. Cambridge. Libby turned to see the white-haired lady hobbling towards her and shaking her cane. "If I were back in England, I'd have the groundskeeper exterminate the whole lot of them."

"Why, Mrs. Cambridge, I didn't mean any harm," Libby called out woefully. "Here," she said offering her hand out towards the old shrew. Gingerly she cupped the bony elbow and supported the elder's bent arm in her hand. "Allow me to help you, these cobble-stones are rather uneven."

"Thank you my dear," lilted Mrs. Cambridge changing her tone to suit her mission. "I hope I didn't frighten you."

"Well, I was a bit startled at first; however upon seeing that it was you who spoke out, I was no longer afraid," Libby said with a smile.

"There, there my child," Mrs. Cambridge professed, patting the young woman's hand in a reassuring gesture that she meant no mal-ice. "Let us walk about," she proposed, stroking Libby like a small rabbit. "You know, this courtyard was once a showcase, a garden that was the envy of Baltimore."

Libby followed her lead and slowly they began to circle about. "Do you see these weeds?" Mrs. Cambridge said, stopping by a clump of unruly and knotted foliage. "My son was the keeper of this courtyard; right in this very spot he planted indigo, the loveliest indigo flowers!"

"I am sure they were beautiful," replied Libby. "My grandmother planted indigo when I was a young child. My mother used to cut the blooms and place them in small vases about our cottage."

Mrs. Cambridge did not reply, but rather winced by gesturing that they move on. Her step was slow and deliberate; Libby clutched the woman's arm supporting her carefully as though she were made of glass. However, it was Libby who was the more fragile of the two.

"May I ask, where is your son?" questioned Libby as they approached the benches. Mrs. Cambridge allowed the young com-panion to steady her as she sat down, positioning her cane for support.

"My son is dead," she said most matter-of-fact. "My brother is my only family and the sole person I can rely upon. You see, he too has been betrayed."

Libby, having now been apprised of this unintentionally solic-ited tidbit of information was overwhelmed with shame for hav-ing intruded upon such a private subject. Mrs. Cambridge saw this admission and realized the she had stirred Libby's emotions, success-fully gaining the young woman's sympathy.

"The plan is moving along quite nicely," the elder thought con-fidently. The two sat quietly, each keeping company in their own thoughts; Libby had been dispirited by her lack of judgment, while Mrs. Cambridge was delighted by her own "tour de force".

Chapter 30

Although it was finally springtime, the little room that had been set apart from the rest of the barn remained cold and damp, offering sparse living quarters to its resident. The room had been wainscoted in oak from leftover timbers and hewn in such a way that when placed side by side, a cool draft could wander in through the cracks where traces of clay had crumbled away between the planks that did not fit squarely. The lodging was modestly furnished providing only the most essential items; a cot, a simple armoire, a small table and chair, a cast iron stove dispensing warmth and heat for cooking, two shelves crudely hanging on the wall with earthenware for storing food, some cookware, a table setting for one, a wooden bin for spuds and onions set in the far corner, an oil lantern, and a basin for washing up before bedtime.

Miss Henshaw pried open the oven's grate with an iron bar and carefully tossed a log into the belly of the stove with mindful aim at preventing any sooty ash from flying out. The seasoned schoolmarm was not a stranger to unpolished conditions. Born and raised on a small Kentucky farm, her bloodline extended from a long line of Kentucky families. Her father was a tall and honest man who prospered nicely from working hard off the land and selling his produce fairly. Her mother was a well-educated woman who craved quiet moments of personal solitude. In the evening when the chores were complete, she would spend her time reading while her husband would entertain himself by whittling small toys or making corn pipes for the neighbors. As soon as they had smoked one to the end, they would always come around again asking for another. As a result, he was never in need of company. Miss Henshaw's mother was one of the only females who didn't take to the pipe in spite of her husband's fine reputation as a pipe maker. So, her daughter followed in her footsteps and too never took up smoking.

Unlike her counterparts that spent most of their solitude reading scripture, Mrs. Henshaw's secret passion was romance novels. Her appetite for reading was such that as the final chapter drew to its conclusion, she would hitch up the wagon and hurry straightaway to the town's general store where she could post her mail-order letter to the Lexington bookshop. She would wait patiently for several weeks, sometimes a month depending upon the time of year, for a package wrapped in brown paper that promised her pages of sheer imagination.

Miss Henshaw stirred the kindling with the poker, now clasping the end with a tattered rag. The heat of the fire penetrated the full length of the iron rod and had become too hot for her hand. Corn cobs were in abundance on the Kentucky farm and burned nicely in the kitchen stove. The only drawback was they did not last long for the fire consumed them with such ferocity. And so, the pastime of feeding the stove became a habitual requirement to all members of the family. Unlike back home, the Tarsons considered wood the only source of fuel; probably because it grew in abundance in this part of the country. She picked up a bit of kindling and broke it up into pieces and scattered the broken twigs into the fire. They snapped and crackled and as they burned they curled inward crying out the sounds that kept the fire alive.

It was some time ago that anyone had referred to her first name. Missus Tarson always called her Miss Henshaw, as did Mr. Tarson, the hired hands, the household staff, and naturally all the students. However, when she was called by her given name it was invariably followed by an additional statement of, "Oh, ain't that the same as the month?" as though she had made a mistake. April, the time when buds and flowers open. Likewise, many kin from her mother's side of the family were named for one of the twelve months. Her mother's name was May and her mother's mother was Grandma June. Then there is Uncle Augusta, her mother's brother, and finally his son, Octavian.

April Henshaw was around thirty-two years old. You see, the Henshaw's never did take much to the calendar since being farming people, the Farmer's Almanac was what they depended upon and specific dates did not seem too important. She arrived during an early frost; a midwife was on hand noting that when this baby was born the crocus knew it was time to awaken.

At an early age April took up the habit of reading and had more of an aptitude for studies than most little girls. Her mother insisted that although she was not a boy education was still very important. When she knew more than the local schoolmaster, she would stay after helping those children that the teacher relegated as "stupid." As time went by, Kentucky could not accommodate her yearning for a formal education so she planned to travel East. However, to her dismay, she discovered there were very few colleges that permitted women to attend. Yet, her resolve nor her spirit could be broken for she was ultimately welcomed at The Oberlin Female Institute in Ohio. Elizabeth Almsworth, the headmistress, propitiously carried forth the philosophy of the school's founder, Mrs. Abigail Postdam, that young women should obtain not just an ordinary finishing school education, but should also be prepared to earn a living.

Miss Henshaw moved her chair away from the fire and sat down at the small table. She pulled aside the calico curtains and looked out of the narrow window that looked upon the main house. She watched for a few moments noticing that one of the field hands must have hacked the new growth of the hickory tree away from the roofline. A collection of cut branches were piled up next to the outhouse. She let go of the curtain and decided that next washday she would take down the curtains and give them a scrub. April glanced around at her paltry lodgings and eyed the ledger where she kept her list of students. She was always neat, almost to a fault, and it troubled her when a student left the class because, rather than scratching out the name that was alphabetically written according to surname, she would rewrite the entire list on a clean sheet of ledger paper.

Joseph Tarson, she had not removed his name from the list. The night of that hideous accident she recalled sounds of commotion descending from the main house. The coming and going of footsteps and the frequent opening and closing of doors prevailed upon her good sense that this was a bad omen. The sky was cold and black. "No," she thought correcting her memory, "it was an angry ocean blue, the color of water that lingers like the prey before the predator storm." Was there a moon that night? She couldn't remember. Was it wrong to have ignored going up to the house and not inquiring about the goings on? April wasn't sure why she stayed in the small room in the back of the barn that night. Maybe it was because the dreams she had were not about the wishes and success of those who came before her. Those dreams passed over her like fog; only to finally dissipate up and away with time. No, the dreams of Kentucky folks were simple and colorless. Their satisfaction was granted with small plots of fertile land to cultivate tobacco or an opportunity to work in a distillery, or ferry new settlers across the Ohio River on flatboats.

April cast her thoughts from the large house on the mound and looked beyond. The sylvan trees had brought her back to the death of her mother. It wasn't clear why, maybe just the foreboding feeling of the moment. She grimaced, turning her lip upward the way she did as a child when she was annoyed or angry. Accidents were frequent and almost matter of fact. Loss came in many forms. May's first born died only days after its birth, buried in the family plot. As for her own death, she too died before her time. Standing on the top rung of the ladder while dusting her books, which were always stacked neatly, their spines facing forward, she lost her balance and fell. It was nearly dark when Mr. Henshaw came in from the field and found his wife sprawled out, face down at the bottom of the ladder, the feather duster still clenched in her hand.

"It isn't that I don't want to be married," April thought reminiscing the years following her mother's death. Despite her yearning to leave home, her decision to stay was strictly based on guilt. It would certainly be premature to expect her father to remain alone. So, she decided to start up a school in the church hoping that after the Sunday sermon the minister could convince the families to educate their children.

Most of the children who were sent to school came from families of disillusioned coal miners. They discovered that the pay for hard labor and dangerous conditions was not very good. Most were living paycheck to paycheck and as time went on found themselves owing more money to the "company store" than they could make each day. The daily struggles created unbearable strife and unless they allowed themselves to get deeper into debt, they were unable to feed their growing families. This was only a minor problem compared to those men who died, leaving behind widows and children. As a result, many families packed up their meager belongings and left. Others that owed money snuck out of the mining camps in the black of night rather than face another day below the earth.

"Had the lives of these poor people actually improved; for now most who ventured away from the mines became sharecroppers." The schoolmarm sighed with this notion and sighed even more deeply with the knowledge that fewer children attended school because they were needed to help in the fields. Consequently, April found that her services were no longer needed. But it wasn't the lack of students that provoked her decision to leave Kentucky. Rather, it was her father's new bride, Margaret Kay, who was with child that granted April the opportunity. True, there was room enough for them all and certainly the new baby would be a blessing for her father, however, April, now in her early thirties, wished to be set free. Margaret Kay, who wanted to be called Maggie, was giddy and easily amused. She was a child bride who was young enough to be her little sister.

The romance novels belonging to her mother were boxed and stacked in the corner of the room. April moved her chair next to the stove and poked at the fire which was barely lit when shouts of dismay rang out from up on the mound. "Miss Henshaw, Miss Henshaw! Come now!" April dropped the poker and quickly unlatched the door to find Grace running towards her and Beatrice, flaying her soup spoon, plodded behind as fast as her heavy legs could carry her.

"Now what's this all about that has you and Beatrice rushing to my door?" questioned Miss Henshaw. "What has you so out of sorts?" Grace stood before her breathless and trembling with fright.

———

Grey clouds prowled overhead germinating the seeds of a storm. "Ya know, kid; I could drag ya down to the river and no one would ever know what happened!" Zachary McNary Rucker folded his sweaty arms across his chest and as he spoke he ran his tongue over his dry lips. He stood almost a foot taller than Alex and used his height as a means of intimidation. Alex remained steadfast, silent, and unfaltering as he listened attentively. He wondered if Zach's entourage thought he was brave to stand up to such a bully. Would they be as courageous if the situation was reversed? In actuality, if given an opportunity, just an inkling of a chance, Alex would have run away. However, as much as he wished, there was no escape for he was stuck between Zachary and the trunk of his apple tree. He had become ensnared by his moral obligations to nature and things that were just, but now he was utterly confused for he always believed that goodness would prevail. Alex was stymied.

"I should make it so's ya never bother no one agin!" Zachary sneered viciously, exhibiting crooked teeth; and as he spoke he blew a hot breath of anger. Alex tried to back slowly away, but soon realized that he had nowhere to go for he had become pinned between opposing forces of good and evil. The sensation of doom squeezed at all sides and the only retreat was to look up at the darkening sky. Pitched overhead several grey clouds melded together by light winds forming images of what appeared to be silhouettes of Delilah and Dandy. They were twirled lazily about the sky, expanding and stretching into other fantastic creations. "What's ya starin' at?" demanded Zachary, now angered with the notion that Alex was paying little attention to this threat. He grabbed Alex's shoulder and shook it gruffly trying to get his attention again, but the only response from the captive was a faint murmur.

"Them," he said and pointed upward. The light of day was veiled by darkening clouds that had turned the horses loose.

The ruffian gaped upward, twisted his head about but could not see anything out of the ordinary. "I don't see nothin!" he growled and complained. "What up there that's got ya so intrested?"

Alex did not reply, but remained entranced upon a renascent vision. Between threads of hazy gossamer was a pair of round dark eyes that held firmly upon Alex, and he upon them. A burst of cold wind scraped the leafless branches. Alex shivered, blinked, and they were gone.

"Go on Zach, let's take' em down to the river and teach 'em a lesson!" yelled Lig, impatiently. "We ain't got all day ya know! Why Dell's already gone down and wait'n on us. He said if we ain't thar soon he's goin' on home before he catches the strap." The taunting voice was an intrusion that brought Alex back among the boys. He heard Lig's eager voice call out as the antagonizer scuffled away, "I'm goin' down to the river, I'll meet ya thar!" And at the same time Alex imagined all three pushing him down the side of the river bank.

Zachary agreed with his friend's suggestion and flourished his dirty hand with a gesture of approval. Specks of dirt trickled upon his nose, and he used his sleeve as a handkerchief. A smudge of dirt was drawn across his face making him look even more savage. Anger had brought the beast out from within and without provocation from his target; Zachary grabbed Alex by his shirt and yanked him away from the tree with sordid intimidation. Surprised by this jolt, Alex stumbled forward, instinctively throwing his hands outward in anticipation of being catapult to the ground. But in contrast to expectations, he felt himself surrender to a violent pull upward, forced to balance on the tips of his boots. Zachary did not let up and with the clump of material grasped in his fist, he kept his prisoner restrained. Alex was a dog on a leash. Zach held tight creeping backwards, scowling into the boy's frightened face. The captive boy tried to hold back tears of anger and fear. He found that it was becoming more difficult to swallow, and as the knot of material was held more firmly it became a noose around his neck. He began to cough and gasp for air, frantically struggling to get free. Trying with all his might to break loose, he clenched his fists, beating Zachary with all his might. But the more he struggled the tighter the shirt was twisted around his windpipe! Alex floundered, gagging, trying to call out but could only deliver a meager moan. He grasped his hands to his throat and tried to rip the shirt from his body, but the more he pushed back, the tighter the grip was held fast. Sheer cruelty stood before him and the horrors of its power were beyond his control.

His life years on earth numbered barely a decade and his finality would become an incandescent flicker in the realm of time. The looming storm clouds burdened by their heavy load sagged overhead. A crack of lightening shot across the cloud as though trying to pierce its thin membrane to release the cataclysm of water it held. Another rod of light, this time even more spectacular, lit up the sky, immediately followed by a low bewailing cry. A threatening snarl and then a deep and menacing growl echoed the booming thunder, and at that very instant the grip loosened around Alex's neck and like a razed tree, Zachary toppled to the ground. Sensing his freedom, Alex raised his hands to his throat and wildly unraveled the twisted shirt, while gasping for breath. At his feet lay Zachary sprawled out in the dirt unable to move for a large angry animal held him by the back of the neck and chided him with throaty warnings.

Pinned to the ground Zachary now trembled with fear, his face flush against the earth. The animal's teeth firmly held his neck motionless. The large jaw was only an inch from his ear and though now, no longer growling, it breathed heavily, inhaling and exhaling through its wet black nose. Between the snorts he could hear a small faint whisper, but was unable to make out what the voice was saying.

"Sergeant, it's you! Why you are a good boy!" Alex cried, crouching down next the dog that had not stirred from his victim. "All alone?' he asked as though expecting a reply. Alex stroked the back of the large soft head and then lifted the long droopy ear and whispered something ever so faintly. Sergeant did not look away from his victim, but wagged his tail with each word from Alex.

The back of Zachary's neck was now wet from saliva. Threads of drool dripped down from the powerful jaw, soaking the boy's shirt. Unaware of what was going on above him, Zachary was certain that this animal that was holding him prisoner must be a wolf or mountain lion and any foolish movement on his part would summon his death. "Alex, don't let it eat me, send it away!" his muffled voice sounded pitiful. But every time the older boy gave the slightest notion of shifting his position, Sergeant bore his teeth down a little more. It was as though the dog delighted in giving Zachary a scare. Sergeant growled fiercely, still keeping his grip and the boy in place.

"Well well, little minute, looks like we got here just in time!" called out a most familiar voice from behind him. Starting round, Alex twisted his head and saw it was his old friend, Tully, sauntering out from the clearing. He was holding the knife that Zachary had dropped during his fall. Alex started up wanting to give him a hug, but thought differently and restrained himself. "Come here and let me look at you," he said. Alex moved towards Tully and immediately pulled open his shirt. "You've got a nasty lash around your neck. Hurts, don't it?" he asked as he took a closer look at the child.

Alex put his hand up around his neck and could feel the circle of skin, rough and scraped. For the first time he now realized the pain, there was a burning sensation as though it had been whipped with a rope and a lump in his throat had formed making it difficult to swallow.

Tully leaned down on one knee and produced a small vile from his back pocket. Alex noticed that the patches had been recently mended for the material did not have time enough to fade like the rest of his pants. The man tipped the open vile and an oily substance dripped out onto a clean piece of cloth. He became more generous with the substance, letting the cloth become fully saturated and then handed it to Alex. "Here, wipe this all around your neck. It's going to sting a little."

Alex did as he was told. The oily liquid adhered easily, not dripping but staying everywhere it was placed. He wiped his neck several times over, winching now and again from the abrasion that stung, but did as he was instructed. Then when he was done, he handed the cloth back to Tully, who stuffed it back into his back pocket. "Release, boy," he commanded. Obediently, Sergeant set the older boy free and then scampered away to chase anything that moved along the grass.

Alex backed away from Zachary expecting the boy to jump up, but rather he remained prone, face down in the dirt still shivering from fright.

"How did ya know I was here?" whispered Alex to Tully.

But before he could get a reply there was a sudden and loud commotion of voices. "Alex, Alex Forester!"

He turned round to see in the distance Grace; pink cheeked and flushed running full steam, her braids flying behind her. Miss Henshaw trailed after and was carrying what appeared to be a shotgun. The wind had picked up and the bleak sky grimaced overhead. "Alex, are you all right?" the concerned woman called out. Her round cheeks were full and puffy, and her hair that was once up in a proper bun was tumbling out of the pins that once kept it neatly in place. "Come on over here Alex, let me look at ya!" she exclaimed as she got into full range of the boy.

"I was so scared, Alex; I thought fer shur they was gonna kill ya!" cried Grace grabbing his hand and pulling him towards the teacher. "I hope ya don't mind, but I had to git help!"

"Course he doesn't mind, now come on here and show me what that hooligan did to you!" called Miss Henshaw, now cradling the rifle against her shoulder.

"What about me? Don't nobody care 'bout what happened to me?" moaned Zachary who had taken the liberty of sitting up. He certainly did not look the part of the menace that he was, but rather with his hair mussed and a crisscross pattern of dirt etched on his cheeks, he looked more like a naughty boy who had been caught playing in the dirt.

Miss Henshaw approached the delinquent, eyeing him up and down as though he were on a store display. "Mr. McNary, I ought to have you hogtied and whipped! I should have thought that you knew better then to bully young Master Forester," she hollered. Grace stood watching for a few moments, then content that Miss Henshaw had everything in control, ran off to find her boots that she had kicked off earlier in the afternoon.

Tired and bewildered Alex backed away. He didn't like to be the center of attention, and he especially didn't want to be fussed over. He cast his eyes upon his resolute apple tree; its thin branches rocked and bent as the wind slapped its twiggy limbs, but it was intact. The grey sky continued to grumble, forewarning a storm. Alex scanned the landscape in all four directions, but Tully and Sergeant were both gone.

"I think you better git on home before the rain. I sent Beatrice on to your folks right before we headed this way," called Miss Henshaw. Alex walked back towards her and found Grace tugging on the laces of her boots.

"You should of seen Zachary run off when he got a look at Miss Henshaw's shotgun! She told him that she had a mind to shoot off his big toe to keep him from stirring anymore trouble! Didn't ya Miss Henshaw?" Grace, now gleeful by the positive outcome, was hopping back and forth on the left foot and then the right, parading about her teacher, who did not feel like a heroine, but rather looked with trepidation at her surroundings. Alex smiled meekly with appreciation and the image of the large boy hobbling along without his toe did lighten his mood.

"Come along children, I don't like the sound of that wind. We better hurry on!" instructed Miss Henshaw handing Alex the old shotgun to carry. Then she began to shoo them along with the hem of her skirt like a mother hen and its chicks. Yielding to the foreboding weather, the three set forth as quickly as their feet would carry them.

Chapter 31

The little sewing room lay tucked away up in the garret where the early morning and afternoon sun generously flooded the space. Although it was small, not more than 10 feet by 10 feet, it was perfectly cozy and well-suited for the most industrious sewer. Everything was in its proper order; a floor to ceiling cupboard had been designed in a most ingenious manner; all one needed to do was to open the door, pull back on a brass handle, and a cutting table would fold down when needed. When this was no longer to be of service, the user could fold it back up and close the cupboard door out of the way. Libby had been sitting before the window mending one of Mrs. Cambridge's quilts. Her fingers flew as she dipped the needle in and out of the soft fabric. It was draped over her lap and across the wooden floor, and she looked as though she herself was donning an elegant gown patterned in gold and silver thread. A large bin of material was stockpiled in the corner and several shelves tumbling full of notions. On the floor by her feet sat a maple sewing carrier. The swing handles hung to the side for as it lay open there was displayed upon the loveliest pink silk lining, a poplar needle case, strawberry emery laden with pins, beeswax, several silver thimbles, a cloth tape measure, a darning egg for socks and gloves, a blue velvet pincushion, and a tiny pair of sterling silver scissors.

Will had promised that he and Nick would be home for supper, Libby reminded herself. "The poor dear has scarcely been able to rest since we arrived," thought Libby as she glanced up from her sewing. The needle was making its closing loop and only a slip of thread remained in the hole to complete its job. The young worker twisted the silky filament and wrapped a tiny knot about her finger, securing the stitch and then cutting it close to the fabric so that only the most meddlesome of lookers would be able to find it. "I am most grateful that we both have found work, and Mrs. Cambridge has been such a kind soul, so much more like family than a proprietor," she sighed contently. Libby found that she felt safe in this sweet room and did not mind the fact that she now spent much of her day bent over a heap of tattered clothes or linens to mend and whenever she wished for some companionship, there was always reliable Marte, the cook, to look forward to; even if it were for just a few moments when she would bring a pot of scalding tea with biscuits or warm buns for her midday snack. Libby unwound the silver strand and threaded the needle once more. Her nimble fingers worked feverishly and never seemed to tire.

The time was about 4:00 in the afternoon when several vigorous raps fell upon the sewing room door. Although there was no time-piece, Libby could tell the hour of day by the length and location of the shadow cast upon the floor. "Libby, I've brought you some tea and biscuits." The voice was not of the broken English belonging to Marte, but instead a richer and deeper delivery by Katrina. Libby turned with a start for Mrs. Cambridge's maid had never climbed the steps unless it was absolutely necessary and certainly never for the purpose of serving her biscuits and tea. However, here stood the unlikely hearty woman extending before her the silver service tray while her large bosom rested upon the edge as though it were a small sleeping animal. The teapot, cup and saucer, sugar bowl, and plate of biscuits had slid to the forefront now making the tray rather unbalanced.

"Oh, Katrina, let me help you!" apologized Libby quickly secur-ing her needle into the soft fabric. "I believe there is room for the tray over here," she said getting up as she spoke and shuffling some odd pieces of fabric aside from the cutting table to make room. She reached over to help, but the woman's large hands remained steady and easily set the tray down without assistance. "I certainly didn't wish for you to come all the way up here, I mean you are so busy with your own work," Libby expressed, regretfully placing much emphasis upon the word "you" as though asking for a pardon from the warden.

"Well, this came in the mail and I thought you might want it, seeing that it's all the way from England," the maid said lifting the plate of biscuits to reveal a letter hidden beneath it. She pushed it with her finger as though it was a bribe to be snatched.

"Did it arrive this morning?" asked Libby as she picked it up from the tray. It was addressed to Mrs. William Piccard, the address listed as Cambridge Arms. She turned the envelope over and noticed that the wax seal designed to keep the contents secure had been broken and then resealed with a drop of wax that did not exactly match the color of the original sealant.

"It must have come yesterday since Mrs. Cambridge gets all the mail first and then hashes it out," Katrina replied wondering what was in the contents.

Libby flipped the letter over again, hoping to recognize the handwriting. It was a bold manuscript, the letters elegantly written, but by no means flowery, probably penned by a gentleman's hand of upper social standing.

"Well, aren't you the least bit curious?" asked Katrina. Both women were standing and the smallness of the room was emphasized by the grand figure of the maid.

"Oh, I'll tend to it later," the petite one replied and slipped the letter into her pocket. "Would you like to stay a bit and have some tea?" asked Libby now realizing that she was negligent in asking the woman to join her. However, no sooner had her invitation been pronounced than did she realize that there was only one chair in the room. "Oh dear, I am not much of a hostess," she laughed and then pointed to the straight-backed chair. "Here you sit down, I've been sitting all morning and I don't mind if I do stretch my legs."

"No thanks, I'll take my coffee with Marte in the kitchen later," came the reply. Katrina picked up the end of the quilt that Libby was working on and fingered it as though she was a buyer in the market.

"Ya like to sew?" she questioned, wondering how anyone really could enjoy such a chore. Katrina laid the quilt back down.

"Oh, I never mind sewing, in fact, I do enjoy all needlework, but I'm not nearly as talented as my mother and grandmother," she replied. Realizing that Katrina was not interested she shifted the conversation. "Are you sure you wouldn't like one of these biscuits?" Libby offered again.

"No, I just wanted to come on up and give you the letter," Katrina repeated.

Libby smiled and began to pour herself a cup of tea. "I do hope you don't mind if I have a little," she said lifting the cup to her lips and gently blowing the surface. But before she could get an answer they were interrupted by a sudden and frantic pounding at the bottom of the landing that startled the young woman so abruptly that she nearly dropped the teacup had she not been holding it with two hands.

"Mercy!" exclaimed Katrina, realizing that the noise was coming from Mrs. Cambridge. "I do wish that woman would have some patience!" Libby smiled and said nothing. "Well, I better get on now," grumbled the housekeeper. "Just bring the tray down to the kitchen when you're finished," she added, and then without any more adieu, bounded away. Katrina's words had been thrown out so quickly that Libby didn't have enough time to thank her for bringing the letter. The stairs resonated with the vibration of clumsy feet hitting every other step; and finally when she reached the bottom landing the banging stopped too.

Libby sat down and sipped her tea as delicately as a hummingbird sips nectar from a primrose. Although she should be hungry, for she barely ate her breakfast, the biscuits did not appeal to her either. In fact, lately, she often found that she was rather dyspeptic and had to force herself to eat during meals since nothing seemed to agree with her. Libby placed the cup back on the saucer and pulled the envelope from her pocket. She hastily tore the envelope around the resealed wax and slid the letter from the satin lined envelope. An elaborately monogrammed "C" adorned the top of the page. Her eyes scanned the handwriting for familiarity and although she tried to remain calm, her heart began to race as her eyes met the words.

My Dear Mrs. Piccard,

How I do love to call you that for I feel rather responsible for your marriage. I am afraid that matters back home in England have not been as agreeable as I would like to relate. I wish to inform you that your Grandmother Analiese has indeed received your letters and continues to cherish each and every word. I know that you would have liked to have heard from her yourself except I regret that she has taken ill. Your father has sent her into London to convalesce closer to the doctors and will remain there until she is well enough to return to the country. Although I disagree with the decision, for I feel the country air is more germane to your Grandmother's temperament, it is not for me to decide. But, even as ill as she may be, she asked me to convey this message to you, "My eyes will always be watching over you and yours."

Be a strong little Englishwoman and keep your chin up, child. Although your mother is too frightened to write you herself, in fear of your father's reprisal, she has you in her prayers.

Regards to William,

Judge Carson

Libby's eyes filled with tears as she reread the line, '*My eyes will be watching over you and yours*'. It was nearly impossible to be strong while the idea that she may have contributed to her Grandmother's ailment fluttered through her mind. "Perhaps," Libby lamented, "if I had not come to America, had I not snuck away knowing it was against father's approval, then just maybe Grandmother would not be ill. I should be back at home to care for her. Oh, what have I done, what have I done?" Tears blurred her vision, and she ached desperately wishing for some reconciliation within herself. Dolefully, she dried her wet lids with the backs of her palms and then began to burrow into her deep pockets searching for a handkerchief when the advent of her quest was suddenly interrupted by a sultry voice.

"What's the matter, honey? You look as though you lost your best friend." Leaning lazily against the door was the most extraordinary woman Libby had ever seen. "Bad news?" asked the woman. Libby looked down at her hands and noticed that she had been clenching the letter in her fist, which evidently the woman must have noticed too. "You're not going to be able to read that correspondence if you continue to squeeze the life out of it like you seem to be," she laughed. "Mind if I come in?"

"Oh, I am most sorry for my poor manners. Please do." Libby, now more flustered, seemed to forget her woes in lieu of making amends for her rudeness and smiled timidly. "Have we met?" she asked with a shade of uncertainty.

The woman sauntered through the portal, pulled a silk hand-kerchief out from her sleeve, and handing it to Libby suggested, "I think you may need one of these." Her voice was soft and tender.

Like a schoolgirl, Libby accepted and as she nervously toyed with the silk cloth it became unfolded, exposing a lilac "W" embroidered in the center. "You're Libby Piccard, aren't you?" she said. "We haven't formally met, but I was told that there was a couple rooming here and since I was up and around, figured I'd make my acquaintance. I'm Wanda Bourdette."

"Oh, it is a pleasure to meet you Miss Bourdette, I have heard so much about you," replied Libby and dabbed her tearful eyes with the handkerchief.

"Yea, bet you have," she replied and batted her long lashes. Libby was fascinated by this woman; in fact it was hard to keep from staring. Her thin lips were painted pale pink as if she had just kissed a rose, and her cheeks had a tinge of vermeil rouge that accented her fine porcelain complexion. Her chestnut hair hung down in ringlets across her shoulders. She was wearing a three-piece gown made of white handkerchief linen, high neck, long tapered sleeves, and an inset with Irish crochet; the train flowed elegantly behind her.

Wanda twirled around once and then curtseyed at Libby. "It's an import from France!" she announced most gleefully.

"Oh, Miss Bourdette, I wasn't, I mean, I certainly didn't intend to stare, it's just that…" Libby was now speechless and could feel her face flush with distress.

"It's okay, Libby, not many around has seen a 'deshabille robe de chamber'," she explained in perfectly accented French. "That's Parisian for 'an undress'. I wear it to be comfortable around my apartment. You ought to get one," she said offering advice and a smile.

"It is lovely, Miss Bourdette," Libby agreed wondering what it would be like to be bold enough to wear such a fashionable garment.

"Call me, Wanda," the woman commanded and moving the conversation along added, "I'm in sort of a bind; I was wondering if you could do a little mending for me on account that my usual seamstress has gone off for an undetermined amount of time." Then, she made an about-face, sauntered out of the door a few feet and retrieved a bundle which resembled a large plumed bird perhaps trapped in red taffeta. Wanda stood by the door and at once shook the bundle violently as if trying to remove any dust that may have been accumulating. A long scarf began to uncoil and as it expanded, tiny red feathers flitted about the room, having been dislodged from the original shaking. Larger red plumes had been sewn up and down the material so that it seemed to flutter whenever the scarf moved; Wanda held her arms up high above her head so that her wrap could be fully displayed. Three quarters of the way down a small but noticeable bald spot, much resembling a plucked chicken, was in clear view. "See why I need you?" she asked rhetorically.

Libby nodded in accordance with this evaluation. It was most evident that there was some mending to be done. Wanda continued, "I'm opening with a new ballad, *All Things Love Thee So Do I*." Then, flipping the scarf around her shoulders, she began to croon with the passion of love-sick entertainer.

"Gentle waves upon the deep,
Murmur soft when thou dost sleep,
Little birds upon the tree,
Sing their sweetest songs for thee,
Their sweetest songs for thee."

"Oh, Miss Bourdette, I mean Wanda," cried Libby, "you have a beautiful voice!"

Wanda shook herself free from her wrapping and handed it to Libby, "So what do you think? Say tomorrow about this time? Of course I will pay you for your work, double since it is such late notice."

Libby examined the scarf and found it to be stiffer than she imagined.

"I do hope you don't think that I would wear this on the street. I am a singer and my audience expects me to be a bit...," Wanda paused trying to come up with some words that would be sensitive.

"I understand, they expect you to be colorful," Libby suggested.

"Why yes, colorful," Wanda acknowledged. She wasn't used to being taken seriously, for most people looked down upon a woman who was not only past the marrying age, but also supported themselves as an entertainer. "You certainly have been busy with mending and sewing, so Katrina has informed me. She tells me much of what goes on around the house since I am sort of a night owl, working such different hours than most," Wanda added as she casually inspected a few remnants that were set out before the young woman.

Libby stroked the scarf gently as though it were alive. "This shouldn't be too difficult; I can have it for you in a few hours, if you wish."

"Oh, my dear, it is already growing late and by the looks of your pale countenance I do think that you are in need of rest rather than more work, and besides, there is something to be said for the unpleasantness in your letter." Then in a maternal manner she placed her hand upon the young woman's forehead. "Why you do feel cold and look absolutely flushed!" she exclaimed. "Come along, it is time you get out of this room and get yourself to bed. Now, how long has it been since you have had a hot meal, hmmm?" asked the singer.

"Oh, I do not think that it is possible, I must get this quilt finished. Mrs. Cambridge wanted it mended straightaway!" Libby confessed as she realized that she had neglected her work.

"Let me take care of Mrs. Cambridge, and now up and away petite jeune fille!" But as she begin to pull, Libby's slight body became limp as though she had not the strength to stand.

"Oh, my, I do feel rather lightheaded," she murmured and folded back into the chair. "Forgive me; I really have not been myself for several weeks," Libby whispered and shrank into her seat. "I just have not been able to eat much and I must admit, am rather tired. I will be all right, please, don't fret about me."

Wanda smiled warmly and bent down by her side, "I don't think that you have anything to worry about, nothing that some tea and rest can't fix," and then she stood up, turned and poured the remaining liquid from the pot for Libby.

The tea was still warm and sweetened to perfection. "You are so kind, thank you. I really don't know what has come over me," Libby explained. She sipped the tea as though she were a sparrow and handed the cup and saucer back to Wanda.

"Is that all?" Wanda asked looking into a half-full cup and set it back on the tray. Then she took her tiny hand and placed it in her two. "You have such a delicate and soft hand," the woman affirmed and turned it so that the palm faced upward. "I do believe that I have never seen such a lovely shape. Hmmm," the woman continued to run her fingers along the outline of the small palm. "Yes, you have the characteristics of grace and delicacy. Look here!" Wanda exclaimed with greater interest. "Your hand is shaped like an almond, wider and round at the base and narrower up towards your fingers." She glided her own fingers up the side of the small hand and moved them to the tip of the index finger. "Your skin is pale in color and these lines are shallow," she explained tracing the thin creases. She picked the hand up towards her eyes and stared into the small palm with more interest than before.

"What do you mean?" asked Libby, now curiously wishing to examine her own hands. "Why do you have that worried look? Did you see something in my palm?" she wondered closing her hand as if to protect it from any bad luck.

Wanda laughed freely, "Worried, oh heavens, do I look worried? Don't be ridiculous!" she remarked. "I have a hobby of sorts. You see, my grandmother was originally from Eastern Europe, and was said to be born of gypsy blood. As a result I have been dabbling in the art of fortune telling, you know, reading palms and tea leaves. I would love to read your palm some time," she offered. Wanda hoped that she had not frightened the girl. Often times the word "gypsy" sent folks fleeing; for just the mention would conjure up horrid images of haggard women stealing children and infants from the arms of their dear mothers.

"That would be rather different, to have my palm read," agreed Libby, "I don't believe that I have ever known anyone who could read the future." The delicate young woman rose from her chair, when suddenly she was overcome by a woozy feeling. She gripped the side and held on to it for a moment before standing without assistance.

"Well, I don't need to read any palms to see that you aren't quite right," cried Wanda who now grasped Libby's shoulder.

"Perhaps I should go downstairs. I suppose I could do with a bit of rest before Will arrives home. I so don't want to have him see me in this state," she murmured in a worried tone. She placed her hand into her pocket and clenched the troubling letter that was waiting for her. Wanda released her shoulder and without taking her eye from the concerned woman watched her slowly advance from the room.

"I'll be right behind you, dear," Wanda said and shut the little sewing room door. Slowly, they walked single file down the narrow and darkening stairwell to the second floor landing.

———

Libby lay upon the bed while Wanda, having insisted that she should remain until the young woman was asleep, sat by her side. She gleaned from their casual conversation that neither Will nor Libby had family in the United States and like many others from Europe assumed that their voyage across the Atlantic was directed towards finding better opportunity. Libby had not divulged their true reason for leaving England and reiterated that they were most grateful to Mrs. Cambridge for her kindness as well as wanting to please her, as she felt obliged for giving them both work. The letter that she received was not mentioned by either woman.

Wanda lit the whale-oil lamp that was sitting upon the small dressing table. It was a particularly elegant lamp and since it was rather expensive to fuel, for whale-oil was quite dear, she felt it was too rich for this grim little room and speculated that it must have been procured with some history attached to it. Perhaps it yearned to tell of the long and hard struggles of crews lost at sea and gale force winds blowing ships through the Indian Ocean. However, it sat without stirring its secrets, the font pear-shaped and the base richly etched like a waterfall held a globe that was throwing brilliant illuminate upon the slumbered. Wanda hastened to lower the wick as not to wake Libby, who had finally drifted off like a docile sleeping princess.

Wanda, her guardian angel, glanced about the room. There was not much more she could do for the girl. She pulled the stool away from the bed and stood by the door before opening it. It was peacefully quiet and only Libby inhaling and exhaling like a baby breathing challenged the silence. "I wonder what it would be like to be so young and fair again?" thought the singer, although she herself was not more than ten years her elder. She began to reminisce about her younger days, how she was forced to leave home and find a job; how she remained alone for so many years, as early as the impressionable age of thirteen, and how it was the company of her audiences that gave her the feeling of belonging to a very large family. Wanda clutched the knob and began to twist it when at the very same time the knob rotated in her palm. Startled, Wanda let go and as she stepped back the door opened revealing a young man, who she assumed was Will.

"Is everything all right?" were the first words spoken.

Will was clearly upset upon seeing a stranger, and he shoved the door open just wide enough to slide past Wanda, who was still standing next to the portal. Somewhat confused, he turned back towards the unknown intruder, searching for an explanation, but her expression did not deem worry for she smiled and said softly, "Shhhh, Mr. Piccard, she is just very tired. You don't want to awaken her. Come out here," she whispered and beckoned to him with her finger. "Let me speak to you in the hallway so we do not disturb her."

Ignoring the request, Will advanced to the side of the bed and lightly touched his wife's warm hand. Upon reassuring himself that Libby was indeed only asleep and not labored in any form or manner, he turned and walked out, leaving the door ajar. "What is going on?" he demanded. Dirty, tired, and agitated by this intrusion, he clenched his palms into tight fists. The impatience for an explanation fueled his distrust.

"Of course you must think the worst. I mean finding a stranger in your room and your dear wife fast asleep even before supper. Actually, I am not a true stranger. I am Wanda, Wanda Bourdette," she said calmly, hoping to ease any doubts in the young man's mind.

Will rummaged through his recollections of recent acquaintances, but the name was not familiar to him. "I am sorry Miss Bourdette, I am still not clear."

"I am the night owl, the permanent boarder, if you will, down the hall?" she wondered if the hints would help. "The singer?" she finally said laughing.

It appeared that the word "singer" did stir his memory. "Oh yes, Miss Bourdette," he repeated her name as though they had known one another for years. "Please explain, what is going on? When I left for work Libby was fine and now I have returned to find you in our room and Libby asleep. I hope she has not fallen ill!"

"Please, put your mind at ease," Wanda suggested in hushed voice. "There is no concern; nothing a little rest won't cure. I was in the sewing room earlier this afternoon to ask Libby if she would kindly do a little mending for me. Of course I will pay her," the singer added for she did not want to appear taking advantage of her good will. "Anyway," Wanda continued, "we talked for a short while when, for what seemed to be no obvious reason to me, she became faint. So, naturally I insisted that she come downstairs for a rest. She had just fallen off to sleep when you arrived home to find me here."

Upon hearing these words Will became less tense; his fists loosened, his arched shoulders flattened, and his furrowed brow relaxed. "Thank you for looking after Libby," he sighed with relief. "She is so delicate; I often worry about her. The smallest amount of stress can be very unhealthy."

"Well then," Wanda added, "see if you can get her to eat. For she needs her nourishment now even more."

"Even more?" he questioned not understanding the significance of her statement.

"Oh, my dear, you don't know!' exclaimed the enthused woman. "Then let me be the first to congratulate. Mr. Piccard," she announced as though he were a contest winner, "you are going to be a father!"

———

"A mother!" gasped the old woman

"That's right, Libby is expecting a baby," trumpeted Katrina. She poured the old woman a glass of port and at the same time looked for any shift in expression from her employer.

Mrs. Cambridge took a long calculated pause after her initially shocked reaction to Katrina's announcement and proceeded to take a sip from her glass. Then, in her usual controlled manner, for she wished not to display any more displeasure, she turned her gasp into a sigh of happy surprise. "A baby! Why Libby is merely a child herself. Well, we will have Doctor Bruner come by, we can't let anything happen to our new boarder, can we?" purred Mrs. Cambridge grinning, and she sipped her evening port with great relish. "That will be all, Katrina," she added and dismissed the maid with a wave of her gnarled hand.

The old woman stared into her glass and sat brooding for several minutes. "Why this does change everything!" she thought, rehashing the message in her mind. "What I don't need is a sick girl and a crying infant! But, it won't be my problem for long," she grumbled and set her glass down upon the wooden table beside her.

"What's that about a problem?" asked Nick, entering the parlor. "Don't tell me a woman with your influence and money could have a problem," he laughed, bending over and placing a kiss upon the ancient's head.

"If I have a problem it would be you, Nick Biddle!" she scolded. "What are you doing sneaking about? I thought you'd be off getting into no good with your new friend."

"Don't change the subject," he provoked. "Did I hear you say trouble?" he repeated, now sure that the elder was avoiding his question.

"It's none of your concern, but," she exclaimed, "if you must know, Libby Piccard is with child," touted the elder.

"Why, that is some news!" exclaimed Nick appraising the announcement over in his mind. "Why, this calls for a celebration drink!" and with great liveliness he swooped up the bottle of port and cradled it in his arms like it was an infant. "Let me call those two down, and we can toast to their good fortune."

No sooner did he proclaim this idea when he was interrupted by a gentle rap on the open door by Katrina. "I beg your pardon Mrs. Cambridge, but a note has been delivered to you by messenger," she announced.

"Ah, Katrina, my lovely Katrina, come and join the party!" and mimicking a ballroom dancer, Nick waltzed over to the large woman and escorted her before the elder.

"Who is it from, Katrina?" asked the old woman reaching for the message.

However, before it could be delivered, Nick intercepted the note, gamboled forward, and began to parade about the room only to create much confusion. All was in disarray as Mrs. Cambridge cackled over and over; "Give it to me!" while simultaneously stomping her cane upon the floor with loud thuds. Katrina, who found Nick's antics to be hilarious, was greatly amused, and laughed with such gusto that tears rolled down her pink cheeks. Naturally this encouraged Nick's buffoonery even more, which he displayed by leaping over the small ottoman, executing a most graceful pirouette, and gallivanting about, but just as he was about to commence around the room again, he was immediately halted by Mrs. Cambridge who managed to strike Nick with her cane and induced a mighty blow at the very moment he sallied by her chair.

"Ouch, what did ya do that for?" he screamed, setting the bottle down upon the floor to nurse his shin.

"Behave yourself, boy," the ancient snarled, shaking her cane at him in a menacing way. "Now, unless you want this across your skull, hand me that note and be off with ya!" and she snatched the paper from his loosened grip like a hungry piranha. Katrina stepped back out of view and desperately tried to choke back her laughter. Finding her composure, she wiped her wet face with the hem of her gingham apron and waited by the door to see what would happen next.

Like a wounded puppy, Nick managed to stand up and set the port back on the table. He was still amazed by the great force produced by this seemingly frail woman. His leg throbbed from the strike and he could feel through his trousers the enormous knot that was growing upon his shin. "I don't suppose you'd have room in your heart to make a man feel better, would ya, Katrina?" Nick whimpered as he limped towards her. Then giving her a wink, he waited for her sympathy.

"Come along with me, Nick, I'm sure we can find something. How about a nice cup of scalding coffee?" she asked and headed out the room.

"Coffee, oh Katrina!" he moaned favoring his hurt leg as he followed her, "I was thinking of something a bit more exciting!"

Mrs. Cambridge listened as the two walked towards the kitchen; with her wolf-like keenness she tracked their footsteps until they were out of range, and she could no longer hear Nick complaining.

Her gnarled fingers fumbled as she loosened the paper away from the sticky seal and unfolded the note. It simply read, "Ship delayed at port of departure due to major mechanical problems, J. Philander." She crumpled the note in her hands and pulled herself up to a standing position. Supported by the cane, she slowly trundled across the room to the fireplace and tossed the balled paper into the hearth. Leaning against the mantle with one hand, she positioned her cane and jammed the paper into the soot, burying it in the dry burned remains. Tiny black and grey flakes sprinkled about while the dislodged ash settled upon the cinders of broken tree branches. She shook the cane allowing any slag that adhered to fall loose and once again stomped it upon the floor, which she often had a propensity to do. Then stooping over the cane, she braced herself and sorely hobbled away.

Chapter 32

"Its 'bout time you learned to use this!" Randle announced, while he displayed the rifle triumphantly. The gun was placed before the child with an obvious implication that it was his to take. Reluctantly, Alex took the outstretched weapon in his hands and braced it against his chest, twisting and then cradling it with bent elbows. It was awkward and heavier than he expected, and he looked down upon at it with enormous trepidation.

"Now Mr. Forester, no good can come from this. What is done is done, but to imply that a rifle could have prevented this unfortunate incident from occurring is really…" Miss Henshaw stopped and paused before speaking again. "What I am trying to say is that no good can come from promoting the prevention of violence with violence. And giving Alex a gun certainly is not an answer."

Randle pushed Alex aside and stepped forward, leering at the schoolteacher. He licked his dry lips and ran his fingers across his unshaven chin. "Mrs. Forester and me, why we appreciate that you were around to bring Alex home safe and sound. No tellin' what would have become of him if ya hadn't. But now, I think you aughta' mind yer own business. What I'm tryin' to tell you is to stick to readin', writin', and teachin'." Randle pulled Alex in front of him and put his hand upon the wavering shoulders as he began to address both the boy and the teacher. "It's time Alex became a man. I think Mrs. Forester's been babying him too long; now it's time for me to take over."

"Well, I still think that maybe you ought to think it over; he has had a very trying day, Mr. Forester," said Miss Henshaw trying to appeal to any sympathetic feelings he may feel towards Alex. Nevertheless, it became clearly apparent that he was immune to this characteristic, for without any more discussion Randle ushered Alex inside the house and following behind shut the open door, leaving Miss Henshaw disheartened and alone.

Alex stood in the middle of the room burdened with his load and yearning to set it down however, he was unsure of what he was supposed to do. He had often seen Randle take the weapon down off the wall or leave it in the corner of the kitchen before it was to be cleaned. "This squirrel rifle ain't perty, but it can sure shoot!" Randle would repeat whenever he came back from hunting. Alex cringed at the thought of shooting a furry little animal with a bushy tail.

"Bring it on over here, Alex," Randle said pointing to the dining table. Still cradling the firearm, he did as he was told and lifted it onto the table. "This gun has been in our house and my father's house when I was not much older than you. Now I remember bringin' home my first possum with this very gun restin' across my shoulder and the possum strapped to my belt. You never have takin' an interest in huntin', have ya boy?"

Alex looked up at the questioning eyes of the man he was supposed to call his father and wondered why he was asking him such a question when he knew what the answer was.

Randle shook his head with disgust. "Well, it's time just you and me go and git ourselves a critter. It's spring and all kinds of new animals are out there in the wilderness for you." He pulled a shammy from his pocket and began to polish the barrel of the rifle. He kept one eye on Alex waiting for some sort of response. Neither the adult nor the boy spoke. A dull silence lingered like stale air. Alex watched Randle and wondered to himself why anyone would bother trying to shine such a rusted looking old gun. Randle spat on the cloth a few times and continued to polish.

The disgusted man threw a glance over towards the boy who stood wide-eyed before him. Surely, he thought, the boy would soon mature and like he had, and his father, and his father's father, and generations of men before, would someday develop that innate desire to control and possess power that is characteristic of all men. Randle put the cloth down and extended the gun out towards Alex. If the boy accepted it, his resolve was firm, if he didn't...

Alex saw the gun move closer towards him as Randle stood up waiting for the child to reach forward and accept it. He looked at the weapon curiously as it was now lying recumbent in Randle's hands. It didn't look very shiny, and he didn't really know what he was going to do with it once he was stuck holding it again. Alex looked away and down at the floor. A very stealth Timothy had quietly entered the kitchen and began to walk back and forth, rubbing his fat body against his leg. The cat meowed loudly wishing to acknowledge his presence. "Timothy, what's ya got there?" Alex asked bending down to stroke the large feline. "Do ya want to go out?" The cat continued to meow with more vigor as though understanding every word. "Come on then," the boy whispered and picking up the large cat, it comfortably draped itself over his arm. Alex walked slowly towards the door, continuing to speak softly to the cat, who was now quite content.

But no sooner did he have his hand on the latch when the room began to tremble with Randle's great bellow! "You are the most exasperating boy I have ever met!" Then with a great fury he sprang to his feet and kicked the wooden bench that the child had been sitting on. Alex turned with a start as the bench violently fell upon the floor with such a ruckus that Timothy leapt out of his arms and scurried back into the kitchen and squeezed behind the butter churn that was resting in the corner.

There was a wild fury in Randle's eyes that Alex had never witnessed. The gun was now straddling his side; his anxious fingers gripped the butt of the rifle with angry intensity. "Git over here, you useless good fer nothin' orphan!" Randle roared in a voice that seemed to have protruded from the back of his throat. Alex's hand appeared to be stuck to the latch, and although he wanted to let go, he dared not for the only thing that supported his legs was the fact that he was now propped up against the door. "I said," repeated

Randle with a low growl, "to git over here!" Alex's fingers trembled as he fumbled with the latch; his eyes were now fixed upon the rifle that had been raised perpendicular against the marksman's waist. Randle took a step forward, his face tensed as he appeared to move his jaw back and forth, grinding his teeth. He kept the gun stationary, firmly planted and pointing towards the direction of the door. "Alex, git over here," he repeated stepping forward again.

Alex tried to mentally measure the distance between himself and Randle. He knew that if the door had been even slightly open he would be able to escape, but could he pull the latch without generating any noise? Never, the old latch had not been oiled since last summer and there was a terminal squeak. Randle stepped forward again, his mouth moving back and forth. The gun had been pulled forward as though leading the man. Alex turned his face and pressed it against door, no longer willing to face Randle. He squeezed his eyes shut and held his body up against the door. When suddenly from the back of the room he heard a shrill cry, "What are you doing?"

The frightened child spun around just in time to see the man who he was to call his father now facing the opposing side of the room. The butt of the gun was pressed firmly against the shooter's right shoulder, fingers were hooked holding the handgrip of the stock, and while his left hand secured the position steadying the rifle, he gently leaned forward taking aim.

It is curious how the human body can store within itself, like a vessel that holds water, anxiety, disappointment, turmoil, and distress. But just as the vessel of water, the human, both man or woman can hold in just so much before it too overflows.

The pad of Randle's index finger effortlessly kissed the trigger and then in a split second, like an overfilled water vessel, he exploded. The barrel of the gun flung upward showering forth a plume of black smoke. A deafening blast shook the room in tandem with a desperate plea of "NO!", which silenced it. Randle lowered the gun and stepped away, revealing to Alex the shattered body of a furry animal.

"How could you?" screamed Betty. "How could you kill that poor animal?"

Alex stood frozen, motionless in the far corner of the room staring first at Betty and then back at the floor where the animal now lay dead in its own puddle of blood. He closed his eyes and quickly turned away, hoping that he would be able to erase the hideous image. "Timothy," he thought, "is he really dead?" Frightened and confused, Alex turned back round wishing to revive the dead animal back to life when he was confronted by his elder.

"See why ya need a rifle?" Randle's gruff voice rang out loudly. The squirrel gun had shifted position and now lay upright against his shoulder as if it were an innocent baby. "Ya know boy, practice makes ya git one every time," he whispered. Alex looked up sheepishly hoping that perhaps Randle's expression might give him a sign that he did not truly blame him for the killing. However, only a determined look of anger could be interpreted.

Betty now sat quietly at her usual spot drumming her fingers upon the table and then, in her customary demeanor, went about her business as though nothing out of the ordinary had ever happened. She removed the basket of rags from the corner and began pulling several from the bin and waved them about needlessly, attempting to free them from wrinkles.

"Betty," Randle said calling to his wife, "Alex is gonna clean up the mess, just let the rags be."

Making no objections, she tossed the cloth back into the basket and shoved it away with her foot. She glanced woefully at the dead animal on the floor and then upon the child, whose duty it was to remove the bloody carcass. "If ya need me, I'll be out huskin' the corn," she declared and tidying her apron, left the two alone.

Alex felt a lump in his throat. He knew that he couldn't cry, he knew that he could never show anyone how much he hurt.

"Go on Alex, carry it out of here and bury it real deep. We don't want no coyote comin' round and unearthin' it. Bein' that its fresh meat no telling what might be attracted." Randle had stepped aside as he spoke and waved the rifle over the dead animal like a magician's wand. Then he turned, balanced the gun against the wall in the corner of the kitchen and walked away.

The pool of blood had grown larger in diameter as the thirsty wooden planks greedily soaked up the liquid. Alex gingerly made his way towards the body. The smell of gunfire was still fresh in his nostrils. "Timothy," he whispered walking cautiously towards the dead animal. "Timothy, I wish you hadn't been in here." Alex could hardly recognize the mangled body. Slowly he held his hand out, as if to touch the cat he was prepared to pick up and carry to a final resting place. With measured prudence, he bent down ready to accept his little friend as never coming back; for it lay so still, so quiet, so final. Alex leaned forward about to stroke its fur when suddenly amongst the mauled body he was able to find a most curious yellow head attached to a long pink nose. He looked at the opposite end and noticed a tail; except this tail was not long and furry, but rather hairless and scaly. Could it be? Was it possible?

"Alex, didn't Randle tell ya to git rid of this opossum?" scolded Betty as she entered the kitchen. The sight of him still pondering the dead animal caused her to raise her voice. "How am I gonna put on a kettle with that thing in the middle of the room?"

Chapter 33

"I guess I just gotta learn to shoot the rifle," Alex bemoaned. Delilah flicked her ears attentively as if to agree. He slid the stiff brush around her neck in a circular motion using short, smooth strokes, releasing a sprinkle of dirt flecks that had clung to her chestnut coat. "You're a fine girl," Alex said, and after several more broad sweeps, he picked the brush clean of debris and started again. Dandy craned her neck over the stall's short partition and nudged Alex with her long nose. "You're a good girl too, Dandy," and placing his check against her soft muzzle he stroked it ever so lovingly. "Ya know I don't want to shoot. I don't like nothin' about guns." Dandy pushed against Alex. "I knew you two would understand." His laconic confession revealed his simple rationale, which needed no explanation or pretext. He continued to contemplate this notion as he brushed Delilah; round and round he gently massaged the animal. Delilah shifted her feet and flicked her tail. Alex dropped the brush to his feet and rested his head against the equine's girth. "Do ya think that I might be a boy on the outside and a horse in the inside?" he whispered. His lids fell heavy and without any effort they folded shut as his body sank against the large animal. "Ya hear that too, Delilah?" he asked in a hush. The quiet and peace of the stable melted together, and he listened motionless as two hearts beat as one. "If only this moment would not pass, if only I could stay here always." He opened his eyes and squinted up into the dark rafters. Instantly, a pair of dark eyes fell upon his. "Do ya see them, Delilah?" he asked quizzically. But as fleeting as a blink, they shyly vanished. "I don't think it was a hoot owl, it's too early for them to be up," the boy remarked with a measure of logical interpretation.

Alex dug his hand into his pocket and retrieved the gold trinket that he liked to carry with him. He brushed one side then the other against his pants and holding it up to the light found that it now seemed to shine a little more brightly. However, when he flipped it over there appeared to be a spot that he hadn't noticed before. "Why look at this, Dandy," he exclaimed speaking to the horse, which also seemed to be taking an interest in what was going on, for she was attentively watching her young master. After a second examination, he buffed it more vigorously against his pants. Alex laid it flat against his palm and brought it up closer to his eye. It was now clear to him that there was perhaps an engraving hidden beneath the dull surface. "See that, it looks like some writin'," he observed and smoothed the area with his thumb. Once again he made another attempt to free the hidden message by polishing it more forcefully, this time against his sleeve. Finding that this method was not working, he scanned the stable for a new plan and found that his opportunity lay at his feet, the brush. Now placing the small disc between his thumb and index finger, he secured it by steadying against the stable railing while brushing with his free hand. Yet no matter how carefully he tried, his efforts went horribly amiss. Several times the disc slipped out of his fingers and more than three times he managed to embed the hard bristles into his thumb. As a result, he ended up with torn skin. "It ain't no use tryin' to see what's on this today," Alex confessed to Delilah and after wiping his bloody fingers on his pants, he slipped the trinket back into his pocket.

"Bring in the eggs, Alex!" Betty shouted as she passed the open barn door, toting a bucket of water. The overfilled vessel splashed water onto the ground each time it hit her ankle as she walked. Heavy breathing and profane grumbling accompanied her awkward stride, for although she was careful with her words, physically heavy chores often brought out exclamations that were considered swearing and occasionally blasphemous in any company.

The irritated tone made Alex quickly scramble about the stable hanging tack and filling troughs with fresh water and feed for the two drafts. "I put a little extra mash in the feed," he whispered to them and then set straightaway to gather the eggs before it grew too dark to see. Now, some would say that chickens, hens, and pullets are the dumbest of all creatures on a farm however; it is possible that Yazhi was the exception. Although she was a full-grown hen her temperament hadn't changed, and she always greeted Alex with a lively cackle, flying from her roost to meet him. No longer was she afraid of the other hens since she had earned the favor of Betty who would now gladly teach each of the barnyard fowl a lesson by flailing the broom high above her head and walloping the very tail feathers of any culprit who messed with her "double yoke laying hen".

The basket Alex routinely used to gather eggs normally dangled from the same low hook, but today he found it clear across the barnyard. Not thinking much about its new location, he simply suspected that perhaps it had been tossed by a gust of wind. He bent down to grab the basket and noticed that a clump of downy feathers had settled beside it and now with each stride several more feathers were lightly tossed about. As if having invented a new game, he would walk, stop abruptly, and watch as more plumes scattered before him, some even settling upon the tips of his boots along with the powder of dry hay and earth. He was not aware of any of the birds molting so he became rather curious as to the source of the feather outbreak. The first time Alex saw a chicken molting he was sure that the animal was in dire straits. "Betty, Betty, come quick, why one of the hens is dyin'!" When Betty finally got to the yard, for she was always too busy to come promptly, Alex had confined the hen in the far corner of the barn. By this time the bird was so mad that it was simultaneously squawking and running about in circles. Her head was bald and pink, on account that her head feathers had fallen out, and looked rather pitiful.

"How'd ya git her in here?" asked Betty stooping down at the mini corral he had assembled by stacking two crates, one on top of the other. "You sure got her real cranky. And can ya blame her?"

Alex looked at the squawking bird who was trying to stick its head out of the uneven slots. Betty lifted the crate that was positioned like a roof and began to laugh with great hilarity for the bird continued to run about the enclosure, never once looking up and realizing that it was free to escape. "Well, I just grabbed her up when she wasn't lookin', but she sure is mean; all I want to do is make her better. Do ya think she'll live?" asked a most concerned Alex.

"Live, why she'll be around a long time, that is until company is comin'!" Betty had stated and pulled the bird out from its confinement. As soon as it felt its legs settle back on the ground it took off towards the light that was streaming into the barn. "Now what's all this fuss 'bout a sick bird?' Why it's moltin'."

That was the moment that he learned about molting. But today's situation was not founded in the same theory, and an explanation about these feathers may not illuminate as favorable an interpretation. There was no easy trail to follow for the downy tufts that now curled upon the ground, though growing in number, lay helter-skelter. Alex picked up several and dropped them into the egg basket. It was apparent that the assortment he assembled was not lost from the same chicken, but rather two or more different birds.

The natural light was struggling in the hour of the day soliciting a feeling of doom. Alex stepped with cat-like tread as he headed towards the usual roosts. His basket did not yield a single egg, and though that was his primary mission, he wished to sift their perches in order to find the answer to the unruly amount of loose feathers that he had gathered. Like a kettle on the verge of boiling, an uneasy feeling was brewing and as much as the boy tried to shake the idea that something was wrong, it was apparent something was definitely amiss.

He dropped the basket at the entrance of the woodshed, a favored roosting location; dry, open, and high enough to be what the hens thought of as 'safe'. "Yazhi, here girl, I've come for yer eggs," he called. But after a quiet moment he called her name again, this time louder. "Yazhi!" Alex opened the small door wider hoping the waning light would miraculously illuminate the dark shed. He peered inside the small entranceway and listened. Intermittent noises were at first interpreted as a hen's cackle, but he thought better of it when he realized the source emanated from several bats retreating from the hayloft in search of their evening meal.

"Yazhi!" he shouted more boldly, hoping to resolve her disappearance. Alex painfully watched and listened, but did not have to wait long for suddenly thrust upon his shoulder a coarse hand grabbed him from behind. Startled, Alex frantically tried to pull away, but the hand had struck like a rattler and was now covering his mouth. "Shhhhh, step back slowly and don't say nothing," he heard a gruff voice whisper into his ear. Then he felt the hand drop away. Instinctively, Alex obeyed. Ever so slowly the frightened boy turned around, and although only about a yard from the voice, his eyes had difficulty trying to adjust in the dimming shadows. There before him he could make out a ghoulish figure of a hunched man. "Git on back to the house, Alex!" he whispered harshly. Alex crept back behind him, but for some unknown reason did not leave; rather he crouched down like a baby lion that watches and waits for the male.

So, there they were, man and boy becoming obscure in the faltering light. Alex observed intently as Randle remained motionless, and he wondered how the older man could stand so still for so long, and he wondered what it was that made him bring the rifle. The vigilant boy shifted position and now leaned on the opposing knee; while he saw Randle stretch his arm out, prop the squirrel gun against the shed, and bend down to retie a lace. Now, no one can be sure of the reason, perhaps coincidentally at that exact split second, a sudden shift in the wind propelled the scent of the man into the shed, or maybe it was the light tap of the gun resting against the wooden shed. Regardless of the cause, for one could continually speculate, a most unlucky and horrific combination of events were united. No sooner had Randle become off guard, did the bleakness of the evening come alive with a ferocious howl. An avalanche of wood came tumbling forward like water escaping from a broken levee. Breaking free from its hiding place in the back of the shed, a grey wolf charged forward and sprung upon Randle like a murderous demon. Instantly, the wolf lunged for his throat, tossing the man off balance and waging his full weight upon him. Alex watched for a second and saw Randle struggling in vain to pull the wolf from his body, and although his scream of agony was tumultuous, his cry was muffled by the incessant growling of the ferocious animal.

It was almost impossible to see man and beast in the dim light for only the stars that dared come out lit up the confused and chaotic scene. Then, suddenly and without warning, there sounded a loud crack so keen that it resonated throughout the land for miles. Randle, who now breathed laboriously and was soaked in blood, rolled the dead wolf from off his wounded body. Alex stood motionless before man and wolf, the gun by his side still smoking from the shot he fired.

———

When the spirit of the man is broken he can convalesce, but to surrender the spirit of the horse, there is no return. Having been covered by months of heavy snow, the frozen ground was finally thawing; only to expose the yellow sprigs of dry grass that had lain dormant beneath an icy glaze. Winter submitted to the overtures of spring and on a frosty cool March day, Pinto Jack and Cally emerged into the streets of St. Joseph like bears coming out of hibernation. Though his heart was burdened by disappointment, it had finally reconciled with his head and the disillusionment of becoming a Pony Express rider had dissipated along with the winter.

"Sure ya want to leave?" Big Pete asked Jack as he led Cally out through the double stable doors. They creaked and groaned as they were pushed open from months of disuse. "Folks tired of beein' cooped up are now talkin' like we're in fer action round here, grumblin' of war brewin', new comers headin' west. Well, there's no account of what jobs ya can git. We still need yer help with them books." Big Pete handed the reins to Jack and stroked the pinto on her long silky nose. Cally acknowledged the affection by rubbing against his large hand like a dog soliciting attention.

"No, it's time that Cally and I move along. Now that Mr. Hendricks is able to get back on his feet and return to his job, you don't need another bookkeeper. I was just glad to have been able to help out. We sure appreciate you lettin' us stay on during winter," replied Jack.

"Well, I reckon havin' you here instead of leavin' Cally behind was good fer us, too. But, are ya sure you don't want to sell her?" he teased knowing full well that a man who had forsaken his dream would never substitute it for a few dollars.

"Hey kid, don't forget this!" Both Pete and Pinto Jack turned round to see Mitch heading towards them. He was waving a quilt and as he got closer to Jack, he rolled it up into a ball and tossed it to him. "I think this belongs to you!"

Jack tried to catch the blanket as it began to unfold in mid-air, but the throw was overshot and Pete, having a much larger arm length and range, caught it as it began to fall overhead. "Where'd ya git this from?" he asked displaying the coverlet like a matador. "It's too soft for a cowboy, even one who is a bookkeeper," he said and trying to provoke a rile he shook it about as though dogging an imaginary bull.

A sense of embarrassment was distinctly dominant as Pinto Jack's face grew noticeably flush. He thought that all his belongings, as few as they were, had been stowed in his saddlebag. Evidently, he had forgotten Cally's blanket; and as grateful as he was for having it returned, he wished it had never been revealed. Actually, he had never used or unfolded the blanket and had only removed it from his saddlebag when he was repacking.

"I must have left it out by mistake," Jack said and began to reach for it.

"Not so fast cowboy, this is one purty blanket!" laughed Mitch, joining the two. "Where'd ya git it? Looks like it was made with a lot of fancy care," Mitch snickered as he snatched the quilt off Pete who was now wearing it like a cape.

The large man stretched the blanket open and held it up in front of him. He fluttered it about and then held it up to his face as though he had taken more of an interest. "Why look, there's a name that's been sewn into the design? Clever, real clever," he admitted, pointing out several letters embedded in the material. Handing it back to the owner, Jack continued to reexamine the blanket by turning it over and following the pattern with his index finger like a miner who sifts through dirt while panning for gold. Sure enough, he was able to find another name that had been judiciously constructed to wittingly blend in with the design. It was evident that the creator of this quilt had spent an abundance of time concealing these names so that they would be perceived as simply part of the pattern. Jack folded the quilt into a smaller bundle and patted the fine needlework gently with more reverence. Just as he had thought before, whoever made this had taken extraordinary care. He rolled it up into a narrow spool and turning towards the saddlebag that lay strapped across Cally's back, he lifted the leather flap open and pushed the blanket down into the large pocket.

"Ya never said where ya got that purty blanket," demanded Pete continuing to enjoy his teasing.

"A kid gave it to Cally," Jack answered. He pulled down on his saddle's cinch making sure it was secured and then continued. "He took a special liking to her right before I left for St. Joseph." Jack cleared his throat after this explanation hoping that both men understood that the gift was not intended for his personal use. However, neither of the men offered a reply which Jack took as them becoming disinterested in the entire conversation.

"So, yer really headin' out," Pete confirmed. "I guess we can't convince you to stay round."

Jack slipped his boot into the stirrup and gripping the saddle horn, raised himself up. How many hundreds of times had he methodically performed this same motion? Countless, he supposed. Beyond understanding he knew this mount was different, not routine or perfunctory, but more deliberate and calculated as if one is about to set out on an urgent mission. He leaned forward in the saddle and slipped the reins into his palm before pulling his hat brim over his eyes in anticipation of a long sunny day. "No, as much as I appreciate all your hospitality, it's time to go," Jack echoed back.

The city of St. Joseph lay before him, the crossroads between East and West. His destiny would be determined by a simple tug in either direction of the reins; and with his pockets holding an entire winter's earnings there was nothing to stop him from selecting the more audacious and adventurous trail. But unlike the spring that inspires the spirit towards freedom and mirth, Pinto Jack's humor was dampened by uncertainty and curiosity. He looked out at the city before him and contemplated which trail to take. Less than an hour ago he was carefree, his choice was as simple as flipping a coin. However, now he found himself indecisive, a feeling that he was not accustomed to, a feeling he did not like. He was a loner and was used to making spontaneous decisions whereby only he would be affected. But suddenly he had inherited a nagging uncertainty that lay heavily upon him. As much as he would like to dismiss his intuition, he was going to have to confront the questions that were foremost on his mind. Could the names threaded throughout the blanket possibly reveal an undiscovered secret or should he let fate take its course?

"Where' ya goin to?" asked Mitch. "After all, we are the Pony Express and maybe you'll need something sent to ya." Jack pulled his hat down again, a habit that he had acquired while trying to block the noon sun. All along he just figured that he'd head west, the direction of opportunity. But now, he wasn't sure if he could be making too much out of a bunch of names.

"Split Rock Station could use a good man," Mitch added while trying to loosen a morsel of fat gristle stuck between his back molars. The more he poked at it with a piece of dry straw the more lodged it became.

"Where exactly did ya say Split Rock was?" Jack asked with renewed interest and leaned over in his saddle.

"I didn't!" the man snapped back in an impatient tone, which may have been instigated by the annoyance of day-old food under his tooth. "Western territory," he answered, "somewhere between Cranner Rock and the south bank of the Sweetwater River. It's rough country, but if you're willin' to take it on, I know that you'd be an honest worker." Mitch paused as though contemplating his hand in a poker game. He continued to fiddle with the tooth until like a hunter that had just speared his meal, he exclaimed, "Gottch ya!" and with much gusto he spit the small wad of dry fat onto the ground. "So, what do ya say?" he asked before sticking his finger into his mouth to massage his gum.

Now, when one thinks of spring one tends to remind themselves of longer hours of sunlight, streams swelling with runoff, blooming flowers, and buds on the trees. The air is cool, no longer burning the insides of the nostrils with the frigid cold. Cally shifted her feet restlessly waiting for a command and took several steps into the outdoors. Jack glanced about what had been his home for several months. Pete had already said his good-byes and was nowhere in sight. Most likely he was already shoeing a horse or pulling out the rotten wood from a stall. Mitch had made him an offer and was waiting for his reply. There was actually nothing to prevent him from moving forward, nothing really at all. A lively wind sent a bramble, devoid of any foliage, brittle and spindly, blowing across the road. Could this stray be a leftover from the summer before? Jack watched as the dry branch was picked up again by the next gust of wind and then land farther along the road. It was too light to be neglected and therefore destined to forever toss and travel with each burst of wind until one day; just perhaps; it becomes tangled amongst other brambles and grows too heavy to move easily with the breeze. He looked until he could no longer make out the long thin shape of the wood for its bleached color blended in with the beige landscape of the earth.

Mitch followed them out to the street and shaded his eyes with his hand even though he was wearing a hat. Jack leaned over and called out to his friend that he had made his decision, "Let them know we're comin, Mitch, let'em know we're heading west."

Chapter 34

Time passes at the same rate-of-speed from moment to moment no matter what hour of day or where you may be, however, depending upon the situation or circumstance, the perceived degree of velocity can fluctuate. Take for example the seven months that Libby has been with child. Some would say that time was passing quickly, while others would view it as dragging by rather slowly. Yet regardless of the idle chatter and empty prattle that fluttered about the Cambridge Arms, Libby never complained either way and made every effort to compose herself with the same cheerfulness as a bright sunny morning after a rainstorm.

Every day except Sunday the young mother-to-be spent her daylight hours in the little sewing room; for Mrs. Cambridge made sure there was plenty of work to be completed. Then, when evening drew near and the dinner plates were cleared, she spent her time in the parlor stitching the quilt that she had started on her voyage from England to America. "I do hope that I can finish this," sighed Libby to Wanda. The "night owl" entertainer was spending this particular Sunday drinking tea with Mrs. Cambridge and Libby.

"By the looks of your work, I don't see how it is a problem?" she replied and then questioned the elder. "What do you think, Mrs. Cambridge?"

Mrs. Cambridge, who usually was rather vocal in most all matters directed to her, seemed significantly indifferent today for there was no reply. In contrast, she was absorbed in the morning paper that lay upon her lap, open to the same page for nearly ten minutes.

"Mrs. Cambridge, Mrs. Cambridge," Wanda set her empty teacup carefully upon a tiny doily that protected the veneer of the wooden table, "is everything all right?" she asked the unusually silent woman.

Libby looked up from her sewing and turned to the ancient one who appeared to be deep in thought. Leaning in towards the elder, she began to fret, "Dear me, we have not been at all attentive to you. Wanda and I have been going on about quilts and the like and never even attending to your needs. Why your cup is empty, too!" Libby, who always put others before herself, set the quilt across the arm of the chair and pulled herself up. However, the enormity of her physique, which appeared to grow exponentially by the day, was exaggerated by the young woman's roly-poly appearance in contrast to her otherwise delicate features, and as she lumbered out of her seat, it was as though she was stuck in mud.

"Sit down, Libby," commanded the elder and lifted her cane as if defending herself. "I don't need a thing, and as for you, Miss Wanda Bourdette," she added turning a sour tongue at the other woman, "I have heard every word out of your mouth." Libby obeyed and with as much effort as it took to get up she sat back down. Wanda, who knew not to take what Mrs. Cambridge said personally, simply shrugged her shoulders. For no matter how acidic the old woman growled, Wanda was always appreciative that she had allowed her to rent a room in the Cambridge Arms when other rooming houses would have banished her from ever stepping foot into their foyers.

Mrs. Cambridge came alive as she pointed to the paper and pressed her index finger against the inky print at the ships' schedule. "You see this," she squawked. "Finally! The Starboard is now one of ours, and she is making her way back from England. We acquired her after a bit of tight negotiations and if there's no trouble, she should reach Baltimore in about two weeks!" By the faraway tone of her voice it was not immediately apparent to either of the younger women if this bit of information was intended for them as part of a conversation that they were supposed to partake in, or if Mrs. Cambridge was merely talking to herself.

Having been brought up with the manners of a saint, Libby felt that she should acknowledge a speaker when spoken to. "Trouble, Mrs. Cambridge, what sort of trouble?" she therefore inquired most innocently.

"The impending war, pirates, typhoons, you name it!" leered the elder. "If this ship arrives safely it will be a miracle!" Neither of the women replied and the silence that followed proved to be louder than any audible response, for Mrs. Cambridge continued to glare at the newspaper and finally, after what seemed to be several awkward minutes, they were thankfully interrupted by Katrina entering the parlor to remove the tea service.

"Katrina, I have a grand idea! What do you think about a dinner party?" Mrs. Cambridge asked, although her remark was more of a declaration than a question.

"A party, what for?" asked the surprised maid. The idea of a party was certainly curious because the Cambridge Arms had lost all its sense of pleasure the day that her son departed.

Ignoring Katrina's question, the elder carried on. "Yes, I believe that we will celebrate the new ship's arrival, in fact, we'll invite the Captain and any guest he chooses. Where is Nick, he always loves a good party? I am sure he will be quite content when he hears the news; unlike the likes of your face," she cried scowling at Katrina.

"Why a party would be lovely, Mrs. Cambridge, certainly I would love to help," said Libby.

"Well, you can count me in, I love a party!" exclaimed Wanda. Her thoughts shifted immediately upstairs to her wardrobe, and she began to envision which gown she might wear. "Unless it's during an evening that I'm working," she muttered and then pouted disapprovingly displaying this notion.

Katrina hadn't moved and continued to glare down at her employer. Her large hands rested on her hips and she cocked her head slightly to the left shaking it back and forth. "Well, I'll believe it when I see it! A party at the Cambridge Arms, just what are you up to anyway?" asked Katrina suspiciously. Knowing she would not get an answer, she picked up the tray with just enough force to allow the cups to clatter into one another and turned away.

But before leaving the room she heard Mrs. Cambridge say, "Let Marthe know that I will need to see her about making up the menu." Whereupon without a response, Katrina simply sauntered out still wary. The sly one never did anything for the simple sake of enjoyment; she always had a motive ulterior to the purpose of its assumed design. Yet Katrina could barely contain her own feeling of excitement at the prospect of a party. It had been a long time since there was any merriment at the Cambridge Arms, a very long time.

———

The negotiations that Mrs. Cambridge had alluded to earlier had been handily transacted by Jack Philander. Will had proved himself a most skillful and industrious worker by heading up a crew of ship's carpenters, his dependability gave way for Nick to move into position of Master Shipwright; the front man, someone who could represent the business honestly and ethically. Besides, years of working in the family business made Nick a valuable asset, for he was trusted by all the workers. The elder needed him to remain unaware of practices that may become for him a moral dilemma. After all, Nick was too honest, too virtuous for his own good.

As for Mrs. Cambridge, she understood that the United States was on the precipice of change and in her typical style, she needed to be in a financial position to take advantage of any situation. During the War of 1812, just off the shores of Boston Harbor, Captain James Lawrence was mortally wounded by British enemy while commanding his frigate the USS Chesapeake. And now, over three and a half decades later, his famous cry of, "Don't give up the ship," still stings the ears of the American Navy. Yet in spite of this loss, years of peace followed the war giving pause to the construction of highly expensive frigates. However, enough time has gone by for the Department of Defense to recognize a need to open a Naval Academy in the backyard of Annapolis. Additionally, the successful blockade at Vera Cruz against the Mexicans could only prove positive that Mrs. Cambridge's success as a business woman was a result of intuitive understanding and her next ingenious strategy. She carefully followed all information regarding changes with ship designs and lapped up the 1839 edition of Admiral Sir Robert Spencer Robinson's book titled *The Nautical Steam Engine Explained, and Its Powers and Capabilities Described for the Officers of the Navy and Others Interested in the Important Results of Steam Navigation.* This could hardly be considered an interesting read for any ordinary woman; but indeed our elder is certainly not ordinary. She invested her time gaining intelligence concerning the Royal Navy and European counterparts that have begun to experiment with the frigate steamer and its use in naval warfare. She could foresee that sailing ships were gradually disappearing from the composition of navies. Difficulty maneuvering in estuaries and other inshore areas was always a problem for the larger sailing ships. It seemed obvious that there was only one logical move; the Chesapeake Maritime Company must acquire a retired English frigate and bring it back to U.S. shores. Once here, it could be retrofitted for battle. And so it came into play, the Starboard, a most mechanically advanced ship with fine sailing qualities was considered in her day one of the finest steam frigates in the world when launched.

"She's 301 feet long and 51 feet abeam, powered by two compound engines and four boilers, giving her 950 IHP." Jack read the telegram to Mrs. Cambridge, who at once had him telegraph her banker to set up the transfer of funds. Large quantities of money during this time were often scrutinized and the purchase of such a ship, even to a shipbuilder was often dangerous, especially if it was interpreted as a sale destined to be used for the illegal transport of slaves. However, Mrs. Cambridge was not politically motivated and wished only to make herself a sizeable amount of money and would agree to sell her ship to the highest bidder. Yes, Jack Philander was the perfect negotiator. He was a man with no scruples, plenty of business connections, and a criminal record that will remain unexplored.

———

Will quietly teetered along the edge of the mattress and bent over his sleeping wife with a gentle kiss. "Oh, you're home so late!" she whispered opening her eyes.

"I didn't mean to wake you," he apologized and lifted his head from her check.

"Oh, dear, I suppose I drifted off while reading." Libby slid her hand across the bed until she discovered her magazine, *The Mother's Assistant*, lying beside her.

Will picked up the magazine that was open and folded back, displaying an article titled, *Parenting Young Children*. "I don't think that you will need any advice from this, you're a natural mother!" he exclaimed and tossed the magazine aside. "Now tell me, how are you?" he asked, and then taking her hand he kissed it tenderly. "I must say, I think you have grown since this morning. If you get any bigger we will have to ask Mrs. Cambridge for another bed!"

Libby pulled her hand away from his and struggled to sit up. Indeed her size made simple movements cumbersome and her ability to be nimble had diminished incrementally each day. "Will Piccard," Libby scolded in her most stern voice that she could muster without snickering, "are you trying to tell me that I am too FAT to sleep with?"

Will laughed at her attempt to be firm and then without warning flung himself upon the bed and plopped down next to her with his face staring straight up at the ceiling. "Hmmm, I think I still have a bit of room!" he said and then moved over so close to her that a sliver of paper could not have fit between them.

"Mr. Piccard, are you trying to be funny?" Libby remarked playfully and both laughed so heartily that they never heard the gentle rap upon the door!

"Libby, Libby," a voice from outside now rose above the laughter.

"Shhh," cried Libby and put her tiny hand over Will's mouth to keep him from laughing. "It's someone at the door," she whispered. Again the knock presented itself. Will jumped off the bed and turned to see Libby trying to stop herself from giggling. She quickly ran her fingers over her hair and pulled the covers up to her chin like a child that was hiding. Will opened the door to Wanda, who was already dressed in her nightclothes.

"Well, look who got home finally? Nick must be workin' you hard!" Wanda exclaimed. "I was just checkin' on Libby to see how she was feeling, she left dinner before dessert."

Will opened the door wider and gestured to Wanda to enter. Libby was now positioned so that she was sitting up against the white linen pillow. A special bond had developed over these months between the two and Wanda's motherly interest in the younger woman was genuine. "How would you like me to tell you if you are having a boy or a girl?" she announced. Will looked skeptical and followed Wanda as she pulled a chair next to the bed and sat down. "Give me your palm, Libby."

Libby pulled her tiny hand out from under the sheet and handed it to Wanda as instructed. Will turned the knob of the whale-oil lamp permitting it to illuminate more brightly. He leaned against the back of the chair since there was just enough room for him to stand. As though he himself were going to interpret the lines in her palm, he bent forward to watch. The small bedroom that had been filled with laughter suddenly fell mystically quiet. An ethereal twist of smoke spiraled up towards the ceiling from the twinkling flame and gradually floated down settling above Libby like an opaque halo.

Wanda's long fingernails gently traced the lines along Libby's right hand, she followed the lines around her wrist and then along each finger. Libby followed the woman's bright eyes, then back down at her hand, and again at the eyes. Will never turned from the tiny palm and wondered how and what the woman could really be interpreting. "It will be a boy, yes, you see this line here?" asked Wanda, "I believe that you are having a boy." Wanda let go of the hand abruptly and stood up. Her face was white as though all the color had drained from her pink cheeks.

"What's wrong?" asked Libby pulling her hand towards her own face. "I know you saw something else! You're so pale, as though you saw something that frightened you!" she cried.

"Don't be silly, Libby, I can't really tell fortunes, why there is a 50-50 chance that the baby will be a girl too," Wanda explained and turned to Will.

"That's true, Libby," he agreed with deliberation and meaning.

"No, I can feel it, something is wrong, tell me Wanda!" she insisted. "I saw it in the way you looked at my hand, I can't explain it, but your eyes were telling me more than your words."

"The only thing wrong is that this room is stuffy and hot," she laughed dismissing Libby. "Now don't you go tellin' anyone that I really can't read palms. Why if I lose my voice someday I just might have to resort to fortune telling for a living; that is unless I can attract a handsome man as a husband."

Libby kept her eyes upon Wanda hoping to see a change in her expression, but the woman continued to keep her countenance so sincere that Libby began to realize that she had overreacted and proceeded to apologize for her misinterpretation. As Wanda left the two alone, Will, who had not said much, was convinced that palm reading was simply an entertainment that should not be taken to heart and maintained an equally silent feeling on the subject. Confident that her husband was correct, the young mother-to-be lay her head down upon the pillow and began to think about her little boy.

———

The intensity of light which calls forth one species of moths to flutter wildly may cause others to retreat. Even the intermittent beams of moonlight may call to play some animals that might otherwise sleep when conditions are dark. Wanda, for most of her adult life, could be characterized as having adapted to the nocturnal characteristics of a domestic kitten; for even on a most cloudy day when others may wish to stay under the covers, she finds the grey atmosphere invigorating. And so it was unusual to see Miss Bourdette in for an evening of palm reading when under most circumstances she would have been out. The reason for her unusual presence was due to the booking she received at a new music hall where she was billed as the

Premier Act on the following evening. Thus depending upon points of view, it would be considered either lucky or unlucky that she happened to be home.

———

Two weeks may seem like a sufficient amount of time to plan a dinner party; however that would be true if all prearrangements fit into their assigned places. All the same, the matter of pin-pointing the arrival of the Starboard could not be precise, for at the very start she was off schedule. Even before the ship left port the latest telegram of regrettable news was delivered informing the reader of an unfortunate accident that had taken place. Two crew members on-board were engaged in a verbal altercation that escalated into a struggle. Several blows were exchanged when suddenly, during the scuffle, they came in contact with the ship's railing. Without warning it gave way, and both men were precipitated into the deep. One sailor was fortuitously saved, while the other ill-fated hooligan was drowned.

"Idiots!" thought Mrs. Cambridge. "Well at least there will be one less troublemaker aboard."

In spite of this small deflection, plans were reignited. Nick Biddle wished to help Mrs. Cambridge with the guest list however, he was a bit disappointed when the ancient one shooed him away with her cane and informed him that he was only invited because she did not wish to have an odd number of guests around her table. When Allister Cambridge was alive Mrs. Cambridge played hostess to the most influential guests; she knew that the dinner party was one of the most reliable methods of drawing and impressing a crowd. Proper dinnerware in which to present the meal was as equally important as the food and drink. Each invitation would be stamped by her alone, using the Cambridge seal that bore the same ornate "C" that hung above the front door.

Katrina began the tedious chore of polishing the silver, for to do a fair job took many days and many linen cloths. Marthe was issued a list of items to procure. Next to each entry Katrina scribbled a small drawing so that Marthe could easily identify what it was that she needed. Although Marthe had the duty of completing the biweekly shopping, this was the first time she was instructed with such an important task. The following morning before setting out on her appointed errands, she made a solemn promise not to dawdle; for a young woman who is not worldly could become easily engrossed in the most trivial of matters. "Ya, Katrina, ya; I vill go straight. I vill not pick the flovers along the vay," she promised when handed the list.

Along the same side of the street as St. John's Church is a cluster of buildings situated upon a large parcel of land once used for farming; here stands a shoemaker's shop, a corn husk depot, a blacksmith and his two small stone buildings, a butcher, and a dry goods store. The Hays Hotel, a small unkempt-looking two story wooden building, sits directly across from the church and is always full the night before and the night after market days, which were Wednesdays and Saturdays. Folks from other counties who live far from Baltimore came to the city to shop. Then, after taking possession of their goods, would drive their wagons back home, simply to return again when supplies ran short.

In the early hours of the morning on market days, a parade of vendors routinely set up shop within the small square of the church grounds in exchange for free food and wares for the clergy. This relationship worked well for several years until one day, a larger-than-most nanny goat, tied to the maple tree, chewed through its hemp tether and upon becoming untied found its way into the church rectory; only to be discovered sitting upon the alter eating the holy wafers. As a result, the vendors have now been relegated to the front of the church where both man and beast can be easily monitored. The availability of goods for sale is arranged in accordance to the season and conditions of the roads. On most occasions there is the usual bounty of fresh produce such as apples, peaches, and plums, a variety of puddings, fresh fish, butter, beer, the highly intoxicating mead, ginger beer, squawking chickens and roosters in coops, baby livestock such as kids or lambs, and an occasional kitten or puppy.

Fish to be bought was detoured to the wharf unless heavily salted and wrapped in enough paper to keep the smell to a minimum.

Marthe, an experienced shopper, scrutinized each product by squeezing, smelling, tasting by way of dipping a pinky into an open barrel, and lastly, bartering. She stringently followed the assigned list, made an order for the next market day delivery, and purchased outright on Mrs. Cambridge's notable credit, for she did not have enough schooling to make change from real money. Afterward, when she had accomplished her appointed task, she strolled lazily back to the Cambridge Arms with not much to contemplate for there was not too much of importance to ponder in her rather empty head.

Chapter 35

No one spoke of Yazhi ever again after that frightful night by the woodshed. Several of the other fowl had too disappeared and the only logical explanation was that they had been systematically devoured. Alex was now assigned to more work around the farm since Randle was confined to bed rest. The wounds inflicted by the wolf were dangerously close to becoming infected even after Betty flushed the area with plenty of water and then cauterized the open gash in his neck with a hot poker. Randle was in considerable pain, but more troublesome was his state of delirium induced by his own paranoia. He shuddered and anguished over the prospect that he could possibly have been infected with a fatal disease from the wolf's bite. Dread loomed over the poor man as he lay in bed filled with the anticipation of developing the most abhorrent characteristic identified with rabies; the imminent prognosis of growing mad. His hands were marked by painful swelling and even the slightest pressure placed upon the wounds received while protecting himself during the attack were likewise excruciating. The worrisome man constantly urged Betty to look into his eyes, for he was convinced that his pupils must be dilated. She placed a spittoon by his bedside to assist with his chronic routine of spitting, a process he designed to rid himself of the "poison". In spite of confinement and rest, a quickened pulse, slight fever, and pain persisted; and though he was no longer in any danger of contracting rabies, it was woefully possible that he was afflicted with blood poisoning.

———

Alex sighed heavily as he finished spreading hay about the stable floor. "Why now that Randle is laid up in bed, well it's just me and Betty to do all the chores." His youthful voice echoed. The great draft swished her long tail, shooing away the flies that tried to settle upon her back. She stiffened her ears forward and turned her head towards Alex, as though listening with great interest. Although the crops had already been planted before Randle's terrible incident, there was no shortage of work. Alex mulled over the short list in his mind: weeding, cutting and stacking wood, carrying water, emptying the slop jars, tending to the animals. As for Betty, aside from the outside work, her inventory seemed to go on forever: cleaning, refilling fuel for lamps, trimming wicks, cooking, preserving, washing, making soap, sewing, mending clothing, and taking care of Randle.

There was one exception to this malaise called work. Betty's prolific herb and flower garden, a living palette of colors, was flourishing. Each variety had been carefully selected and planted with the sole purpose of being used to dye the drab cotton and linen materials and put some glow into her sewing basket. The weld flowers, marigolds, and indigo were mature and ready to be picked. The tall straggly leaves of the henna shrub were also ready to be pulled from their spindly branches, while the madder herbs' roots needed to be separated from the plant and soil. Alex was instructed to clear a small area of the barn where Betty could dry the plants and leaves. Reminded of this latest task, he surveyed the barn and concluded that if he rearranged a few crates that had over time been misplaced, and restacked them against the opposing wall, he could make enough room to suspend the tightly corded hammock from two opposing beams. Betty could reach up and hang or lay the plants from above, using the hammock as a support.

The old wooden ladder, still missing a middle rung, lay on its side horizontally against the wall. Its ill state of repair stemmed from too many times being soaked by the rain or having been forgotten outside, only to be covered by snow during a heavy winter storm and should have been retired long ago. However, without a suitable replacement Randle decided that chopping it into kindling was not prudent. It was a long awkward ladder for one man, let alone a boy to maneuver and attempting to set it upright was most difficult. Alex contemplated his predicament, paced back and forth for a few moments, and then wrapped a wad of muslin that had been balled up in an empty crate around his hand, grabbed the top rung, and began to drag the ladder into position next to the first beam.

"What's ya doin', Alex Forester?" a chipper and familiar voice asked. Grace, who had entered the barn without being noticed, was standing upon a beam of light and had come in so quietly that if it were possible one would have thought that she had drifted in with the sunshine. Alex dropped the ladder and smiled. "I ain't seen ya in a long time," she said confirming what they both were thinking. "I heard 'bout Randle, sure sorry," she added. She moved out of the light and walked towards him. She was wearing the same boots that she always wore, but today they were laced with new rawhide and crisscrossed all the way up to the top. Her too long pinafore covered her plain muslin dress and, except for a large sash, was most ordinary. "Here, this is fer you," she said handing him a square package covered in brown paper and secured with a piece of twine that had been wrapped around the bundle twice.

"What is it?" he asked almost too shy to take the package.

"Miss Henshaw said that if ya ain't comin' back to school then she'll bring school to you!" Still holding the bundle in front of her she waved it about as though coaxing a dog with a bone, gesturing for him to take it.

Alex reciprocated with a reticent "Thanks," and upon accepting the gift placed it by his ear and shook gently as though expecting the contents to rattle.

Grace watched and giggled. "It ain't gonna break, silly," she said. "Go on, open it!" she urged. It took only a small tug to untie the tiny bow, which instantly caused the brown paper to unfold on its own like a lazy flower bud. Alex, who was not used to receiving anything, slowly peeled the wrapping away to uncover the contents of the parcel. "Isn't that Miss Henshaw the best?" exclaimed Grace, who was eagerly waiting for Alex's verbal reaction.

But somehow Alex did not share the same enthusiasm. He let the paper fall to the ground as he separated the stack into two. He held one item in each hand. *Lessons in Spelling and Reading*, a small plain book with 47 pages that had obviously been used many times for directly over the "p" in the word "Spelling" there was a dark grease stain which made the title read, Lessons *in Selling and Reading*. His other hand held a slightly larger, thicker, and newer book titled *Ray's Arithmetic* by Joseph Ray. This book wore a cover that displayed the idealistic schoolhouse; a well executed illustration of four interested students attending to a properly dressed schoolmaster who was standing beside an oversized globe and solving an arithmetic problem written in chalk upon an ornately framed blackboard. Grace swayed back and forth as Alex stared at the books for what seemed like a very long time.

"If you want I can help you! I mean not that you need any help," Grace explained. But then realizing that her intentions may have provoked hurt feelings she annotated her remark with, "What I meant to say was, on account of the fact that you've been away from school, you might need a little catchin' up."

Alex looked up at her sincere face. He placed the smaller of the two books under his arm and began to skim the one about arithmetic. Grace remained silent and watched Alex; by parsing his expression she hoped to gain an understanding of his genuine impression of the book. Nervously she swayed back and forth as he mechanically turned the pages. The further he headed into the middle chapters the number of difficult problems and concepts increased. He wiped his forehead with the sleeve of his shirt as though exhausted by the mere presence of the material set before him. Grace stopped swaying and began to amuse herself by trying to stand on tiptoe like a ballerina, which proved to be futile in her clumsy boots. Being still was not something she enjoyed and waiting was not something she enjoyed either.

Alex stacked the pair of books together in his hand in the same manner they were received, picked up the fallen paper and rewrapped them as though they were a flounder in the fish market. "Ya think I need a little help?" he asked in a most boisterous voice.

Grace fell back on her flat feet startled by his outburst for this was the first time that she actually felt frightened in his presence. Had she overstepped their friendship by insinuating that he may need some schooling? After all, it was really none of Miss Henshaw's business. Suddenly Grace grew angry at Miss Henshaw. Why did she butt in where she had no business? "Now everything was ruined, everything!" she thought. If only she had said "no" when the teacher asked her to bring over the books; she and Alex would still be friends. Grace could feel her face grow hot and flushed from both the anger at Miss Henshaw and the fear that once again she had lost another person in her life; someone she cared about. "There, I admit it, I do care about Alex Forester," she confronted herself and in the secret place that no one was permitted to enter. She wanted to take back what she did and start all over again, take back those minutes when she had handed him those stupid books. Grace imagined grabbing the books and running away from this most dreadful situation. "I'll get on a boat and become the wife of a pirate's son, and we'll find an island and live off the coconuts and live in a little hut made of palm trees and never set foot near this farm ever again," she decided. The mind's ability to work so fast and conjure up stories in a matter of seconds is truly a most remarkable ability as witnessed by Grace's fanciful and youthful imagination.

However all this trepidation, panic, and guilt were suddenly exterminated by Alex's abrupt outburst, "A little help?" he exclaimed. "Why I could use a heap of help!"

"Alex Forester!" Grace shouted, not knowing if she should be mad at him for putting her in this state or mad at herself for being so silly. "So ya ain't mad at me fer bringin' ya the books?" she asked.

"Why would I be mad at you?" Alex wondered aloud, and then to avoid her fawn-like eyes, he looked awkwardly down at the package and began to fumble with the paper.

"I'll come by in a few days to see if ya need any help with the arithmetic," she said giving extra emphasis on the last syllable. And then without waiting for a reply she announced, "Well, I gotta git goin," and turning quickly away she skipped out of the barn on the same sunbeam that she flew in on.

Alex balanced the pair of books on top of the stacked crates and retied the loosened twine. He wasn't unhappy or disappointed that he couldn't go to school, actually he was quite pleased. The events that had just transpired allowed him to surrender himself to a feeling that perhaps a change for the better would come as a result of these books. He set out moving about the barn, undaunted that a dark pair of eyes stared down from above. They were his silent chaperone, watching as he rewrapped the piece of muslin around his right hand like a bandage and dragged the ladder into the correct position before attempting to lean it upright against the wall. He closed his eyes and listened for a moment, then calmly looked up and searched above the highest beams and over to the hayloft. Nothing seemed out of the ordinary, at least anything that he could see. Alex wiped his forehead with the back of his sleeve and continued to work.

Heading homeward along a ragged trail, Grace skipped and scampered and all the while scolded herself for letting her imagination get the best of her. "Why life with a pirate's son would be dreadful!" she exclaimed to a small ladybug that happened to be resting upon one of the tiny dandelions that she choose to pick. "I just don't know what I could have bin thinking!" Then setting the ladybug back onto the ground, she stuck the flower into her pocket and skedaddled away towards the Tarson's home.

Chapter 36

"I think it is quite sad that Mrs. Cambridge is estranged from her son," Libby sighed. "Family is really all we have in the world!" she added smiling meekly at Katrina who had just dropped onto the rug in front of her an assortment of items that were in need of mending.

"Be careful with this one," the maid cautioned fumbling through the pile until she exposed a linen tablecloth. "Start with fixing this appliqué; we may use this for the party." Katrina pointed to a finely stitched rose that was missing half of a green stem and a pair of adjacent leaves. "Word of advice, Libby, I wouldn't go around talkin' aloud about her son. That's a dead subject, literally."

Libby stopped threading her needle. "Oh, I had no idea that he may really be dead!" she exclaimed.

"Dead or not, it's not open for discussion, besides, these walls have ears and so if ya don't mind," Katrina whispered, "I'd prefer changing the subject."

"Of course," Libby agreed most apologetically.

"No harm done, I can see why you're all sentimental," she said acknowledging her condition. "It won't be long now. What ya got, a month or so?"

Libby looked down and realizing that she could no longer see her feet unless she poured herself forward, nodded in agreement. Then she asked, "Katrina, do you believe in fortune tellers?"

Katrina stopped at the door and laughed, but when she saw that the young woman was serious she stopped. "Let me guess, you had your palm read by Wanda."

Libby flattened her hand wondering which lines held the secrets to her future; were they all interconnected or just randomly stationed going every-which-way without any real direction? "Oh, never mind, I'm just being silly," she replied and closed her palm. Then she reopened it again repositioning her statement. "It isn't what she said," Libby added, "it's just a feeling I have that Wanda saw something bad and is not telling me."

A cautious reminder tickled Katrina as she became unusually stoic. She needed to use the utmost care when delivering her response for it was only days ago that she gave Wanda her word never to disclose their conversation, the conversation that included what Wanda really saw in the tiny palm, the conversation that predicted doom. So when Katrina was presented with Libby's sensation of foreboding uncertainty, one should ask whether this was merely coincidental or the destiny of fate? For if it is fate we will prescribe to the belief of an inevitable outcome, sometimes personified by the goddess Moirae who spins the thread of life after birth. But, if it is a coincidence, we will prescribe to the belief that there has taken place an accidental occurrence between two circumstances. However, being most pragmatic, Katrina did not have time nor curiosity to decipher Libby's feelings. "You should know better than to listen to Wanda, she's an entertainer! Now, git on with your work so I can do mine!" and with that Katrina sauntered away hoping that Libby believed what she said after asking, 'Do you believe in fortune telling?' She didn't need to ponder Libby's question, there was no doubt in her mind that trouble was heading the younger woman's way. The only thing that mattered now was when, and that would only be determined by time.

———

Time is often lamented by those who see it as lost or squandered. Nature's time is a cycle of expressions defined by colors, hues, distinguishing smells and sounds emanating from its four seasons. The white birch tree, an example from winter, cracks the snow's skin with a fallen branch that becomes kindling for an evening's fire and the grey smoke lingers up through a chimney and out into the sky. New grass blades, an example of spring, emerge from dried seeds cracking the earth's crust as it stretches upward while below the ground its root-like tendrils dig deeply and take hold.

For Tully time was hardly a notion that was ever forgotten and therefore did not need to be remembered. Only on occasion did he find himself thinking about the past. But tonight the view above was revealing itself most differently; it was taking on a persona that was found not in present time, but rather in a long ago memory. Tully stood outside his soddy and gazed upon a sky that continued to distinguish itself in a most artificial manner. The appearance of a greenish glow splashed across the blackness and gave him reason to take particular pause.

Sergeant, who took no particular notice of the sky and besides may be color-blind and therefore would be unable to see anything peculiar, slept restlessly by his feet. With every hoot and rustle of the wilderness he would perk his large head up, sniff the air, and then lay it back down. The man stretched out next to the dog and stared upward watching the viridian hues begin to dissipate as they were slowly absorbed by the vast darkness of night. How many years had it been? He didn't keep track, for there was no relevance; the loss was the same regardless of years, months, days, hours, minutes, seconds. He listened to Sergeant breathe, snorting between every other breath; he exhaled as though trying to dispel an insect that had decided to rest in one of his nostrils. Tully closed his eyes and slowly began to drift off to sleep. He often dreamed and tonight was no exception. He saw himself walking on familiar grounds; Sergeant in front with his nose to the ground in his usual exploratory method of sniffing. He saw himself stop beside markedly pastoral country, not a clearing nor a mountain pass, but rather it was a rolling cemetery laden with headstones. Sergeant waited by the small gate while Tully entered and headed directly towards one of the gravesites in an unceremonious way, just as if he had done it many times before. The air became uncommonly cool as though his arrival had beckoned perfection. He couldn't make out the etched name, but dug into his front left pocket and then coming up empty reached into the other one and pulled out a circular object. It was a ring, a wedding ring. He knelt down and with the utmost care placed it upon the ground in front of the headstone and buried it deep into the earth until it was no longer visible.

Tully slept soundly and comfortably. The night air respected his presence by sending intervals of light breezes that carried the notes of the allusive whip-poor-will; time was part of the murky blackness of the sky and would announce itself tomorrow in the color of day.

———

Marte delivered the invitations to the office of the American Letter Mail Company, a reputable service of delivery. As instructed, she wrapped two freshly baked biscuits in brown paper; an incentive that the letters go out without delay. And so, the small but noteworthy guest list had been established. The elder's rat-a-tat echoed as she hobbled about the first floor, designating specific tasks that were to be performed. She had the finer china set out for inspection as though reviewing the troops before battle. The pattern was plain in comparison to others that were set on Baltimore's society tables. Many years ago, when a much younger Mrs. Cambridge first set eyes upon the lovely dishes in the shopkeeper's window, she knew her decision would be easy. A single table setting and tea service was enough to entice the right buyer. Each dish was white with a scalloped edge defined by a golden accent. Only the combination of a finely crafted boar's hair brush and the steadiest hand could have painted with such accuracy. The central design was a bouquet of crimson roses, a spray of blossoms in full bloom and a few florets of tiny buds. What a shame to cover such a masterpiece with a helping of potatoes and fatted veal. It was the young Mrs. Cambridge's fascination with the Empress Josephine's rose collection at Malmaison that had sealed the purchase. It was revealed that the French Royal Garden contained every species of rose ever known, and the very bouquet drawn upon the humble design was a duplicate of the favorite flower that flourished solely for the Empress.

Mrs. Cambridge looked upon her table and spotted the twelve teacups and saucers. The last time she used them a clumsy Mrs. Dartmouth had stirred her tea so loudly that it produced a resonating tone which was quite annoying to all the other guests. Pulling the cup out of line she noticed that there was indeed a small crack, a hairline fracture that traversed a tiny bud. Her gnarled finger ran across the imperfection and then placing the cup up to her eyes, she wrinkled her nose in disgust as the tiny fissure was confirmed to be real. The cup was repositioned upon the table, setting her off to ruminate on life's imperfections, many of which fell into the category of disappointments. These were generally manufactured by human error or most likely stupidity.

The grey woman rested her cane against the table, freeing both hands in order to pull the chair from its nesting place. Slowly she lowered her bowed body into the seat and plucked a folded parchment of names from her pocket. It was not a long list, but a dinner party did not need to invite many to be entertaining. What mattered was the quality of guest and the disposition each would bring to the table. Pouring over every individual name, her mouth formed an audacious grin while her head nodded approvingly with small spasmodic movements that one would expect from a chicken. Everything was in its place, nothing could go wrong now, that is unless some misfortune would perchance doom the arrival of the Starboard, however as much as one could anticipate, nothing but an unusual act of nature would keep it from docking safely. Timing was everything and with the element of surprise on her side there was no reason to believe the plan would not be a total success. She had waited a long time for this chance and now she would only have to be patient a little longer. Mrs. Cambridge refolded the list and returned it to her pocket. Smiling wickedly, she enjoyed being alone with her thoughts.

———

There were only three days until the party and still Libby could not find a thing to wear. She had outgrown just about everything and certainly owned nothing that would be suitable for such a fancy affair. Fortunately, Wanda had a trunk full of gowns and an armoire just as generous; so when she knocked on the door of the little sewing room with an arm load of taffeta and silk, the entertainer was determined that there had to be something in her pile for the young woman to wear.

Meanwhile, Nick was assuring Will that there was no reason to feel out of place and that he had been at the Cambridge Arms long enough to know that it was positively going to be a night to remember.

Katrina hired extra help to work in the kitchen for the next few days, a small sensible woman who had come highly recommended by Parson McCormick's wife. "She can and will do anything you require, except serve," Mrs. McCormick had announced. "Just don't ask her to serve," she reiterated, but this time in a whisper and looked about before continuing. "You see, she's missing a thumb on account that her mister accidentally chopped it off when she was trying to steady a carcass for him. I suppose he got too zealous with the cleaver." So with the assurance of the Parson's wife and the fact that the butcher's wife was ample in the area of preparing not only meat, but fish and crustaceans too, Katrina had no choice but to acquiesce.

The following morning Lillian Stark, the butcher's wife, arrived with the sun by way of a horse-drawn delivery cart with a hand painted sign which read 'Meats and Sausages by Stark'. Lillian, a small, stout, ordinary woman kissed her husband goodbye, climbed down from the bench seat, and kissed the horse with the same amount of passion that she gave her husband. Lazily the cart traveled away and she remained vigil, waiting by the front gate for someone to admit her. And she would still be waiting outside if Katrina had not just happened to open the front door to sweep the stoop.

———

"I'm beginning to wonder if Admiral Ringgold is ever coming back to our shores," Mrs. Cambridge remarked to Katrina. "I would believe he were dead if I didn't receive his rent money every six weeks. He's never missed a payment yet," she added.

"I miss his stories," Katrina confessed as she dusted about the parlor. "He does like to spin a tale," she mused to herself.

"That's exactly why I would have liked him to be with us at the dinner," agreed the ancient one, who rarely agreed with anyone.

"There will be an even ten for dinner, Mrs. Cambridge; the Doctor and Mrs. Bruner have sent their reply and will be joining you." Katrina reached into her apron pocket and retrieved an elegantly penned note acknowledging the acceptance to dinner along with a clumsy excuse for the late response. It appears that the Doctor had just returned from a medical convention in the capital whereby their social engagements could now be resumed.

"Medical convention, that old quack," the elder snapped after reading the note and handing it back to Katrina. "He only goes to those things to get away from his shrewish wife and drink the free liquor!" she proclaimed adamantly.

"So, why did you invite them?" asked Katrina, the only individual who could get away with such a flippant question.

The grey lady laughed for a moments and then sallied forth, "Because they're always cheap entertainment!" Although as truthful a statement as this may seem, it was a declaration that divulged only a half-truth; for let it be known that in spite of Doctor Bruner's lack of skill and sparse moral dignity, he had bought his way into Baltimore's elitist's society and therefore was a man everyone wanted on their dinner party list.

Chapter 37

Miss Henshaw paced up and down the narrow rows and listened while the children recited their weekly poem.

Bright and tiny in the dark
We look upon you like a lark
Lights above in the night
Are they heaven's little lights?

Back and forth she strolled, hands clenched behind her back, each step she took was measured in the same beat and rhythm as the verse. If a child stumbled upon a word it also broke her stride, and she would hesitate until the word caught in the back of the throat was reassembled correctly and both child and teacher could move along.

Rumblings of an impending war kept enrollment of the older children down and only on occasion did one decide to return to school. Zachary McNary Rucker and his band of hooligans had all joined the army, although Elijah forged his father's signature because the recruiting officer did not believe that he was of age. "Perhaps they will find glory, heaven knows that they were not destined to amount to much," Miss Henshaw thought as she filed past the back succession of empty seats. However, this was not the only group that no longer attended; there were a few families that were too proud to send their children because they simply did not have proper school clothes and their honor was more important than an education. Yet the biggest deterrent came during those few weeks that little Elmer Syth was home sick; rumors of putrid fever spread although he was only laid up with a croup. But nevertheless, the mere notion that a child would be in the close proximity to impurities from another allowed the infiltration of acute paranoia to take precedence over school. And although Elmer returned fully recovered, the majority of his classmates did not recuperate from the rumors.

Miss Henshaw paced up and down, every now and again stopping before a student to rap her yardstick upon the wooden bench; roaming eyes were not a way to learn and discipline was her ally. She tried to appear interested as she made her trek about the schoolroom; but even her own mind began to wander outside these bleak walls. How long would it be before her services would no longer be needed? "Miss Henshaw," an eager hand went up. The teacher nodded with approval for the child to continue. "Do you think that the lights in the poem are stars?" asked Elmer Syth, who rarely asked a question unless he was absolutely sure he was correct.

"Why I believe that is a very good answer, Elmer," she replied nodding approvingly.

Miss Henshaw looked about the room for another response when she noticed a small hand fluttering about like a butterfly caught in a net. It belonged to Grace, who impatiently waited her turn to speak. "Yes, Grace, you have an idea?" the teacher asked.

Grace pursed her lips together before speaking. "Miss Henshaw," she exclaimed as she rose from her seat. "Ain't it possible that the lights in the poem are really tiny torches that the angels carry so that they can see their way when it's dark?" Grace sat back down convinced that she had given an excellent interpretation. Elmer's answer was too obvious, but her idea showed true understanding of what the poet was trying to say. "Ain't that so, Miss Henshaw?" she asked again. Yet as she waited for her teacher to anoint her with the praise she had earned, for no one else had thought up such a clever meaning, screams of laughter exploded filling the room with pandemonium.

"Why that's the stupidest answer I ever heard!" roared Arnold, a slovenly ten-year-old who looked at least twelve and being much larger than his peers seemed to get the attention of the others even when he was wrong, which was most of the time. Again the class rose to the occasion with yelps and howls followed by giddy laughter. Now there was a time, not too long ago, when sweet little Grace would have become deeply mortified by this show of ridicule; to such a great degree that hiding beneath the seat boards and tunneling her way out would have been far better than having to face the class. However, she was no longer the same timid child that sat in this same seat so many months ago and with a thrust of energy that could only be described as astounding; she leaped over her seat, like the goddess Artemis in swift pursuit, and flung herself upon the culprit with as much force as she could muster. It was quite obvious that Grace had learned more than reading and writing during her schooling.

For a split second Miss Henshaw toyed with the idea of disappearing outside for a bit of fresh air, ensuring Grace an opportunity to demonstrate her feminine prowess. But, thinking better of herself, she succumbed to her dutiful schoolmarm side and immediately pulled Grace off the crying boy who threatened to tell his mother and father, and anyone else who would listen, how unjustly he had been treated. Grace emerged victorious, as for Arnold, he sniffled his way through the day nursing his embarrassed pride more than anything else. Only the fact that school was dismissed early seemed to make him feel better.

The same lively spirit that possessed Grace had once dominated Miss Henshaw's own youthful disposition until time had become a tick filling itself with her sanguine optimism and leaving her ambitions anemic. She sat in her small room and pulled the curtain aside and stared up at the Tarson house. Belle Tarson, once noted as the outspoken brash woman who brought Eastern etiquette Westward, was now rarely seen in public. The death of young Joseph had changed the mother into a morose and melancholy woman. The schoolteacher wondered what would happen if her position was no longer warranted. She was not concerned about her own welfare; she was self-reliant and there were plenty of communities that needed teachers. No, her uneasiness was for Grace. She had grown fond, perhaps too fond, of the child.

———

Although Grace did not have the patience nor the tenacity to keep her mind on sewing, Beatrice was intent on giving the child the basic skills that defined her gender. It had been neglected too long and now that she was becoming older, it was no longer optional. Knitting, crocheting, and sewing were not only a necessity, but may later become a trade whereby she would earn wages. However at the rate the little girl was going, Beatrice was not sure how successful the child would ever become. Her many attempts to try and teach crocheting failed miserably; the thread constantly slipping off the needles after only a few stitches, upon which Grace took that not as a failure, but rather an incentive to produce a cat baiting invention. Consequently, the woman's patience was wearing thin, evidenced by a display of disapproval when she used the needles to truss the stuffed turkey for dinner, while mumbling expletives that was not fitting for a child's ears. Grace did not see why she was so upset when the cat device proved to be fail-proof.

Though in spite of a few setbacks, a corner of the kitchen was set aside with a sewing basket filled with colorful threads, sampler patterns, and a stool. "How come I can't go outside and help Tod with his chores? I much rather help him with his chores than be in here?" bemoaned Grace as she watched Beatrice's younger brother by the water pump. Beatrice turned around to answer her, only to see that the wooden stool had been repositioned in front of the window, most likely, the woman supposed, during her churning of the butter.

Beatrice sucked her teeth under her breath, a habit that Grace had become used to hearing when the woman became annoyed. "Grace, you'd better be careful of what ya wish for. Ya might just find yerself doin' all of Tod's chores!"

Yielding to her fanciful ways, Grace jumped down off the stool, sauntered over to Beatrice, and stuck her finger in a bowl of newly creamed butter. But her attempt to sneak another taste was immediately squashed by a sudden whap of the long wooden spoon on her behind. "Git yer fingers out of my butter," scowled Beatrice.

Grace licked the glop off her fingers that she had managed to dip into the bowl before getting caught. "What' ya mean by sayin', I'd be doin' Tod's work round here? Is he goin' somewhere?" the playful child asked as she wiped her sticky hands on Beatrice's apron.

"We all might be goin' somewhere!" she exclaimed, while skimming her hand across the flour barrel and scooping up a fist full of flour. With a lightly clenched palm she waved it over the table top and slowly sprinkled streams of white powder. When her full fist had surrendered all its contents, she clapped her hands together, which released a white flour cloud that always managed to fly up and land on her nose and cheeks. All this was in preparation of kneading a bowl of dough that had been set out to rise earlier that morning.

Grace, trying to recreate the surface of the moon, plunged her index finger in and out of the dough that had risen like an inflated balloon. She watched as the soft pasty blob slowly reshaped itself back to its original form. "Goin'? Yer talking in riddles; who's goin'?" the child asked and turned to write her name in the neatly dusted flour.

"Grace, git yer fingers out of my bakin'!" scolded Beatrice as she grabbed the little nymph's arm and led her back to the sewing corner. "Now, I've been talkin' too much as it is," she complained with an extra air of disgust and picked up the partially stitched sampler from the sewing basket. A feeble attempt had been made to complete several rows of stitches. "Now you finish this row and I'll let ya go out!" Beatrice commanded pointing to the work. Thereupon, she showed Grace how to tighten the hoop and when feeling that it was sufficiently taut, toddled back to her side of the kitchen.

Dutifully Grace bowed her head and pulled the threaded needle up and back through the tight material making a tiny "x" that resembled a cross-stitch. She continued to follow the lightly drawn design, a cluster of very ripe strawberries encircled by small twisting stems and leaves. Grace had no clue as to why anyone would wish to own such a thing, but decided that to ask Beatrice would have been futile. She perched herself back up upon the stool and peeked out the window. Tod was no longer in view. She wondered what he might be up to; probably chopping wood, she thought, someone always seemed to be chopping wood. She looked down at her work, only a few more stitches and freedom would be hers!

———

Betty continued to care for Randle, who had barely made any improvement since the attack. The latest diagnosis confirmed that the bedridden man had not contracted rabies; however the old physician couldn't give a reason why the patient still carried on as though he was not right in the head. Having returned to check on his recovery, Dr. Foy found himself sent away before the examination by a castigation of threatening assaults and being lambasted by a voice from beneath the bed sheets. "Git him out of here!" shouted Randle in a fit of rage, "I don't need no stranger comin' in and tryin' to take my land!" So, unless he took a turn for the worst, Dr. Foy decided to keep his distance.

"There ain't much else to do now but give him time to git the poison out of him," the doctor had announced and prescribed a bottle of liniment to apply four times a day. But even with hope and medicine administered, when three months passed, Betty was tired of 'giving him time'. Randle refused to leave his bed, and if he was not having conversations with himself, he was sleeping. It was his hands that were a constant, the great reminder of the dreadful assault. Neither had returned to a normal size remaining pink and inflamed. The swollen flesh was hot and painful if touched, no longer could he make a fist, so he kept them in a claw-like position resembling a fat pair of mittens.

Alex peeked into the bedroom several times a day, but like everyone who attempted to pay a visit, he too was met with squalls of anger. "Now, don't think that he don't like ya, Alex," Betty said on the afternoon that Randle swore to tear Alex in half if he tried to come in. "He just don't know who ya are. He ain't right." So, Betty suggested that they establish a signal; if the door was partially open that meant the tyrant was asleep, and Alex could go in without fear.

The morning distinguishes itself into thirds, three observable time periods lasting the first six hours of the day. The first third we will call sunrise which is characterized by a low hanging sun in the eastern sky and any shadow cast is considered long. The second third we call midmorning when the sun begins to rise higher in the sky and any shadow cast begins to grow shorter. The last we call midday and is the time when the sun is at its highest point and any shadow cast is of the shortest length. But the time when the signal failed was an hour before the first third, before the sun crept up from the horizon. It was an hour before the eastern sky was bathed in reds and oranges. It was an hour before the shadow was so long that it stretched out upon the awakening land; it was the hour all too familiar to those who are restless sleepers.

And so, unbeknownst to Betty, who was sound asleep, a brisk wind blew down the chimney flue and whistled loud enough to wake Timothy, the cat. Like all cats, for they are notoriously sneaky, he interpreted the partially open door as a signal of his own and barged in without being detected and settled comfortably next to Randle. Purring contentedly, the very heavy cat repositioned himself by elongating with a great stretch and sprawled across the man's legs; it was here that the cat's carelessness began. Ordinarily one would not be wakened by the stretching of a fat cat such as Timothy; however, Randle was awake for he was one of those restless sleepers that lies in bed waiting for the first third of the morning.

How Betty did not hear what took place next can only be attributed to her extreme fatigue. But sometimes it is what is not heard that awakens the deepest sleeper, for it so happened that with the absence of heavy snores the room became uncommonly quiet. Betty opened her eyes and peered about the darkness trying to readjust to the limited light. "Randle?" she muttered and then stopped to listen, but heard nothing. She repeated his name a bit louder. "Randle!" she beckoned, except this time when she received no response she feared the worst. Jumping up from her narrow cot she rushed over and threw her hands upon the rumpled sheets blindly feeling for life. "Randle!" she shouted as though demanding an answer. Her heart was thumping in her chest so hard that her temples throbbed; suddenly she could only think the worst. She tore the blanket from the bed as though lifting it off would miraculously make him reappear, "Randle, where are you?" she screamed with the terror in her voice that signified he was gone.

It was now the start of the first third of the morning when the subtle transformation of dark to light ensues. Alex, having been woken by the outburst, stood by the open door. "Here, take this," Betty said and handed him the lit lantern. She grabbed her shawl that had been hanging over the chair and covered her shoulders, tying it loosely in a large knot so that her hands would be free. "I don't know how long he's been out," she said sullenly. The air was brisk, cold, but invigorating. Betty followed behind Alex and the flickering lantern. He held the light out in front and wondered what would have made Randle want to go outside. He looked on the ground and pointed to prints, footprints of bare feet. Alex lowered the lantern so Betty could see and then slowly, like a scout, followed the trail. At first there seemed to be no real relationship between the destination and the feet because they were haphazard, going left, then right, then left, but soon the journey to nowhere suddenly was leading them further away from the farm. Betty rewrapped her shawl several times and trudged behind Alex. She placed her hand upon his shoulder keeping her eyes upon the ground as they walked single file down a narrow path between tree and brush.

"The only thing down this way is an old well, and it's been dry for ten years or more!" Betty recollected as they followed the prints that now had become less identifiable as feet but instead resembled the markings of a person sliding rather than walking. Round another bend they rambled when suddenly they were besieged by a muffled cry of an animal like a prelude to the macabre. Before them stood an enormous silhouette, an elongated shadow of a man dangling the strings of a gunny sack that writhed and twisted in his claw-like hand.

"Timothy!" shouted Alex. "It's Timothy!" he shouted once more raising his voice above the howls of the trapped animal.

Randle stepped away from behind the shadows of his darker alter ego. As though all the blood had been transfused out from his body, he now was a ghostly pale white. The empty eyes gazed upon the followers as though he had abandoned his soul along the way. The gunny sack persisted to explode with life as a constant blood curdling shriek called from within.

"Randle," Betty screamed, "Randle, give me the sack!" But undaunted by their reactions, he continued to dangle the bag over the open well as though he was going to let it go. The bag wiggled in the air all-the-while howling with fear. At one point it appeared as though it was filled with a live cactus for Timothy's sharp claws punctured the coarse material displaying needle-like tips which clung fiercely to the outer surface. Alex set the lantern aside and crept behind Randle however, he thought better of doing anything bravado in fear that Randle could lose his footing and fall into the well.

"It's me, Randle, come on home with me!" Betty pleaded and put her hand out for him to take. Alex remained kneeling several feet behind and contemplated how he could grab the sack without harming Randle or Timothy.

Although it was still the first third of the morning, the sun appeared more golden and more illustrious than it had been in a very long time. "Betty," he asked looking at her as though recognizing her for the first time. "Betty, take me home," he whispered and with an outstretched arm he handed her the squealing sack. His foot was cut from having stepped upon the barbed brambles in the raw earth, and as he hobbled along heading down the path, he left behind a trail of blood.

———

It was the second third of the morning. Timothy, exhausted from his experience, found refuge by squeezing under Alex's small cot. Betty applied the liniment to Randle's hands that now had swollen into much larger mittens and raised them up on several pillows hoping that they would drain. She washed his foot and dressed it with the same liniment before tying a cloth bandage. Unscathed by his ordeal he slept soundly, but not before announcing, "That cat and that boy, trouble, they're nothin' but trouble."

———

Alex unlatched the barn door and pulled it open just wide enough to enter. "It's me," he said walking towards the stables. Delilah and Dandy hung their faces in his direction in anticipation of his morning arrival. "These are fer you," he said digging into his pocket and retrieved a half-dozen sugar lumps. He counted out three, laid each across his flat palm and fed Delilah first. Then, he did the same for Dandy. "Taste good, don't it?" he asked and rested his head upon Dandy's forehead. "I think Randle's lost his mind," Alex whispered and lifted his head away from the horse. He took turns stroking each velvet nose. "Don't worry, he ain't gettin' in here, I'll protect you with my life," Alex promised.

He stopped stroking and stood perfectly still. He closed his eyes and could feel the light breath of the animals upon his face. He breathed in and out sharing the same hot moist air. There was the sense of peace growing within him and as the quiet of mind and body connected to the horses, he became one with them.

Chapter 38

Bad news and bad luck are often the catalyst by which people that ordinarily do not socialize come together to commiserate. It may perchance be accredited to human nature or the proof that misery loves company. Whatever the reason they choose, such a posture was taken up between Belle Tarson and Betty. And although they were more than acquaintances, but not exactly friends, they had formed a relationship that found itself amidst a fitting opportunity to resuscitate their individual spirits.

Beatrice led Betty to the sunroom; a section of the Tarson home that was seldom visited. In spite of its name, this was really an open porch shaded by a low beamed roof whereby the early morning sun poured in making it uncomfortably hot during the summer. "Why these are so unusual," exclaimed Betty as she ran her fingers across the back of one of the twin rocking chairs.

"There used to be a little one just the same as these two, but Missus Tarson had it burned right along with the garbage right after…," Beatrice stopped talking and put her hand up over her mouth before going into too much detail.

"I know," Betty replied understanding what the woman wished to say. Betty bent down and lightly pushed one of the chairs allowing it to gently rock. It was a most lovely pair of chairs crafted from willow rods bent into curlicues and spirals. And although invited to sit, Betty was reluctant, for being a large woman she feared her weight was too much for the delicately woven seat of willow twigs. Noticing the visitor's trepidation to follow her gestured invitation, Beatrice stood over and pushed down with all her might upon the seat convincing her that it was much sturdier than it looked.

Most certainly Belle Tarson had forged her attitude and style far from her current surroundings as evidenced by the chairs and collection of oddities displayed upon a wooden shelf that extended along the opposite wall; the likes of which Betty had never seen. It was apparent that much time had been sanctioned to identify each item, for placed beside the dried sea creatures and groupings of shells were handwritten labels. Betty counted at least a dozen blanched starfish and bleached sand dollars that were meticulously lined up in size order, from largest to smallest. She wished to examine them closer, but dared not for they looked particularity brittle, and she didn't want to be blamed for cracking or breaking any. On the other hand, the sea shells were considerably more hearty, and she readily fingered some of them by flipping a few over, concluding that they must not be too rare for although varied in design, there were so many of them. The angelwings looked like their namesake, identical shells attached in the middle, ribbed with a cross-hatched membrane, nice but nothing out of the ordinary, and the calico scallops, white with rust colored mottling were the prettiest. Betty poked around the room as she waited for her hostess. Resting in the corner was an anchor encrusted with a small colony of barnacles. Having never seen these before, she tried to chip one off, but it had secured itself with the utmost tenacity. A bronze ship's bell mounted on the most curious mahogany stand occupied a smaller and narrower wooden shelf. Deciding that she would probably not break the rocker, she sat down and found herself enjoying this unusual room and wondered if anyone ever came out here to sit in this nautical museum anymore.

One would not call Belle Tarson attractive however; she was the type of woman that a person could not help but notice. Perhaps it was the fact that she took up a lot of space in the room since she tended to wear her hats tall and her skirts layered and wide. Her clothes were not homemade and everything she purchased was either from back East or imported from Europe. "Been a while hasn't it, Betty?" Belle remarked as she entered the room. She bent down and kissed her guest upon the cheek, a gesture that Betty had not recalled ever receiving before. Perhaps her grief had softened her usual hard exterior. No, Betty reconsidered; it was most likely that she enjoyed the fact that someone else was miserable.

Belle sat down in the opposing rocker looking out of place in such a provincial piece of furniture; to such a degree that Betty asked her, "Are you comfortable?" even though she was the visitor.

"Quite," was her reply. She sat stiff backed and rigid, refusing to allow the chair to move freely, but rather locking her knees and crossing her feet so it could not commence on its own. "I hope that Beatrice offered you something to drink."

"Oh, yes, but I didn't care for anything," Betty lied, trying to remember to accent the "g" in the word "anything" as she spoke; and although it would have been nice to be sitting here with a lemonade or sweet tea, why make mention of it.

"Why don't we get down to the real reason for your visit," Belle remarked and stood up. Betty wasn't sure if she should stand too, so she remained sitting. "I know that Randle is not..." Belle paused trying to infuse the right word and then rephrased her comment, "that he is not feeling well."

Betty laughed and started to rock, "You can say it Belle, he's plum goin' crazy!" she smiled and watched for Belle's reaction, but the mistress of the house did not return any and remained stoic in features and response.

"Regardless of what we shall call his condition, I know you wish to see him recover. I have made inquiries back East as you requested and have secured a spot for him in the best sanitarium." Now it was Belle's turn to watch for a reaction. "I heard what he tried to do to your dog," Belle added.

Betty corrected her, "Cat, it was our cat, Timothy." She rose and walked over to the shelf where Belle now stood.

"You know, I found these many years ago along the coast. Did you know that this sand dollar is actually a skeleton?" Belle asked holding a medium size one flat upon her palm. "It is actually greenish with tiny little legs when it's in the sea."

"No, can't say that I did know that," Betty answered. Then rerouting the conversation to the original discussion she continued, "I have his things already packed. Not too much 'cause he won't need but a few items, I suppose. It sure is nice of you to let him travel with you. I don't know what I'd do with the farm and Alex if you hadn't come along with yer offer."

Belle turned to her, "You know, it may take him years. You may not even recognize him when he returns."

"I know," Betty sighed. "How long are you goin' to be gone for?"

Belle's eyes had now taken on a look that had become almost all too familiar; it was a far away gaze that Betty often recognized in Randle. "I don't know," Belle remarked as though speaking to herself, "but I do know that I must leave as well. There are too many ghosts and too many memories." She smiled timidly and then slowly closed her hand permitting the sand dollar to fracture and break into many tiny pieces.

A startled Betty gasped when she realized what had been done.

"Don't worry, dear," mumbled Belle. At once she exposed her open hand and let the tiny shards fall to the ground. "There are many more of these where they come from," she mused.

Betty knelt down and began to pick up the broken pieces. "Leave them!" Belle commanded pulling Betty's arm away from the floor. Dutifully, the obliged woman stood up and placed the few broken pieces that she had collected back onto the shelf. "There now, no need for you to dirty yourself, Betty, I'll have Beatrice tend to this later," the hostess remarked with a forced smile. "Come along then, we both have things to tend to." Without any more discussion, she led the way out of the sunroom and into their own private darkness.

———

The hustle and bustle of activity that emanated from the Cambridge Arms kept all the residents in the area of Washington Mound quite entertained with curiosity since most all of the three hundred and sixty four days were met with the same humdrum routine, excluding Christmas. Katrina, tired of having to answer the bell's constant peal to open the secured gate, let it remain unlatched while preparations for the dinner party were going on. The smells from the kitchen were as individual as the tastes that were arriving, for within and on top of the large pig iron stove, pots brimming with delicacies were being stewed, boiled, baked, or awaiting their turn to be cooked. Lillian Stark proved to be as commendable as Mrs. McCormick promised; an expert cook who washed her hands often as well as having the ability to follow both written and oral instructions; so between her and Marte they divided the work equally.

"Katrina!" the ancient one cawed as she settled her cup of tea upon the saucer, "I wish to remind you that we must maintain the structure of the meal, and to do so it is necessary that each dish be served accordingly." Mrs. Cambridge gestured for the woman to sit down. "I am assuming," she continued, "that everything is in order for this evening."

Katrina obeyed and teetered upon the edge of her chair, quite content to be off her feet. The old woman offered her one of the buns that had been brought in earlier, but she declined. The house-keeper pulled a sheet of paper from her apron pocket and began to read it aloud. "We are startin' with raw oysters and champagne," Katrina stopped reading and turned her nose up at the mention of the bi-valves. "Are ya sure ya want this first?" she inquired.

"Perfectly sure," the ancient one replied and waved her hand for her to continue.

Katrina shrugged her shoulders and followed the list, "After the oysters we will ladle beef consommé from the large tureen. When the last person finishes, the bowls and soup spoons will be cleared. This will be followed by baked cod in port wine sauce, saddle mutton, and puree of fowl nested in a wall of mashed potatoes, accompanied by applesauce."

"Russet apples?" the elder lifted her eyes upon the woman and repeated, "Russet apples, they are the best."

"Russet applesauce," she replied, "and candied carrots." Katrina grinned and quickly continued. "Both white and red wines will be offered with dinner." She paused for a moment and turned the page over. "All glasses and dishes will be cleared and I'll wait for your nod before we to proceed with dessert." Katrina set the paper on her lap and stated, "Ya still haven't decided between the fruit pudding in wine sauce or apple crisp pie, and its gettin' late."

"The pudding," the old one retorted, "and of course be sure to have fruits and cheeses on the trays. We'll then retire to the parlor for port." Mrs. Cambridge reached for one of her breakfast buns and pondered for a moment before selecting the plain dough with sprinkled sugar.

"I don't think all ten will fit in the parlor," Katrina said.

Mrs. Cambridge scowled and wiped her hands on the cloth napkin. "I may be old, but I'm not stupid!" she sneered as though ready to hiss and sting. "If my calculations are correct ten will never make it to dessert!"

Katrina boldly raised her eyes and she stood up with a piercing curiosity. "You're acting pretty cagey, pretty cagey indeed," she mumbled. But knowing better than to wait for an answer she simply shook her head and continued to prepare for the evening's event.

———

Jack Philander turned to the left then to the right, twisted his head as far around as his neck would allow in an attempt to get a better view of his back in the mirror. He picked up his walking stick, faced frontward again, bent his right knee slightly and advanced his foot, leaned his body back and posed. Nonchalantly he rested the stick to his right side. "Now what to do with the free arm?" he thought looking down at it as though it was a loose appendage. He held it stiffly, then relaxed. "A bent elbow perhaps," he pondered giving it a try. He knew that the mirror told no lies, unless it was deliberately slanted back, the old carnie trick to make someone look taller and thinner. "Excellent, excellent," he grinned. His eyes ran up and down the image of a well-dressed man in a severely starched white shirt, the high collar turned down slightly over a bow-tied cravat, a tightly fit frock coat and low vest tailored perfectly. He had spent too much money on his new clothes however; this was not a concern, for after tonight's dinner party, he would be richer, much richer. He shifted his body trying to secure a casual and leisurely stance. "Time?" he mimicked aloud and reached into his vest pocket. "Why yes, I do," he said and produced a gold pocket watch that would be the envy of any gentleman. He practiced snapping it open to expose the delicately filigreed face. "Half past the hour," he mocked and allowed the gold watch fob to dangle fashionably.

He stood for a few moments studying his stance in the mirror. "No one will notice this," he grimaced fingering the watch. Finely engraved initials, T.C. had been etched on the back. With his thumb he flipped the front cover shut and returned the watch into his pocket. A loose thread stuck up out of a shoulder seam, but when it wouldn't tug free he wet his fingers with a little saliva, moistened the rogue thread, and flattened it down with several pats of his hand. All thoughts drifted towards the mission that awaited him; for it was his responsibility to escort the guest from aboard the Starboard to the Cambridge Arms. He put on his hat but shuddered with the way it appeared, so drab and warn. "It will have to do," he thought as he practiced tipping it first to the left, then to the right, and then settled it upon his head. Hastily, he grabbed his walking stick and gave a last look at himself in the mirror. "Why Jack Philander, things are falling nicely into place," he cried aloud. A long maniacal laugh followed which echoed throughout the pitifully small room. "Indeed they are," he repeated in a low voice, "indeed they are."

―――――

As the afternoon drew to a close, Libby put away her last bit of sewing and went downstairs to see if she could help before the guests arrived. She had barely gotten the words out offering her assistance, when Katrina ushered her into the dining room to supervise the table setting. According to "de rigueur', strict rules of social decorum, a multitude of silverware and drinking glasses were waiting to be separated and placed at each seat. There were small forks for oysters, medium sized ones for fish and vegetables, and larger ones for meat. Wide mouth spoons were designated for soup, tiny ones for tea, while mid-size allocated and set aside for dessert and side dishes. The blunt edge knives were for buttering and sharp cutlery for cutting. Crystal tulip shaped glasses were appointed to accompany the first course oysters and to be filled with a Brut Champagne. Each guest needed a water goblet and two different wine glasses, one for white and the other red, upon which all of these instructions had sent poor Marte into hysterical confusion and tears.

"There, there, dear," Libby's voice was most gentle and assuring. "You go back to the kitchen and let me set this table," heeded Libby, trying to cheer the housemaid who had been crying for some time. Indeed, Marte had reason to be upset for she had never set a table with so many dishes, glasses, and eating utensils, and the more she tried to figure it out the more she realized how little she knew.

"Yah, are ya sure?" she whimpered, wiping her eyes with the hem of her baking apron.

"Of course I am sure, now go on! I know you have plenty more to do," the young mother-to-be insisted and encouraged her by gently stroking the back of her head, while Marte buried her face in her apron.

At which upon hearing the suggestion, the woebegone maid reappeared wearing a smattering of chalky flour, except for the tip of her nose which was quite red from crying. "Oh, Missy, thank you, thank you, an angel, you var an angel!" Marte sniveled between small sobs of despair; and she continued to repeat the word, angel, angel, all the way down to the kitchen.

"She's an idiot!" an annoyed voice cawed. "A complete idiot!"

Libby turned with a start to see the ancient one stooping over her cane in the open doorway. "Oh, Mrs. Cambridge, I didn't hear you come in!" the younger woman gasped. Libby glanced at the crystal goblet she was cradling and set it back upon the table, fearful that she may drop it for her hands were still shaking from having been startled.

"I trust that you know how to set a table?" called the old woman as she peered into the room. Not waiting for a reply, she continued. "As soon as you're done in here why don't you go upstairs for a bit of a rest before preparing for our little dinner party?" her voice now saccharine sweet. "You look tired, my dear," she added pursing her thin lips into a smile. "I do believe that it may be a longer and more eventful evening than you are used to."

"Yes, why thank you, Mrs. Cambridge," Libby agreed. "I am a bit tired."

"And Libby," directed the elder, "why don't you call me Auntie, that's what Nick calls me. Mrs. Cambridge is so formal. After all, I have grown so very fond of you and Will."

"Why thank you, Auntie," Libby exclaimed giving the new name a try, "you have been so very kind."

"No need to thank me, my dear," she answered hastily and leaving Libby to her work she started down the hall towards the kitchen. Rat a tat tat, her cane beat against the hard wood floors as she hobbled. Libby listened for a moment and wondered if perhaps she heard a rhythmic beat, a lighthearted tap that she had never noticed before coming from the old woman's stride.

———

"Ya can always tell something about a guest by the way they arrive," Nick remarked. "Now, let's take Dr. Bruner and his wife; they will hire a coachman and hansom, something we don't see too often. Or, they might just hitch up the Doc's horse to the buggy and drive over themselves. Tell ya what," he said turning to Will, "let's make this interesting, how about a little wager, buggy or hansom?" But before the transaction could even get started, they were interrupted by the crinkle of taffeta.

"Why, Nick Biddle, are you trying to cheat Mr. Piccard out of his hard earned money?" asked Wanda as she sauntered down the stairs. "Now tell me, just what are you two boys up to hangin' round here? Don't you have anything better to do?" she teased.

Nick reached for Wanda as she approached the last step. Gallantly he took her hand and kissed it as though she were regal. "Ain't he just grand?" she laughed and turning to Will added, "wait til ya see Libby, she's as pretty as they come."

"You don't look too bad yerself!" remarked Nick, who hadn't taken his eyes off a surprisingly prim Wanda. She lightly tossed a saffron yellow shawl over her pale shoulders and arranged it so that it draped elegantly down her back.

"Yes, you look very lovely," echoed Will. However, as Nick and Wanda exchanged flirtatious glances, Will was confronted by a notion that his presence was definitely an intrusion, as he was suddenly besought by a feeling of awkwardness. "Perhaps I should go up and see what's keeping Libby," he suggested. But as he began to excuse himself in his usual courteous fashion, a most heavenly image emerged like an apparition at the top of the stairs. It was an enchanting form of iconic pageantry amidst the dark and gloomy corridor. A flowing satin gown, which concealed pale satin slippers, offered an illusion that this angelic creature was floating. Libby carefully held the banister as she glided down the stairs towards her husband like a delicate snowflake.

"Now look at the four of ya, standin' around like there was nothin' to do!" Katrina complained, eyeing them as a policeman fixed upon loiterers. "Now, I'm bring'n down the Duchess," Katrina said using her most sarcastic tone referring to the euphemism of royalty, "and don't let her catch you dillydallying at the bottom of these stairs."

"We're off then, my dear Katrina," agreed Nick. "Come along now," he said turning to Wanda, "let's see if we can cajole someone to give us a sample of dinner," he suggested; and taking Wanda's arm he led the way.

The soft spoken Libby reached out to Katrina, "In what manner may we help?" she asked.

"Well, if ya can keep Nick from makin' Marte too nervous that would be a start!" the woman groaned and giving a wink she started up the stairs.

Directly after the death of her husband, Elizabeth Cambridge had her sleeping quarters renovated to meet her personal needs. Although the room had been constructed to be well ventilated and exposed to natural light, for a spacious bay window monopolized most of the exterior wall, she rarely permitted the curtains to be drawn open. Rather, she preferred to keep the room lit by a cut-glass chandelier of concentric rings that was suspended on a brass chain. Beneath the chandelier there stood an imported dressing table from France with an attached triple folding mirror of beveled and floral engraved glass. A silver monogrammed brush set, a wedding gift from a guest she couldn't remember, and a silver hinged pillbox laden with a porcelain floral spray, occupied the left side of the table.

The ancient one sat hunched forward before the mirror trying to decide which of the three perfumes to wear. In her younger days she knew that a woman's perfume deployed at the right time could be used as a powerful weapon. A partially completed cup of cocoa tottered alongside of her sweet scented ammunition. In the mirror's reflection she caught sight of the matching silver-top vanity jars upon a silver tray. She remembered when she had received them; they had been wrapped in the most glorious box with the largest purple satin bow. The boy was only twelve when his father took him shopping, allowing him to choose a birthday present for her. "I can't give them to you empty!" the child had exclaimed after she had unwrapped the gift. So he ran outside and plucked the blossoms off the garden roses and filled one with crimson petals and the other with pink. She brought her mind back to the present and wondered why she had kept these jars sealed ever since that day. Perhaps it was because like harbor lights in a dense fog, they were the only splendor left within the cheerless and monochromatic room. However, to believe such a warm design had come from such a hard old woman would be to misinterpret her character. Mrs. Cambridge lifted one of the jars; her gnarled fingers barely clasped the slippery glass. Carefully, she turned it upside down. Several of the petals lightly tossed about the empty space. Then, she turned it right side up and set the jar back upon the table with its mate. To this day they remained sealed; never having been opened since that celebration so many years ago.

For this evening's affair she had selected the same gown that she wore on the evening of her birthday, but unlike the rich colors of the petals, her pink chiffon had faded with age. She looked into the mirror and saw an old acquaintance staring back at her, a gold bordered cameo brooch still pinned to her dress. "So that's where you have been all these years," she remarked talking to the elegant woman resting on her shoulder. "And I thought that you were lost, not pinned to this dress stuck in the back of the armoire. Tut tut tut," the old woman continued, "but you certainly have not lost your beauty."

Katrina peered into the bedroom chamber after announcing herself at the open door with a light rap. Without turning around, for the elder could see who was standing in the portal by way of looking into the mirror, she beckoned with a crooked index finger to enter. "Good, you're on time," she said to Katrina. "Now help me with this," and handed her a strand of sea pearls. Katrina placed the necklace so it fell just below the thin wrinkled neckline and began working the mechanism on the gold clasp. It was a most intricate design made of inset coral and carved to resemble a tiny cherub.

"What a lovely string of pearls," Katrina said admiring the necklace after it was fastened. The elder nodded approvingly at her own reflection.

"Now," she added turning towards the maid, "why don't you proceed down before me and let them know I will be along in a moment." Then gesturing for her cane, Katrina handed it to her and left the room as instructed with the voice of the old woman still in her ears.

Mrs. Cambridge fell silent as the stir of feet moving and doors opening found their way up the stairwell and into the bedroom. She could hear a man cough, "Probably Admiral Ringgold who has brought back with him some dreaded croup from the Pacific," she pondered, still surprised by his return. A chorus of laughter followed by a woman's high pitched squeal, "That is surely the doctor's foolish wife and her empty babble," she thought with disgust. Pulling away from the dressing table, she leaned against her cane and stood up. Bit-by-bit she hobbled to the open door and grasped it with her free hand as another means of support. The obtrusive noises of the guests intermittently penetrated the corridor. She slowly made her way to the top of the stairs and peered down. Before a hunt the predator recapitulates the action it shall take and so she did. For a few moments the huntress conjured up an image of victory she had long been conspiring. Her left hand clasped the banister as the right guided the cane. She fixed her eyes upon the stairs as she plodded her way down step-by-step towards the dinner party and those who awaited her arrival.

———

In the animal kingdom the young quickly learn which beast is friend and which is foe. However, humans are not always as well prepared. Ill fated are those who are regarded as trusting and benevolent; for like the fly that had become entangled in the spider's web, they may find themselves unwillingly the victim of a carefully orchestrated snare.

———

Emanating from the corner of the dining room the mahogany clock rang out seven long consecutive chimes. Mrs. Cambridge, escorted by Nick, led the trail of hungry guests into the dining room. Several resounding refrains of "oohs" and "ahhs" were exclaimed as the party gathered round the elegantly set table. In preparation of the gastronomical marvel to be served, the glassware was lined up on top of the sideboard like votives on an altar and sparkled generously in the candlelight. Katrina helped Doctor Bruner and his wife to their seats as the other boarders occupied their usual places at the table. Nick pulled the chair at the head of the table out for the ancient one and waited while her angular figure was seated comfortably. Only the seat at the opposing head of the table and the chair to its left remained empty. "Nick," the elder whispered as she tugged on his jacket, "go tell Admiral Ringgold that the empty seat across from him will be occupied, two of our guests will be arriving later."

"And who may they be?" Nick asked; for he had never known her to be so accommodating for a late arrival.

"Well, if you need to know one is Jack Philander; he is bringing the passenger from the Starboard," she said in a soft and most pleasant voice she could muster.

"Jack Philander!" exclaimed Nick in a louder than intended cry. It was obvious by his tone that he was questioning her judgment. The other guests, already engaged in trivial conversations, turned their heads towards the hostess with prying eyes hoping to uncover the reason for such an intrusive exclamation. Mrs. Cambridge smiled and waved her hand casually indicating that there was nothing of substance going on at her end of the table. Upon taking her cue, the others resumed their chatter, all but Libby who now began to sense that something wasn't right. However, when Admiral Ringgold struck up a lively discourse about his travels to California and his experience with gold prospectors, the party soon became enamored of his wild tales.

Nick, realizing that he had made an unintentional scene, kneeled besides the old woman and whispered, "What are you up to, Auntie?"

But as he spoke she squeezed his hand with the greatest of force and harshness, revealing a direct contradiction to her anatomical appearance of being housed in a frail shell of a body. Her eyes glared angrily as she exhaled venom, "If you do that again," the miserable woman threatened in a very hushed voice, "I'll wrap you around my cane and I don't care who sees me!" Then smiling sweetly, she repositioned her stick and signaled for Katrina to bring round the first course of champagne and oysters.

They had scarcely begun to eat when Nick, who was sitting in his usual place next to his Auntie, rose from his seat. "Excuse me," he called out to the party. "Everyone, may I have your attention?" he exclaimed more emphatically than before. He waited for a moment until all had directed their eyes and ears to him. "Let us now come together and raise our glasses; let us toast to our grand hostess!" And as he elevated his champagne flute in the direction of the ancient one, the others quickly mimicked the custom. "To Mrs. Cambridge," they thundered in an almost perfect unison.

The Doctor, who wished to demonstrate his own refined couth added, "To good health," and again the glasses were raised and all chanted, "To good health!"

Wanda responded with a witty salutation she had picked up while among other less-refined acquaintances, "Come, fill up a bumper and let it go round, May mirth and good fellowship always abound!" Everyone chuckled with this bit of off-color humor. Katrina, who had placed herself by the sideboard, busily filled the champagne glasses for a third time. Except for Libby who did not partake in the evening's libations and Mrs. Cambridge, who had instructed Katrina to pour a minimal amount into her own glass, the guests drank heartily. In short; the party was in excellent spirits.

About the time everyone was ready for the next course, Mrs. Cambridge cast her chilly grey eyes up at the old timepiece as eight long chimes rang out. No one seemed to take notice of the hour except for Libby, who at the very moment the hands changed, just happened to detect the ancient one leering at the clock. Wanda was half-listening to Nick and Will discuss the political climate of the country as well as eavesdropping on a heated conversation between Mrs. Bruner, Mrs. Bruner's husband, and the Admiral concerning the dreadful situation with the French monarchy. The singer was growing tired of politics and turned her attention to Libby, who she found now sitting very quietly while moving her food about the plate. So fair and youthful, like an alabaster china doll, one could hardly imagine that she could be old enough to be having a baby. The entertainer was transported back to the evening she read the tiny palm and shuddered under the prospect of the undisclosed prediction. If there was ever a night when such a prophecy could come true, this could be it! Wanda was suddenly overcome with a feeling of grave uncertainty. "Nick," she whispered leaning against his arm, "we have to get Libby out of here!" But no sooner did she try to recount her concerns to her companion, who was unable to hear her for the room was consumed with uproarious laughter and conversation, did Katrina return from the kitchen requesting Libby's assistance. Mrs. Stark, who if you remember remains short one finger, and Marte were being overrun with dirty dishes, so much so, that they were in desperate of need of having more help with the serving of the prepared meal. Once these platters were brought out to the dining room, there would be plenty of room in the kitchen to stack the mess.

"Of course, I will help," Libby graciously answered and politely excusing herself from the table, she followed Katrina back to the kitchen where the grand feast was being perfected.

The savory scents of cooked meats and yeasty smell of baked bread followed a large steamy soup tureen out of the kitchen, and mixing with the elegant fragrances of the cut roses, the mélange of aromas perfumed the air. In the midst of the meal, when the party was in high gear, the eminent arrival of a hired hansom presented itself in front of the Cambridge Arms. Jack Philander stepped down and paid the driver, while a second individual dropped his bag into the street before descending from the coach. It was a dark starless night and had Jack not been fiddling with his gold toothpick, which caught the light tossed from the corner streetlamp, both persons may have easily blended into their surroundings. The hansom drove off leaving the two standing alone in the quiet street. "Are ya ready mate?" laughed Jack. "That is what you English call each other, mate, ain't it? he asked.

The man took his time mulling over the question before coming up with the reply. "That's what we would call each other if we were chums," he answered. Jack shrugged his shoulders, picked up the man's valise, and motioned for him to follow. The stranger's gait was slow and deliberate, for he had not rid himself of his sea legs, which he acquired during the ship's long and arduous journey. They passed through the unlatched gate and upon approaching the front entranceway, Jack straddled the bag between his legs and placed several light raps against the door with his walking stick.

Mrs. Cambridge, who still possessed the keen hearing of a wolf despite her age, was the only one who heard the knocking amongst the engaged dialogue. "Will," the elder called gaining the attention of the young man, "do you mind answering the door? I believe our second party has arrived, and dear Katrina is so busy."

But only a moment after the appeal had been issued did Nick respond by setting down his spoon and jumping to his feet to oblige; for he knew too well of the traps often set by the scoundrel who made the request. "No reason to disturb Will," he cried. "I'll go."

"Sit down, Nick." the old woman commanded politely, however unbeknownst to the others, she simultaneously kicked him under the table with her foot. "Why, you haven't finished your soup," she cajoled feigning concern. Nick sat back down like a scolded child and proceeded to rub his hurt shin.

Will, more than happy to avail the old woman, for he was uncomfortable in this formal setting and more than ready to stretch his legs, pulled his chair away from the table and excused himself to the others. He turned, thanked Nick for the offer, and gave him a hearty slap on the back as he passed behind his friend's chair.

"Isn't he such a nice young gentleman?" Mrs. Bruner said as Will left the dining room, "and that Libby, a perfect darling."

At once a firm hollow knock struck the door, but this time proclaiming more impatience than the original tepid raps. Mrs. Cambridge picked up her spoon, dipped it into the bowl, and sipped the hot soup. Then, dabbing her wrinkled lips with her napkin she turned to her guests and rhetorically asked, "I do hope you are all enjoying my little party." However, rather than listening to the complimentary replies which shadowed her question, she ignored them all and tuned her ear to the foyer where she listened as Will made his way to the front door and started to unlatch the lock for the awaiting guests.

Chapter 39

Now that the Tarsons had decided to go east for an undetermined amount of time, legal arrangements were drawn up giving April Henshaw provisional guardianship over Grace. As the custodial parent, it became necessary for the teacher to move out of her present living quarters and into the big house on the hill. Not leaving anything to chance, Missus Tarson also hired William Beasley, a business acquaintance with impeccable references, to take over the day-to-day affairs. The extra room once occupied by Miss Henshaw became a natural fit for the new employee's occupancy. Belle Tarson anticipated that his belongings would be transported from St. Louis at once, allowing the man to take up her rent free proposal straightaway. But, his first impression of the intended living arrangements was not favorable for he found the tiny room much more rustic and modest than he was accustomed to. Mr. Beasley, who liked to be called Mr. Billy, proved to be a most convincing little fellow and renegotiated for an increase in the original salary. The terms of Missus Tarson's contract were agreed upon by both parties, especially since Belle had little time to find another suitable person for the job. So, it was on the very day Belle's carriage departed down the winding road did Mr. Billy's wagon find its way up.

At first it was hard for Grace not to stare at him because she had never met anyone with a hunchback, even though it was a small hump. But having been brought up with good manners, she soon found herself disregarding his stooped posture and labored limp. The little man had never been married, perhaps because of his slight deformity, and seemed to take a greater interest in work than being sociable. He was not accustomed to being around children; however found Grace an exception to the rule for her demeanor was quiet, polite, and not meddlesome.

Beatrice retained her position as head of the household staff and found that she was able to get most all the chores done more quickly now that she did not have to contend with the usual interruptions from Belle. As for Miss Henshaw, she too had acquired more free time because there were days when Grace was her only student. The little girl continued to prove herself to be a bright and fast learner, so much so that Miss Henshaw could excuse her before lunch, allowing the child time to help Beatrice with the afternoon chores. Much to Grace's chagrin this was a frequent event. "Idle hands make idle minds," quoted Miss Henshaw whenever there would be the tiniest fuss about having to hang clothes on the line or assisting with the dipping of tallows. Only when Grace went off to teach Alex Forester a new lesson was she excused from what the child coined as, "Dumb woman's work!"

And so, such a day was today when the schoolroom sat empty. Grace had completed all her lessons in the first part of the morning and as much as one would like to think that this was a gloriously sunny day with birds chirping and cool breezes pushing billowy clouds about the sky like a light load in a wheelbarrow, it was sadly quite the contrary. On this rainy and most gloomy day the sky was as grouchy as Grace who found herself miserably bored and not the least bit interested in darning stockings or completing a needlepoint. She just couldn't understand how a little rain was preventing her from being able to visit Alex Forester. Even if he wasn't much interested in school, she was dying to show him how to use a quill pen. The fact that she could write on something other than slate had opened up a whole new world of creative ideas.

Beatrice was in the middle of baking bread and not likely to tread across the rugs with an apron dusted with flour, the busy housekeeper surely would not come in to check on her work. With this in mind, Grace decidedly pushed the sewing basket into the corner of the room and as softly as a snowflake lands on a twig, sat down at Belle's writing table. It had always been off limits to anyone except maybe Mr. Tarson, and even then he left all correspondence to his wife. There was an almost lonesome feel about it, as though the austere desk was yearning for company. "Such a grand desk this is," Grace thought and ran her fingers across the smooth wood finish. Dubiously, she looked behind her just to make sure there was no one around. Beatrice could be heard talking to herself while kneading the dough.

"This desk has its own history," Grace said mockingly in her best imitation of Belle's voice. "Every child in my family, as far back as 1760 learned to write his or her name on this desk." Grace slid her hand along the edge and tried to recollect if Joseph had ever had a chance. The desk wasn't very long by some standards of fancy desks and stood on tapered legs made of turned wood that resembled a pair of woolen stockings. Along the front were twin drawers decorated with a delicate foliate motif of lighter colored inlaid wood. Grace pulled on the new brass rings that had recently replaced the original wooden knobs. The former had been accidentally broken off when the desk was moved away from the window to its present location. Belle had insisted the sun would damage the natural wood. The young impersonator removed a sheet of parchment paper, a small bottle of ink, and a duck quill from the open drawer and placed them side by side. "Now, what will I write?" she thought as she tried to pry open the full bottle of black ink. As one would suppose, it would seem most probable, even presumptive, that Grace, in her youthful enthusiasm to write, may surely become less than careful and upon the first dip of the quill tip, topple the inkwell. But that would be too obvious a mistake for although Grace was a child, she was by no means a dolt. On the contrary, she thoughtfully doused the tip as she had been instructed and allowed her hand to take over, gliding the quill across the paper like an ice skater, twirling and swirling with the most glorious penmanship. This calligraphy for a child her age was something to admire and as she wrote she became submerged in her own world.

Dear Alex Forester,
    You are invited to a picnik this Saturday at noon. Please meet me under the apple tree.

From your frend,
THE one and only Grace Tarson

She gently rolled the blotter back and forth over her work, taking care not to smear any of the newly written letters. She reread her note aloud putting particular emphasis on the phrase, "from your friend", but scrunched her nose up as she reviewed a few of the words. Although she was a good student she was not sure if her spelling was all correct, but disposed of these doubts figuring that Alex wouldn't mind a few mistakes since he was far worse than she was. She puckered her lips and lightly blew across the note, trying to accelerate the ink's drying time.

"What in heaven's name are you up to little missy?" exclaimed Beatrice.

Grace jumped up from the writer's desk, for the sound of Beatrice's gruff voice startled her. The chair came crashing backwards due to her quick response, adding to the commotion. Instinctively, she hid the note under the blotter. Her heart was fluttering as rapidly as a bumble bee's wings. "Beatrice, you scared the wits out of me!" she moaned and placed her hand over her heart while fanning herself with a blank sheet of paper for a dramatic effect.

The flour dusty housekeeper kept her distance and stood with arms crossed in front of her like a fairytale genie that had just emerged from a magic lantern. "What are you up to?" she repeated; her tone demanded a solution.

"I was just practicing my writin'," the child answered and crossed her fingers behind her back even though this didn't seem like a fib because it was a half-truth. She picked up the toppled chair and slid it back into place.

"You know that Belle don't want nobody fussin' with her belongings!" Beatrice humphed and then with a crooked finger beckoned, "bring me what's under the blotter."

"Under the blotter?" Grace remarked coyly and searched about the desk as though pretending not to understand.

"Now, don't go tryin' to fool Beatrice!" the woman announced and as she pivoted forward a plume of flour followed her. However, after taking only a few steps into the room she hesitated and declared, "Don't make me mark up these floors neither!"

Reluctantly Grace lifted the blotter and picked up the hidden invitation. "It's private," she said walking over to the woman and handing her the paper. "It ain't bad, just private," she reiterated.

It took a moment for Beatrice to extract a pair of round rimmed spectacles from her apron pocket and put them on. Tilting forward she slowly read the invitation. "I see," she remarked, trying not to show any emotion. "And tell me, what are you gonna put into your picnic basket?" she asked, handing the note back to Grace.

Grace leaned her head to the side and with a slight shrug of her shoulders gave her answer. "I ain't sure," she mumbled meekly.

Beatrice stood erect for several minutes and shook her head with disapproval. "Well, I believe we got some work to do if we want to fill this basket, don't we?"

Grace looked away and back down at the invitation, aligning the edges so it would be perfectly folded in half. "So I ain't in trouble?" she asked and offered a smile up at the large woman.

Beatrice glared upon the inquisitive face, pouted her lips, and just nodded left and right for a few moments. "Do ya think Alex likes boiled ham?" she inquired. "Don't know nobody that don't like boiled ham." Then without waiting for an answer from the child, the large woman turned and sauntered away leaving behind a gossamer of flour.

Grace stood in the threshold and listened to the wind howl while the rain roughly pelted the roof. Suddenly this gloomy day seemed to offer more light than the previous morning of sunshine. She unfolded the note and smiled at the neat letters, pleased with her penmanship. She remained absorbed in the happy reflections of the future. "Now, if I can just get Beatrice to let me deliver this note!" she schemed and playfully skipped towards the kitchen to forge an amicable plan which would suit her elders.

———

Finally after several hours and many more cross-stitches later; Beatrice found time enough to pay attention to Grace. After some wrangling, it was agreed that the note would be carried to Alex Forester the following morning by way of Mr. Billy, who happened to be heading in the same direction as the Forester's. Without much delay to his own business affairs, he could stop off and make the delivery. Naturally this plan was contingent upon fair weather. "But why can't I go myself?" begged Grace hoping to change the reluctant woman's mind. Yet no fussing or pouting made any difference; the matter was closed. Since Mr. Billy was already scheduled to leave directly after sunrise and his morning coffee, there was no reason for Grace to miss any lessons with Miss Henshaw on account of a 'silly' invitation.

"Go on now; I believe Mr. Beasley is in the dining room having his midday meal. Ya better give it to him now before he leaves to do his work," cried Beatrice and shooed Grace along with the business end of the broom as though she was a pesky field mouse.

Now as was said before, Grace was a bit shy when it came to Mr. Billy and the idea of asking him to hand-deliver something so personal was more than she could muster. Softly, on cat feet, she padded into the hallway and stopped directly to the right of the open doorway. She listened as the sound of a spoon hitting the side of a bowl clanged; then there was a long slurp as the lips touched the edge of the silver and the hot broth sloshed its way into his mouth. Again the sound of the spoon hitting the bowl was followed by a long and contented slurp. Grace peered round hoping that he would not look up. She craned her neck so only her head would appear in the doorway when suddenly, to her dismay, at the very moment she thought the coast was clear, he looked up from his crouched position over the bowl. "My dear, please enter!" he said and wiped his mouth as though it were a delicate flower. He turned his face towards her and smiled compassionately as the hump too moved forward as though wanting to see her better.

Grace edged into the room and stood before him. Her heart began to thump and she felt herself unable to speak, as though if she tried, the words would become garbled and unintelligible. Then for some reason, she knew not why, she grabbed the hem of her skirt with her left hand, for the other was holding her prized note, she pulled the calico away from her legs and she curtsied. It was not a small delicate curtsey, oh no, it was one that would have been suited for a queen; a low, deep and knee bending, a one foot forward curtsey. As such, all might have gone well had she not been wearing her over-sized boots, which were by no means the correct pair of shoes that one wears while making such an elegant gesture. And as luck may have had with the very deep bend, she just happened to tip a bit too far forward and toppled head-over-heels creating a most unfortunate stance.

"My dear child!" the deformed man wailed upon seeing Grace lying prone upon the floor. "Are you all right?" However, before he could get himself away from the table she had quickly scampered up on her own two feet and was dusting herself off even before he could rise.

Now, Mr. Billy may have been a quiet and reserved fellow, but he was by no means insensitive to the feelings of others and could tell that her pride was more wounded than her knees or elbows and changed the subject from her fall to the reason for her visit. Grace reluctantly explained that she needed him to stop and deliver her note, adding that she was perfectly capable of such a task however another person, whom she was not to mention, had other plans for her. Then, she handed over her invitation to the little man, all the while trying desperately not to allow her eyes to wander towards his humped back.

"I see that your letter is not sealed," he said and placed it upon the table. "Perhaps I may be of help. It just so happens that I have been completing some correspondence for your step-mother, she is not your birth mother, is that so?" he asked.

Grace nodded her head "yes".

"Then," he continued, "if you wish, I can seal it shut from any prying eyes." In a rather decisive advance, he pushed his chair away from the table, stood up, as tall as a hunched-back man is able, and limped to the opposite end where several piles of neatly stacked documents were aligned. Setting Grace's invitation upon the table, he meticulously refolded it so the opposite ends met in the middle; whereupon he rolled a warm pea-size ball of wax upon these two edges and with a stamp firmly pushed down until a thin circular rim curled up around the seal he was holding. Grace watched as he held the paper with one hand and gently pulled the seal away from the crimson wax. The letter was now tightly secured. Grace admired the embossed impression; a carbon copy pressed into sticky wax. Was it a letter 'B'? She couldn't make it out at first. She picked up the invitation to examine its elegant addition. But as her small index finger hovered over the wax preparing to touch what appeared to be irresistible strawberry taffy, she heard an explicit, "No, my child, allow it to harden!" The small man tugged the note free and held it away as though if she were to touch it she would turn into a pillar of salt. "Have you ever seen one of these before?" he asked and abruptly handed Grace the metal seal to examine. "I used to work for an enchanting family and 'B' is their initial, just as it is mine. I suppose that I forgot to give it back when I left!" he mused.

Grace rolled the small object over in her palm. It was the fanciest initial she had ever seen; most undoubtedly it belonged to a very important person indeed. One day she would own a very fancy seal, but as her mind wandered she found that she couldn't decide if it would be a "T" for Tarson or maybe an "F" for Forester! Suddenly, she felt her cheeks flush from this daydream and quickly handed the seal back to the rumpled man. She patted her cheeks with her palms hoping that her thoughts were not transparent.

"Oh, where are my manners?" she said aloud and began to back away from the table. "I better be getting back to Beatrice or she'll have my hide! Thanks fer yer help and fer deliverin' my note tomorrow, Mr. Billy." Then taking particular care not to look at his hump, she smiled meekly and started away.

The small hunchback placed the invitation upon a stack of documents that were meant for his attention and limped back to his place at the table. He sat back down and picked up the spoon that he had left tilted in his soup bowl and commenced to finish his meal.

Chapter 40

Mitch was right, the terrain was anything but hospitable, however when they finally arrived Pinto Jack knew he had made the correct decision to head west. He soon learned that Split Rock Station was not only used by the Pony Express as a relay, but was a reliable stopping off point for emigrants in Prairie Schooners and Conestogas heading northwest. Unlike other stations, this one was noted for its hardy log structure that was situated at the base of the gnarly wall of rocks.

"These here have saved many a folk, yes indeed!" claimed Llewellyn pointing to the rocks. Pinto Jack listened intently to the old man. Llewellyn was the stationmaster who had been a fur trapper and trail guide before becoming hired by the Pony Express as the relay station's most 'interesting' employee. "See that one, the real pointy craggy-edged rock?" he asked squinting into the sun. "Granite, that's what it is, granite." Jack nodded hoping the old man was getting to the point. "Split Rock, it ain't just a name," he stated and looked directly into Pinto Jack's eyes to be sure he was listening. "It's a lifesaver, salvation, a spot on this earth that the good Lord placed so that man would find his way." Llewellyn stopped, cleared his throat and then asked, "Now, what was I saying?"

Jack assisted, "You were saying that the good Lord..."

"Oh yes!" the elder interrupted with much fervor. His wispy grey hair fluttered about in the light breeze as he spoke. "Now, this very spot is a well-known landmark, those wagons comin' from the east are guided for a whole day. Those going west can turn round and see it fer at least two days. Never thought that a rock would be yer guardian angel, did ya?" the old man cleared his throat again, but this time relished the moment to spit.

When Pinto Jack first arrived he wasn't sure why the main office in St. Joseph needed another man at Split Rock however, he soon realized that in spite of Llewellyn's great wealth of knowledge, he did have a certain drawback; he had a tendency to fall asleep during the most inopportune times. It was not uncommon for him to be in the middle of a conversation during supper when, for no apparent reason, his chin would fall upon his chest as his neck drooped forward in a most relaxed and limp state, whereupon his head would swoon with no more rigor than a rag doll, and no matter what may be in its way, which included a plate of perfectly prepared victuals or hot broth, he simply collapsed into a deep and unwakeable sleep. On the other hand, Llewellyn knew every nook and cranny of the Wyoming territory and provided the new express riders with pertinent information. He was their symbol of assurance, a steadfast guarantee that if they heeded his advice they would have a good chance of making it to the next relay station alive. Unlike other stationmasters before him, Llewellyn knew as much about the land as the Shoshone and Crow that inhabited the hills and beyond.

"Did I ever tell ya 'bout a fella named Theodore Grant?" Llewellyn asked Jack. "Yep, a most intriguing man; he was heading west from…" the experienced elder paused and then started up again. "I believe it was Massachusetts, yep, that's it!" he remarked. "A most intriguing fellow indeed," he repeated as though in deep contemplation.

Jack sat down and waited patiently hoping that he would find out more about this Theodore Grant before the storyteller fell into one of his sudden slumbers. Jack gave the man a little nudge, which seemed to have started him up again.

"Now, what was I saying?" he stroked his wispy-haired chin as he pondered.

"You were telling me about a fellow from Massa …"

But before he could say the entire name of the state the old man blurted out, 'Yes, Massachusetts, Grant, Theodore Grant! Well, you'll never guess what load he was carrying in his Conestoga!" the man shouted and with as much energy as he began he halted his story abruptly. "Well?" he demanded wishing for an answer.

Jack looked inquisitively. Not expecting that he was supposed to guess he said, "I really have no clue."

"Guess!" shouted Llewellyn with a most emphatic reply.

Jack was on the spot. "Chickens?" he asked.

"Chickens! What kind of guess is that? No, he wasn't takin' no chickens! Well, maybe he had one or two, but no, that ain't right! He was takin' jars, sixty, that's right sixty jars! He had crates full of jars!" the old man expelled with gusto. Then, as though severely irritated, he plopped down upon the rickety rocking chair situated in the corner of the large room, pulled out a torn handkerchief and mopped his face. When the last drop of sweat was dried, he stuffed the filthy rag back into his rear pocket and leaned back. The tired rocker creaked as it carried him back and forth. Being as he was not a large man, he was able to keep the chair in motion without too much effort.

Jack was now curious and had become quite intrigued by the story. "Jars, what was in these jars? Why did Theodore Grant feel compelled to load his wagon and drive them all the way from Massachusetts, Westward?" he asked enthusiastically, wishing the answer to this mystery be divulged. Nevertheless, after posing his questions, he waited for a few moments more, and soon realized it would be awhile before the answers were revealed. Unfortunately, the old man had fallen into one of his intolerable states. Resting his grey head now comfortably upon the wall, for the chair had finally given up without his momentum, he was completely relaxed and had settled easily into a midday nap.

Jack shook his head as he stared at the sleeping man. He was indeed a paradox. Sometimes you can tell a man's age by how many white hairs he has lost or by the amount of wisdom he has acquired. Llewellyn was a man that had accumulated all of the aforementioned including the harshness of the sun's weathering upon his skin. "Perhaps he is younger than he appears," Jack suggested to himself. "Maybe this seemingly old fellow wears only the façade of an ancient ruin." Jack dismissed this notion however, for he had become acutely aware that this old timer's knowledge extended decades beyond his peers. Jack watched as Llewellyn shifted positions, appearing to be engaged in a most delightful dream; for upon his face was an expression that transcended from a smile into distinct laughter. "It must be nice to be so content with oneself," Jack mused and walked out of the cabin to tend to Cally, who was waiting for her mash.

———

Alex looked down at his hands and rubbed the newly formed calluses that landscaped his palms. "It's been hard since Randle's been gone," he whispered to Delilah and Dandy. "It's not so bad for me, but Betty, she sure don't say nothing anymore. She wasn't one fer talkin', but now she just keeps to herself." Alex stuck his hands into his pockets and searched for a small treat, only to discover tiny bits of sugar bonded to the coarse material. He tried to pick some off with his fingernails, but they simply pulverized into even tinier specks. "I ain't got much," he explained apologetically and turned his pockets inside out so they could see that they were empty. Granules of dislodged sugar crystals sprinkled freely onto the ground. His fingers were sticky, and he wiped them back and forth along the sides of his pants until they were less gummy. "One day, just one day, you two won't have to work so hard; one day, you'll see, I promise!" Alex stroked their long smooth noses. Each horse returned the affection by deliberately nudging his shoulders. He closed his eyes and sighed. This was what was meant by peace; this was the only true peace he knew. A few tears began to trickle down from the corner of his eyes upon his dusty cheeks. He quickly wiped them with his sleeve and turned his face away from the four brown eyes that were watching him. He had lied, he never lied, but he felt that he couldn't tell them what he really knew. "Oh how could I have said that everythin' would be right?" he distressed. "How can I tell 'em Betty is always tired; that she's threatnin' to sell the land and the house and everythin' on it?" Alex crumbled to his knees and dug his hands into the hay and dirt that he knelt upon. He bowed his head as a sudden rush of grief tightened inside his chest. Maybe he could die right here in this spot, at this very moment and leave the world so he did not have to feel this agony of deception. Alex lifted his head and looked beyond the stalls; then he slowly closed his eyes hoping that when they opened he would be somewhere else, miraculously transported into another gentler realm.

———

On that craggy chilly hilltop everything below appeared bleak and still. Sergeant, unscathed by the happenings around, scouted the area. His black nose skimmed the ground while his tail wagged feverishly like a hapless puppy. Upon the discovery of every moving leaf and branch, he unearthed six-legged creatures and romped after those on four. Tully turned over the year in his mind and although leaving matters of others that did not concern him concealed, he began to approach the situation before him differently. He descended cautiously with Sergeant now romping by his side and whenever he stopped the dog stopped. Tully crouched down and leaned heavily against one knee while Sergeant lay by his side waiting for the command to continue either back up or down the trail. His eyes followed a horse-drawn wagon straddling the dusty track. The driver hunched nervously forward trying to keep the wheels steady as they rocked and quaked between the well-traveled grooves that had been etched by so many wagons and carriages before. Tully shifted his position leaning forward, his eyes perched upon the driver. Sergeant sensed his movement and opened one eye, only to close it when he saw his master did not make any attempt to move in either direction.

A well-tailored individual pulled the reins back, set them down, and then clumsily dismounted. It soon became quite clear that the limping man was a hunchback and had arrived at the Forester's with a delivery.

Tully watched the events unfold; Betty's monotone voice was carried by the wind as she exchanged informalities with Mr. Billy. Although he was asked to come in for coffee, he declined cordially accepting a future invitation, handed her the note with a simple explanation, and hobbled back to the wagon. His first attempt to ascend proved to be futile for the ground he stood upon was positively uneven, and he happened to be standing in a very low spot. Betty waited as he pulled the wagon forward, finding higher ground, which allowed his second attempt to be a success. Settling back onto the seat, he turned towards the tired woman, tipped his hat, pulled the old mare round, and rode away. Betty sat down upon the steps and wearily leaned against the wooden post dropping the invitation beside her. A cool unconventional breeze stirred. She looked up and wondered how long she had been sitting; a minute, an hour, a day? Without moving her head she glanced down and noticed that the note was no longer visible. Had she dreamed the entire event; the horse, the wagon, the hunchback? The wind stirred again bringing the sealed invitation into the foreground. She reached forward and without much effort retrieved it just as Alex was walking toward her. "Got somthin' for ya, boy," she said as he approached. She wiped her face with her apron and handed him the letter. "It's from the little Tarson girl," she continued. "Mr. Billy brung it round not too long ago, I think," Betty remarked.

Alex smiled as he turned the letter over in his hand.

"Mightly fancy writin'," Betty said grinning with curiosity. "Look at that pretty stamp, it sure looks special. Mr. Billy told me that you've been invited to a picnic by the little Tarson girl."

Alex stared at the spot where the letter had been marked by wax and wondered if he should open the note in the presence of Betty or wait until he was alone. Something about the elaborate seal stopped him from cracking it apart. Betty changed the drift of her conversation. "Ya done with the chores?" she asked.

Alex nodded, "yes".

"Well then, why don't ya go round back and fetch water to wash up with?" she suggested and pointed to the wooden bucket as though it was his first time. The boy agreed and systematically folded the note and stuffed it into his pocket. Then, just like every afternoon that had proceeded, he commenced with the end of the day rituals. Betty sat back semi-dormant under the shade of the porch roof. She purposely gazed straight ahead. She decided awhile ago not to look up on account that the roof needed so much patch work that she didn't need reminding. She could hear Alex shuffling towards the water pump with an occasional knock of the bucket hitting his leg with every other step. Timothy crept up from behind and with the usual audacity of his kind, tried to settle into her lap for a rest. "Well, Mr. Timothy, you better not get too comfy, some of us got work to do!" Betty scolded and gave him a great shove, pushing him off her apron. Resuming his feline disposition, as though he had been unreasonably maligned, he quickly scampered away while Betty lumbered to her feet. Reluctantly, the big cat set out to the corner of the porch, took several laps circumnavigating the same spot until suddenly, as though he had found the ultimate point in the imaginary circle, lay down and fell asleep.

As the day dragged itself away from the sun and succumbed to the moon both the boy and the woman finally retired for the night. The dimly lit shadow of the house drew Tully closer to the Forester property. He continued to observe the comings and goings of its occupants. The man sat at the bottom of the hill with Sergeant by his side. Life had been simpler in times past, but as circumstances changed his occasional encounters with the boy had become more and more frequent. The observer leaned back on his elbows and planted himself into the earth, while Sergeant lay comfortably leaning against his master like adhesive. The night lingered with restless stirs that slowly awakens a keen man's senses. The bleak stillness that had appeared earlier on top of the craggy hill was moment by moment becoming transformed and agitated by the nocturnal creatures of the night. Tully reached over and petted the grand dog upon its large head. The tail thumped with gratitude for several wags and then changed its beat as though deliberately trying to keep time with the rising chatter of the katydids.

Alex sat back and leaned against the wall with his feet dangling off the edge of the cot. He pulled the note from his pocket and turned it over in his hand. Earlier in the afternoon Timothy had crept into his room and now slept peacefully on the tattered quilt folded at the foot of the bed. The cat's large head rested comfortably upon its two front legs that were stretched out before him. The wax seal had become an object of curiosity for Alex ever since he first examined it. He just couldn't recall why it looked so familiar; he was sure he had seen one like it before. There had been several letters and documents that belonged to Randle but no, no stamp quite so elaborate and ornate ever was used. Alex slipped his finger along the seam and pulled upward cracking the seal. Bits of splintered wax flipped up into the air and landed on the dusty floor. He spread the note before him and noticed how finely it had been written. He read each sentence slowly, his lips stumbling on a few mispronounced words. Saturday, noon, apple tree; his mind raced from one image to another and with each picture he conjured in his mind an emotion followed like harmony in a duet. He had wanted to visit the apple tree, but ever since Randle had taken sick it was near impossible to steal time away from chores. Betty had started taking in more piecework, mending and darning for the neighbors; not because she needed the money but because it helped her pass the lonely nights. It was in the midst of those deserted hours that overwhelming unhappiness filled her heart. It was during these moods of melancholy that she formulated elaborate schemes of selling all her possessions and property and moving back East. With prospects of a new future she would become momentarily energized. But could she really leave, she wondered? Perhaps it was better to stay here with memories of what was, than to move forward and face the ugly unknown.

Alex lay upon his cot with his head resting upon the lumpy blanket he had crumpled into a makeshift pillow. He aligned his legs and feet along the wall, trying to be especially careful not to annoy Timothy who was completely relaxed and taking up way too much of the tiny bed. His thoughts flitted about like a moth as he tried to design a workable schedule. So far his best plan would be to get up at least an hour earlier on Saturday to get an extra start on his chores. But the more he thought about it the more it didn't seem like a very good plan; it was hard enough to wake up at the usual time. Besides, he would have to ask Betty to wake him, and he couldn't do that. Perhaps he could get up at the usual time, but work later into the evening when he returned from the picnic. Fortunately, Betty was not one to care as long as everything got done. Alex turned the invitation over and picked at the remaining half-broken seal which clung to the paper. "Why is this so familiar?" he asked himself. "Where have I seen this before?" Timothy looked up as though he was going to answer, stretched, and then fell back to sleep. Alex remained numb and silent; he listened to Timothy breathe, noticing the large feline took two breaths to his one. It was so much quicker than his own. The boy tried to breathe at the same pace as the cat, watching the up and down motion of the cat's large body. And then, without warning a voice inside his head, one that he had not heard for so many years announced itself with a single, "Here." It was not the kind of "here" that signifies a location, no, it was the "here" that someone says before handing something to you; like "Here, you may have this."

Alex sat up, got off the bed and knelt down and peered under. The cot's thin wooden frame now sagged from both time and the gradual weight increase from his growing body. A curious sensation of one who is setting out on a discovery overcame him. "Why hadn't he looked into this for so long?" he wondered and positioned himself on all fours. Leaning on one hand, he bowed his head, facing the underside of the cot, and tugged on the leather handle with his free hand. He recollected the first time he peeked under the cot. Now, almost seven years later, he would pull out for only the second time the old carpetbag that he had stashed so faithfully on his first day. It wasn't that he had forgotten about it. The truth was that there was nothing in it that he needed. He continued to yank with more might, but now found that he had managed to wedge it between a bowed plank and a small rise in the floor. Alex lay flat against the ground and wriggled like a snake under the frame until he could stretch his right arm and reach with his fingertips. Finally, unlike seven years ago, he was able to maneuver the carpetbag so much more easily in comparison to the time he had originally shoved it into this hiding place. The bag appeared so much smaller now; how difficult it had been to carry. He remembered disembarking from the orphan train and never letting go of its handle, lest he lose the only familiar item he possessed. Alex sat on the floor and placed the bag before him. It was older looking too; time had yellowed its fabric like the sun that etches years upon a face. He tugged it open, releasing a hint of lilac; a fragrance that he had only inhaled once since he was a very young boy. He held it open and rummaged about until he felt what he had been looking for. "Here," a voice in his head stated; it was crystal clear who this voice belonged to.

Alex retrieved the object from the bottom of the bag and began to reexamine it with greater interest. "Here," his father had said, "this is an heirloom from your mother's side of the family." In the fading light Alex began to rediscover the signet ring. He placed it up to his eye turning it towards the last stream of daylight. The stone's decorative carving; the single initial "C" was placed in the center, suggesting that the ring's other function was that of a seal. Alex twisted it to the side and followed the inside and outside of the ring. He saw that it was marked "10K" on the reverse of the band. The back had been set to allow light to bleed through the red stone. He slipped the band on his ring finger and then his index finger; however found both were still too slim for it to fit securely. Trying again, he placed it on his thumb and decided that it was way too uncomfortable. He turned the ring over in his hand, rolling it along his palm. His mind drifted about and wondered how something so important could be packed away here in this tiny dusty little room. He closed his eyes and tried to remember his father taking the ring off. Did he toss it into the bag carelessly or was it hidden with the intention of concealing it from those who came and took him away? Nothing was clear, just a blur in a moment of time choked with anger and resentment, a moment in time heaped with sorrow and pain. He held the ring up to his eye as if to reexamine it and then decided not to put it back into the valise, but rather he stuffed it into his pocket.

The deliverance of dusk was accompanied by a low mournful hoot hoot. Perched on low limbs in the nearby woods and along forest edges the small owl swoops down on prey or catches insects in flight. Timothy awoke abruptly and as though attending to its call, leapt off the bed, sat before the closed door, and proceeded to meow with great impertinence. Alex obeyed. He slid across the floor like a crab and cracked the door open to release the prisoner. Timothy wasted no time and scampered away with the attitude of a caged lion.

Yellow candlelight spilled over from the kitchen into his tiny cubical by traversing the exit space created by Timothy. Alex folded the handles and shoved the bag back beneath his cot before Betty could happen along and ask him what he was up to; even though he wasn't really up to anything. The tired boy now lay upon the lumpy mattress and placed his hands behind his head and shut his eyes. Everything was back in its place, everything except for the lingering smell of a lilac. Then, without much effort he turned on his side and wearily drifted off to sleep.

Chapter 41

Whoever was behind the front door continued in their efforts to gain the attention of the rooming house occupants. There sounded another heavy knock followed by several impetuous raps with the butt of a stick; this time markedly louder and more deliberate than the previous attempts. "I'm coming!" cried Will to the impatient visitor as he tried release the latch. However, no matter which way he turned the knob the door did not want to release itself. Again there was a rap from outside, this time coming from the adjacent window. Will slid the curtain aside and looked out upon a dark figure peering in. "The door latch, it appears to be jammed, give me a moment!" shouted Will, endeavoring to crank open the casement window to relay his message.

"Well hurry it up, sport!" grumbled Jack, shaking his walking stick at the window.

By now, Mrs. Cambridge, not known for her tolerance, was beginning to grow thirsty with impatience, but not wishing to draw attention to her irritable standing, drew her bony finger at Katrina and beckoned service. Upon seeing the elder, the housekeeper quickly served up another hot dinner roll to the Admiral, who had personally polished off half a dozen himself, before setting the dish back upon the credenza.

"My dear," whispered the ancient one as Katrina lowered her head, "go see what has happened to our dear Mr. Piccard. I believe that our front latch has decided to stick again."

"Is the rest of the company finally here?" asked Katrina, although she knew full well the answer.

"It is Jack Philander and a guest from the Starboard," Mrs. Cambridge uttered.

"Jack Philander? I never could understand what ya see in that good for nothin'," muttered Katrina under her breath and then without hesitation stomped towards the foyer.

"It appears that my front door doesn't wish to open to our late arrivals!" said Mrs. Cambridge to her dinner guests. "It can be rather sticky," she added.

"Oh, we had a similar problem with ours," Mrs. Bruner piped in, "that is until one night, after several glasses of whiskey and a losing streak in poker, my husband made an impetuous decision with an ax and well, let us say, the front door had to be replaced straightaway! Remember dear?" she asked turning to the scowling husband who grimaced with disapproval that such a story had been repeated in good company. "Never you mind," she added patting his pudgy hand, "it was a rather ingenious way to rid ourselves of it."

"You see!" hushed Wanda leaning into Nick, "it's an omen! That the door won't open on purpose, I tell ya! We're wasting valuable time right now listening to giddy old gossip; we got to get Libby out of here!" However, when she looked about the room for the younger woman, she barely caught a glimpse of her ruffled skirt floating back into the kitchen.

"Here, let me help ya! This door and I go back many years, we understand each other," claimed Katrina, and she gently pushed Will away. "Go on back to the company and finish yer dinner," she commanded and fumbling about her coiled bun with the same commitment as a bird gathering twigs for its nest, she pulled a long hairpin out from behind her head and began to shimmy the lock like a thief.

"If you insist," replied Will and knowing better than to argue with her, he backed away.

Katrina mumbled as she continued to wangle the hairpin in no less than a dozen contorted positions until finally there was a finite click signaling her success. "Now Mr. Jack Philander, what kind of no good shines are ya up to?" She yanked the stubborn latch and pulled the door open wide enough to see him standing before her along with his annoying presumptuous disposition.

"Ah, my favorite lady!" cried Jack tipping his hat to the side, and picking up a rather new looking valise with his right hand, took a step forward. "I was wondering what was takin' so long; been standin' out in the street like a vagabond!"

"That's where ya belong, you scoundrel!" she grumped. "Well, come along now, since you are an invited guest. And ask yer friend to close the door behind him, this ain't a barn ya know!" she reminded. Her eyes pierced the darkness as she tried to see who was standing in the shadows of the night. But no sooner than these words left her lips did a taller and more elderly man come up from behind.

"Beg yer pardon, Sir," apologized Katrina, "I thought ya were an acquaintance of Jack's, but I can see by your attire that you're a gentleman." The man said nothing in return, but cast a cold somber stare upon her uneasy face as he filed past.

"There's something evil in his eyes," whispered Katrina to Jack. Forging ahead she turned her back on the two men and headed down the small corridor towards the kitchen. The younger man gestured at the coat rack and upon hanging their coats and hats; he motioned the elder to follow him.

Lively chatter was emanating from the dining room as Admiral Ringgold, between mouthfuls of rare beef and buttery potatoes, entertained the guests with his inflated yarns of sea-faring pirates that preyed upon the ships commanded by the less experienced. Wanda wiggled in her seat as she tried to keep her mind on the merriment of the party, but found that she was consumed by a feeling of dread. Breaking into a whisper she tugged at Will's jacket under the tablecloth. "Get up and find your wife!" she exclaimed in hushed tones.

Will was perplexed at the request since he knew exactly where she had been assigned, and could see her coming back and forth from the kitchen.

"Wanda thinks your better-half is in some sort of danger," cautioned Nick, leaning over to his friend and watching the ancient one with his other eye while the astute woman was keenly attending to the dining room door.

"Danger?" replied Will. "What kind of danger?"

"Don't ask questions; just make sure she's o.k. I can't say why, I just got a feelin'!" Wanda interrupted.

The urgency in her voice gave Will reason to pull away from his seat. At the same time a trail of footsteps, one set heavier than the other, could be heard nearing the dining room. "Well, I believe it must be our late arrivals, I hope they are hungry!" said the hostess and smiled graciously at those seated before her. The dinner guests began to turn fidgety attention towards the door like an audience waiting for the final act of a play. Wanda sat forward in her seat; her eyes fixed directly ahead, her heart pounded fast, so fast that she became almost breathless. Nick slung his arm around her shoulder, while Admiral Ringgold continued to ramble on about things that now seemed so meaningless. The candles flickered wildly as though possessed by some terrestrial force.

"I've come to see Libby!" bellowed a coarse voice, and with a sudden thrust on the door it swung open revealing the speaker. Could it be? How could it be true? But the face was unmistakable. Will pushed the chair from the table and stood up to get a better look at the man who was standing on the opposing side of the room, when suddenly all present became aware of a pitiful gasp of a woman's lament coming from the kitchen; for upon hearing her name, the young mother-to-be had peered out into the dining room to see who it was that called. Heeding her cry, Will turned towards the portal of the open door just at the very moment that Libby pushed it open. Her pale white hand clasped over her mouth, her brows furrowed, and her eyes widened in terror. The grip she had on the knob appeared to loosen and as the door began to close, he barely caught glimpse of the dear woman as she tumbled to the floor.

"Mr. Piccard, come quickly, it's your wife! I believe she's fainted!" cried Mrs. Stark peeping out from within its threshold. Mrs. Cambridge remained utterly composed as the room transposed into a series of vignettes. The Doctor and his inebriated wife continued to eat noisily as though nothing out of the ordinary had occurred; for having been brought up with impeccable manners, they did not want to appear nosey. This did not prevent Mrs. Bruner from craning her neck to the left every few moments hoping to catch a glimpse of what was happening in the kitchen. Admiral Ringgold took delight in the fact that more guests had arrived and gestured for Jack to sit down in the unoccupied seat. However, the scoundrel was being verbally accosted by Katrina who demanded to know the identity of the tall elderly grey-haired man. Mrs. Cambridge possessed total repose and only the curl of her lip seemed to waver. Her sharp eyes flickered back and forth from the intruder to Will, and she became amused as she watched the younger man obviously go from shock to concern. His emotions were evident as he tossed his chair aside and hurried round the table towards the closed kitchen door. The unexpected visitor stood before the elderly hostess while a thick wall of ice formed between them. Wanda Bourdette's instincts took charge as she quickly followed Will, with Nick at toe. The stranger, undaunted by the comings and goings, reached into his vest pocket and produced a smudged pair of spectacles with which he vigorously rubbed with the rolled hem of his silk handkerchief before putting them on.

Mrs. Cambridge was the first to speak. "I haven't been called that in years," the ancient one said and picked up her glass of water. She sipped slowly. Katrina came round to replenish her glass, but was stopped with a quick motion of the bony hand. "No one," she continued brashly, "has referred to me as Libby since we parted." The old woman looked up from her glass and directly into his chilly stare. Like a pair of daggers their eyes met. The dining room that was earlier filled with the chatter of festivity had now become heavy with frosty uncertainty; and like a winter storm that blankets the landscape, the solemn mood began to smother the household.

"You're looking well, Elizabeth," the elder man noted and without asking he reached over and retrieved an empty wine glass. "That is the name you go by, isn't it?"

"Don't flatter me, you were never very good at it," the ancient one sneered. "Sit down," she commanded, "you needn't be standing like a gatekeeper; besides, you must be hungry after having traveled for so long. I hope you found your journey satisfactory?"

Jack Philander did not wait to be asked and had found his seat at the table. He listened intensively like the lapdog that he was, and while he waited for any commands from his mistress he placed his dinner napkin on his knee and prepared himself to eat with gusto as the assorted plates of food were being placed before him. "Ya better have a good reason for all this meddlin'," Katrina whispered in his ear and deliberately issued a severe pinch upon the scoundrel's lobe before dropping a hot potato onto his plate.

"Please, don't keep us in suspense! Ask the fellow to introduce himself," the intoxicated Doctor Bruner called out to his hostess.

"Yes," Mrs. Bruner cried clapping her hands with glee, "tell us who this mystery person could be! I do say he has caused quite a stir; I mean sending half the table scurrying into the kitchen."

"Yes, Libby," the man nodded in agreement with the animated woman. He paused for an instant to clear his throat. "Elizabeth," he said correcting the name. "While you're at it, explain why you paid first class for me to cross the Atlantic aboard such a grand ship as the Starboard. No, better yet, tell us all, what is the surprise that you baited me here with?" the man gruffly questioned as he approached the elder. Katrina, now most curious in the affairs of her mistress, came courting answers by pretending to take an interest in the man's well-being and began to fill his wine glass each time he set it back down upon the credenza.

"You really don't know, do you?" Mrs. Cambridge scoffed. "Didn't you notice our illustrious guest when you first entered the dining room?" she cross-examined.

"Nay, I was not wearing my spectacles when I came in; but as I look about," and he did so as he continued to speak, "I know not a soul present, that is except for you, and even now, I do not really know you very well, now do I?" he mocked.

"My, my, this is quite a party, my dear hostess. I had no idea that we would have such melodrama," Admiral Ringgold called out from the other end of the table.

The elder hurled a glare of distain and sharply snapped back, "Shut up, you drunken fool!" upon which the large man recoiled, cowering back into his seat like a fat puppy in the corner of room and began to gnaw on another dinner roll. Then turning away from the shamed man, she spoke in a more gentle tone to the standing guest. Leaning forward, she pushed aside the half-eaten plate of food that had been left by Nick and beckoned for the grey man to sit down beside her. "Come, sit down here and have your meal. I remember that you take your gravy under your meat, unlike other men who like it poured over theirs." With her gnarled fingers she picked up the gravy boat that had been placed before her and generously poured a reservoir of sauce upon an empty dinner plate. "What was it that you always said?" The ancient one hesitated and set the porcelain back on the table. "Ahh, yes, you would say that a fool is one who trusts the cook without question; for with blind allegiance, he would deserve a dead rat smothered in thick gravy."

The man obliged his hostess and pulled the chair away from the table. All eyes were now upon him as he sat and maneuvered about trying to find a comfortable posture. The top of his knees rubbed against the table so he repositioned himself by slinking down into his chair with outstretched legs that reached forward interfering with the opposing floor space beneath. Even so, he sat tall among the others, almost a head above the Admiral and Doctor. They fit into the category of squat or portly. He tossed the linen napkin aside, not upon his lap, and bent his head down into his plate to eat rather than bringing the fork up to his mouth and waiting for the food to arrive slowly and deliberately. His hands were stained brown from working the earth and although he must have frequently attempted to remove the dirt from under his fingernails, there was a shadow of dark residue permanently encircling the cuticle.

"Katrina, do see what is taking the others so long," Mrs. Cambridge told the maid who was rounding the table with another full platter of mutton.

"Put that right here, young lady!" the Admiral commanded and pointed to an empty spot on the table.

Dutifully she plopped the covered dish before him and sauntered past, but not before Jack Philander could catch her eye and cast towards her a taunting wink.

"To the devil with ya!" she muttered as she whisked past the good-for-nothing and pushing her way into the kitchen; he smiled like a wolf in gentleman's clothes.

The guests now had quieted down, not because there wasn't any food or drink left, but because there was too much. Jack leaned back in his chair and seemed to impersonate the Admiral and Doctor who had initiated the relaxed stance. Mrs. Bruner leaned forward, resting her head in her hands as though it was too heavy to be propped by the thin neck. Every few moments she would mumble to her husband, "Oh, I shouldn't have drunk that last glass of sherry."

Mrs. Cambridge, wondering what was keeping Katrina, for she had been sent off on a very menial errand, ignored the others while she watched the Starboard guest polish off the last of the applesauce. Finally, he lifted his head from his plate and looked at her, noticing that she was staring at him. "Your son was a great disappointment to you, wasn't he, Elizabeth?" the man caustically announced and carelessly wiped the suet from his lips. He tossed the linen cloth back on the table and proceeded to predict her forthcoming reaction to his statement.

Stunned by the remark a bemused Mrs. Cambridge glared in horror. Her initial instinct was to strike back like a defensive cobra. It had been a long time since she had been around a formidable enemy; she had forgotten what it was like to in the presence of an equal. In her earlier life the grey man had been a sparring partner of parallel prowess. But now, it was necessary that she not let her guard down. Without giving into his verbal joust, she pondered her next move like a player in a game of chess. All remained strangely quiet. The only sound now was the clatter and rattle of pots and dishes in the kitchen. The grey man cocked his head to the side, removed and wiped his spectacles clean with the skirt of the tablecloth, and returned them to his face.

"Ahh, this is too easy," the ancient one thought to herself and sipped from the crystal glass. A few water droplets fell upon her lap that had accumulated round the base. She was pleased that they fell upon her napkin and not the lovely dress she had decided to wear. "I could say the same about your daughter," she said with a smile. "By the way, did you ever find out where she ran off to? Such a disappointment, such a shame." Mrs. Cambridge watched knowing that she had won this round, check.

However, if one knows the game of chess, the term check is not a resounding conclusion that the game is over; for there are many variables that can come into play. If one's opponent is more adept then it is simply a time, shall we say, to regroup and take a new line of action. Yet, it is possible that the player who called checkmate had played out all the possible moves in his or her head and hence forth, the game was indeed won. But the game that was about to take place did not exactly come to the conclusion that the ancient one had planned, it was not checkmate.

Abruptly the kitchen door opened and Katrina called out of breath, "They're gone, the whole lot of them!"

"Gone, who's gone?" the Admiral questioned sleepily as though waking from a quick nap. "You don't mean that lovely young woman who is with child do you?

Mrs. Cambridge, ignoring the seaman turned to the grey man with a sneer. "Well, it looks like she has outsmarted you again, and I was so hoping that you would have a chance to see her one more time, dear brother!"

"Brother!" shouted Katrina. "Mrs. Cambridge, this man is your brother?"

"Elizabeth, what are you talking about?" the stranger demanded leaning forward. "Who is gone?"

"Who am I talking about?" she shrieked, her eyes widened wildly. "I am talking about your only child who married that inferior boy so beneath her ranking! Your only child who ran away from you! Now, she belongs to me!" Mrs. Cambridge jabbed her crooked finger at him and wagged it violently like a stinging needle.

"You're a liar!" he screamed and grabbing the old woman by the shoulders held her firmly. He could feel her thin skeletal frame through the light material of her gown and like the bones of a bird, knew with only a slight bit of pressure, he could easily crush her with his bare hands.

"Well, if you don't believe me, go!" she exclaimed. "Look for yourself, in the kitchen, your own flesh and blood, find your precious, Libby!" the old woman cried.

"Is it true? Tell me wretched woman!" and he began to shake her by the shoulders!

"Get your hands off me, you animal!" she scolded and drove her sharp fingernails into his arms. Obediently, he pushed her back and rose to his feet like an angry bear. Katrina moved aside as the man approached and swung the kitchen door open. He peered inside and first came upon Marte, sniveling in the corner while Mrs. Stark stood leaning against the cupboard as though frozen in time, a dripping soup ladle clenched in one hand continued to drizzle broth upon her boots.

"Where is she, where is my daughter?" he roared looking from one woman to another; however they remained speechless hoping he would leave without provocation. "Where is she?" he called again more firmly and grabbed the young maid by the wrist. "Tell me quick or I'll snap your arm in two!" he threatened.

Too scared to talk Marte whimpered even more loudly and tried to pull free from his grip, but was met with forceful resistance. "I'm so sorry, Miss Libby," she cried and trembling with fear, she reluctantly lifted her free hand and pointed towards the cellar door.

Chapter 42

Will cradled Libby's hand as though she would wilt if he dared let go. She had tried to convince him that she could follow Nick down the narrow passageway without help, but he would not hear of it. "I'm quite all right, I promise you," she implored, but when Wanda insisted that she take his hand the young woman decided to abandon her insistence. Libby's mind was whirling with questions. Although having only caught a glimpse of her father as she had stood before that open kitchen door, the sight of him was enough to send her into a timorous state. It seemed hardly possible that he could have found them; especially when she and Will had been so careful to avoid leaving behind any evidence of their whereabouts. Even her letters to Grandmother had been secretly delivered by the Judge and all correspondence to her mother had been eliminated. And now, Libby wasn't even sure where she was going, just that Will assured her that she would be safe.

The air grew colder as they descended towards the basement and into the dark corridor. "The root cellar is down here," Nick said holding the tallow in front of him and stopping to explain their underground destination. "But we're not going there. You see, when you both first arrived I snuck Will around. As I was reminiscing about my childhood I showed him an obscure passageway that used to be a great hiding place for me and Marcus Cambridge. Its original opening was almost too slight for even you, Libby, to squeeze through, especially now. But I have since enlarged the entrance and it will be perfect for you to hide in. Trust me, not even the Duchess knows of its whereabouts!"

"Well stop your talkin' and git goin'!" Wanda complained. "I don't like the looks of this place," she muttered and slipped her fingers into the folds of Nick's jacket tail.

The approach to the hidden nook was apparent to only those who were privy to its location and even Nick would have begun to wonder where it was if he hadn't most recently visited the spot. "Quickly," he whispered and handing Wanda the flickering tallow they all gathered round, waiting in the dimly lit tunnel. There was a moment of nervous silence as Nick skimmed his palm against the damp earthen walls and slowly felt about until he came upon a loosely fitted wooden board. He dug his fingers around two opposing edges and shimmied it towards himself until the board was set free from the wall. Small chunks of earth were dislodged and crumbled to the floor. "There," he announced as he set the board against the wall and crouched before the burrow. "It isn't much, but it will keep you safe," he said.

Wanda knelt before the opening and held the tallow out before her, allowing the glow to resonate into the dark hollow. She let out a small gasp as she peered inside. "It's a tomb!" she cried. "They'll be buried alive!"

"Shhh," Nick whispered! "I'm not going to leave them for long and besides, they can have this tallow!" he said. "As soon as we get above, I'll open up the passage from the outside, they can escape tonight! Now hurry!" he commanded. "The old man will be coming down the cellar in only a matter of time. But, if you keep very still, no one will find you in here."

Wanda stood up and handed Nick back the flickering candle. Her hands were shaking as she released the copper holder into his. She knew that this could be the last time they would all be together. "Now you know," she whispered trying to hold back her sadness, "I ain't much of a softy, but Libby, I love you like a baby sister." Streams of tears began to flow as she leaned forward and embraced the delicate young woman.

"I'll never forget you, Wanda," Libby whispered back. "I'll never forget you!"

Wanda released her tender friend and turned to Will. "Now you take good care of her and that new baby!" Wanda demanded and held onto the man with great compassion. And then overwrought by sadness, she turned away from her friends and buried her face into her hands.

"Quickly!" Nick called out as he handed Will the lit tallow and ushered them towards their dark hole of safety.

Libby peered into the small cavity; hesitating for a moment she found herself barely able to move on. She understood that she must go forward into the blackness of the tiny sanctuary, but the sensation of fear welled up as she was suddenly reminded of earlier times; the punishments of her father. He would lock her in the storage closet under the stairwell or in the shed; sometimes overnight, sometimes as long as several days. Angry hands and fire in his eyes were all a warning to keep still, not to call out to Mother. "I must be strong," she now thought, "I must be strong," she repeated again as she followed Will. Her wistful feelings slid past the narrow portal and as she turned round she could see Nick lift the board and begin to seal the entrance shut, but this time with the intention of making sure it could not be easily found or opened. Libby followed Will to the corner of the tiny room and sat upon one of the wooden crates that were set before them. The tallow flame flickered with all its might and hovered round her like flecks of glitter. At first glance, the tiny room would not admit to its role as a child's hide-away. However, as their eyes began to adjust to the dim light, with little imagination one could fantasize a pirate's hideout or Medieval Knight's secret refuge.

Although the ceiling was low and the ground damp, there was a curious coziness about the nook. It was not much larger than a pig's sty and so one had only to traverse a few feet across to reach the opposing walls. "This is where we will escape from," he said turning to Libby. "You see?" he asked and pointed at the whitewash to exhibit the area of departure. "These boards have been sealed from the outside," and giving them a few raps with his knuckles they produced a hollow tone. Libby nodded in agreement and smiled meekly. Will continued to examine the little room and peered into the corners, bending down, and brushing the floor with his hand. Then he took the tallow from off the crate where he left it and lowered it to the ground. "Now, what do we have here?" he asked tipping the tallow more closely. The hot wax began to slide down the taper and dripped carelessly upon the very spot that he was engaged in.

"What is it? Libby asked curiously as she watched her husband scout the little room.

Will poked about the bare ground. "I believe that we may have found a bit of treasure!" he answered and brought the item to Libby. "Here," he said. "What do you make of it?" and placed the prize into her dainty palm.

Presented with a discovery in such unusual circumstances, she approached her inspection with great earnestness. Slowly she turned over what appeared to be a ring. "Why look, Will!" she exclaimed, "it looks like the letter 'C'," and pointed to an ornate initial. "Who do you think it belongs to?"

"Probably Marcus Cambridge," he answered as he placed the ring on his own finger to see if it fit. He gave it a little tug and was satisfied that it would not fall off.

"Oh, it couldn't have been his," she said, "Why Marcus was just a young boy. Why, look how well it fits your finger. No, I bet it belonged to a man; probably his father, Mr. Cambridge. Why, this ring must be at least twenty years old." Will took the ring off and placed it back in her hands. He moved his crate beside hers and created a small bench where they could sit side by side.

"Are you scared?" Will asked as she leaned her cheek against his shoulder.

"I'd be lying if I told you, no," she said and paused for a moment's reflection. "What will happen if my father finds me?" she asked meekly.

"He won't, I promise, I'll keep you safe, Libby: I'll keep you safe until the day I die," Will whispered and gently kissed her head. Libby took the ring and placed it upon his finger. She stroked his hand gently. "It won't be long now. I am sure that Nick is going to be setting us free straightaway!" he said reassuringly.

"Perhaps," she murmured.

———

The snorts and snarls that were emancipated from the stairwell below sent shivers through the household staff. Mrs. Stark did not stay long enough to be paid for her services for after her initial encounter with the grey man, she ran from the house, deciding to take her leave before the brute returned. Marte spared herself with an excuse that she needed firewood for the wood stove and held up for the night hiding in the woodshed. As for the rest of the guests, the Admiral retired to his room, happily fed and intoxicated while the Doctor and Mrs. Bruner went home believing that the entire event had been a well-staged dinner show for their night's entertainment.

Only Jack Philander remained with Mrs. Cambridge.

"There's nothing down here!" Mr. Dowling shouted as he came storming up through the cellar door and back into the dining room.

"Not even whiskey?" asked Jack Philander, half kidding and half serious as the man reentered the room. Mrs. Cambridge sat back at ease in her seat and sipped her cognac. She said nothing.

"Not anything down in the cellar but preserves and rotten potatoes!" Anger oozed from his pores like sweat. "I demand to know what you've done with Libby!" he shouted.

"Demand!" Her ears perked up upon hearing the word. "You have no demands here, my brother. This is a Cambridge home, not a Dowling. As for Libby, she is not a Dowling anymore. What is her name, now?" the ancient one asked toying with his anger.

"Piccard, ain't it. Piccard?" Jack piped in.

"I'm warning you, Elizabeth, you better give me back my daughter!" His howl tore across the room as he systematically began to throw over the dining chairs.

Jack jumped to his feet alarmed by the elder man's fit of rage; however he made no attempt to stir from his place for like a vessel anchored in a cove during the storm, he maintained a safe distance from the ire on the opposite side of the table.

The white-haired hostess remained resolute. Steadfast in her desire to demonstrate her superiority, she spoke slowly and deliberately. "I have waited years for this moment, little brother, but it seems that your memory has failed you too!" she pointed out. "Do you not remember how you threatened to destroy the life of a man whose only crime was to love me? Oh, no!" her voice now lowered becoming more acrid and bitter. "You could not bear the truth that your older sister was going to have a baby out of wedlock. So, what did you do? You took it upon yourself to terrify him with lies and blackmail; despite my protests you continued with your intimidations and threats."

Katrina, speechless, peered round the outside of the kitchen door like a mouse watching a cat. The expression on the grey man's face as she spoke these words remained hard and tense. Only the muscles that held the jaw firmly appeared to pulsate as he clenched his teeth. "He was not a strong boy, he was no match for you," she added. "Finally, you drove him to commit the unthinkable. How I hate the very sight of you. No, hate is too weak a word," she sneered. "I loath you!" The elder woman's hands trembled with rage, and she placed them upon her lap so that they could not be seen wavering; for any signs of quivering would be interpreted as weakness. She constricted her palms into fists and steadied her nerves once again. "I have waited years for this moment," she continued, "years anticipating our meeting; and then, like a gift, a most remarkable opportunity came my way. Do you think I did not keep my eyes and ears open to your every move? Even though we were across the Atlantic from one another I kept my sights upon you; waiting for the right opening. And then, when I learned that your child had run away, I knew this was the perfect opportunity to make you suffer; except your loss is not dead, but she might as well be to you! You made it so easy to lure the unwitting child into my arms. How ironic, Libby here with me, and there is nothing you can do about it!" she laughed mockingly. "But, I have saved the best for last," she exclaimed as her eyes widened, and she paused with a sense of ultimate triumph. "Did you know that you will be a grandfather? So sorry you will never get to see the baby. Ironic isn't it? And reunions are supposed to be so joyful."

Jack listened attentively. Not wishing to disturb this soliloquy of vengeance he edged softly forward; he did not want to miss a single word. Mesmerized by the ancient one's finesse he knew he was in the midst of a master, this artist of deception was at work. And to think that he, Jack Philander, was her protégé.

Libby's father spun round on his heels and lunged forward. All the pink from his cheeks had drained away until his face appeared a chalky white as though he had seen the ghost of death. "I will not let you have her!" he roared, placing his hands back upon the ancient one's shoulders and handily gave her a firm shake. The old woman's neck snapped back, and she unleashed a horrified wail. Katrina watched as the old woman appeared stunned.

"What are you going to do?" shrieked the elder, as she glared into her captor's face. "Kill me too? Kill me too?" Furiously, her question grew shriller and she plagued him again with her badgering. "Kill me too? Kill me too?"

His muscular hands had crept away from the pair of bony shoulders and were securely placed around the elder's gangly neck like a human necklace. "Tell me, where is my daughter, where is Libby?" he shouted as he continued to rattle the old head. Her pallor deepened, her pupils rolled back into the sockets, and the whites of her eyes were mottled red as the pressure of his tawny hands round her throat slowly increased while he took pleasure in choking her. "Where is she, what did you do?" his voice echoed in the ancient one's ears. Frantically she gasped for air! Reaching upward, her gaunt fingers clasped his arms and with unyielding desperation shoved and pulled. "I'll squeeze the truth out of you!" he grimaced savagely as he peered down at an expression that was growing more foreboding with every instant; she was trapped in his menacing grip.

"Stop, stop!" cried Katrina, and she grabbed the assailant round his waist. "Jack, do something!" she demanded and while yanking back with all her might, she tried to pull him away from her mistress. Feverishly Jack grabbed from behind and tugged at the broad shoulders. "Get off her!" Katrina continued to howl. "Get off her!" she screamed more violently. However, the more they tried to make him heed the more firmly he remained rooted like a sturdy oak. The anger of "Brother Cain" continued to germinate until it blossomed into a rage that surpassed the strength of both Jack and Katrina. Was he under the spell of an external force, a force that was supernatural in strength and power? Or was his deafness to the frenzied commotion that surrounded him fueled by his own abhorrence. Impervious to the poundings they lodged upon his body, he would not loosen his manacle-like grip from round the ancient one's neck; all the while groaning and moaning like a rabid dog. It was not until the clock chimed twelve steady peals signaling the hour of midnight that the hideous man was set free from his trance and released Mrs. Cambridge. Suddenly, she fell limp in his hands, and as he backed cautiously away from the chair they watched her tumble to the ground like a broken mannequin.

"She's dead, you've killed her!" Katrina cried out in despair and dropped to her knees beside the old woman. A full moon had risen and broke through the window with a vengeance. "You killed her!" repeated Katrina pointing up at the grey man.

Was this terror finally ending or just beginning? It all depends upon one's point of interest. For some it had ended with the great matriarch having been murdered by her hateful brother. At the same time the terror was just beginning for our innocent Libby, an angelic victim in the revengeful retribution of sibling rivalry.

Katrina wailed wildly as Jack tried to wrestle the attacker to the ground. But the older man was too powerful a match for the wily fellow and managed to out-maneuver his opponent by running from the house and back into the shadows of darkness; leaving behind the ancient one in a stone dead state.

Chapter 43

The once dry fields were now verdant grassland speckled with wildflowers tipping their colorful top hats. Grace raced up the hill, one hand swinging the picnic basket, while her other hand grappled with her boots that she had removed; now too small for her feet that seemed to have grown into canal boats during the long winter months. She set the basket down upon the ground and pitched her hand above her eyes like a sunshade, but as she peered ahead the glare from the sun inhibited her from being able to see much farther up the hill. "He must be there," she thought and crossed her fingers just for good luck. Grabbing the basket, she started up again, this time pacing herself more slowly, making her way to the precipice where she finally caught sight of the apple tree. At first glance Grace was not sure if she had perhaps walked up the wrong hill for the tree that she thought she vividly recollected could not possibly have grown so. For here a grand burly fellow stood before her with a canopy of healthy green leaves and sturdy boughs stretching upward, supplicating towards the heavens. Grace scanned beyond the apple tree, but still did not see her friend. However, as she approached she noticed that Alex was concealed by the tree trunk and had in fact been watching her closely; for as soon as she advanced in his direction, he stood up from his resting position under the shade and walked towards her. He reached out and took the picnic basket from her small hand. "I was afraid ya might not of come!" Grace remarked as she released the basket. "On account that ya got so

much to do; but I figured ya would of sent word if ya couldn't of."
She smiled happily.

"I got all my chores done early," he admitted favorably. They
strolled silently back to the tree; Grace now swinging her boots along
her side by their laces. The air was crisp and cool, a most remarkable
day for a picnic. Alex set the basket down and waited while Grace
bent down and released the leather straps. She pulled from its contents a red gingham tablecloth that had been neatly folded. Pinching
it on two corners, she tossed it lightly, setting it free from its folds so
that the thin material flew up gently, catching the air like a parachute
and floated to the ground landing in an almost perfect square. She
knelt down and like a storekeeper setting up a display, removed from
the basket all of its contents. A proper helping of diligence was present as she began to assemble what was a most hearty lunch upon the
cloth: boiled ham, a crusty loaf of white bread, a tin of milk, sliced
gingerbread squares, a pair of matching cloth napkins, a knife, two
forks, a spoon, and two tin cups. Alex stood idly by watching her
timidly. "Come on and sit down, Alex Forester!" she said, and with
a slight wave gestured for him to find a place under the shade of his
tree. "Ain't ya ever been on a picnic?" she queried. It was evident that
he had not and looked about wondering if he was supposed to sit
directly on the cloth or just close to the edge.

"Can't say that I have," he announced, but taking Grace's lead
he promptly sat cross-legged upon the cloth. He allowed himself
to relax and looked upward, remarking on the grandeur of the tree.
"It's a beauty, ain't it?" he sighed.

"Why I don't think I've ever seen such a grand tree as this!" she
stated. He looked back at her and smiled shyly.

Grace handed him a tin plate upon which she had generously
piled a sampling of each dish. Then she served herself. The skittish
wind picked up bits of dry grass and stray burs and scattered them
upon their tablecloth. Alex ate and listened while Grace, between
swallows, chattered happily, telling him about her days at school and
at the Tarson's. When she was finished and had nothing new to relay,

she sat back, resting on her elbows, and asked, "So, Alex Forester, what have you been up to besides chores and more chores?"

The question rumbled through his mind like a runaway train. "What have you been up to besides chores and more chores?" Her words echoed as he tried to think of something out of the ordinary. An endless list of mundane jobs was easy, but what had he really done that was different? Was life with Betty really all work and drudgery? His most meaningful times were spent with the two draft horses, but no, that was not what she had in mind.

Grace grinned cunningly. "Why Alex Forester, I can't imagine that you don't have somethin' new to share." She leaned forward fumbling restlessly with the bits of grass that had blown onto the tablecloth.

"Well, I did find somethin' the same day that ya sent the invitation," he said and dug his hand down into the corner of his pocket and retrieved a small object. Grace leaned toward his flattened palm to get a better look. "My real Pa gave this to me. It belonged to my real Mom," Alex explained, placing an extra emphasis on the word "real".

"Well, looky here," exclaimed Grace picking the object up. "It's a signet ring and a stamp just like the one I used on the invitation!" She placed the ring on her finger and admired it by donning her hand out before her. Then she removed the ring from her finger and handed it over to the owner. "Why does it got a letter "C"?" she asked.

"Don't really know," he mused and shoved it securely back into his pocket.

"What ya gonna do with it?" Grace asked. "Bet it's worth a lot of money. Why with all that money ya could do anythin' ya wanted!"

This thought had never occurred to him; he could sell it. But, what would he do if he had money? Lots of money, not a few dollars he might earn from selling eggs or fixing broken fence rails, but lots of money. "I don't rightly know," he honestly admitted.

"Well, I know what I'd do! I'd go to school to be a teacher. I'm purty good at it, don't ya think?" Grace asked hoping that Alex would be encouraged to agree. "But some folks think only old maids can be teachers, and I sure don't want to be an old maid!"

"I think yer real smart," Alex agreed nodding his head. "You'd make a fine teacher and ya ain't gonna be no old maid." Alex reached back into his pocket and removed the ring again. He had never thought of himself as ever being in a position to have his own money, but this afternoon under the shade of the apple tree suddenly made it seem possible. "I know, I'll take care of Delilah and Dandy!" he exclaimed.

"Do what?" Grace asked impertinently. "With all that money you're gonna spend it on a pair of work horses?" The suggestion seemed absolutely ludicrous. "What are a couple of work horse gonna need money fer?" she laughed. However, it soon became clearly evident that Alex did not find this amusing. "Ya mean it, don't ya?" Grace questioned; this time answering with genuine compassion.

"Betty's gonna sell the property, the house, everything someday. I gotta be prepared to take care of Delilah and Dandy," he explained.

Grace suddenly was stricken with a pang of horror. If Betty were to move why she'd take Alex away with her! "Do ya really think she might leave?" Grace's tone of concern was directed not for the horses, but rather for herself.

"Don't know fer sure, but I best be prepared." He shoved it back and tapped his pocket where he could feel the ring's contour. Alex lay back leisurely and stared up into the tree where he grew more peaceful than he could ever remember feeling. Legions of branches, some thick, some thin, crisscrossed over one another creating a web of sticks and leaves. He was glad that Grace had invited him. Besides, other than Delilah and Dandy, she was the only human being that seemed to understand him. She didn't question or ask anything of him. She accepted him for who he was and who he was becoming. Alex closed his eyes and listened while Grace put back into the wicker basket the lunch remains. She was humming to herself; nothing that he recognized, but rather a carefree tune that perhaps she had learned in school or maybe something she made up.

"Alex, did ya ever want to know yer real last name?" she asked.

He thought for a moment and replied, "What good would it do?"

"Guess no reason 'cept just because," she answered. "Sometimes I get kind of curious, but I suppose yer right, what good would it do?"

"Why do ya ask?" he said.

"Well, it on account of the ring, maybe yer real last name starts with a "C" like Carter, or Callahan, or even Charlemagne. Why if ya were related to him, ya just might be a prince!"

Alex rolled over on his stomach and broke out with laughter. "Do you really reckon I'm kin to a king?"

"Well, I suppose it is a bit far-fetched, but ya never know!" she exclaimed. Grace smiled meekly and then looked away. Amusing herself, she began to fiddle with the strap on the basket. "I guess I better be gettin' on home," she remarked in a most gloomy voice. "I promised Beatrice that I'd help her with the wash." She turned her hands over after she said this and looked at her palms. She had begun to worry that they were going to become red and scaly like most of the older women she knew. Reluctantly, she reached over and began struggle with her boots as she tried to get them on; all the while remembering to keep them unlaced so that they would not be too tight.

Alex rolled off the cloth and stood up. No longer needing the table covering, he picked it up and shook it gently, allowing any clinging dirt and grass to fall back to the ground. He draped it over his arm and handed it to her. "You better fold it; I ain't too good with stuff like that," he admitted shyly.

Already feeling like a hostess, she handily folded the large gingham into a neat square and plumped it down into the basket. "When are ya comin' back to school?" she boldly asked, knowing that this was not the most favored subject to discuss.

"Don't know. Betty needs me. Seems like there's always work to do," he reminded her.

The beautiful afternoon enjoying the apple tree was waning. They stood face to face, Grace cradling the basket as if she were boarding a train for the last time. Moments became painful hours. "If ya do have to leave, ya better tell me first, Alex Forester!" Grace moaned. "Ya promise?"

"I will," he promised. The quiet that stood between them seemed interminable. Alex shuffled the grass with his feet and then broke the awkward silence. "And Grace, thanks for the nice picnic."

She looked up and smiled, "See ya again soon?" she asked.

"Yep," he answered. Grace sighed and hesitated for a moment before turning away. What she really wanted to do was to give him a hug, maybe even a kiss goodbye, the kind of kiss between friends, a light peck on the check. But she drew away before doing something she would regret and started her little journey homeward. If Alex felt the same about Grace, he did not reveal his intentions. He stood and for what seemed like a very long time watched as she trundled down the hill. When she was almost out of his sight, he noticed her turn and wave. He smiled and waved back as she continued along the path until she disappeared below the horizon.

The shade of the apple tree spread out before him like a cool dark blanket. He sat back upon the ground and he leaned against the trunk. The notion that he could be someone other than plain old Alex Forester had never crossed his mind. But now he couldn't waste time on "what ifs". He wanted to find a way of selling the ring. Alex tilted his head slightly and looked upward. There between the leaves amongst the tallest branches he felt as if something or someone was looking downward. Sure enough he spotted a pair of dark eyes staring back into his. Were these the same eyes that he had seen on several other occasions? Then, as mysteriously as they appeared they instantly vanished. Alex rubbed his face with the sleeve of his shirt. He tucked his legs up and rested his head upon his kneecaps. His weary brain tormented him for several minutes; how would he find someone to buy his ring? When out of the quiet he heard a rustling in the grass. A figure making a wide circuit round the trunk before formally approaching appeared out of nowhere.

"Won't be long before you'll be needing help harvesting apples!"

Startled by the presence of another, Alex immediately scrutinized the voice as belonging to a most familiar person. It was Tully!

"Mind if I join you?" he asked and without waiting for a response he started to sit down beside the boy.

"I ain't seen ya round much," Alex said. "Where's Sergeant?" he remarked wondering the whereabouts of the dog.

"Oh, he's scouting the grounds; probably sticking his nose where it doesn't belong," Tully suggested and leaned back against the adjacent side of the tree's trunk that the roots had so obligingly formed in the outline of a seat.

The relationship between the man and boy was as natural as taking a breath; for no effort was needed to sustain their friendship. They sat quietly, neither speaking but rather staring out at the grassy knoll and beyond; each accompanied by his own thoughts. Tully had never mapped any particular route to follow; being guided by his innate power to reason and adapt. He valued self-preservation, which he sought, and cultivated his own natural disposition of compassion. Perhaps this is why he understood the boy better than anyone else; for he had discovered a part of Alex, a character and moral sense, which was unnatural to their imperfect world. Alex never questioned the fact that Tully appeared and disappeared in and out of his life. He never wondered why the man would mysteriously emerge in times of turmoil or why no one else ever saw him. Was he a figment of a lonely child's acute imagination? Alex had been born with a spirit of simplicity and sensitivity. Today he was seeking help outside his own person; he would take a step that was foreign to his being.

"I gotta show something to ya," Alex whispered in an almost inaudible voice. He dug his hand into his pocket and retrieved the signet ring. He placed his open palm before the man as though presenting a crown jewel.

"What's ya got there?" he asked showing little interest. Worldly objects held little or no interest to him.

"It's a ring; I was hoping you'd sell it for me!" Alex replied meekly. It was obvious to Tully that there was much trepidation in the small voice for as the boy spoke he sounded unsure and with great reservation. Alex brought his flattened palm closer to the man hoping he would pick it up and take it like a fish swallowing a worm.

Still the man appeared uninterested. "Sell it?" he asked as though still unclear. "Now what do you need money for?" he questioned.

Alex sat up on his knees and rolled the ring about in his hand as he proceeded to explain his situation. Like a lawyer to the jury he pleaded his case, expressing his desire to sell the ring that had been given to him by his father; for enough money, he explained, so he could follow out his plans of saving the two horses from a dreadful life of misery. Tully listened attentively as a most convincing Alex completed his woeful soliloquy. "So, can ya help me?" he asked. He reached forward and handed the ring to Tully, who now readily accepted it. Curiously the examination began. With a bowed head the ring was turned and rolled about in his palm. A few moments later, it was brought forward into the sunlight where it could be appraised more critically. Evidently this chance exchange from hand to hand was enough for Alex to detect that there was something inexplicable about this ring, for the man's usual bronze complexion was becoming strangely pale. Tully shook his head as he reexamined the object, bringing it closely to his eyes and squinting so he could peer around the inner parts of the band as though looking for something that perhaps he missed. Finally, after several minutes he sat back against the tree and lightly tossed it up and down; first catching it in his left hand and then his right hand, his left hand and then his right, rhythmically back and forth like a juggler.

"The pirate's ship is home to me
So cast your fate and go to sea
Fight with swords, sharp and bold
And steal your fortune, coins, and gold!

We'll drink your rum, your grog and ale
A skull and crossbones marks our sail
On shores by night on shores by day
Heed warning now or your life shall pay!"

Arguments over who was going to be held captive in their secret hide-away and what treasures would be buried in the top layer of the cellar floor took up childish afternoons. Much of the excitement was looking for objects from around the house that could be confiscated for this game of piracy! Tully laughed to himself as he remembered sneaking about, hunting through desk drawers and entering do-not-disturb rooms without being detected by an adult, especially his mother.

"I think your ring is valuable," Tully remarked as he handed it back to Alex. "But not in the same way you would like it to be. You said that your father gave it to you?" His face had returned to its natural bronze coloring.

Alex lifted himself up on his knees and shoved the ring back into his pocket. Then he settled back down cross-legged. "Yep, but not Randle, it was my real Dad." Alex wanted to be sure that Tully understood and for the second time today emphasized the word 'real". He tried to interpret Tully's reserved expression. "I can tell ya don't think it's worth much money?" Alex remarked doubtfully.

Now, if there was to be something said of Tully, it was that he was honest. "Well, I can't say for sure, but it is valuable in a different way. If I were you I'd keep your ring and not try to sell it. Someday it will help you find out who you are," the man replied. After he spoke, he closed his eyes and recalled his own decision to relinquish and abdicate his punitive name; it had become meaningless to him. He stretched his arms over his head lazily. Then, as if raising a load, he stood up and bent his legs trying to get the kinks out for he had become stiff from sitting for so long. "Sergeant!" his voice rang out loudly. "Sergeant!" he called again. His voice harsh and gruff, but to the dog's ears it was a heavenly call. "Come on, boy!" The animal obediently rambled up the hill, its tail wagging happily for he was duly thankful to be in service to his master. The dog panted heavily for he was tired from running, and a pool of saliva dripped evenly from its long tongue. He extended his front paws out as though clumsily bowing and then dropped with all his weight and lay down under the shade of the apple tree. His sides heaved up and down, and he waited patiently for he knew Alex would respond by placing continual pats upon his huge soft head.

"Good boy, Sergeant, you're a great dog!" Alex began and smothered him in affection. He leaned his head upon the dog's burly neck and stroked him for several minutes repeating gently, "You're a good dog, you're a good dog."

A breeze stirred up the grass sending a cooling message that the afternoon was coming to a close. He and Sergeant lay upon the ground together. Unaccustomed to spending time lazily, Alex found this moment of tranquility particularly soothing. The dog finally began breathing at a normal rate; Alex could hear him exhale and inhale as the large chest moved up and down, up and down with long even breaths. The boy sat up on one elbow and rested his head on his palm. An occasional gnat flew around them settling on Sergeant, but was quickly shooed away with a swift slap of its tail. Like a theatre curtain that is slowly lowered to the stage at the end of a performance, the sun was drooping languidly down the afternoon sky. Alex lay back beside the sleeping dog and decided that he would stay for a little bit longer.

Chapter 44

After leading the momentous escape to the secluded chamber in the cellar, Nick instructed Wanda to sneak back up to Libby and Will's room where she was to pack a few articles of clothing, toiletries, and bedding. A nervous shiver ran down her spine for she was expected to find her way back alone through the dark chamber by means of feeling the damp walls to the left and right of her, all the while she reminded herself to be brave for the sake of Libby. Her feet must have hurried more than she remembered for as she proceeded upward the blackness surrounding her was becoming remarkably diluted by hues of white. Navigating more clearly through the gloomy grey haze, she felt a sudden pang of relief; for a stream of light was seeping under the kitchen door like compote dripping from an overstuffed pie crust.

Emulating the gestures of a thief, she slowly pushed the door ajar, waited, and listened. Adding to the young lady's anxieties were the muffled sounds of intermittent shouts and fits of commotion coming from the enclosed dining room. However, Wanda did not allow herself to become distracted from her main objective and having surfaced like a mole in spring, she snuck unnoticed all the way upstairs and into the Piccard's room. Here she found a carpetbag under the bed and with haste indiscriminately rummaged for what she thought would be appropriate accouterments for their secret journey. Had the entertainer known that a murder was being committed, she certainly would not have been in such high spirits in anticipation of the couple's escape.

At the very same time, Nick aptly secured the inside chamber and without pause immediately turned his objective towards preparing the prompt and safe liberation of his friends. Catlike, he followed the corridor back towards where he came from but turned to the right rather than to the left, which led to the kitchen whereupon he noiselessly unlocked the cellar door and padded up the small set of steps to the street level. He then prudently forged a small trail through a thicket of overgrown brush that had flourished in such grand twists and gnarls that the burgeoning plants masked from view the very wooden planks that he was so intent on removing. Here and there brambles and spiny branches caught his jacket like pinchers on a crab; he was scratched and cut, but found that the path he was able to clear had been tamed by his tenacity and sharp machete, and its wicked foliage would not be able to place even a solitary prick upon Libby's fair skin. Time and nature had made his job easy for the boards that once were bolted fast had decayed and rotted from years of exposure to the natural elements. With a minor disturbance and a few hearty tugs, Nick handily ripped the boards free, revealing a rather substantial exit whereby the two runaways emerged from their concealment and easily escaped as night descended upon them, fleeing towards their deliverance.

The elder Dowling growled like a ferocious animal as he sprang free from his evil misdoings into the street. Jack followed in quick pursuit wielding his walking stick like an armed soldier. Such a circumstance could not have been timelier for at that very hour a police officer on his nightly patrol happened to be standing beneath a nearby streetlight enjoying his evening cigarette. He inhaled deeply, savoring the taste of the tobacco, and then slowly exhaled, idly watching the smoke drift towards the flickering globe of light when suddenly, he was roused by the fitful shouts of, "Stop, murderer!" being expelled from the good-for-nothing's lips. An echoed cry even more pronounced was taken up by Katrina as she peered out from behind the opened door like a frightened child. Farther down the road, like dogs working themselves up to a feverish pitch, the pair pounded the street, one in pursuit of the other. Though this order could not be noted as good stalking evil, for Jack Philander was not an honest fellow, one could not help but wish him speed in overtaking the murderous devil before him. Summoned by instinct, the policeman tossed his cigarette butt into the street and listened for where the cries were coming from. Springing into action, he seized the moment and boldly intercepted the assassin as he was fleeing round the corner. Now Jack, who generally made it his business to keep his distance from the law, stopped his pursuit and hid behind a large shrub while the policeman wrestled the assailant. All the while the scoundrel wondered if he should reveal himself or keep out of sight. The rogue made a calculated decision; for being a betting man he wagered odds and abandoned his initial instinct to elude the policeman. Concluding that this was an opportunity to be viewed in a favorable light; he made himself present and assisted with the capture of the perpetrator.

A most shaken Katrina contributed to the night's final performance by relaying details of the brutal murder to the local detective, which was quickly transcribed by a reporter, who skillfully recreated the affair in time for printing the early edition of the *Baltimore Daily News*. As flies take to garbage, the parade of investigators and snooping neighbors had attracted quite a bit of unsolicited attention. By the time the first cup of coffee had been poured, the city was abuzz by the scandalous events that had taken place at the Cambridge Arms. A quick sketch drawing of Jack Philander adorned the article heralding him as a hero for assisting the police. As for Nick and Wanda, they had returned to the boarding house just in time to see the coroner's horse and carriage slowly plodding towards the morgue. Both provided the police an abbreviated version of the dinner party, which collaborated with the others in attendance. As a result of the evidence found at the scene, and the testimony they had collected, the police were content in their findings. They had their criminal in custody and were in the process of obtaining a full confession. As far as they were concerned, the murder had been committed by an estranged brother, a family feud escalated out of control, regrettably ending in the demise of Mrs. Cambridge. All guests and household staff were exonerated.

Meanwhile, poor Will and Libby; their escape was so successful that having traveled night and day they were unaware of the heinous crime they left behind. Obscurity of the truth such as this can be considered a blessing; for had the sweet Libby learned that her father was a murderer; one can never be sure what grave consequences the shock may have provoked upon her delicate nature. On the other hand, their decision to forgo any contact with their past may be a decision that will later be regretful. Obscurity of the truth can also tempt fate's reproachful irony. No longer is it necessary for the Piccards to remain in hiding now that Libby's father was safely locked away from society awaiting execution for the murder of her old aunt, Mrs. Cambridge.

———

Americans are a restless people who find pleasure and adventure in traveling; so much so that their rugged and feral land is rapidly being domesticated. Footpaths and narrow trails once difficult to navigate have been bridled and broken. Traversed with iron rails, miles of track are being stretched across the country connecting one line to another to form an elaborate and elongated means of transportation for people, goods, and articles of trade. Rivers and large lakes are populated with steamboats, some as grand as 350 feet long that grant their passengers a romantic view of her picturesque landscape. Stately bluffs with their craggy escarpments of limestone stretch from point to point in solitary opulence on either side of the river. At first glance these steep banks appear to be painted in hues of green that transition from light to dark depending upon the angles of the sun and shadows. But as the boats chug closer to the bank, the general contour and silhouettes are visibly conspicuous and what once resembled a distant landscape now becomes a botanical garden. The demur elm bows low aside the deep curtsey of the courtly willows that extend their long elegant branches of green lace as the steamboat coronation parades past.

The common method of travel, a passenger coach pulled by a team of six gallant horses, was becoming less routine as the thundering sounds of the locomotive snort and holler through the country; its enormous wheels shake the earth beneath the rails, and its whistle out-screeches the most obstreperous fowl. Like some sort of mythological creature, it often frightens those who happen upon it for without any former warning, many are sent running for safety. Passengers press their faces and noses against smudged windows and in simultaneous amazement watch as landscapes disappear in a flash of speed that was once not even conceivable in one's dreams until now. Was man meant to travel at such velocity and in such large groups?

Cities like Philadelphia, Boston, Baltimore, and Charleston continue to prosper, but none quite as remarkably as the transformation of New York, which has become the commercial nerve center of the East coast. Steady financial success and worldwide notoriety has prompted and triggered the construction of grandiose projects. Granite and marble buildings were designed with stately Greek columns, lavish vestibules, and palatial halls. Brownstone buildings with impressive pinnacled entrances inspired by Gothic architecture mingle with counting houses of granite post and lintel construction. Places of worship erected with lean towers that project above steeply pitched gable roofs are adorned with pointy arched windows; hovering above the entry portal, beams of patchwork colors bleed upon the parishioners as they enter. Land consecrated by the Church of England now touts the tallest point in the city. Graced with a Neo-Gothic spire and crowned by a gilded cross, ships many miles from harbor set their sights upon its stately pinnacle, which guides them safely into port.

However, those glamorous scenes of New York City, the ones that are plastered on crumbling walls or stuffed in vest pockets of dreamers were merely disguises to bait the naive. For once you journeyed into the workings of the great city only then would she unmask, revealing her true identity. Like fish caught in a net, idealists were dumped out upon her shores and floundered about hoping and looking for a means of survival. The lucky could often find work; some as shipbuilders, many as factory workers and shopkeepers, while others gave up and ventured Westward or Southward in search of a chance to prosper.

"I was the head stoker in the boiler room where there were three of us working the furnaces," an angry man cried out to anyone that passed his way. He was a large dirty man with swollen lids and mud-crusted hair. His clothes were tattered and his cap was too small for his large head. He paced up and down the streets, making a small track in the dirt like a caged bear. "She was a beauty of a ship, the work-horse of the river. Her name was the "Perseverance", and that was what she did, persevere! We kept her coals glowing red and her steam firing high; the heat radiated like the devil himself was down below with us. We were workin' in a coffin. I sweated so much I wondered where all the water was comin' from. The wailing of the machinery kept us tremblin'. When I left the river and the "Perseverance" I was sure I was finished with that black soot and grimy air. But I was wrong!" his voice cracked with rage. "'Cause I'm still in that inferno, this city is the same hell! It don't matter; summer or winter, it will git ya, it will git ya!" For those who did not heed his advice and judged him by appearance alone; for those that regarded his words as the ranting of a madman, they became easy prey for criminals who fed on the innocent like a piranha in the Amazon River.

And so as this aspiring city grew, its populace was equally swelling like a tumor, infested by corruption, poverty, gangs, and filth. The downtown streets were frequently muddy, often littered with horse manure, while trash accumulated in wooden garbage boxes or scattered on the sides of the streets, until the "cartman" would make his collection and wheel it away. It was a game of survival and all able-bodied, regardless of age, were expected to earn wages. Families sent their young children into the city as rag-pickers or hired them out to those who needed help, while the youngest or infirmed trailed alongside their working parents. Formal education was not required since schooling was not mandatory. To that end, bickering, bartering, and fighting were simply a part of the daily existence. The chattering and clacking of foreign tongues reticulated throughout the streets and dwellings. Poverty was so prevalent that many in prisons were merely vagrants and not criminals. Some were sent to the almshouse, a three-story building equipped with sixty rooms, two dining halls, and a chapel. This was the reservoir for the disenfranchised.

Housing for the poor was often confined to the cellar where subterranean dwellings lacked light and ventilation. Many found a place to live by renting in single family homes whose owners reconstructed space within its premises. But even these wooden framed buildings were inferior. Wet laundry was pinned on lines across the rooftops or strung between the buildings like telegraph wire. But this solution to drying was not always encouraged; often thieves made off with the clothing making it necessary to dry them inside. Occupants shared a hydrant, water closet, and sink in the courtyard. Slop, water, garbage, and human excrement runoff was channeled through open ditches.

The evolution of New York City housing was conforming to its growing population. Squatter shacks and row houses of substandard size rapidly multiplied, transforming the landscape and devouring every inch of grass with the ferocity of swarming locusts. Construction of two rows of six tenements called "railroad flats", because of their resemblance to cars in a train, contained two dwellings each measuring ten feet by four feet. In the cellar were water closets and sinks. But, as time and populations burgeoned, these buildings were either added to or subdivided. Rear yards were eliminated and only rooms facing the streets received light. On cloudy days those rooms that had a window now faced a dark alley and lamps needed to be lit continually. Tenements called "rookeries" that were located in the inner and middle rows were now built with only one foot of air space between them, and its window would face the brick wall of its neighbor. Lack of sanitation, lighting, and ventilation continued to plague those who resided in this city. As living conditions became deplorable for the poor these parts of New York were coined by health authorities as "fever depots" and "dens of pestilence."

———

Four harsh winters had passed since Libby had given birth to a son. She looked lovingly upon her little boy. This was not the life she had pictured for him, but for now it was the best that her world had to offer. The young mother lay prostrate upon her bed like a limp rag doll, yet tried to maintain a cheerful disposition for the sake of the child. As though kneading dough, she pushed two pillows behind her frail body; and with this support propped herself up against the wrought iron headboard. But in spite of this charade to appear on the mend, her once rosy complexion had all but disappeared beneath a sullen pallor revealing to anyone who looked upon her countenance that the woman was gravely ill.

On the floor beside her bed the young child, unaware of his mother's serious condition, sat upon his quilt and played contently. Scattered about were his favorite articles; a wooden spoon, a metal sauce pan, a tin cup, and an assortment of wooden blocks ranging from small to large. He was a particularity quiet child who rarely complained. He turned his face every now and again towards his mother to cast a sweet smile in her direction, and then went about his playful business of stacking the blocks, knocking them down, rebuilding the tower, and once again knocking them all to the floor. This activity would go on for some time until he would choose another diversion. The mother wistfully gazed about their shabby room. How she longed to release him from the bondage of the city. She wished to see him romp freely about a flowering pasture or poke the beetles that hid under autumn's fallen leaves. This was their fifth rooming house since escaping into New York City that dreadful night many years ago; a disquieting reminder of the passing of time.

The grayness of the room was solemn except during the early morning hours when the sun shot a radiant beam through the solitary window targeting the pane like a winged arrow. The wooden sill, rough and splintered, was wide enough for Libby to grow a trio of herbs. Here the sunlight settled upon the small pots of sweet tarragon, Italian oregano, and blue rosemary, which she generously fed a compost of tea and potato peels. Her sill garden flourished into a chromatic wonderland in contrast to the dull smoky view on the other side of the glass

Libby rested the back of her hand upon her forehead and woefully stared up at the blistered ceiling. She found herself following the maze of fissures and cracks that stretched from corner to corner. Her mind drifted away from the tiny cubical as she settled her thoughts upon the first time she and Will filed down the sea stained gangplank onto the shores of America; how they innocently strolled along the tired streets of Baltimore unaware of their future. Perhaps that was the last time they walked leisurely, taking an occasion to delight in their new surroundings. If only she knew back then what was ahead she never would have been so flippant and frivolous with her time. She never would have squandered away the hours like a starving man devours a meal and tastes not a single bite. Instead, she would have hoarded each moment, nurturing and embracing it like the lovely morning glory that blooms in the first hours of day; considering that by the shade of the afternoon the gentle flower fades and curls until it is dead by dusk. In lieu of all her desires the young family was forever running, hiding, looking behind them for any signs of reproach incurred by her father's hatred.

Libby wiped away the tears with the corner of her apron. "If only I could get well, then I could go to work again," she silently lamented. But her recurring cough just didn't want to subside. Her fitful attacks made people afraid to be around her. They feared she was contagious: and so she was denied employment until given a clean bill of health by a doctor. Maybe it was just as well; Mrs. Grady no longer wanted to watch the child; afraid that he too might be carrying the sickness. A collection of the neighbors' clothing sat heaped in the corner of the room waiting for Libby to stitch. Each item completed would mean adding a few coins to their meager coffer. But with each day that passed the tired woman found that she was growing weaker, barely able to muster the strength to get her sewing completed.

To lessen the city's visual assault, she would shut her eyes and create a temporary blockade by conjuring up distant memories of her English home with roving landscape; however blocking city noises was not as easy for sounds have a way of affixing themselves to the consciousness by jarring and jolting anytime day or night. Simple sounds such as the clopping of horse hooves, the rumble of boilers, street conversations, wailing children, shouts, whistles, the out of tune song of the drunk, the clatter of horse-drawn street cars moving along uneven streets, when combined with the intermittent clanging of engines, the hawking of produce, yelping of chained dogs, and the ramblings of beggars and vagabonds; when all sounded together, its summation would total a boisterous climate that would awaken even the most restful of sleepers. Water was brought in for baths and washing, and she heated small amounts on the stove for the boy's warm bath. The coal burning stoves made everything sooty, but regardless of how tired she made sure that the dust and dirt were swept up each morning and night.

As for Will, for two years he never saw sunlight on account of the fact that he walked to work before the lazy thing would rise and ambled back well after it had set. At first he told himself that he would become accustomed to his job in the brick factory however, as time moved on he felt within him an inexplicable sense of dissatisfaction. His present working conditions chiseled at his childhood memories, leaking hard times and misfortune like a bleeding wound. As a poor child he had been relegated to the dark cheerless factory; "So perhaps," he thought, "this is why I find my present situation so detestable." But being a good father and good husband, he would never reveal nor allow his true feelings to interfere with his obligations.

Now it so happened that almost two years to the day, during the fairest part of the morning when the streets are comparatively deserted and the silhouette of the city is outlined in dust, the young father was threading along his usual work route when in the not too far off distance he heard the frustrated prattles of an old man. "Damn ya, beast!" shouted the voice. "Damn ya!" A rickety looking delivery wagon leaned haplessly to one side. Standing in a gossamer of thinning clouds was a grey-whiskered man, at least forty years his elder and a thin blinkered nag. Evidenced by the taut reins, the horse could not stretch forward any further for its neck and head were strained and elongated by the forward motion and leverage that was being place upon it. The tattered deliveryman was using all the physical strength he could muster and had assumed what appeared to be the lunge position of a fencer. His right knee that was bent in a perfect right angle prepared to absorb the weight and motion of his body's forward momentum. His front foot rocked forward while his back leg straightened behind. Only his left heel, which lifted from the ground, seemed to waver in anticipation of his next move. Intervals of ten seconds would pass and then he would lunge forward, pause, and then violently jerk back on the reins with all his might. This seemed to go on for several minutes as the fellow desperately attempted to get the animal to move and set the wagon right. Yet the long-faced horse refused to obey, and the harder it stood its ground the harder the old man tugged.

"Need a hand?" Will called out.

"Damn you!" the man grumbled, but still the horse would not move.

"Maybe I can help?" Will proposed again. However, when his invitation was heeded only by angry mutterings, he decided to survey the situation more closely for himself. It appeared that an accident had occurred during the early fog when the old man steered too far to the left and landed in a deep gully that was not meant for wagon wheels, but rather water runoff. Will rounded the wagon and curiously peered over the sides, which exposed a full load comprised of a half-dozen or more galvanized iron cans all equal and conical in size. Having once been lined upright, they now toppled against one-another leaning towards the fallen side of the wagon. As a result, the wagon was now unequally balanced in weight, for the left side bore the burden of the load.

"She ain't worth the hay I feed her!" grunted the man tugging more fiercely on the reins. "Why this is my last delivery and she can't git it right. Well, it's off to the slaughterhouse when we git done.... hardly good enough to boil down for tapers or cat's meat!" The old man leaned forward again and tripping upon a stick that happened to be lying on the ground before him, he angrily picked it up and swung it over and back ready to beat down upon the poor horse.

Fortunately for the beast Will was a compassionate man and would not stand by and allow the driver to strike. Coming up from behind, he grabbed hold of the stick and snatched it free. Then he seized the reins away whereby he stood between the man and his horse.

"Git from here! Ya got no business, I got delivery to make and the milk will spoil, I'll lose my money, too. The hell with ya!" shouted the man and lifted his fists in rage.

But in that moment as if ignited by gratitude, the old nag acknowledged that she had been delivered to her savior and suddenly finding new courage, she whinnied long and loud which startled the old man so greatly that he nearly jumped into the rut himself and now held his hand over his heart, gasping for breath as though he were about to die. "My milk," he cried, "my milk! I'm ruined!" Whereupon in disbelief, Will saw the old man sit down in the middle of the road and begin to cry like a baby.

Now the sight of the weeping old man tempered Will's ill feeling against him and the harder the old fool cried the more his unhappy affairs surfaced. Finally, after he was all cried out, a grave calm came over his tear-stained face, and he began a woeful explanation. Several years ago, having been left a bit of money by a rich aunt, he had invested all of his inheritance in a dairy farm located in the pastoral section of the city, a bit uptown. For many years he lived quite comfortably, for as his investment prospered and the dairy farm grew, he was able to employ several men to care for and milk fifteen of the finest cows ever to have been bred in New Jersey and live in New York State. However, his good luck turned sour when his wife of thirty years suddenly took ill and died.

The old man blew his nose with such vigor that Will thought his head would explode. He wiped his bloodshot eyes with his dusty shirtsleeve and added a low sigh of despair before he continued.

It was only a day after her headstone had been placed and the bouquet of lilies lying across her tomb had begun to wilt that a salt and pepper-haired bank proprietor visited him at home. The well-groomed banker placed before him a stack of papers and brought to his attention a most unfortunate situation. It seems that his wife had been, for many years, borrowing small amounts of money against the farm and squandering it on frivolous spending sprees. To make matters worse, although he didn't know how it could happen, she spent the money from their personal savings as freely as one sips water from a riverbank. Although her intentions were seemingly harmless, she never returned the borrowed sum and the years of mounting interest against the accounts had grown into a substantial debt. All said and done, the widower was deeply and horribly in trouble.

The old man groaned, shook his head wearily, and went on with his miserable story. For several months after the visit, he tried to challenge this preposterous claim, but having no money for an executor, for what little remained was taken by the bank, he was forced to sell off the farm to satisfy all creditors. His only remaining assets were paltry in comparison to what he had once accrued. Two black and white cows, the old stubborn nag (a pell-mell mixture of breeds), one large milk cart, his delivery route, and a small two room hovel were all he owned.

Upon completion of the story the old fool began again to cry, but this time with such sorrow that Will believed that if it was possible the man would drown in his own tears. Yet, the great mishap that had befallen the wretch this morning may have not been all misfortune for had he not broken-down at the very moment that he did then most certainly he would not have been approached by such a hospitable individual as Will; for there were very few honorable men that strolled the early streets of New York City. Having been caught in a flurry of despair for so long, the younger and elder now considered the scene set before them and recognized a most favorable combination of circumstances could prevail whereupon each might be able to benefit from the other's melancholy. For years Will had only wished to find a job in the open air and longed to be free from the sweltering furnaces of the brick factory, while the old fool cursed his life, believing he would forever be relegated to toil behind the reins of his milk wagon. But like an unexpected shift in weather that sends an unseasonably warm breeze to melt a snowy passage, on this unassuming morning a new path had been set that would alter the day-to-day drudgery for both men. So upon arriving at an amicable consensus, a symbiotic relationship was formed. Will would give notice at the factory and take over the dairy route in addition to looking after the few remaining cows. In exchange for a weekly salary set aside from the meager profits, the elder could remain at home to smoke his pipe and read the local paper. Sealing the agreement with a hearty handshake a new chapter for each would begin; that is, as soon as the wagon was steadied back on the road.

Chapter 45

Libby sat at the little oak table by the open window seemingly oblivious to the outside noises. The peddlers' rickety carts stopped and started along the street as they permitted laughing and chattering washerwomen carrying their loads to cross in front on their way to the public pumps. As they dilly-dallied back and forth, boisterous exchanges of sentiments, often crude and flirtatious in manner, rolled in and out of windows with the hot breeze. A torn scrap of newsprint, having been fingered and folded at least a dozen times, lay rumpled before the young woman like a worn piece of ribbon. The words creased along the folded lines were markedly lighter than the rest of the dark print. "Death Notice: Analiese Helm... died at her family country home. A private burial will take place on Sunday..."

The announcement had been snipped from the *European Times* eighteen months earlier, but the painful reminder was as fresh as if it had been clipped that morning from a corner newsboy's first edition. Libby raised herself away from the table and with a gentle sweeping motion the scrap sailed into her hands as though performing a magic trick. Then, carefully retracing the creases, she refolded the little piece of paper back into the size of a sugar cube. Padding across the room like a night watchman, she opened the doors of the oak armoire and reached up to the top shelf. Her right hand slid beneath the neatly stacked linen, while the left supported the pile from toppling over. Feeling about for a few moments, she retrieved a palm-size, brown leather pouch that was drawn closed by a charcoal silk ribbon. With a light tug, Libby loosened its knot and like a fledg-ing waiting for its daily rations, she dropped the bite-size paper down into the throat of the pouch and felt it sink to the bottom, secured the top with a fine bow, and carefully slid it back beneath the linen from where it stayed hidden.

The young mother pulled a lace handkerchief from her apron pocket and coughed into it several times. A small amount of blood and spittle splattered the cloth, and she quickly crumpled the evi-dence into her palm. It had been decided that Will should take Lexy to work with him each day, and although it pained her to wake the child so early each morning, she now admitted that she was too weak to care for him properly. "You should see him!" Will exclaimed to Libby after the very first evening when they arrived back from work. "He's a natural with the nag. I couldn't get her to put the bit in her mouth; no amount of pressure on the bar would get her to open her stubborn jaw. Well, right when I was getting pretty frustrated, since there was a full load of milk and we needed to get going, I saw the cross-ties being tugged upon. Straightaway the old nag obeyed the advance and bowed her neck towards the ground. On my right was our son stroking her long face and whispering into her ears. Libby, I swear she understood what he was saying. Her narrow eyes and tight pinched mouth suddenly relaxed. I dare say she was smiling. Well, lickety-split, the old horse gave me no trouble; minded me better than she ever had before!"

Libby smiled and wearily sat back down, drawing her elbows up as she drooped her head forward into cradled hands. She pictured her little Lexy embracing the horse's velvety muzzle, teetering on tiptoe while whispering into its long tapered ears. "What a spirited child I have!" she mused to herself. "For the stubborn old nag to take a liking to anyone is a true testimony to the boy's kind-hearted disposition." But sadly her thoughts were quickly squelched as she began to consider other alternatives, for although the child enjoyed spending days with his father, it was not the most suitable routine for a youngster. A pang of urgency overcame her senses, and she felt herself begin to swoon. She leaned back in the chair as if to catch herself from falling forward and sighed deeply. If only the neighbors minded their own business things would set themselves right in due time, but knowing that someone had reported them to the authorities only created apprehension of impending troubles. Evidently someone who did not have the courage to come to the Piccards themselves had seen a downy-haired child walking with a man during the grey part of the morning when even the gutter rats were still asleep. "He was the size of a sprite and smelled of farm animals!" the authorities were told. "Imagine at the wee hours before even a hint of daylight!"

"Who were they to decide what was best for our child?" Libby lamented and pondered the following incident.

It was around noontime when she had heard a loud and emphatic knocking at the door. She remembered wondering who it could be, for the constant rat-a-tat-tat of impatient knuckles upon the wood had a deliberate air of authority. Even from behind the closed door she knew that the caller was not on a cordial visit, but rather a stranger on business; urgent business. She remembered the smell of starch waft into the apartment when she cracked open the door. A small, well-dressed woman wearing a finely crafted hat introduced herself as a Mrs. Westly or Wesley; she spoke so fast and with such short staccato tones that Libby had a difficult time following her train of thought. She announced that she was from the New York City ..... or was it the ...... "Heavens," Libby said aloud, "how is it that I didn't write it down!" She recalled how the woman went on to explain that a complaint had been lodged by a neighbor that her son was allegedly being neglected and that New York City was filled with people like she and her husband that couldn't care for their children. Libby remembered feeling frightened and made every attempt to fully explain the situation; that she was not feeling well and had been sick for a long time; how Will was only caring for the child until she was better.

It was humiliating to have the stranger inspect their home, but most curious that the woman placed a particular interest in seeing where "the boy" slept. She was directed to the tiny cot in the corner.

The bed was neatly made with fresh linen; his quilt was folded squarely across the pillow. Libby chastised herself for not having straightened up the dishes that were still stacked on the table from breakfast. However, this bit of untidy evidence did not appear to concern the stranger for she walked past the mess directing her full attention to the child's sleeping arrangements. The woman examined the cot with sterile hands, tugging at the sheets, unfurling the blanket, and shaking the pillow as though expecting to disclose something insidious. Having been granted all opportunity, her only act of discovery was a child's nightshirt stitched from blue gingham rolled up in a ball inside the linen pillowcase. Libby followed behind like a handmaiden to a queen, refolding and replacing each item after inspection. The strain of being up and about had begun to take its toll upon the poor frightened mother, but she would not permit the somber woman to see her compromised; so she remained standing.

Finally when "her majesty" seemed to be content, the woman leaned against the chair while her hawkish eyes roamed the room as though in search of prey. Libby found herself glancing about the room too, wondering what more the woman could possibly wish to see when suddenly a pair of brown-banded cockroaches scurried across the floor, one after the other, fleeing towards the opposite wall where they happily disappeared into a thin crack in the plaster. Libby held her breath praying that the impertinent woman would not notice these squatters who now began to flit in and out of their hideout as though playing hide and seek. Hoping to pull the woman's attention onto her and away from the "buggy" side of the room, Libby remembered that she had nonchalantly strolled over to the only window and pulled open the drawn curtain whereupon a sudden explosion of sunlight flung itself upon the investigator. Like a vampire unearthed during daybreak, the proper woman lost all composure and recoiled with horror, cowering back and hiding her face behind her gloved hands. A most startled Libby instantly apologized for the sudden intrusion of sunlight by pulling the curtain closed again, but not without leaving behind a most foreboding premonition. For the first time since the unwelcome arrival, Libby felt a gut wrenching fear. For although Mrs. Westley, or Wesley, left satisfied that the child's home was not in violation of any heath code, that he had sufficient amount of living space, a fair amount of food, and enough clean clothing; she was not yet convinced that he was cared for properly with a respectable day-to-day routine. "These are merely tangible items," she had informed the mother. "As far as the allegations of neglect; that is still to be determined. I promise to keep an eye on the child's lifestyle."

Libby pitched forward again and placed her hand over her forehead and wiped it feverishly with her handkerchief. Even after having thought back on this intrusion, she continued to wonder who could have called the authorities; but still came up with a blank. She shook the lace hankie until it opened like a tiny parasol and covered it over her mouth while she coughed into its finely embroidered flowers. Although weary and fatigued, she knew that extra careful precautions must be taken. The thought surged to her head like blood flowing through her veins and with a sharpened instinct to protect; she pulled away from the chair and went to the cupboard where she removed from the shelf a large ceramic soup bowl and the jar of matches. She wadded the handkerchief into a ball and flattened it down into the middle of the bowl. With a quick strike against the flint, she lit the match and placed the flame upon the material. At first it did not seem to want to accept it, but in a matter of a few moments the entire cloth ignited and was engulfed in smoke. Small bits of soot flew up into the air as tiny pieces were separated from the whole. The lace border went first; the embroidered pink roses charred by the flames turned yellow and then brown, until there was nothing but sooty ash left in the bowl. "If only the disease was as easy to get rid of," Libby thought as she dumped the mess into the garbage pail. Exhausted, she glided away from the table, pulled a clean handkerchief from the armoire and wearily went back to bed.

———

For the next five months the Piccards were victims of unwarranted scrutiny by an invasion of meddlesome neighbors. From morning until night they peppered the young family's life with thorny annoyances, pilfering away at their privacy. Pairs of nosey eyes peered through the cracks of open doors and slatted peepholes as father and son left for work. They followed the two during the daylight hours from open wagons or passing by on foot, and again when the man and boy returned home in the evening. There was always an observer loitering on the front steps or hanging about behind the stairwell landing. No matter the temperament of the day, may it be cold or hot, windy or rainy, falling snow or tenebrous fog, the father and his child always left in darkness and returned in darkness. At first, Will thought that he may have been imagining being watched; that perhaps he was acting paranoid to believe a few unwelcome glances were really laced with malicious intentions. But as the months passed exaggerated yarns of the boy's ill treatment seeped their way into the streets and the markets. Distorted stories describing firsthand accounts of child neglect freely scattered about the neighborhood and were hungrily consumed by prattling gossips. Like squirrels that hoard nuts in the winter, accusers deposited the rumors into the largest burrow in the forest; the City of New York's authorities.

It is not without surprise to presume these impertinent intrusions escalated Libby to her present condition; but regardless of the reason, the dear woman was now confined to her sickbed. Her bright eyes that could always inspire happiness and sunshine upon even the most down trodden and despaired seemed permanently lost behind the languid effects of physical suffering. And in spite of the assured doctor's attentiveness, his diagnosis grew bleak, for each day her condition seemed to worsen contrary to all his well-meaning intentions. The little boy watched as he administered the latest treatments, but in the squalor of the city the doctor himself may have unknowingly transported the illness of another from house to house; producing a somber situation with little or no chance for improvement.

In just a few months the sickly woman had become a bed-ridden invalid. The only solace Libby found was with her son. Occasionally, when she felt fit enough to lean up against the headboard, the child would come and sit by his mother, and she would tell him a story or two; however with each passing day the effects of her illness had become more grave and were taking a severe toll upon the young woman. The concerned doctor instructed the boy to keep his distance, therefore prohibiting the child from entering his mother's room. Displaying no outward reluctance, Lexy set up a little camp of toys and played outside the shut door hoping by chance to catch a glimpse of her whenever it was opened and closed. But as time went on this restriction did not stop the child, for when his mother and father were asleep he would drag his blanket from his little cot into her room and lay upon the floor next to her sickbed. With a view of her sleeping figure garbed in a white dressing gown with tiny lilacs, he would happily fall asleep.

———

Bouquets of flowers lay before the gated walkway like a massive funeral wreath. Freshly cut lilacs and roses were tied with silky ribbons while pansies and daisies had been bundled together with twine. Handwritten condolences with misspelled sentiments were scribbled on torn scraps of brown wrapping paper and tucked between woody stems. In contrast to this homage were those of more refined manner. Folded sheets of linen parchment were elegantly addressed "To the Deceased".

Now, although the ancient one had never paid much attention to following any church doctrine, this did not stop the followers of "the Lord" from displaying their convictions, for as the weeks passed so grew the roadside memorial. An assembly of religious enthusiasts had wired a gilded cross upon the entrance gate inviting an impromptu eulogy to be conducted by the Reverend Hubert Glass, a minister with a flair for the theatrics. "Here at this gathering of neighbors; friends and kindred come together to pay a last tribute of respect to her memory!" the Reverend exploded; his clenched Bible held close to his chest. He sighed deeply, looked about to be sure he was being heeded, and then bowed his eyes into the heap of wilting flowers. A small crowd of followers assembled about him and watched as he bent down and plucked a daisy from the pile. Then, with a fever of exaltation, he sprang forth and raised his Bible towards the heavens. "What further can I say concerning that gentle, kindly spirit, that she was a goodly neighbor, fond and devoted patron of Baltimore, and believed in the Golden Rule of doing unto others as you would have them do unto you? Is not that the sum of virtue?" he shouted. In perfect harmony there was a cry of affirmation, "Amen!" A young disciple, not much older than a child of ten, was sent forward to ring the gate's bell. And although it was merely a tinkling of light peals, it was produced with as much enthusiasm as though tolled in the grandest of Europe's Cathedrals.

The crime that had been committed attracted the gathering of uninvited visitors before the locked gate of the Cambridge Arms. Each set up stations hoping to catch a glimpse inside the dark house, but all that was visible was the tired stoop that held out its stony banisters like outstretched arms. The hideous events that had transpired courted many who were not satisfied to simply saunter by the boarding house, but rather took it upon themselves to appoint the residence a destination on a sight-seeing tour. "Look at the window, there's a face!" cried a nosey neighbor from down the road. "It's her, it's Mrs. Cambridge back as a ghost!"

"Where, where? I don't see! What's that yer lookin' at?" shrieked the fish monger's wife. And as the crowd thickened, a chorus of shrills and rumors began to bubble, spreading freely like gravy over a free turkey dinner. "It's the old lady! See in the window?" Men and women, the young and the elderly began to push against the gate and along the surrounding fence. Some peering over on tiptoe, as though rising a few inches higher would allow them to get a better glimpse of the dead woman, while others squatted down on bent knees and pushed their faces between the metal slats like jailed prisoners; and the more the crowd cried out with curiosity, the more people came round to see. The rows of flowers that had been so neatly laid were now being trampled and crushed; carelessly cast aside like overgrown cuttings.

"What are ya doin'?" a boisterous shrill spilled out of the foyer window as it was suddenly flung open. A simultaneous shriek of horror was expelled from someone in the crowd! "Get away from here, all of you!" cried Katrina, and she shook her fist with vengeance.

"It ain't the old lady!" shouted a man. "Why it's just the maid! See, I told ya, there was no ghost!" he barked with dissatisfaction.

"Be gone, all of you!" Katrina called out again. "Where were you when she was alive? What good are you now? What good are you now?" Cranking the casement closed, she retreated behind the sealed window, ridding herself of the intruders, even if it only meant temporary seclusion.

Disappointed that the face in the window was not the ghostly apparition of Mrs. Cambridge, the crowd slowly dispersed, but only to return later with a fresh lot of curiosity seekers.

As a result, it would have been impossible for the wretched Jonathan Dowling to get a fair trial in Baltimore, for not a single soul who lived in the city had the opinion that he deserved one. But since the law was the law, and all men were considered innocent until proven guilty, a change of venue was granted and a trial date was set to begin in the city of Chicago. So weeks after the murder, as a heinous crime had been committed, the trial, which began after a month of the change, soon was but a footnote in the *Baltimore Times*; and when the jury found him guilty of murder just a fortnight after it had begun, the sentencing of "death by hanging" crept its way to page three.

A patch of sunshine splashed upon the white linen as the window drapes moved freely in the early morning breeze. A pool of yellow light trickled back and forth upon the table like the ebb of a tide. The two friends sat at the large table as they had done so many times before except Nick placed himself in the chair that had once been reserved for the matriarch. "The Cambridge Arms belongs to her son, no matter what she thought of him," Nick reminded Wanda.

"It's just that I haven't a clue as to where I can find him. For all I know he could be dead."

"Oh, don't say such a thing!" Wanda shuddered. "Didn't we have enough death for one month; I simply can't think of anything morbid; all those dreadful people trespassing day and night. It is high time the news has finally turned its attention to someone else's catastrophe besides ours. Maybe now Cambridge Arms can have some peace!" bemoaned Wanda. "Besides, the only thing on your mind should be to get me to the station. My train leaves in a little over an hour."

"Are you sure I can't get you to change your mind?" Nick asked and leaned closer. "I know the ancient one wouldn't have minded if you stayed on."

Wanda looked up from her teacup and wrinkled her nose with disapproval. "Mrs. Cambridge was a lot of things, but approving of a ...," Wanda paused for a moment. "Now what did she call me? Oh yes, a sassy salon singer, I think that was the term. Anyway, don't be ridiculous, I've made up my mind. Besides, it took almost a week to haul my things out of this place." She put down her cup and reached across the table for Nick's hand. "Promise me that you'll come and visit, why California is the most exciting place in the country!" She took his hand and squeezed it in hers. "I know!" she suddenly exclaimed shaking her hand free and jumping up. "Why don't you come with me right now? Katrina can manage this place especially now that it's only the Admiral, and he's away most of the year. And don't forget, there's Marte! What do you say?" She slinked over the back of his chair and draped her arms around his shoulders like a fur tippet.

"I can't," he replied shaking his head "no". Then he leaned his neck back and stared up at her inviting and enchanting expression. "Someone's got to look after the business; anyway, what does a shipbuilder like me do in a gold-crazy city like San Francisco?"

"Nick Biddle, you are the most exasperating man I know. Sometimes I wish you didn't have such high scruples!" Wanda complained as she abruptly surrendered him from her embrace. But in spite of her disappointment she couldn't remain angry; after all, it was his honest convictions that made him the man he was. "Oh!" she exclaimed, her sigh peppered with a bit of annoyance, and headed towards the door, when suddenly, she stopped, turned round, and shook her head side to side as though he had been a naughty little boy. Nick looked back at her and for a moment wondered how he could let her go, but before he could tell her that he had changed his mind, she threw a seductive smile at him as a reminder that she wouldn't want him any other way. "I'll go up to change," she said, "I won't be long," and slowly she sauntered away.

Nick listened to her heels make a tap, tap, tap up the long set of stairs, and then the creek of the door closing behind her. "Am I making a mistake?" he wondered. He glanced around the large dinner table, at the dining chairs, and the silver tea service that had not been employed for over a month now and folded his hands behind his head. "Have I made a terrible mistake?" he asked himself again, but having no answer, he got up from the table and proceeded out the door.

———

The new Jack Philander posed back at the old Jack Philander wearing the latest men's fashion. The tailor that fitted him had double checked the inseam at least twice before marking the measurement on his paper, and he was shown at least a half-dozen different kinds of fabric until he settled on a conservative black velvet. He leaned back on one leg and admired himself while stroking the smooth material up and down like a boy petting a kitten for the first time. "Fine, yes this is exactly what I wanted," he thought adoring his new garment in the mirror; a single-breasted jacket reaching mid-thigh, accented with patch pockets, a small collar, and short lapels. He tugged at the shirt collar that folded down as compared to those he was used to wearing that were heavily starched in order to stand up around the neck while he made several attempts to flatten his wide cravat from springing up like a poppy flower. Jack turned to the right, then to the left, and questioned if perhaps the color was even a bit too garish for himself. However, the tailor had explained that the color was exactly what all the European's were wearing, and it often took time for Americans to become comfortable with the newest fashions. So, against better judgment, he agreed, though he still thought a red cravat was much too flamboyant. The dandy pulled his watch fob from his vest pocket and decided that he had time enough to pour himself a shot of whiskey before departing.

Less than a month ago he was a lonely ferret slinking around corners and dodging the law. "Being in the right place at the right time makes all the difference in the world," he thought as he pulled the cork out of the bottle. He had poured himself a drink from the same bottle several times before, however today's libation was exquisitely different. The brown liquid had a golden tinge, and when he held it up to the open window, he swirled the glass about so that it caught the light, and he was sure he could see it sparkle. He placed the rim to his nose and sniffed, inhaling with the same exuberance one places upon a bouquet of spring flowers. "A sign of things to come!" he thought and staged himself once again before the mirror. He stared for a moment at the new Jack Philander, raised the shot glass above his head and toasted, "To me and the future!" and with a gallant gesture, he threw the whiskey to the back of his throat in one swig.

Two steamer trunks stood side by side and handily fit all his belongings, for he didn't have much to his name except for his new tailored clothes and the first class ticket to Washington, D.C. All had been procured with the reward money he had been allotted. He bought at least a dozen newspapers and filled the empty spaces in the trunks with the accounts of his heroic effort. "Local hero risks his life!" and "Hail to the Hero of Baltimore!" But his favorite was the *Baltimore Sun*, which had quoted the police captain as saying, "Yes, thanks to the heroic efforts of our city's own son, Mr. Jack Philander, the killer was apprehended and safely taken into custody."

"Now, that's a turn of events!" Jack laughed thinking about the irony of it all. Picturing himself only a year ago eluding the very same policeman brought a sinister smile to his thin lips. He reached back and turned the whiskey bottle over, but to his dismay only a few drops managed to find their way out and fall into the shot glass. "Damn," he said and shook the bottle up and down as though the vigorous movement would miraculously release several more ounces of spirits into his glass.

"Mr. Philander," a knock at the door sounded. "Your hansom cab is here, Sir. May we get your trunks?"

"Sir? Ahh, I can get used to this," Jack thought and opened the door for the caretaker's two sons.

"Good morning, Sir," the younger of the two men greeted. Jack opened the door wider and stepped aside to let two wiry young men into his room. He gestured towards the trunks and stood idly by as they each grabbed a leather strap and started to drag the trunks away. "Anything breakable?" the scrappy fellow asked as he continued to slide his trunk towards the top of the landing.

Jack shook his head "no" and heard what he thought was a faint reply of "Good." He leaned his head over the banister and watched as the two trunks were manhandled down the stairs with not much degree of reverence for their contents. He waited until he saw them push the first trunk across the threshold of the front door and then hurriedly walked back into his room. For the very last time, he gave it a once over before putting on his hat and taking his walking stick from the corner. He looked at himself in the mirror and tipped his black bowler so that it was just slightly tilted to the left. Then, he laid an I.O.U. upon the table and shut the door behind him without looking back. After all, old habits are hard to break.

Chapter 46

B etty was sitting outside on the steps of the front porch when Alex came trudging down the side of the hill. She was leaning against the second stoop with her long legs tucked up under her colorless skirt resembling a huge mushroom. Her hair, usually pulled back into a tight bun, had loosened during the day and wisps of grey fell free from the hairpins that were meant to keep it fastened up and away from her face as she tended to her chores. At night she wore her hair plaited in a long braid that hung down against her nightgown like a horse's tail. Alex had lived at the Forester's for almost eight years, and Betty hadn't changed the way she wore her hair for as long as he could remember; except that now it was more grey than brown. Timothy had taken up residency in his usual comfortable position on the rocking chair. His large body dominated the entire seat, furnishing the illusion that this lump could be a fur covered cushion. It was only his paws folding down over the edge of the seat like a pair of limp mittens that divulged his true identity.

"Where ya been?" Betty called out as Alex's silhouette approached. Her voice was tired but still strong, and he wondered where she mustered her strength from. The sleeping feline, startled by the abrupt interruption in sleep, lifted his head in disgust to see what the fuss was all about.

This was quiet time in the late afternoon and except for an occasional cackle from the hens or turkeys beginning to roost for the night, Alex was conscious of his own breathing. The closer he advanced towards the house the more he noticed how everything before him appeared grey and brown. "Remember, I was on a picnic," he called back. Dust kicked up in front of him as he scuffled along. He didn't hear her answer and supposed she couldn't hear what he had said either. The boy made his way quickly, rejoining her as he melted into view out from the hazy background. He sat down on the step next to the tired woman. "Remember, I was on a picnic," he replied again and started to shake one foot at a time trying to toss the loose dirt from the leather creases in his shoes.

Betty continued to stare outward into the open afternoon as though fixed in a trance. "That's right, with the Tarson girl wasn't it?" she asked continuing to keep her eyes fixed on the hillside before her.

Alex looked over at her and then down at his feet. "Yep," he replied. He waited a few moments thinking that she was going to talk, but she leaned against the post and sighed. Alex turned his head in her direction, but she remained anchored on the hill before them.

Finally she spoke. "I got a letter today from the hospital." She paused and fiddled with the hairpin trying to get the strays to go back up. "Randle ain't doin' so good," she added. "He ain't never comin' home."

Again silence. Alex wanted to say something, but he wasn't sure what. "Never?" he asked as though not hearing her the first time.

"I don't believe so, that is unless it's in a box." She turned her face towards the boy, and he wondered if her seemingly callous remark meant that she was only kidding, but there was no laughter in her expression. "It's better off we think of him as gone," she continued, "cause the man I married is gone. If anybody asks, you might as well say he's dead."

Alex was the one who now turned his face away. He felt a sudden pang of sadness, but it was directed towards Betty, not Randle. It took courage for her to finally come to the realization that Randle was never coming back. They sat together like they had done times before, but today there was something far removed from the ordinary experience. Betty remained in a faraway daydream that was becoming part of her usual persona, while Alex tapped his feet restlessly waiting for her to say something. Timothy stirred in the rocker. It shifted lightly back and forth until the cat finally found itself another comfortable position, and it no longer rocked.

"Do ya need me?" Alex asked and stood up. "Cause if ya don't, I'm gonna clean out the stalls."

"Ya know," she remarked very matter-of-fact, "I think you like them two drafts better than people." She raised her face up at him and offered what he thought was a smile, but the dusky light of the late afternoon had restricted him from understanding her expressions. "Go on then, but don't take too long," she added not waiting for his answer.

Alex stepped down from the porch and started for the barn. He took a few steps and then turned around, "Sorry about Randle," he called out. He waited for a minute assuming that Betty might say something. In the distance a low rumbling of thunder resonated through the stillness and high overhead there was a faint hollow booming. Startled by the noise, Timothy jumped down from the rocker and scampered back into the house. A sudden flash of lightening lit up the sky for nearly a second. It was a curious scene now on that lonely porch; the earthy browns of the farmhouse had taken on the pale blues and greys of an ocean landscape. The cat's sudden lunge had set the rocking chair in motion and like a ghost ship rolling up and down along the waves; it was tottering back and forth, back and forth without any visible help. A few drops of rain sprinkled from the dark clouds and then a heavier drizzle began to fall. Alex turned his attention to Betty who looked like a pale corpse leaning up against the porch. She hadn't moved at all, so still, so lifeless. At first he thought perhaps he should go to her, but instead he decided to let it alone. He quickly jogged towards the barn trying now to keep from getting too wet, for the rain was now falling more heavily and as he pulled open the door he began to wonder if he should plan on fixing himself some supper later that night.

———

Alex woke up to the sound of raindrops. It was not coming from the outside, but rather the plop, plop, plop of water dripping down from a leaky roof. Delilah was standing over him, her large brown eyes staring into his face. "You're hungry, ain't ya?" Alex remarked and reached up to pet her long soft nose. He rubbed his eyes and recollected the events from last evening. The rain had come down for so long and so hard that he had decided to sleep in the stall. Alex sat up and tossed the woolen blanket aside. He looked like a porcupine with yellow quills and began to pick off the hay that had, without invitation, stuck to his clothes. "I know, you're hungry, too," he said to Dandy that had walked over to see what was going on. "Well, you ain't the only one." She gently nudged his shoulder with her nose as though prodding him to "hurry up" The two horses stood side by side and waited patiently as Alex quickly set out to work.

"Ya know, I told you before, you're my family, and I ain't ever gonna let nothin' happen to ya," he whispered. He worked quietly now, tending to their needs; never straying from his tasks. When he was finished, he lay down a fresh layer of hay and smoothed it out as though it were fresh linen on a bed. "I gotta be gettin' back to the house and wash up," he told them as he rested his head along Delilah's thick strong neck. He placed his hand over her mane and stroked gently as she chewed her mash contently. With closed eyes he listened to her breath for a few minutes more. "If only I could stay here forever. If only I never had to leave." The boy opened his eyes, shedding a great sigh, for he knew this would be the last moments of pure tranquility until he returned to the stalls again.

———

When Alex walked back into the house he expected to see Betty; however he didn't expect to see her sitting at the kitchen table amidst three neat stacks of papers. Reminiscent of a schoolboy's caricature, she was balancing a pair of Randle's old reading glasses low on her nose. At first he wanted to laugh since they changed her appearance to the likeness of a weasel, but by the very stern expression on her face, he decided that perhaps he would not bring that to her attention. Besides, she didn't ever seem to have a very good sense of humor. Instead he gingerly said, "Mornin'," and approached the woman with caution. He stood beside her and waited until she finished reading from the sheets of paper that she pressed firmly in her hand. Her tight grip had created permanent wrinkles in what must have been expensive parchment. Finally, she put the papers down. Her eyebrows and forehead furrows moved simultaneously with the same upward motion as she peered over the rims of the spectacles, giving her an expression as if she was frozen in the moment.

"I don't know why these lawyers have to make it so complicated," she exclaimed in disgust and tossed the reading glasses on top of the papers causing the whole lot of them to topple into one large pile. Then, acknowledging Alex, she stood up and pushed the entire pile to the center of the table, while the glasses got buried below. "Sit down, I'll fix ya some grits," she commanded and without waiting for his reply, pulled a bowl from the shelf and ladled several thick scoops of mush into the bowl. She dropped the dish before him, handed him a large soup spoon, and continued to ramble in such a glorious fury that she spoke without ever taking time for a breath.

"When Randle was around we ate like kings, oh maybe not kings, but certainly lots better than most folks. Now look at us, mush and grits for breakfast and if we're lucky we got eggs and fried dough at supper. Now I ain't complain'in'!" she continued, "but, to tell ya the truth, well with all this talk of war I read about, I don't know what else to do." Alex slid his bowl aside suddenly not very hungry and watched her now more intently. He knew that things had not been easy, but this was the first time he had really ever seen Betty so intent on the negative. She scurried about the room and looked into his bowl. "Ya didn't finish!" she grumbled and pushed the bowl back in front of the child.

"I'll work harder," Alex suggested. "Ya need me to work more? I can work at night if ya need?" But, he really had no idea what else he could do.

"It ain't you, Alex" she said and lightly tapped her finger against the brim of the bowl as a subtle reminder that there was more to eat.

"Alex?" she never called him by his name, it was always, 'boy'. Now he knew this was serious.

She sat down across from him and pulled the papers closer to her. The shift in position revealed the reading glasses from beneath the pile. "I got an offer, and I'm gonna take it," she remarked and then started to restack the papers into neat piles, page by page. She put the reading glasses back on and slid them down along the bridge of her nose until they settled in the low weasel-like position. Keeping her face perfectly still, she lowered her chin down towards the table so they would not slip off and continued to make the piles.

"What offer?" he asked softly, for he was afraid of what he assumed would be the response. But before he could get an answer the sound of a carriage rolling up to the farmhouse sounded outside.

"It's him, he's early!" Betty announced and sprang away from the table. Without asking if he were finished, she plucked Alex's bowl up and poured what he had not eaten back into the cook pan. Then, fumbling behind her back, she tugged at the apron strings trying to unfasten the covering, but she only managed to make the knot tighter. "Here, get this off me!" she whispered harshly and turned her back towards Alex, employing him to untie the apron knot. However, with all her fussing and fidgeting, what would have been an easy request turned into a big wadded mess for the more she told him to hurry up the more his fingers seemed to flounder in all the wrong directions. Every time he appeared to have untangled much of the knotted mess, Betty would pull in the front and undo all his progress by retightening the connected strings. This went on for several minutes until suddenly they were interrupted by a knock on the door. It was not a loud knock, but rather two short and cursory raps, as though saying, "Excuse me for intruding."

"Never mind this!" Betty exclaimed, and without notice pulled sharply away from Alex, reached for a kitchen knife and with one quick motion sliced the sash in two, letting the apron fall to her feet. She breathed slowly, taking in deep breaths as though she had just removed a noose from around her neck. Remembering the apron, she picked it up from the floor and tossed it over to Alex, practiced a happy smile, and nonchalantly opened the door for the visitor with the grace of a queen.

———

Mr. William Beasley, who liked to be called Mr. Billy, tipped his bowler, wiped his feet on the welcome mat, and exchanged the usual courteous salutations with Betty. "Won't you come in and sit down?" she asked the hunchback. Betty was a tall woman, but standing next to the poor deformed fellow made her feel like an oak tree beside a shrub.

"No, thank you, I've got to get back to work," he said declining the invitation and handed her a brown leather portfolio. "Now, as soon as you get Mr. Forester's signature, well, we can close the deal. Of course take your time and read everything over, but I believe you'll find that they are in the order of business that we discussed."

She took the case from the hunchback and forced another smile. "I suppose you've become accustomed to the Tarson place. It has been a while now since Belle put you in charge," Betty said fishing for gossip.

"To tell you the truth, I keep to myself. Of course there's Miss Henshaw, she takes care of the child, and Beatrice, runs the house like a matron in a prison. So I guess you could say that I have the easiest job of all!" he chuckled heartily, thinking that he had made a funny joke, but found himself standing there laughing all alone since there was no reaction either way from Betty. He started in again, but this time in a more businesslike tone. "Yes, well, just send your boy up when you get back the signature and well..." he stopped and tipped his hat again. "Well, see you again, Mrs. Forester," and turned to leave.

Betty fixed her eyes upon the little man with an unseeing gaze before shutting the door and then rested her head against the wooden frame. She gripped the leather portfolio and twirled around in complete exuberance only to see Alex sitting at the head of the table in Randle's chair. A sheet of white paper was placed in front of him with freshly drying ink. "I never asked ya for anything," Alex announced in a voice that was unfamiliar to the woman. He started again, "I never asked Randle fer nothin' neither. Ain't that so, Betty?"

She looked at the child and saw something in his face that she had never seen before. His gray eyes seemed to penetrate right through her casual glance, and his cold stare almost made her shudder. He was as determined as she had ever seen anyone and for a moment she felt as though she did not know who he was.

"You look so serious," she remarked and sat down across the table. She put the portfolio to the side and nervously fiddled with its leather string.

"I ain't asked you fer nothin', have I?" he repeated.

"No, can't say that ya have," she replied. Still his stare was icy.

"Then, if I ask ya fer somethin', then ya can't really be angry can you?" he asked.

"No, I suppose I can't," Betty agreed, nodding her head in unison with her answer.

"I know that Mr. Billy's gonna buy the farm, ain't that so?" Alex remarked and then added, "I don't care 'bout that, it is yers to sell."

Betty was quite curious now and couldn't imagine what had made the boy so serious. "If it's the farm yer worried about, well don't you fret. He's gonna let us stay on. Why we'll live here as always, just that we won't own it," she explained, making her answer light and carefree.

"I don't care 'bout the farm," he replied again more firmly. His monotone voice continued to be strangely calm. He looked straight at her and didn't flinch. "It ain't the farm, it ain't you, it ain't Randle, it ain't nobody. I have only one job in this world, and I can't let you sell it away."

"Tell me, what do ya want?" she asked, with a searching glance.

"I want ya to turn over Dandy and Delilah to me. I don't believe in owning another life, but I need to know that I'm in charge of their well bein'. Let me take care of them." Alex's face remained rigid and the only thing that moved were his hands sliding the newly written paper towards her. Before Betty took it up to read, he began to explain. "I wrote out a note that says you and Randle have put me, and only me, in charge of Dandy and Delilah. It says that nobody can buy or sell them. All I need is fer you to sign it."

Betty smiled after hearing the explanation. "Is that all? Why Alex, Mr. Billy ain't gonna take them away; why you can care for them," she remarked, however the infliction she placed upon the words was more patronizing than sincere.

"No," Alex interrupted, "I promised! I cannot have you sell them."

"But, don't you see, Alex," Betty implored, "they are part of the sale, why they go with the farm, like the hens and the chickens."

"Promise me, Betty, sign the paper, ya can't sell them two. I am telling ya, if you sell them, well ya might as well sell me right along, too." Alex pushed the paper further towards her. She glanced down at the perfectly formed letters, each one neatly scribed, each word carefully executed. Then she looked across at his hands that now seemed to have become so much larger than she remembered.

The confused woman stood up and placed her hands across her forehead. "Well, I don't know, after all the papers have been all put together." She picked up the portfolio and pulled out the documents. "You're just a child, you don't understand these things." She started to pace the floor and shake her head while waving the papers about as though they were a Chinese fan.

"Promise me, Betty; don't let them sell them horses. I don't care fer nothin' else." He paused for a moment and swallowed hard. "I gave my word," Alex replied again with a startling sound of conviction.

She sat back down and reached for the inkstand that was sitting in the center of the table. "Okay boy, you can have them!" she said and wrote her signature next to her name. "I'll even get Randle to sign, too." Then she placed the blotter over her signature and rolled it up and down making sure that it dried evenly. Without hesitation she placed his paper on top of the others and put them all back into the portfolio.

Alex watched her every move with the suspicion of distrust. But, she had given him her word and with that promise he had to believe her; after all, he had no other choice.

Chapter 47

Will rose from the bed, lit a fresh tallow, and watched as the flimsy wick accepted the flame. The glow of the candle swooned in the stillness of the evening. He folded his hands together and sank into his thoughts which received him like a kindly friend. He turned inward and tried to imagine what his son would look like; did he favor his mother or his father? He wondered if the child would recognize him now after all this time or worse yet, perhaps the boy had forgotten about them altogether.

Will fixed his eyes forward on the cheerless room; and with the heart of a mourner kneeling before the grave, found little peace. Though he had no true cause for self-reproach; he raised too many reasons not to chastise himself. "What could I have done differently?" The hurt rolled over and over again. His lamentations were the tolling peals of the funeral bell. Will forever rehearsed the horrible scenes time and again in his mind, chronicling each conversation and recreating the details hoping to uncover a different ending; however the conclusion was always the same, tragic. He drifted away from the bed and sat down at the table by the window shoving aside the ruminants from last night's meal. Disgusted, he began to slide the dinner plate towards the edge, but thought better of himself and tipped it closer to the center again. He expelled a somber groan, mechanically placed his elbows down upon the table, and leaned forward to rest his weary head in his open palms. Burdened by his troubles, he closed his eyes and once again began to relive the nightmarish past.

It had been an early Sunday morning when they stole his son out of their home. The matron of the court held a firm grip upon the boy in the same way one would carry a squealing piglet even as the terrified child hollered out in small fits of terror, wiggling in pure desperation so that she might set him down. His outstretched arms were flailing wildly as his tiny fingers opened and closed as though trying to grasp the last bit of hope. But his assailant's cement-like hold was too effective; for being a master at her job and having performed this same act numerous times before, she knew how to quickly usher a child away from its parents while creating the fewest unnecessary disturbances as possible. Yet in spite of her rapid departure, the child's deafening screams tangled with Mrs. Wesley's demanding stifles of "Shhh, shhh". All the way down the dingy corridor and round the narrow stairway this disharmony of cries and hushes echoed up and down the building until finally it was barely audible, for she had safely deposited herself and the boy in the carriage that awaited them on the street below.

"Somebody stop her, she's stealing my child!" bellowed Will as he frantically started to bound for the door; but to his immediate dismay, his escape was thwarted. All attempts to leave had become obviously futile since standing between him and the outside were two powerfully large men each helping to bar the exit. "Someone must have heard my plea and at the very least the wails of my son," Will thought as his eyes feverishly darted from man to man. "Someone will come to his rescue!" His mind was working judiciously. He listened intently like a watch dog, shifting his head from side to side, but no one surrendered themselves from behind their locked doors, no one approached from outside to help.

"She's not stealing him, Mr. Piccard," announced a calm callous voice. "Only taking him to the train. Why, he's off to a good family where he'll be well cared for, get plenty of fresh country air and open space to play in."

"Here that?" snapped a whisper from across the hall. "They finally got around to it."

"To what, what's going on?" demanded the higher pitched response. A neighbor's creaky door gingerly edged open, and a pair of yellowish eyes glared across the narrow hallway. As customary in a crowded city dwelling, any distraction from the day-to-day doldrums lured the curious and meddlesome out from their quarters. "They finally grabbed that Piccard child," the acrid voice replied. "Want to bet he'll be screaming all the way to the train?"

"Where?" asked the inquisitor. "Let me see!"

"Hush," grumbled the husband and put his finger to his pursed lips as he inched the door until it sealed shut. Then, pushing his ear against the wood, he waved his hand at the hag for silence. "It's the Children's Society, they're sending the boy to another family, shhh!" the impatient man repeated, hoping to extract more information from the goings on across the hall.

"Sending him where?" the inquisitive wife petitioned again and planted her ear beside his to listen too.

"Away, they're taking him far away!" was the disagreeable reply. The passage of time remained motionless except for the ticking of the old clock as the two meddlers listened intently, hunched up against the door like two old hares in a rabbit hole.

———

Will's unforgettable scene of confusion haunted him, while at the same time he feared that the elapsed time of years may have permitted him to lose precious details. He locked his fingers though his hair and pulled back over his scalp as he called to mind that detestable morning. Caustic insults had spewed out of him like a madman. Was he insane? Did he temporarily loose his mind? He had picked up a chair and threatened to kill the officer, but was swiftly struck down by the stout faced burly man that sported a neatly cropped beard as red as his cheeks were ruddy. The larger of the two men had squatted beside him and pressed a yellow document into his palm. "The City of New York does not look favorable upon parents who neglect their children. Your child will be better off with another set of parents now," he growled and pointed towards the closed bedroom door. "Mind you better take care of your wife and let the child go without trouble." But regardless of the large man's commanding voice there was nothing he had said that would keep the father from jumping up again.

Will rubbed his knees as though the fall had just occurred rather than having taken place many years ago. He remembered that he had managed to struggle to his feet, all the while lashing out at the two men and like a tormented bull gores the picadors, his blows were impelled with vengeance. "Get out of my way!" he roared. "Move away or I'll kill you both!" Yet, as enraged and determined as he had become, the multiplied force of the two men overpowered all of Will's greatest attempts to overthrow his combatants. They held his arms behind his back and demanded that he settle down or they would break his limbs. But he was deaf to their threats. Will twisted and kicked like a savage animal; sweat streamed down his forehead and trickled into his eyes stinging them with salty perspiration.

"Hold up," yelled the large burly fellow, who fiercely grabbed Will by the shoulders and with a rugged shove pinned him against the wall like a mounted butterfly. "Listen man!" he shouted and leaned in closely while extending a menacing look. His hot breath smelling of stale cigars flew from his lips like rotting July garbage. The officer offered no explanation, but merely pointed his fat finger towards the overwrought man and dug it into the confined shoulder blade with several hard taps in concert with threatening whispers, "Don't try anything too heroic when we leave 'cause if ya do Englishman, we'll deport you and the missus on the next ship back to where ya came from." He stepped aside and added wickedly. "And I don't think the little wife would make it alive."

A bitter smell of melting wax permeated about the room rousing Will back into the present. He tilted his head and rubbed behind his neck with his calloused hands. He shifted towards the burning tallow and picked off a thin piece that had melted down the side of the taper and began to roll the soft wax between his fingers. "What should I have done differently?" he questioned himself. The silent response was echoed by another recollection. There was no time for even a tearful goodbye. Only a few hasty moments were permitted for the oppressed father to surrender some of the child's belongings into a carpetbag before the impatient intruders hurried away. They had assured him that Lexy would receive his property. "Did he, had they?" The word property was so cold, so impersonal, especially for a child. The unknowns were remote.

In comparison to his culpable and miserable existence, Libby had been living in a dream world where all actions and thoughts were manipulated by illness. Fevers induced periods of deliriums; and in her weak and fragile condition infrequent spells of recognition mirrored a continuum of the past. Perhaps the only good that had come out of her frail mental state stemmed from the fact that she never thought her child was gone; for as she continued to flow in and out of consciousness, so did her son drift in and out of her thoughts.

The tallow flickered brightly. He turned away and saw a counterfeit image of himself, a silhouette that leaned against the wall with the quivering of the light. He repositioned the candle so that he no longer could see his own bent shadow mimic his every move; if only he could remove the feeling of despair as easily as he slid aside the tarnished candle-holder. For a full year following their son's removal Will had prayed for a miracle, wishing and hoping that Libby would recover. He was not a religious man, but in his desperation he tried to strike a deal with the heavens. He promised that he would never ask for anything ever again, that he would turn his life over to ecclesiastics and walk on his knees to the alter every Sunday, giving all other days of the week over to earn wages for the poor and the impoverished (even though he himself was a member of that unfortunate population). And lastly, he vowed to remain bent and stooped, pronouncing to the world that he was humbled and reverent by the great powers of the almighty. So, upon making these proclamations, Will watched and waited by Libby's side for any minute sign of recovery. For two weeks he believed that when he went to sleep *this* would be the morning that he would be awakened by her light caresses, the gentle stroking of her hands across his forehead; he was sure that when he opened his eyes he would be looking up into her bright shining visage, her cheeks pink and rosy, and forever rid of her languid and pallid complexion, that finally he would be able to reclaim his wife as being cured and well.

But at the start of the third week it became clearly evident that bargaining did not bring forth his intended appeal, so he turned his faith towards the doctors, to which he had grown even less adherent. Nevertheless no suggestions would be ignored and desperation triumphed over discretion; he relied upon their medical opinions and their administering of conventional medicines; but still again, no recovery. With no other options to avail himself with, he approached Mrs. Grady with enough of a financial incentive that she agreed to watch Libby while he was away at work. Adding to the growing list of treatments and elixirs, the elder woman concocted her own herbal remedies claiming that in her experience these old-fashioned medicinal potions would restore the young woman back to health. Yet even after several weeks her treatments were of no help and as Libby's health continued to decline the oppressed man found himself drowning in debt.

As the evening exchanged positions with night, the shrinking candle inexplicably continued to illuminate the room with the tenacity of two lit wicks. Will was intoxicated by memories like a drunken sailor. The past was the only thing keeping him company. "It should have been a damp and dreary night, but it wasn't. On the contrary, it was specifically glorious," he mumbled. He walked over to the open window and leaned against the frame; his mind rewound to four years after his boy was taken. He knew not what made him suddenly aware of these thoughts, noting only that he was relapsing into his former self as he arrived once again back in time.

His wanderings deepened through a solitary trail. He remembered that he stopped to buy a bouquet of spring daisies from a street vender. He hadn't paid much attention to the flower woman before, but for some reason that evening she drew him in. "Buy these, they are the freshest," she exclaimed in a raspy voice and thrust a full bouquet forward nearly knocking him over. Her hands were coarse and leathered by the sun; unusually large and rugged looking for an elderly woman; perhaps hands that once had worked the fields and farms. These were muscular hands used to hard work. There was something else that seemed a bit contrary for a woman of her age and social status; she displayed a full set of teeth. "Here, deary," she cackled, "take these, they will surely be one of the last your missus will enjoy!" And with a wave of her large hand, she flaunted the oversized bunch before him like a conductor's baton. But rather than enticing the buyer with their beauty, her message was perceived as a startling and dark premonition of the future. For as Will's startled expression grew morbidly grim, the old hag hastily added, "I'm moving my flowers uptown, the business here ain't as good as it once were," and without care, wiped her sullen checks with her coat sleeve that was stained with the brown earth of one who had been digging in a garden.

Recovering from his thoughts, Will slid the curtain aside so as to expand the confines of his quarters. A timid breeze blew past him arousing his memory again.

It had been a chilly evening; beautiful, clear, and cloudless. The air warmed by the early morning sun had risen at noon and had gradually fallen, dissipating into the graying sky; and although the temperature was beginning to grow cooler with a shift from late afternoon to dusk, it was not nearly cold enough to warrant a heavy outer garment. Yet the flower seller was wearing a dusty woolen topcoat, which she kept unbuttoned, exposing a tired and battered woolen jacket. Her knit cap must have been too small for her head for she had stretched and yanked it over her ears and wore it down upon her forehead so it kissed the top of her brow. Every few minutes she reached down and pulled up one of the two pairs of baggy stockings that kept sliding below her knees. The stockings were old, having been darned at least half a dozen times with coarse yarn from skeins of different dyes, and when she leaned back against the brick wall her long skirt hiked up slightly, which revealed the thicker and ill-matched patches above her boots. If she was uncomfortable, she did not seem to mind for she smacked her lips in a way that resembles one who has been satiated by a good meal and nodded her head in unison with the smacking.

Set before her large tired feet was a brown wicker basket covered with pink gingham where small clusters of daisies were strewn one-on-top of another. Will remembered how diligently she had reached into the basket and lifted the cloth as though uncovering a newborn baby. "This bunch is special," she whispered; her voice was low and raspy as though divulging a secret. "The first growth of the spring season," she added with a grin. Independent of her cunning expression, her misty light eyes hinted cheerfulness in spite of the dilapidated conditions surrounding her.

Will shook his head as though he were shaking lose some new episode that he had forgotten. He walked away from the window and over to the narrow shelf on the wall and picked up the empty vase just as he had done four years ago. He had arranged the daisies in the yellow china vase and placed them on the windowsill next to the pots of herb plants so they would be one of the first things Libby would see when she woke up. How particularly quiet and peaceful she looked that night while asleep. She was Persephone, fair and selfless; carried off by death from her earthly home too young and too soon. Only this Persephone, unlike the one of ancient myths, embarked to the heavens without pagantry, and as a hermit crab leaves behind the abandoned shell, she too left her body where it lay.

Several white petals had fallen from the daisy's yellow center and lay scattered upon the table as though it had been disturbed by someone or something. The calendar date read the fourteenth day of the month; the timepiece chimed 11:00 P.M. He wondered if she ever saw the flowers on the sill.

Libby was dead and although the distraught man was forever consumed with grief, he never permitted himself to lose focus. "Close to five years alone and over six since Lexy was taken," he remarked as he counted time on his fingers; the same amount of years spent saving and scrimping. Beneath a load of doubt and despair, he stared out the window and his eyes followed a few scattered people straggling to and fro. The gas-lights were set low and most of the streets that generally swelled with noise were noticeably still except for a sharp crack of the waggoner's whip farther down the street. Will sighed. Finally, now, he had enough money. All bills and debts were settled. He was free. He wasn't exactly sure where to begin, but he knew that he must find Lexy, he knew he would reclaim his son.

———

Miss April Henshaw had great plans when she left Kentucky, great plans that had been set aside for a small town and a country school that had diminished in size from a community of students down to a handful of boys and girls. She looked about the Tarson's place and wondered what it would have been like to be the mistress. It wasn't much to look at by European standards of a manor house, but at least there was a sturdy house and rich land. Miss Henshaw glanced down at her hands and remembered how she had spent most of her girlhood days pulling weeds and sowing seed. She watched Grace stitch her petit point tapestry and admired the child's tenacity to sew tiny, neat stitches. With each thread that entered one side of the canvas she pulled it up from the other until the thread became too short to knot, and then she had to pull it back through the same hole that it started through. Despite her reluctance, Grace had become quite adept at sewing and had become an even more skillful embroiderer, however the child did not enjoy either task and claimed sewing was a boring chore and her nimble fingers would much rather be shooting marbles. Miss Henshaw turned her attention to the letter from Missus Tarson that was resting on her lap.

"What's ya got thar?" Grace asked as she noticed the woman holding something that looked like a letter. She was most eager to put her needlepoint down, for she always looked for an excuse to set it aside, and sallied over to the rocking chair. It was a lazy kind of day, a perfect time to be in the sunroom, which Grace called "the ocean room" because it was decorated with shells and dried sea animals from the East coast.

"It's correspondence from your mother," Miss Henshaw replied. "I don't suppose you'd like me to read it to you?" she asked and then winked in her direction for she knew the child was always longing to hear from anyone outside her little world. She patted her hand on the adjacent rocking chair inviting her to come and sit down. Grace happily abided the invitation and tucking her legs beneath her long skirt sat cross-legged ready to listen.

Dear Miss Henshaw,

I set down to write and inform you of our situation here. Mr. Tarson is in his usual good health except I have not been as well and taken with a cold, which has left me with a bad cough. All and all I am on the mend. I expect that these lines find you enjoying good health, which is one of the greatest blessings we can have in this world. I have been traveling quite a bit and both Mr. Tarson and I have found that this time away from the farm has done us quite a bit of good. I am afraid that is not the same for Mr. Forester. I have written Mr. Beasley myself and asked him to stay on, we are going to acquire the Forester property together and therefore we will need additional help.

Upon hearing the last sentences Grace's ears perked up like a rabbit in a forest at night. "What's that 'bout the Forester's?" she asked.

"Well, it appears that your mother is in the process of taking over the Forester property with Mr. Beasley," she answered confirming the information. "Should I continue?"

Grace nodded "yes" and started to propel the chair forward and back.

I have been inquiring about some finishing schools for Grace and will speak with you about my choices when we arrive. I am a firm believer in a good education for girls as you know by your position with us. Please inform Beatrice that

although we have eaten in many inns and establishments, I still prefer her cook-
ing. By the time this letter reaches you, we will be on our way home.
    Regards,
    Belle
    P.S. Tell Grace that we have purchased her a lovely bonnet, which was made
all the way in Paris, France.

Grace unfolded her legs and continued to reel back and forth. She didn't say anything, but by the gradual increase to the rocker's momentum it was evident that something was on her mind.

"You're rather quiet," Miss Henshaw said. "A bonnet from Paris, now that's something!"

Nevertheless, the child did not seem impressed with the idea of her gift and continued to stare straight ahead and just rock, however, with a bit more vigor. "I ain't got nothin' to say," she replied smugly.

"I haven't anything to say," repeated Miss Henshaw, placing a greater stress on the words "haven't" and "anything".

Grace turned and repeated, "I haven't anything to say."

The schoolteacher decided that she didn't want to press the matter and sat back in her chair enjoying the sunny room. She rocked gently up and back, fastidiously folding the letter into fourths. She ran her fingers along the smooth edge keeping tempo with the movement, while inattentively creating deep grooves in the linen parchment. "What do you say that later we go and pick some blueberries? I bet Beatrice would make blueberry muffins if we did," she chimed; her voice laced with sweetness.

"If you want," Grace agreed sullenly, and then with disconcerted directness allowed her feet to hit the ground so that the chair would come to an abrupt halt. Escorted by gloom, she got up and moped back over to the needlepoint whereby the dispirited young lady commenced to sew, pretending as though nothing had happened. Miss Henshaw watched as the child looked down into the tapestry that was stretched tightly between the wooden hoops. The only tell-tale sign of displeasure was the pursing together of her lips as though something was horribly sour.

———

"I ain't goin' and they can't make me!" stormed Grace. "I just ain't goin!"

Alex heard the small angry voice several yards behind him as he pumped the handle up and down. A vigorous stream of well water poured into the bucket with such great force that he held tight upon the rim with his left hand to keep it from toppling over under its own weight.

"They can't make me and that's that!" squealed Grace; her face was flushed and her eyes bloodshot from crying. He turned around and let go of the pitcher pump's handle; a final trickle of water emptied into the bucket.

"You been cryin'?" he asked. He placed the ladle in the water and offered her a cool drink.

"I ain't been cryin', I'm just mad!" she explained, half lying about the crying. She reached forward and put her lips to the stream of cool water that continued to dribble slowly out the spigot. Alex took a sip from the ladle and then hung it back on the hook.

"Comin'?" he asked and hoisted the bucket up. A silent groan was expelled as he took a step and started towards the trough. It was awkward and heavy, and although he managed to lift the vessel to the height just below his knees, he was forced to walk very slowly for no matter how careful it was nearly impossible to keep the water level. It sloshed recklessly from side to side, spilling over as he trudged across to the feedyard. "We don't have many animals anymore, but there's still a sow, her piglets, and a couple goats." Alex lifted the wobbling bucket and poured its contents into the trough and set it to the side. Water that splashed over the edge was immediately devoured by the dry earth

"Where are they?" Grace asked, looking about the vacant yard for some signs of animal life.

"Sleepin'," the boy replied and pointed towards the inside corner of the pen. Sure enough, under the shade of a low wooden lean-to there was an ungainly pile of animals massed together with the corpulent sow taking up most of the shade. One could readily assume that the bristly piglets were sleeping somewhere between her plump folds of skin, for they were never far from her side; and while the black and white goat peacefully rested its long knobby head on the swine's back, the brown goat nestled contently next to its brother. The only lively animals were the pullets. They were content to peck about the ground unearthing grubs and stumbling upon food that had fallen out of the others' mouths.

Grace tagged behind Alex. They passed through the open barn doors into another world and breathed in the scent of warm dry hay. He hung his hat on the nail and wiped his forehead with his sleeve. Sunlight shined on the dark timbers, on the wooden stalls, and on the yellow bed of straw. Both large horses had been put out to graze. Grace looked towards the ladder that rose up into the loft; it seemed to go on forever. She let her eyes wander about the barn and then back at her friend where she watched him set out and prepare the brewers grain and meal as though he was preparing the holy sacraments. There was a mystical air of spirituality that she had never noticed before, and as she followed him she was filled with reverent admiration. She wanted him to tell her that everything was going to be all right, that she didn't have to go off to school, that she could stay here. But instead she shrank away from her fantasy and suppressed this deep yearning, surrendering to the reality that was placed before her.

Grace climbed up and sat on the top stable rail. She lightly tapped the second wooden bar with her boot as her feet dangled restlessly. "Miss Henshaw got a letter from Belle; it said they're gonna send me East to a girls' school." She nervously glanced over at Alex anticipating a reply. She was used to his quiet nature and hesitated to pry him for an answer, but right now she needed him to say something. Silence loomed like an impending storm as he went about tending to his chores. Grace tapped the rail harder. "I didn't tell them, but I ain't goin!" she announced again. The silent minutes between them lingered like hours.

"Ya gotta do what they say, it'll be good for you," he finally replied, and climbed up on the rail to sit next to her.

His reply stung like a freshly cut switch. After all this time of anticipating and rehearsing in her head what he would say after her proclamation, this certainly was not the answer she wished to hear. "Good fer me!" she gasped. "How do you know what's good fer me, Alex Forester?" she demanded. And with a sudden surge of adrenalin, her broken heart began to thump with an unanticipated flood of anxiety. She jumped down from the railing and stood before him shaking her head in dismay.

Now, one must wonder what is stronger; the desire for truth or the desire for illusion? Alex always gave his honest opinion, but by Grace's reaction he was finding out that sometimes an honest answer is not always what has been petitioned. "I only meant that yer too smart to be hangin' round here," he explained with a tincture of apology. Now it was his turn to wait for an answer.

Her anger towards him was quickly dampened by his words, which she inferred as a compliment; he on the other hand meant it only as candor. "Ya really think I'm smart?" she asked. The sun had shifted positions and was pirouetting around her as she loitered before him.

"Sure," he said. "It'd be a waste if ya didn't go, besides, it ain't forever," he remarked.

True, it wasn't forever. "I suppose yer right, I didn't think of it like that." She paused and flitted about the stalls like a fairy. "Not forever," she reminded him, "and you'll be here when I git back!" she exclaimed with a sudden inspiration towards the future.

For Alex there was only stillness and little revelry. He surveyed his surroundings and sighed heavily. Then with an unexpected turn of interest, he jumped down off the rail and dug his hand into his pocket and retrieved a small object. "Here," he said and stuck out his clenched fist.

Tipping forward, she responded and opened her hand. Alex dropped the signet ring into her palm. She picked it up and then clasped it tightly. "I can't!" she protested and tried to hand it back to him, but he wouldn't take it. "Please!" she exclaimed, "it's too valuable." But he only shook his head no.

"Tell ya what," he said in a compromising tone, "you can give it back to me when you return. Just keep it now for good luck." Grace ran her eyes over the ring and didn't know what to say. She was always filled with chatter, but now couldn't think of the words. She was afraid that if she spoke she would make a fool of herself and say something that would ruin their friendship, especially if she made the mistake of telling him how she really felt. She knew this would be the last time she would see him for a very long time.

"Okay, Alex Forester," she whispered and clutched it snugly in her fist. "I'll take good care of it." Then like the little nymph with enormous feet, she ran out the barn towards the sun-stained hill.

Alex stood alone with his heart heavy. "Take care, Grace Tarson, take care."

———

If there had ever been a pure love it was the bond between Will and Libby; pure in the sense that although she was gone her soul could not be taken from him. She appeared before him only during his deepest part of sleep, and they would lay together in the still darkness of the night, she could hear him breathing, his skin was warm, and she would nestle close and lay her head beside his until morning when he had no recollection of them being together and he was alone. In utter silence he could hear her flitting about the kitchen or humming a familiar melody. Sometimes he sensed that he was being watched, as though she was looking down at him. But he knew that wasn't so because if she could see from above she would not be tending to him, but rather watching over Lexy.

With a familiar click of the latch, he shut the door behind him for the very last time. Now there was only one more act to perform. For the past four years all daily activity was performed by means of automation; his actions were merely perfunctory routines however, it was his sense of self-preservation that provided him the stamina to wait for the right time, to be able to detach himself from those around him and maintain his focus. Will wiggled the latch and acknowledged it was securely locked. The dairy route had been reverted back to his elderly partner who found a promising young apprentice to take good care of the old nag. Everything had been sold except for his personal possessions, which he stuffed into a steamer trunk and could store in Mrs. Grady's cellar for a small sum. The young widower had learned that that there wasn't anything the older woman wouldn't do for the right price.

Will walked out onto the sidewalk and glanced around the great city. Two dirty looking little children were throwing pebbles into the murky water that was lying stagnant in the open ditch. One was stooping along the edge while the other was running up and down the street preparing a stock pile of ammunition. He strolled past with mixed emotions as the two urchins turned their attention to a distant peddler hawking his goods. It was a beautiful cool day and although Will had enough money in his pockets to treat himself to a carriage, he preferred to walk.

———

"Flowers mister, want some flowers?" the vendor called.

"Have you any daisies?" Will asked.

The eager man fumbled around in the back of his wagon and pulled a sparse but respectable bouquet from one of the several wooden buckets. "Nice and fresh," the merchant promised and shook them up down. Plump drops of water flung onto the ground like tears falling from the thin stems. Will reached into his pocket and exchanged a few coins for the flowers. The seller tipped his hat and climbed back up into the wagon to wait for another buyer as the customer turned down the narrow path and passed between a pair of stone pillars into a silent retreat of high ridges that looked down upon the same ocean that George Washington had settled upon as a military fortification during the Revolutionary War. Will weaved around and about the gravestones as though he was on a garden walk. But despite its Arcadian setting, this cemetery, with all its amplitude and grandeur, could not distract him from seeing only one marker.

He laid the daises before her tombstone and brushed the marble lightly with his hand, and then he rearranged the flowers again so they were settled together in a tight bunch. "Libby, I'm going to find Lexy," he said. He knelt down and bent forward so she could hear him. "I'm going to find him and take care of him," he whispered and then paused as though waiting for a reply. "I paid off everything and everyone. I bought a ticket to St. Louis. Don't worry, Libby, I have enough money to buy a wagon, a horse, and I'm heading west." He paused again. "I brought you some daisies. I love you Libby, I love you forever."

He stood up and brushed the raw earth from his knees. Then he pulled from his vest pocket a small, framed image of the young mother taken several days after their boy was born. He remembered how Mrs. Grady had scolded him for disturbing the dead, for he had cut several strands of Libby's hair the night she died. Now tucked behind her beautiful photo, he had placed a lock of her hair. He secured the daguerreotype back into his vest pocket and placed a kiss on his two fingers, which he laid upon the marble headstone. Slowly, he backed away.

He was a prisoner of the city no more.

Chapter 48

Mr. Beasley sat at the table opposite the graying Betty. Neither spoke very much after the papers were signed. It was an amicable arrangement; Betty could stay on as long as she wished, while Mr. Beasley would remain living on the Tarson property, although he would be assisting in running all aspects of the farm. If however, luck turned her way and she came into a windfall, Betty could buy back the property at fair market value, but with an added incentive of 1% below the current interest that the bank was offering. Belle was not an unreasonable woman, just one who knew a good business proposition. The Forester property had growth potential; she was not going to let it slip by her nor would she take advantage of the distressed seller. As for the two draft horses, Belle gave full ownership to the boy.

Betty rose from her seat and placed the newly signed document under the glass paperweight that had been recently assigned to oversee the stack of bills. "Coffee?" she asked the hunchback and moseyed slowly over to the cook stove. Her wool shawl hung limply across her broad shoulders like a droopy pair of wings. Her eyes clouded with pity at the deformed figure sitting at the table.

"Don't mind of I do," replied the little man, and he cast a coveted glance about the room and then out the window that led to a small colorless herb garden.

———

"It's been a month since Grace and Miss Henshaw headed to the East," Alex whispered to Delilah. The large animal majestically laid its head against his shoulder as though trying to comfort him. "I ain't sad," he remarked and stroked the velvet muzzle. "It's good she got out, what would a girl like Grace gonna do around a farm?" The horse nodded as though agreeing. "Besides, one day you, Dandy, and me, why we'll git our own farm, and who knows…" But the boy stopped short of answering that question for he didn't have the faintest idea of what his future would bring.

Alex led the doughty workhorse into the stall beside Dandy and carefully removed her weathered halter. Having completed his afternoon chores, he decided it would be more comforting to stay by the two horses for a while longer rather than going back up to the house. Both drafts rested idly, shifting from one leg to the other and swooshing an occasional pesky fly away with their long tails. He hung the halter back on the hook and then sat down, leaning against the stable post. He slid his feet towards his body and pulled his knees up like an upside down "V". His tired boots had disturbed the loose pieces of hay strewn about the ground exposing the coarse brown earth beneath. Settling comfortably he crooked his neck back and with half-curiosity gazed aimlessly up into the rafters. He saw himself on the hill by the apple tree. The wind was rustling through the branches of heart-shaped leaves. He placed himself in the shade and recounted his life from the time he first planted the seed until the last time he spent a lazy afternoon beneath its boughs. A persistent gnat landed on his arm and as he swatted it away he was transported back to the barn. The dry warm scent of hay, the fragrance of leather and horses, he closed his eyes; will heaven be like this? He opened them again, but in the midst of the solitude he recognized the outline of two dark eyes peering down. He twisted his neck and craned forward, but was too lazy to stand up and readjust his position to get a better look. "You ain't a screech owl, are ya?" he called up. It responded with silence. A healthy feeling of slumber fell upon Alex, a restful lull reinforced by dwindling sunlight. His mind was cobwebbed with fatigue. He strained through the obscuring daylight in hopes that he would catch another glimpse of the mysterious vision. But a quick glance likened by a flicker was all that was granted; for like every single time before the dark eyes retracted well above and beyond the rafters; they were gone.

Ordinarily even those with the most spirited personalities would find themselves chilled to the bone by this strange vision. Such a dark and mysterious pair belonging to neither a head nor a body that distinguished itself by floating freely about like an apparition or ghostly demon would certainly set teeth chattering or send fearless men cowering beneath their bed coverings like whimpering dogs. Contrary to what one would expect from this innocent youth, for the boy had not been exposed to much worldliness beyond the farm, he never felt the least bit afraid of his unidentified voyeur. In fact, he sensed a strange familiarity in those eyes, as if he recognized them from another time and place. It was quite possible, if you believed such a thing, they were not the eyes of a living being, but perhaps belonged to a higher order; perhaps the soul of something unearthly.

———

Timothy lit into the barn and headed toward the nearest hiding place; a too small burlap sack with just enough room for him to wriggle into. However, if his intention was to elude someone or something, he certainly had not made himself a very well secured decision, for his plume-like tail stuck out of the opening, while the cloth lay upon his fat body tracing the outline of two distinct humps: the head shape being somewhat rounder and smaller than the higher and lumpier wide body. Alex wondered what had provoked the cat into moving so fast and just assumed it was one of the old hens. They were not as big as the large feline, but could put up quite a fuss if he had gotten in their way.

"Come here, Timothy," Alex called. "Come on, don't be scared." Slowly the tail swooshed back and forth along the ground like a metronome. Alex leaned forward and called forth again, "Timothy!"

Again the tail marked the same spot along the barren floor. Alex shifted his position and edged forward, resting his weight on his right knee and speaking ever so gently, but this time rather than calling the animal's name, he recited a poem.

"Whiskers long and smooth
form pointed arrows,
It tiptoes on clouds of silver,
hunting with dark eyes that shine
like the moonlight on the sleeping prairie."

The lyric must have had an alluring effect, possibly as magical as the Pied Piper himself, for slowly the sack began to reanimate and like a molting snake shedding its skin, the creature began to emerge. First the rumpled tail backed out, followed by rear legs, a set of meaty haunches, a long fat body, a broad pair of shoulders, a thick neck, and an oversized head, until the whole cat came into view. Lured from his hiding place, Timothy hastened over to Alex, whereby he rubbed his face against the pair of dusty pants. The boy scooped the four legged beast up into his arms and placed it across his crossed legs. Contently, the cat poured itself into his lap like custard in a pan and promptly fell asleep.

"There there, Timothy. Why you ain't got nothin' to be afraid of." Alex peered down upon the sleeping cat and then looked up and over at the two large horses. Now on most occasions, generally speaking, Alex would have felt nothing but peaceful bliss sitting in the barn surrounded by the innocence of the animals, but for some reason today he felt different. There was an air of uncertainty; an ominous disposition lingering about like smoldering embers after the fire is extinguished. He stroked Timothy between his pointy ears. The cat lay motionless except for the rhythmic vibration fostered by its noisy purr; all sense of enjoyment exuberated from this happy throaty whirr.

In the fading light of the dull afternoon when fatigue presents itself by hanging upon tired shoulders and aching feet swell within the confines of leather boots, Alex bowed his head wearily as he pet the contented cat sleeping heavily upon his lap. That poem, where had it come from? What part of his brain extracted these lines with so little effort? Timothy stirred. His long tail now restlessly swished back and forth indicating that at this moment he was ready to move on. The wayfaring memory was at first treated with little respect; a little ditty that was passed over in the hand-me-down pages in Miss Henshaw's schoolroom? Alex looked back upon the time when he first began learning to read, but soon determined that this poem would have surely tripped up his tongue into making sounds that would never have resembled those that had just before come out of his mouth. He now concluded that the poem had not originated from school. Alex rolled the animal off his lap anticipating the cat's expected action of leaping forward, using his thighs as a springboard, whereupon the needlelike back claws would surely have been extracted to produce a spirited, but painful exit off and away from his master.

The unhurried mood of the day was welcomed. Alex got up from the ground and walked towards the open barn door. He stopped and with a thoughtful countenance looked out upon the sun-scorched land. A dry grey haze speckled the sky like a gossamer veil shrouding the old farmhouse that sat before him. He found himself idling over to the water pump and drew a cold drink. He slowly sipped the water from the ladle before setting it back beside the pump. Then following the direction of the hilltops, the gigantic ball of the sun was balanced upon the horizon like a Japanese lantern, and the whole earth was turning a fiery blaze of orange.

The poem came alive in his head like the humming of a few bees that had wandered away from the great hive. It grew more pronounced, and as he walked towards the pale farmhouse, it fell from his lips.

"Ears short and erect
form tiny triangles
It leaps over twigs and clover,

hunting with dark eyes that glimmer
like the sunlight on the awakening meadow."

'What's that you say?" A shrill voice called out from the open window. Alex walked up to the front porch and sat down upon the dusty steps. "Is that you, Alex?"

He twisted his neck round and called back towards the open window, "Yep, it's me." He bowed his downy head and ran his fingers through his hair finding it rather curious that she wondered who it was since visitors, except for the hunchback, were so infrequent.

"What's that you say?" she repeated in a louder voice. The front door yawned opened and the smell of fried dough rolled out of the portal. Betty stood before the open doorway wiping her hands on her gingham apron. Stained with grease and smelling from the thick odor of fat rendering that had impregnated the material; the smudged apron must have stirred the interest of Timothy, who was now circling her feet and affectionately rubbing his face against the hem of her smock. "I can't make out what ya said!" she declared again.

"It was just somethin' I remembered. Nothin' important," the boy added softly, attempting to dismiss her question. He himself had wondered why after so many years he would suddenly recollect this poem.

"Well, come on in, supper's 'bout ready," she announced, while continuing to wipe her hands across the front of the smock and seemingly not interested in what he did or did not remember. Her hair loosely assembled behind her head in a twisted bun now began to fall, and she wiped the few rogue strands that had managed to free themselves from the regimented army of hairpins with the back of her hand and away from her face. She gazed for a moment as though having something to say, however, with a gentle swat of her foot, she pushed the fat cat away and traipsed speechlessly back into the house.

Alex obeyed, but not before turning his attention to the splintered timbers of the porch roof and catching a glimpse of the pair of dark eyes. He blinked and at first the pair melted into the beams disguising themselves with the other knotholes that infected the tired wood. But soon the eyes distinguished themselves from the rest and their irresistible ebony pupils implored him to dig deeply into his memory. "Lexy," a sweet voice whispered in his head. "Come sit beside me." Could it be? Alex continued to look up and then fell down upon his knees and clasped his hands together so tightly that he could feel his nails digging into his palms.

"Mom?" There was an enormous pause, and he held his breath fearful that if he uttered even a single breath his question, which was now floating above his head, would promptly drift away. "Mom, is that you?" he asked again. With the quiet resonance of paper-thin whispers he spoke decisively but ever so gently and so lovingly that had an angel heard him, it would have surely picked up his question and carried it up into heaven and placed the words before the mother. He could feel his knees begin to tremble beneath him as he leaned his head back as far as his neck would stretch, and he stared wide-eyed trying not to blink. Now, if you have ever tried to keep yourself from blinking, you may well remember that this involuntary action is more than impossible to suppress for longer than several minutes. However, despite the odds, Alex held steadfast and with such anticipation that one could believe Raphael, the great painter, would have embraced the boy's rapture on canvas.

"Alex, what in tarnation are you doin'?" A sudden cold breeze fell over him like a winter frost over a dogwood blossom. He could feel Betty's luminous shadow smothering him, and bowing his head slowly forward, her dark silhouette rumbled again. "What are ya doin' down here on the ground?" she demanded. Alex unfolded his hands and raised himself up. He carelessly dusted his knees and shuffled toward Betty who was now visibly impatient. "I thought I told you to come on in. I got supper on the table and what do I see, but you out here stuck on the ground!" she grumbled gruffly. Placing her hands upon her hips, she created two perfectly symmetrical right triangles with her pointy elbows. Her intolerance resonated with a thump, thump, thump of her right foot tapping upon the wooden planks.

The boy shifted his weight back and forth; not quite sure what to say. He knew that right now any explanation he gave would be misunderstood, and so he made the decision that "nothing" was the best answer. Betty waded through a few more silent moments and continued to bark. "Randle and me always knew that you were different, the way ya talk to them horses, dogs, and people ya don't see! But now..." she stopped in mid-sentence and expelled a prickly "humph". At a loss for words, Betty regarded the boy in disgust; her eyes roaming over him as though searching for a defect; all the while her head bobbed up and down with displeasure. "There's no use talkin' to this boy," she thought to herself and making the conclusion she didn't have anything to add, she sighed deeply, shrugging her shoulders in exasperation

Now although the elder was a woman of commanding presence, her most recent tongue lashing unleashed upon the young man did not alter his calm demeanor, and the more she tried to stay annoyed the more she realized that she was beginning to look upon him quite differently, as if for the very first time. "After all, what had he done that had vexed her so?" She chastised herself with this thought. Whereupon, she now discovered that her proclivity towards criticizing his actions had changed; for although she wanted to be angry, his doe-like eyes were so innocent that she found herself submissive to his guileless nature.

Night was falling gently upon them both and the first evening stars were poking out from behind a once hazy mist. "Come on along now, boy. Come on in and git yer supper," she said; her tame voice trailing behind as she beckoned for the child to follow.

An emotion apart from the usual stirred. Alex quietly shadowed after except this evening he knew something was going to happen; he wasn't sure, but for the first time he actually sensed a feeling of hope.

———

When supper was finished and the last of the dish water had been tossed outside, after Betty rekindled the hearth with several fresh logs, she sat down to darn her stockings, knowing perfectly well they were far too worn out and shabby for even her fine stitches. Alex excused himself and headed out to the barn. He held the lantern directly in front of him and followed the light like a moth. He hurried along with brisk steps since he had been too lazy to fill the lantern again and knew that if he dawdled it would not have enough oil to keep burning for the rest of his obligations.

He remembered that he had closed the large barn door for the evening, but when he pulled it open and entered, he sensed that something was different. He raised the lantern high up above his head and searched the rafters, but only the regular roosting birds, undisturbed by his intrusive light, stirred on their perches, ruffled a few feathers, but remained peacefully content. The two draft horses greeted him with gentle neighs, and he returned the greetings with several broken pieces of sugar lumps that he had stashed in his pocket. "I got a good feelin', Delilah," he said and stroked the horse's long nose. She exhaled and released a warm breath that tickled his hand like a downy feather. "I counted that I've been here for almost seven years, and now for the first time I got a sensation like I never had before." Another neigh of agreement came from Dandy that was still enjoying her sugar. He could hear her back teeth grind together as she carefully mashed the sticky treat, and the horse drowsily closed its eyes as she ate.

This was Alex's sacred place; with all his treasured possessions around him, he remained sure that his hunch was well-deserved. The lantern flickered timidly, its light was waning. Alex glanced around and wished he had taken the time to add more oil into the brass fount and scolded himself for being lazy. It wasn't as though he was afraid of the dark; it was just that he wanted to be sure that he didn't miss anything that might come about.

Tired, but filled with too much anticipation to sleep, he sat down on an empty crate; its wooden base made a suitable seat. He edged forward as he listened with the same intensity as a huntsman in the woods. Taking heed, he inspected up and around the rafters, then into the loft, but it was too high and dark to see anything beyond the first few rungs of the ladder, so he scouted downward and was soon drawn towards the barn door. Without any disturbance it had swung slowly open, and with very little warning he heard a familiar bark which was followed by a generous yelp. Within moments of this exuberant greeting the boy suddenly felt himself being trounced upon and then over-powered by a strong and weighty animal that commenced to give him several slobbering kisses with its long tongue. Wagging his tail with the fury of a whip, the dog had Alex pinned to the ground and was licking him like a mother cat. "Yuck, Sergeant, stop it!" cried Alex. "You're getting me all wet!" he exclaimed laughing playfully, while at the same time making great attempts to push him off. But the huge dog didn't obey, and its happiness to see his dear friend was only interrupted by the powerful hand of Tully who lifted the canine up by its collar and pulled him away.

"Sorry about that, little minute," the man calmly said. "That darn dog gets carried away sometimes." Warily, Sergeant rushed back beside his master and sat patiently, waiting to be pet. And although he remained attentively still, the tail continued to wag furiously, giving the ground a grand beating. Tully grabbed the boy's hand and helped him to his feet. Regarding his wet condition, Alex began to wipe the slobber from his face with the back of his sleeve and then knelt down to give the dog a righteous hug. "You're a good dog, Sergeant," he cried and locked his arms around the hound's thick neck. "A good old dog, ain't ya?"

Tully stood over the two and watched the reunion of the dog and the boy as they greeted each other with the same affection that one would expect from life-long friends. "We've come to say goodbye," Tully began.

Stricken by a sensation of misunderstanding, Alex let go of the dog and looked up. Several long seconds of silence hung between them until it lifted like fog. "Ya never really said "goodbye" before!" he fretted, and rose like a young warrior that had just been wounded in battle, for the words imparted had been received like a weapon. The boy's legs seemed unwilling to support his shell-shocked body;

though he managed to stand and face Tully. Anxiety ensued and as his heart beat faster, a small lump formed in his throat.

Tully nodded his head in agreement. "You're right. All those times before, we were never gone for very long; but this time, it's for good." He paused and then continued. "It's only right to say good-bye to a friend when he intends to leave."

Alex listened intently; his head turned upward as he watched the man's earnest face. The boy tried to swallow, but the lump in his throat had become larger and more pronounced. He tried to shake his head with understanding, but his youthful heart began to race and its distinct pounding, like hooves on bare earth, extended up his neck and stampeded towards his temples.

"There's something I got to ask you," Alex remarked, trying to get the words out without choking. He cleared his throat and shifted his feet uncomfortably. "It has to do with when I see you. I mean, it's just that other people…" Alex hoped that his lantern would not burn out now; he hoped that he would not be suddenly standing in the dark. He felt cold, and empty, and his palms were sweating. He rubbed his hands nervously against the sides of his pants.

Tully bent down and began to pet the dog. Alex stared at them both and tears began to well up. "Don't tell me," he blurted out. "I already know!" Then, he wiped his eyes on his already damp sleeve. Tully reached into his back pocket and offered him a handkerchief. Alex dabbed his lids and handed the cloth back.

"Keep it," the man said. He stood up and smiled reassuringly.

Alex put the cloth to his face and dried the tears from his cheeks. But, he could no longer hold back his emotions and like a mountain of snow smashing free, an avalanche of unhappiness broke loose. All he could feel was the intolerable pain of loneliness, that dreadful sensation of terminable loss. "Let me come with you, let me go, too!" he whimpered.

"You're going be o.k., now, Alex. Everything will turn out the way it should." Tully put his hand on the child's back and patted him lightly. A gentle nicker came from the stables, and Sergeant gave a hearty bark back and set about to investigate.

Alex looked up and tried to understand. "Where are ya going?" he asked. "Are you goin' back to live in the soddy?" His thoughts suddenly became flooded with the memory of their first encounter; the damp dwelling dug into the side of the hill, the animals, and the solitude of nature.

"We're going back from where we came from," Tully answered. Silence fastened itself to this hollow and quiet place in the barn. Tully turned towards the door and called behind him, "Come on, boy!" Within a moment, Sergeant came bounding out beside him.

"Wait! Tully, please!" Alex cried. "There's still somethin' I gotta ask you!" he shouted breathlessly.

Tully turned round and looked back. He stood directly between the open door's portal, framed between the barn and the outside. The man's face looked ashen in the dim light of the lantern and for an instant Alex felt as though he could see right through his body, as though he was just a figment of his imagination. "Never mind Tully, I just want to say, thank you." Tully nodded his head with gratitude, turned back round, and then simply walked out.

Feeling very desolate and confused, Alex picked up the lantern and ran to the door. Miraculously the lantern seemed to be reenergized, it was alive with the radiance of a thousand candles. He lifted the lamp before him and watched the man and his dog as they strolled along the edge of the road until they approached the bend, and with a final glimpse of the two, they disappeared into the darkness of the night. The boy waited for a few minutes patiently anticipating their return, however the reminder that he was alone came only in the impatient gesture of the lantern that suddenly extinguished itself, leaving Alex standing in the shadow of the moonlight.

Chapter 49

Time had been kind to St. Louis and St. Louis was kind to its visitors. Commerce has changed her landscape and ever since the discovery of gold in '49 she established herself as the gateway to the West. The first railroad west of the Mississippi was under construction. The St. Louis Fair Grounds was in the final stages of showcasing one of the world's most ambitious agricultural exhibitions. If there was ever a time to rejoice, it was now, for the city was engaged in a boom of economic prosperity. Oh yes, there were grumblings of political division, some politicians were claiming discontent, but for the average citizen, they were not minding the discourse of uneasiness brewing in Washington, and as for a war...these were simply back page stories hidden amongst the editorials.

Against the hurly-burly landscape of the most prosperous city in the Midwest sits the gigantic Planters' House Hotel. A grand beauty by all accounts; her four-story frontage flaunts opulence and splendor for anyone who wishes to stay. Considered one of the finest hotels built, she is recognized as the quintessential meeting place that entertains the most interesting guests. Within her 300 rooms, gamblers, river boat captains, politicians, and the wealthiest travelers take refuge from their long and arduous travels. At the corner of Chestnut and Pine, all four directions of the compass rose converge. East and west, north and south, all meet at one vertex to drink mint juleps and gin cocktails, while others that become boisterously inebriated from too much dark whiskey chaw the end of Havana's La Caronas. Politics are debated, women are courted, and many graying goatees are stroked. The establishment keeps secrets of those who had slept in her beds and exchanged gossip in the colossal dining room. Where else can one find seductive dishes and trade secrets while dining in the greatest detailed replica of the Temple of Erechtheum in Athens, Greece?

Yet, in spite of its grandeur, luxury, and fine service, Will wasn't ready to give up his hard earned wages, and although a room per night included four meals, he felt that $4.25 was far more than he could afford. He had been keeping track of his provisions ever since he left and arrived in Missouri knowing his limitations. The fact that Charles Dickens and Daniel Webster had spent many comfortable visits in the fine hotel certainly made the establishment tempting, but he remained unwavering.

The Englishman's eyes searched past the sun-scorched street for any sign that might lead him to his son. Indeed, there were those paltry clues obtained from the prattling of meddlesome women who had related their knowledge about trains bringing children from the East. Early in his arrival to the city one such woman even brought him to a small church that was used as a meeting place to bring together adoptive parents and the children; which only gave in to his disappointment for he soon learned that the deacons and clergy all appreciated his problem however, they were trained in the art of discretion and could not divulge any particular specifics. The orphans, all wards of the courts, came and left without too much fanfare, and as far as having any recollection of a child that resembled the young Piccard, well there were just too many children for anyone to clearly remember in such a short time. Besides, so many years had passed and the boy would certainly have changed over time.

Will sauntered up into the Planters' House Hotel and wandered about until he found himself entering one of the smaller restaurants that occupied the first floor. He removed the tiny portrait of his late wife from his pocket and held it in the palm of his hand as he scanned the establishment with the minute possibility there might be someone who remembered a boy that looked like his beautiful

Libby. The restaurant was occupied by only a few patrons. Seated at a too long rectangular table covered in the white signature linen of the hotel was a party of four burly men. Each man occupied the opposing sides of the table and was heavily engaged in a muffled exchange of conversation, cigar smoking, and whiskey drinking; a sorted combination that often led to either brotherly love or short tempered provocations. If they did not intend to be secretive, their body language gave them away, for they tipped their chairs and leaned their torsos forward into the center of the table. A musty chain of cigar smoke slowly lingered upward from the stubs of lit butts, twisting lightly over their heads until it grew too thick to hold itself up and crawled back down, engulfing them all in a shroud of stinking smoke.

"Prospectors," whispered the maître d'.

"Excuse me?" Will replied, not hearing the man clearly.

"Those men you were looking at, they are prospectors from Boston; quite easy to spot. I can always smell them out by the way they talk; as though no one ever before them had ever heard of going west for gold," he whispered sarcastically. "If I were you, I'd find myself a local guide." Then he winked and left Will standing idly while he hastened to seat another party that was waiting by the door.

In contrast to the table of men, a well-groomed, middle-aged woman was sitting alone at a small table surrounded by a silver tea service roosting upon a nest of lace doilies; and although she was quite refined, she possessed a presence of someone that invited gossip. Having exhausted most all the leads the city had to offer, Will glanced about the restaurant for the maître d' in hopes that he would acquaint him with the curious woman, however the fellow was nowhere to be seen. Had his matter not been so grave, then perhaps Will would not have wandered over to her table and introduced himself. Yet his task did not prove to be as painful as projected and after several moments of awkward introductions a small exchange of conversation erupted, for the woman was quite talkative, and the passive man found that his intuition was correct, for she cheerfully invited him to join her.

"What's done is done, my dear man," stated the refined woman who was a guest of the lavish hotel. She sipped her tea like an Englishwoman, steadying her cup upon the bone china saucer, balancing it with one hand, while in perfect harmony cradled the cup handle with the other. "Once those papers are signed by the new legal guardians and the new parents are declared suitable, well I am afraid even the Queen of England couldn't get them away. It appears that if this is the fate of your son, and from what you tell me it sounds quite possible, the child legally belongs to the new family." The woman took a long hard look at Will and added, "Take my advice and go back to where you came from." Although her answer was curt, he hated to think she could be right. After all, unless the boy was dead, he wasn't going to believe that there was no hope.

The woman waved her hand and summoned the waiter. "What would you like? You look as though you could use something strong," she said implying that Will accompany her in a drink. The matron prattled on; she was Mrs. Jackson Thurston and was thankfully on her way back to New York City. She had enough of the dust and trouble associated with the West and couldn't wait until she returned to "civilization". "Is there anyone you would like me to look up for you when I am back in New York?" she asked Will, and dispensed a warm and sympathetic smile.

A sudden hush of strangeness fell upon the newest visitor as he felt a need to retreat from the conversation. Somehow talking to this stranger on terms of such personal concerns was highly unnatural. Will quickly declined her invitation and stood up from the table. He thanked her for the advice, backed away, turned, and hastened out, still clutching the photograph.

"Strange sad man," Mrs. Thurston thought, and then with little more concern than one has for a stray cat, she sipped her tea and waited until the coach heading east was announced.

———

Will stepped out from the hotel and walked slowly in the direction of what he believed was the way to the livery. He was making leisurely progress as he wandered along the sidewalk lined with both culinary and decadent delights; a tailor, barbershop, cigar maker, saloon, dry-goods store, and a weathered vendor selling local fruits and vegetables from a rickety wooden pushcart. The middle-aged man was chattering aloud in Italian, rearranging his fruits and vegetables and wiping his brow with a handkerchief; for the sun was hot and the rays beat down upon him with no mercy. At first glance it appeared that he was complaining to the bunch of long yellow zucchinis that he had just aligned in size-order; however, upon taking a closer look, one could see a short-legged terrier with triangle ears and a low fat belly lying beneath the shadow of the cart. Its dusty coat was coarse and wiry, making it look more like a miniature boar than a dog. The small dog was tethered to the cart with a thin strip of twisted hemp and was the recipient of the man's constant gabble.

A young dandy dressed in a fine woolen suit studied the merchant and his dog as he leaned lazily against the storefront post sucking on the seed of a peach. His jaw moved back and forth as his back teeth removed any flesh that remained on the pit. He was keeping himself cool under the shelter of the building's overhang and fanned himself with a newly purchased bowler. The man's eyes grew menacingly wide as Will approached, and he spit the pit into the street. "What are you lookin' for?" the Irishman asked. He stopped fanning and hoping to draw attention to his stylish hat, he lightly dusted the brim with several wide scooping gestures of his palm before he put it upon his head tilting it down slightly towards his eyes. A hat such as his was worth more in the envy it brought than in comfort.

"The livery," Will replied. The man studied Will's face as though he didn't clearly understand the response, and then suddenly broke into a most crude form of laughter. His sniggering and snorting was loud and boorish. As if he had just delivered the punch line of a joke, he shook his head wildly up and down and held his arms across his abdomen in such an attack of hilarity that had he not been propped up against the pole, he may have fallen over.

Not really understanding the jocularity his inquiry had provoked, Will waited while the man gained his composure.

"Oh, oh, you're a funny one!" the fellow exclaimed, and with a flip of his hat the gent pointed at the structure across the street. Attending to the gesture, Will saw the reason for the uproarious fit. The blunt irony of the situation was disclosed as he raised his eyes. Set before him a clearly painted sign above the building read, *Livery Stables.* "English, eh?" remarked the Irishman. Will nodded, understanding that his own accent had revealed his identity just as the Irishman's brogue had revealed his. The two men exchanged curious glances, summing each other up like a pair of dogs. Satisfied that he had extracted as much entertainment as he wanted from this greenhorn, the dandy sauntered away with an air of superiority, obviously uninterested in Will's particulars and pulling out a coin from his vest pocket, he tossed it to the street vendor in exchange for another peach.

Will had always thought of himself as observant, however any effort to understand how he could have ignored his own lack of surveillance towards his surrounding was quickly dismissed and now taken up with the ponderings of his next undertaking; should he buy a secondhand wagon or should he buy one that was new. He was convinced that if the boy wasn't in St. Louis then it was logical that he may have been picked up at the railroad station and taken further west with his adoptive parents.

The West, a place where land was deemed untamed and ruthless by both those who knew it well and those who had never crossed over from the eastern side of the Mississippi. Will quickened his pace towards the distinctive wooden structure across the street. It stood several stories higher than the neighboring establishments and was set apart from the others by its distinguishing end walls of free stones that had been collected during the original land clearing. The gambrel roof dated back to the first owners who were of German decent. They had decided to emulate their barn construction when building the livery and engineered the slanting design of a pitched roof that strategically allows the rain and snow to fall off. The two part wagon-door was pinned back with leather straps preventing it from swinging shut and lay flat against the wall. However, what distinguished it the most from other places of business was the air emanating from the entrance. Thick, rich, and pungent, a notable mixture of manure, hay, and damp leather clung to the insides of the nostril, while a half-dozen or more pesky horse-flies loomed above the entrance; making themselves a nuisance to anyone they came in contact with. Four strips of 7.5" x 6" fly-paper dangled from twine, which was attached to the lintel by four oversized rusty nails that clearly produced more support to the paper than needed. Each morning it was the duty of the youngest livery hand to soak fresh sheets of the poison-treated paper in a plate of water and brown sugar solution and after permitting several minutes to pass, he was to set it out to dry for an hour or so, and then replace the old with the new. But despite the advertisements' promises of deadly results to the flies, it appeared that the mettlesome insects only seemed to find the paper a useful rest stop on route back and forth from the manure piles.

Will peered curiously into the dark abyss of the livery stable and found himself immediately challenged by the contrast of light. Forced to make a quick adjustment to the windowless interior, it took several minutes for his pupils to become accustomed to the ill-lighted station. He entered as cautiously as a blind man and slowly made out the forms of a smoothly hewed hitching post stationed to his immediate left. Two horses were tied to the timber by loosely slung ropes. They were standing idly side by side, as though waiting to be tended to. Directly before him were the makings of a black-smith shop and the enormity of the livery continued as far back as the next block. He could see a brick forge and its massive anvil; it was far larger than any he had ever seen before, and beside it was a tall barrel that he assumed was filled with water to cool the iron the blacksmith was working on. The walls were arranged with wheels of all sizes, yokes, and chains, while on the shelves were bins of nails and horseshoes. Beyond the forging area was a loft to store hay, and at least four stalls hooked together for livery guests, the horses and mules. In the farthest back there was another set of open double doors, which exposed at least one Conestoga wagon and a yard filled with junk. It looked like a well-fitted livery, except for the fact that it was void of workers.

The larger of the two horses was a handsome black Morgan stallion, probably having been purchased in the green hills of Vermont where most of this breed had originated from. The other smaller horse wore a mottled coloring like those so favored by the Apache. "Hey, there girl," Will called lightly as he sauntered up to the pinto and stroked her nose. The horse looked over at the stranger and nudged her head against his arm. "Why you're friendly, aren't you?" he said fondly and gave the soft nose another gentle stroke. The horse lowered its head seeming to enjoy the attention. "You are pretty," Will exclaimed and moved along to the side of the animal. He rubbed the crest of her neck and ran his hand down along her withers, awarding her a few gentle pats. "Where's your rider, in the back?" The pinto wriggled her ears and shook her head as though answering his question. "Must be happy to get that saddle and blanket off too," he remarked noticing the tack that had been strewn upon on the ground just a few feet away. "I bet you haven't been here long either," he said continuing to talk to her. The pinto swished her long tail trying to flick away a large black and blue fly hovering overhead. Will removed his hat and tried to swat it, but soon discovered that contrary to what one may think that its large size would make it slow and an easy prey, it was in reality quite quick and his attempt to crush it proved most ineffective. Unfortunately, he only managed to keep the fly at bay for a few moments; returning again with an entourage of several more blue-winged pests.

Will turned and scanned his surroundings for something to use as a fly swatter, but when he found nothing immediately suitable, he found himself eyeing the blanket and saddle lying on the ground. For some curious reason, yet unknown to him, he was strangely drawn to this spot, and although he reminded himself that he had seen many other saddle blankets, this one was of particular interest. Will moved away from the horse and knelt down. He parted the folded blanket and rubbed his thumb and forefinger between the edges of the material. It appeared to have been made from a fabric far softer than any other saddle blanket he had ever felt. The pinto neighed lightly as though asking for more attention however; Will's interest in the pony had suddenly waned. He brought the corner up towards his face. The light of day was obscured by the windowless walls of the livery stable adding to the somber interior of brown and gray enclosure. He held a patch of the blanket firmly in his fist and reeled it toward him so that little by little it began to slide off the saddle. The young father stood up and pulled upon it gently, and it obeyed. Just as an armadillo uncurls itself, the blanket unfolded and came creeping forward. Will cradled the entire blanket in his arms like a swaddling cloth and stroked the quilted patterns with his fingers. He looked upon the fine stitchery of the quilt in the same way one recognizes the countenance of a forgotten acquaintance.

"Hey, Cally, looks like you made a friend," exclaimed a voice that was no more than a few yards behind him.

Startled by the intrusion, for he was sure no one was so near, Will twisted round to encounter a face-to-face with the owner of the horse and the saddle. Will held the blanket out before him. He tried to keep it all bundled in his arms, but it remained unbalanced and draped over his hands and down to the floor. "This quilt," he exclaimed, "where did you get it?" Will demanded. His anguished cry spoke volumes beyond these miserly words.

The dusty man looked upon the ghostly expression of this stranger who seemed to be wearing a death mask. He immediately sensed that something was deeply wrong. "A boy," said Pinto Jack, calculating his words very carefully. "A young kid gave it to me. What's it to you?"

"What was his name?" Will asked now bringing the blanket back towards him. He ignored Jack's question and pressed further. "Tell me, when did you get it?" All color had drained from his face and

Will's pallid appearance looked especially ashen against the stands of black hair that fell down upon his worried brow.

Pinto Jack was not too sure what to make of the situation and frankly, he was unconvinced that the man was in his sane mind. For the stranger standing before him was holding on to a horse blanket with the same embrace a child clings to his mother's skirt, and yet a reasonable explanation for such a sentimental display had not yet been revealed. The cowboy decided to proceed cautiously. "You got a mighty good grip on Cally's blanket," Jack replied and held his hand out hoping to retrieve his property back. "Mind if I ask, why?"

The unfortunate man at once found it difficult to speak. His voice began to quiver as his emotions were beginning to get the best of him. "It's been over two thousand, five hundred, and eighty-five days," Will stated. "That's more than seven years." He consciously cleared his throat and began again. "It's been seven long sleepless years since I lost my boy, and this," he said pointing to the object of contention, "this is the first clue to his whereabouts that I have uncovered since we've been separated!"

By now Jack was feeling pretty awkward and didn't exactly know what to do or what to say, when happily he found unexpected relief from this somber soliloquy by a chorus of buzzing flies flitting about his horse, whereby he stepped away from the present drama to shoo away the pests. But after several unsuccessful attempts to crush the flying vermin, he returned to the problem at hand. "You're English, aren't you?" he asked confronting the stranger again.

Will smiled at him cautiously. "You're the second person today who has chosen to remind me of that," he remarked. "Look, I don't mean to be trouble, but I think this is my son's," Will replied shaking the quilt.

Jack remained pensive. "The boy that gave me the blanket, he didn't sound or talk like you do," he explained.

Will clenched his fist and trying to compose himself calmly shook his head "no". Then, he inhaled deeply and exhaled very slowly. "Mister," he continued, "I haven't seen or spoken to my son in years. He was just a little boy when he was taken; stolen away from his poor sick mother, too."

Jack removed his hat and wiped his forehead with his sleeve before putting it back on. This was a lot to take in. Could it be possible that this man was indeed telling the truth? But then again, St. Louis was a big city riddled with swindlers, tricksters, and thieves. The "Gateway to the West" was also the "Entrance Way" for frauds and cheats. But then again, what could this man gain by claiming the blanket belonged to his son? After all, if he was telling the truth then it was quite possible and even logical that the boy may have picked up a new inflection and lost the English accent of his birth parents. Seven years is a lifetime for a kid. But then again, perhaps this Englishman was an imposter who was claiming to be this boy's father.

Jack was confused and weighed each conclusion back and forth in his mind as Will waited anxiously with the knowledge that his fate was in the hands of a drifting cowboy.

"I can't help you," Jack finally said decidedly. "All I can tell you is that this is my horse's blanket, a kid gave it to her, and that's all. Now if you don't mind, I think you better drop it before you leave."

Will's expression changed from sadly woeful to firmly resolute as sorrow was transformed into condemnation. He clutched the blanket and remained steady. "Can't do that," he retorted angrily.

Now on most occasions Jack was a man who was eager to compromise and to him one blanket was as good as the next. However under the circumstances that he had obtained it, there wasn't really any room to bargain. "If I hadn't given my word to the kid, I'd let him keep the blanket," the cowboy thought. "Listen fella, I don't want any trouble, and I'm sure neither do you. I've been traveling from St. Joseph to out west, spent time at a relay station, then back again, and now I'm here in St. Louis headed east. Let's just say I'm tired and don't want to fight. But if it's a fight you want then I'll tell ya right now, me and those livery hands out back will give you a beating that you'll wish you'd never seen the likes of that blanket!"

But regardless of the threat, Will didn't flinch. Rather, he replied in a cunning tone that was cold and calculating. The pitiful sorrow he had once displayed had turned to a controlled rage stoked by years of frustration. He would never relax his hold on the blanket. "Do you think you can deliver more pain upon me than I already have received?" So grandly vehement was his question delivered that it lingered in the air like smoke. The two foes stood glaring at one another for several long silent moments.

For Jack, the conclusion to this predicament would have been quite straight forward if this man had a Machiavellian face, a grizzly face, even weatherworn or scarred, but instead he was met by a pair of gentle eyes, a clean shaven muzzle, and honest countenance. Although angry and bitter, it was a rather handsome face indeed.

"What's ya doin' there, Jack?" A strong and gruff voice boomed to the front of the livery. From behind a half wall there stood a heavy built man wielding a branding iron above his head.

The cowboy called back without turning around, "Got someone here that may need some help."

"Be right there," the man griped and kneeled back down behind the short wall that kept him hidden from view.

This moment of disturbance had now given way for Jack to reconsider his actions and as he redirected his attention back to Will, he now felt that perhaps he should give this man a chance to explain. Taking a step forward, Jack pointed to the blanket and asked, "So, what proof have ya got that this is your son's?"

Will was silent. He reached into his pocket and pulled out the photograph of Libby and surrendered it.

Jack rolled it over in his hand. "Mind if we walk out into the light?" the cowboy asked.

Will nodded approvingly. The crusty voice of the blacksmith echoed behind them wanting to know if he could help. Jack turned around and signaled that everything was all right. The large man grumbled from having been disturbed and lumbered to the front of the livery to tend to the pair of equines that had been waiting so patiently

Will received the sunshine like a hibernating bear after winter. He tilted his head and welcomed the mild breeze as it brushed against his pallid cheeks and forehead. It warmed his neck, arms, and legs, while rekindling vitality back into his miserable humor. Like a rose bud limp from morning dew that becomes awakened by the early sun; Will felt cleansed by the warmth of the rays that poured over him and with quiet repose. he was rejuvenated.

In contrast, Jack headed directly into the cooler shade of the building's overhang where he gestured for Will to follow, and both men sat down upon the steps. The cowboy turned the photograph of the dead wife over in his hands and then back again staring intently at the lovely face. Will removed his hat and ran his fingers through his sweat-soaked hair. He lightly struck the brim several times against the bottom step. Dry dirt and soil flew up into the air and landed back down upon the ground. "It returns from where it once began," he whispered.

"What's that?" asked Jack turning to the Englishman.

"Nothing really," he mumbled and put his dusty hat back on. Will glanced up the street and tried to capture what it must have been like for his son when the child first arrived; if indeed this was the city the boy had been sent to. He imagined him being alone and terrified. Will winced at the distant wailing of a mourning dove. It resembled too much of a human voice. He put his hands over his ears blocking out the mocking of the bird until it stopped. His thoughts fell upon the notion that it was feasible the child could have tried to act bravely and held back all his tears until he was alone at night and wept softly in his pillow. Will clenched his fist, loathing the conjured images of his son's predictable anguish. Provoked by his restlessness, he began to fumble with the quilt as it lay in a rolled wad. Stretching his stiff-ened limbs, the blanket began to trundle off his lap until it fell along past his knees. He glanced down upon the partially unfurled bundle. Blocks of patched material revealed beautiful patterns that were visibly more colorful in the bright light of day. Bit-by-bit he followed the patterns until he began to salvage a lost part of himself. Fervently, he flung the quilt out before him and leaned forward starring at it as though he were deciphering the Rosetta stone. "There, right there!" he shouted. "Here is your proof!" and with a wild exclamation, he gathered the quilt up and pointed to a most elegantly stitched design.

Jack's eyes went from the counterpane to the man's pained expression before he hung his head sheepishly as though admitting something horribly shameful. It was on the morning that he had made the decision to go west, the time in St. Joseph when he had almost forgotten Cally's blanket, when at the last minute it was hastily retrieved. He remembered stuffing it into his saddlebag, but not without first detecting that stitched within the patches of the quilt were names. At the time he was in a hurry and had not made anything out of it and certainly not any connection of great importance. But today a voice from within finally woke up and validated the uncertainty he had once lightly questioned.

"Piccard, you see!" exclaimed Will and traced his finger along the swirling letters. "And here, look at this!" He placed his index finger along another swatch of the material and spelled the name as he traced out the ornate letters: L-e-x-y Piccard! That's my son! And here, here is Libby, my wife. And me, there!" Enthusiastically, the Englishman confirmed the details by outlining his own name. "Will Piccard! You do see it don't you?" he asked. "My wife embroidered the names into the design!"

"Your son's name is Lexy?" Jack asked.

"No, that's the nickname we called him. His name is Alex, Alexander Piccard!" Will stood up and positioned the quilt over his shoulder. "You believe me now, don't you?" he insisted peering down at the cowboy.

Jack was conscious that his feelings of miscalculation regarding this current episode were indeed promptly reconciled, and he quickly resolved to assist by helping reunite the boy and his father. It was now only a bare matter of admitting his wrong. "If it means anything to you, I am sorry for doubting you. My name is Jack, they call me Pinto Jack on account of Cally," he said returning to his feet. With this resolution taken, his usual lightheartedness partially returned.

"Will Piccard," returned the Englishman's introduction. "But I guess you know that," he added referencing the name in the quilt

Jack smiled at the half-joke. The cowboy looked at Will and like a man in a confessional spoke up, "I know where your son is," he said handing the father back the photograph. Jack had all the proof he needed. There was now no doubt in his mind, the resemblance of this woman and the boy could only be that of mother and son. "Will, your son is safe," he said softly. "And, not too far from here," he added reassuringly.

The hopeful anticipation of this information brought forth an immediate response of delight, and without paying any attention to prior feelings, they acknowledged their new friendship. Will accepted the outstretched hand and locked his tightly into the other's palm, and then with a vigorous handshake the two men sealed their silent bond.

Chapter 50

Early pioneers that were brave enough to venture into the unknown journeyed with only their wits and the constellations above. Rounded swells of prairie grass and dense wilderness often became an invincible barrier and with only the horizon as a guide, a man unfamiliar with the territory often made erroneous decisions and subsequently found himself in dire straits. However, for the two men now venturing together the trails and roads had been etched by years of previous travel made by wagon wheels hauling heavy freight and loads. Now long after these journeys have ended, deep grooves and narrow furrows remain as a map-less route for others to follow.

Arrangements had been promptly made for the trip out of St. Louis. Cally would stay behind at the livery, for having been on the trail for so long Jack concluded that the rest would do her good. Will purchased from the blacksmith a sturdy farm wagon, sporting a canvas hood that promised protection from inclement weather and a "span" of two patient mules; although oxen would have been the favored choice if they were taking a longer and more arduous journey. But being as their destination was not too far away, and neither man had much to carry, they didn't need the extra strength possessed by such powerful brutes. As for the mules, such a purchase was not an arbitrary choice, but rather a well-grounded and calculated decision. For even though these beasts were noted to be slower than their athletic counterpart, the horse, their appetites are less hearty, they endure the harness for a longer period of time, and have been found to be most skillful and sure-footed on rough terrain. Will spent his money readily, and it spilled into the palms of the livery hands as easily as an overturned milk bucket. He ensured that his departure would be ready the next morning by securing a guarantee with dollar notes for each greedy hand that required enticement.

A goodly part of the evening had been spent in the hotel dining room where Will presented Jack with a multitude of questions regarding his son; and when the latter had delivered all that he knew and remembered, the father found a willing audience in the cowboy. His dark hair fell down upon his brow, and he pushed his long bangs aside, smoothing the stray locks with his hand. In the dimly lit room his large brown eyes expressed the temperament of a shy boy and for the first time since their meeting, Jack could see the family resemblance, although it was quite clear that Alex's sweet looks had come by way of his mother. The waiter sallied round several times to offer up dessert, only to be waved away by Jack, who now was fully absorbed by the storyteller whose soul was fully consumed in his tale. "I shall speak quite candidly," confessed Will as he slid the tiny paraffin lamp away from the center of the table to the side. It was hard to imagine that such a small vessel could distribute such a somber atmosphere. The waiter passed by the table again, but this time his offer of whiskey was not ignored. And as the night fell past the last dinners served, Will told Jack about Libby, their escape from England, the events that led to their living at the old woman's home, and the fact that Mrs. Cambridge was sister to Libby's cruel father. He recounted his friendship with Nick, and did not forget dear Wanda. It wasn't until the maître d' politely requested they take the conversation elsewhere, for it was notably an hour after closing that Will's incessant eagerness was satisfied for the night.

It was fog, thick and still which the morning light could not pierce. Will arrived at dawn outside the livery stable and although he had not slept very much, his enthusiasm canceled out any fatigue. The morning haze rose and fell, heaving heavy sighs as it obscured the capacious wagon. From around the corner of the building a figure appeared, parting the damp mist with his body as he ambled towards him. "You here fer the wagon?" a surprisingly young voice emerged out of the white vapors; he seemed to be sleepwalking. Will had lowered the wagon's rail and was fumbling with the supplies. The livery hands had kept their promise; the wagon had been stocked with general provisions of eggs, bacon, coffee, water, dried beef, cooking utensils, and a barrel of water. The boy shuffled past and around to the front of the wagon where earlier he had harnessed the pair of mules. Both stood at attention awaiting their orders. The boy pulled a dried zwieback from his pocket and gnawed at it with his front teeth, allowing only tiny nibbles to be shaved free. He pecked at the cracker as though hoping that if he ate it slowly it would miraculously regenerate. He then shoved the uneaten half back into his pocket and wiped the crumbs on his shirt. The two mules watched and ground their teeth against the hard bit. They followed the few crumbs roll off the boy's shirt and disappear into the fog. One of the mules lurched its head forward anticipating catching the tiny morsel of food that had been captured in a web of mist; only to be disappointed by finding nothing.

Jack arrived at the livery just as the moon slipped from white to silver blue, camouflaged in the pale morning sky. "Ever shoot one of these?" he asked Will and handed the Englishman a plains rifle.

Will took the gun and nodded 'yes'. "I wouldn't exactly say that I'm an expert, but I have had some practice shooting cans and targets," he said.

"This is a sure bet for you, then. I'd say with adequate aim, you'll be able to get in a range of at least 80 to 100 yards," he remarked and then added, "and most likely get what you're gunning for." Jack tossed a bedroll and a saddlebag into the back of the wagon and went round to the front.

"If ya don't need nothin' else, I'm gonna head out," announced the boy who had made himself noticeable as he shuffled forward.

"No, you run along," Will said with an approving nod.

The boy started away, but stopped and turned abruptly as though he had forgotten something. The fog was now a pool of misty haze. "Better take care, Mister," he warned. "It's might different once ya git out of the city. If ya don't mind me sayin', you look like a greenhorn."

"Greenhorn?" Will laughed at the term. "Now tell me, young man, just what is a greenhorn?"

"Why, that's a fellah with not much experience," he explained, and shaking his head as though he were an old sage, he slowly canvassed Will up and down. "Let's just say that ya seem like a nice man, and I sure wouldn't want you to git tricked."

Will wasn't sure whether he was grateful for the advice or if he had been insulted by a boy that probably wasn't much older than Lexy. "I appreciate your concern, but I think I'll be fine."

"Well, just watch out," he cautioned and walked back around the corner of the livery from where he came.

———

The wagon was barely large enough for the two men to sit side-by-side, and the canvas cover had been mended more than once as evidenced by the mismatched patches dripping with dew like a leaky spigot. Jack hunched forward, his heels dug into the floorboard, and his hands clasped lightly around the reins. He pushed his body forward as though helping the pair of mules pull the large beast of a wagon. And they plowed forward. Out of the mist and back into the mist, they traveled and though it was after dawn when the sun should be burning off the low clouds, the sun would not shine. It was a bleak morning, a curtain of dense fog cloaked everything and all they could hear was the heaving of the mules and the clopping of feet. They were traveling exclusively by instinct.

Jack pulled back on the reins and the two mules immediately halted as if in a battalion of infantrymen. "What's the matter?" asked the Englishman with noticeable annoyance. "What did you stop for?"

"It would be foolhardy to go on," Jack replied. "Look ahead, why I can't see beyond the ears of those two mules," he exclaimed, wondering why something so obvious had to be explained. He set the reins down and readjusted his hat, giving himself a moment to come up with a plan that would appease the impatient father. "Listen," he suggested, "we're barely a quarter mile out of the city. Let's turn around here where the road is at least wide enough for the wagon. We can go back and get some breakfast while the fog lifts. Besides, we'll be able to make better time a little later than if we try to fumble our way now; and if one of the mules trips, then we'd be really out of luck."

Will knew that Jack was right. He could barely see his own hand let alone a trail that he was unfamiliar with. "I guess you're right," he mumbled. "But just till the fog lifts!" he insisted assertively.

"I won't even unhitch the mules," Jack agreed and handed Will the reins; then he jumped down from the wagon and felt his way to the front of the team. Following the outline of the left mule until he caught the edge of its bridle, he slipped his hand through the cheek-piece and gently pulled the obedient animal to the left, allowing it to follow his lead. The road was uneven and at the same time rough with loose stones, and he hoped that he could steady the animals enough so they could keep the wagon from sliding in either direction. They hadn't traveled long enough to come upon a ravine, so he knew there wasn't any fear of toppling over into the gorge. No, the worst thing that could happen might be a wheel rolling over a rock and having to be pulled out of a furrow. He winced at that thought and skimmed his foot over the ground feeling for any large object that may be in their path. "Slack up on the reins," he called out. Will let the reins slide down and held them limply in his hands. He could hear the old beast creaking as it was turned slowly round like a mule powered gristmill. When they were fully repositioned back towards the city, Jack gave each mule a good pat on their foreheads, told them they had earned their keep for the day, and climbed back up into the wagon. "Don't worry, Will," he said as he interpreted the man's silence. "We'll get to your son soon, don't worry."

Chapter 51

"Now, aint't that nice," mused Betty, peppering her sentiment with a blend of curiosity and sincerity. She held the letter up to the open window and flipped it over in her hands. But the paper was too thick to see through the envelope, and the only disclosure of its contents came from the sender's address on the back.

"What have you got there?" asked a mildly interested Mr. Beasley. He dunked his biscuit into the coffee and quickly retrieved it with the skill of a man who had performed this epicurean feat many times before. Lifting the soppy dough out of the liquid, he bit off the wet piece in a single chomp, while not a crumb infiltrated his cup!

"It's a letter for Alex from Belle Tarson's girl, Grace," Betty replied and placed the envelope on the counter. "More coffee?" she asked. The hunchback waved his hand "no" and as though prompted by her request he picked up his cup, emptied it, and pulled himself away from the table, noisily settling the crockery back on the saucer.

"Well, I better be getting along. I received the o.k. to hire a new man, and I want to see which section of the field to start him out in." Betty smiled as though she cared, but actually she took a casual interest in such affairs now that she was merely an occupant and not the owner. Besides, she wasn't being paid to be a full caretaker and only had to tend to the chores she was able to muster as well as those she relegated to Alex. The graying woman untied her apron and threw it over the bench before opening the door for the bent little man.

Mr. Beasley had become a regular visitor and their friendship was kindled by the man's laziness to prepare meals and Betty's new found interest in cooking. Theirs had become a companionship of convenience. And ever since the transfer of her ownership of the farm to Belle Tarson, she no longer had to worry about keeping the property up or losing it to the bank. Taxes and mortgage were torments of the past.

Betty watched the crooked man hobble out towards the field and exchange greetings with Alex, as the boy was walking back to the house from the barn. The boy didn't mind the small man and in fact he was rather pleased that Betty had someone that could keep her company, for now she seemed to regularly be in a more cheerful mood.

"There's some biscuits left if ya want," she said. "Just try not to drop any crumbs on the floor, I just finished sweeping." Alex nodded and set out to wash his hands while Betty removed the used dishes off the table.

"Oh, this came for you," she announced and handed him a linen cloth to dry his hands. She dangled the letter loosely as though it was bait and he was the catch.

"A letter?" Alex wiped his hands and sat on the bench. He took a pale biscuit off the plate and picked at it carefully over the table. Several crumbs fell onto the oil cloth and he brushed them into a small pile away from the edge. Betty sat across and placed the letter down between them. For a second time this morning she considered its contents. Alex finished the biscuit and wiped his mouth with the linen cloth that he still had in his possession.

"More?" she asked. He nodded "no" and reached for the letter. "It's from that sweet Grace Tarson," blurted Betty at the same time Alex was reading the return address.

He looked up, smiled meekly, and drew away from the table. "Thanks for the biscuit," he said. Then with hurried reference to the time, he walked out, leaving a rather nosey Betty still wondering about the contents of the letter.

———

Several months had passed since Grace had left on her trip East with Miss Henshaw, and the only news the boy received was by way of Mr. Beasley. Had it not been for those occasional updates, Alex just assumed that he would never have heard from her again. After all, why should this situation be any different? Most all people that came into his life seemed to stay around for awhile and then suddenly take leave. But this letter, it was a new twist that he was unacquainted with.

Alex felt lighthearted as he skipped into the barn and held the letter up over his head. "Look what came for me?" he shouted and hurried to show Delilah and Dandy. "It's from Grace, you remember her don't ya?" he asked and tucked his head along the soft smooth neck of Dandy. A gentle snort was exchanged for his affection, and while satisfied with the response, Alex climbed up and sat on the stall railing. He slit the envelope with cautious enthusiasm and wriggled the letter free. It had been written on fine white linen and when he noticed how his hands were dirty and a small thumb print had already soiled the envelope, he balanced the letter on the rail and wiped his palms across his clean shirt. Then, he picked up the elegant linen again and as though it were porcelain, he unfolded it and began to read it aloud.

Dear Alex,

Baltimore is a city with so many people that if I don't hang on to Miss Henshaw I will surely get lost. Yesterday, we took a ride in the grandest carriage and came across a most curious thing. Not more than a haystack away from the road was a house with a fine gate and a small path leading to the doorway. The windows looked all shut up and dark and the weeds were growing up onto the stone wall. But that's not what I wanted to tell you, my fingers got to keep up with my mind…that's what Miss Henshaw keeps telling me. Anyway, above the doorway, on what she calls the façade, is a large letter C, and it's scrawled just like the one on the signet ring you gave me! This place is actually someone's home. It's called Cambridge Arms.

Miss Henshaw tells me the C is a coincidence, but I told her it can't be. She is making me send the ring back on account she thinks it is too valuable. She wrapped it up and it's on the way. Do you believe in fate? I do. I know I won't get to see you soon so I might as well let you know, I think you are the most wonderful boy in the entire world! There, I've said it and now I can go on with my life knowing that I won't die thinking that you never knew. Goodbye, Alex Forester, I hope someday we will meet!

Your friend forever,

Grace

P.S. Miss Henshaw helped me with the spelling.

"Now what do you suppose P.S. stands for?" Alex asked the two horses, and then refolded the letter and stuffed it back into the envelope. He wasn't sure what to make of the contents. Did this mean that Grace may come back to the farm? All he could tell for sure was that she was in a city called Baltimore and that she was sending back the ring. Alex smiled when he thought about her. He jumped down and balanced the envelope on the rail. The large horses shuffled their feet restlessly. He leaned his head against Delilah's velvet neck and stroked softly. He could hear her breathing with a gentle rhythm. He lifted his head away and whispered so quietly that even the horse bowed to hear him. "Someday, we'll go away, too," he explained. "I don't know when, but I'll always take good care of you both. I'll never leave you, never! I promise."

———

A fairly large dog lay in the middle of the sidewalk where the pedestrians would have to maneuver around him. He wasn't any particular breed, just a plain yellowish tan with a curled shaggy tail and triangle ears that stood up and folded in with a slight curve. He must of have belonged to some owner for around his neck he wore a brown leather collar. He appeared to be a rather well-mannered dog and didn't seem to mind being near people; for every now and again you could hear someone make a comment or two.

"Oh, look at that dog! He sure looks peaceful, just sleeping the day away!" someone would say to another while pointing at him; and then he would thump his tail happily and collect cheerful smiles from passersby. However, it wasn't until he looked for a more comfortable spot by the main entrance of the Planters' House Hotel did the poor old dog find himself in a rather unfortunate situation. For let it be told that not all persons like animals and on this particular morning, a robust and unshaven individual with this particular dislike came upon this very sleeping dog.

At first when the man approached he gave the dog a light kick, encouraging it to move out of the way. To his surprise the animal did not move, but simply wagged its tail as if with approval. Again the man lifted his heel, but this time producing a much swifter blow, whereupon his contact with the dog was in such a great manner that the animal growled deep and low with all the intent of scaring the man away, but not once did it ever bar its teeth. Suddenly, in a fury that is generally displayed only by the mad, the brute struck the dog again and then swooped down hovering over it and yanked the yelping animal up by its leather collar. By now the man was embroiled in a furious rage and the veins in his neck were pulsating with venom. "Take that you dirty mongrel!" he snarled and with a mighty heave threw the dog into the street. The moment it hit the ground the animal scrambled to its feet and trembled away until it was long out of sight.

Now, if anyone was witness to this ghastly incident they did not make mention nor make eye contact with the unshaven man, and if anyone had any pity for the dog, no one dared speak up for fear of crossing this terrible temper.

———

Inside the hotel restaurant Jack and Will had already been seated and served their breakfast, all taking place during the same time that the poor dog was scampering far away. Mrs. Thurston, of whom Will had made an earlier acquaintance, was sitting by herself at her usual table and by her reappearance this morning, she had either changed her mind or had missed the coach she was scheduled to take back to New York. She was sipping tea poured from the same porcelain teapot and picking at what appeared to be a breakfast of rather large portion for a woman of her demeanor. Her plate was stacked high with griddle cakes glazed with sticky maple syrup, and after each mincing bite she would dab her lips lightly with the linen napkin. It was apparent that she did not notice either of the two men, for she was sincerely engaged in reading the morning paper with her breakfast. There was a light chatter of conversations flitting every-which-way between guests who were dining or those waiting to be served. Waiters scurried like worker bees as the hive of activity seemed to heighten whenever the swinging door leading to the kitchen brushed open and the clanging of dirty dishes in soapy washtubs and the trill of teakettles screeching for attention escaped into the already noisy room. And so it was on this dreary grey morning that if anyone found themselves in a hurry, it was apparent that they would have to be patient for although it was quite early, most all travelers had made the same decision as Will and Jack; deciding to wait until the fog lifted rather than venturing outside.

No one seemed to take notice of the unkempt man when he entered the hotel dining room. He wasn't particularly large, more robust than burly. The city of St. Louis was used to visitors of all kinds and the fact that he was in need of a shave didn't seem unusual. However, as he leaned against the wall under a decorative light fixture, his coarse countenance illuminated and the days of chin growth showed their black stubbles as ornery as thistles. He wore a patina of dust that adhered to his clothes in the ordinary manner of a man that had just returned from a long trip; and his boots were still covered with dried mud, except for a spot on the top of the left boot which had been dusted clean when he kicked the dog.

As he waited he scanned the room, a predator on the prowl. When finally satisfied that he was not in the company of anyone he knew, he moseyed up to the maître' d. "Sure could use a drink and some vittles," the bounder clamored, and when he smiled the teeth he exposed wore a brown veneer of tobacco stain.

"Of course, Sir, as soon as a table is free," the courteous man replied.

The unkempt brute paced a bit with impatience, and then taking several steps forward, he sashayed away and started about on his own hunting expedition.

"Perhaps you would like to wait in the saloon," exclaimed the maître d' scampering up behind as he pointed to the exit. In a most genteel manner he added, "I can have one of the waiters come and get you when there is an available seat."

"What's wrong with that chair over there?" the lout demanded, and with a great shove pushed the little man aside and bounded towards the corner.

"Sir, Sir!" an exasperated voice called out, still trying not to draw attention to what was already becoming an embarrassing scene. But before the black-suited man could stop him, the unshaven thug had already made himself more than comfortable by leaning against the chair of Mrs. Thurston. Rather unscathed by his presence, the refined lady looked up from her paper, folded it, and coolly placed it down upon one of the empty chairs. "What may I do for you?" she asked politely.

"Why I'm sure you won't mind sharing a meal with me, now would you pretty lady?" the gruff fellow remarked. "Matter-of-fact, I sure could use something more than a hot meal!" he roared and with a grotesque chortle, he bent down low and whispered something into her ear.

A long and exaggerated shriek fell out of the dear woman's mouth as she put her hand over her sticky lips. "How dare you, how dare you be so impertinent!" she screamed. Yet, as loud as Mrs. Thurston sounded, it did not intimidate the intruder.

"Come on now, I think you can handle that little order," and without being invited, he pulled the spindly chair away from the table, tossed the paper aside, and settled himself down like an over-stuffed turkey in a pan. Mrs. Thurston looked stunned; her hand still remained over her mouth as though protecting it from what she predicted was the man's next intention. His crude voice bounded shamelessly across the room, "Waiter! Bring me something stronger than this," and with a howl he lifted the teapot above his head and tilted the spout towards her delicate china cup, allowing the last bit of liquid to overflow and drip out onto the table. "Whiskey, make it two; one for me and one for the lady!" he bellowed and set the pot aside. Attending back to the dumbstruck matron, he smiled wickedly with a toothy grin that bore the resemblance of an alligator. "Now, what do you recommend?" he asked sarcastically.

"This is outrageous!" muttered Will; who like all the other diners unwittingly was privy to the goings on at the corner table. "Why doesn't somebody from the hotel throw him out?"

"I'm sure someone has already notified the manager," Jack replied as he turned his head towards the scene that was taking place just across the dining room. "This kind of thing happens all the time; he's a scoundrel that has been out on the trail too long."

Will glared across at his friend surprised by the callous response. Disgusted, he dropped his fork into his eggs and pushed the plate towards the center of the table. "Then I don't suppose you think there is anything wrong with what's going on over there?" the Englishman suggested, pointing to the brute.

"Now, I didn't say that. I just mean that these fellahs are a kind of common thing round these parts. Look, you don't want to stick your nose in another man's business, that's all I'm saying."

Will glanced over at the table across the room and shook his head with reproach as the unshaven man leaned across the table and muttered something to Mrs. Thurston.

"You are an animal!" she squealed in horror, but when she tried to get up to leave, the boorish man placed his dirty hand on her shoulder and pushed her back down with such a force that her tiny hat tipped to the side. Her face, already pale, was now chalked white. Her entire body seemed to be trembling as she righted her hat.

"Well, if no one will do anything, that's their business, but I certainly will not be a party to such brutality!" cried Will as he pushed himself away from the table.

The traveler's remark lifted Jack to his feet and he jumped up and quickly stood in his friend's way with the intent of blocking his departure. "Sit back down," whispered the concerned companion. "You don't want to get involved!"

"Involved, this is not a matter of getting involved, this is honor!" Will exclaimed and before Jack could pull him back, he shoved him aside and was marching away from the table and directly into forbidden territory.

A blanket of tension cloaked the room as Will approached. The entire establishment had now grown silent and only the chuckles of the unshaven man and the muffled sighs of disgust by Mrs. Thurston were audible. Even the kitchen help seemed to hold their breath as faces appeared round the corner like children playing hide and seek. Anticipating a confrontation, all patrons remained at bay. "What do you want?" snarled the fiend, and he contorted his lips into a menacing scowl.

Jack, recognizing trouble, hurriedly followed from behind. "Will, come on back to the table!" he commanded.

However, dismissing any danger, Will remained defiant to the order of his friend and continued to exercise what he believed to be the appropriate action. "I couldn't help noticing the situation from across the room," he stated and gestured to his table. His voice was deliberately calm, almost reverent. "I think that the lady would like to finish her meal alone. Isn't that so, Mrs. Thurston?" remarked Will as he addressed the troubled lady. But before the woman could acknowledge her response with either a yay or a nay, the unshaven man sprang to his feet, and what a malignant spectacle it was; for his unwholesome form and threatening glare created a toxic stir that vibrated across the entire dining area. Like woodland creatures that sense danger, the patrons scurried away from their tables and took refuge around the walls of the room as though waiting for the start of a boxing match. No one wanted to participate, but all were eager to see the show. Only Mrs. Thurston remained steadfast as though nailed to the seat of her chair.

At this point by a simple appraisal of the situation, Jack silently lamented that he had entered the restaurant without his firearm. "I think there is a misunderstanding," claimed Jack, addressing the antagonist. Then with a jovial approach he continued, while motioning his arm towards Will, "Why, you can tell just by my friend's accent that he is not from here and clearly does not understand." But the light humor did not seem to appease the unshaven man for his dead cavernous eyes revealed no emotion.

In any event, if Jack's statement was true or not, Will took no heed and remained unruffled by the flaring of nostrils of the larger man he confronted. "Not so," said Will, correcting his friend, "I am English, that is true, however, this woman, may she be here in America or across the Atlantic, is clearly being harassed." And although it is unwise to poke a resting grizzly bear, the devilish man's size and aggressive posture seemed to be of physical insignificance to Will. He then turned again to the aggressor. "Sir, I believe that you should find another table and respect this fine woman's privacy by allowing her to finish her meal in peace and solitude."

Will's response was followed by silent gasps of expectation as his words were received in the manner one interprets the tolling of the bells.

"Let me get this straight!" roared the opponent. "You're tellin' me to get lost on account of this rich dame? Are you sure?" and as his first question resonated around the room the subsequent words echoed from one ear to another, and the entire gawking population shuddered as though they were standing upon a fault line.

"You're not gonna take that from a foreigner, are ya?" cried out a voice from amongst the ring of people. Savagely the hideous man lunged forward to see who in the swarm had taunted him, however, the silent crowd formed such a tight chain as they stood shoulder to shoulder that he was unable to identify the coward.

It had grown uncomfortably warm in the stuffy closed room. Several of the men had taken a table in the far corner of the restaurant, each placing a wager on an anticipated outcome. A slither of rich cigar smoke rose over their heads and penetrated the atmosphere leaving behind the stench of mendacity. Then without a second thought and with unbridled hatred, the prickly man reached into his dirty boot, pulled out a bowie knife and savagely plunged the blade into the Englishman.

"He's got a knife!" screamed a patron. The crowd simultaneously squealed in horror, for no one had thought that the verbal dispute was going to take such a dramatic turn, one so quick and so brutal. As coldly as he struck, the beast swooped in and retrieved the weapon he had just used in the savage attack; its sharply tapered blade still dripping with the innocent blood coated the elaborately etched slogan, "Death to Traitors".

Jack frantically grabbed at the fleeing attacker, struggling to keep him from making an escape however; the vicious man was now as angry as a tormented hornet and knocked the cowboy over with a chair. Effortlessly, he pushed aside and toppled over several large oak tables, blocking any easy egress to catch up with him. A few men grappled at the assailant as he plowed through anyone in his way, but the mere strength of his hands could crush the skull with the pinch of his forefinger and thumb making their attempts futile. Everyone saw him run out through the back doorway of the restaurant, yet no one could stop his flight.

Confusion and tumult continued to reign. Morning diners who were unaware of these most recent happenings were ushered away as cries of "catch him, somebody stop him!" sounded from both the front and rear exits. Those who were bystanders at the front door ran down the street in chase of anyone that looked suspicious for the cries to apprehend were so desperate that anyone hearing the instructions felt compelled to follow orders.

Within the restaurant itself the scene was bleak and morose. Horrified patrons ran about screaming for a doctor. A red and white gingham tablecloth was used as a blanket, and as they waited for the surgeon Jack anxiously tried to find his friend's pulse. He placed his fingers upon the side of the wounded man's neck, yet all he could feel was his own trembling heartbeat. Will lay motionless; the floor was soaked in crimson and with each minute that passed the pool around the prone body grew larger in circumference. The young man kneeling beside his wounded companion called to him with frantic appeal. "Will, Will, hang in there! Can you hear me?" he begged. "Will, Will, hang in there, the doctor's on his way, Will!"

"He's dead!" shrieked the maître d', when finally reappearing from the kitchen pantry where he had taken safe refuge.

"Shut up, shut up!" demanded Jack. "Keep your mouth still! Do you hear?" Jack looked beneath the blanketed tablecloth and then tucked it up around Will's shoulders. He wanted to check the open wound, but was afraid that it may do more harm than good. Blood was crawling slowly into every crevice and fiber it touched, while delivering a putrid smell of fatality. A growing circle of both woman and men surrounded the two friends with their morbid curiosity of getting a good look at the injured man. They exchanged hushed exclamations, whispered sympathetic quips and eyewitness reports, all of which did nothing to improve the grim situation.

Finally, a raspy voice from the entrance hall called forth, "Here comes the doc, stand back, let the doc through!"

———

Out the backdoor the attacker eluded capture despite the lineup of kitchen staff and waiters standing clear so as not to be stampeded. A noble chase was valiantly underway by a few of the more athletic men however, once outside, the escapee had found immediate asylum as he disappeared behind a tapestry of grey fog and mist, as though melting into the raw and gloomy day. A dreary sprinkle of cold rain began to fall hampering any hopes of following the man's tracks he may have left behind. A light gust picked up and diffused a scent of the hunt, and although the anticipation of a capture was assumed, with each passing minute it was becoming more imminent that the vicious assailant would escape.

Not more than a block from the hotel, hemmed in between several nearby buildings, a keen wind carried the wail of a howling canine. At first gathering it sounded like a solitary wolf, however the longer it yowled the distinction became clearer; for this was not the mournful cry, but rather the vicious growl of a predator. A violent breath of air exhaled with interrupted hiccups of sharp dog barks. But soon the short staccato bray transformed into a long thunderous and vicious threat and the animal thrashed out and terrorized, until in the distance its master's voice could be heard in unison with the fitful demands of the hunted. The dog slinked, pacing back and forth, its gaping jaws nipping at the air with any slight movement. Its muscular body and sharp teeth of a hunter continued to show impatience as it pinned its prey between the building and itself. The trapped man sat upright against the wall, his sticky palm tightly clasping the coffin-shaped handle; his single focus was to slit the throat of the animal. Sweat began to fill the creases on his brow, and as he wiped his forehead with his shirtsleeve it left behind a paste of brown dirt. Edging his hand forward, he slid his fingers against the earth slithering the appendages like baby rattlers however, to his dismay even this minute show of movement created enough of a stir to propel the dog forward with such fine elocution that it managed to slice a piece of flesh from his brutish neck with its sharp incisors.

Instinctively the attacker dropped the knife and grabbed his own throat with a new found terror. He gnashed his teeth in pain and swore at the dog demanding it be sent to the devil. The mutterings of his filth were barely audible for all the while the hound continued to snarl and bar its teeth with the same hatred. Snorting and screaming with anger, the wounded man tried to stand free, but this time the dog seized him by the leg piercing the skin with its muscular jaw. The fierce dog held on to the limb like bait for a shark as the fiend tried to free himself, striking violently upon the animal with his fists. But the harder the man hit the deeper the dog's teeth penetrated. With a thunderous grunt the man howled in both agony and anger as the dog continued to grapple and growl; its saliva dripped freely with the victim's blood.

"Sergeant, let go!" commanded a firm voice. Reluctantly, the dog released his grip whereupon the wounded attacker reached for the knife, only to find that it had been apprehended by the dog's master.

"Get up or I'll kill you!" was the instruction as the blood-stained knife slit a seam in the fog exposing the full gesture of the blade. The assailant leaned forward holding his leg in pain. "Get up!" the voice demanded again.

With one eye on the knife the defiant brute slid back and began to raise himself up using the wall for support. Pushing upward with his unwounded leg, he snorted and groaned until he was finally situated upright and leaned miserably against the wall. "When I get free, I'm gonna kill that dog," he snarled.

Panting happily, Sergeant sat beside Tully wagging his tail upon the sloppy ground. Mud splattered freely as the thumping unsettled the slippery muck. "Good boy, Sergeant!" he said petting the top of the hound's head, "very good dog!"

The rain trickled lightly and fell upon the mud leaving behind small impressions like sweet peas falling from the sky. The wet man and his wet dog stood guard until a sudden barrage of noise clamored into the alley. "Look! It must be him!" shouted the policeman. Several men following close behind, bearing rifles and un-holstered revolvers, trundled forward to view the captured man along with poor Mrs. Thurston who seemed to be equally curious for she pushed her way ahead of the rest. The hem of her white and pink gown was stained with mud, and the velvet shawl hung limply about her shoulders. The rain-sodden lady reached into her small satin purse and pulled out an embroidered handkerchief and blotted her damp face. Then, she put on her lace gloves, slipping them on as methodically as one would before a ride in the park. Water droplets fell from the tips of her lashes and sprinkled upon her rose colored cheeks. And like everyone standing in the misty morning, all eyes were upon the brute, but especially intent was Mrs. Thurston.

"Excuse me," she whispered to the policeman and pardoned herself to get a better view.

Minding his best manners, the officer stepped aside making way for her to see the devilish criminal. "Be careful there, Ma'm, he's mighty dangerous."

"Oh, thank you officer, I will," she said smiling agreeable. Like an actor on stage the arrogant attacker didn't mind the attention and licking his lips he grinned wickedly upon the sight of the unfortunate lady. Mrs. Thurston returned his smirk with an icy stare and without any provocation or annoyance once again dipped her hand into her silk-lined purse and carefully removed a small, but efficient derringer. "This is for killing the only gentleman in St. Louis," she calmly explained and with the accuracy of a marksman fired two deadly shots directly into the murderer's heart.

The bullets discharged with a deafening blast sending everyone within range shuddering with surprise however, it was the thud of the large brute soundly dropping to the ground that was most startling. Leaping to his feet, Sergeant began to bark fiercely at the man now strewn face down in the mud. The brown muck beneath the motionless body quickly liquefied as a rapid discharge of blood oozed from the bullet holes that had been blown straight through to his back. Mrs. Thurston stood statuesque as a puff of smoke whispered upward from the barrel; the small pistol still aimed in the direction of where the man once stood. For a moment it appeared that the woman may have been so startled by her act that by the very sight before her, she had become frozen with fear. But this was not the case, for when she watched a bystander put his fingers on the toppled man's pulse, feeling for life and then declare he was dead, she serenely surrendered her gun to the policeman and as methodically as she had put them on, she removed her gloves and tucked them back into her purse. The morning was a palette of misty grey and crimson red. A wet blanket of despair draped over the city and confusion, death, and turmoil collided with any hope.

"It's o.k. boy!" Tully said and eased the dog back. Sergeant turned his barks into muffled whines as he sat impatiently with a lack of understanding.

Mrs. Thurston wiped her damp hands on her wet dress and stared blankly. Her wrap was soaked with rain and lay heavily across her shoulders. "I must be a mess," she chimed and waited as those around her appeared to know what to do. She tugged upon the end of the shawl, and as she pulled, it crawled off her neck like a slimy reptile. She held it lengthwise and began to wring it out, as though it was a washrag, before slipping the shawl back on. Several men were calling for a wagon to cart the body away, while the police officers huddled together with several other important looking figures.

"Yes indeed, purely self-defense!" cried the small balding fellow as he walked away from the group and toward the dead man. He stopped and gave the lifeless body a small kick with his foot.

"No choice but to shoot, no choice at all," agreed the policeman shaking his head up and down. Using his authority as a law enforcement officer, he bent down beside the body and reached over to examine the smoky black holes that exposed the deadly wounds.

Mrs. Thurston turned to Tully who had chosen to remain silent. "What do they mean?" she asked.

"Why it's obvious, everyone here saw him," interrupted the policeman pointing to the lifeless body. "We all saw him reach into his pocket, no tellin' what he was going to do!" The policeman yanked a tattered cloth from his back pocket and mopped his wet face. "Yes, everyone here is a witness to the incident. It was self-defense." The officer looked down at the confused woman and gave her a crooked smile.

Mrs. Thurston pondered what she had just been told. Was this true? Is it possible that she was so intent on her own action that she had failed to notice the killer was reaching for a weapon? Did she fire in self-defense? But if that was true, why hadn't he used whatever it was that he possessed on the dog?

"Here, let me escort you back to your hotel," suggested the bald man walking up beside the heroine. "You have had quite a frightful encounter. No need staying around here," he remarked and gestured that they take leave.

Nodding approvingly, Mrs. Thurston acknowledged his proposal with a coquettish smile, dipped into her purse, and put back on her gloves; but not before shaking them lightly for they had become slightly smudged with gunpowder residue.

"Where is that man and his dog?" she solicited, while employing considerable effort to wriggle her fingers into the soggy gloves. However, the bald man either didn't know their whereabouts or hadn't heard the question for she was quickly swept away from the crime scene. As for the man and his hound, they had disappeared from anyone's recollection without leaving behind even a single paw print.

Chapter 52

Silent thoughts meandered like water downstream. Alex lay on his back and stared into the solemn darkness. He didn't dare move his feet for Timothy remained sleeping along the far end of the cot. The boy had awakened with a strange feeling, he couldn't pinpoint what it was, just a notion that something was lost. He turned on his side and shifted his foot. The cat stirred, stretched, repositioned its fat body, and deposited its tail upon his legs. Alex pet the long tail ever so gently however, it whipped up like a startled diamondback, reminding him that it didn't like to be disturbed. The boy shifted over and lay on his back again. A buttermilk cloud swayed past the moon like a pendulum and released a patchy beam into the dark room. He stared wide-eyed at the path of light and chanced upon a tiny object scurrying across the floor. It was too small to be a rodent, and besides, Timothy would have smelled it before it had a chance to escape. He looked down at the cat that lay contently. Resting his arm over his forehead, he brushed his yellow curls away from his brow. Again, that sensation of loss ascended, and he shuddered as if by a windless chill. "Yes," he thought, "something is gone forever." He reached down and stroked the cat, this time it batted him with his paw. "Timothy," he whispered. "Timothy," he whispered again.

The drowsy cat extended its legs, rose with the same energy as a water-logged sponge, and crept towards the head of the cot. "You're my good cat, Timothy, you're my good cat," Alex murmured. He slid closer to the wall and secured a larger space whereby the animal lay down beside the boy and dozed with contentment. As it breathed

Alex counted each breath, counted them slowly, very slowly; until perhaps he didn't remember falling asleep.

———

If ever there was a time for the tolling of the bells, it was now; one for the righteous and one for the evil. The death knells made no distinction between the rings; that was left for interpretation and consolation. All that knew the innocent claimed they pealed for his eternal repose, while others prayed the evil one would now receive true justice. Finding the harmony of these bells might dilute the dissonance in such disharmony, but such a keen ear was rare indeed.

———

The Planters' House Hotel had always been crowned with the most interesting throng of travelers however, today its restaurant was receiving all recognition not by virtue of its fine cuisine and hospitality, but rather because of the sudden notoriety it had just acquired. And although the kitchen was closed for service, uninformed patrons who had set out looking for a good meal, unknowingly happened upon the hustle and bustle of police activity. Forgoing their hunger pangs, which were willingly exchanged for morbid curiosity, the meddlesome paced deliberately up and down the street in hopes of securing a souvenir story to carry back home.

Like an artist's still life, Jack's half-eaten breakfast remained in the original position that he had left it, along with Will's plate, which occupied the center of the table; fork turned down with prongs resting in a broken circle of egg whites. The mortified cowboy wandered outside the restaurant unable to reconcile any of this morning's incidents except with rueful remorse. His chance meeting with Will was undeniably a brief encounter however, with as few hours as they had spent together, it felt as though he had known the dead man all his life. Will had poured out his life story, a narrative that was as sad as any man could recollect, and as much as Jack didn't want the responsibility, he had become the moral custodian of the tale and was obligated to see it through to the end. Only moments ago the doctor ordered Will taken to the morgue, coinciding with the news of his murderer's capture and demise. A fitting end? Jack wasn't sure. Did he make the right choice to stay behind with his friend while others hunted down the killer? He should have joined in the chase, although if he had then the murdered man would have died alone. Only earlier this morning he was kneeling beside the fallen victim barking orders for him to live, but if there was any fire left in his voice it hadn't been enough to reawaken the dwindling breath that had been stunted to the point of imminent mortality. All around a quarrelling pitch fueled discourse; people were running this way and that as a disorganized muddle of police activity amplified the commotion coming from the shoving and repositioning of toppled furniture. How could there have been so much irreverence? Where was Will's final moment of peace?

Jack removed his hat and slapped the brim against his leg. He fumbled with the tiny portrait of the dead man's wife that had fallen to the ground beside the victim and secured it in his pocket. Was he a thief for taking it?

The sheer stillness in his brain stopped with an abrupt slap on the back. "There was nothin' more that you could do except take the blade yourself," exclaimed the lieutenant coming up behind Jack. "I know how ya must feel, but that sure won't bring your friend back." Like an old crow on a clothesline, he positioned himself along the outer plank of the raised sidewalk. He teetered lightly with the nervousness of a drifting rowboat rocking to and fro. His long arms oscillated up and down, up and down, making any bystander who was watching him seasick. He was a clean shaven man, particularly well-groomed, and his symmetrically arranged hair was slicked back firmly against the sides unless provoked by the wind or the barber's comb.

The man's pity stung. Jack didn't reply and looked out into a lightly misted street. He didn't know when the fog had lifted. The wagon and mules were waiting in the same position, and he could hear the drip, drip, drip of water trickling down the sides of the canvas.

"Well, there isn't much more to do here," the officer mumbled as he kept up his irritating sway. The muttering of his conversation soon took a pause by the appearance of a large dog walking down the street. Every few yards it would stop to sniff its immediate area and when satisfied that there was nothing of particular interest it scurried along looking for interesting things.

"Why look at that!" shouted the swinging-armed lieutenant who had now altered his attention away from Jack by announcing the obvious arrival of the hound. "You're the talk of the town," the lawman exclaimed merrily and stopped swaying as he bent over to give Sergeant a pat on his head. The dog acknowledged the salutation by returning it with a zealous tail wagging. "Officially, I would say that you saved the day, I mean by cornering that culprit the way you did. Where's your owner?" he added, and as he praised the canine he glanced up the street. Sergeant panted happily as he listened to his commendations by the officer.

By now Jack had stepped back and was listening to the accolades as he examined this very unassuming hero. Several long seconds passed with neither he nor the officer saying anything, and now the awkward silence began to reek like old fish. "Well, I guess I'll see what's happening at the morgue," he said aloud, appearing to take an interest in the dog more than the cowboy.

"Morgue!" Jack winched at the word. The lieutenant gave the obedient hero another pat on his head and sashayed away. The miserable man stood alone on the sidewalk as the narrow figure of the lieutenant headed down the street. In the meantime, the large dog decided to take an investigative lap around the unattended wagon. The mules hinted some impatience for having been waiting all morning during the unfortunate incident; they restlessly shifted their feet as the dog sniffed around the spokes and wheels. Finding nothing of interest, it crouched under the wagon, but after a brief exploration, the four-legged detective exited the opposite side with the sudden urge to discontinue its ground level investigation. Assuming the position of a hunter, the dog stopped to sniff the damp air. With such grand intensity did the nostrils quiver as it lifted its wet black nose up and towards the sky. As though attached to an angler's pole, the nose led the hound along to the back of the wagon where he sprang up, leaning his front paws upon the side and peered into the wagon-bed with the same regard as though he were the owner. Suddenly, with the springy action inherent to a cat and not a dog of this one's large size, it bound into the back of the wagon and began to nose around the belongings.

Jack had not taken much of an interest in the dog for his morose state of being had dimmed all his senses. His lack of concern for his surroundings was in direct opposition to the dog who had now discovered the bag that contained the item it wanted. With the same intensity of a woman that is looking for her favorite scarf, the dog began to pillage. Things that had once been packed neatly were now strewn about the wagon, clothes that were clean now wore muddy dog prints, until finally the sound of a commotion that was undeniably the rummaging about of personal property alerted the bereaved cowboy.

"Get out of there" shouted Jack upon his first notion of the dog. However, as much as he was alarmed by the sight of the wagon, the dog was doubly startled by his presence and quickly leaped out of the wagon still clenching its prize in his mouth.

"Stop! Stop!" screamed Jack, and set out in chase. His quick sprint matched his determination to catch up with the thieving dog; but to his dismay, this was a most elusive opponent.

———

The dog was impervious to the pursuer's commands and ran as fast as its four legs could carry him, and although it was not used to the bricks and stones of the commercial city, it used its keen instincts to try and elude the chaser by taking a route that included a few sooty alleyways. Jack rounded the bend following the beast that had now lost its firm grip on the contentious item and from its mouth a long portion dragged freely along the ground.

With an energy that drives a stricken animal away from its foe, the dog charged the corner whereby the trailing object nearly tripped a starchy businessman wearing a very gloomy frown who happened to be waiting for the next scheduled omnibus. "Brute!" the elder man shouted and raised his cane in an expression of disapproval as the chase continued. At last it reached the end of the street where the hound's innate ability to locate its master at all times, a testimony to the canine's allegiance and highly developed senses, brought the dog to the finish line. A lone sycamore tree with mottled bark and limbs flaking in great irregularity grew next to the livery. It was the kind of tree that appeared to have outgrown its bark and like wearing a too-small sweater; it burst at the seams shedding its skin like a molting snake.

Panting excitedly, the canine thief dropped the pilfered property at Tully's feet as though it were prey from a great hunt. "What's this?" the older man asked and picked up the unraveled object. It lay limp across his hands, soggy in the middle where it had been secured in the dog's wet mouth and muddy on the lengths that had been towed through the streets. "Where'd you get this?" he asked again. The dog sat up at attention and wagged his tail emphatically. However, when it did not receive the positive commendation expected, he lifted his paw and hit the quilt.

"I ...can tell you.... where he got.... it!" called out a rather winded Jack, pausing every few syllables to catch his breath. Jack hustled over to the tree and like the dog, panted heavily however, unlike the dog; he held his side as if in pain.

"Cramp?" asked Tully.

"I'm not too used to running down the city streets after a dog," he replied rather sarcastically. He let his hand fall from his waist and inhaled slowly, hoping this would help the ache subside. Sergeant, having completed his task, took advantage of the cool shade and stretched out comfortably. His large narrow head lay upon the ground and the thin drooping ears were so long that they folded up on the edges like a pair of velvet wine coasters. It was the first time all day that the curved tail could relax. The noble beast took in a mountain of deep breaths.

Tully rolled up the quilt and handed it in the direction of Jack. "It seems that my dog has taken an interest in your blanket," he remarked. "He isn't usually a thief unless there's a good reason."

Jack retrieved the quilt and pondered the answer. The man had a point. It did take considerable effort on the dog's part to go to such great lengths.

Tully resumed his explanation, "Generally, a dog like Sergeant gets interested because of something they smell." Jack lifted the quilt to his nose and then shrugged his shoulders, allowing the gesture to speak. Tully continued to clarify, "Not usually anything we can smell, but something a hound like Sergeant can recognize."

Jack nodded in agreement acknowledging a well-known fact that they are tenacious trackers. It was now only logical that he ask a question. "Am I to assume that you and your dog knew Will Piccard, the owner of this quilt?" Although, how reasonable a question it may have been, under these circumstances, it was affirmed that Tully had only heard of the murdered man today.

Jack surveyed the situation and silently agreed that it was rather a curious act committed by the hound. Now in the midst of this unusual meeting he realized that he had not introduced himself. He offered his name. "My name's Jack, most know me as Pinto Jack," he said presenting his name.

"Tully, and this here's Sergeant," the scruffy man said offering his identity and that of the resting dog. "You and the dead man friends for long?" he asked. A kind of friendly attitude occupied the same space as this man. The old timer exuded a trustworthy countenance and although rugged on the exterior, he possessed a strangely polished quality that could only have come from a more refined and educated upbringing.

"No, met him only yesterday, but I got to know him pretty well in a short amount of time. Darn shame, his death that is. I just happened to know his kid. He hadn't seen the boy in years and I was going to take him this morning when the fog was too heavy and we had to turn on back. That's when the fool decided to be a hero and…" Jack stopped and realized he had been rambling and probably wasn't making too much sense.

"And?" asked Tully with some added interest, conceding that he was following the story quite easily.

"And, well, he put his business where it didn't belong and got knifed," the cowboy bluntly explained. Tully nodded with understanding, but offered nothing more to this one-way discussion. "You from around here?" Jack asked. His decision to change the subject was initiated by Tully's face showing no trace of curiosity to the rest of his narrative.

"No," the older man said in his usual unemotional and simplistic manner.

"Well, I'll be heading up into the countryside; I got to get Will's belongings to his boy. But I got plenty of room in the wagon for you and the dog; that is if you need a hitch that way."

"Can't say that we do," Tully replied. His pale grey eyes turned away and scanned the full breadth of the sycamore tree. Several large limbs stretched up into the sky like a pair of extended arms holding up an umbrella of leaves. "Sure is a beauty," he remarked and then with a short crisp whistle, he woke the sleeping dog. "Come on boy," he beckoned. As alert as a sentinel the hound scrambled to his feet and immediately began to follow Tully however, after only trailing a few paces behind, the noble canine stopped as though he had forgotten something. Raising his nose into the air, he let out a long and unexpected howl. Quite noticeably upset, the dog proceeded by tossing his head about and commencing on a barking attack that was directed towards Jack; who at this time had no idea what had initiated this hostile provocation. Both eyes were directed upon Sergeant while the cowboy backed up as the animal moved forward. It lunged toward the innocent man and with playful ferocity, snapped at the blanket that he now held up against his body like chain mail.

Jack hoped that the snarling dog would tire of its game since if it was not appeased soon he knew he would be forced to draw his gun.

"Sergeant, sit!" grumbled Tully and as quickly as the dog had leapt forward, so did it obey the command and sat obediently by his master's side.

"It's this quilt!" exclaimed Jack. "The dog hates this quilt."

"On the contrary," said Tully, "I believe he wants it."

———

Together the two wanderers and the cowboy walked back towards the wagon with Tully carrying the quilt. By way of the main street they arrived with little distractions and activity; which was most welcome. Several hours had passed since the horrific murder and although the air was abuzz with gossip and accounts of both killings, the restaurant and the hotel wanted to put the incident as far behind them as possible. To entice dubious and dissuasive travelers back to the establishment, a hand-written sign was posted out front promising free ice cream with every meal.

Tully tossed the quilt into the back of the wagon and the dog whimpered. "Funny," the graying man said, "I don't suppose there's something about that quilt you're not telling me?" Tully eyed Jack with a new suspicion without voicing exactly what he was proposing.

"If you believe it was used in a crime you got it all wrong, fellah! Here, take a look!" and with full indignation the cowboy reached over and spread it open like a picnic blanket. "See, not a trace of blood!"

"Mind if I take it out into the light?" Tully asked. He pulled the blanket from the back of the wagon, but as soon as he hung it over the wagon's side-rails, Sergeant sauntered over and rubbed his nose playfully against it as though it was another dog. The sunlight which had remained elusive for most of the morning now shined gloriously, exposing the elegant colors and patterns that accentuated the grandeur of the quilt. "Looks like it says something, right here," said Tully and read the name aloud. "Lexy Piccard," he affirmed. Then in an almost inaudible utter he read another name, "Dowling..." but this time his voice drifted off as though he was unsure of what he read. Tully dropped the edge of the quilt. "Just who does this belong to?" he asked with guarded interest.

"Will, Will Piccard," Jack repeated. But after this blunt reply he momentarily interrupted himself, for if he wished to be explicitly correct then he must change his answer. "No, to be precise, it's my quilt, but in the true sense of who the original owner is, well, it's not really me. Actually, it belongs to the dead man's son, Alex, Alex Forester."

A subtle smile fell upon Tully's face, and he grinned with an air of supreme understanding. He leaned over and laughed lightly while petting the dog. Sergeant wagged his tail as though taking part in his master's realization. Finally the bitter day was gradually becoming restored. The wanderer spoke and the words glided out of his mouth as though he was offering a blessing. "Alex Forester," he whispered, "Alex Forester."

No matter how determined we are to solely travel by way of passages deemed secluded and remote, it seems that our fates are destined to converge somewhere along the journey and eventually in the near future; we will intertwine. Perhaps it is because the earth is round, for while its circumference begins at a point in space, it also too shall terminate at that very same place.

The dialogue between the two men continued as the tired dog found a bit of respite beneath the wagon. The history of Will was roused again and as Tully became more informed the events became littered with remarkable coincidences. Sergeant's tail thumped up and down every time the name Alex was mentioned and with each landing of the curled appendage, shards of dry earth were sent airborne and sprayed out from beneath the wagon like a miniature sandstorm. Jack leaned his elbow against the splintered side-board as he illustrated the circumstances of his encounter with Alex. He related how he had acquired the boy's quilt, how it had been sewn by the unfortunate boy's mother, Libby Dowling, and how the fate of the woman turned even more tragic when the child was taken from them.

The appearance of the quilt's cryptically-sewn message had given a new role to the naturally modest man, and he was prepared to relieve Pinto Jack from the burden of driving the dead father's articles back to Alex. So invested was he in helping, that the very private traveler was prepared to divulge a bit about himself, if it was regarded as necessary to set his plan in action. Tully's situation was no common occurrence and though his impulse was to remain anonymous, he could not overlook this circumstantial evidence. All indications pointed towards the fact that the boy he had nicknamed, "Little Minute", most likely was his very own flesh and blood. Marcus Tullius Cambridge, a name this man had denounced; it was a bitter mouthful he cringed at with every syllable. And although he had surrendered the surname of Cambridge for another of unassuming obscurity, today it was miraculously resurrected under the guise of Dowling, his mother's maiden name, the surname of Alex's mother. He had chosen the moniker Tully, abandoning Marcus after his service in the Texas Rangers, but now his secluded journey was becoming densely overpopulated.

Tully cautiously mulled this over. The bond between him and the boy had already been galvanized for so many sunrises and sunsets. They shared a unique alliance that scarcely any other soul would recognize. Each was a consoler, a listener, and a receiver; each could hear the wind when there was none blowing, summon the horse when it was sleeping, and with a whisper comfort the frightened dog. He and Alex were deeply perceptive and Tully needed no prompting to understand that this unnatural talent was not merely a twist of fate, but a relationship that retained its connection to the past, present, and future.

With that reflection Tully turned to Jack; he did so with an exclamation of relief. This was a powerful pause in the man's life and he imagined himself returning back to the Forester's home, to the bleak lodging, the brown and tawny land, and the quiet boy.

It was soon agreed upon by both parties, the dog having no say, that the cowboy would remain in St. Louis in order to tend to the details of Will's final resting place for neither wanted the young father to be buried in the pauper's graveyard. "What are you going to tell Alex?" Jack asked, after having discovered this most remarkable addition to the saga.

He expected that he would be plied with an astute and judicious disclosure to his question; however the elder man only offered a stony glare and simple reply, "I'll tell him the truth."

In front of the restaurant's ornate entranceway several hungry patrons loitered about chattering idle incidentals before entering the establishment that was now serving midday meals. With very little clean up the restaurant was fully operational, and except for the maître d' who had set out for home to calm his shattered nerves, the gas-lamps were lit and the pace of the day was remarkably normal. There was no longer any reason for the police to patrol about the area seeing that their routine investigation was complete and the final report was ascertained as purely an act of indiscriminate murder. Enjoying a bit of celebrity status, the small band of officers reluctantly dispersed and scattered themselves about the narrow streets and open spaces of the city. Sergeant dragged his nose along the ground looking for morsels of molasses and oats that perchance dropped out of the greedy mules' mouths that Tully was feeding them as he prepared for the journey.

The smooth-faced young man and the scruffy elder both cared about the welfare of the unassuming boy, and when it was time for each to take leave there was a flicker of remorse and uncertainty. Like a pesky fly at a picnic, its appearance was quite unwelcome and decidedly needed to be eliminated. With that in mind the two men kept their small talk positive and brief. Although the quilt had dominated most of the morning, it was now folded and packed back into the bag. Neither questioned whether it should be returned to Alex, even though he had given it away as a gift, for it was determined that its worth as a family heirloom far outweighed any practical reason to leave it behind.

Sergeant jumped into the back of the wagon and up towards the front where Tully was now perched. The dog, not accustomed to riding, showed his glee with an abundance of tail wagging and excited barking. In response, the mules, not used to having a passenger with four legs, showed their dissatisfaction by pulling their ears back and in disharmony brayed like a rusty old saw across a wet log. "Sergeant, lay down!" Tully commanded and then with a gentle but firm, "Gidup" the boisterous animals followed his lead. Moving like a chorus line they turned in unison toward the left until they were parallel with the open street. Tully let up on the reins. The large mules methodically plodded and as they pulled the wobbly-wheeled wagon it rattled back and forth, and as the mules continued to keep a steady pace the harness they wore jingled against their bony backs. Tully kept his eyes lowered and pulled his hat low over his brow. The frequent rattle and jingle of the wagon quieted the restless dog and like a lullaby courted it off to sleep. In a few minutes the old wagon passed the livery where Jack returned to look in on Cally, but Tully didn't turn around so he never knew that the cowboy was standing and watching as he and the dog rolled towards the outskirts of the city, heading on their way to the Forester home.

———

For some there was a certain romance attached to traveling, especially for those who were coming west for the very first time. The sight of freighted flatboats piled high with grain, paddle-boats with their enormous wheels, and new steam-wheelers chugging up and down the Missouri River reinforced America's ingenuity and highlighted the possibility of exploration and opportunity. For the financially advantaged it linked the prospect of their endeavors becoming even more lucrative, and for those who dreamed of independence it proved they had traveled to the right place. The time was ripe for those who worked hard and had the courage to pursue. Some came from the Appalachians and traversed the Ozark highlands in the southern region looking for new settlements. However unlike those who were thinking of the future, Tully was contemplating his past as the wagon trundled along the rocky pass. He was a man who long ago had relinquished his place with the upper crust, a life that allotted him financial benefits. Living what many called "the good life" did not come without a caveat and although having high-powered connections furnished him a physically comfortable existence, it was laden with rules created by pretentious society who are not driven by the heart, but rather by purse strings.

The mules moved slowly and with their lumbering steps they rocked the shaky wagon with an even but bumpy tempo. The tawny man slacked up on the reins and wiped his sweaty palms on his handkerchief. "Funny," he thought. "Me having kept these monogrammed handkerchiefs." He glanced at the ornate C that took up a corner of the cloth. It was now barely recognizable for the once hand-stitched family emblem was worn away from years of use. He knew perfectly well why they had not been discarded. He was a proponent of austerity and practicality; he never threw away things that might be useful. He laughed at this irony; he was still carrying around that "C". Sergeant lay on his side and stretched his long legs forward, but finding little room to extend their full complement, he curled them at each independent joint like greased hinges. The dog was a faithful companion and like its master, savored independence. Tully's decision to live by the rules of nature, a way of life that had been effortless to conform to, was presently under attack by a foe named destiny. Destiny, neither man nor woman; silently stealth, it circles both the day and the night; infiltrating without a knock or a ring, for no one is exempt from delivery, and then without notice you blindly fall, surrendering to the host.

It was routine for Tully to take mental notes during long walks and rambles. The hollow sounds in the forest warned of blustery winds, bats swarming back to their hiding places cautioned bad weather. When the temperature grew hot and dry the spiders would spin long silky webs, and if the flowers tucked in their petals like a folded fan, it would rain. Tully glanced up to the west; the mist had cleared and he was able to read the clouds. No longer was it the same dreary grey morning. Splinters of pale blue and white glazed the sky; a light stream of wind stretched the clouds like strands of spun sugar transforming this into a perfectly good day to travel.

Chapter 53

B etty pitched back in the old rocker. It creaked weakly against the tired wooden planks of the front porch. The ritual of shelling peas was the art of dissection. This was a chore she could perform blindfolded; pinch the pod wall, disengage the fibrous thread, pull down, and rake the peas into the bowl. A handful of pea pods rolled safely to the middle of her lap. Beside her chair and wedged against the stubby wooden bucket set aside for the discarded hulls was a yellowing bowl. It was lined with plump sugar peas that hid the scars the porcelain bore from years of mishandling. Betty wiggled her tired fingers and laughed silently thinking about how many times she had tried to get Randle to help her, but he always said it was "woman's work". He had a knack of dividing the chores into two categories, those for men and those for women. It was times such as these when she really missed him.

This was a damp afternoon with the merging of dark clouds into blue skies; a sure bet the day would end in a torrent of rain. It was a slow process, removing the peas. Betty rocked longing for a change. Maybe she'd go visit Belle Tarson, not that they were good friends, but it gave her a destination to think about. California was supposed to be nice. No, not until that railroad was built would she think about a distance of such magnitude. Timothy scouted around the chair looking for stray peas that may have bounced out of the bowl when they were dropped too roughly. Being familiar with the cook's ritual, he knew that there were some escapees that he could find and bat about. With restless eyes he stalked the bowl, crouched low in an attack position and remained very still except for the shifting of his pupils. But no sooner had he set his sights upon a rogue pea did Betty promptly shoo him away with her apron string. "Get on away from here, you pesky cat!" she cried. But instead of obeying, the playful feline simply turned her threat into a game and leaped forward trying to grasp the flaying tie. "Come a little closer and you'll find ya tail flattened," she warned and with a gentle shove pushed the cat away from the rockers. With a spirited movement, he scampered down the steps and headed in the direction of a pair of cranky hens. The lively flickering of the red wattle and lobes baited his attention as they pecked about the barnyard scratching for grubs.

"Ya better be careful, Timothy!" Alex warned, and he stopped for a moment to watch the exchange between feline and fowl; but scarcely had he paused, when he heard Betty call out.

"Got somethin' for ya, Alex!" She was waving a small package wrapped in brown paper that she had placed under the rocker. It had been delivered by Mr. Beasley, who had picked up the parcel and a few letters when he was in town. Betty set the remaining pods into the bowl, laying them on top of the shelled peas. She had tired of this chore and was pleased to have a distraction. "All the way from Baltimore!" she exclaimed, handing him the package as he wearily dragged himself up the steps.

"Thanks," he said in a tone that betrayed his fatigue and took a seat on the porch landing, keeping one eye out towards the barn-yard. The fussy hens were still pecking about, but now there was no sign of Timothy. "That doesn't mean he ain't' stalking them," Alex thought. "It just means he's too smart to be seen." The boy stretched his legs over the last two steps noticing that his ankles were sticking further out of the pant legs than he remembered.

Betty must have noticed too for she remarked, "Looks like you better let me tailor your pants so I can add another inch round the bottom. You're growin' faster than I can keep up with the sewin'!" A thin exasperation sliced through her words, but her eyes were glint-ing with approval.

Alex pulled his knees back towards his body and rubbed his legs above his ankles as though having just realized he was taller.

"Remember how Randle would measure you up against the hay-loft ladder? Why he'd count how tall ya were by the rungs. When you first came, you weren't even four rungs high," Betty mused.

Alex rested his head on his knees. A sultry breeze collected dust and tossed it freely. He peered down at his boots and flicked the dirt that had settled between the cracks in the leather. It was always dusty unless it rained, and then it was muddy. Betty's chair creaked as it rocked back upon a loose plank. He listened as she wheezed slightly. He didn't remember her breathing that way when he was little, and he wondered when she had developed this annoying habit. It wasn't always noticeable, only certain times like when she was concentrating or thinking. He twisted his head around to see what she was doing. The bowl was now balanced on her lap, and she was shelling peas again. "When are you goin' to open the package?" Placing emphasis on the immediacy of the task, her voice created a curious strain.

Alex turned away. A descending trill from a nearby branch delivered several energetic bars of a familiar twitter, and he listened as if understanding the wren's language. He picked up the rumpled package he had set down next to him with casual curiosity. It was wrapped with far too much twine for its size and had the markings of an amateur packer. "Grace," he thought and smiled to himself.

"There won't be any peas for supper unless I get these shelled," grumped Betty. "But you won't mind since you don't like them any-ways," she added commenting on Alex's lack of enthusiasm for the vegetable.

"I like 'em okay." he replied. It wasn't that he didn't like them; he just didn't want the big helping she expected him to eat. Every now and again he was tempted to drop a handful on the floor for Timothy, but he knew the cat would merely play with his mishap and then desert them about the floor only to be discovered in a corner, under the table, or splat against the sole of a boot by the cook. Now if Timothy was a dog, the greedy beast would surely have come to his rescue by licking them up and gladly beg for more.

Betty rocked silently; she lowered her eyes upon her lap, furnishing the illusion that she was asleep. Her glasses balanced on the center of her nose, slipping gradually downward and every few minutes she would have to nudge them back up the bridge, readjusting their position before they began their coast downward again. She gathered up the pods and then one-by-one dropped them back on her lap as she counted aloud, twenty-two; there were twenty-two more pods and another pile waiting in the kitchen. As soon as she was finished with this heap, she promised herself a nice glass of sweet tea. By now Betty had forgotten about the package and was delighting over her reward. She was going to add a sprig of peppermint; in fact, she was going to clip a few leaves from the herb garden just as soon as she finished shelling; then she'd make the tea. The graying woman passed her days with simple rewards; she would say to herself, "When I finish making the soap, when I darn all the socks, or when I mold five more candles…" after which she would promise herself some sort of prize; something sweet or sticky to eat, or time stolen away from her chores to flip through the pages of *Godey Lady's Book*. However, the treat she looked forward to the most was spending an afternoon with the crooked Mr. Beasley. It was simply a matter-of-fact that she found herself missing a mature male's companionship, and plainly speaking, he was the only bachelor around.

Alex fussed with the parcel, tugging on the twine, however as soon as he pulled on one loose end, expecting it to obediently unravel, the opposing line would tighten, pinching the brown paper.

"Still haven't got that open?" asked Betty liberating the greens from her lap and tossing them into the bowl on the floor. All his rustling was like a mouse in the cupboard. "Go on in and git the paring knife," she commanded sourly.

Alex did as he was told and returned with a short, but notably sharp knife. In an instant she hooked the string around the blade and slit the twine. Betty dropped the knife into the bucket and handed the small parcel back. Its broken threads hung limply like a dead daddy long-legs. Slowly, the paper came alive, unfolding itself like petals of a morning glory, and then when it had lost its momentum, it settled with the repose of a burgeoning water lily. Alex poked around, probing for more valuable contents, but found only more paper. As though removing the inner leaves from a head of cabbage, he systematically peeled back the crumpled paper, revealing in its core a folded parchment letter and a small object secured by a swatch of silk. Alex laid the silky bundle next to him and opened the note.

Dear Alex,

Here is the ring Miss Henshaw is making me return. It isn't that I don't like it; it's on account that she is making me give it back. I hope someday it brings you good luck.

Your friend forever,
Grace Tarson

"What is it?" exclaimed Betty with overtures of curiosity mixed with a tinge of impatience. She had resumed her work and commenced to snap the pods with a sort of heroic energy.

Alex folded the note back along its creases and removed the ring from the small piece of cloth. "It's a ring," he answered bluntly. "Just this ring I had fer a long time." He twisted around so he could show her, lifting it up in the air.

"Ring?" Betty questioned taking a more conserted interest. "What kind of a ring?" The peas rolled about in the bowl as she shifted forward in her chair and inadvertently pushed the dish with her foot.

"I think it's called a signal ring," he said and stood up to hand both the letter and the ring to the woman. Betty removed her glasses and wiped them clean with her apron before putting them back on to examine the parcel's contents.

"Signet, it's a signet ring," she muttered, dropping it onto her lap, and then read the note. When she was finished she handed it back to him. "So, where did you find this ring?" she asked in a tone that was reserved for matters of more importance.

"I had it ever since I came here. It was in my bag all this time." Alex's answer dropped off at the end of the sentence. He wasn't really sure why all the questions, the ring was just that, a ring, and now that it was back in his possession he was going to return it to the bag under his cot.

Betty rolled it over her wrinkled palm that looked like a fallen autumn leaf and then slipped the ring on her index finger and held it up to appraise. The ring appeared large and clumsy. "C?" she mused curiously.

Alex shrugged his shoulders.

Although the elder woman was keenly interested, she was quite perplexed by the whole matter however, nothing about this peculiar boy surprised her. "Perhaps we should put it somewhere safe, that is until you're old enough to wear it," she said, slipping it off. Even though it did not belong to her, the decision of what to do with it was one that she decided was hers to make. She continued, "Take it inside and set it on the shelf in the living room; you know, the one with all the cups and saucers."

Alex shook his head affirming he understood. He didn't see how the ring could possibly fit in with a display of teacups and china ornaments, but being the good boy that he was, he would obey.

"C?" he could hear Betty carelessly talking to herself as he moved away and hesitated between the two doors.

———

The shelf used to be too high for him to see over, but now he could clearly make out its contents. This was the "no touching" shelf, the shelf that even Randle never fussed with. "If ya know what's good fer ya, you'll keep away from this shelf," he was warned. Once he saw Timothy sitting underneath it, not doing anything, just sitting. But the mere sight of the cat near the shelf sent Betty lickety-split out with the broom and chased that poor feline out into the barnyard, all the while threatening him with the broom like it was a stick and he was the ball. After that, Timothy didn't go back into the living room for a full month.

Alex stared. There was a set of eight matching cups and saucers decorated with green ivy and gold filigree trim; the kind that are only used if important and fancy company comes over, like Belle Tarson. They were all lined up, a hairpin apart from one another, looking dangerously fragile. Directly behind, one could see they were also in the company of two china figurines; a posed ballerina dancing in a peach-colored tutu with gold tipped toe-shoes and a yippy looking little dog with a sharp pointy nose lying on a silver frosted pillow. Alex frowned disapprovingly at the shelf. It was already quite full, but as much as he wanted to just keep the ring in his pocket, he pictured Betty's sour expression and hastily reached over and set it down beside the ballerina. No sooner had he moved his hand away, then did the boy plainly think it would be safer next to the mean little dog. He lingered for a moment and suddenly disproved of this idea since this placement would be too close to the edge of the shelf, and besides, the mean little dog's head and nose was tossed upward and certainly couldn't guard anything with that haughty attitude.

"Alex, what are ya doing in there so long?" cranked Betty, claiming his attention. The boy jumped with fright, for the tone of her voice was so startling that he suddenly wondered if the mere presence in the same room with these items had alerted something inside her, signaling that he had over stayed his welcome.

"Nothin!" he called back and with a little shove of his finger pushed the ring a bit closer to the ballerina and hurried away.

In contrast to the city, Tully found the natural countryside a most welcome rendezvous. At first the mules took a slow flat meander, but soon there was a noticeable lively change in their pace as the road narrowed and the landscape widened exposing dark soil, green vegetation, and untamed streams. The richness of the surrounding land remained true to the character of the region; this was where homes abut with mountains, where the air was perfumed by wildflowers, clover grew freely along the embankments, and slumber came before the evening stars. No words were needed; just images and smells and sounds created this poetry.

The mules pulled the wagon with a holiday stride. Sergeant placed himself alongside of Tully and sat as though he was a commissioned scout. As far as the eye could travel the palette used to paint the land was green; a moist wet green of fields in the dewy morning or fields after a rain in the late afternoon. Tully scanned the sky and hoped that his earlier observations were correct. According to the sun and the clouds, they should be arriving at least a few hours before the weather could turn against them.

The afternoon sun was falling, shedding magnificent hues of deep purple and sharp blue shadows. Rattling and jingling, the wagon rolled along; the wheels clattered as they twisted up and around the country road. Betty pulled the gingham curtain aside when she heard the distant rumbling and called out, "We got company," even before she could see what was rambling down the road. Lost behind its own dust cloud, it took several minutes before the travelers were close enough for her to take an accurate reading. "Looks like a dog and an old tramp," she exclaimed, her nose pressed hard against the glass. She took off her spectacles and squinted to get a better perspective. Then, she picked up the hem of her apron and wiped the window with a circular motion, cleaning it as though it were a hand mirror. "Pair of horses pullin'....," but suddenly, she stopped mid-sentence and clarified the error. "No, pair of mules, good lookin' plow mules pullin' a wagon. Mighty sad lookin' wagon, though!" she proclaimed with a new found exuberance in her voice.

Alex touched her arm lightly and peered out. "Wonder who it can be?" she inquired as the wagon came to a halt directly in front of their house. It was driven by a grey man with a short scruffy beard wearing a leather hat that obscured his face from the onlookers. Alex stepped back with a sigh of gladness. "What do you make of them?" Betty asked, while she continued to spy at the newcomer. The driver unmistakably noticed the curious occupant peering out between the cotton panels because he tipped his hat precisely in her direction.

"Good heavens!" she muttered, and quickly the woman turned away from the window and drew the curtain partially closed; obscuring what was left of the day's sunlight.

Tully set the reins down on the bench and stretched. His body arched like a cat after a long nap. The mules flicked their ears as though interpreting new and unfamiliar sounds. Without hesitation the driver stepped down and whistled lightly to the dog. As soon as he heard his call, Sergeant scrambled to his feet and lumbered out, nearly tripping over his own four paws. His tail wagged wildly, gliding his nose against the ground in search of anything of interest. He was a curious sight, hobbling around the wagon, for his joints were stiff and legs wobbly from being cooped up so long.

"Stay," commanded Tully, as he approached the old porch. Leaving the dog sitting at attention to wait at the bottom of the landing, the man sprang with light strides as he directed his steps up and onto each weathered plank with the same fortitude as a man half his age. However, he had hardly pressed his knuckles to the door when it flung open and standing before him was Alex Forester.

"I knew you'd come back! I knew it!" the boy cried and making a brave attempt to subdue his exuberance, he gave way to his emotions which he was unable to suppress. Tears of happiness forced their way down his cheeks, but he didn't muster the courage to give the man a hug.

"Little minute," the elder announced and drew the child toward him with his subdued smile. Alex looked up and without hesitation shook free any timidity he may have harbored and grabbed the man around his waist.

"I knew you'd never really leave!" he whispered. But poor Sergeant, it was barely more than he could do to contain himself. His tail thumped almost as hard as his heart, and he squirmed impatiently awaiting the command to "at ease".

"Look who's waiting for you," Tully said, and turned the boy in the direction of the dog.

"Sergeant!" squealed Alex. "Come here, boy!" Yet, as though nailed to the ground, the poor animal would not leave his post.

"Okay, boy," Tully conceded, and as though opening a flood gate, the hound bounded forth releasing such a high-spirited bark that it discharged Betty, who was listening discreetly from behind the open door, out onto the open porch. A more serious appearance she could not have made for she aimed Randle's old shotgun right in front of her. But as soon as she saw Alex in a full embrace with the dog, she lowered the weapon, resting it up and against her thigh.

Tully eyed the gun first, and then removed his hat.

"Alex," cried the lady, "it is clear that you are the one who has company," and casting a cautious smile towards the scruffy man, extended her hand, while keeping the other fixed firmly on the barrel of the shotgun.

"Don't mean to intrude," explained Tully, shaking her hand. He noticed that she had a good firm handshake, the kind of grip that was accustomed to doing manual work. "But, I have some news that is of importance to the boy," he added. His eyes addressed the woman with earnestness.

"This boy?" she questioned, and released her skepticism. "Now what could you have for Alex?"

Alex was just as surprised by these words and drawing himself away from the dog was silently drafted into the conversation around him.

Betty placed her free hand on top of Alex's shoulder, "This boy," she repeated, but not as a question, but rather a declaration of understanding.

"Yes, Ma'm; may I come in?" Tully asked. But when he saw that her face showed worried uncertainty, he added, "I assure you, I have only good intentions."

Betty was at first taken aback, for although he looked like a vagabond, his command of the language and good manners surpassed many folks claiming to be born into higher social standings. But even more convincing was the sincerity in his voice, a stern yet persuasive tone that had an almost calming effect on her.

"It's true, Betty," Alex piped in. "Tully is my friend."

Betty tossed a glance from the man, to the dog, to the child, and forming an opinion, upon which she had nothing more to go on except blind faith, she set the gun behind the door and stepped aside.

"Sergeant, outside!" Tully ordered and leaving the dog behind, followed the woman. Reluctantly, the hound turned and scampered away, but not too far for it turned back, parked itself halfway across the porch, all the while keeping its head facing inside the house and its eyes resting upon his master until the man was out of his sight.

———

Tully declined the offer of a chair and leaned casually against the wall, easing slightly forward in a relaxed stance. He watched as the woman fumbled awkwardly with some loose knitting that was occupying Randle's favorite chair, and decidedly placing it in a wicker basket, she sat down. Alex walked about idly until Betty pushed aside the tidy hassock that was stationed before her and gestured for him to sit. Immediately he complied, and as though perched upon a toad stool, for the seat was as bulbous as a bloated mushroom, he pitched his elbows on his knees, rested his chin in his hands, and waited. There was a slow wash of peace that now settled over this room that he had so often spent time in, yet never had felt before. But amid all this tranquility, a ripple of suspense rolled about like an undercurrent, irking his curiosity. He had never known Tully to be so approachable towards others and wondered what matter of such importance would have drawn this reclusive man out.

"So, Mr. Tully," Betty was the first to speak.

"Tully, just Tully," he said correcting her.

"Well, Tully, what have ya got that's so important to Alex?" she asked.

Tully said nothing, but simply pulled a small object from out of his pocket and walked across the room. He bent down beside the boy. "Here," he said and handed a tiny photograph over to him.

Alex cradled the object in his hand and stared hard. At first there didn't seem to be any recognition, no signs of identification as to who the photograph of the woman was. But within a few seconds a glimmer of remembrance surfaced. "The eyes," he said. He turned to Tully for some kind of acknowledgement, but received nothing that would confirm his instincts. His thoughts passed silently across the picture again and then back towards Tully, but this time he stared deeply into the man's eyes as though he were walking into his soul. Clutching the photograph, Alex got up and went to the window. He strained for the last light of day, but the sun was unforgiving, and it had grown dark.

"Betty, can you light the big lantern?" he asked.

"Alex, you know we can't waste no oil," she humphed. "What's the matter with the one we got lit?" she wondered and pointed to the smaller lantern on the table. There was a film of disgust coating her voice, and when she spoke her mouth turned downward with sheer disapproval.

"Please, Betty," he pleaded and with his petition so soft and so divine, she immediately followed his request as though she had been heavenly commanded.

The light slowly feathered up from the glass bulb and as she turned the little wheel it illuminated the room casting a spiritual glow. Alex brought the photograph over to the light and confronted it with a sad recollection. He moved it away from the lantern and tried to give Tully back the small framed picture, but the man refused to accept. "I know these eyes," Alex said, his hand still out stretched and the object taking up most of his palm balanced naturally. "I've seen them lots of times." He drew his hand back and then stared directly up at Tully. "And you," he whispered, "why you've got the same eyes," he confessed in a state of awe.

Tully put his hands in his pocket and shifted his weight casually to the other foot. "And so do you, Alex," he remarked.

Alex looked deeply at the picture. "Mom!" he proclaimed. "It's my Mom." And then rotating the wheel on the larger lantern until the flame was extinguished, he turned to Betty. "I don't need it no more," he explained to the woman, "I don't need the light."

"Well I do!" demanded Betty and as though warned by the shrill of a policeman's whistle, her suspicion to distrust this man was suddenly provoked. "Let me see that!" she said; and put out her hand with the same emphatic gesture of having one's palm read.

Urged on by her prickly voice, Alex attended to the woman and dropped the small heirloom into her rugged palm. She pulled herself up by the arms of the chair and shuffled back to the big lantern, placed the small photo on the table and struck the flint. Her usual steady hand quivered slightly as she relit the smoldering wick. A tiny flame floundered, and as the suspicious doubter coerced the little wheel round, a glow of mad excitement extended out towards the four corners of the room. Alex watched the woman's face. She bent towards the picture and glared. She reached into her apron pocket and put on her spectacles. Her lips pursed together as she tipped the frame to the bulb; the glow showered the lovely picture which seemed to confuse her. "Do ya' mean to tell me that the woman in this picture is Alex's mother?" she asked. However, without any verbal confirmation, the similarity was undeniable. Betty returned her glasses to her pocket and lowered the flame to a dull flicker. Her face was pocked with shadows reflecting off the dwindling light.

Alex remained silent. Tully leaned casually against the wall. Betty handed the photo back to the boy. She glanced at both and shook her head and took a long pause. "Come now," Betty remarked, "how did you come about getting this?" Her voice, suspicious and accusatory, demanded a defensive rebuttal from the scruffy man. "After all," she asked raising her voice as she pointed vehemently at the photo, "how do I know you didn't steal this?" She glared at the rugged man with an anxious eye, but reading his expression noticed he did not appear a bit insulted or disturbed by the accusation.

"Why would I?" Tully asked plainly.

Betty was confounded, and she had to agree that there was really no good reason for the man to have stolen the picture. But what remained an enigma was how it came to be in his possession, and of course, what did this now mean for Alex? She had been told upon receipt of the boy that his mother was on her deathbed, and the father, well he had been unfit to care for him. Could this man be the father reclaiming the boy? No, impossible, he was far too old. Betty's thoughts were interrupted by a small tug on her apron. "Can I have it back now?" Alex asked. His hand outstretched as though wishing to receive the holy sacrament.

Betty turned with a start. "Of course, Alex, here you are." She smiled and handed the boy back the photograph.

Tully waited; he knew that he was now going to have to explain the rest of the story, the sad and true story, but hated formality. He glanced around the room with restless curiosity and noticed the "unapproachable" shelf hanging on the wall, caddy-corner to where he was leaning. He meandered over to it and with certain idle watchfulness took a half-interest. With his back towards the others he perused the items that were arranged so carefully. There was a certain amount of uncomfortable stillness mingling about the room. Alex turned and with guarded caution watched Tully. He shuddered at the thought of imminent reprisals which may occur if Tully accidentally mishandled one of the precious items. He glanced back at Betty, but she seemed detached from the goings-on. Tully removed his hands from his pockets and picked up the signet ring. He turned it over in his hand before placing it back on the shelf where he found it.

"I know who you are!" Betty suddenly announced. Her voice dispensed an eagerness, and she began thumping her foot up and down as she spoke. "You're that hermit that lives up in that soddy. Why Randle believed the stories that you were there; but since nobody ever saw ya, I just figured he was as big a fool as the rest." She shook her head and laughed mockingly at herself. "I'm right, ain't I?" she goaded, directing her probe at Tully.

If her words were to act as a signal for acknowledgement, they only initiated a smile and nod from the unprovoked man. Alex shrugged his shoulders not understanding why all the fuss. Betty smacked her lips with satisfaction and laughed heartily.

"It's late," Tully quietly said.

"But we've only touched the surface!" Betty exclaimed wishing to continue. There was urgency in her voice. This was the first time in so many years that something of interest had happened. Like leaving off in a book, she wished for the chapter to continue. Nevertheless, there was nothing more that Tully was going to do that evening.

"I'm going to leave the mules and wagon, everything," he declared, "all here with Alex." Then he turned to the boy, "That's okay with you, isn't it?"

Alex nodded approvingly.

"Well then, I better be getting along," he announced. "Alex, need help with them mules?"

Alex shook his head, no.

This was all the man needed. With a slight nod of approval he replied, "I'll be back."

Betty remained frozen as she watched Alex happily trail behind this very unusual man. She wasn't really sure what to make of all this, but it had become clearly evident that this Tully was no longer going to divulge any more of the tale. But as far as she was concerned, wherever the story led, there were two more mules heading into the barn than she had before; plus a wagon. "This will make Mr. Beasley very happy," she thought, "very happy."

As soon as Tully had departed there was much to think about. Alex listened to Betty flutter around her bedroom before finally seeing the light under her door extinguish, which was accompanied by a long deep sigh. He remained vigilant, but heard nothing more except an occasional creak as the old house stretched. The excitement he was supposed to put aside only made the boy too restless to sleep. He tried rolling over, refolding his blanket, and flipping onto his back; but as hard as he tried he just wasn't able to put his mind at rest and lay awake much of the night waiting for daybreak.

———

Perhaps it was only Alex that noticed the glow in the eastern sky. Changing colors and hues, it spread downward like spilled paint; first gold, then orange, and finally pink. It rinsed over the farm-yard and spread into the open door of the barn where it gradually

crawled and crept and stopped. Timothy was laying across the doorway on top of a blanket of sunlight and flatly refusing to awaken
unless provoked. Alex approached and walked softly towards the
lazy cat that acknowledged his presence with a flicker of its tail. He
ignored the annoyed feline and deliberately walked along the fresh
tracks that led to a rather large obstruction, far too big to be housed
inside the barn. He came up alongside of his new acquisition and
eyed it with fascination; not because it was so odd looking with its
patched canvas and weather-beaten planking of mismatched wood,
but because it belonged to him. He knew that Tully was a man of
few words; but even in the light of day the man's statement still
didn't make sense. "The mules, the wagon, and everything in it are
yours."

The boy circled the wagon as though it was the first time he had
ever seen one, and when he had rounded it twice he pulled himself
up and climbed in. He remained standing while he looked about
the barnyard as though surveying the property; he twisted left, then
right, before sitting down and trying the spring-seat out for size. He
planted his feet squarely on the footrest and leaned forward. One of
the floorboards was buckled, so he traced his foot along the wood
slats that had been pieced together in order to fill in previously broken sections and gaps. He picked up a pair of pretend reins and
motioned for the invisible mules to "giddyup". For a few innocent
moments, he became wrapped in the spirit of a real child; he imagined he was traveling west, following trails that were long, rocky,
steep, and dangerous. "How many others before him may have sat
where he was now?" The question stuck in his mind and for a few
minutes this game of make-believe amused him, until it no longer
remained a fantasy. Suddenly the only image he could conjure up
was himself in a wagon, but he was not in the country; he was in a
city. There was a horse, a thin nag, tramping along so slowly. It was
in the dark of the morning before anyone else was awake. A lantern
hung from a tall pole, and it juggled as the poor old horse walked
ever so diligently. Alex turned his head to the left and stroked the
bench. He stared in the direction of the empty seat and noticed it

was occupied by his imagination. "Dad," he thought. "I remember, I was with my real Dad." Alex shivered and turned his face towards the front. He leaned over and bowed his head as he recalled what Tully had explained, "Everything in the wagon was his." He sat up and peered over the side of the wagon. Timothy was still sleeping, but had moved to a new position that aligned with the sun. Alex scooted around and with ease crawled into the rear of the wagon to inspect his claim.

Beneath the shade of the canvas were several boxes and a leather valise. Alex pulled the bag towards him and sat on his knees. A small beveled plate made of bronze with the initials WP etched on the surface had been stitched to the side pocket. Alex flipped the bag around and tugged at the strap that fastened it shut. The leather was stiff and the holes were small so it took several attempts before he managed to slip the buckle free. Like the jaw of a great sea bass, the bag opened its mouth wide, allowing its contents to be displayed. "What's this?" Alex exclaimed and pulled from the top a most familiar article. "How did this git here?" he asked and unfolded the same quilt that he had given Cally. He stared at it for a few moments wondering why it happened to come back in this wagon, but without an explanation all he could do was wait to ask Tully. He tossed it lightly aside and without looking, he drew his hand into the bag and retrieved the next article. It was a flimsy leather bound book with a stamped title. His first reaction to the book's title was of little interest, for not being the most proficient of readers; he believed it was about farming with cows for he read, "Dairy". However, after leafing through the first few pages he realized he had made a mistake; for the unsparing memories on the pages were a series of personal letters, and the book was actually someone's diary, not dairy! Alex turned the pages and leaned into the book. He scanned the writing for identification of the owner; something that would bear the name. It wasn't until he worked his way backwards and turned to the beginning page that he uncovered the rightful owner, WP; the same pair of initials that were stamped on the bag. Alex closed the book and held it close, "WP; Will Piccard," he said sinking his voice into what was a whisper. Alex stared at the book in amazement. "Alex Piccard," he said aloud. "I am Alex Piccard."

———

From the side of the hill, which was gentle and rocky, he could see the farmhouse, the barnyard, over the roofs and down the road towards the fields, but he couldn't hear the anxious crow of the old rooster, or the complaining bleats of the goat, or even the soft whinnies of Delilah and Dandy. From this side of the hill he could only feel the wind wresting him forward. He began to run, and without taking notice found himself drawn to a small clearing of Queen Anne's lace that had turned the slope into a wintery coverlet. As if nature herself had crocheted each flower, whenever the wind would blow the round heads looked like thin sticks waving lace doilies. For the remainder of the walk Alex's mind did not follow any particular pattern, but wandered from one idea to the next. He thought briefly about Betty and was heartened that she had insisted he continue his schoolwork even after the schoolhouse had disbanded. "Finally, all this readin' was going to come in handy," he announced to himself. Aside from Betty's books, Mr. Beasley's newspapers, and the few letters from Grace, he hadn't really found anything that he needed to read until now. He passed sweet clover growing along the road and thought about Delilah and Dandy, and when he placed his hand into his pocket and felt the small framed photograph, he thought about his poor sweet mother. And then there was the quilt he had given Pinto Jack for Cally turning up in a wagon driven by Tully; just how did all these things fit together or did they? In the course of having pondered over the circumstances, he concluded that perhaps some inspiration would come over him under his apple tree. A loitering population of butterflies was flitting from dandelion to dandelion, some resting upon golden petals and others unleashing a sprinkle of wispy seeds into the air from feathered crowns of the dried flowers. Other guests surrounding the tree were hidden between the blades of grass, under rocks, and beneath the soil; for although there were miniature colonies of tunnel-working beetles, fastidious ants, and hungry aphids, they did not make themselves visibly present, and Alex found himself quite alone.

It was a grand tree, a still-life painting that changed with the seasons. Except for the wind's jostling, it stood as majestic as a queen in a coronation, steadfast and regal. The canopy, a green crown made of tussled leaves, and the emerald and russet jewels, her marble-size fruit, and an elegant gown flowing down and along the ground, she had grown into a beauty. To the north, south, east and west, it gestured with out-stretched branches and welcome shade. It was not hard to understand why aside from the barn, this was Alex's favorite place. With a renewed sense of interest in the book, Alex settled himself. With one knee up and his back resting against the trunk, he lay the book down and opened to the first entry.

Monday

This has been a beautiful day. Libby and I took a walk and talked about our new home, Baltimore. However, ever since meeting Mrs. Cambridge never have the thoughts of leaving England come so vividly to my mind as they have since our introduction. There is something very odd about this woman, yet I do not have a desire to bring any fear upon my dear Libby, for she has already had such a difficult time. My Libby never complains, however I am sure she is homesick for her grandmother and mother. I am very grateful to have met Nick Biddle; he seems like a square chap and knows his way around. I have a feeling that Nick and I will become good friends.

Alex roamed the page like an explorer in uncharted waters. Up until now the boy had never seen his father's handwriting. The letters were well-formed, not too curvy and not too fancy, quite neat and deliberate. The words were all written on a slant however, the letters that needed to be crossed or dotted, such as the T and I, rested on the horizontal, which allowed the sentences to remain conservatively uniformed. "He must be a very smart man," thought Alex admiring the fancy style of the manuscript. The eager reader shuffled through the diary as his eyes glittered restlessly upon the pages. He skimmed to the middle of the book where a particular entry caught his attention

I am overpowered with grief. My vision of any hope has died when they took my son, my precious little boy.

The passage had not been dated and the handwriting was not nearly as neat, but rather scrawled across the page with the taller letters loosely penned, while the points and the arcs of the smaller letters, such as 'c' and 'e', were scarcely as round. A teardrop fell upon the page and created a tiny pool over the word "boy". Alex wiped his face with his sleeve and carefully dabbed the book with his shirttail. A small black stain of grey formed around the letters as though they had bled. He remembered that if you get dry ink wet, it can ruin everything. He blotted the area again and then leaned over and lightly blew with his breath until it dried. He squeezed his eyes shut and refused to let the horror of that day enter his mind. There was something tingling in his fingertips like a fast burning twig of kindling. He fanned the pages and they fluttered like the release of a hoard of winged creatures until he came upon the last entry. All pages thereafter were blank.

Tuesday
For the first time in years I have reason to be optimistic. Although I have grown hardened by my losses and disappointments, perhaps finally all my years of saving and working and hoping have paid off. I have meet a cowboy, Pinto Jack, (he is named for the horse he rides). He had given me Lexy's quilt. He seems honest and has no reason to lie, although I remain skeptical with his claim of knowing where my son is. If it is so, then my prayers have been answered. At last my wife will finally rest peacefully, for I may be only a day or so away from finding our child. Can this be the miracle that I have been waiting for? I have bought a wagon and two sturdy mules. Tomorrow, Jack will take me to the Forester's and I will reclaim my boy! Tomorrow I will be reunited with my son!

The optimism of the final entry could be observed not only by its content, but in the handwriting; it had been written in the same orderly penmanship as the earlier entries. Alex closed the book, setting it down beside him. He sat up on his knees and pulled the photo of his mother out of his pocket and looked at it again. In the light of the day she seemed even younger and lovelier than last evening. He put the photo to his lips and gave it a kiss and then stretched it before him so he could see it clearly. "You see, everything will be all right," he whispered. He stared at the miniature face as though it were going to reply. "Dad says so right here in his book," he added and tapped the diary. "Don't ya worry none 'bout me, it's gonna be fixed." The wind prowled lightly, rustling the leaves and carrying with it the sweet aroma of hickory.

"Who are you talking to?" Standing behind the tree was Tully being closely trailed by Sergeant. Alex turned round when he heard the voice and quickly stuffed the picture in his pocket.

"Just kind of talkin' to myself," he answered shyly. He wasn't sure how it would sound if he confessed that he was having a one-sided conversation with his dead mother.

Sergeant dropped a stick next to the boy. Alex read the dog's mind and tossed it as far as he could throw. "He found that on the way and has been carrying it. I believe he knew you'd be here," Tully remarked and parked himself next to the boy. Sergeant bounded back with the stick in his mouth and promptly dropped it on Alex's lap with the intent that he wanted it thrown again. "Sergeant, go play!" Tully shouted and tossed the stubby branch several yards beyond Alex's original throw. "That should keep him busy," he said. The dog turned at once and charged after the stick until it fell to the ground. Toying with it, he prodded the end and pushed it along the ground with his paw, gave it a sharp bark, and then picked it up in his mouth and carried it about until he found a suitable spot, whereby he sat down and began to gnaw on the end.

"He's a great dog!" Alex remarked, smiling. The elder man nodded. "I got the stuff from the wagon," Alex said. His tone grew with positive intonations as he spoke. "I read some of my Dad's diary," he continued and securing the book, opened to the last entry. "Look! He's comin' for me. Tully, he's really comin' for me!" expounded the boy with unmistakable exuberance and tilted the diary, inviting him to read. Tully took the book and glanced down. Alex watched as the elder man scrolled the entry and then surrendered the diary back.

"I have never been so excited! Do you think he'll recognize me? I mean, I ain't the same little kid anymore!" Alex grinned; half expecting Tully to smile, but all he received in exchange was a sullen expression. As the seconds ticked by the boy's mind waded through pools of darkness and all hope was slowly flickering out like dampened kindling. "What do you know, Tully?" Alex asked, as he interpreted the absence of alacrity as trouble. "What ain't you tellin' me?" There was a new tremble in his voice, and he made himself clear his throat hoping that the lump he felt would slip away along with this undercurrent of pessimism he was feeling.

Alex watched the kindly man as he shifted his hat back from his brow and immediately bending forward spoke. "You know Alex," he said gently. "I've always been straight with you." Alex nodded affirming this statement. The boy looked nervously around; he looked past Tully and beyond until he found the dog peacefully asleep in the sun. The day had started out so positively, but suddenly it was becoming more and more unfavorable and very possibly turning out to be a disaster. Alex drew his eyes back to where he was sitting. Tully hadn't changed position and was still wearing that somber expression. The brightness of the morning contradicted the dark message about to be imparted. But no amount of waiting or skirting the inevitable would diminish the pain. "I am afraid," Tully remarked, his voice resolutely direct, "he's not coming back."

"Not coming back!" Alex recognized the sincerity in Tully's tone, but gleaned only betrayal. "But the diary!" he exclaimed, "it said he was comin' for me!" Alex was confused, he knew what he had read, the words were in his father's own handwriting and penned only days ago! He snatched up the book and skipped to the last entry. There was no mistake, it was right here in writing. He thumbed through the final pages, perhaps he had missed something, but they were, as he remembered, completely blank. His heart pounded furiously, and he suddenly felt as though he was going to throw up. He could feel his face growing crimson and his big doe-like eyes welled up with tears; tears of anger and tears of disappointment. Easily the heart confuses the mind, wondering which emotion is which, as it was doing at this moment.

Tully drew a breath. He considered the atrocity of the murder and decided to forego any details; all that needed to be revealed was the final outcome; Alex's father was forever gone. "I'm sorry, little minute," Tully concluded. "Your father is dead."

Cruel words; as lethal as a dose of poison. What antidote could sooth this broken heart? Alex dropped the book as though it too had died. Did the author intend for the boy to have read his last words? Only a day ago things were simpler, not easier, but rather presumed in order. Now his order had been displaced. Alex didn't know where to look or what to do. If he dug his hand into his pocket, his mother was there, if he looked at the book, his father was there. He drew his knees up and buried his head into his folded arms. He didn't want Tully to see him crying, he didn't know why, but he just didn't. Every trace of hope that ever had existed was blotted out. Suddenly, it seemed one could go a whole lifetime and never feel alive.

Tully followed the direction of the horizon as it stole the sunlight and laid it upon the verdant land. "There's no shame in feeling sad," Tully remarked. "Wouldn't be natural if you weren't."

Alex turned his head and peeked up at the man, contemplating his prudent words. He found himself drifting away from his own terrible sadness and mapping an imaginary route about Tully. Then with intense politeness, he asked most peculiar question. "Ever been married?"

Tully glanced over to look at the boy. He laughed at the question, and then grew more serious. It was a subject that pierced like windowpanes flooded with sunlight so bright that it hurts to look at them. "Yes, but that was a long time ago."

Alex retreated. He placed his head back down on his arms. But no sooner did he find a moment to ponder did he pop back up again like a worm being pulled out of the hole by a sparrow. "Where is she?" he asked with innocent curiosity.

Tully slid back and leaned against the tree. He closed his eyes and folded his hands across his chest. "Shhh," he whispered with genuine emotion. Buried in silence the two sat listening to their own breathing and the rustling of leaves overhead. After several long minutes the chanting of a distant wind hummed through the branches. "There," he proclaimed softly, "that's her."

Alex nodded his head as if he understood. He inferred that the woman was dead, but he also knew that she remained alive. "How do you know so much?" Alex remarked.

"I don't," he said. "I just only know what is not true."

Tully shifted around and dug into his own pocket and pulled out his handkerchief and opened it so that it remained flat over his palm.

"You gave me one of these,' Alex said, wiping his eyes with his sleeve. Tully nodded. Then he turned it over and pointed to the monogram.

"It's got the C!" Alex remarked. He twisted his head to the side as though he were contemplating something very difficult. "Is it the same C as ...," but before he could finish Tully interrupted the sentence.

"As on the signet ring? Yes," he answered.

"Then Grace was right!" Alex became wide-eyed. "She said she'd seen this on the house in Baltimore! It's got to be the same one!" he exclaimed; immediately struck with the exuberance of a winning lottery number.

"And the same as in my name," Tully revealed. "Cambridge."

"You mean the Cambridge that my Dad wrote about?" Alex asked, as he tried to fit all the pieces into place.

"Yes," he added. "And that is where I grew up as a boy."

Chapter 54

The events narrated were as leisurely as they were cautious. It was a strange collection of fate that needed to be sorted out as carefully as fitting broken crockery back together. There were no rules, no precedence to follow, only time. During the hours that followed Tully took apart the diary, impressing upon the boy Will's unbridled commitment to find his son. He relayed the tale that had been imparted upon Jack and then to him following the untimely death; how his parents were foiled in their attempts to be completely happy and how their poverty and undocumented ability to maintain a suitable home led to Alex's hasty and cruel removal. However, Tully never diminished the Forester's goodness and simple naive nature. "Betty is a good woman," he reminded Alex; upon which the child simply nodded.

The astonishing flight of his parents from England to Baltimore grew more extraordinary and as Alex learned the relationship between himself and Tully, the forlorn boy's spirits returned. Tully was Marcus Tullius Cambridge, the son of Alex's Great-Aunt Elizabeth Dowling Cambridge, and cousin to his mother, Libby.

For Tully, he learned of his own mother's demise at the hands of his uncle within the pages of the diary, however unlike the boy who was stricken with grief at the loss of his father, the elder man felt no sadness, no remorse, nor any feelings of a son's affection for Elizabeth Cambridge. The brother and sister tie between Libby's father and Tully's mother had remained a secret until now. Yet, if someone had taken the time to look more discreetly, they would have sensed that although they lived most of their lives oceans apart, their cruel and unscrupulous ways were undeniably related. "Tully Cambridge," Alex repeated and smiled. But the elder did not see anything humorous in this revelation and looked at him with a grimace. "Maybe I'll call myself Alex Piccard," the boy said thoughtfully. "Or maybe just Alex."

Tully closed the diary and let it rest upon his knees. He looked up into the canopy and shut his eyes. "After all," he remarked, giving pause. The wind blew and he turned his head as though being pushed by the breeze. "What's in a name?" he declared expressively.

Alex exchanged an appearance of not understanding.

"Shakespeare," Tully said clarifying the boy's gesture of inquiry, "it's a line out of a play that was written a long time ago."

The boy shrugged his shoulders and added, "Who?"

Tully mused. "I'll tell you 'bout him some time," he said and then stretched his legs lazily. "There's lots of stuff I'll tell you about."

A cloud had swallowed the sun. Unsettled shadows now partitioned off the hill into a patchwork of light and dark. Sergeant awoke after these memorable accounts had been successfully relayed. The reinvigorated hound sprang to his feet and again attached himself to his owner's side by wedging himself between the boy and his master, and habitually lay his head down, conforming to the space he now occupied. A long drawn-out yawn, repeated by an agreeable groan, detached itself from the mouth and throat. Then, without caring that he had just woken up from a rather long nap, the canine respectively fell back to sleep.

Alex rubbed the dog on its large head and scratched behind its ears. There was a long silence, the pensive quiet of those who are the benefactor of another's enlightenment. "We just might get apples this year," Tully said volunteering the information with an air of accuracy. He cupped his palms over his knees and speculated the tiny fruit peppering the branches above.

"We!" the word sang in Alex's ears like a hymn, and he smiled to himself. There was something very permanent in the way Tully had said "we". "I never had no kin before, except my ma and pa," Alex whispered, and then collecting his courage he added, "I'm glad me and you are real blood relation."

For a moment there was silence again as the story-teller turned over in his mind the dramatic changes. Tully tapped the boy on the shoulder with a gesture of approval and said wistfully, "It's been just me and Sergeant for so long, it sure will be strange having someone else around; a good kind of strange. I don't suppose Betty would mind if we took a trip to Baltimore and took a look for ourselves at Cambridge Arms. You know, there was a garden I used to tend to. I imagine it might need a little work."

Alex's eyes widened at the mention of a trip. "Do ya think, Tully," his voice raised with excitement. "Could we really? Maybe we could take Delilah and Dandy with us; why they could pull a wagon better than those mules!"

Tully smiled at the prospect. "I bet they could," he agreed with a laugh and rested comfortably against the tree.

Sergeant moaned peacefully in his sleep and as he exhaled it disturbed the ground around his nose, creating a little path of dirt.

Alex leaned back on his elbows, his knees arched, and his head facing upward. He hunted about the branches counting the tiny russet and green pebbles, so immature, but so promising; they would be the very first apples! He reveled in his find and with his eyes continued to climb the tree, branch by branch. Rocking his head back, he found himself along the highest bough, a sturdy limb with an elongated and elegant reach. He inspected the branch faithfully; threading from leaf to leaf, until in the midst of the tangled stems he stopped at what he believed was a pair of dark eyes staring back at him from amongst the foliage. In the perfection of the day and under the coolness of the canopy, he yielded to the sight that drew him upward. He regarded his find intently; and as he mingled with his thoughts, the boy soon realized that he had been mistaken. He blinked and looked again, and within that flicker miraculously discovered that what he presumed to be two eyes was in fact four. Radiating aloft, nestled in a bed of green leaves, two pairs of dark eyes were watching over him; and then like always, in a flash, they disappeared.

———

The trail to the house remained the same. All paths led to the barn, and he sat down upon the yellowing hay and surrendered himself to the moment. "Tell me I'm an orphan no more," he whispered. Restlessly the two drafts shuffled their feet and lashed the air with their tails. Alex smiled, and he waited.